PRAISE FOR *PEOPLE OF THE BEAR MOTHER*

"Joseph Campbell taught us the inner dimensions of the heroic journey which we are all to take. In People of the Bear Mother, *Austin tells us a story that reveals the origins and meaning of ancient cave paintings and we learn about the power of initiation through the animal envoys of the unseen powers that still inhabit our universe. This is truly a mythic tale that will remain in the imagination for a lifetime."*

—Dr. Jonathan Young, PhD. Founding Curator, Joseph Campbell Archives, Center for Story and Symbol, Santa Barbara

"The stunning discoveries of Chauvet Cave, upon which Austin's fictional account is closely based, have revolutionized and up-ended all earlier conceptions of art history and life in the European Upper Paleolithic. Austin gives us a perfectly plausible interpretation of Chauvet's masterpieces of animal art that are the earliest known examples of the magnificent burst of creativity that began to be expressed in the painted caves of Western Europe some 35,000 years ago."

—Dr. Theodore Telford, PhD. Adjunct Professor, Department of Sociology and Anthropology, University of California at Riverside

"This story of a young woman's adventure of initiation within one of the great painted caves of Stone Age France will resonate with everyone who is faced with the choice of how to live a truly human life under any circumstances. Little Bear's encounter with her own wise mentors provides some surprisingly universal answers to such questions of human existence as how we are to acknowledge and balance the feminine and masculine energies that are a part of each and every one of us."

—Marsh Engle. Author, *Amazing Women Amazing World*; CEO, The Envision Network and Amazing Woman's Day Seminars

Great Cave of The Bear Mother

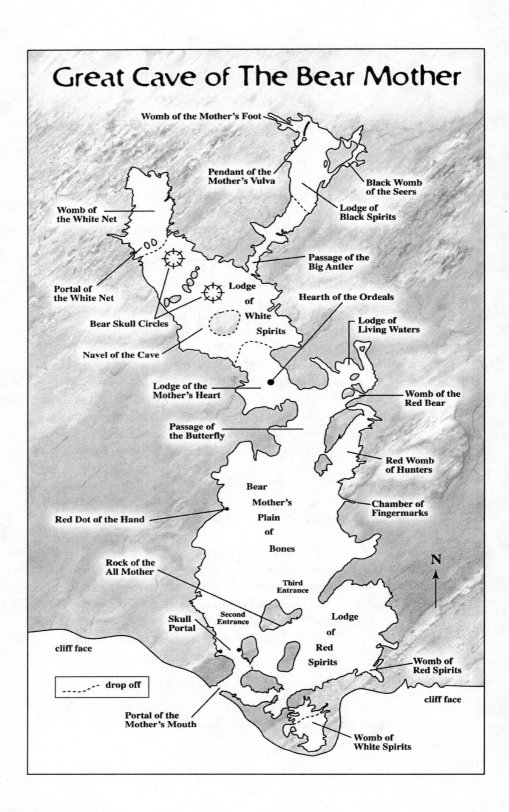

Womb of the Mother's Foot

Pendant of the
Mother's Vulva

Black Womb
of the Seers

Lodge of
Black Spirits

Womb of
the White Net

Passage of the
Big Antler

Portal of
the White Net

Lodge
of
White
Spirits

Hearth of the Ordeals

Lodge of
Living Waters

Bear Skull Circles

Navel of the Cave

Lodge of the
Mother's Heart

Womb of the
Red Bear

Passage of
the Butterfly

Red Womb
of Hunters

Bear
Mother's
Plain
of
Bones

Chamber of
Fingermarks

Red Dot of the Hand

N

Rock of the
All Mother

Third
Entrance

Lodge
of
Red
Spirits

Skull
Portal

Second
Entrance

cliff face

Womb of
Red Spirits

- - - drop off

cliff face

Portal of the
Mother's Mouth

Womb of
White Spirits

PEOPLE OF THE BEAR MOTHER

A Novel

T. D. Austin

Eloquent Books
Durham, Connecticut

PERIPLUS OF THE SEA OF SOULS
BOOK I: PEOPLE OF THE BEAR MOTHER

Cover photography courtesy of Dr. Jean Clottes, Director of Chauvet Cave Excavations, France

Periplus of the Sea of Souls is a trademark of T. D. Austin

Eloquent Books
An imprint of Strategic Book Group
P.O. Box 333
Durham CT 06422
www.strategicbookgroup.com

ISBN: 978-1-60860-380-0

Book Design: Bruce Salender

Printed in the United States of America

Dedicated to the wise teachers of all time
and to the enlightened artists, bards and scribes
who have passed the universal truths of all the ages on to us.

CONTENTS

PROLOGUE

THE ORACLE SAID this would be my last lifetime. She must be correct because this transition is completely different from any other passing. Maybe it feels different because this lifetime was unlike any of the uncountable lives I have ever lived. And not just because of the cremation. My body has been burned many times before. In fact, sometimes while I was still alive.

In truth, I think I prefer returning the molecules of a no longer useful body to the winds and waters of Mother Earth with fire. It is so clean, so quick. A pure and seamless rejoining even at those times when the flames have scorched my living flesh and smoke from my own clothing has seared my gasping lungs.

As shockingly painful as being burned to death is, it is over rather quickly even when I have been slowly roasted to prolong the agony of a reviled heretic. I find the fearful anticipation of the dissolution of the body and descent into the Abyss is always worse than the actual going over. That is because it means the end of separation.

It is the end of loneliness and isolation in a blood-filled bag of skin and bones. Compared to lingering deaths from cancer, or the slow-motion suicide of addiction, with a burning the soul is liberated instantly to the light-filled condition in which I now find myself yet again. So freeing, so serene, so blissful it is! The soul is released from its ponderous swim through the deep pool of golden, sticky-sweet honey that is a body of flesh and blood into this middle space of absolute tranquility.

I almost said *this place*. But I suppose that is mere habit of thought for one so recently dead. This is no place. This is no time at all. On the contrary, it is that oh-so-familiar middle ground between a life just lived and a new life yet to be. To be out of body is to be out of every place, outside of all time and to be without a name. It is having been and about to become. And so I have no name in this ethereal between-space. And yet, I have a thousand names having been known by one or another, in one body or another, for as long as I have been drawn to rebirth after rebirth as one of the human tribe.

The smoke arising from my disintegrating flesh has no name. But as I see my ashes scattered by those I have left behind, I pass through the Veil of Remembering and all the memories of a thousand, thousand lifetimes are alive and present and here and now in me. Out of the midst of inconceivable darkness and bloody suffering I now pass into incomprehensible light and peace. Unimaginable bliss, a knowing of all that has gone before surrounds and penetrates this being of light that I am. The spark that is me now soars higher than any bird, flies faster than any flame-belching rocket to speed me in an instant to every time and place that I have ever lived.

I have met those who say they have had few lifetimes on this Planet. But I love life so much here that I have returned again and again and again to this blue-green orb floating in the endless blackness of star-spangled space. This Mother Earth is my soul's true home for I have come out of her fertile body, shielded by Sky Father's protecting blanket of air. And now I see them all—every existence on this Planet I have ever had—happening all over again and all in the same moment. Each lifetime is distinct as a snowflake. They swirl, they merge, they are coming into focus and then slipping away again. Each is unaware of all the others but they are pushed in the same direction by the formless storm of which they are a part.

While in the flesh, memories of these myriads of past lives are always as if covered by heavy fog. They are fragments of a dream in the night—at least for most of us. Only beings like the Oracle or this soul now drifting in the middle place of numinous light, are conscious enough to be aware of any other existence except the one they are in the midst of living.

Only now, having passed through the Veil of Remembering, do I see the complete periplus—the navigator's guidebook—of my own soul's twisting and winding journey to the center of my own labyrinth and to the oneness that I am with all Creation. Only while in this middle space can I see how this life was different from all the others, yet part of the same arc of life now linked to, and a culmination of, all the others I have ever lived.

I have lived lifetime after lifetime endlessly repeating the same opera, playing the same roles, mindlessly treading the same paths with forgotten loves, births, deaths, joys, sufferings, initiations, sorrows and dissolutions. There have been lessons rejected and lessons learned. And there have been far too many withdrawals from the light offered to me by gentle teachers, impassioned lovers and bitter enemies alike. Whenever I managed to awaken in some small way to the Oneness within all things, I have blazed a new path and a new ending. I changed the odyssey of my own soul by choosing to take this path and not that, to a destiny that was mine alone.

What made this lifetime different from all the others I have ever lived? The answer to that question, in part, can only be explained if all the other souls, with whom I have played the game of life over and over again, open their minds to me in this between-world. Only then could I see with perfect clarity. Since many of those teachers and lovers and adversaries have not opened their souls to me or are still stuck in the thick ooze that is a body, I can only see as through a glass darkly, so it is said, even here in this world of peaceful, welcoming light.

In this light-world of all the lives that have ever been lived, only my own memories are crystal clear. For me to see the part others have played in my own soul-saga, whether still in body or in spirit, all those others must choose to open their minds to me and I to them for us to see our shared experience in its completeness. Only then will we become the Formless Union that is the spark at the heart of every soul.

Just because we are dead does not mean we have learned enough through hard experience, inspiration or revelation to see clearly and be open to those who would reveal all else to us. That is the life-task of every embodied soul while we are alive. Even in this body of radiant light I see there is still some degree of separation. I know I have not yet chosen the Eternal Light where all things are inseparably one, where the past, present and future is one and beyond even the idea of "one." I know this because in this middle-space of the soul I continue to think the thoughts, "I" and "You."

Still, this condition, this consciousness of past experience, is all I am and all I have. This consciousness of experience past is not so much a higher or lower consciousness compared to all other living things. It is simply a different consciousness. My soul has a distinct awareness of surroundings and self from the bacteria that survive within the living stone of the earth beyond all light and pressed by enormous weight. I have had different experiences. As a consequence of a myriad of lives lived, I have had much more experience and so my consciousness is different.

In this middle-space, I see that the entire Universe is alive and has a consciousness and a way-of-knowing all its own. Who has ever beheld a cascading stream or an erupting volcano and, for at least one split-second, not thought the stream of water or snaking river of lava were alive and aware? Who has ever gazed into the shining brown eyes of a dog, as it cocks its head from side-to-side in understanding, and has not seen the Infinite Soul of all souls in those limpid, loving eyes?

The exploding galaxy knows how to gather its atoms to form stars and planets. The water knows to obey the law of gravity and flow downhill. The virus floating on a speck of dust knows how to find the kind of living cell it needs to reproduce. The plant knows where the sun is and turns its leaves to face the life-giving rays. The animal knows how to find the grass or meat its body needs to survive and find a mate and continue in existence. The Neanderthal knows how to make a spear and reverently bury the dead with gifts of fragile shells and flowers.

Our tribe of Wise Humans knows how to tell the stories of what has gone before. Today, we imagine our tomorrows so that we may plan where we will go to find sustenance for our bodies, our minds and our souls. We alone, of all the creatures of this world, are those who make love face-to-face while looking into the eyes of the other. And we, of all the creatures of this fragile little Planet, are most capable of seeing the Divine Spark of oneness in the other and in ourselves, if we but look for its glimmer within. We alone can look forward and make choices in this moment that will forever shape our destiny.

All of these consciousnesses are within my soul just as the genes and chromosomes for all of those other creatures are within my disintegrating body. All of this is within each of us: each and every body, each and every soul. We are made of the same stuff as the stars. We are made of earth and water. We are made of fire and air. We have virus, plant and animal genes within us and we share all of these same genes and chromosomes with our primate and our extinct human cousins. Once all is said and done, we are one with all of life regardless of the appearance to the contrary.

I have moved from body to body to body to body, from consciousness to consciousness to consciousness for eons of time. And through the experience of all these consciousnesses interacting with one another, evolving one from the other, awareness has evolved as surely as the body has evolved over my millions of lifetimes.

That being so, *I am* the stars and *I am* the planets. *I am* the earth and *I am* the water. *I am* the virus and the fungus. *I am* the grass and the trees. *I am* the reptile and the fish. *I am* the elephant and the flea, the sparrow and the whale. *I am* the ape that walks the earth upright. And *I am* that creature who looks into the water and sees itself and knows that I and the Universe are one.

In this middle-stage I feel I am one with all things in every way. It is all part of my consciousness because my soul has experienced it all. The very memories of those myriads of bodies are now hidden within every gene and chromosome. With the kind of awareness that has evolved in me, *this* voice is become the voice of the Earth. *These* eyes are become the eyes of the Earth. *This* heart and *this* soul *are* the heart and soul of the Earth. How else could it be?

Having evolved the consciousness of a human being, life after life my soul has followed and learned from their tortured and joyful living wherever I have gone. And from all of these myriad lifetimes, I know the human consciousness is the same for every soul embodied as a human being. The kind of consciousness we share as humans is made possible by our bodies and brains and by the evolved human soul within each of us. In the end, it is only that soul which continues and grows and evolves forevermore.

Every human soul that has ever lived, or is living now, has the same brain and the same mind. Each has the same heart. We have the same passions, desires and fears as all those who have lived before or will live after us. And we all have our soul-lessons to learn and our soul-lessons to teach. We learn the truths of the ages by experiencing as many lifetimes as it takes to teach them to each soul. And so each lesson is endlessly repeated until, at long last, it becomes part of the soul's deepest awareness, programmed into our very bodies.

This life of mine just passing has been lived in an age of mechanical miracles the likes of which I have never witnessed. It is also an age that has forgotten its humble origins as evolved bacteria utterly dependent upon this tiny speck of dust floating in the infinite blackness of the Cosmos. This is so in spite of all the science that teaches us where our bodies have come from. What is most damaging to the growth and illumination of our souls is that our marvelous machines have added to the appearance of apartness and separation: separation from each other, separation from the earth that gave us birth, the sky that protects us and separation from the other creatures that feed us with their bodies. Our wondrous tools have separated us from the awareness of the very survival needs of our bodies which tie us inexorably to all else in this glowing Universe. And it is a world turned upside down: the rich lusting for the thin bodies of the desperately poor. The utterly destitute coveting the fatness of the distressingly rich.

Most now have no idea where drinking water or meat comes from. Nor do we know the source of any of the other substances that sustain our bodies. We foolishly think we are separate from, and are masters of, the very Planet that gives us life. In this age, all we know is that water flows out of a tap from some unseen source and meat comes from the grocery store.

We are so apart from the shimmering aliveness of the Planet that very few of us have ever had to take the life of a sad-eyed doe with our own hands, to pour her blood upon the ground, to turn her flesh into food and her skin into clothing and shelter. Few of us have ever delivered our own blood-drenched children into this world of endless suffering. So miraculous is our medicine that few must plead desperately with a reluctant deity for the body-lives of our beloved ones in the face of incurable plague.

At the end, we do not wash and shroud the bodies of our loved ones with our own hands as all the ages before us have done. We pay money to a stranger to do what we should do out of respect for those beloved ones having left us. And so we become even more apart and separated from those who have given our bodies birth and our souls rebirth through the wisdom of their own marvelous experience.

And yet, all that we are, all that we feel, all that we fear, all that we love, all that we pray for to the Unseen Powers of the universe is no different from all those who have ever lived before us or who will ever come after us. Awash in a tsunami of noise, distraction, the demands of the head and the urgencies of the body, enlightenment of the heart can only come when we cease looking outside ourselves. Only then may we find and grasp the lifeline of that within us which is also the heart of all hearts and the soul of all souls. Too often have I come to that shining place only to fear and reject the light as something not a part of me.

The lifetimes which have spurred my body's and my soul's evolution, the lives which have set my path in this and not that direction, are alive within me now. And they will live within my soul forever and ever as long as this tiny spark of the Unseen Power within keeps hungering for existence and keeps returning to more and more life and more and more experience. I now realize the people I encountered and the experiences that seemed, at the time, to be occasional and merely peripheral occurrences with no real importance, have actually been critical turning points. They have been life-altering awakenings. They have been little epiphanies opening essential pathways to some destined meeting or some lesson-to-be-learned necessary to find the center of my soul, the center of my own labyrinth.

Looking back, it all seems to have had a plan. It appears that some part of me had a navigator's periplus to guide my steps, to alter my course when it should have been altered. But having lived a myriad of lifetimes, I see now that it is all by chance and moved out of the will in the universe which is *my own will*. And so the odyssey of my soul has wound round and around to finally bring me to this single center of all being that I truly am.

So which were the critical forks in the road? Who were those great teachers, impassioned lovers and implacable adversaries that have shaped my very soul? What were those insignificant insights, occasional encounters and tortuous sufferings that have changed my soul's course? When were those casual meetings that brought me to this particular kind of awareness and consciousness? How have I come to where I am now, on the verge of choosing between more life among the human tribes or going into the Eternal White Light? Am I now to leave the luscious experience of the flesh forever behind for the eternal bliss of Oneness? Is this life-just-lived to be my last to savor the delicious suffering that is a human life?

I only have to ask the question and I know all of those turning points. I see them all. I live them all again here and now. Soaring at the speed of thought, I fly to every remote corner and distant time-gone-by of this endless universe. I gently cradle the very cosmos in my arms as a mother does her infant. I see now that the truly soul-changing experiences and sharp turns in the winding path to the center of my own labyrinth are really very few and very far between.

This periplus of my soul is the guidebook and ineradicable record of those innumerable stories. The periplus of my soul tells not only the paths I have taken but warns of the dangers of hidden reefs, contrary currents and terrifying storms that have threatened to block my passage. It tells also of the beacons of light and of the beauties along the way. My periplus tells of the paths and lovers accepted and rejected, of adversaries struggled with in defeat and in victory. My periplus is the guidebook to consciousness awakened, no matter which choices were made.

And so I pass back through the Veil of Forgetting to one of those lifetimes, to one of those crucial turning points along the way. I know this life will be a story of lessons repeated until *this* soul has learned what must be learned to realize the oneness of it all.

CHAPTER 1.
IN MY MOTHER'S LODGE

THE OLDEST SHAMAN OF THE BEAR PEOPLE never comes to anyone's lodge unbidden. But here he is, thrusting his head and cropped, white beard through the flap, past the door post and into the glow of our hearth fire.

"I would speak with your daughter, Little Bear. It is a matter of great importance to the whole People," the head rasped brusquely in my mother's direction.

Completely startled, my mother sat stone silent in the seat of honor directly opposite the doorway across the little cooking hearth of our lodge.

It is difficult to come upon the Grandfather anywhere in the camp unexpectedly and not immediately react with some degree of fear. Everyone is terrified of this oldest of the Bear People's shamans and seers. Shamans with such power are always formally addressed as "Thrice Born" because they will have lived at least three lifetimes as an Ecstatic One. I knew also that between one life and the next, they would have been nurtured by their animal-guides in the highest shaman-nests of the All Mother's great Tree of Life. We may be frightened of them, but their awesome presence is always required at times of great loss and tragedy. Or those times when the powers must be approached for whatever reason.

There is no one of the Bear People who has not been told the story of our young cousin and his sad end, when, in the midst of innocent play at the River, he tossed a stone at a cavorting otter killing the Grandfather's animal-companion unintentionally. As I sat silently watching my mother's startled reaction to the old man's sudden appearance, I could not help but instantly picture the whole tragic affair. Accident or not, our cousin's belief he had killed the Grandfather's personal guide, and possibly injured the Grandfather himself, was enough for the boy to sicken with fever and return to the Mother at the age of only eight seasons.

The Grandfather himself had been called for the healing rites. The old shaman was also there to assure the boy he was forgiven the offense of killing the Grandfather's otter-guide. Everyone knew the Grandfather's appearance at the boy's sickbed was to assure one and all that he had no ill-will toward the boy or his family, ill-will that might have been a cause for the evil use of his powers. The old shaman's promise that he had not been in trance when his animal-companion had been killed by the boy, and so could not have harmed the Grandfather, was not enough to prevent our cousin from returning to the Mother.

The ways of the spirit-powers are mysterious to us all and so we hold all the shamans and seers of the Bear People in great awe. They bridge the worlds by their very presence. In times of need, a shaman will even enter the world of the spirit-powers to rescue and heal the souls of the People. I knew this is why every shaman displays some sign of their special animal-messenger so that no deliberate harm would come to those so close to the Mother. Each animal-companion is considered to be an extension of the shaman's very body and must not be injured while the shaman is in a holy trance. Everyone knows that is why the Grandfather wears his otter skull necklace and otter fur hat. It is also why he always carries a medicine pouch made from a whole otter skin. The face of the animal itself is cleverly designed to fold over and close the top of his shaman's bag of mysteries.

My youngest brother, White Fox, originally sitting opposite me across the hearth when the old man appeared, had already scuttled to the back of his sleeping platform to get out of the great and fearsome shaman's way. White Fox, with just five seasons, covered all but his eyes with a sleeping fur and began to whimper. His reaction is typical. Even other seers and shamans would do anything to avoid looking directly into those all-seeing eyes, if for no other reason than respect.

Since the old buzzard was looking at my mother and speaking to her directly across the hearth while I was off to her right, I could look at him as directly as I had ever dared. In the glow of waning embers the Grandfather's head hung suspended between door post and flap staring at us above the rawhide draft screen which rises up from the floor between the entrance and the cooking hearth. The liquid eyes of a young man as black and shiny as a raven's feather were out of place in a face this old, weatherworn and wrinkled. My mother was so startled by the sudden appearance of the disembodied head with its lengths of unruly, white hair sticking out from that famous otter-fur cap, she continued to stare bug-eyed at the Grandfather without uttering a sound from her slack-jawed mouth.

After what seemed like days, my mother finally recovered her composure and stammered, "Welcome, Grandfather. Please come in. Please come, Great Seer of the Bear People. We are honored by thy presence, Thrice Born."

Still paralyzed, she inexplicably failed to move toward the entry to courteously hold the flap and help the old man with his boots. My mother was so immobile I began to wonder if I shouldn't get up and help the sour old fart myself. In truth, I was as if frozen in my place as well. So in awe was everyone of this shaman that no one would dare speak his name out loud to his face. Indeed, I would guess there were few among the whole of the Bear People old enough to even remember his personal name. But among the seers and shamans who must surely know his secret name, they do not speak it out of reverence for him. I certainly have never heard it spoken. Out of respect, he is always referred to by his honored place among the Nine Kin as "the Grandfather." This place he holds by virtue of his age, his great wisdom and his closeness to the powers. On that, everyone agrees.

But to me, he just looks like a shabby old man who I am required to treat with respect out of common good manners. My mother must be doubly nervous about inviting the old shaman into our lodge to address him with such honorific words as "Thrice Born" and "thy". And here he shows up unannounced when no one is ill in my mother's lodge, when my father and brother, Little Ibex, have already left with the other men of our camp for a Great Hunt that could last many days. Besides, the scary old man arrived when he must have known that my mother was unprepared to offer the best we had to give such an honored person. He had to know that all the food we had gotten up so early to prepare this morning had been taken by the hunters. What remained of the food had already been finished off by the three of us who stayed in camp. What was there left to offer him?

To entertain such awesome spirit-power without any preparation made my mother's hands shake. Finally, hesitantly, she got up, went to the door and pulled back the leather flap to reveal a dark, hulking, bear-like presence outlined by the first rays of the coming dawn. My belly sank as he bent over to enter the low doorway. He supported his weight on a bird-headed seer's staff hung with a small bundle of feathers taken from those birds that shamans are said to ride in trance. Big wing and tail feathers of owls, swans, ravens, eagles—among other birds I could not identify from a single feather—adorned the wooden rod that came up to the his shoulder.

The old man leaned his staff next to the entry. And to my complete dismay, my mother even failed to greet him with her forehead pressed to his as all guests are to be welcomed upon entering a lodge! Seeming not to notice the lapse of good manners and assisted by my mother's hand beneath one elbow, he began to hobble on what looked like crippled legs around the left side of the draft screen. Eventually, he was escorted to the honored seat in front of the hearth facing the entry where my mother had just been sitting.

The dry pine boughs beneath the lodge's floor skins and rush mats crunched faintly as the old man made his painful way around the draft screen to the head of the hearth. Sinking slowly at first, then more rapidly, he dropped to the fur-covered floor with an audible cracking of joints. With a whoosh, a rush of pine scent found its way from beneath the floor coverings into the lodge to combine with the heavy aromas of wood smoke and leftover food.

His face had not been fully visible at the portal of the lodge, but lit by the flickering glow of the small fire just in front of him, it is now. He adjusted himself stiffly to sit cross-legged at the head of the hearth. I shifted nervously and watched with growing discomfort as my usually unflappable and completely self-assured mother all but scurried like a frightened mouse toward the clutter that remained from the morning's cooking. To my utter surprise, she began frantically trying to bring her usual order and neatness to the untidy mess upon and around the low work table that backed up to the draft screen.

"Let me prepare the Grandfather something to eat," my mother stammered weakly. She began rummaging through the disorder of cooking baskets, wooden cups and dirty bowls.

"I did not come here to eat, One Doe," he said with impolite sharpness.

"At least a cup of hot herb water to warm you, Thrice Born," she offered. "There are already heated cooking stones. It will only take a moment," my mother mumbled in a barely audible voice.

She continued to rummage among the bowls and cups and bone plates, obviously embarrassed by the messy clutter. Finally realizing how upset and distraught my mother was at his sudden appearance, the old man spoke my mother's name gently and held out his hand to her.

"One Doe, my Daughter," he said. "Come now, please sit and calm yourself. There is no need for your kind hospitality or formalities this day. I have come only to speak with your daughter, Little Bear."

Relenting, she put down the utensils and dishes and sat dejectedly to the old shaman's left. I sat directly across the hearth from her to his right. Strangely, she did not look up at me, but dropped her eyes to the hearth fire. Still waiting for someone to say or do something, we both sat dumb, daring only to keep our eyes averted from the Grandfather. He sat quietly, apparently gathering his thoughts or resting his legs. I could not tell. Occasionally my mother and I looked in each other's direction, our mutual apprehension barely masked. We sat nervously wringing our fingers and breathing rapidly until the Grandfather finally raised his head slowly, seemingly with great effort, to gaze across the faintly flickering embers of our morning cooking fire toward the door flap.

I took a furtive sidelong glance to see what he was doing. It was hard to tell whether or not his inability to raise his head all the way up or to turn it to either side to look into either of our worried faces was due to a permanent bend in his neck and back. I thought maybe the heavy otter cap and thick robe with its heavy bison-ruff collar worn against the late winter's morning chill prevented his head from sitting squarely on his shoulders as he sat cross-legged before our hearth. The flames wavered silently, warming and softening the deep wrinkles surrounding clear black eyes gazing out at us from depths and dream-visions we could only imagine. But nothing served to calm the churning anticipation in my stomach now that I knew it was I the great shaman had come to speak to.

Still looking ahead, the old man proceeded to slough his ancient bison robe from his shoulders. He pulled off his fur cap revealing a flattened bush of almost pure white hair the color of the full moon. I watched as the dirty robe fell to form a puddle of bison wool and fur around him. Now, without the heavy robe and thick otter cap, he sat up much straighter. The old man began to busy himself with smoothing out his shoulder-length hair.

Soon, he turned his head to stare directly at my mother. He spoke mysteriously, "I would speak with your daughter Little Bear ... alone."

My mother reacted to this request by leaning back sharply as if she had been shoved. With wrinkled brows and a concerned frown, she began to voice her opposition to the whole notion. But the look in the old shaman's eyes told her there was only one possible answer. Without a word of courteous agreement or a polite request to be excused from his presence, she stood up, pulled White Fox off his sleeping platform by the arm and wrapped him in the fur he had been hiding under. She moved toward the lodge entrance, wrapped herself in a heavy bison robe from a peg near the entry, grabbed their boots and moved as quickly as she could through the leather flap out into the slowly brightening dawn.

Sitting alone with the Grandfather, I pushed all apprehensive thoughts away to think only about where my mother might go and how far away she would be if I were to call out for help. I wondered what she would tell my Auntie, because Auntie's lodge was surely where she would take my toddling brother on such a chilly morning. I was not the slightest bit comforted by the knowledge that she would be within earshot of any screams coming from this lodge just because Auntie's lodge was the nearest to ours.

"My Granddaughter. Look at me," he said quietly.

His words were softly spoken, but I still jumped a little at this voice that startled me out of my idle musings. It was not the high-pitched bark of his otter-companion or the voice of a great and powerful shaman speaking with the low rumbling of the Great All Mother's voice. I knew *that* sound as I had heard him speak with that terrifying voice while he was in the deep trance of the Blissful Ones—the shamans of the Bear People. No, this was the voice of a kindly old grandfather.

I did not realize my eyes had been locked on the flames of the hearth until he began to speak to me softly. "Don't be afraid, my Daughter. You and I have a wondrous journey to take to that place where the skin between the worlds is very thin. Look at me, Little Bear, Daughter of My Heart."

Such an unexpected endearment gave me the courage I needed to raise my eyes to his. The ruddy glow of the embers softened the deepest wrinkles on his face and suddenly he did not seem so terrible—or so old. Still, his seer's marks stood out on either cheek and to look directly upon the face marks of any seer is always unsettling. I'm not absolutely sure, but I thought I saw a faint gap-toothed smile peeking out between his cropped white beard and moustaches. Somewhat assured, I looked up. I smiled at him and fell headlong into his magic eyes—sooty black and yet clear as a lake of deep, still water.

I heard my voice say, "Yes, Grandfather. What would you have me do?" as if someone else were speaking.

"Come sit beside me. I will tell you of the adventure we will take together, my Daughter Little Bear. No one else must hear and you must never tell any of the People. Sit closer," he whispered conspiratorially.

I shifted around the hearth and sat down again close enough to smell the accumulated smoke and dust and sweat of many seasons on his ancient bison fur robe. It certainly hadn't been properly cleaned for a very long time. As I leaned closer to hear his whispered secrets, I expected to smell the breath of an old man's rotten teeth and last meal. His breath was as sweet as the mint that he must have been recently chewing.

"Daughter," he said. "I want you to vow by the All Mother that you will tell no one of the things I reveal to you, nor the secrets I will show you in the Great Cave of the Bear Mother."

I knew nothing of making promises to a shaman, but I knew something of the Great Cave because all three camps of our Bear-kin—both up and downriver from the Middle Camp—are Guardians of the Cave. It is only a short climb up the south-facing cliffs that curve around behind the Middle Camp to the east where the entrance to the Great Cave is found.

I knew something of the Grandfather as well. I knew he had no lodge of his own but kept his sleeping skins in the Shelter of the Solitaries, a shallow dry cave behind and above the Middle Camp. The Shelter is where the Grandfather shares a hearth with others who have no families to hunt for them. Most people are so afraid of the old vulture that they're happy to have him and the other solitaries and misfits out of the way.

Unless, of course, they are needed to speak to the animal-messengers of the All Mother or to heal the sick or those possessed of many spirits. Just the mention of the Great Cave, where so much of the unseen power of the All Mother comes into our world, filled me with dread. I had to swallow hard more than once to force the rising fear back down into my liver from where it insisted on rising.

"The Great Cave?" I asked dumbly.

It had been seven seasons since I was initiated as a woman of the Bear-kin in the Cave's Lodge of Red Spirits only a few moons after my own moon-blood began to flow each moon-circle. My head raced trying to imagine what could possibly take me to the Great Cave a second time? After one's Moon Blood Ceremony, only seer-initiates enter the Great Cave a second time, and I had definitely not heard the Mother's voice. I saw no visions of animal-guides. I had no dreams. I was no seer of spirit-powers, let alone one who had taken the shaman's journey! There was no reason for me to re-enter the Great Cave.

16

Then, as if the old man could hear my thoughts, he answered me. "You have not been called by the Mother in the same manner as your Auntie. But you will become Seer of the Bear People and you will assist me with a most holy task in the Lodge of the Dark Mothers. You will become my apprentice, but only if you freely choose to do so. But whether you decide to become Seer of the Bear People or not, you must never reveal what I will tell you now with *any* of the People—except for initiated seers and shamans. Do you agree?"

The Lodge of the Dark Mothers! That is in the deepest part of the Great Cave! I became more than a little alarmed just hearing the words. Soon I began to panic and could not keep a cold fear from rising up through my liver, emptying my stomach and heart, racing up my throat and draining my face. The old shaman apparently saw the color leave my face and, concerned I might actually fall over in a faint, began to speak more calming words to me.

"Have no fear, Daughter of My Heart. I have had a dream-vision of the All Mother herself! Together we will do a great work that will bless uncounted generations of the Nine Kin of the Bear Mother. I have watched you draw the animal-messengers in the sand, on tree bark, and on flat rocks with the colors your Auntie has taught you how to make. The Mother knows your heart and it is the Unseen Hand which guides your own when you make spirit-animals. Daughter, I have seen the hunters of our Bear-kin come to you to draw the lines for them on their spirit-pendants and plaques so that they may carve the shapes of their special companions and carry them to the hunt. I have seen that you will also follow your Auntie's path as seer and healer," he said without taking a breath.

It is true that I am already well-known in the Middle Camp for my drawings of animals, fish, birds and even the bugs we see around us every day. It was my own hand that painted the images and signs upon the entry portal of my mother's lodge greeting all who enter. It was I who painted a spiral in the center of the translucent rawhide draft screen. It was I who made my father's kin sign, the Ibex, to the left of the spiral and my mother's kin sign, the Bear, to the right of the spiral, all in red ochre.

It is also true that my Auntie became shaman as a young mother when she nearly died in childbirth. She began to see, to have dreams, to commune with the powers in trance-visions and to treat with herbs and mixtures and healing chants. It is she who taught me how to make charcoal in a special hearth covered over with earth to slow roast the wood into hard, black coals instead of turning into ash. It was she who taught me that pine is the only kind of wood ever used to make charcoal for drawing the lines of spirit-animals or making black paint. The pine is Earth Mother's tree, green with life in both winter and summer seasons. Everything I know of such things my dear Auntie has taught me. In truth, she and I have become more like sisters and age-mates than aunt and niece. It was Auntie who showed me where the best red and yellow earth is found and how to crush and mix it with water or animal fat for body painting and for making lines on stone or leather. It is true that many of my uncles and cousins who are not skilled at drawing or carving have asked me to make bison or aurochs or fish or birds on pieces of especially beautiful stone or ivory that seemed to me to already have those shapes within them. After I make the drawings with my finest brush, they incise and shape the stone or ivory with sharp flints and rubbing stones to carefully follow my lines. Some have brought their partly finished amulets back to me so that I could redraw the lines before they finished the shape of their spirit-animal with more carving and polishing sand.

They all say my lines give strong spirit-fire to the ivory. They always carry the images in their medicine bags or around their necks. They tell me holding an image of their guide with them assists in a successful hunt. I don't know about all of that, but I do know I have a skill for making lines and drawing animals. My soul flies like a shaman bird when I see the lines of a bison looking over his shoulder or some other animal already in the cracks of a piece of ivory or the bumps in a rock that I hold in my palm.

The seers tell us that all animals and birds are messengers of the Mother, they are all her children, and to make a stone or ivory spirit-animal brings the spirit-guides near to us. The ivory becomes a living spirit-animal. Or so we are told and so it seems to me.

"Could I be a seer and not know it?" I whispered to myself in the tiniest voice, sure that the Grandfather could not hear.

Every sound can be heard through the bark and rush walls of our lodges. Everyone can hear when anyone is joining in sex, having a conversation or farting, let alone when having an argument. Seeming not to have heard my whispered question, the old man leaned closer. He spoke so softly that even someone with their ear pressed to the gap of a door flap could not hear what he had to tell me.

"Daughter, you are Seer in your secret heart and in your soul. If you are willing to accept the Mother's call, go to your Auntie and she will prepare you to enter the Great Cave as seer-initiate at sunrise. She will help you prepare the special Mother-ochre and show you how to collect embers from your mother's hearth to ignite the flame of your initiation. Your mother will prepare your father's oil lamp and she will prepare the uncooked root foods you will take into the Cave. But you must prepare your own charcoal pencils, brushes and colors," he whispered in a hush, his excitement growing.

"How many days will we be gone, Grandfather? My father has just left for the hunt. Will we return before the men?" I asked practically in a small whisper

I failed to even notice that my paralyzing fear of the old shaman and the Great Cave had vanished with the anticipation of such an exciting secret adventure.

The Grandfather answered with the most honorific words of address that have ever been spoken to me. "Dear One," he whispered patiently, "I cannot walk as fast as I was used to, but the three days and two nights of the puberty ceremony is the same length of time required for a seer's initiation. You must first be initiated as hunter and then as Seer if you are to enter the Dark Mother's Lodge in the deepest part of the Great Cave and do what my dream-vision has revealed that we must do."

A sickening chill ran through me as I realized what he was saying. I rudely broke in, "Me? A seer?" I whined. "I have not been called by the Mother. I do not see or speak with spirit-powers. I am only eighteen seasons! Why me?" I pleaded.

"Yes my Daughter," he broke in, cutting off my protests. "*You.* Even now I see the boiling fire of life surrounding you. But you must be initiated as a seer-apprentice to go into the deepest, most powerful parts of the Cave of the Bear Mother. There we will enter upon our quest together."

"But I, I, I ..." I stammered. The Grandfather continued on as if he hadn't heard me. Maybe he didn't hear me because his eyes had glazed over and he seemed to be drifting and dreaming as he spoke.

"You will become a great healer. You will see the powers in dreams and in trance-visions. Your gifts will heal and bless the whole People of the Bear Mother in all the worlds to come," he muttered in a singing chant.

Then, rocking slowly back and forth, he mumbled unintelligible words in a low voice as if someone outside the lodge, who was not prepared to be seer or shaman, might overhear. I was dumbstruck at the idea that I could possibly have a seer's spirit-fire surrounding me. For many seasons thereafter I would look at myself in quiet pools of still water wondering where is this boiling fire of life? In truth, I could not see the fire surrounding me or any other shaman or seer—even the Grandfather or my Auntie.

But who can argue with the Thrice Born? Who can go against those fostered in the highest branches of the Tree of Life? Who can deny one who sees the spirit-messengers and speaks with the voice of the Mother as this old shaman does? Certainly not one such as this girl called Little Bear. This old man still frightened me but I saw no way around doing what he asked.

I nodded in resigned assent. All the Grandfather had to say to me was, "Good."

"What shall I tell my mother, my father?" I mumbled weakly, as if they could get me out of this.

"I will tell your mother myself that I have had a dream-vision and my spirit-guide has told me you are to be initiated as Seer, for that is what I have seen. She can tell your father when he returns from the hunt," he replied curtly as if that would resolve everything.

He could see the questioning concern on my face and tried to comfort me further. "Daughter, you know that a seer is called by the Mother to see and to heal as the Mother sees fit. None of us have deliberately chosen to be seers or shamans. But I *have* had a dream and you *are* to become Seer. You *do* have a great work to perform but only if you willingly accept the Mother's call to take this path. Regardless of your decision, and above all, you are sworn to absolute secrecy. No person, not since the People came to this Valley of the Bear Mother, has ever added a single spirit-image to the walls of the Great Cave. This is a great honor for you, Little Bear. Accept the Mother's call with gladness and gratitude," he cajoled.

"Is that what I am to do, Grandfather? Paint a spirit-animal in the Cave? How can this be? How can I be the one to do this thing that has never been done?" I pleaded.

Lowering his voice again he said, "Your Auntie and all the other seers and shamans of the People have already agreed that my dream-vision is truly of the All Mother. You must understand that we refuse the Mother's gifts at the peril of the whole People. For generations to come, the lines you make will be seen as the living spirit-animals of the Great Cave. If you will take this great adventure with me you must swear by the All Mother that you will never share this secret with another living soul who is not now Seer of the Bear People."

Awestruck hardly described my feelings. But I was already becoming caught up in the conspiratorial thrill of knowing something no one else of my tribe would ever know—including my mother and father.

After thinking on it for only a few more moments I said, "Yes, Grandfather, I swear by the All Mother."

I knew that in seasons to come I would have long conversations with Auntie about this moment and what it was I was to do in the Great Cave, the most terrifying and power-laden place in the People's experience. I was certain even then that in those conversations I would discover new respect for my kindest-of-all Auntie and her deep wisdom.

My Auntie was initiated rather late in life. Most shamans are called by the Mother long before they have even had my eighteen seasons. Those who become Ecstatic Ones are most often touched by the powers as sick children. Sometimes they are touched during the initiations of men and women in the Great Cave. My Auntie's kind, gentle heart and formidable healing powers are well known, even in the camps of the Nine Kin upriver from us and far down the river to the Plain of the Mammoth Mother. She has sometimes traveled great distances to help with birthing a baby, setting a broken bone or dispelling a fever. My Auntie was called by the Mother, her spirit-guide began to speak to her, and she was healed from a terrible illness following the difficult birth of her only child. The infant died soon after being born and so, almost, did my beloved Auntie return to the Mother. It was the Grandfather and other shamans-of-healing who brought Auntie back from the worlds of the spirit-powers with their great healing skills and true sight. In her illness she took the shaman's journey and only after that was initiated as Seer.

Surely such a one as my Auntie has a very bright spirit-fire. But never had I seen a "boiling fire of life" surrounding her. She did, subsequently, confirm the Grandfather's observation of my own glowing spirit-fire. But as I said, I never did see it despite peering often into any smooth pool or puddle of still water.

"Help me up, my Daughter," the Grandfather said in his full voice.

The Old Man's voice made me jump after all the whispering. I hurried to snatch his staff from where it lay against the wall near the entrance portal. While he pulled his otter cap back over his chock of white hair, I held the staff in my left hand within his reach then extended my right hand to help him to his feet. As he stood waiting, I hefted the heavy bison robe and wrapped it around his shoulders. Standing behind him, he seemed so small. No taller than me.

He began to hobble stiff-legged toward the entry of my mother's lodge and said, "Run ahead to Auntie's lodge and fetch your mother back to me, my Daughter. I would speak with her before you help me back up to the Shelter. It is already dawn so you will be safe returning by yourself in the daylight," he said with genuine concern.

First of all, I was astonished the crafty old geezer even knew where my mother had taken my little brother. I imagined his otter-guide whispering to him quietly in one ear as we spoke to each other. My mother later told me the truth of it. While she was help-ing him to his seat, the Grandfather had given instructions for her to go to Auntie's lodge and wait until she was summoned. So much for a guardian's voice in a shaman's ear. He certainly could have said all of that to my mother with the faintest of whispers while my head was elsewhere. Maybe I was just paying more atten-tion to the glowing hearth than what was going on around me.

The only other puzzling thing was the old man's concern for me walking alone through the Middle Camp of my own Bear-kin. Whether day or night, I was never afraid to go anywhere in the camp, even as far as the river, to the drinking spring, or all the way to the hot springs of the Serpent Father completely alone. What did he know and have concern for that I did not?

After sending my mother back to speak with the decrepit old shaman, I stayed with Auntie and flooded her with more questions than she possibly could have answered in the time we had before the Grandfather was finished speaking to my mother. My dark-haired, reddish brown-eyed Auntie had already descended into the Black Lodges of the Great Cave. I knew that because she was an initiated seer who bears the marks of Lion Mother upon her shoul-der. Certainly my Auntie would know the secrets of the Dark Mother's Lodge. But no sooner had I begun to question her, my mother appeared at the flap telling me the Grandfather was ready to go.

* * *

The Grandfather was safely, if slowly, escorted to his lodge with barely a word spoken between us. The trail up to the Shelter zig-zags back and forth to make for an easier climb up the sloping broken rock and dirt. The trail slants away from the cliffs toward the bark lodges of the camp and our River below. People from other camps always say the Bear-kin have the most fortuitously sited camp of all the Nine Kin. The protective cliffs are behind with the River running in front of all the south-facing lodges. That includes the south-facing dry cave of the Shelter of the Solitaries itself.

At the top of the trail the view from the entrance to the Shelter overlooks the Eye of the Mother—a huge arching rock with a gigantic hole, through which the River of the Bear Mother flows. From the mouth of the Shelter the rocky, tree-spotted hills to the south and east are also visible. That is where our little river runs out to join the huge River of the Mammoth Mother upon the great Plain of the Mammoth Mother.

Off to the east, I could also see the mouth of the Great Cave almost at the same level as the Shelter. The curving line of cliffs follows an old, mostly dry, river bed that once flowed around the Eye of the Mother. Whenever the river runs high, as it is now, all of the water does not fit through the stone arch of the Eye. When it is this high, the water fills the dry bend as it flows around the Eye before running back into the river downstream from the Eye. This bend in the river is very wide, and because of the flooding, is rich with water plants, rushes, grass, flax, water birds and all kinds of roots. Fruit bushes and nut trees are numerous in the flooded bend and these are always harvested upon our return to the Valley at the end of each summer season.

This sight of the world of the Bear-kin is so beautiful, but it is rarely seen by the people of the Middle Camp because we have little need to climb up to the Shelter of the Solitaries. Or even to the Great Cave, for that matter. The Shelter of the Solitaries has its own spring flowing from a crack at the base of a precipice only a short walk along the face of the cliff in the direction of the Great Cave. Getting water is no problem for those who have their sleeping skins and cooking hearths within the Shelter.

"They must live a strange and lonely life without family to care for them," I thought out loud.

I suppose that is why all the people of the camp bring a share of the hunt to these oldest and wisest of our Bear-kin. It is Auntie who tells me that there are eight solitaries in the Shelter. Only two are seers or shamans: the Grandfather, who is the oldest of all the Bear People's shamans and there is one other woman shaman who has never taken a husband. She is not as old as the Grandfather but is a skilled seer of spirit-powers and a maker of masks, drums and oil lamps. The other six solitaries are either old men or women who have no husbands to hunt for them or daughters to care for them. That is so except for one young two-spirit man who is, as yet, unmarried.

Whether initiated seers or not, all the solitaries make, repair and keep the whole tribe's spirit masks, fur and feathered head-dresses, carved figures of the Mother in all her disguises. And they keep the special fur robes used in our dance circles and gatherings. They also keep and repair the spirit-drums and bone flutes of the dance circles. And within the Shelter there are supplies of healing herbs, ocher powders and special oils. In a way, this little rock shelter is the center of the life of the whole People. No one begrudges what is brought and shared with the solitaries, however much we may avoid them because of their oddities.

When I am up here I realize it is small wonder that the Shelter is on a level with the Great Cave. Together, these two places of great spirit-power, along with the great Eye of the Mother, watch over and bless the Middle Camp of the Bear-kin below. The Grandfather did not ask me to enter his lodge—there was no reason to do such a thing. He bade me farewell at the mouth of the Shelter with a surprisingly affectionate pressing of foreheads. He told me that my mother had instructions to prepare me to enter the Great Cave at dawn the next morning. The very next day? Great Mother of us all!

The only thing I could think of was getting back to Auntie's lodge as quickly as possible.

But soon I found myself daydreaming my way along a path and through a camp that looked strange and suddenly unfamiliar to me. It was not just the late winter sun that had risen above the cliffs leaving the camp still in shadow. Somehow, the air seemed clearer, the sky bluer, the sun warmer and the new shoots greener than I had ever seen them. A thrill of excited anticipation raced up and down my spine and I found myself twirling in dancing circles and singing a child's song:

> *The bunny goes hop, hop, hop,*
> *The raven cries caw, caw, caw,*
> *The salmon goes flop, flop, flop,*
> *The baby cries wah, wah, wah.*

I felt I was flying. I certainly was in no hurry to come back down to Earth Mother. As I approached Auntie's lodge, she was already standing in the path as if she had been waiting a long time for me.

"Little Bear, come inside. I would speak to you," she said with an irritated tone.

I had never seen Auntie without a smile for me. A foreboding followed us through the flap and hovered about as we sat facing each other across her barely glowing hearth. The sun still hung low over the eastern cliffs but a good deal of light would soon be flooding through Auntie's south-facing door and the smoke-hole above it. But Auntie had closed the flap leaving me almost blind in the dark. She stoked the fire for more light.

Auntie's bark lodge was identical to my mother's except for the unkempt storage areas on either side of the entrance. They were crowded with stacked baskets and racks of herbs and medicinal roots in addition to the usual food storage containers and cooking implements. The strings of drying herbs looping above our heads clearly marked the lodge of a healer, as did the three big-hipped women drawn with simple lines in red upon Auntie's draft screen. A shaman-of-healing like my Auntie is Thrice Born and heals body, mind and soul. The three faceless, sinuous figures were made side by side, their protruding buttocks in profile and arms gracefully raised in dance. These three Mothers is the one sign given to those entering my Auntie's lodge that they are entering the lodge of a Thrice Born servant of the All Mother herself.

The air of Auntie's lodge was always filled with a confusion of indistinct aromas and perfumes from many different kinds of plants layered on top of the usual scents of wood smoke and cooking food. It had, in fact, been the lodge of generations of famous healers—my well-known grandmother in particular. It was my mother's mother who passed this lodge and all its contents to Auntie upon her return to the Mother. That was when I was too young to remember anything about her. I probably had not even come into the World of Light at the time my grandmother returned. This was the first time I had ever wondered why my mother, as the eldest sister, had not inherited this lodge of my grandmother?

Crowded as the front of the lodge is with all the paraphernalia of a healer, with no children in the lodge there is plenty of room for pack frames, extra sleeping furs, clothing, gathering baskets and herb drying racks along the east side of the lodge on top of and beneath the unused sleeping platform there. There is another sleeping area on the west side of the lodge immediately in front of the leather-draped sleeping space where my Auntie and Uncle Bright Wolf keep their sleeping furs. The grass-filled pads and furs of the west sleeping platform are used by visiting kin. Sometimes the west platform is used by those who need daily care in their healing. Auntie's stoked hearth fire began to give us just a little more light. In spite of the somber mood she had set, I was full of questions.

"Too many questions!" she complained. "Slow down, slow down! Your mother is very upset. Do you know why?" she asked with a scowl.

"I have never seen her so confused and her tongue so thick," I admitted. "She was very rude to the Grandfather too. I have no idea why she would be so upset by all of this."

"Then let me tell you, my true niece, because you had not yet come into the World of Light when your strong-willed mother and your stubborn grandmother struggled with each other to make all our lives what they are," she began. "If you are to become Seer of the Bear People, it is time you learned your family's secrets."

I leaned what I thought was imperceptibly toward my Auntie in startled anticipation. That was Auntie's signal to begin.

"Your grandmother was a powerful shaman-of-healing. She, herself, was the daughter and granddaughter of honored healers, seers and shamans. Many believe the Mother's call to become shaman does not come to those who have neither men nor women shamans among their forebears. And so your grandmother be-lieved. She was more than fond of telling anyone who would listen that her line—our line—goes all the way back to Red Bear, the first Grandmother of all seers and shamans of the Bear People. She was determined that her eldest daughter, your mother One Doe, would succeed her and inherit not only her lodge but also her skill in healing and seeing. And, if the Mother wills it, a shaman falling into blissful trances."

"What could possibly be wrong with having pride in honorable ancestors," I asked innocently.

"Little Bear, you must know that to force anyone into a path for which they are not suited, and which is not in their heart, is the surest way for that person to take another path in resentment and anger. The truth is, no matter how many shaman ancestors you may have, the call to take the shaman's journey and descend into the Abyss comes without warning and without regard to the desires of those around you. Even your own desire to become a shaman does not result in becoming one, no matter how sincere or well-meaning you may be. One Doe was so resentful of all your grandmother's efforts to make of her a seer or shaman that in her anger your mother took a vow that she would never take your grandmother's path. She swore upon the All Mother's great breasts that no one of her family would ever follow the ways of the seers if she could prevent it."

"Why would she do that?" I asked. "How could my mother be so angry at her own mother to make such a vow?"

"The path of seers and shamans is not an easy trail to follow. Taking the shaman's journey into the Abyss sets one utterly apart from the People even more than initiation as Seer. If one is a gifted healer, many will come to be treated and to be advised in their own life-path. If the results are not as they wish, they become angry at the seer. A healer cannot say 'No' to those in need even when their own families are suffering from want of their mother's care, attention and love. Can you understand that?" she explained.

I thought for a moment before I replied. "Well, I suppose so. But my mother has always been there to care for us. I can't imagine what it would be like for her to be constantly away from her own lodge helping others," I reasoned aloud.

"That is why you must consider well and long what accepting the call of the Mother will mean to you and to all those around you before you choose this path. I have no children so it was easier for me to take the path the Mother sent her animal-messengers to bring me to. Let me tell you now that One Doe was so overwhelmed and angry at having to be mother to me and our brothers—your own true uncles—that she vowed she would never learn the ways of the seers and shamans or even the ways of a healer. It is as simple as that. So hurt in her heart was your mother, imagining she had been abandoned and cast off by her own mother, that she refused to learn anything about herbs and plants, except those used in cooking and those used in the simplest of remedies all the People know."

"Do you mean like willow bark for pain and fever, cherry bark for coughs?"

"Yes, the kind of thing you learned before I began to show you the ways of a healer. As my elder sister, and one who had been mother to me, One Doe also put that same hatred of the path of the seers in my heart. I was only called to the way of a shaman after your grandmother returned to the Mother. I lost my only child and almost returned to the Mother myself. In my fever I was called by the Mother's Voice and I became shaman. That call no one can refuse unless they wish to go mad trying to run away from it."

"Can you tell me something of the coming of your animal-guide, my Auntie?" I asked, genuinely desiring to hear her story.

"Yes, Little Bear I can tell you. The All Mother came to me in the shape of a dove to guide me beyond the seer's path to make of me a Blissful One. It was only after I took the shaman's journey did I become a healer. Try as I might, I could not refuse it—to your own mother's great distress and sorrow. So ill-disposed was One Doe to your grandmother's life as a shaman-of-healing, she refused to marry a seer-apprentice of the Horse-kin who was not of her choosing. Your grandmother wanted One Doe to marry the young man so she could apprentice him as a son of her own lodge. Your mother was so angry at being forced she deliberately, and in opposition to your grandmother's wishes, took your father as husband of her lodge. Your father, Roe Bear, was considered by your grandmother to be an ill-conceived match—a son of poor, upriver Ibex-kin of no fame or honored name and beneath marrying any daughter of hers. One Doe married your father in spite of her opposition, and until she returned to the Mother, your grandmother always said our family had been cursed with too many boy children and too few girl children who could learn the ways of our honored shaman ancestors. That was all before you were born and so you have been unusually favored by your mother in many, many ways."

"I had no idea, Auntie," I said, my mouth completely empty for words.

In that moment, I realized that I *was* the only girl born to either of my grandmother's two daughters.

"Is that why my mother seems so resentful of the time I spend with you learning about healing herbs and plants?" I asked with a glimmer of knowing flickering up inside my completely oblivious head.

"Yes, Little Bear," she said with a sadness she could not hide.

"Do you think our family is cursed?" I asked in complete disbelief.

"No, Little Bear," she replied. "I do not believe the All Mother gives to some and withholds from others. The Mother gives alike to all her children, to the ant and to the mammoth. The Mother values each alike the other and does not respect the honorable above those with little honor as we of the human tribes do. The All Mother only gives as we are able to receive and feel gratitude, but the All Mother withholds her abundance from none that are willing to receive."

"But why would she say our family is cursed, Dear Auntie? I am confused."

"That was surely your grandmother's anger, disappointment and wounded heart speaking. But some, including your mother, do believe such things because it was spoken by someone she loved, respected and, I am sorry to say, feared as a powerful shaman of the People. Know that your dear mother has only tried to protect you from what she sees as harm. One Doe has thus always tried to prevent you from taking any interest in matters of the spirit-powers or even of the skills of a healer. Here is your first lesson as an apprentice, dear Little Bear. Whatever is desired with the heart or spoken with the mouth into the ears of the Mother is returned to us many times over. The All Mother is a pool of clear water reflecting back to us only what is shown to her. If you speak curses, more curses will return and if you speak healing and abundance, more healing and abundance will return. This is so because the All Mother never sleeps. She is always present and hears our every thought because the Mother is within us and all around us. This you must always remember as you begin to learn the ways of a shaman-of-healing. You must learn that whatever you bless will be blessed and healed. Whatever you curse will be cursed and injured as surely as the Mother is the mother of us all."

Suddenly, I saw my whole life through my mother's eyes and I began to pull the scattered pieces together.

"Then why has she allowed me to become virtually your apprentice healer?" I asked.

"Little Bear, your own mother knows better than anyone that no one can be forced to do anything they find repulsive without great hurt and anger coming from it. She would never be married to a man not of her choosing and neither could you be forced to go to what you have no gift for or to love that which you hate," she explained.

Auntie moved around the hearth, took my hands in hers and looked directly into my eyes.

"I love my elder sister as my own mother and nothing can change that. You are my true niece, the daughter of my elder sister, but you are also the Daughter of my Heart because I love you like the girl child I will never have. I only have you to teach the skills of healing with herbs and mixtures and no other. You are the only kinswoman who can receive this knowledge and pass it on to her daughters. When you showed an interest and love for such things, I knew it was the Mother who was calling you to this destiny, though you didn't know it. But I knew not in what way or when you would hear the Voice and whether or when you would be called to take the shaman's journey," she said earnestly pressing my hands with hers.

"Can you not take other apprentices? I am pleased to learn the gift of healing from you, Auntie, but am I the only one able to pass your wisdom on?" I asked innocently.

"The only other seer-apprentice I have is a boy of the Upper Camp. His song has the power to heal the mind but he has none of your gifts for healing the body with herbs and potions. He certainly does not have your gift for making spirit-animals and may never be called to take the shaman's journey. As much as I want you to choose freely, you must consider that if you do not choose this path, our ancestor's great knowledge and wisdom will be lost forever. Entering the deepest parts of the Great Cave is only for those who have such gifts as yours and are willing in their hearts to become Seer."

"But Auntie, I am already learning to heal with plants and roots. Why is it necessary to do anything else, to go any further?" I asked.

"Learning which plants and herbs and animal parts have healing powers, learning how to set broken bones, to midwife a baby and to sing the healing chants are all skills of the head. Since you are very intelligent, you learn quickly and remember everything. Because of the brilliant powers of the head which you possess, I can teach you anything with only a single hearing. With these gifts alone you may be initiated as Seer. But you must understand that to be a healer of the body and a seer is not the same thing as being a shaman-of-healing. It is the Mother who calls to one's soul to become a healer of minds and spirits in addition to healing bodies by sending that one upon the shaman's journey into the Abyss of Silence. Having taken the perilous descent into the darkness of our own souls, a shaman can then descend in trance to rescue the souls of others. We can locate the hidden centers of poison and disease and draw them out from those who are sick in body, mind or spirit by sucking on that spot. Do you understand the difference between a seer and a shaman, dear Little Bear?" she asked.

"Well, I never thought of it that way. But I suppose you are right," I said. "I know I have not been visited by the Mother as shaman—or seer. I have certainly not been called in the manner you were, dear Auntie. What does a shaman's journey of initiation involve?" I asked cautiously.

"A shaman's initiation is nothing like your Moon Blood. Neither is it like the initiations of hunters or any of the rites of the Great Cave. It is an initiation of one's self by one's self. A shaman descends into the center of their own soul through the inward space. It is not a ceremony that can be performed for you by another. It is a journey that only you can take, a door that only you can open. The shaman-initiate is torn to pieces by the powers hidden within the Abyss of their own soul. The initiate's soul is then fostered and nurtured by some animal or bird spirit-guide who will join with and utterly transform the initiate into an altogether new creature which is part human and part animal-guide. The shaman's guides become the shaman and the shaman is guided by her familiars forevermore. Should you take the perilous shaman's journey, even when there are no other seers present to help sing you back to life, your animal-companions will bring you back to the World of Light from the Abyss of the deepest of trances. That spirit-animal becomes your guide and constant companion in your holy service as shaman to the People for the rest of your life."

"No one has ever spoken to me of the shaman's journey as an initiation, dear Auntie. How is it different from the trances I have learned to do? Why does everyone speak with such terror of the shaman's journey?" I asked with a sincere desire to know.

"Every shaman's ordeal is intensely one's own and is never the same as any other shaman. Telling of one's own journey often brings to mind such terrors that we do not wish to ever speak of them again—with each other or with the uninitiated—without the highest and best of reasons. We also do not speak of our private journey with others because it is not wise to lead any initiate into expecting to see or hear or experience anything within the trance-dream in particular. What one shaman sees upon his journey may be completely different from what you will see upon your own journey. In the trance and in the shaman's journey, often we only experience what we expect to experience. Such things are best left unspoken to the uninitiated so that they may see what they may without interference. But I love you, Little Bear, as my own daughter and if telling you of my own journey will help prepare you for what dreams and visions may come, then I will tell it. My wish is that it will help you decide to follow the way of a seer or not. But know that to take this seer's path in your life could take you upon the shaman's journey at any moment when it is the least expected. Do you understand my words, dear Little Bear?"

"Yes, Auntie, I understand. I do want to know and I want to understand even more before I make my decision."

"Very well, Daughter of my Heart. I will tell my shaman's journey. I will tell you of the call of the Mother's Voice to serve the People as shaman."

* * *

"I was near to returning to the Mother after the hard birth of my only child. I was extremely feverous. Though I was burning and delirious in my body, I soon became aware of those standing and kneeling around me but I knew that my body was asleep. I floated above the birthing bed as if I were a roll of skins suspended from the lodge roof for the summer season. I could see who was around me—the Grandfather was there. My sister One Doe, your mother, was there crying and dabbing my fevered face with a wet chamois. My mother—your grandmother—had already returned to the Mother and I could not see her anywhere in her spirit-body or otherwise. 'Abandoned yet again in a time of need,' is all I could think of her with a very heavy heart."

I stared at my Auntie as she spoke trying to imagine what it would be like to watch one's own body die. The more she told, the more far away her voice sounded. It was as though a filmy curtain had descended over my Auntie's face, her voice devoid of all emotion. The words seemed to drop from her lips unbidden.

"Two other seers had been called in to assist," Auntie continued. "They were trying to staunch the bleeding. The lifeless baby and afterbirth had already been taken away. I could clearly hear all of them singing the songs of healing. But the song of healing came from your mother's heart and not just through her mouth. All this I could see and hear, but I could feel no pain. Then I heard another faraway song and I felt compelled to seek its source. I began to fly very high, climbing strings and ropes of light hand over hand. And then I was moving into the earth, into a dark and watery void. Falling, falling, forever falling. As I fell, suddenly my mother's face appeared but she did not speak. She frowned at me with great disgust and then the very flesh of her face fell away to reveal a bare, white wolverine skull who began to speak with my mother's voice. Tatters of dry flesh and stringy hair were blowing in a gale of terrific force. Others of my shaman ancestors were there—some in the shape of people, some in the shape of their animal-guides, some only half-transformed. But all were in the shape of lions and hyenas and birds of prey. My mother began to shriek in a loud voice and they all began to claw at me and stab me with hunting spears in my head and body. The animal shapes began to tear at my flesh with claw and tooth."

Speechless and wide-eyed, I could not have spoken if I wanted to.

"They cut me up with flint blades, took out all my organs and spread them upon the ground as if I were a butchered animal upon the hunt. They stabbed me in my anus with a heavy spear shoving it all the way through my belly. The belly that had just given birth to a dead child. My guts spilled out on the ground and the screaming monsters began stretching my entrails out to the horizon in a long thin line. They ate my flesh raw. They drank my blood uncooked. They cut my joints, separating each bone and spreading them all out on a hide. They began counting the bones one-by-one. Suddenly the bug-eyed, slavering bony monster who was my mother said with a terrifying screech: *My daughters both resist the call of the Mother! But only one daughter is missing a bone and may not become a shaman. Count the bones! Count the bones! Count the bones!* The monster who was my mother continued to howl like a ravening wolf, laughing like a crazed hyena. Having counted the bones they all began to cackle: *All the bones are here! All the bones are here! All the bones are here! With all her bones complete, this daughter may now be nurtured as shaman!* The half-wolverine, half-human skeleton who was my mother shrieked so loud it hurt my ears. And just when I thought I could bear no more a beautiful dove appeared. She flapped and spread her wings to surround me with healing love. The pure white dove rode upon the back of a huge black aurochs bull. The great bull stamped his hoofs like thunder. He snorted and charged with his curving horns at the skeleton who was my mother, tossing her high into the air. Then the dove gathered all my scattered bones with her wings and, together, the dove and the aurochs carried me to the great Tree of Life. My animal-companions placed me gently into one of the many nests among the great tree's spreading branches. Then the aurochs-guide and the dove-guide killed a mammoth cow. They began feeding the red meat and red blood to my mother and the others who were still there circling about the base of the great tree that now sheltered me. Then my animal-guides began to feed the meat and blood of the mammoth to me. They lovingly wrapped the mammoth's skin about my bones and fed me with the mother mammoth's ample hump of white fat."

I blinked my eyes in horror, unable to say a single thing.

"Once they were covered with the mammoth's skin, all of my organs began to grow until I was whole once more. But my intestines and heart were no longer red. They and all my entrails had become white, clear-water crystal through which the sun shines and becomes the colors of the rainbow. It is just as the spirit-fire of the shaman shines through to bring light and healing to the People. With my new body of crystal and mammoth hide, I rode my soaring dove up, up and up and up until I reached again the World of Light, my still sleeping body surrounded by all the healers and seers."

She paused, returning from what was clearly a terrible ordeal. I said nothing in awe of my astonishing Auntie. Noticing the horrified expression on my face, Auntie reached out a comforting hand and placed it upon my own.

"There is a little more to tell and I will be finished, dear Little Bear," she said softly returning to herself.

"I cannot remember anything after that. But when I finally awoke, to the astonishment of all, I discovered I had been asleep for several days. I was still very ill and feverish. I was in great pain. Your dear mother cared for me for many days. But all the while I refused to sing the songs my guides had taught me as they nurtured me upon the shaman's Tree of Life. I stubbornly refused to accept my destiny as shaman and it was many more days of illness before I relented. Finally, I accepted what the Mother had called me to do and began singing the songs I heard while upon my shaman's journey. I recovered quickly after that and became the Grandfather's apprentice. When the season had turned and the time was right, I was initiated in the Great Cave as Seer of the Bear People. But I was already a shaman and forever more would be so in my heart and soul."

* * *

"But Auntie," I asked. "I have never had such visions or dreams. How can I be initiated in the Great Cave?"

"One becomes Shaman when they know that they have taken the shaman's journey, but one does not need to be a shaman to become a seer of the People, as I have said. Many have gifts of following the trails of animals. Some know all things with the unspoken knowledge of the Mother and some are skilled with herbs and setting bones. There are those who can see the glowing spirit-fires of a body but none of whom may ever have taken the solitary journey of the shaman into the timeless Place of Dreams. Those who have any of the gifts of a seer may enter the Cave to be initiated as Seer. It is as simple as that. You already have many seer's gifts and should the Mother call you to become a shaman during the seer's initiations, or even after that, no new initiations in the Cave are necessary. Do you see, Little Bear?"

"Yes, Auntie, I understand. But are you sure that my meager gifts are such that I could even be honored as a seer? The Grandfather only wants me to do something for him in the Great Cave, not because I have been called by the Mother to be seer or shaman. Why should I become seer if he only intends to get me into the Cave for his own purposes?" I questioned.

"I am sure the Grandfather sees many gifts in you, just as I do. He will take you into the Cave with the hope that the seer's initiation will also foster the shaman in you. In addition, as a woman you must also go through the initiations of a hunter. If you become the oldest seer, you may one day be given to lead the rites of the boys to become men as the Grandmother of the Rites. In the seer's initiations, if one has not yet been called as a shaman by the Mother in sickness, trance or through a dream, everything will be done to encourage the powers to come forth during the initiations. If they do come forth, that is good. If they do not, that is good as well. You will still be Seer and prepared to bless the People in your own way. The discovery of and communion with personal spirit-guides involves heavy trials to the body and deep revelations to the mind and heart during the initiations. And so will you be tested in the hunter's and the seer's initiations to bring forth your shaman guides, if they would come forth. Did none of your Sisters of the Moon Blood meet their spirit-guides in trance during your initiations in the Lodge of Red Spirits?" Auntie asked.

"Well, there was one girl among my age-mates who had some kind of vision during the rites. White Lynx had violent convulsions and made terrific screams that echoed throughout the Red Lodge. It terrified all of us. The seer-assistants present went to her to calm her and to help her adjust herself to the spirit-powers visiting her, or so we were told. Do you not remember, Auntie? You, yourself, took her away to another part of the Red Lodge of Women."

"Yes, I remember the girl. How could I not? I was your Mother of the Rites and you were told correctly, Little Bear."

"She lives alone with her father in our camp. Her mother is returned," I volunteered.

"Yes, Little Bear, I know. Since her elder brother joined his new wife's lodge, her father suffers from fevers and terrible coughing. He has not been able to hunt very often. I have treated him many times with White Lynx's assistance. Do you ever speak with each other? Are you friend or gift-giver to White Lynx?" my Auntie asked quietly, questioning me with one upturned eyebrow.

"No," I said straight out. "Although she is the only Moon Blood sister I have who is of the Middle Camp, she is strange and distracted. She smells bad too. She always seems to be talking to herself or to someone who is not there. And she doesn't seem to want to do anything with the other women of the camp. I have tried a few times to speak to her as an age-mate, but all she wants to talk about is becoming a hunter. She dresses and acts more and more like a man all the time. She doesn't even want to talk about the boys in the camp let alone about bringing a husband to her lodge. I decided not to spend any more time with her."

"Dear Little Bear," Auntie said looking directly into my eyes with a kind but exasperated expression. "There are no other women in her lodge. She is without a mother to dress her or comb her hair. How could she be expected to know how to act and dress like a woman with no other women in her lodge and without even her own Moon Blood sister to befriend her?"

"Yes, Auntie, I never thought of it that way," I said, suddenly feeling ashamed for shunning one of my own Sisters of the Moon Blood.

"Little Bear, do you know what it means to become Seer of the Bear People? Do you know you will have to learn compassion for all the People no matter how strange they may appear to you, no matter how fearful of you they are and no matter how much they might shun *you*? Or even how they smell?" she chided me.

"To become Seer, do you know that even as you give of yourself to help and heal it will mean you will become more apart from others than even your Moon Blood sister White Lynx?" she asked in a solemn tone that broached no disagreement.

At this moment, Auntie's seer's marks looked like tears running down from the saddest eyes I have ever seen. Certainly the saddest eyes I had ever seen in my Auntie. I suddenly got very serious.

"No, dear Auntie, I do not know any of these things. But I have already promised the Grandfather I will be prepared by dawn to be initiated in the Great Cave. He made me swear not to discuss it with anyone. What makes you so sad that I should be honored thus?"

After a long and thoughtful pause, my Auntie began to speak. "I am not sad for you, Little Bear. It is only fitting that you should receive so great an honor. But one of the first lessons you must learn as Seer of the Bear People is humility. The second lesson is compassion for all those who come to you for healing or guidance. If you are to become a river carrying the Mother's abundance to bless the People with your many gifts, you must be content not to stand above any of the People. Never treat anyone as if they are less than you in any way. And you will have to learn never to act as if you are special in any way. Otherwise, jealousy and fear of you may arise. When you are Seer, never try to stand above or place yourself above another."

"What do you mean by *fear of me*, dear Auntie? I am only a young woman. What would anyone have to fear from me?" I asked.

"Many people will be fearful and jealous enough of your position as Seer even when you do not deliberately hold yourself above them. You may not be Thrice Born, but just the fact of initiation as Seer will cause many to fear you. Many will pull away and avoid you no matter how young or pretty you are. Your mother and grandmother's experience should teach you that fear can easily turn to anger and discord. As a seer, you will be expected never to react in anger when you are mistreated or when your honor is diminished and belittled in any way by anyone. Even when your position goes un-respected by your own mother, your father or your husband and children, you must not react with anger. This might be difficult for you to do, Little Bear, because you are often very headstrong and insistent on having your own way in things. You are very much like your mother, One Doe," Auntie said, her little smile returning.

"You must also know that the All Mother will withdraw from you if you ever use your power to hold yourself above another or if you ever attempt to use your gifts to harm instead of heal, to curse instead of bless. Shamans and seers who are believed to be using their powers to harm others may be driven out of their own camps. In truth, that is not because the Mother has withdrawn from them, but because they have withdrawn from the Mother by speaking curses instead of blessings into her all-hearing ears. When you say, 'I do not want to be hungry,' the Mother only hears the word *hungry* and so gives back to you more hunger. When you say, 'I do not want to be cursed,' the Mother only hears the word *cursed* and returns that to you. Do you understand, my Dear One?"

I remembered my own fearful reaction to the Grandfather's sudden appearance in my mother's lodge and I immediately saw the truth in her words.

"Yes, Auntie, I understand. I will learn to be humble and speak only abundance into the Mother's ear if you will continue to instruct me in the ways of a Seer of the Bear People," I said with growing conviction.

Then Auntie continued, "Yes, my beloved niece, I will be most pleased to continue your training as a healer. Just remember, while the seers and shamans may live among the People, and do all the things that the People do, we are not the same as others. The Mother calls us to do great works and bring healing among the People, but you must always be humble in this. As Seer, you must also realize you have spirit-powers others do not have, so always honor yourself and know the Mother blesses the whole People because of and through you. As your skill and knowledge increases and you become more and more aware of the power of your thoughts and words and songs, you will learn, like every seer, to be more careful of what you say and think than those who have not learned the ways of the seers and shamans. The more power you see your words as having, the more power will your words come to have to bless and heal those who do not realize this power of the All Mother is within all things. It is always within those you are healing, though they may not know it. This is a difficult lesson for all of us to learn because we are exactly like everyone else and have the same joys and pains as anyone."

"Auntie, why was I so frightened when the Grandfather first appeared, but when he had finished speaking with me I felt he was a kindly old man and not so scary after all? Why was that so?" I asked.

"People are always afraid of what they do not understand, Little Bear. When our spirit-messengers are invited to come forth to heal and bless or when we are in the company of someone like the Grandfather who descends into the Abyss to save a sickened soul and bring it back to the World of Light, the People hold themselves apart from such great power because they do not understand it. The powers and spirit-fire of the Unseen can frighten the People with their brightness because it is not what they know and do not understand it. The awesome powers the People see shining from us can lead many to pull away from us out of fear. They do not understand that the same powers lie dormant within themselves. They do not know it is they who heal themselves and not our songs, our suckings or massagings. It is not our herbs, our amulets or our potions and teas that heal but the Mother within each that does the healing. This is the greatest of all the secrets of seers and shamans," she explained carefully.

"Little Bear, as Seer, what you must learn is that the power of the seers and shamans comes from our practiced ability to throw ourselves into the trance at will in order to bless the People. With initiation and training, we are never victims of the trance to be tossed about and terrified by the visions and dreams that may come. Whatever dreams and visions appear to us, we know they are just that—dreams, visions and illusions of the Place of Dreams. Our own souls decide what will happen and what we shall see within the dream. And with this knowing, all fear of the illusions before us will dissipate like fog before the morning sun. By our sounding of the hoop drum, singing the healing song, taking the trance plants or doing the dance, we send our souls into the Dreamland of the Abyss and we call forth our companion-spirits to assist us and guide us in our flights and battles of healing and blessing. With practice, seers and shamans command the dream-trance as a bird commands the air in its flight. We know that we must not fear the dreams and visions that come forth from our souls just because the People cannot understand them."

"But Auntie, if we are healing and doing good how can the People fear us," I asked, still having difficulty grasping her teachings.

"Little Bear, here is a great secret: it is not the darkness that the good and honest People fear the most, it is the brilliance of the spirit-fire within that causes many to draw back and reject us. And I am sorry to say, some of those who have been given the wisdom of the seers will even pull back from the spirit-light that comes through as we do the work of the Mother. But when the Mother calls, we must answer. We must take that life-path even though walking it changes everything, just as it changed everything between your mother and me ... as much as I desired it to be otherwise. If your heart tells you that you have been called by the Mother to the way of the seers, then you must choose the path of your soul's change and transformation. You will soon learn that change is more fearsome than almost anything else in life, my dear Little Bear. Many are so frightened of the change that the exercise of our power brings, our lives as seers will be lived apart from others even when we have husbands and children. Remember your grandmother in this. And remember, too, the fear hidden deep within my soul of my own mother which the shaman's journey revealed to me. Except for our seer's marks, we appear to be like any one of the People, but we are not," she said, sad longing filling her quavering voice.

Then Auntie said something that shook me to the bone. "Dearest One, I see your gifts of making lines, of telling the stories of our People as you make the lines: how the ibex got his marvelous horns, how the bison took a woman to wife and all the other stories of the People we love. I see how you love to make spirit-images and can do these things so easily and with such beauty and spirit-power. That tells me they are the Mother's spirit-gifts of the heart. This *is* the Mother calling you to her service even though you have not been called to make the shaman's descent into the Abyss. I see it is so, Little Bear my Beloved, and full awareness of this in your own heart, together with all you have learned of herbs and healing potions and helping the mothers of the People to bring forth new life will make of you a great shaman-of-healing. This will be so whether you are guided by the Mother in the shape of an animal-companion or not. Even now I see the boiling yellow life-fire of a shaman-of-healing surrounding you. You must accept this visitation of the Mother and do exactly as the Grandfather tells you, but *only* if it is what is truly in your heart. Do not do this thing for any other reason or for any other person. If you hear the Mother's voice calling you to this great undertaking, then it is very good. Go with the Grandfather and learn all he has to teach about the Great Cave and the spirit-powers. You should know that he tells the seers and shamans he will not be with us for many more seasons before he returns to the Mother. The Grandfather is very anxious to pass his wisdom on to me, and now to you, before it is too late," she concluded.

"Yes, Auntie, I can see the wisdom of your words. But why does that strange old man want me not to tell anyone about this?" I asked innocently.

"Little Bear, you must always speak of the Grandfather with great respect. *The Grandfather* is the most honored one of the People and holds that respected title as the eldest shaman of the Bear-kin. He is the most respected one of we Bear-kin, who are the Guardians of the All Mother's Cave, and of all the Nine Kin. You must always honor him with every word and deed for he truly is Thrice Born and the most powerful shaman of the People. Only seers and shamans know his secret name and we never call him 'old man' even behind his back or out of his hearing. He is a most wise, kind and powerful shaman and he will teach you well and instruct you as no other. Honor and respect him as you would the All Mother herself. He owns all the wisdom of the Ancients. He will train you well, and with kindness and patience. It is good you do not fear him as so many do, otherwise his lessons would be far more difficult to learn."

Suddenly ashamed of my disrespect, I said, "Thank you, Auntie. I will do as you ask out of respect for you and the Grandfather. I would not have agreed to go into the Cave and become a seer if I were afraid of the Grandfather," I lied, knowing full-well how terrified I was of this old man. "But why must this all be kept so secret?"

"Because that is the way of the holy knowledge of seers and shamans," Auntie replied. "You should know the Grandfather has given all the seers of the Bear People his dream and we all agree it is a true vision. We also agree your quest must be carried out within the Great Cave, but only if you freely choose the life of One Who Sees because you will do what no other Seer of the Bear People has ever done. Regardless of your decision you must keep the vow of secrecy, which you have surely taken, because respect for the All Mother demands it. If you are to willingly take on this burden, your sworn silence about what you will do within the deepest chamber of the Cave will forever keep you apart from the People—including the husband you are sure to have one day. Choose with the unspoken feelings of your liver *and* with the waking thoughts of your head before you agree to go with the Grandfather. If you listen to both head and liver, you will be choosing with your heart and that is the only voice to which you should pay heed in this matter—certainly not to me or the Grandfather. The small voice of the heart *is* the Mother's Voice speaking to you and only to you. Now is the time to choose the path of your life, so consider well this decision. Know that once you set your feet upon this path there is no turning back, not in this world or in all the worlds to come."

* * *

Now I was becoming very nervous, indeed, and the heaviness of my decision began to weigh down upon me like a heavy pack. As I pondered this choice, other questions began to well-up like bubbles in a spring.

"Is this why the Grandfather lives alone? Without any wife or children to care for him?" I asked cautiously.

"Only in part," Auntie began. "The Grandfather's terrible story is never told by any of the People and he will never speak of it. But yes, he has lived alone ever since the day we do not speak of for fear it will bring the same tragedy upon the People again." Auntie's brow began to wrinkle in pained creases.

"Whatever do you mean, dear Auntie?" I asked, growing more and more alarmed by the moment.

"I will tell you the story, but you must never allow the Grandfather to know that I have done so. Nor should you discuss his story with anyone without the best and highest of reasons. Will you agree?" she said with a lift of both eyebrows.

I probably shouldn't have agreed to this, but I *had* to hear the story, especially if I was expected to go alone into the Great Cave with this old vulture.

"Yes, Auntie, I agree," I said with just a little too much eagerness to settle my destiny as Seer of the Bear People.

"Very well," she began. "The Grandfather was a powerful shaman-of-the-hunt who always knew where the herds would be and which direction the animals were going. He was always selected by the men as Leader of the Hunt and so entitled to the leader's extra share in the division. Some say he could even put a trance on the animals that were to give themselves to the hunters—the easier to return them to the Mother with the least amount of suffering. It was because of his great gifts and obvious closeness to the spirit-powers that he could never find any woman brave or big-hearted enough to mate with him and take him to her mother's lodge. He was already a mature man when your own grandmother's youngest sister loved him. She asked her mother—your famous shaman-grandmother—to arrange the match without ever having joined with him in sex. You can probably guess how elated your grandmother was that such an honored and powerful shaman-of-the-hunt would become mate to her own younger sister and thus become one of the Uncles of the Middle Camp. But none of that mattered to your great aunt. She willingly married the Grandfather because she alone had courage enough to become wife to so powerful a shaman—a shaman said to be able to command the winter storms."

"Can he *really* do that," I questioned rudely.

"Perhaps," Auntie replied, her familiar smile returning. "It was enough that the People believed he could command a storm to make everyone fear and avoid him except when they needed his gifts in the hunt. Every shaman has a few quick-finger tricks or practiced knowledge to awe the resentful and to teach a beneficial respect for the shamans among the good and honest people. Perhaps that is what the Grandfather did with his knowledge of storms upon the Plain. Anyway, your grandmother's little sister was young and strong and very beautiful. And like you, she refused all the hunters who asked to become her husband for several seasons after she became a woman. I can only suppose it was the dangerous excitement of mating with a man so much older than she and a man with such wide fame and prestige that drew her to him. No one ever doubted the heart-love that grew between them. They joined and quickly had a child—a daughter. Your grandmother and her aged mother, still living in the World of Light at the time, were both so pleased with the marriage to such a great shaman-of-the-hunt and the birth of a daughter that a new lodge was made for them in the midst of the Middle Camp."

Auntie paused, took a long deep breath, rubbed her hand a few times across her forehead as if her head ached and continued her story.

"A few seasons on, at the end of one particular winter season, the food stores began to run low. All the men left the camps for a great hunt on the Plain of the Mammoth Mother, just as our hunters did this very morning. Then, as now, few grown men or even older boys remained in the camp. Your brother, Little Ibex, has gone with the men even though he has not yet been initiated as a hunter, has he not?" she asked.

Breathless, I nodded and she continued.

"Only one shaman of full seasons remained in the Middle Camp, but he was mad from knowing too many spirit-powers at the same time. He lodged in the Shelter of the Solitaries and wore only ragged, tattered skins for clothing. He had dirty, matted hair and yelled at a myriad of unseen powers which tormented him constantly. Because of his disquiet and the chaos within his soul, the hunters would not allow him to go out with them—even as a bearer. The People called him 'shaman' because he fell in ecstatic convulsions and was a seer of spirit-powers. But his gifts could never bless the People."

I was already in a half-trance with her increasingly somber tone and did not dare interrupt. I could hardly breathe as she went on with the tale.

"Only days before the hunters were to have returned from the Plain laden with meat and hides, in a fit of jealous rage at all the Grandfather had—a beautiful wife, a daughter, the respect of the Nine Kin, a love-filled lodge with abundant bison robes, full storage pits and all we accept as the Mother's abundance without ever thinking about it—the madman burst into the Grandfather's lodge with the strength of the many powers struggling within him. He smashed the child's head upon the hearth stones and choked my beautiful Auntie, your grandmother's youngest sister, to death before anyone could come to her aid. By the time the women, children and old men of the Middle Camp were roused by the noise and came to her lodge, the mad shaman was raping her lifeless body."

In wide-eyed surprise I prodded Auntie to tell more of the tale because she had stopped speaking. "What happened next, my dear Auntie?" I asked in a whisper when I could tell she didn't want to go on.

And go on she did. "The whole camp began screaming and weeping and beating the madman with sticks to drive him out of the camp. No one ever saw him again—a lone man, even a great hunter, is a dead man without his kin and hunter-companions. But the terrible damage to the whole of the Bear People had already been done."

My drop-jawed astonishment did not even cause Auntie to look up as she stared into the glowing hearth reliving the entire story. I did not dare interrupt her to ask how old she had been at the time. From the telling of it, I knew she had seen it and had been there.

After another long pause she continued. "By the time the Grandfather and the hunters returned, the whole Middle Camp was in full mourning. Each lodge had already begun performing ceremonies for cleansing and the restoration of harmony. Hearing the clamor of the drums, flutes and the singing from as far away as the Eye, the hunters all must have known something was very wrong in the camp. When the Grandfather reached his lodge, he found within the two bodies shrouded in bison robes awaiting his return. The Grandfather howled like the wounded wolf he was ... such a terrible sound no one had ever heard before. He stayed inside the lodge where his pitiful young wife and little daughter lay dead and closed the flap to one and all. His cries of grief and desolation continued for a very long time and not even your shaman-grandmother dared approach. Days passed without the usual rites for those who have returned to the Mother. Finally, the Grandfather emerged from the lodge completely naked except for his otter-skull necklace."

Auntie took another long pause, then continued.

"The pine branches and rush mats, all the furs, skins, clothing, baskets, sleeping platforms, rush walls, and the bent saplings of the roof covered with bark were ablaze. The Grandfather sat upon the ground in a deathlike trance before the burning lodge. He stared with dry red eyes while the fire collapsed the roof, consumed the walls and the flames turned everything into ashes. No one dared to approach a shaman in such a state—not even your grandmother. When the last ember had died, the Grandfather arose and without a single word climbed the path to the Great Cave. He did not emerge for several days. When he did, he walked along the cliff-edge to the Shelter of the Solitaries and he has been there ever since. The Grandfather never again was acclaimed as Leader of the Hunt. In fact, he never again went out upon another hunt or killed another animal—to this day."

A long, sad silence followed. Neither of us spoke until I asked, "What happened to the burned ones in the lodge?"

On the verge of tears, a long sigh issued from my Auntie's lips. "While the Grandfather hid away in the Cave, the whole Bear-kin gathered at the burned-out lodge to sing the farewell songs of return with drums and flutes. All three camps of the Bear-kin gathered in a dance circle around the ashes. You know that our celebrations of one's return to the Mother are happy and joyous. The Rites of the Return are always full of gratitude for those gone from us. They are full of forgiveness and comfort for those remaining. And so it had to be with those two and for the madman and his grieving family as well. Always the songs of return are songs of the good things each person did while they were alive—including the poor mad shaman. You do not know how very difficult it was to do so under such tragic and unhappy circumstances."

"Yes, Auntie, I can only imagine. It must have been terrible for everyone," I volunteered.

I tried hard to put myself in her place on that awful day so long ago. I also found myself putting myself into the Grandfather's boots. He was, after all, just a man like any other with all the hopes and fears, loves and losses, happiness and suffering of any other man. My respect and love for him grew to fill me up, no more space for fear of him to hide within my heart.

"Yes, Little Bear. It was even more terrible than you could dream in a nightmare. There were no bodies to wash and lead by the hand to the Place of Return as a mother leads her children. There were no pieces of liver to share among close kin. There were no clothes in which to impersonate the departed with funny skits of the Trickster. The attempt to do the pantomimes with borrowed clothing only left everyone more heartbroken. So, after the remembering and the Celebration of the Returned had been completed, the seers went into the ashes to find whatever remained of my beloved aunt and her infant daughter. They carried the burned bones wrapped in the life-renewing skin of Bison Mother from the burned lodge. They took them to the River for their Return. But in truth, the Bear-kin sent four souls back to the Mother that day because the Grandfather was never the same man after that. The place in the camp where their lodge once stood has never been trod upon again."

After another long and thoughtful silence I asked, "Is that the forbidden, unclean place in the midst of the camp? Where the grass and brush grows tall because it is never walked upon?"

"Yes, Dear One," she said sadly.

"Auntie," I ventured cautiously. "I have one question for you about the mad shaman."

"Yes, Dear One, ask what you will," she said simply.

"How is it that one who takes the shaman's journey returns to bless the People and another is mad and brings such tragedy and sorrow to the People?"

"That is because the shaman's journey to the depths of their own souls is unique for each one who takes that journey. What leads one shaman to madness and another to union with the Mother is taking the journey and believing the apparitions and monsters that appear are real and are to be joined with in the heart. I have said that a true shaman commands the trance and knows that the dreams and visions that come are but illusions coming forth from within one's own soul. In the trance, we are to know that the chimeras and creatures that appear to us are messengers of the All Mother, the Source of all there is, including these creatures who are to become our guides. We do not join with them in order to take on their powers. Instead, we are to join with the Mother and know that we are one with the All Mother. To join with the animal-guides that may come in the dream is to mistake the Source for the creature and in that lies madness when the shaman returns to the World of Light. Can you understand that, Dear One? For if you can, when and if you take the shaman's journey you will become master of the trance and not its victim."

"Yes, Auntie. I will think on this. I begin to understand what you are saying."

"And there is one more thing you should know before you choose to embark on this journey into the Great Cave with the Grandfather."

"What could that be, dear Auntie?" I asked, afraid of the answer.

"I told you that you looked like the Grandfather's young wife, your own great-aunt. What I did not tell you is that she also famously possessed the right eye of Lion Mother, just as you do. The darkness of the Great Cave may not reveal your lion's eye to the Grandfather. But if he does become aware of it, you should be prepared for how he might react. Go now and think on these things I have told you and prepare yourself to enter the Great Cave tomorrow if that is your choice. One last piece of advice I have for you, Dear One. Never think that because the unseen powers favor you and speak to you and heal through you that you are above and apart from all the suffering and the pain of life that the service of the All Mother will bring."

"Yes, Dear Auntie and thank you. I will remember all you have told me," I answered, still astonished by all I had heard.

My mind raced to sort it all out. I held Auntie's hands in mine and looked into her eyes for a long moment but she had nothing else to say.

Chapter 1. *In My Mother's Lodge*

I returned to my mother's lodge in stunned silence to prepare for my initiation as Seer of the People of the Bear Mother.

I have made my choice.

CHAPTER 2.
MAKING A SHAMAN

MY MOTHER SHOOK ME AWAKE with a steady rocking motion long before the first light of dawn. The day before had been so full of excitement and emotion that I had collapsed and slept the long, dreamless sleep of a hibernating bear. For just one moment I did not know where I was. Then I remembered.

"No food for you this morning," she said matter-of-factly.

My mother sat on the sleeping platform next to me, her legs hanging over the edge.

"Even if the hunters had not taken all of the traveling cakes, the Grandfather said you may not have any food—only a little water. But you should know that from your own initiation as a woman," she chattered on still trying to wake me.

My mother never failed to irritate me by telling me things I already know And then repeating them again! But as she went on and on with more and more things I already knew, I heard the tension and nervousness in her voice she could not hide with idle chatter. Still rubbing my sleepy eyes, I pulled my reluctant self up and out of the sleeping furs. Soon we both fell silent as she began to pack my leather shoulder bag with all the things the Grandfather had instructed my mother to prepare for me.

My bag was packed with bone containers of red and yellow ochre powder and some fully burned chunks of charcoal that could be ground into powder along with a few partially burned sticks of charcoal still hard enough to sharpen as pencils. I would draw narrow guidelines with the pencils. A flat piece of rock with a shallow depression—to grind charcoal and mix paints with water or oil—along with its small round grinding stone were wrapped together and packed next. Everything that was to go into my satchel was separately wrapped in soft fur or flax cloth. I pushed a ball of fire-making tinder into the satchel. Next, my mother handed me a few carrots and turnips from what remained in the root storage pit. I was touched to see that she had also taken the trouble to dig a few fresh cattail roots for me. All the roots were wrapped together in a piece of bark paper and packed away in the rapidly filling bag. These few roots were the only food the Grandfather would allow me to take into the Cave.

Next, the All Mother's Ochre was brought out. A generous dollop had been spooned onto a piece of stiff bark paper then folded into a packet and tied securely with a braided hemp cord. The packet of Mother-ochre had been prepared by Auntie and brought to our lodge the night before. As the eldest female seer of the Bear-kin, Auntie holds the blocks of All Mother's Ochre in her exclusive keeping.

"Have you ever seen Auntie preparing the Mother-ochre?" I asked, breaking the silence.

I already knew what my mother's answer would be. I had been shown how to prepare it more than once by Auntie but I knew my mother never had, not being a seer and all. Having heard all my family's secrets, I began to understand why she avoided all things having to do with seers and shamans.

"No, I have not," she replied with more than a hint of indignation. "Only seers may be involved in such things. Only the most honored female shaman may prepare and stand guardian over this special ochre bursting with the Mother's life-force," she said, gently and reverently handing me the packet.

She may have hated living the life of the seers and shamans, but she certainly respected them, however grudgingly.

"It is only used in the girl's Moon Blood rites and in the initiation of seers," she continued, again restating what I already knew.

I had always wondered why Auntie would share such a powerful secret with me. Several times she had shown me how the All Mother's Ochre was made.

Once she had said to me, "You have the eye of the lion powers, Little Bear. With that eye you may be shown all the secrets," leaving me to wonder exactly what she meant.

Now I begin to understand.

Then, as now, I have no idea what Auntie is talking about— the eye of the lion-powers? But sharing such a powerful secret with the one person I loved the most excited me. Only now had all the broken pieces begun to come together.

"The All Mother-ochre is made from newly gathered red clay of the darkest, blood-red hue. Ground to a fine powder, it is moistened with the urine of women in their moon-blood and with their very moon-blood. It is formed into a rod shaped like a man's penis and then dried in the sun," Auntie had explained to me.

Auntie keeps the reddish-brown clay block carefully wrapped in a finely tanned piece of delicate reindeer skin—the same kind of skin from which we make our softest, finest clothing. Only chamois skin is softer.

"Little Bear," Auntie had said the first time she showed me the red block as long as my forearm. "You must learn how to prepare the Mother-ochre should you ever become the Grandmother of the Nine Kin after I return to the Mother."

At the time, I thought it terribly odd Auntie would be speaking to me of being a seer and of her returning to the Mother. It does not seem so odd now, especially after learning about the right eye of the Lion Mother I have possessed from birth.

"See the three-cornered sign of the All Mother's vulva inscribed on the top of the block?" she had whispered reverently as she peeled back the last fold to reveal the darkest red ocher I had ever seen.

It was the color, almost, of dried blood.

"The block is inscribed with these three signs shaped like a woman's three-cornered pubic area. It is marked thus so that you will *never* use this great power of the All Mother for anything except that for which it is made. Do you understand, Little Bear?"

As I had answered, "Yes, Auntie," she removed the longest, whitest, most finely made flint blade I had ever seen from alongside the red shaft. She began to carefully shave pieces off the back end of the sun-dried block. It *did* smell faintly of urine. I knew she was taking off pieces from the "back end" because the head of the penis would be the last of the block to be shaved off. The shaved pieces were then placed in her grinding stone—deeply grooved from long use—to be reground into a fine powder. Using one of the smooth black stones from the river as her grinder, she carefully worked the red chunks and shavings into the finest powder to which she added small amounts of tallow from an oil horn marked with the lines of the Mammoth Mother of Abundance.

"This is the holy oil of Mammoth Mother respectfully rendered from the fat of mammoths who have given themselves to the Nine Kin," she explained as she worked the oil and red powder into a smooth paste.

"Like the All Mother-ochre, this special oil is used for initiations and for healing. Use it sparingly as Mammoth Mother does not often give herself to the hunters of the Bear-kin," she had instructed further.

It is from my Auntie that I have learned to grind the different ochres, chalks, black-stones and charcoals into fine powders and how to mix them with water, spit or oil for different uses. I had not seen my Auntie prepare this very packet of All Mother's Ochre, but I could imagine her grinding and mixing just enough for my initiation on this very dawn. I knew she would have worked it into paint as smooth as mink fur. She would have poured and pushed the paint from the mixing stone into the packet with her fingers. The hemp cords binding the packet are still stained red with this special ochre from her fingers as she tied the knots.

"Take these cedar bark lamp wicks with you too, my Daughter," One Doe suggested helpfully as she enfolded them with another piece of bark-paper. "The Grandfather said he would provide the wicks and torches. But he is getting old and might forget. Now we should complete the rite of washing."

"Yes, Mother," I said compliantly.

She began to help me out of the flax-cloth sleeping clothes I was still wearing leaving me naked as a new baby. I sat cross-legged in the seat of honor before the hearth while my mother took a few cooking stones from the fire with wooden tongs and dropped them one by one into a large cooking basket half-filled with water. Each stone hissed in protest as it touched and then disappeared into the cold liquid. As the ceremonial cleansing water heated, she brought out my best whitened doeskins from the finely woven storage basket where they were kept beneath my sleeping platform. I would wear them on this special day as I would someday wear them at my marriage.

"Come, stand up and let me brush your hair while the water is heating," she said with complete resignation to the path I was setting my feet upon.

Standing behind me, my mother began to comb out my long, dark brown hair. After a few strokes of the combing thorn followed by her smoothing hand, in a quavering voice filled with deep emotion she said quietly, "I knew this day would come. I have feared it all my life. Now my only daughter will be taken from me in spite of everything I have done to prevent it."

"No, Mother," I protested gently. "I will always be your daughter. Nothing can change that. Even when I marry, I will be the daughter of your hearth and I will bring my husband to be the son of your hearth."

"That is where you are wrong, Little Bear, my Dearest One. We wash the newborns receiving their names and we wash those who are marrying and we wash those who have returned to the Mother. From birth to the Return they will always be our sons, our daughters, our parents, our friends. Nothing ever changes that— we will always call them husband, father, son or daughter. But when you come out of the Cave you will no longer be One Doe's daughter. You will be Seer of the Bear People. Forever more, I will call you 'Sister' out of respect for what you have become.

"Oh Mama, don't say such things. I will still be your daughter. I will always be your daughter," I said trying to comfort her.

"No, Little Bear, you will no longer be my daughter with the duties and respect a daughter owes her mother. You will have become a peer and an equal as if we had been initiated together as age-mates and Moon Blood sisters. You will have a new seer's name that I will never know. I will never speak the name Little

Bear again." I knew without turning around that her tears were flowing like rain.

"I hated it when my shaman-mother abandoned her children. I hated it when my younger sister became shaman and was taken from me. And now that you have chosen this path I will hate it that you have been taken from me too," she whispered.

I turned to see the welling tears glistening like tiny yellow stars in the flickering hearth light. Unable to bear it, I turned around again so that I would not begin weeping. I stared straight ahead toward the lodge entrance trying to push down the feelings of my liver and heart.

"Yes, Mother, I know what you are saying," trying to comfort her and to keep myself from crying. "Auntie has told me the story of your life in your shaman-mother's lodge. But no matter what comes, I will always be your daughter in my heart. I will always love you and respect you. Will that be enough?" I asked with pleading in my voice.

She stopped combing and stroking my hair and turned me around by my shoulders to look into my eyes. "Yes, Little Bear, my beloved daughter. I love you and that will be enough," she replied with resignation for what I was about to do.

Still gazing into my eyes she continued. "It was enough for me to love your Auntie and your Auntie me as true sisters to this day. It would have been enough if your grandmother had ever given any care to the children she left to grow up by themselves without her guidance and love. It would have been enough if she had ever said the words I have said to you. It would have been enough," she said, with a bitterness I could not understand.

She hugged me, pressed her lips against both my cheeks. She then pressed her forehead to mine with great tenderness, eyes glistening with tears about to flow over again.

Turning toward the warming water and to practicalities she said, "The rinsing water is warm enough. For one last time, let me bathe you as I did when you were a little daughter cradled in my arms."

My mother dipped a small bowl of warm water from the heating basket and handed it to me so I could begin squeezing and dipping dried soap flowers into it to make fragrant foam. As she began dipping a small piece of chamois skin into the bowl of soap flowers, I felt small again as if I really were a tiny baby. My liver and heart were full of many emotions as my mother began wiping my body with the warm, cleansing water. She dipped another piece of chamois skin into the warmed water to rinse the flowery film from my arms, legs, back, breasts and belly.

When she had almost finished she said, "Lift your hair so I can rinse your back and underarms," all emotion in her voice now gone.

The washing and rinsing completed, it was time for her to help me dress. She helped me loop and tie the straps of a fine, absorbent chamois loinskin around my waist and between my legs. Then she held up the pure white, knee-length tunic so I could put my head through the neck opening and my arms into the long, soft sleeves. This was my most beautiful dress, made by my mother from the softest, whitened reindeer leather. The dress was as supple and smooth as chamois, sewn only with unmarked and unscarred doeskins. Buckskins often have many scars and blemishes because the males fight each other with their antlers at the time of mating. And this dress had been further whitened with chalk after bleaching making it truly the whitest, most beautiful dress I ever could have imagined.

My mother has a gift for making fine leathers. Her love of working with skins and furs shows in the beauty of all the clothes she makes. But she does not like the difficult, smelly work of making the white and finely dyed hides. She passes off this nasty work to the rest of us whenever she can. The clay-lined urine basket placed near the latrine always has enough old sour piss sloshing in it to strip the hair and whiten the hides she chooses to make into fine clothing. Her gift-givers and close kin value her leathers above all other gifts. But as I said, it usually falls to me or my brothers to scoop the rotting, foul-smelling stuff into the watertight, clay-lined baskets she uses to soak the carefully selected hides that would be transformed as if by magic into cloud white leather as soft as rabbit fur.

My younger brothers both seem to actually enjoy treading the soaking skins with their bare feet, squealing and splashing the acrid liquid all over the place as if it were some kind of game. The stench makes my head swirl in circles, so I am glad to have younger brothers when it comes time to bleach a skin. The skins my mother chooses to dye dark brown with steeped nutshell coloring, yellow or red with different shades of ochre and ground up black-stones for black leathers, are always bleached with urine first. Then they are scrubbed with ash-water soap to remove all the oily, fatty parts before they are soaked or rubbed with the coloring. She taught me this would ensure that the colors will always come out rich and even.

When it is abundant, my mother always saves poor quality fat to make the ash-water soap so that she always has enough on hand to clean dirty, oily skins and furs of all kinds. My mother may not have learned to be a healer but the clothing she makes is highly prized by all her kin, friends and gift-givers. She offers the gift of her leathers and clothing as if she is making a song or chanting the healing words—I see that now. Along with my father's beautifully made flints, our family's friends and gift-givers are always extremely pleased with the presents they receive from us because they are made and given from my mother's and my father's hearts as well as from their skilled hands.

Of course, all I know of making clothing I have learned from my mother. Now I am putting on a tunic I had helped her make with my own hands. My mother cut this dress to fit my form closely around the chest and hips upon my request. The neck has a three-corner opening running past the bottom of my breasts. If I had any bigger breasts they would bulge through the cut and I probably would have to add some laces to hold everything in. I often wish I had bigger breasts—the better to attract and please the men. But I have my mother's small breasts as well as her dark brown hair and brown eyes flecked with yellow and red. The dress was put over my head and we shifted it back and forth to pull the top into place. My breasts were pushed up and together and clearly showed through the three-cornered neck hole.

I was just thinking how my breasts must have grown since I last wore the dress—it is definitely much tighter than I remember it—when my mother said, "Your breasts are growing Little Bear. And your hips are getting wider! The top is now tight enough to give you a very pretty woman's cleavage too. We may have to alter

59

the tunic if you get any bigger before you do the marriage dance with a husband," she said, lightening the mood.

I smiled as she rambled on absentmindedly about the dress, my growing breasts and continued to adjust the beautiful tunic into place over my newly discovered woman's curves. My mother is considered to be beautiful of face. Even though she is very strong, she is rather slight in her body. My father has given me his height, I think, though not his light brown hair and pale, sky-blue eyes. I am taller than my mother—and heavier too—or so it seems. It is clear my breasts are growing to match the rest of my body and this long tunic will definitely have to be altered—especially if these breasts or hips get any larger!

But I love this simple white dress just the way it is with its red-painted zigzags across the front beneath the bust, around the edges of each sleeve and the bottom of the skirt. I have always thought the most unusual and beautiful part of the dress is the fringe made of long mammoth hairs running up the back of each sleeve and across the upper back. The braided mammoth hair, from which the fringe hangs ingeniously, covers seams of fine sinew.

The Great Ones are seen in many different shades from almost white to reddish brown to a dark brown that is almost black. My mother tells me this mammoth-hair fringe and the hair that makes the apron-style, long fringed belt, was specially selected to match the color of our reddish-brown eyes. None of my brothers have brown eyes. Only my mother and I do. If ever I find a husband to bring to my mother's lodge, I will be married in this dress. Then I will decorate it to my own taste with whatever shells, beads or quills I can acquire. But today, this will be the simple white doeskin dress of my initiation as Seer of the Bear People.

"The paths are so muddy. I hate to get my doeskin boots dirty," I complained.

I looked about for the fine foot coverings anyway, discovered them already put out for me on the sleeping platform, and sat down to slide them on. I tied the drawstrings at the top of each boot that reached almost to my knees.

"Never mind that," she said matter-of-factly. "You will only be wearing the boots as far as the Shelter of the Solitaries and the mud on the trail is still frozen this morning. Speaking of foot coverings, I have made a new pair of grass sandals for you as the Grandfather required."

The sandals, made of soft plaited grass were brought out and stuffed into my bag.

"Let me fix your hair, Dear One," she said softly as if I were just a little girl.

I turned around so she could pull my almost waist-length hair out of the back of the tunic. Pulling out my thick, long hair actually made the top fit a lot more comfortably. But those growing breasts would still make alterations necessary one day, I am sure of that.

My mother combed my hair one more time and tied it in a horse tail with a short lace of red leather. "There is one last item you will need—your woman's necklace," she said.

My mother lifted the bone and tooth necklace over my head. She pulled the horse tail out of the loop so that the necklace settled around my neck reaching almost past my bosoms that were still crowding out of the neck hole. The necklace was the very one she had given me when I became a woman in the Great Cave, six or was it seven, seasons ago?

* * *

Bathed and dressed in my finest clothing, wearing my best boots and ornaments, I was ready to go. Running through my head the list of things I would need, I remembered one more item and asked, "What about the lamp?"

"I haven't forgotten it," she comforted. "The Grandfather has requested you bring embers from our hearth fire and that they be carried to the Great Cave in the lamp," she explained. She handed me the stone lamp wrapped in a piece of soft rabbit fur.

The lamp is my father's most valued possession and was already an ancient lamp used by generations of hunters when it was given to him by his father. This oil lamp was only used for special occasions like entering the Great Cave or for smoking the hemp in council. Other, more ordinary lamps are used for lighting our lodges or lighting our feet to the latrines at night. As an initiated seer I would possess such a lamp of my own one day. But as a hunter, my youngest brother will be the most likely one of my mother's lodge to possess this lamp when my father returns to the

Mother. That is, unless my father keeps the lamp when my brothers marry and leave our mother's lodge. In that event, I might still be the one to receive my father's most unusual and beautiful lamp—we shall see in good time. Every lodge has at least one such special lamp. But in our Middle Camp, more than one can often be found. That is because the Bear-kin have become famous for the fine lamps made from the smooth, flat river stones that come from the rapids below the Eye.

This lamp of my father is beautiful and very unusual. It was not made from a river rock but from a yellowish-brown stone my father says can only be found far up our River beyond, even, the camps of his Ibex-kin. It is extraordinary because of the large bump on one side that has been smoothed and polished into a handle. My father's lamp can be held by the handle-bump without your thumb slipping into the oil. The flat bottom of the lamp is also exceptional because it is engraved with a beautiful ibex ram, his long, gracefully curving horns arching all the way over his back. The horns on the lamp are just like the unusually long pair of huge ibex horns my father has placed over the entrance to my mother's lodge.

I say "unusual" because my father's personal guide is not the ibex. It is the raven. The most common outside decoration for a lodge is the sign of the animal-guide of the Uncle of the Lodge. I was sure the ibex was not his animal-companion because I had once asked my father about the ibex on the lamp. Of course, that was before I learned of my stubborn mother and her headstrong marriage to this man of the Ibex-kin who is my father, Roe Bear.

"My father possessed this lamp before me," he had told me in answer to my question. "I married your mother from the Ibex-kin and upon my coming to the Bear-kin and your mother's lodge, my father wanted me to remember whence I had come. My father had the ibex engraved into the base of his special lamp to forever remind me."

"But my brother Big Ibex did not engrave a bear on his lamp when he married away to another camp? How does one decide?" I had asked.

"When a new lamp is made or given as a gift, we inscribe our animal-guide, sometimes our first kill, upon them if that is the hunter's desire. We can make our kin signs or we can leave them without marks—it is completely the man's choice. Every father wants one of his children to have his lamp when he returns to the Mother so they will remember him. My own father wanted me to remember where I came from and not who his animal-guide was. How can a father put his guide upon the lamp and then give it to his son? No father has the same animal-companion as his son. Besides, it was done before I even had any sons to give it to. It is what it is," he had said curtly, thus ending one of the longest conversations I ever had with my father.

Having learned the story of my father's marriage to my mother, I began to understand his obsession with the ibex-power.

"Little Bear, take the small bone spoon and find a few bright embers from the center of the hearth fire and place them in the bowl of the lamp." My mother's instructions brought me back from those times of visions past to this time and this place.

"The embers are to be taken from your mother's hearth by your own hand. The Grandfather says these will be used to light a holy fire at the Great Cave. The new flames will give fire to your lamp and the torches of your initiation," she explained unnecessarily.

"What is left to pack?" I asked after I dug the brightly glowing coals out of the ashes and tipped them gently into the lamp. "The embers will die before we get to the Great Cave," I protested.

Even as I spoke, my mother handed me a smooth river stone that covered the lamp like a lid. The flat bottom of the lamp was already beginning to warm to the touch as the coals gave life to the rock I held in my palm. The fire of the glowing coals actually reflected through the thin, translucent stone with a lovely, soft yellow light, as if the very soul of the lamp itself were shining.

"Take this leather strip and bind the lamp to its cover as tightly as you can before placing it in your bag. The embers will still give fire for a very long time after you do so," she promised.

I did as I was instructed and then wrapped the warm little bundle in its rabbit fur covering. Nothing remained to pack in the bag so I slung it over my left shoulder to hold it firm with my hand under my right arm.

"There is one more thing you need to take with you, Little Bear."

My mother's voice began to quaver again with emotion as the time drew near to leave the lodge one last time as her daughter. I would return Seer of the Bear People, her daughter no more. I understood better than I ever had before how this tugged at my mother's heart and made her sad. As I considered the significance of it all, my mother moved to the west side of the lodge and removed my father's special tallow horn from its peg. She hung the leather cord over my right shoulder so it would rest beneath my left arm.

A tallow horn is always carried close to the body to keep the rendered fat warm enough to pour easily. If it were not kept warm, it would not pour smoothly for use in lamps, for mixing paints or even for starting fires quickly. This special bison horn is stopped in one end with a wooden plug and carved all around with skillfully made reindeer, bison and salmon. It was from studying the carved lines on this finely engraved oil horn that I taught myself to make spirit-animals.

"Come, Dearest One," my mother said, a catch in her throat.

My mother enfolded me with a warm bison robe around my shoulders. She turned me around and tied the thongs made from narrow strips of leather so it would not slip from my shoulders. I am ready to go.

"It is time to go," she said, a suppressed whimper in her voice.

Then, leading me by the hand as a little child, out we went into the cold dawn. We set our feet upon the path upward to the Shelter of the Solitaires where the Grandfather and all the seers of the Bear-kin would be waiting for us. The climb seemed to take no time at all.

As we approached the entrance to the Shelter of the Solitaires, I dropped my mother's hand to turn and look once more at the world I was leaving behind. The sun was yet to rise and promised only by a band of pale yellow sky above a level band of dark horizon in an otherwise starless, gray sky. As everyone at the entrance waited in silence, I stood for a long moment gazing at the most astonishingly slender crescent of waning moon I had ever seen in my life. Impossibly thin, it hung just above the yellow band of sky, its slivered horns pointing up. I knew this would be its last appearance in the sky before a new moon-circle began three days and two nights hence. It was the sign of the end of my life as a good and honest woman of the Bear People. When I reappeared from the Great Cave after three days and two nights, it would be the beginning of my new life as Twice Born Seer of the Bear People.

Still wondering what it all meant and doubting the choice I was making, I turned and took the last few steps. At the mouth of the Shelter, the Grandfather awaited to begin my initiation as Seer of the Bear People.

* * *

The Grandfather was dressed in the most astonishing clothing I have ever seen. He wore a short, long-sleeved tunic of burnished red leather with trousers made of the same shiny skins. It was fine clothing my mother might have been responsible for making. His famous otter cap and bag were, of course, present. But the deep red tunic and trousers were not the most astonishing items of clothing he wore. In addition to the usual otter skull around his neck hung a marvelous necklace of enormous bear claws. The teeth were interspersed with extremely rare pieces of smooth yellow amber and polished beads made from short lengths of the hollow leg bones of some kind of large bird.

But what took my breath away was the long robe draped around the Grandfather's shoulders. It was made of the pure white fur of a kind of bear I certainly had never seen before. I knew it was a bearskin robe because the ties looped in front still had claws attached to them. This was indeed the true garb of the Thrice Born Grandfather, Oldest Shaman of the Bear People. I had never before seen the robe worn by the Grandfather at a dance circle, which means it is only taken out during such important and power-filled occasions as the initiations of seers and shamans. To think that my initiation was the cause of all of this overawed me! Before such a spectacle, I could feel myself shrinking in size into utter insignificance.

"Welcome, our Daughter of the Bear People," he intoned loudly and formally so that everyone in the little crowd on either side and behind him could hear.

He held out his hand to me. As I took the warm hand in mine, the little crowd parted and he led me up into the wide mouth of the Shelter. We turned to face the little audience gathered before the entrance.

"This is the dawning of thy initiation as Seer of the Bear People," he said formally, still holding my hand. "If thou, my Daughter, or anyone present, believe that our Sister, Little Bear of the Bear-kin, daughter of One Doe's lodge, should not become Twice Born Seer of the Bear People, let them speak now or forever keep their words."

I looked to the side where my mother was standing still as a stump, no expression on her face. I knew she fought back her tears and I was sure she would blurt out an angry objection in spite of herself. But not a word came from her mouth to save me from all of this.

After a few more moments of looking over the faces of the crowd and waiting for an objection, the Grandfather announced in a loud voice, "No one objects to Little Bear's initiation as Seer of the Bear People. Come thou forward and prepare thyself, Daughter of the Bear People."

The Grandfather then led me away from the little crowd deeper into the Shelter followed only by my mother. That must have been a signal because Auntie came forward from where she had been standing within the Shelter and began disrobing me. My mother, the Grandfather, two other seers from the nearby camps of the Bear-kin and a few other inhabitants of the Shelter of the Solitaries looked on from within the threshold of the Shelter. The seers assisted Auntie by taking my clothing as each piece of it was removed. Soon I stood naked in front of them all with only my woman's necklace, oil horn and bag slung about my neck. To my increasing embarrassment, I had not so much as a loinskin to cover my three-cornered pute!

As I stood there, alternately chilling from the late winter air and flushing from naked embarrassment, my mother was handed a carefully folded black fur robe by the two-spirit keeper of ceremonial objects. She must have retrieved it from a cache of holy objects somewhere at the back of the Shelter. In turn, my mother reverently handed the robe, its shiny fur cleaned and oiled, to my

Auntie. I could see it was also a bearskin because the front legs and claws of the Bear Mother dangled from one end as a tie just like the white bear robe of the Grandfather. Auntie held the folded black robe up with both hands.

"Oh Great Mother of all things, hear the words of my mouth! We ask thee for permission to enrobe thy human daughter in thy Holy Skin for she has freely chosen to become Seer of the Bear People and thy servant. We thank thee and know thy permission is already granted." Auntie intoned the solemn words of an invocation I certainly have never heard before.

She placed the ancient robe around my shoulders. Turning me slowly to face her, Auntie looked into my eyes with a beaming smile of tremendous pride and began to loop the strips of front paws around each other to keep the robe from slipping off. What a relief to be covered and warm again! What a relief to remove my body from all those staring eyes gawking at me. Not many of them had been looking at my face either!

The use of such rare and holy bearskin robes was only the first of many jolting surprises I would receive during my initiation. It is forbidden for any of the Nine Kin to kill Bear Mother in her own Valley—it is her own lodge. Using a bear's teeth or claws found anywhere in the Valley as power charms or as part of a necklace, let alone taking its skin and tanning its hide for everyday use, is also strictly forbidden. These white and black Bear Mothers must have given themselves to the hunters during one of our summer journeys to the Northland for the express purpose of being used in such important ceremonies. Maybe they had been given as gifts by some distant tribe? I had no way of knowing. If so, it must have been long ago as this robe was already very old and I had no memory of any bears giving themselves to us in my lifetime. But then, I am still very young. The skin of a bear that has died of its own accord during its winter sleep in the Great Cave or any other cave of the Valley of the Bear Mother could not even be used in this manner. Such found Bear Mothers would always be left to rot into skeletons where they lay and return to the Mother without disturbance. These were indeed holy skins of the All Mother. A signal from someone facing the crowd must have been given because the little group of spectators at the mouth of the Shelter began to sing the Song of Abundance.

Without a word, the Grandfather took me by the hand again and led me through them, to the descending trail and out into the brightening dawn.

* * *

The black bearskin robe seemed to weigh down on me with unnatural heaviness as we made our way out of the Shelter and down the path. The Grandfather leaned stiffly on his bird-headed staff— a duck, most likely. But it could be a goose, I thought, as I followed blindly behind. I was naked except for the robe so I pulled it in closely to keep my body warmth inside. My feet began to get very cold on the frigid earth of the trail. The old man was barefoot as well, but at least *he* had warm clothes beneath his robe. I did not have so much as a loinskin to cover my pute hair!

By the time the two of us reached the bottom of the steepest part of the sloping path, we began following a trail that took us above the camp, eastward toward the Great Cave. The sliver of crescent moon had gone down and the sky was getting brighter making the trail visible. It was not necessary to carry any fire to see well enough to walk it. The coals from my mother's hearth were blessedly warming the leather of the satchel riding on my hip. As we moved along the path taking us downriver directly toward the Eye, a trail branched to the left. It clearly led up the hill to the Great Cave, but it was not taken.

"Grandfather," I spoke up, breaking the silence. "This trail leads up to the Cave. The other leads to the Serpent Springs. Why are we going there?"

"We will bathe and purify ourselves before entering the Great Cave, my Daughter," he replied without emotion. "The Serpent Springs are not just for the relaxing and the enjoyment of the body. The power-filled, hot pools are for cleansing our souls as well."

The hot springs of Serpent Father emerge from the ground near the base of the cliffs beyond and below the entrance to the Cave. The steaming waters flow in the direction of Chamois Creek and its joining with the river just downstream from the Eye. The hot springs are often visited by the People at the time of the Great

Gathering. We also use the waters at other times and not just for purification before encountering the powers. In winter, bathing in the hot waters is one of the greatest joys of living here in the Middle Camp.

Another of the joys of the Middle Camp is that the brush thickets and large trees lining every stream, spring and river in the Valley provide lots of cover for couples sneaking away to be alone with each other away from prying eyes and listening ears. Young and old alike enjoy taking the hot waters during the winter cold. I just did not know until now that the hot springs played any part in a seer's initiation. I was impatient now to get to the pools before I froze to death, barefoot as I was in the frigid air. The Grandfather hobbled at a turtle's pace, but just one thought of all he had suffered returned my patience along with a little compassion for the dear old man.

"Is it permitted for me to go ahead of you, Grandfather?" I asked impatiently. Staring at the Grandfather's back and not being able to see where I was going made me very anxious.

"Of course it is permitted," he mumbled, struggling to move along more quickly.

I knew he was trying to move along as fast as an old man could, but being out in front, I could at least see the trail disappearing into the willow thickets and brush ahead. I was surprised to find being in the lead only made me more nervous and uncomfortable. The words of the Grandfather's warning of the day before echoed oddly in my head.

"Are there any bears in the brush or leopards in the trees, my Grandfather?" I worried aloud. I turned my head to hear his answer better.

"No, Daughter. The bears are still sleeping and the leopards stay in the thickets of the Plain where there is more game than the few deer they will find here in our Valley," he said with a twinkle in his eye and a wry smile. "Besides, no leopard would attack creatures that look like two big shaggy creatures as we."

Both wrapped in heavy robes, we did look like bears or some kind of half-human, half-animal monsters with human arms and feet poking out of these bulky fur robes. As I turned to laugh at his little joke, the sun just rising over the cliff tops shone full on his face. I saw for the first time that his eyes were not black at all. They were the soft bark-brown of an ancient pine tree flecked with the dark green of mature pine needles. The smile lines radiating from his mouth and the corners of his eyes obliterated all other wrinkles and temporarily distorted his shaman's cheek marks as he squinted into the rising sun. Wisps of pale hair escaped from his otter hat like white-spirits fleeing into our World of Light, hinting at the powerful shaman enfolded in a dazzling white bearskin. No dirty, smelly, ordinary old man at all was this.

I was transfixed by those shining eyes and began backing up along the trail until I nearly tripped and fell. Catching myself, we both laughed out loud at my backward-walking clumsiness, returning me to my senses. We resumed moving slowly along the path without speaking until we reached the largest of a series of hot pools that began with a scalding spring near the base of the cliffs. Pools of different sizes were strung out like the stones and teeth of a necklace as the steaming waters meandered in the general direction of the Eye. Where the water first emerges from the cliff it is far too hot to bathe in. But by the time these waters of Serpent Father reach this pool, they have cooled enough to soak as long as one cares to. Other pools lie further on all the way to the marshes along the dry bend in our River. The streams and pools of hot water are lined only with low brush along them—the large trees do not seem to like the steaming water.

"Help me with my clothing, Daughter," the Grandfather said, as he sloughed his robe to the large flat rock upon which we stood at the pool's edge.

The Grandfather placed the amazing bear-tooth necklace, his staff and his otter bag and cap atop the white skin after withdrawing his own grass sandals from his bag.

"Then remove your things and help me into the water. Please place our sandals close to the pool. When we emerge from the waters, we will step directly into our new grass sandals so the soles of our feet will not touch the ground until we enter the Great Cave. Do you understand, my new Apprentice?" the Grandfather asked through his gap-toothed smile. Flattered to be addressed as the Grandfather's Apprentice, I smiled as broadly as he.

I replied, "Yes, I understand."

I was hearing what he was saying and I knew what it was I had to do. But I really didn't understand what was happening to me.

"Help me with these shirt laces," he ordered sharply, clearly irritated. "These mother-humping fingers do not work for me anymore!" he cursed under his breath.

I could understand his anger at stiff and swollen joints, but still I was surprised to hear the Grandfather curse this way. I loosened the laces and helped to pull the red tunic over his head. Then I loosened the drawstring of his trousers for him.

"As Seer of the Bear People, you will always ask permission of the spirit-powers before entering their special lodges. This is the holy Lodge of Serpent Father," he instructed, his composure returning. "Ask Serpent Father for permission to enter his holy waters, my Daughter," he directed as he pulled off his trousers and untied his loinskin.

I dropped my robe to the icy rock, un-slung my horn and bag and, both naked, we raised our arms together to the rising sun. The yellow rays had yet to touch the steaming pool which remained almost completely obscured by cloud-like billows hugging the water as if shrugging off the cold morning air.

I intoned in the most self-important voice I could muster, "Oh, Great Serpent Father, we ask for permission to cleanse ourselves before entering the Great Cave of the Bear Mother," I improvised. "We thank you for your healing waters, Serpent Father." I completed the request as best I could with a quick glance toward the Grandfather for some sign of approval.

Without looking at me he prompted, "And we know thy permission to enter is already granted."

I repeated, "And we know your permission to enter is already granted."

I turned to help the naked Grandfather into the pool—naked, that is, except for his otter-skull necklace. The heat seared my ice-cold feet as I backed into the pool while helping the Grandfather down the gentle slope of the big rock into the water. Our sun-browned faces were oddly dark next to our pale bodies—almost as white as the white bearskin, it seemed to me. Our hands, too, were stained dark brown—in my case from the brown liquid of soaked nut shells and tree bark my mother uses to tan and dye her dark brown leathers—and from the sun too. Neither the soap root nor the soap flowers we use to clean our bodies and hair—not even ash-water soap—can do anything to remove the brown stains that come from dyeing leather or exposure to Grandfather Sun. In the old shaman's case, his hands were almost certainly dark from many seasons of sun and wind and skinning animals and preparing ochre and making flint blades. But I could only guess.

The unwrinkled skin of the Grandfather's pale body was in startling contrast to his face and hands. As swollen as his joints were and hunched his back, I was astonished to see that his is the body of a powerfully built younger man. I could not help thinking he must have been very handsome in his youth. The scars I could see on the front of his body were those of a daring and skilled hunter who made his own flint tools. He has the same fine scars as my father does from striking off a flint core or from flaking a spear point on his bare thigh.

The first-kill mark at his throat was very faded, almost indistinguishable. To my surprise, the scarcely seen mark of the mammoth appeared there. Most young hunters have a deer of some kind as their first kill—like my father. It is a courageous and clever hunter who can claim such an animal as a mammoth for his first kill. Clearly it had been many years since the marks had been made, or refreshed, as some men like to do to keep the black color bright.

His body had little or no hair except around his penis. And that was as white and grey as the beard on his face and the hair on his head. Judging from the boy cousins and naked Uncles of the camp I have seen, not a bad penis either! At least it looked like his beautiful wife might have had plenty to enjoy for the short time they were together. Just before his penis slipped beneath the sulfurous steam and water of the thigh-deep pool, I caught a glimpse of a curious blue dot near the end of his man-rod.

With one great *Ah-h-h-h-h-h* in unison, we lay back into the steaming waters up to our necks. Stiff joints, aching muscles and freezing feet yielded to the soothing heat. In a long, sublime silence with only the plaintive calling of a lone robin far off in the trees to be heard, we drifted side-by-side in the warm and gentle buoyancy of a watery dream. I was thinking, "It's kind of early in the season for a robin. If not a robin, what kind of bird could it be?" Mostly, my mind just wandered aimlessly.

Finally, the Grandfather began to speak quietly. "Daughter, remember all you see and hear this day for you will become a great seer. You will initiate many to the mysteries of the Great Cave and to the ways of the spirit-powers."

"Yes, Grandfather," I replied in the same hushed tones. "I remember everything I hear and see. After only one hearing I can repeat the stories of the dance circle or a hunter's newly made first-kill song word-for-word," I explained unnecessarily. The Grandfather had already told me he knew of my ability to remember the Bear People's stories and songs and chants. Still, I felt I had to say something about my gifts.

The Grandfather spoke no more and when I could tolerate the heat no longer I asked weakly, "How much more soaking, Grandfather? My skin is cooked and ready to eat." I thought a silly joke was the best way to subtly bring up the topic of getting out of the pool.

He did not answer. The Grandfather had gone far away into some warm and secret place.

When I could barely breathe and was about to ask to leave the pool again—this time a little more insistently—he said suddenly, "Come, my Daughter, get out of the pool. It is almost time to go. As you get out of the water, step directly into your sandals. Do not let your purified feet touch the ground. A few more moments for me and we will continue. Please bring my sandals closer to the water's edge."

I did as I was instructed. Shod in new grass sandals I stood waiting, my naked body releasing smoking clouds into the air like the steaming fog lifting from the surface of the barely moving waters. As I began to get dry and cold again, I wrapped the soft, warm bearskin robe around me and waited for the increasingly wrinkled old man to get out of the water. I squatted on my haunches atop the robe so that no part of me would touch the cold rock or be exposed to the still icy air.

"It always seems to be colder just after the sun rises," I thought out loud.

Eyes closed, in another world and muttering something I could not make out, the Grandfather soaked and soaked and soaked as if preparing himself for something. Just when I thought he would at last shrivel to a dried berry, he stirred, opened those magical eyes and stood up straighter than I had ever seen him stand. Rivulets of water ran off his otter skull necklace and his smooth, steaming chest and arms. Water dripped from his pubic hair, from his flaccid but partially swollen penis and his disturbingly low hanging man-eggs. The red head of his penis was visible now making what had been a single blue spot become two.

"Just as I suspected. His companions in sex would have enjoyed all of that for sure," I commented quietly to myself. I was comparing it to the relatively tiny penises of boy cousins I had played with. I could feel myself blushing but not out of any lack of respect, and not because I had seen the Grandfather naked and close-up. It was because the sight of him naked aroused something deep within me that I wanted to push away from me.

Still muscular and strongly built, only his sun-browned, wrinkled face, his swollen joints and knotted, scarred hands looked old. I thought how handsome he must have been and how easy it would have been for my grandmother's little sister to be so captivated by the man and not the shaman. It was not a Great and Powerful Shaman that now stood naked, steaming and dripping in front of me, but a red-bodied man I could not keep myself from staring at.

"Give me your hand, my Daughter. Help me from the pool," he said, completely oblivious to the unacceptable thoughts I continued to force from my head and liver.

The Grandfather barely finished speaking before I knelt to push his sandals toward the water's edge. I stood up and my hand went out to help him up the small rise to the top of the flat rock, the touch of his hand in mine hotter than the steaming springs. The sun was shining directly onto my face now. As I helped him from the water, he looked up to me and his gaze fixed immediately on my right eye. His eyes grew big as full moons in amazement. His hand began to shake in mine and I knew he had seen my lion's eye.

I lowered my face to break his gaze. Without his asking, I knelt down to put the sandals on his dripping feet. Then I moved away to retrieve and hand him the bird-headed staff. I helped with his loin cloth, shirt, and trousers without ever looking at his face. Neither of us spoke a word. All that remained was to replace his magnificent spirit-necklace, hand his oil horn and bag to him and wrap the thick white bearskin around his shoulders. Then we were on our way again … in silence. A palpable tenseness crowded around us that would not abate.

Returning the way we had come, we soon came to the fork in the trail. This time, we took the path that led up toward the Great Cave. We began to climb the winding path that would take us to its entrance.

* * *

As we made our way haltingly up the increasingly steep trail toward the Cave, I stopped at a brook of bubbling, clear water to the side of the path. But when I bent to drink—the hot spring waters had made me terribly thirsty—the old man stopped me short.

"Having been purified to enter the Great Cave, we will not drink of any water but that which comes from the pools and springs of Living Water inside the Cave," he cautioned me.

"Yes, Grandfather," I grumbled, my tongue still tasting the cold, clear waters. The little stream chattered with high-pitched, laughing voices over the rocks on its way down to the River.

The further away from Serpent Father's hot pools we went, the more we seemed to return to our Great Shaman-with-Apprentice selves. Soon he was talking to me again and began testing my knowledge of the lore of our People. The uncomfortable tension between us melted away as soon as he began asking his questions.

"Do you know the tale of the People's coming to the Valley and the discovery of the Great Cave, my Apprentice?" he asked.

"Yes, Grandfather, I know the story," I answered.

"Can you sing the story to me now, my Daughter?" he asked.

"Oh Grandfather, you would not want to hear my magpie's cackle of a singing voice. In my whole life I have never been visited by a sweet song or rhyming chant of my own making. Even if I had, I have not the voice to do anything but speak it without everyone laughing at me. A song bird's voice is not a gift the Mother has given this woman, I promise you, my Grandfather! But I will be pleased to chant it for you."

"Very well, my Apprentice. We should all know what our gifts are and what they are not," he chuckled, to my great relief.

So, as we climbed the path to the Cave I began to chant the tale. But as we moved upward along the trail, and as I began chanting the rhythmic words, in no time I was singing the story in my poor voice. Absentmindedly, I began miming the characters in the story along with the hand movements and dance steps every good storyteller uses when telling this tale.

It is a story every child can tell of how the People first came from the far north beyond the Plain and the Great River of the Mammoth Mother to our home in the Valley of the Bear Mother. I began the telling the way all stories begin:

At a time long ago, in a place far away, the Bison People roamed the great plains of Mammoth Mother. They knew not that a home had been prepared for them in a rich and abundant river valley far, far away. That is, they knew not until a dream was sent by Bear Mother to her shaman-daughter, Red Bear, the Grandmother of the Bison People. The dream called the Bison People to Bear Mother's place of abundance if they would but hear and believe. "I have had a vision in a dream!" cried the Grandmother of Seers to her People assembled in a Summer Gathering upon the Plain of the Northland. "It is a true vision of my very own bear-guide. Give ear, Oh ye people of Bison Mother and hear the words of my mouth! The Mother of us all has given this dream to me! Bear Mother has shown me the rich and abundant valley to which she will lead the whole of the Bison People. Give ear and hear me now, for I will follow the Bear Mother to this place no matter how long the journey. I will lead all those who are willing to live in Bear Mother's bounteous lodge and to become a new tribe, the People of the Bear Mother," Grandmother Red Bear cried out in a loud voice so that all could hear.

Grandmother Red Bear sent out runners to find other bands of the Bison People scattered upon the Plain who had not come to the gathering. Those who believed in Grandmother Red Bear's vision came. But there were many of the Bison People who did not believe Red Bear's vision from the Dream World and would not come. And so there were many who would not follow where Red Bear led. They said to Grandmother Red Bear, 'The Plains of Summer are full of the Mother's many children. Bison Mother, our Guardian and Guide, never ceases to send the herds to us, for which we are endlessly grateful. Old woman," they said, "why should we follow you to the Mother-knows-where only to starve to death?" Thus, many of the Bison People did not believe and would not follow. These are the tribes of unbelievers in Grandmother Red Bear's dream who still roam the Plain as the Others.

I chanted and sang dramatically to the Grandfather as if I were telling the story for the first time to a group of children.

Those who did believe Red Bear's vision followed her and they began their long, long journey to the blessed place the Grandmother's animal-guide showed her in nightly dreams. Every night Grandmother Red Bear would dream a dream of her animal-companion. In the dream-vision Bear Mother would cross a certain stream, walk toward a specific hill or climb over a certain mountain. When she awoke the next morning, the Grandmother would lead the People in the direction she had been shown in her dreams. Night after night after night after night the Grandmother dreamed and Bear Mother led. Day after day after day after day the Grandmother led and those among the People who still believed in Red Bear's dream followed. Moon after moon after moon after moon the dreams were dreamed and the Grandmother led the People.

One day, when the exhausted People were all ready to turn back in disbelief, the Grandmother came to the very place where our River runs out upon the Plain of the Mammoth Mother. Some said, "Surely this is the place of plenty you have dreamed of, Grandmother Red Bear? Look at the abundant water and herds and flocks of birds and the many nut trees and bushes full of berries. Look at the jumping salmon in the rivers and streams! See the protecting hills and cliffs for our winter lodges!" they shouted together excitedly. "Surely this is the Place of Abundance in your dream, our Grandmother," they said. But the Grandmother cried loudly, "No, this is not the Place of Abundance. Bear Mother has sent more dreams to me and we must continue on to the Place of Abundance!"

Many believed the Grandmother and followed her, but some of the People would not. They said to Red Bear, "We are now the People of the Bear Mother for it is she who has led us to this, our new home. We will stay here in this place of abundance. We are happy wherever we are!" All those who would follow the Grandmother no further shouted in unison and stopped where they were. And so they became the Bison-kin who still have their camps where the river runs out upon the Plain to this very day.

Then others of the People said, "Look yonder at the bounteous land across the river, Grandmother Red Bear! It is lush with grass and shrubs that Mammoth Mother loves. Certainly many mammoths will give themselves to us here in this abundant place. Its streams are full of salmon and there are many trees with which to build our winter lodges. Surely that is the Abundant Land of your dream-vision, there, just across this river!" And so they would go no further. But still they said, "We are now the People of the Bear Mother for it is she who has led us to our new home. Here is where we will stay. We are happy wherever we are!" And so these people who would follow Grandmother Red Bear no further became the Mammoth-kin who still have their camps across the River opposite the Bison-kin to this very day.

"No!" cried the Grandmother. "That is not the Place of Abundance of my dream-vision! Follow me, those of you who believe in my vision, to the true Place of Abundance." And again Red Bear led those who would follow her up the river, which is our River, away from the Plain of the Mammoth Mother. As the followers of the Grandmother ascended the River they found wide bends with a great abundance of roots and rushes to be collected. Some places had caves and springs and warm winter rock shelters. Some had many nut trees and fruit-bearing shrubs. All had the salmon in the river and many deer and boar in the thick forests. All had abundant chamois and ibex in the surrounding hills and high valleys. At each well-favored spot some of the People decided that they had found their Place of Abundance and would not follow the Grandmother any further. But, in turn, they all declared that they were the People of the Bear Mother for it was she who had led them to their new homes of abundance.

First, the Reindeer-kin found their place and they all shouted, "We are happy wherever we are!" Then the Aurochs-kin found their place and they all shouted, "We are happy wherever we are!" Next, the Horse-kin found their abundant place and they all shouted, "We are happy wherever we are!" Further up the river, the Red Deer-kin found their abundant place and they all shouted, "We are happy wherever we are!" The Musk Ox-kin found their new home next. Still the Grandmother insisted, "No, this is not the Place of Abundance!" for her guide continued to appear nightly in her dreams to lead her further and further up the river, deeper and deeper into the Valley of the Bear Mother.

One night, on the first appearance of the slivered crescent of Grandmother Moon in the western sky, Bear Mother had one more dream to send to her daughter, Red Bear. The very next day, those who still believed and still faithfully followed Grandmother Red Bear were led, first to the great stone arch of the All Mother's Eye, past Serpent Father's hot springs and on to camp beneath the entrance to the Great Cave. Red Bear climbed up a difficult path strewn with many stones and boulders to the Portal of the Mother's Mouth, wherein the Grandmother's animal-guide had disappeared. As Grandmother Red Bear stood at the mouth of the Great Cave overlooking the Eye and the wide, dry river bed that is now the home of the Bear-kin, she called down the path, the very path we are on at this moment (I improvised) *to all those who still believed and had followed her faithfully to the Great Cave.*

Grandmother Red Bear said in a loud voice to those below, "Give ear and hear ye the words of my mouth! Bear Mother, the animal-guardian and spirit-guide of our whole People, has dreamed us to this true Place of Abundance. She has entered her own Holy Lodge and will not come out again. This is the Place of Abundance for all the worlds and is our new home because, in my dream, I have seen Bear Mother herself enter her Great Cave, her very own Holy Lodge, and she does not come out again. She leads us no further to any other Place of Abundance!"

And so it came to pass that all those who believed in the Grandmother's dream-vision and who had followed her faithfully from the distant Northland began to build their lodges in the river bend below the Great Cave. They became the Bear-kin by all acclaiming together, "We are the People of the Bear Mother for it is she who has led us to our new home, our true Place of Abundance. We will stay here. We are happy wherever we are!"

But even then, a very few of those who had believed the Grandmother's dream and had followed her throughout the long, long journey from the Plains of Summer began to complain. They said to Grandmother Red Bear, "What if there is an even more abundant place further up the river? We will not stay at the Great Cave. We will not become Bear-kin as you have all acclaimed yourselves. We will travel on still further up this river to find an even more abundant place!" Grandmother Red Bear just looked at them sadly and said, "Do as you will my Children, but there is no better place in all the World of Light. None are as full of the Mother's white spirit-power and her red-abundance as this place of the Bear-kin!"

And so those who did not believe that the richest and most abundant part of the Valley of the Bear Mother had been reached went on. They ascended almost to the very source of the River of the Bear Mother in the Mountains of Snow. But in the end, they were disappointed in their search and were forever known as the most skeptical and doubting of all the Bear People. These people descended again almost to the camps of the Bear-kin at the Great Cave. They decided that this is their Place of Abundance, no matter how poor it actually was. They acclaimed together, "We are the People of the Bear Mother for she has led us to our Place of Abundance! We are the Ibex-kin and we are happy wherever we are!" Of course, these are the People of the Bear Mother who live further up the Valley than any of the other Nine Kin.

So bountiful and so abundant is the land of the Bear-kin around the Eye and the Great Cave that, in time, the Lower and Upper Camps of the Bear-kin were made by people from the Middle Camp. And this is the story of how our People were led to the Valley of the Bear Mother and how we all became her children and lived happily where we are to this very day.

I finished the tale with the usual ending just as we completed our climb to the Cave to stand in the very place the story tells us the Grandmother of all Seers stood so long ago.

"Very good, my Daughter. You left absolutely nothing out of the story!" the Grandfather praised my storytelling. "All we needed to make the telling complete was a dance circle with all the spirit-masks and costumes to sing this Tale of the Nine Kin that you have spoken and sung so well. Your singing voice is very pleasant, Little Bear. I do not think it is a poor one at all," he said smiling his gap-toothed smile.

"Thank you, Grandfather, but my voice is not that good. I prefer to chant the story in my telling," I said modestly.

"Nevertheless, thank you for your excellent telling of the story of Grandmother Red Bear and the coming of our People to this Valley," he said smiling broadly.

I can never tell this tale or hear this story without being amazed at how our ancestors came to this beautiful place to find it completely abandoned, the Cave exactly as it is now. Like me, no one hearing the story ever failed to wonder why the Ancient Ones would abandon such an abundant and beautiful valley as this? Why would they leave such a place as full of the spirit-power of the Mother as the Great Cave with her single, All-Seeing Eye before it?

As we reached the top of the trail and the mouth of the Great Cave, we turned to the wide view that could only be gained by climbing above the trees lining the river below which covered much of the ground around the camp from the cliffs down to the river. The Middle Camp, spread out in a half-moon shape below us, was mostly on ground that had been cleared of trees so the winter season sun could warm our lodges during the day. There was still a lot of grass and patches of low brush between the lodges where storage and cooking pits and smoking racks are placed. Among the bushes, the latrines could also be screened from each other and from the bark lodges. The tree-dotted cliffs and hills stretched out from the Eye as far as our human eyes could see. Out there, to the south, lay the vast Plain of the Mammoth Mother and the Great River into which the relatively little stream of our River fed. In the summer season, the Great River and the Plain were the very life of the whole Bear People. It is during the summer season that we all move down our River and spread out upon the Plain in small bands of close kin, gift-givers and friends to follow the herds to the Northland. The Northland is the very place from which all of the People had originally come, led by a dream. And now we collect the rich plant food that grows here and we fish the rivers and hunt in the hills in the very Place of Abundance to which Grandmother Red Bear led the People. Or so the story is told.

At times, our little summer bands reach the very banks of the River of the Mammoth Mother where we can see all the way to the Mountains of Ice far off to the northeast. I have even seen the camp smoke of the Others on the opposite side of the Great River. We never cross, as that side of the Great River is theirs, just as this side of the Great River is ours. But not all of the Others live on the other side of the Great River. Otherwise, we never think of the people who may live in other parts of the World of Light or how they might live that is different from the People. In some seasons, several of our bands will meet at a place of rendezvous for a small Summer Gathering or for a bison jump. Occasionally, there will be bands of other tribes who do not have the same speech as the People. Still, we come together to trade or to share in a great killing of the Mother's children, joining our hunting bands for a short time in a Great Hunt. Because of that, all the People learn the hand-talking so that we can communicate and trade with the Others we encounter while traveling upon the Plain. Still, with all the Others upon the Great Plain, it is always such a mystery to me why there was no one in this marvelous Valley of the Bear Mother when, as the story is told, Grandmother Red Bear and her followers arrived here in this bountiful place of abundance and shelter.

I could not help but think about the old story I had just told and how it helps to explain the different character of our Nine Kin. The Ibex-kin of my father are always thought of as too skeptical of everything. The Ibex-kin will not believe the evidence of their own eyes and they do not recognize a good gift when they see it or a good trade when they make it. They are always second-guessing their exchanges after a Great Gathering. Little wonder my grandmother thought of my father as "poor" and looked down upon him and his Ibex-kin. After all, my father did come from one of the Nine Kin who, in the legend, passed by the rich river bends of the Bear-kin for the narrower, poorer lands upriver.

And yet, the Ibex-kin are closer than we are to the numerous ibex, chamois and mouflon coming down from the high mountains. Maybe they are not as poor as people say? The Bison-kin and Mammoth-kin certainly have a reputation for being more concerned with the things of the World of Light—rich hunting close-at-hand and trading with the others of the Plain—than with matters of the spirit-powers as we Bear-kin are. I suppose it is to be expected that the Bear-kin's seers and shamans are the most numerous and that I have the curse or blessing—I have yet to decide which—of being born into such a family as mine. I think whether the path of the seers is a curse or blessing is a question that I am about to answer for myself. Or so it seems.

"It's marvelous how all of this can be seen from the mouth of the Great Cave," I said to the Grandfather as I scanned slowly from horizon to horizon.

I was thoroughly enjoying the view and exulting in the stillness of the morning air and the brilliant red, yellow and orange bank of clouds far off on the horizon through which the sun continued to rise in this most beautiful and abundant of all places.

"It *is* beautiful, is it not?" the Grandfather asked as he looked at the same glorious panorama.

"What memories of the Plain and the many seasons he has spent there as a shaman-of-the-hunt must the Grandfather have?" I wondered to myself in words. Together, we continued to gaze out toward the Plain where, at this moment, my father, my brother, Auntie's husband and all the hunters of the Nine Kin of the Bear People were in the midst of a Great Hunt.

"Yes, Grandfather, it is very beautiful. But why would any people leave this place with its abundant salmon, nuts, roots and seeds to be collected? Why would they leave the spirit-filled Cave and the abundant winter hunting of deer, ibex, and chamois? Why would they leave the sheltering cliffs that protect us from the fierce storms of the winter plains?" I asked, not really expecting an answer.

"That is something I cannot tell, my Daughter," he replied simply. "Let us just give thanks to the All Mother that we have such abundance in this Valley. All I know is this is the best of all places and the most filled with the powers of the All Mother. This Great Cave is the very belly of Earth Mother and was made to instruct us and give us experience of the worlds of the spirit-powers—and for you to be reborn as Seer. The presence of this Cave is why we have become the People of the Bear Mother since our Ancient Ones were dreamed to this place by Grandmother Red Bear," he said, his voice becoming hushed and pensive.

"The very cave wall is the invisible barrier between our World of Light and the unseen worlds of the powers. This is the place out of which all the abundant life of the Mother comes and it is the Void back into which all life goes. That is why we have come. Now let us enter the Mother's Great Cave and begin the great adventure we have come here to experience together."

Without saying anything else, we both turned to climb the last few steps to the gaping mouth-like hole that was the Portal of the Mother's Mouth, the entrance to the Great Cave of the Bear Mother.

CHAPTER 3.
INTO THE CAVE OF MYSTERIES

THE MOUTH OF THE GREAT CAVE remained in deep shadow at the base of white cliffs rising straight up into the cloudless blue of the late winter season sky. Everywhere, the stony hills were spotted with stunted evergreens and leafless shrubs clinging to the rocks like children clutching at their mother's breast. The cliffs above the entrance were steep so the sun would not begin to shine upon this only opening to the Great Cave until well after midday.

But since the entrance portal faces southwest there would be times in the winter season when the sun could shine directly into the entrance, and, for only a moment, shine narrow shafts of sunlight into deeper parts of the Great Cave. Or so the seers told us during our Moon Blood rites. Supposedly, the rays of the setting mid-winter sun shine right into the Lodge of Red Spirits. There, the spears of sunshine light up the Rock of the All Mother before which many of the women's rites are carried out.

I don't know how anyone could say that because the People never go into the Great Cave in mid-winter. Unless a seer is being initiated, there is no reason for anyone to enter the Cave and there could be no one to see such a marvel. I know from my own experience that during the Moon Blood, always held just before the People leave for the Plains of Summer, some light does shine in through this only entrance from the World of Light into the Cave. At least there is enough sunlight to see where it is coming from, for sure. But it never lasts very long before the women's Lodge of Red Spirits is completely dark again. My curiosity was killing me and so I had to ask.

"Grandfather? Is it true that the mid-winter sun shines upon the All Mother's Rock deep within the Cave?"

"Yes, my Daughter, it does. In fact, it shines upon the Rock for a few moments two times each winter season. The shamans-of-time tell us that some ten days before and ten days after the winter sun stops moving further and further south, the setting sun will shine for a few brief moments through the Portal of the Mother's Mouth and through the First Entrance to shine upon the All Mother's Rock. If there are seers to be initiated, that is the pre-ferred time to enter the Cave so that the apprentices may see the marvel for themselves during their initiation. I am sorry that your initiation will not be marked by such a miracle. That should not concern you, my Daughter, because you are certain to take part in some future seer or shaman's initiation one day and you will see the marvel with your own eyes."

"Thank you, Grandfather, for telling me that. I will look for-ward to the time when I can see the miracle with my own eyes," I said, comforted that I was not being told a children's tale and that someday I would see it for myself.

The path to the Great Cave's entrance had been cleared long ago of the large rocks and stones that had fallen from the cliffs above the Portal. But we still had to clamber up a steeply sloping pile of small loose stones and dirt to the entrance itself. The Portal of the Mother's Mouth yawned like a gaping monster with a maw ten paces wide. It is little wonder everyone speaks of entering the entrails of the Mother when going into the Great Cave through this mouth-like opening.

After helping the Grandfather up the last few feet, we paused at the entrance where the ground flattened out. Exactly in the cen-ter, and just back a little from any stones that might fall from above, appeared the mammoth ivory image of Earth Mother. The yellowed and cracked figurine of the Mother—no taller than the length of one's hand—marked this cave as the Holy Lodge of the

85

All Mother herself. Her great breasts bulged out and both arms curved around her belly as if to hold the ponderous bosoms up, offering one and all to come and suckle. This little ivory Guardian of the Cave also had a huge three-cornered vulva etched between wide, fat hips. I have always thought a much grander ivory carving should be placed here. This carving is so very ordinary for a grand entrance to such a place as this. But the carving is obviously so ancient that no one dares to replace it. The figure's faceless head, completely veiled with a tightly woven net, is no larger than, nor does it vary in any significant way from the ivory carvings of the Mother that are pushed into the soil by their short, pointed legs near every hearth of every lodge of the People. The All Mother's image at the foot of my mother's hearth, just beneath the low work table, is finely polished and still pure white—the mark of a recently made ivory. But this carving looks so old and weather-worn as to have been placed here by Grandmother Red Bear herself so very many seasons ago that no one could ever count them, not even the shamans-of-time.

"Join hands with me, Dear One," the Grandfather's voice broke the silence of my thoughts. "We will enter the All Mother's Holy Lodge together as we pass over the ivory Guardian of the Portal."

"Yes, Grandfather," I said grasping the Grandfather's outstretched hand.

Only a few footsteps further on and we were inside the Great Cave. The Grandfather motioned me to follow behind as we began our slow descent along a gently sloping ramp of dirt and dusty rocks that had rolled in from the outside. We soon reached an almost flat area that branched into three passages leading to the deeper recesses of the cavern. The cave mouth behind us was already above our heads as we moved slowly down into the gathering gloom.

The Grandfather stopped our descent at a flat area and said quietly, almost reverently, "Daughter, do you remember which passage to take? Straight ahead, to the left or to the right?" He gestured toward the three possible entrances.

"Yes, Grandfather," I said confidently. "I remember. The passage to the right is almost completely blocked with stones and allows no entrance. Before us is the First Entrance to the Lodge of Red Spirits through which the sun may shine but through which we do not enter or exit from the holy lodges beyond."

"And the passage to the left?" the Grandfather asked.

"That is the way to the Skull Portal and the Plain of the Bear Mother," I answered without hesitation.

"That is good. I see you have a gift for finding your way and a fine memory. With such gifts of the head, you would have made a good hunter, my Daughter," he commented with an approving smile and nod. "Come, I will lead the way. The Cave grows darker and the fire of your initiation must be ignited there at the Skull Portal to light our way."

The Grandfather took a sharp left turn into the deepening shadows of the entrance passage and led the way to the Skull Portal several paces on. The Skull Portal itself had been placed just where the stone walls of the passage narrowed slightly. I knew this spot marked the formal entrance to the Cave of the Bear Mother from my Moon Blood initiation as a woman. The twin bear skulls of the Portal faced each other across the entrance. Each was painted with red and black stripes and signs on white, skinless bone. And each skull of the Portal had an upright leg-bone half buried in the dirt of the floor before each skeletal snout— guardians at the door posts of Bear Mother's own holy lodge.

"Kindling and firewood has been placed for our use," he said, pointing to a pile of firewood, dry-leaf kindling and pine torches in a small niche in the left-hand wall.

"Prepare your mother's hearth coals and ignite your tinder here in this holy hearth in the center of the Portal so we may light our lamps and torches for the journey of your initiation," he instructed.

As I pulled the ball of fire-weed tinder and the packet of warm coals hiding within my father's stone lamp from my bag, the Grandfather sat down stiffly against a large boulder to wait for me to light the fire. With kindling and a few sticks of wood from the niche, I laid the firewood in the stone-encircled hearth that had been carefully placed exactly in the center of the ten-paces-wide Skull Portal. The Grandfather had barely gotten comfortable upon his stone seat and the flames were leaping. The coals had only taken a breath or two to fire the tinder and for the kindling and wood to release their light. The fire began to crackle and leap up as I added more small pieces of wood. The fire of my initiation began casting a warm yellow glow over the two guardians of the Skull Portal to the Great Cave and the great opening into the utter blackness beyond.

"Clean the ashes from your lamp and hold it out to me with both hands as if you are presenting a gift," the Grandfather instructed.

He pulled three thick wicks of twisted tree moss from a packet in his otter satchel and handed them to me. He removed the wooden stopper from the oil horn hung about his neck and stood waiting to fill my cleaned lamp with tallow oil. After brushing the last of the ashes out with a corner of my robe I held the lamp out to him.

"Will I not use the oil from my father's tallow horn, Grandfather?" I asked.

As he carefully poured my lamp just full enough that it would not slosh out too easily, he answered, "No, my Daughter, your tallow oil will have other uses. Use all three of the moss wicks. I have more as they are used up. Moss wicks provide a little more light than the cedar wicks the People use. The scent of burning tree moss, reindeer fat and the pine smoke of our lamps, torches and hearth fires are pleasing to the Bear Mother. You must already know that Bear Mother loves anything that grows on or comes from the pine tree. Have you never seen a bear scratching its back on the rough bark of an ancient pine? That is true joy for a bear," the old man prattled on.

I slid the three wicks into the oil, moved them around to the front edge of the lamp and touched a stick of flaming kindling to each. While doing as I was instructed, I was thinking, "Any scent should be pleasing to Bear Mother!" The dank, moist smell of mushrooms, musky old animal fur and dry, throat-clogging dust combined with the faint odor of wet rocks and long decayed flesh wafted out of the darkness. The foul smell came toward us on a barely perceptible breath of chilly wind coming from somewhere deep inside the Cave.

The Grandfather took a few of the torches of bound strips of pine bark sticky with resin and wrapped them in thick birch paper from the little cache of kindling and other supplies. He placed them inside his bag and we turned to face the solid gloom that lay just beyond the Skull Portal. Side-by-side we looked out over my little fire into the sooty darkness that stretched endlessly beyond the yellow circle of our warming flames. Here, at the Skull Portal, only the faintest glimmer of sunlight reached us from the entrance around the corner, already far above and behind us.

"Now place your lamp upon Earth Mother and raise your hands in reverence to Bear Mother, speaking the words of entrance three times," he said in a soft whisper.

I stood with my hands raised while the Grandfather moved off to the right side of the Skull Portal where a large mammoth leg-bone rested beneath a thin, wavy wing of rock protruding from the wall and rising all the way up to the roof. I may have been in the back of the line of boys and girls and mentors when I last stood here, but I did hear and I do remember the words of the Song of Entry. As we sang the first request to enter together, I never expected what the Grandfather would do next because it had not been done during the puberty rites.

"Oh, Great Bear Mother, hear the words of my mouth! We ask thy permission to enter the Lodge of the All Mother and we know permission has already been granted," we sang together.

To my surprise, after each request the Grandfather struck the wing of stone with the mammoth bone to send a body-shaking vibration through me. The unearthly tone reverberated and echoed back from the darkness, slicing through the very center of my body like no drum I had ever heard. The Grandfather and I sang the second request followed by yet another booming chime felt more in the gut than heard with the ears. By the third request and the extended ringing of the stone, I could tell by the shift in his voice that the Grandfather was already in a half-trance. Holding his bird-staff in one hand, the Mammoth Mother's bone hammer in the other, he stood—eyes closed and in silence—for several moments before he replaced the bone hammer against the wall along with his bird-staff. He moved the few footsteps back to the hearth where I stood shaken by the ringing to my very liver.

No words were spoken as he retrieved one of the torches from his bag and slowly removed the bark paper wrapping from its tip.

After adding the bark covering to the fire, he touched the torch to the flames. Turning, the Grandfather raised both arms again toward the blackness. Clearly, we were not finished with our request to enter the Great Cave.

"Oh Great Mother of us All, hear the words of my mouth! I am Flying Otter, Grandfather of the Bear People," his voice boomed like the ringing of the stone chime. "I am come to initiate thy Daughter, Little Bear, as Seer of the People. We thank thee, Mother of us All, and we know thy permission to enter is already granted," he concluded his invocation.

It was the first time in my life I had ever heard the Grandfather's secret shaman's name uttered out loud by anyone. I thought it was my cue to proceed and so bent over to pick up my lamp. But before I could take a single step forward, the Grandfather grabbed the edge of my robe and held me in place before the fire and the Skull Guardians of the Portal.

Intoning with the growling, rumbling voice of the All Mother which, disconcertingly, combined the sounds of a grunting bear with the terrifying crack of Sky Father's voice of lightning and in the most honorific form of speech ever addressed to me by any respected elder of the People, the awesome Voice spoke through the Grandfather's mouth.

"I am the One beside which there is no other! I am thy beginning and thy end, Beloved Daughter Little Bear. I walk with thee in the midst of all thy joys and sorrows. If thou wouldst freely enter my Holy Lodge as a welcome and honored guest to take the path of Seer of the Bear People, remove the sandals from off thy feet for the ground upon which thou standeth is holy to me. Remove thou, all that stands between the soles of thy feet and the wisdom that will come to thee of this, my Holy Lodge. Enter now into my peace and my joy," the other worldly voice commanded.

I kicked off my sandals before the Voice was even finished speaking. Without a pause or even waiting long enough for an echo to return from the depths of the Cave, the Grandfather, now also barefooted, led me by the wrist over the fire, between the two Skull Guardians and into the Cave of the All Mother in one smooth movement.

* * *

Only a few paces past the Skull Guardians, we stood on the flat, moist, clay-covered floor of the vast Plain of the Bear Mother, the hearth fire of my initiation and the Skull Portal behind us. In every direction, the portions of the floor falling within our little circles of yellow light were covered with bear bones, skulls and circular dens dug into the ground where mother bears had passed the winter season in sleep and where they had given birth to their cubs. This part of the Great Cave was certainly well-named as Bear Mother's Plain of Bones! But in spite of the chill, the freezing ground and the disconcerting display of so many bear skeletons, it was actually warmer here than in the icy air outside. As we moved deeper and deeper into the Cave it remained the same chilly, but hardly freezing, temperature. Truly astounding!

"Do you know the way to the entrances of the Lodge of Red Spirits, my Daughter?" he asked, speaking in his own voice again.

"Yes, Grandfather," I replied. "From the Skull Portal, the initiates separated into two lines—the boys went to the left and the girls followed the right-hand wall."

"Follow the right-hand path then," he instructed. "We will begin your initiation as Seer in the women's Lodge of Red Spirits."

Finding the way to the Second Entrance was no great feat of memory. The hard and darkened path—trodden by countless feet for innumerable initiations—clearly curved to the right. I knew only ten or fifteen paces away I would find the Second Entrance to that part of the Cave where the girls became women in the Moon Blood.

As we approached the western portal of the Second Entrance, the Grandfather ordered abruptly, "Stop here. The first holy round of the Red Lodge for girls begins here at the west portal of the Second Entrance. For your seer's initiation, we will enter the Red Lodge by the west portal of the Third Entrance as you have already become a woman. But first, I have something to show you, my good Apprentice," he said with unusual glee in his voice.

And so begins my instruction as Apprentice at the knee of Flying Otter, Grandfather of the Bear People.

"Learn well, my Daughter, for you may one day become the Grandmother of the Nine Kin. When you do, you will be called upon to initiate hunters as well as women," he began. "And you will instruct new seers and shamans, too, when you are the eldest and wisest of the seers. Remember as much of what I tell you as you can, Dear One."

"Yes, Grandfather, I promise to remember all you tell me," I replied.

And so began the vows and promises of an Apprentice to her wise Teacher.

"The Plain of Bones is Bear Mother's own Lodge and is especially holy to her as a place of her white spirit-powers. The bones, teeth or claws here may not be collected for necklaces, talismans or for any other use. And only Bear Mother may make marks upon the walls with her great claws here in the Plain," he explained with a solemn warning.

As the Grandfather spoke, he raised his torch to cast the light as far up the wall as possible.

"See here? High up on the walls that are the very entrails of the Mother?" he said, pointing with the flaming tip of the torch. "See where Bear Mother has stood up on her hind legs like one of the human tribe and scratched the soft clay covering the hard white stone beneath with her long, curving claws?"

"Yes, Grandfather," I said, my mouth gaping at the sight of the deep claw marks so high up above our heads. "I can see the marks. They are made so high!" I whispered reverently. There was a growing recognition of why both men and women born of the Bear-kin all have the five-clawed mark of Bear Mother made upon their right shoulders.

I remember well passing by this very spot on the way to taking the first holy round of my own Moon Blood initiation. We girls moving toward the Lodge of Red Spirits for the first time were definitely not shown this spectacle of the claw marks. We were all terrified enough as it was having just entered the Cave for the first time. The sight of these marks high above our heads would have unnecessarily frightened us even more than we already were. In spite of myself, the hair now stood up on the back of my neck and prickled along my arms. I felt the eyes of a gigantic bear standing on her back legs taller than two men lurking somewhere in the indescribable darkness behind me.

"Are there any bears sleeping in the Cave now, my Grandfather?" The high-pitched nervousness in my voice bounced back to me from the almost vertical wall of stone.

"There may be. But there is nothing to fear, my Daughter. Now that we have been given permission to enter Bear Mother's Cave," he replied calmly, but with a smile audible in his words from a mouth I could not see.

"In truth, Dear One, any bears sleeping in the Cave will have already awakened this late in the winter season. If there are any late risers, we only need respect their slumber and quietly move around them," he said.

Hardly comforted by the idea of sneaking around a giant sleeping bear, I did feel better about staying out in front with the Grandfather protecting my back from whatever bears or unknown monsters were out there skulking in the darkness. Stalking us.

Only a few paces on, the path forked to the right. Here, it began to curve around toward what would be the western portal of the Second Entrance—the place of first entry for uninitiated girls into the Red Lodge. The Grandfather had already said we would not be entering by this portal so I knew I was to follow the other path which led straight across the Second Entrance, past its eastern portal and on to the Third Entrance beyond.

"You will begin your seer's initiation at the Rock of the All Mother," he said, acknowledging that I knew where I was going.

The Second Entrance was just a few paces across, but beyond it the Cave stretched out with many, many paces of almost flat, soft clay-covered walls. Occasional claw marks stretched up and arched out over our heads into the utter darkness of a high roof. The wall I was following ran approximately northeast, and then it made a sharp turn to the south, followed by another sharp turn toward the east where we soon arrived at the western portal of the vast Third Entrance to the Lodge of Red Spirits. The eastern portal of this Third Entrance could just barely be made out across the darkness at the extreme edge of the Grandfather's torchlight. If I had not already been there during the holy rounds of my own Moon Blood, I would not have known to look for the eastern side of this Third Entrance.

Since the Grandfather was walking behind me with the brighter of our two flames, shadows danced out ahead of me and the cracks and crevices of the walls seemed to come alive with movement and rapidly changing shapes. The flickering light chased shadows from the depths only to have them dart into another shadowy refuge as we passed by. Regardless of the twists and turns, I could always sense in what direction we were moving.

In truth, I *did* have a gift for finding my way out of the camp and back home again—a gift of a hunter, so the Grandfather said. Somewhere deep in my gut I could *feel* the change in direction even in this place with no sun or stars for finding one's way. I *knew*, from having just come into the Cave, that the entrance to the outside and the World of Light opened to the southwest. I knew that the Cave's entry passage was running to the northeast where the First Entrance lay. I knew that the passage had turned sharply to the north where the Skull Portal gave entrance to the Plain of Bones. Now, as we stood at the western portal of the Third Entrance, I knew that it opened into the completely blacked-out Red Lodge. I also knew we stood at the east end of the great Rock of the All Mother, which runs almost exactly east to west, facing toward the south. The Rock faces the same direction as our bark lodges, which would, at this very moment, be busy with all the usual early morning business of the Middle Camp.

As we slowly made our way around the Third Entrance's western portal to the Rock of the All Mother, the light brown clay floor of the Plain of Bones turned dark red—the very color of the Mother's lifeblood. It is little wonder this part of the cave is called the Lodge of Red Spirits and is the place where the Moon Blood rites of women take place. Wherever there were no large rocks or hard, wet crusts of stone, the flat clay floor of the Lodge was so red it could have been used to make the many red marks, dots, spirit-animals and handprints that almost completely covered the Rock of the All Mother. In the rites of the Moon Blood—mostly performed beneath the high roof of the Lodge of Red Spirits before this great, red expanse of stone—each girl brings a drawstring bag of finely ground red ochre which she pours out upon the already blood-red floor at different points on the three holy rounds of the Moon Blood. These red powders are a thank-offering to the

Mother and a sign of the lifeblood every woman pours out upon the ground with each moon-blood of her life. Whether the Red Lodge's floor was always the color of dried blood, or it has become dark red from the countless bags of red ochre poured out here from the time of the Ancients, no one can say. But the extent of the red-stained floor in front of and far beyond the massive Rock of the All Mother is truly astonishing to everyone who sees it.

I knew from first-hand experience that uninitiated girls always enter the Red Lodge for the first time through the Second Entrance, which we had just bypassed. The Second Entrance is actually on the extreme western end of this great expanse of stone. The All Mother's Rock stretches for more than twenty-five paces of fairly flat, almost vertical, stone running between the Second and the Third Entrances inside the Red Lodge. The Second Entrance is marked only by a single red pute-slash in the center of the entrance. The vulva-slash mark is a sign that the unitiated girls should follow an against-the-sun path to the right around the edge of the roughly oval cavern to begin their first holy round of the Lodge of Red Spirits. In making our first entrance into the Red Lodge through the Second Entrance, none of us girls saw this grand, red-painted Rock and the vast red floor before it until we had completed our first holy round, which, of course, ended at the very place where we now stood.

Much of the Red Lodge is filled with fallen boulders and huge tree trunks of stone that appear to be holding up the Cave's roof. In many places, undulating drapes of white stone and hardened cascades of rock descend from the roof of the cave to its floor. It is around and between these marvelous stones that the three rounds of the Red Lodge are walked by all the girls and their mother-mentors. At the end of the girl's first round, a small fire of initiation is kindled, and it is here, before the All Mother's Rock, that many of the rites of the Moon Blood are enacted. As the girls enter the Second Entrance, their mother-mentors take the path we have just taken and wait at the Rock for the girls to complete their first holy round. While the mentors stay near the Rock and its Hearth of Initiations, the way of all three holy rounds is led by the Mother of the Rites, the oldest female Seer among the three camps of the Bear-kin. That the Mother of the Rites should come from one of the camps of the Bear-kin is only fitting as more female seers are known among us than among any of the other Nine Kin. And, so it seems, I am now to become one of them.

At my initiation as a woman, I was proud my own Auntie stood as Mother of the Rites. A woman Seer always officiates at the Moon Blood unless there is absolutely none other to lead the initiations of women. Such a situation has not arisen in living memory because most seers of the Nine Kin are, in fact, women. The Mother of the Rites leads in telling the stories of the animal-guides. And she teaches the chants and songs of our People as part of the rites. She also shows the entrances to side-chambers and alcoves where we were encouraged to return later. That is, if we choose to do so as moved by the spirit-powers of the place. Of course, the Mother of the Rites teaches us about the ways of men, joining in sex with them, getting with child and having babies. The Mother of the Rites uses words and speaks of important things for women to know in a way most of our own mothers will not.

I began wondering what the Grandfather would do now since my initiation as Seer will begin in front of the Rock of the All Mother rather than end here as the Moon Blood ceremonies do.

Again, the Grandfather spoke to me as if he had been hearing my thoughts. His voice was so filled with kindness I felt I *was* a beloved daughter.

"Dear One," he said. "You have already been reborn as a woman in the Moon Blood. We will not need to light a hearth fire here for your initiation as Seer as is done for the Moon Blood of girls. But we will repeat the anointing and blessing of that initiation as a woman to begin the rebirth of your soul as Seer of the People."

I understood what that involved. Knowing from experience that such blessings are always done facing east—the direction of Horse Mother and her rising yellow sun—I turned to face the Grandfather across the cold, ash-filled hearth of the girl's initiations.

"Please place your lamp upon Earth Mother to your right. We will have flames to our left and right hands, to the north and the south of us," he directed.

As he stuck his torch into the soft, reddened earth between the hearth-place and the Rock, I let my robe drop to the ground.

"Before we begin your anointing and our walking of one round of the Lodge, I will give you a seer's understanding of the Mother's Great Cave," he began. "Turn 'round with your back to the All Mother's Rock. Now raise your left hand straight up to your side. Good," he said as I followed his directions.

"When you are standing in this place, you are facing toward the south and your left hand is pointing to the place of the rising sun. In the World of Light, that is the direction of the Sun Hunter of the star herds and flocks which flee before him and to whom they give their red-bodies. Whenever we circle to the left, we are moving in a sun-wise direction, which is the direction of the white-spirits of men, the direction of the Sun Hunter. Whenever a circle is taken in the sun-wise direction anywhere in the Cave, or in the World of Light for that matter, it is to bring to mind the eternal, unchanging circling of the white-spirits of Grandfather Sun, which *is* the Sun Hunter."

"Yes, Grandfather," I said. "Is that why the boys circle off to the left and the girls move to the right as we enter the Cave?"

"That is correct, Dear One. Now raise your right hand and you will see it points toward the west, the direction of the setting sun. When you move to the right, you are circling against-the-sun. You are moving in the direction of the ever-changing, forever dying and rebirthing red-spirits of Grandmother Moon. And just as the herds of red-bodied animals are hunted and returned to the Mother to be born again, so are the white-bodied star herds and flocks of birds reborn as the blood-red sun sets each day. Whenever you circle to the right, you are moving against-the-sun and so you should be mindful that it is always a sign of the red-spirits of rebirth, which is the spirit-power of women and the Mother herself. The rounds of the Red Lodge or any of the red-spirited wombs of the Cave are always walked by circling to the right. The white lodges or any of the white-spirited wombs of the Cave are always walked by circling to the left. If the passage is too narrow, then one walks the side-chamber up the center. Do you understand, my Daughter?"

"Yes, I do understand, my Grandfather," I replied formally.

"Very well, then. We may proceed. Please retrieve the Mother-ochre you have prepared and hold the open packet in both hands in front of you as if you are offering a gift," he directed.

I rummaged in my bag and found the packet. But before untying it, the Grandfather helped to remove my bag and oil horn from around my neck to place them upon the bearskin robe nearby.

I untied the cords of the packet and he began to speak. "Dear One, you have already been blessed with the abundance of the red-body in your Moon Blood rites as a woman. This day, your woman's red-body has been washed and purified by the hands of your own mother. This day, your white-body has been washed and purified in the living waters of the Serpent Father. Now you will receive the anointing and red blessings of the Mother's Abundance which all seers, whether man or woman, receive at the Rock of the All Mother. Say, 'I thank thee, Mother and I accept' after each blessing," he instructed.

Holding up his left arm, palm facing toward me in blessing, he dipped one finger of his right hand into the packet of red ochre spread open upon my palms. He began to draw a single red line from my throat, between my breasts and down my belly to scribe a red circle around my navel.

As he made the lines, he chanted blessings that were not exactly as I had received them during the puberty rites. "Blessed Daughter of the Bear People, I mark thy throat that thou wilt always speak the truth of thyself and to speak only truth and abundance into the ear of the Mother."

"I thank thee, Mother, and I accept," I whispered in low voice.

"Blessed Daughter of the Bear People, health in thy belly and blood to thy bones, thy navel shall always receive and be nourished by the food of the Mother's spirit-power as thou wert nourished by thy mother's red-body through the cord of life," he sang again.

"I thank thee, Mother, and I accept," I answered, closing my eyes.

Again he dipped his finger in the ochre and drew a large red circle on and around each of my nipples. Both nipples were hard from the frigid air making the intimate contact with the Grandfather's finger uncomfortably and embarrassingly stimulating.

"Blessed Daughter of the Bear People, I mark thy breasts to be full of the Mother's spirit-milk to nurture the souls of the People as thy body-milk nurtures and feeds the children of thy womb," he spoke softly.

In turn I repeated, "I thank thee, Mother, and I accept."

The Grandfather proceeded to mark the insides of my thighs and across the top of my pubic hair with a three-cornered pute. Then, uncomfortably, he made a vulva slash down the middle almost to the bottom of my pute.

As he painted the three-cornered vulva on my body he intoned, "Blessed Daughter of Bear Mother, I mark three corners of thy womb that thou wilt always give new, abundant life to the hearts of the People as the womb of thy body gives red-life to thy children."

As the Grandfather marked two large spots on my knees he continued to sing solemnly. "Blessed Daughter of the Bear Mother, I mark thy knees that thou always submit to the Mother and yield always to the Small Quiet Voice in thy heart."

After each blessing I continued to answer with, "I thank thee, Mother and I accept."

Finally, he dipped his finger in the smooth, blood-red ochre and I raised my face to receive the marks of a seer. But first, he carefully marked one short line running from mid-forehead along the bridge of my nose. As the Grandfather began to make the seer's mark on my right cheek, he looked directly into my lion-eye. He stopped abruptly. I knew he would be unable to see it in the dim light, but his finger began to shake and his eyes brimmed with tears.

"What do these quivering hands mean? What do thee tears mean? Certainly not lust for a naked girl ... something else," I asked and answered silently.

We all know men are like rutting aurochs so it is best not to be alone and naked with any of them, especially not a full-grown shaman. I have heard the stories! It is why women initiate the girls and men initiate the boys, I think. I also think it is why initiations of seers are carried out by more than a single shaman. Only now did I begin to understand just how unusual, how out-of-the-ordinary, this initiation is and just how singular is our whole adventure together in this dark, dark place.

"Knowing all she knows, why was Auntie not even more anxious and concerned for me to be alone in this place with an unmated old man?" I thought in words to myself.

After a long moment of staring intently into my lion-eye, the Grandfather haltingly completed the marks and the blessing.

"Blessed Daughter of the Bear People, I mark thee with seer's marks that thou may always see clearly with all three of thine eyes and give the People thy wisdom."

His voice quavered slightly as he continued peering directly into my right eye, visibly straining to see the vertical black rod that could not have been there in so little light. I knew he was trying to decide why the black rod was only visible in bright sunlight. I was also sure with only torch and lamplight that it would appear as any other eye—wide and black and reflecting only the yellow flames.

To my utter astonishment, the brimming tears the Grandfather was straining to hold back began to overflow. They tracked down the seer's marks on either cheek like tiny streams about to overtop their banks. The tears glistened in the flame light as the Grandfather's heart flew to other places and other times. But not a word did he utter, nor did I dare speak.

As he continued to gaze into my eyes, some small voice inside told me he was looking at me but he was seeing my grandmother's little sister. I felt that he was seeing the face of his beloved wife come back from the Mother again and standing before him. Without his even touching me, the heart-love coming out of him was palpable. This look in his eyes suddenly made me very uncomfortable.

"I thank thee Mother and I accept," I said and looked away to break the trance.

The Grandfather quickly regained his composure.

"What love is this that crosses lifetimes? That goes from world to world?" I asked myself in astonishment.

It was at that moment I realized my great aunt had not feared this great and powerful shaman. Neither do I fear him. *That* is what we two lion-eyed women have in common. And yet, here the Grandfather is, heart-to-heart, across the Abyss of Silence believing that he is standing with his Beloved once again. All I could think was how was I ever to find a love like this? Would I ever find a heart-bond with another such as this in my own life? Would I ever find one who would love me above all others as the Grandfather obviously did my own great aunt? It simply could not be that my soul had ever lived such a tragic life with this man in the red-body of my own great aunt! How was that possible? Surely I would have some faint memory if, in any world, I ever had the same love for this man as he surely had for that woman who just happens to be my close kin?

But before I could end this moment, my heart and soul went out to him.

With eyes still downcast, I asked in a gentle whisper, "Grandfather, do I look like her?"

Already knowing the answer and knowing he would understand who I was asking about, he said simply, "Yes, Dear One. It is your lion-eye that gives you away. Like your shaman-grandmother's beautiful sister, it is only visible if one looks directly into your eyes in full sunlight. It disappears in the darkness of the Great Cave. Few will ever enjoy the magic of that experience, I dare to say, my Daughter."

"What is the meaning of a lion-eye, Grandfather?" I asked before I could stop myself.

"Allow me to complete the marking and the blessing, then I will tell you, Dear One," he said.

"Yes, Grandfather, I am prepared," I replied, already covered with red ochre marks from forehead to knees.

"Health to thy navel and marrow to thy bones," he began the blessing. "Peace to thy heart, wisdom to thy Single Eye and children to thy womb in this world and all the words to come! The Blessing is completed," he intoned then began busying himself by handing me the oil horn and satchel and helping with my heavy robe.

"And the lion-eye, my Grandfather?"

"It simply means you have the special favor of Lion Mother. Or it may be that one of your undiscovered animal-guides is the lion. Whether it is the red, white or black-spirited Lion Mother which dwells in your heart that, you will discover as you seek her and the part of you which *is* Lion Mother."

Such words! They left my head swirling in thought.

"The seer's anointing and blessing is complete. Let us now walk a single round of the Red Lodge to begin your initiation as Seer," he said, bringing us both back to the present and to the task at hand.

"You must not be afraid to ask questions of everything you see and do not understand, my Daughter. That is the very meaning of the word *seer*. It is one who sees in truth, finds the All Mother within the heart and one who, because of that seeing, then blesses the People with the Mother's wisdom. Do you understand?"

"Yes, Grandfather. I understand and I am ready to begin," I said resolutely.

We turned as one to face the Rock of the All Mother.

CHAPTER 4.
THE LODGE OF RED SPIRITS

"PLEASE SING THE SONG OF THE ALL MOTHER," the Grandfather asked as we gazed toward the great expanse of reddened stone known as the Rock of the All Mother. The eastern end of the Rock—to our right and nearest the Third Entrance where we had just entered the Red Lodge—was covered in red ochre handprints, finger dots, clouds of blown-on ochre, smudges and indistinct animal shapes. At the center of this roiling red spirit-power appeared a mass of ochre that the Mother of the Rites tells the initiates is an image of Earth Mother's liver. The liver, of course, is the source and seat of all the loving and nurturing feelings and urges which arise from our red-bodies and are felt within the heart. I know also that the liver is the source of all the angry, hateful emotions and desires of the gall bladder and spleen as well.

And rising up and above this swirling mass of red life-fire erupting all about, appeared the crossed lines of the All Mother—the same as the shaman's marks I had just received on my cheeks to make of me seer-apprentice. To the right and left of the central cross, barely visible through the masses of red ocher all about, spouted fountains of red lifeblood shooting up in outward-curving streams. Everywhere I looked, the Mother's abundant life seemed to be coming into the red-world of women directly from the womb-walls of the Great Cave.

To our left, on the western side of the central cross, a barely visible spirit-bison head emerged out of the rock in a flood of birth blood and water like a calf coming from Bison Mother's great womb into the World of Light. As directed, I began to sing the song we had all learned as girls in our Moon Blood. It is a song which speaks of the course of our body-lives as women:

> *I am the sun*
> *I am the moon*
> *I am the stars above.*
> *I and the Mother are one.*
> *I am the fire*
> *I am the water*
> *I am the earth below.*
> *I and the Mother are one.*
> *I am the girl*
> *I am the mother*
> *I am the wise woman within.*
> *I and the Mother are one.*

"Yes, very good, my Apprentice," the Grandfather commented. "I hear your Auntie's teachings in this song of yours."

Taken aback, I shot back rudely, "What do you mean my *Auntie's* teachings? Is every girl and every seer not taught the same songs and chants? Do not all the People receive the same initiations?"

"No, my Daughter, they do not," he said directly. "Every Grandfather or Mother of the Rites teaches their initiates according to their own understanding. And each initiate sees and hears only what they are willing to see and to hear. The stories and chants and songs and images, indeed, even the Great Cave itself, are all meant to bring us to the brink of the Abyss and bring us to an experience of the Mother from within our souls. No one can take the final step into such wisdom but us. And that step is only possible when we are prepared in our hearts to do so. What is taught by the mouth of a wise mentor may be felt in the heart, but feeling the Mother and hearing her voice within cannot be taught.

It can only be experienced within each heart and within each mind. Because you were initiated by Auntie as Mother of the Rites it could be no other way," he explained calmly, taking no offense at my brash question.

Not quite satisfied with his answer, I stood gazing at the astonishing red Rock before me trying to understand it all.

"What do you see when you look at the All Mother's cross above this pouring river of red lifeblood?" he asked quietly.

He turned his head to look at me. I stood quite still, I am certain, with a puzzled look on my face. My eyes searched every corner of the mute stone in front of me for answers.

"I see, I see ..." I was stalling, trying to give myself time to think and remember what Auntie had indeed taught me about the Rock.

After a few more moments of thought I answered. "In the cross of red I see the sign of the Four Mothers of the directions: the red Bison Mother of the west, the white Mammoth Mother of the south, the yellow Horse Mother of the east and the black Reindeer Mother of the north—the Mother's children we most depend on for our food. Their red-bodies are all being born out of the Mother at the same moment as a Cross of Red," I said, exhausting my memory on the subject.

"Yes, my Daughter, that is correct. But what most initiates do not remember is that there are Five Mother's of the Red Lodge— the same number as the fingers of one hand and of the senses of the red-body. So who is the Fifth Mother of the Center where the four arms of the cross come together?"

The Grandfather questioned gently but I knew I was being tested.

"A Fifth Mother?" I asked, perplexed at the question. "Well, well ..." I stammered, trying to think quickly. "The Mother of the Center must be Bear Mother. This cave is the center of our whole world and the Great Cave is Bear Mother's own lodge," I stated flatly.

"Good answer, my Apprentice," he commented with a little smile. "But where are *you* in all of this, my Daughter? Who is it that sings the Song of Abundance every morning as we greet the sunrise? Who sings the Song of Abundance every day as we go out to

hunt or dig the roots or collect the nuts or grind the seeds or work
the hides or cook our food or snare rabbits or make baskets or
work the fish traps? Who is it that dances and sings and lives the
life of the red-body?" he queried insistently.

With these words, the Grandfather had given me all the hints I
needed to answer. The words of the Song of Abundance ran
through my head to give the final clues:

> *Abundance before me*
> *Abundance behind me*
> *I am on the Mother's path.*
> *Abundance to the left of me*
> *Abundance to the right of me*
> *I am on the Mother's path.*
> *Abundance above me*
> *Abundance below me*
> *I am on the Mother's path.*
> *It is a good day to live*
> *It is a good day to die*
> *I am happy wherever I am.*

"It is I, Grandfather. I am at the center of the Cross of the
Five Mothers," I replied with feigned confidence. I couldn't decide
how I *and* the Bear Mother could be in the center at the same time.

Still, these were the songs and the words that had been spoken
to all my age-mates while standing on this very spot. I could remember almost everything, but I was not sure if Auntie had taught
us about the Fifth Mother of the Cross of Red. I decided she had
not, so new and strange did the idea seem to me.

Narrowing his eyes, the Grandfather looked at me with his
head tilted slightly to one side while nodding in agreement. Then
he spoke quietly in a tone I was already learning was the voice he
used when he was about to impart some important teaching to his
new Apprentice.

"Daughter, move forward and place your hand against the
stone upon any image or part of the Mother's Rock you feel
moved to touch," he instructed.

"Yes, Grandfather," I said cautiously.

I was wondering what the crafty old shaman was up to even as I moved around the hearth toward the Rock. I slowly began moving my hand back and forth over the expanse of bumpy, rough, red-stained stone trying to feel something, anything. Finally I placed my right palm firmly against the mass of blood-red ochre that did, indeed, look like a large liver.

"Now, tell me what you *feel*, Daughter of My Heart," he said.

"What I feel? What I feel? What does that mean? I feel cold stone! What else would I feel?" I thought to myself, completely exasperated.

That was too harsh an answer to give to the Grandfather in words, I decided. Still, I had to answer *something*. My hand was getting chilled holding it against a stone that, judging from its shape and color, should be hot as fresh blood. Nothing spoke to me and no answer would come.

After several long moments I gave my reply. "I feel nothing, Grandfather, nothing but a cold rock." I answered honestly but with just a little disappointment in myself.

"It is of no great importance, Dear One," he said comfortingly. "You will learn … in time … I am sure of it. Just be patient and when you see anything in our rounds of the Cave that you do not understand, ask. At every sign or image, just let go of trying to think it all out with your head and open your liver and your heart and let them speak to you. As Seer, you will learn to allow the powers to speak to you through your heart and less through your head or through your liver."

"What do you mean by hearing through my heart, Grandfather?" I asked, truly not understanding what he meant.

"You will never hear the voice of the powers through your ears or see their forms with your eyes. You will only experience them or encounter them in dreams or trances or through a quiet, gentle whisper to your heart. You cannot feel them with the tips of your fingers because the powers are a part of you. They are all inside you. Just quiet your senses and let them come to the awareness of your heart. If you would listen with your heart, you must relax the noisy thoughts of your head which always crowd out the gentle voices of the powers within. Let them speak to you through the hidden senses and secret impulses of your heart," he explained.

"Let's try again," he said brightly. "But this time clear your head of all thoughts by taking three deep breaths. Hold each breath for a moment and then slowly let the breath out through your mouth. When you have released the third breath, hold your palm just above All Mother's Liver without actually touching it. And close your eyes when you do."

I did as the Grandfather directed. After taking three long, deep breaths, I held my hand only a hairbreadth above the crimson liver while closing my eyes.

"Good," he said. "Now concentrate on your hand and imagine the Mother's lifeblood flowing there. *Be* the stone. *Be* the pulsing blood. Continue breathing deeply and slowly," he said in a soft whisper next to my ear.

To my complete astonishment I began to feel my own heartbeat pulsing down my arm to fill my warming fingers with tingling flames of life-fire. It seemed as if my whole body had gathered together in just the palm of my hand. The heat began to increase to the point I felt I was holding a hot coal from a hearth fire in my hand!

"Tell me what you feel now, my Daughter," his voice whispered again.

"I feel the life-fire of my own body, the life-fire of the Mother," I said in amazement.

My eyes remained closed while I just reveled in the soothing warmth.

"Yes, Dear One. That is exactly what you are feeling. It is the heat of the Mother within you coming to touch the spirit-fire of the All Mother through the hair-thin barrier between the Two Worlds that is the stone wall of this Great Cave. The pounding of your own heart is the beating of the All Mother's heart, just as the drums of the dance circle are the beating of her One Heart. This is the Mother speaking to you, but not through the desires and urges of the liver or the thoughts of your head. The Mother is speaking to you through the hidden senses of your heart where the white-spirited powers of the head come together with the red-spirited powers of the liver in harmony and cooperation. In her hidden voice, the Mother speaks to thy soul without words or sounds of any kind as the liver and head come together in love within the beating of your own heart. Do you begin to understand, my Daughter?" he concluded.

Too astonished to make any comments I said simply, "Yes Grandfather, I understand. I do understand."

"Very well my good Apprentice. As Seer, know that finding a balance between listening to the stirrings and urgings of the liver and the words you hear through your ears into your head is difficult for everyone. But the meeting and balance of the two is the Voice of the Mother within your own heart. It comes without effort to the few who are truly ready to listen and to see with the single eye of the Mother's wisdom rather than with the two eyes of the red-body. This is the one thing we come to the Mother's Cave to learn and to experience. As Apprentice, know that it does not come to everyone at the same time or in the same manner."

"Is the Great Cave the only place to know such things, my Grandfather?" I asked.

"No, Dear One, the Mother may speak to us at any time and in any place because she is always within and around us. But seers must learn to hear this Silent Voice within the heart because it is the same Voice of Stillness you will hear in trance and in your dreams as well. It is the Silence beyond even the All Mother that you experience when you touch the Mother without pressing your hand to the stone. It is the Silence every hunter in harmony with the Mother experiences in preparing to throw when he takes the same deep breath you took and casts his spear to the killing spot at the very moment of utter stillness. Now that you have begun to be aware of the Mother's Presence, I will share with you the deeper meaning of the Cross of the All Mother, a teaching many seers do not understand. Are you willing to learn, my good Apprentice?" he asked.

"Yes, Grandfather, I am willing to learn whatever you are willing to teach," I said completely entranced by the prospect of learning yet another secret of the seers and shamans.

"Very well, Daughter of my Heart, I will instruct you in the signs of the Red Lodge," he began. "In this women's Lodge of Red Spirits, the Mother's Cross of Red is the sign, to all those who see it, of the four directions of the horizon and the 'fifth direction' of the center of the red-world, which is the world of your own body and its five senses. Wherever we go with our bodies, to the north, south, east or west or when we stand still in the center, our five senses guide and direct us. Each one of us stands at the center of our own body-lives thinking with our heads in response to the senses of the entire body. The Mother of the Center is the special guiding spirit-power of each person, which is often revealed to our hearts within this Holy Cave. Each stands in the center, no matter who they are or which animal-guide may speak to them. We all respond to all things from that center. The red-world is the world of the senses and of changing conditions; the shifting shapes and forms and the names of things. It is the right-hand circling of all things. The red-world is forever being born in the bloody pain of mothers, lives by the unending shedding of blood, and is forever dying as the lifeblood ceases to flow in the veins of all the Mother's children. And yet, all of it *is* the Mother. As Seer, you must learn that this blood-drenched world of pain and suffering *is* the face of the Mother everyone sees for every day of their body-lives, though many do not realize it. The red-world is also the world of the hunters who must go out to the four directions to hunt and bring the body-lives of the Mother's children back to us so that the red-bodies of our human families may all continue to live. All men and women must learn this about themselves and about all the Mother's children. The horizontal arms of the Cross of Red are the signs of the coming in and going out of the red-world of Light above us here in the belly of the Great Cave. The Above World is that world of the five senses out there in the light where we live the dream of our body-lives. It is that red-world in which we move and live and continue in our being. It is the world we experience with our bodies and its sign here, in the Great Cave, is the color of red. It is the red-world upon which the sun rises and sets every single day of our lives. It is the red-world, when the Return to the Mother approaches, we look back to and wonder if it was all just another dream," he explained carefully.

"Then what does the long, vertical arm of the Cross of Red represent, my Grandfather?" I asked, eager to hear more.

"The arm pointing up represents the upper world of the white spirit-powers. It is that space of the unchanging, eternal light of nothingness within each one of us which cannot be seen or heard or felt by the red-body. It can only be known and experienced in the mind—in the head—which is connected to and directs the lower world of the red senses of your own body. That is the 'Below' of the red-world that is directed and controlled by the white-spirits. At least, we must strive to have the 'Above' in charge and directing our lives. The 'Below' world, which is to be guided by the 'Above', is the long arm pointing down to Earth Mother. This is why actively seeking the white-spirits through your five senses is doomed to failure because it is seeking the white-powers as if they are outside of us and can be known through the senses. The senses of sight, smell, taste and hearing are all located in the head, but the eyes and the other organs of the senses go searching for that which is made welcome to some part of the body or another, including the head! Only if the upper and lower powers have been joined within a heart that has been awakened will the eyes and other organs of the head seek and find that which is welcome to the heart and not just that which is welcome to the belly, the organs of joining in sex or even of the head itself," he explained. "I see the puzzled look on your face, my Daughter. Am I not answering your question?" he asked.

"No, Grandfather, I don't think I understand," I said.

"Then let me try to explain it to you this way," he began. "The first time you touched Earth Mother's liver you were trying to feel with the red-senses, with the touch of your hand—the horizontal arm of the Mother's Cross. But the second time, you were able to experience the emptiness that is the hidden senses of the white spirit-powers of the Mother—the vertical arm of the Mother's Cross. It seemed to come from within your own self, and yet, not through your sense of touch. Did it not?"

"Yes, Grandfather. It did seem to be coming from inside my body and then I began to feel it in my hand."

"I know this sounds confusing," he continued his explanation. "But by closing your eyes and holding out your hand to thin air you were surrendering to the Mother just as if you had knelt before her upon those knee-spots of red ochre. By paying attention with your mind to the empty spaces between deep breaths and closing your senses by shutting your eyes, you are hearing the Silence of the white-spirits of the Above, the vertical powers, of the Mother.

And when you practice being quiet, what you will soon discover is that *you*, my Daughter, are the single place where the two worlds of the red-body—the changing world of the rising and setting sun upon the horizon—and the unchanging, formless world of the white spirit-powers of the mind—come together. They only come together in this very moment and within you—that is the opening of the black spirit-powers. You *are* the Center of all the Worlds and they come together, even if for only this moment, within your heart and only within your heart. As Seer, you will also learn from experience that the upper, white-spirited powers must never put themselves in complete control, just as the lower, red-body urges and desires must not put themselves in absolute control if you are ever to find peace and joy and abundance in your life. Instead, the two must be joined and harmonized in the heart so that the upper powers of the head may guide and balance the lower urges of the liver. In this way, we all come to line ourselves up with the Mother's abundance. Do you see, Dear One?"

"Is this why the seers and shamans always say, 'As it is above, so it will be below?" I asked. Finally, I was beginning to pull the stampede of my thoughts back together into a proper herd.

"Yes, my Daughter, that is exactly right. In surrendering to the Mother by feeling the Stillness within, you say 'yes' to whatever shape the Mother takes in the World of Light. You are opening yourself to the vertical powers that live within your own heart. As you open yourself to the white spirit-guides of the Above, they are balanced with the red spirits of the Below within you. Together, they will guide and lead you with the quiet, small voice in the heart. So if you would bring these two powers together in harmony and love and if you would experience the timeless, never-dying soul within you, look to the Stillness that lives between two breaths. In doing so, you will hear the Mother's Voice within your own gentle heart. To live in balance is to live in the center of your own harmonious life. That point within each heart where the two arms of the Mother's Cross come together is the present moment. It is the place where the ear finds nothing to hear and the eye finds nothing to see, and yet all is heard and all is seen. In all things, try not to rely too much on the many things of the World of Light which make claims on the body senses and those things your head desires. Listen always to the whispering in your heart," he concluded and patted me affectionately on the shoulder.

"Oh Grandfather," I pleaded. "How will I ever learn to do this? To live a balanced and harmonious life of a seer?"

"You will learn to do this by thinking about it and practicing it. As you live your life, always remember that you stand at the center of all there is. Like the Star of the North, around which all the star herds and star flocks circle, so does everything around you turn about you protecting, supporting and giving you what it is you need. As the four Star Mothers circle the Star of the North in the center, so will four women support you on the left, on the right, before and behind as you squat to give birth to your own children. All these are the lessons of the All Mother's Cross which you will take with you all your life and which, when you practice them, makes of you a true Seer."

I must admit that no matter how confusing, I am astonished by these teachings. I am even more eager to move on and see what new revelations await in the parts of the Cave I have never seen before. The Grandfather allowed me a few more moments to continue looking at the All Mother's liver and the Cross of Red to ponder the wisdom he had just imparted.

Finally, the Grandfather said, "It is now time to begin our single round of the Red Lodge. You will lead the way, Little Bear, but stop where you will and ask me any questions you may have."

With these words the Grandfather moved a few paces further on to stand at the western end of the Rock. Here, another mass of red smudges, marks, handprints and dots made with the palm of the hand covered a huge pute-shaped stone pendant. Many red palm-dots ran up and onto the rocky ceiling overhead. The western end of the Rock of the All Mother ended with another blurry head of the red Bison Mother of the west, beyond which opened the dark gap of the Second Entrance. It was as if this huge stone vulva was giving birth to the vast Rock of the All Mother with its cross and liver of red and bloody masses of spurting red spirit-fire and birthing animals stretching away to the eastern side of the Rock all before our eyes. The Rock was so massive its eastern edge was already fading into the darkness as we moved further away to begin walking our holy round of the Red Lodge.

* * *

I had already come this way before during the triple rounds of my Moon Blood. We could only move at a turtle's pace now, and not because the Grandfather walked so slowly. As the wall of the Red Lodge curved around past the Second Entrance, the cave floor dropped steeply in short stone steps as we reached the place where the First Entrance should have been. The First Entrance was well above our heads and the wall so steep here that it would have been very difficult, indeed, to either enter or leave the Red Lodge by this entrance. That is, unless one's animal-guide were the sure-footed ibex or chamois!

It seemed best to let the First Entrance remain as Grandfather Sun's winter entrance into the Cave when, for one brief moment, the Mother's Cross of Red would be illuminated by one slender beam of yellow sunlight coming through the opening. That is how I imagined the miracle looking never having actually seen with my own eyes. Even now, some light was showing faintly through the First Entrance. It was not bright enough to illuminate our downward sloping path with its large rocks and stair-steps. The trail simply could not be negotiated any faster than I was moving and keep the lamp from spilling its oil. Directly overhead, on the roof above us, I could see the four large red spots that mark the First Entrance. These red dots must indicate the path of the sun's winter rays on their way to their brief visit at the All Mother's Rock. I completely understand why only the Second and Third Entrances are ever used to enter or leave the Red Lodge.

I also knew that off to the left of the descending path we were on we would soon come to an expanse of white, wet stone which appeared to be flowing like frozen water from the cave's roof to its floor. This mass of white rock is known as the Cascade of the Mammoth Mother. Some seasons, it is said, the water does not run down the rock as it is flowing now. Small rivulets of water trickled down in a shimmering stream covering the whole left half of the cascade of stone in a sparkling sheet of wetness. The glimmering water gathered in pools at the bottom of the Cascade before disappearing into the ground through unseen cracks and fissures between the boulders on the ground. Water glistened everywhere in our yellow light as we moved toward the center of the Cascade.

When we reached the middle of the great expanse of rippling wet stone and turned to face it, the almost vertical wall of the Red Lodge was only a foot or two behind us, so narrow had the passage become.

"Daughter, if you are thirsty, you know it is permitted to drink from the pools beneath the Great Ones," the Grandfather encouraged.

I realized I was *very* thirsty, which only made me wonder why I was not also very hungry. No one ever seems to get hungry while in the Cave. Auntie told me once the fear and excitement of coming into the Cave for any reason is enough to make all hunger flee away from us. And so it is with me.

"I am very thirsty, Grandfather," I said, stating the obvious. My mouth was truly parched and dry for lack of water. I realized I had drunk nothing at all since leaving the hot springs—before that, even!

"All you need do is ask Mammoth Mother's permission, my Daughter," he reminded.

I barely had, "Oh, Great Mammoth Mother of the South, may we drink from your wellspring and I know your permission is already granted," past my lips before I was on my knees cupping handfuls of clear, icy water into my mouth.

The Grandfather was also very thirsty and soon was at my side drinking the truly delicious waters of the Mammoth Mother of Abundance. He must have been either extremely thirsty or he thought the permission given to me to drink was also permission for him to drink. Somehow I knew the asking of permission or the singing of entry songs did not have to be voiced to be heard by the powers. The Mother hears our songs of gratitude and hears our thoughts of joy or sadness even if they are never spoken out loud. A new lesson learned at every turn, it seems.

We again began making our way along the Cascade of the Mammoth Mother and I was reminded why the Ancients had chosen this particular place to bring the mammoth-powers out of the rock. The Cascade also marks the southern end of the Red Lodge. In fact, this was the most southerly point in the whole Cave—except for a side-chamber whose entrance was only a few paces further along the path.

As we moved along, our lamp and torch lights flickered against the huge expanse of shimmering white rock. The light cast rolling shadows across the white stone to reveal an entire herd of mammoths following behind their mother-of-the-herd. The leading mammoth's back, head and long curving trunk had been emphasized with a single graceful red line. The hazy image, as if covered by a thin layer of stone, was completely devoid of a mammoth's long curved tusks. As we made our slow way along the path, the whole herd seemed to move with us, running behind their mother-of-the-herd as our flames danced off the glistening, gushing waters. The further we went along the trail in front of the wonder, the shadows revealed more and more members of the spirit-mammoth family in a herd following behind their leader. This was always a moment of magic on the rounds of the Red Lodge. The Cascade of Mammoth Mother was a never-to-be-forgotten image for all the girls whose first experience of spirit-animals in the Cave was of this herd of shadowy, marvelously alive and moving mammoths.

"Take the right branch of this path to the entrance of the Womb of White Spirits, my Daughter," the Grandfather directed from where he doddered close behind me.

"As seer-initiate you must enter this place," he said mysteriously with a slight narrowing of his eyes.

I am beginning to catch on to some of his shaman's tricks of voice and manner. This time, the tone of his voice failed to alarm as it had once so disturbed me with the promise of deep and dangerous mysteries to come.

I followed the right-branching path and in no more than ten paces we arrived at the narrow entrance to the Womb of White Spirits. The Womb's left-hand portal is marked with two horses cut into the stony wall. They appear to be nibbling each other's necks as horses love to do. It is a moment of gleeful harmony and enjoyment between the two playful horses captured in a few carefully scratched lines. I was amazed at the skill with which they were made the first time I saw them. Now, I only appreciated them more. The wall to the right of the entrance also has signs, including various marks in red along with the scratched claw marks of Bear Mother.

"Did any of your age-mates enter to commune with the powers of this place?" he asked without emotion. The Grandfather was looking directly at the playful horses.

"Yes, Grandfather," I said. "White Lynx was brought here by Auntie after she went berserk during the third round."

"Ah," he said knowingly, "The two-spirit girl from Middle Camp—unfortunate name for a girl. The lynx is such a solitary animal," he said, thinking pensively out loud. "Did something happen at the end of the third round? It was during the ceremony of the Hymen Stone, was it not?" he mumbled the answer to his own question.

"Yes, Grandfather. It was terrible. She frightened all of us near to returning to the Mother. We had learned the Women's Song to Dispel Fear but White Lynx kept holding to the back of the line of girls. When the end of the line came and it was her time to receive the hymen stone she suddenly began to shake all over. She fell to the ground screaming and crying. She spilled her lamp's oil all over the place. It took Auntie, the other seer-helpers and White Lynx's mentor to hold her and quiet her enough so that Auntie and White Lynx's mentor-auntie could take her away. She did not return for a very long time. When she did rejoin us at the All Mother's Rock, she was big-eyed but calm. She did finish her initiation, I think. Except for the hymen stone," I explained.

"Do you know why White Lynx would behave in this way at the hearing of the Song to Dispel Fear and the presentation of the hymen stone? Do you know why Auntie would bring her here, to the white-spirited womb within this women's Red Lodge?" he asked.

The words of the Women's Song to Dispel Fear ran through my head as I searched for an answer:

Fear not the winter storm
It is only the Mother's embrace.
Fear not the summer drought
It is only the Mother's embrace.
Fear not the breaching child
It is only the Mother's embrace.
Fear not the fevered brow

It is only the Mother's embrace.
Fear not the pain of loss
It is only the Mother's embrace.
O Noble One
Fear is the killer of peaceful hearts.
Therefore, let go thy fear
Be one with the Mother.
It is only the Mother's embrace.

I sang the words of the song in my head and I remembered that White Lynx had watched her own mother die in childbirth. In fact, her mother had returned only a few seasons before we were brought into the Cave for our Moon Blood. There must have been much bleeding. I know that now from helping Auntie with bringing in newborns.

"Is it because White Lynx saw her mother die in childbirth? Was she afraid to give birth as a woman?" I ventured.

"That is certainly a large part of it," the Grandfather answered, nodding slightly. "But it may have simply been the time of the powers calling to White Lynx, like your Auntie's time was in her fever unto death. Only White Lynx can know the truth of that. The powers call us to be seers and shamans with many voices and in unexpected places. The Trickster's call to our own true way is among the sharpest of turns we will ever experience in our meandering path of life. As Seer, you will learn that nothing can stop the call of the powers when the proper time has come. When it does come, we can only choose to accept the call or reject it. But never can we hold back the Mother's Voice when the time has come," he said with faraway thoughts crossing his sad face.

As he spoke I thought of my mother, her mother, my Auntie and all I had been told about their lives. I began to understand why they have made the choices they have, why they have taken the paths they have. Am I making the right choice? Has the Mother's call really come to me?

Lost in my own thoughts, I came back to the present when the Grandfather continued his instruction. "Some powers choose the puberty rites to come forth and begin speaking to us. But then, much of the ceremony of the Great Cave is intended to make that happen. If the time has come, the initiate will hear the Song of the Mother in their hearts and nothing can stop it. As Seer, you should know that when the powers call to us, it is always terrifying. All of us will try to reject the call because hearing the Mother's Voice changes everything in our lives. The brightness of the light which dawns never makes life easier for any of us and so our first reaction is always to push it away and deny that the time to change our path has come. We all fear change of any kind and of not knowing what is coming. But, as Seer, you will learn that those who have heard and still reject the Mother's call do so with a shriveling of the soul."

The Grandfather paused for a moment for both of us to ponder what he had just said before going on. "In denying the Mother's light when it shines, we will also fail to bless the People with our gifts, Dear One. Though set apart from the People, our gifts are always and only given to us to bless and make the People abundant."

"Yes, Auntie has told me of the apartness that hearing the spirit-powers will bring," I agreed.

"Your wise Auntie is teaching you well, my Daughter. In White Lynx there is another great lesson to be learned. When a visitation of the powers comes during the puberty rites and the girl appears to have a terror of the blood of childbirth, or if she clearly fears joining in sex with men, she will most often be brought to this white-spirited place. Sometimes, as the Mother of the Rites is guided, the girl will be led to another womb of the Cave depending on what kind of healing is required. Some girls have been ill-treated by their parents or abused by the Uncles of the camps. They will be those in greatest need for a healing of the mind and the heart. It will also depend on whether the spirit-power that has come forth is red-spirited, white-spirited or black-spirited as to which womb they will be taken," he explained quietly.

"Red, white and black spirit-powers and wombs?" I asked. "What does it mean to have different colored wombs, different colored spirit-powers, my Grandfather?"

Without waiting for an answer I blurted out, "Grandfather, I am becoming very confused. You have already given me so many teachings and none of them are in rhyming songs, chants or stories. I am sure I will not remember the half of it. How will I ever learn all you are teaching me?" I pleaded on the verge of tears. I have always been so good at remembering things but now I was becoming confused.

"Dearest Little Bear, do not concern yourself with this. These teachings will be repeated many times over before we leave the Great Cave. You are now my Apprentice and I will be with you, together with your Auntie, to answer whatever questions may arise as you walk the path of Seer. When you will teach your own apprentices and initiates, understand that everyone follows the trail their hearts lead them upon at a different pace. But everyone is more or less open to the wisdom of the Mother when they are in the Great Cave. Teach what you are moved to teach in your heart and your apprentices will learn and remember what they are prepared to accept and to bring into their own everyday lives. Does that make sense to you, my Daughter?" he asked kindly.

"Yes, Grandfather, it does make sense. I will do my best," I said, somewhat reassured.

"Then we will continue with your question of the red, white and black wombs. The worlds of the powers are divided into three parts just as the worlds of our body-lives in the World of Light have three parts. Above, Grandfather Sun moves through the sky during the day, and at night, moves through the dark waters upon which the Middle World floats. The Middle World of the human and animal tribes, the Above World of the sky and the Below World under the ground, these are the three worlds of flesh and blood. These are the worlds of all the things we see and hear and smell and feel and desire in the organs of the body. These powers are centered in our livers. These three are all parts of the same World of Light and *is* the red-world of women giving birth and nourishing the bodies of their children. It is also the white-world of sunshine and rain coming from the father-powers of the Above which are centered in our heads. And it is the black-world of life-giving springs coming up from the deep waters of the Below. These are the three worlds of the life of the body and they may be signified by the colors red, white and black."

"Yes," I thought to myself. "Everyone knows that." I began to grow impatient as I am with my mother who tells me what I already know.

But the Grandfather continued on. "The worlds of the spirit-powers are also three in number: a white-world of the active, thinking, giving, male spirit-powers and a red-world of the receptive, still, feeling, female spirit-powers. When these two line up with each other in harmony they give rebirth to our hearts, which is the world of black spirit-powers. Black is the sign of the joining and oneness and aligning of the red and white spirit-powers within the blissful and harmonious heart. You have already seen these two worlds represented in the vertical and horizontal arms of the Mother's Cross of Red. Think on this and know that within the Great Cave we will yet encounter a Cross of White and a Cross of Black, signs for each of the three worlds of the spirit-powers."

"Yes, Grandfather, I think I understand. But how does combining red and white result in black? As one familiar with colors, mixing red and white does not result in black paint."

The Grandfather smiled one of his little smiles at me and chuckling softly said, "For now, my good Apprentice, just remember that black crosses, images and spirit-animals are all signs of the union of the red and white powers within the heart. It is not a mixing of paints, but is a mixing and balancing of unseen spirit-powers. As Seer, you will learn that the heart is the place of the union of head and liver, body and mind, red and white and when they are in harmony—in a line with each other—the color black will be a sign of that. In fact, black is the center of the Mother's Cross of every color because when you are at the center, you have balanced the red and the white parts of you. You will have harmonized the seen with the unseen powers which will no longer be struggling with and in contention one against the other. Know that black *is* the Great Cave itself in which the powers of red and the powers of white are found to be in harmony and joining in blissful union."

The Grandfather paused and took a deep breath. I hung suspended and breathless in anticipation of the rest of the teaching.

"This Great Cave within the bowels of Earth Mother is the place where we come to meet the all the powers of initiation face-to-face. Here we are to experience the birth of those powers within us just as the light world above is the place of the birth and rebirth of the flesh and blood lives of all the Mother's children. The spirit worlds of each of the Mother's crosses *are* the sign of the joining of the white-worlds above and the red-worlds below. The center spot of every cross sign *is* the black world where opposing things come together in love within our hearts—body, mind and spirit-power symbolized in red, white and black unified as one, which is to be joined and balanced within one's own heart. Even though these signs and colors have this meaning for many, it is still yours and yours alone to decide within yourself what any sign or spirit-animal of whatever color means to you and whether it speaks to you or not. As Grandfather, I can give you clues to the meaning of signs and spirit-animals, but it is your own heart that will understand the meaning, or not, regardless of what you have learned from others or what you have learned about your own soul. As Seer, you will do the same for others and that is one of the blessings you are destined to give the People," he concluded.

"Why are some caverns called *wombs* while others are not?" I asked.

"We call these side-chambers and small caves-within-the-cave *wombs* because these are the especially powerful places where animal-guides are born into our hearts to make us anew as Seers of the People. As you live your life, you will learn that even without teaching of any kind and without any specific experience which turns one's life-path into a different direction, that women possess the red-powers in abundance. In a similar way, men possess the white spirit-powers in abundance. The Cave was given us by the Mother as a place where both men and women may learn this crucial lesson about themselves. Each man and each woman must recognize the contradictory powers active within and deliberately choose to balance and harmonize those spirit-powers in their hearts to live a good and honest life among the People. As part of your initiation this day, you will enter all of the wombs of the Great Cave. From this you will learn which of these special lodges of the Cave an initiate should go to in order to experience the powers which are manifested in abundance there. As Seer, you will attempt to guide them to that holy place where they might find harmony between the red and the white spirit-powers within themselves. While in the Cave, we are all to seek out and commune with the powers that have called us to bless and heal the People. Can you understand this, my Daughter?" he asked, his eyebrows lifting up into a question.

"I think so, Grandfather," I replied. "If I have more questions I will be sure to ask them."

Still, I couldn't help wonder why *I* was here at all to be initiated as Seer? In all my life I had never felt nor heard nor seen nor even dreamed a white, red or a black spirit, whatever they are.

Again, as if the Grandfather had heard my very thoughts he answered the question. "Do you know the meaning of figures and signs scratched through the soft clay of the cave walls to the white stone beneath rather than painted in red?" he asked softly as I turned my attention again to the two affectionate horses engraved on the left-hand entrance portal of the Womb of White Spirits.

Seeing the puzzled look on my face, the Grandfather began to answer his own question before I could say, "No, I don't."

"Spirit-animals or signs engraved or scratched into the cave walls *are* the white, active, giving, thinking, male aspects of the animal-powers. The white horses on the left indicate a place where the mind-healing powers of the white Horse Mother are predominant. The nurturing, head-healing powers of the white Bear Mother are also here in abundance because her white claw marks appear upon the right portal of this entrance passage to the White Womb and in many other places. This is how you must learn to read the signs and symbols of the Cave to become Seer and initiator of girls to be women and perhaps even a shaman-of-healing. Do you understand the difference?"

"Yes, Grandfather, I am beginning to understand. But if this is a place of white spirit-powers, why are there red signs here as well?" I asked, pleased I had given the Grandfather a difficult question to answer.

"The various red marks and signs appearing at the portal and within the White Womb should say to you that the red, passive, receptive, feeling, female aspects of the animal-powers are still present, even though the white spirit-power is dominant in this special place. Always, the white must be balanced with the red and the red with the white if the healing of the mind and the body is to take place as they become one within the heart of the person you are healing. As a shaman-of-healing, you will not only allow the white-spirits of the head to work through you to heal the minds of the People but you will also allow the red-powers of the liver to give you the healing touch for the bodies of the People. As shaman-of-healing you will also be able to heal the very souls of the People in addition to their minds and their bodies. For now, know that Seers are Twice Born and so have skills to heal the red-spirited body and the white-spirited mind. As Seer you should always remember that the two must always be treated together if true healing is to take place. When a girl like White Lynx shrinks in terror from a red spirit-power, as Seer, you will realize she is in need of healing from a harmonizing white spirit-power. Now take the torch and enter this Womb of White Spirits as seer-apprentice and open yourself to allow the powers of this place speak to you, if you will but hear."

The Grandfather pointed to the shadowy entrance with his torch.

CHAPTER 5.
HOLY ROUNDS OF THE RED LODGE

WITHOUT SAYING ANOTHER WORD I placed my lamp on a flat stone beneath the joyful white spirit-horses and reached out an unsteady hand for the torch. "I am terrified to go in alone, Grandfather," I admitted.

"All is well, Daughter of my Heart. Have no fear. Remember always that nothing the Mother has made will ever hurt you. The Mother would only be harming herself!" he said with a broad smile as if he had just told some hilarious joke.

Seeing that I was not laughing, the Grandfather became more serious. "If your uncertainty gives rise to apprehension speak the Song of Dispelling Fear and enter with courage. Know that the Mother always stands within the shadows keeping watch upon her own. You may not feel it yet, but you *are* her own, Dear One," he tried to comfort me.

"I'm still scared to go alone, Grandfather," I pleaded. "I never went into any of the side-chambers to quest by myself during my Moon Blood."

"I know you are afraid, Dear One, but there is nothing to fear. Our bodies and minds may suffer and feel pain, but wherever we are, the All Mother stretches out her arms to gather us to her great bosom to comfort us as every mother does her beloved child. We may be fearful and we may stumble and miss the mark, but always there is the Mother's Voice, forever whispering peace and refuge within our ear. We are happy *wherever* we are and whether we are alone or with others. We may appear to be alone, but the Mother is with us always because she is within us and all around us. If we but listen to that soothing gentle voice, she forever sings and sings and sings," he said, already flown to some faraway place of dreams.

I was still terrified, nonetheless. I waited for the Grandfather to finish speaking and hand me the torch but he just stood there staring into the blackness of the entrance to the White Womb.

I touched his hand and called quietly so as not to startle him, "Grandfather, Grandfather?"

Abruptly roused back to the present moment he said, "Yes. Ah, yes, my Granddaughter. You may continue."

He handed me the torch and, grudgingly, I asked permission of the white Horse Mother to enter. I started moving through the opening between the two sidewalls of the wide entrance higher than me by half. A few paces on, the roof of the passage soared up even higher. To my right, I could see a faint glimmer of sunlight coming through a small opening high up near the roof. It had to be the blocked passage at the Portal of the Mother's Mouth. That meant that I was very close to the cliffs nearby the entrance to the Great Cave.

I continued moving through the passage in what I sensed was a southwesterly direction. The passage dead-ended after only fifteen paces, so I backtracked on a faint trail that had been trodden by very few feet. I easily found my way back to a place where the wall curved inward to reveal a tiny opening. I got down on my hands and knees to crawl through.

"I see why he gave me the torch. All the oil in a lamp would have been spilled by now and I would be in the dark just getting through this hole as tight as a little girl's pute!" I thought to myself. "Oh, I get it now!" I said out loud, the Grandfather already well out of hearing.

I continued repeating the calming chant as I emerged from the very low and narrow entry passage to see how the White Womb opened out into a much larger space. The cavern here is large but the roof is so low I could not stand straight up until I reached a ledge that dropped down to a lower level. The same red clay covered the floor here just as in the main part of the Red Lodge.

When I looked up, I noticed a line of five big red dots on the roof directly above the ledge. Obviously, the five dots and the ledge are a dividing line between the red and white parts of this womb-chamber. I slid over the short drop where I could see that the lower level is covered with a hard white surface—no more red ochre on this ground. The rock-like floor reflected little yellow sparkles of torch light back to me and the walls here have many niches and deep crevices. Whatever flat wall spaces there are have no images at all, except at the very back of the ever-narrowing chamber at least twenty paces deep. I could tell it was running in a southeasterly direction. I reasoned from that I had to be very close to the outside World of Light.

Sure enough, when I reached the very back of the chamber, there were many tree roots coming in from the outside. I looked but I couldn't find any opening, however small, to the World of Light. I thought of all my friends and family who went about their daily rounds even as I crawled about on all fours in these damp and stony chambers.

"Could these be the roots of the Tree of Life the shamans are said to follow to the spirit worlds in their trances?" I wondered aloud.

Upon reaching the back of the White Womb, I could see the walls contained only a single engraved, and therefore, "white" Mammoth Mother. This mammoth had no tusks but was accompanied by a single engraved ibex—a male with huge curving horns.

"Is this the union of male and female spirit-powers?" I wondered aloud. "I will have to ask the Grandfather when I get out of this stuffy, musty hole in the ground!"

The only other marks on the back wall I could see were some bear claw marks and a group of black dots—black spirit-powers—the sign of the union of the red and white spirit-powers which I had just learned about, no doubt.

"Interesting," I said aloud, finding some comfort in the sound of my own voice. "The Cave begins to speak to me in signs and symbols."

The Song to Dispel Fear worked well enough to calm me, but all I wanted was to get out of this place. Immediately turning around and running straight back to the Grandfather wouldn't look good, so I went back and sat down on the dividing ledge just to see if a power of any kind or color would come to me. Even with deep breaths and closed eyes nothing came. And it was nothing coming to me for what seemed a long, long time. It is time to go back.

The Grandfather didn't need to ask if I had communed with the powers of this white womb. I had remained barely long enough to talk to myself, let alone to commune with an animal-guide. The Grandfather was just standing up from his seat on a large rock near the entrance when I reached him. I handed back the torch and picked up my lamp once more.

"Let us continue on our circle of the Red Lodge," is all that the Grandfather would say to me. Moving on is fine with me.

I wondered why he hadn't asked me anything of my short adventure into the Womb of White Spirits. But then, I had not asked anything of him even though I did have questions about the black signs at the back of this white womb-chamber.

* * *

The wall along which we began to pass had plenty of flat spaces to make spirit-animals. But none appeared until we reached the opening to a very narrow and deep side-chamber. There, at the entrance, on the left-hand wall, the first image to be seen was a small red bear. It is my namesake, if nothing else. Some kind of a deer— probably a big-antler without any antlers—had been made in red on the right-hand side of the entrance.

At this deep niche the Grandfather stopped and asked, "Daughter? Did any of your age-mates come to this place on a personal quest to sit with the animal-guides here?"

"Maybe," I ventured. "I'm not sure because after the incident with White Lynx, I was too afraid to leave the Rock, the hearth fire and my mother to go anywhere on my own. I don't know where my other Moon Blood sisters actually went to quest by themselves. A few sisters left the group and went to other parts of the Red Lodge. But most of us stayed near the Rock of the All Mother to sing and drum and dance and tell stories until it was time to leave the Cave. I suppose this could be a place one of my sisters might have come to sit with the spirit-powers," I guessed.

"This narrow split in the cave wall is called the Women's Womb of Red Spirits," he began. "It is one of the red wombs of the Great Cave to which some girls are drawn in their quest for a personal animal-guide. See how the right-hand entrance portal is marked with a red-painted deer lacking any antlers? Within this side-chamber are only female or hornless spirit-animals in red. As I have already instructed you, my Daughter, the Women's Red Lodge is a place where the red-powers predominate. Girls who may feel that the often overbearing white spirit-powers of the head may be in need of balancing can sit with the red-powers here. Such girls should be directed to this womb if they are questing and trancing for a guide of the red-spirits," he said with a pointed look in my direction.

"Please step inside the portals of this Red Womb and tell me what you see," he instructed patiently.

"Before I do, my Grandfather, I have one question."

I was stalling again because I would probably feel as uncomfortable in this place as I had in the White Womb.

"Why does this big-antler deer have no horns? It's clear it is a stag that has shed his antlers for the winter," I commented as I pointed to the red image.

It marked the right-hand portal to the narrow chamber into which my feeble lamplight barely penetrated.

"Did no one instruct you on the meaning of such a spirit-animal?" he asked.

"No, Grandfather," I replied, wondering why Auntie had forgotten to pass this bit of information on to me.

"I'm sure I would have remembered if I had been told, Grandfather," excusing my lack of an answer.

Actually, I was thinking, "Maybe Auntie forgot to tell us with all the turmoil of White Lynx? I suppose the instruction we receive in the Cave *could* be different."

"My Daughter," he began. "After the three holy rounds of the Red Lodge, if you did not feel moved to quest and meditate in this place by yourself, you would not have been brought here and given instruction. Let me say now that this great egg-shaped cavern is a place of women. It is the Lodge of Red Spirits and so none of the spirit-animals here have horns or antlers, except those where both males and females have them, like the bison, the rhino or the ibex. Though they have horns, their spirit-powers are said to be neither overpoweringly male nor female. They are said to be both male and female and so are a sign of the perfect harmony of red and white spirit-powers. Since they balance the white and red aspects of themselves they may appear anywhere in the Great Cave as red, white or even black spirit-powers because males and females will be almost indistinguishable one from the other. When animals like the mammoth are made here, since the giant tusks of bull mammoths distinguish them from the smaller mother mammoths, Mammoth Mother is made without any tusks at all here in the Red Lodge."

"But Grandfather? Why a big-antler without his gigantic horns here, at a place of entrance?" I asked.

"At the entrance to this and other wombs of the Cave, the presence of this stag big-antler deer that has shed his horns is to instruct and caution us. If you wish to enter and commune with the animal-guides of this red womb, you must leave behind what you think you are, what you think you want, what all others say you are and open your heart to the red spirit-powers of this place. Only then may you discover who and what you really are in your heart and soul. Having left behind all you believe yourself to be, your personal animal-companion may then come forth and show itself to you to be your guide and companion for life. By leaving behind the thoughts of your head about yourself and even the desires of your red-body, only then will the spirit-power at the center of your being come to you and reveal to you what it is you really want and who you truly are in your heart and soul. Do you understand, Dear One?" he asked.

I really didn't understand but I said, "Yes, Grandfather, I understand," anyway.

"Very well, my Apprentice. Go in and tell me what you encounter."

After hesitantly asking the powers of the Red Womb for permission to enter, I moved forward a few paces into the narrow entrance of the side-chamber, actually, a huge crack in the cave wall. I walked in a southeasterly direction further and further back into the little cavern. I stopped at a spot almost to the end of the crevice where I could make out a buttock-sized depression in the dark red clay floor. The little round hollow had obviously been pressed by many girls' bottoms over many seasons, each one sitting on her robe to commune with the red animal-powers of this place.

"I see two red ibex and three big red bears. They are all coming from cracks or shadows in the rock in the direction of the mouth of the side-chamber," I shouted to the Grandfather over my shoulder.

"Sit and contemplate for a time, my Daughter," he called back, his voice muffled with distance.

Grudgingly, I sat trying to find the butt-depression through the thick bearskin robe. As I placed the lamp on the ground just to my right, a stiff breath of unexpectedly fresh air snuffed all three wicks leaving me dead blind in the dark! Blackness like I had never experienced descended around me in a suffocating blanket as heavy as a wet bison robe tied around my head.

The terror of the unseen and the unknown grabbed my throat. I began screaming, "Grandfather, Grandfather! Help me! Help me! The darkness!"

I could not move even my little finger I was so paralyzed with fear. The unseen and unseeable cave walls closed in to smother me.

I screamed again, "Grandfather, Grandfather! Come get me! I am afraid!"

Still no response. Then I heard in a small, muted voice as if it were coming from across a valley, "Calm yourself, my Daughter. The Mother is always with you and I am here. Slowly take in the Breath and I will come for you," the Grandfather's muffled voice came like a soothing balm.

I began to breathe in and exhale slowly. Then the anger began to rise up from my liver. The Grandfather had stranded me in this darkest of dark holes by design! He knew the little breeze from the outside would snuff my light!

"Curse this old man and his shaman's tricks!" I shouted silently in my head on the chance he was actually coming for me and would hear if I cursed him aloud.

A touch on my shoulder made me jump. I didn't even know I had my eyes tightly clenched shutting out even the Grandfather's torch light, I was so furious and frightened.

"I am here, my Daughter," he said without emotion. I turned on him glaring as if the look in my lion-eye was a spear to his cold, dark heart!

"I see you are angry, Dear One," he said, a broad smile spreading across his face. "Did you really think I would fail to come to you?" he chuckled.

I was still too angry to answer.

"From the telling of your Moon Blood, it seemed as though you had never experienced the full power of the darkness of the Mother's Great Cave. Should you be initiated as Seer without ever having experienced the complete and utter blackness of the Cave as all hunters and seers are expected to feel for themselves? If only for a few moments?"

My anger, my fear really, began to subside as I understood the Grandfather was just testing me again.

"If you had been rescued too quickly, you would not have learned how easily fear can shift its shape into anger, my Daughter," he said with a knowing smile and raised eyebrows.

"Yes, Grandfather," I said simply, my jaw still half-clenched in anger. "I have decided that my 'heart' is telling me I have a lot more important places in the Mother's Cave to be than here," I replied sarcastically.

"Fair enough," the Grandfather agreed with a slight nod.

Still with a wide toothy grin on his face he said, "Let me ask you a question, Dear One. Now that you have entered these two Wombs of the Red Lodge, why do you think White Lynx was brought to the White Womb to heal rather than this Red Womb?"

He asked the question and immediately began moving on down the path.

I should be able to sort all this out, I thought. But I really had no idea why, so I just had to admit, "I don't really know, Grandfather."

He stopped and I waited to hear what he had to teach me next. As the Grandfather began to speak, I let the remainder of my anger float away into the darkness from whence it had come.

"To learn what it means to be two-spirited, my Daughter, you must understand that what our own soul longs to be and what we desire to join with in the World of Light, is what we are in our hearts. But that is rarely how we appear in our bodies to others or even what we think we are in our own heads. Know that every creature possesses a male power and a female power within. Because women are said to have a red spirit-power and men a white spirit-power does not mean women are unable to think with their heads and men have no passions of the liver. How could a woman ever learn to recognize the plants that will nourish or heal us and distinguish them from plants that will poison or sicken us if women could not use the senses of their heads? How could you be so intelligent as to be able to memorize the stories and songs and chants of our People if you did not use your head, which is where our memories collect? All of us, men and women alike, have skills and learning of the head we use every day. But it is the silent urges of our red-bodies, the passions of our livers, which really move us. Even while our livers drive us on, our heads may only be aware of what is actually going on when we are awake. But when we dream or trance, we are going down into the silent world of the secret urges of the liver and we can see the desires of the different organs of the body made into shapes and forms. The head, only aware of the waking world, is completely unaware of the hidden senses of the world of dreams without special effort or concentration."

"Yes, Grandfather. I know that to be true," I volunteered.

"Then you might also know that most of us have one power within that predominates. Sometimes we are born with one spirit-power controlling the urges and desires of the body which is not the same as we appear to others—on the outside. Many things are hidden within us all and are never shown to those around us for fear they will not love or respect us. Always within Mammoth Mother's full moon is hidden the Bison Father's horns of the new moon. So, which is the moon, male or female? Father or Mother? I will tell you, Dear One, that it is both and neither all at the same time. It depends entirely upon what it is you wish to see in yourself and what you choose to show to others. As Seer, you must learn to see below the appearances of the body and never to judge another before you have looked with your soul and listened with your heart. Because two-spirit men and women are much more aware of these opposing powers struggling within every one of us, it makes them closer to the Mother at their very birth. Two-spirited animals and birds, by their very souls, are closer to the Mother and so are often the spirit-companions of shamans and seers. In our questing and in our trancing, we are to learn what and who we really are, to balance the opposite powers within and live our lives from that balance and harmony. Does that make any sense to you?" he asked.

"I think I can understand how that could be, my Grandfather," I agreed. "So White Lynx has one spirit-power in her liver and a different one in her head? Is that right?" I asked.

"So it seems, my Daughter. We come to the Great Cave for its trials and revelations, in part, to learn who and what we are. We are to allow whatever aspect of us which emerges to open a new life for us that will bless all the People. In your Moon Blood you came to this Great Cave as a girl and left knowing you are a woman, equal to the Earth Mother giving birth and nurturing all new life, is that not so?"

"Yes, Grandfather, that is true. We girls leave the Great Cave different persons than we came in," I agreed.

"In the same way, the boys come to the Cave and leave as men and hunters. But if two spirits continue to fight with each other inside us to be what we show to others, only confusion and chaos and madness can result. Only sorrow, unhappiness and suffering come if we do not follow our heart's true desire. It is the heart which balances and unifies these conflicting powers of the head and liver within us. As Seer, you must be able to discern which spirits are fighting within each person causing imbalance and sickness if you are to restore harmony and heal the mind and the body. White Lynx did not know she is two-spirited, but the Cave has revealed it to her because, like all two-spirits, she is holy to the Mother and is full of her spirit-powers. All two-spirits bring together opposite worlds because they have one foot in each, just as the swan has her feet in the water and her wings in the clouds. I will tell you that White Lynx has a blessing to give to the People by following her own path. But the only way for her to know, in her heart, who and what she really is and for a spirit-companion to guide her to what she might become, was to bring her to the Womb of White Spirits *because* she was fearful of the red-powers which fill the Red Lodge to overflowing. To be so fearful of something within us that is an inseparable part of us is the surest way to unhappiness and suffering. Even her name tells you the White Womb is where her soul wished to go."

"So does that mean by bringing her to the White Womb she found her special spirit-guide?" I asked.

"That is uncertain. Whether or not she found herself in the White Womb and discovered her spirit-guide while there, only she can tell. All you can do as Seer is to point the way and bring the seeker to the brink of wisdom. You cannot force anyone in any direction just because you think it is the way they should go. Do you understand, my Daughter?" he concluded.

"I think I am beginning to understand, Grandfather," I ventured. I was thinking again of all I had learned about my own family.

"So if White Lynx was terrified of her female—her red-spirited—side there is certain to be another power, a male spirit there? Is that what you are saying, Grandfather?"

"Yes, that is what I am saying, my intelligent Apprentice. As Seer, you must not assume you know what is happening within someone else's head or liver—it is difficult enough to know that for ourselves. The white wombs of the Cave are most likely to speak to those girls who are fearful of the red blood of life and the Middle World of the living. Their destiny often lies with the worlds of the spirit-powers and they frequently take the shamans' journey. Other girls and boys will be drawn to the red wombs of the Cave during their initiations as men and women. Even a few will find themselves with the deep desire to go into the black-spirited wombs of the Cave. As I have said, the black wombs are places where the spirits of the white and red-worlds become as one within the heart, a most difficult and sometimes dangerous path to choose. There are powerful connections and pathways between the white and red-worlds of the head and the liver that are only to be discovered by those who have the courage to face their true selves and enter the Lodge of Black Spirits, which is the Lodge of Lion Mother within the deepest part of the Great Cave. This is why the destinies of you and I are to be found in the black wombs of the Cave and not here, Dear One," he concluded.

"I think I understand, Grandfather. That is why the Womb of White Spirits has many tree roots. The roots connect the world above and the spirit worlds below and make a pathway the souls of shamans can travel in trance. It is why the entrance has two white horses, why the red dots of the Five Mothers divide the White Womb in two parts. I think that is why the white Mammoth Mother, the white Ibex Father and the black dots are at the back of the White Womb. All three worlds are connected in that one place. And that is why there are only red spirit-animals within the Womb of Red Spirits. I see, I see!" I cried, enthused at my brilliant insights.

"Very good, my Daughter, you are my excellent Apprentice," he said with much less exuberance than I was showing but with a satisfied smile nonetheless.

"What will happen to White Lynx now? Is she a seer?" I suddenly had so many questions.

"No, she is not yet ready to become a seer. That may never happen for White Lynx. Each must open to the powers in their own way and in their own time. Here is a great lesson for you, my good Apprentice: at any given moment, each is moved by different urges and life is lived according to the desires of one organ, one part of the body or one way of thinking of the heart or head. Which desire guides any person at any given time in their life is only to be discovered by quiet observation. It is not to be discovered by giving judgment on what appears on the outside. I am sure you have known people who live only to eat the fattest of meats and those whose only desire is to pleasure themselves by joining in sex. There will be those you know and love who are always fearful and only live to tell others what to do in the effort to protect themselves from imagined harm and pain. Some happy souls will act only out of concern and kindness and compassion for others. And for you, my Daughter, there may come a time when your whole life-path will be only to speak the truth of the All Mother through song and story. You may even know those, perhaps like your Auntie, who live out of the kindness and compassion of a truly loving heart. A Seer is to open their own soul and become a true seer who sees all things with the Mother's Single Eye, which distinguishes between what is true and what is beautiful and what is not. And, if you have opened your heart completely to the Mother, you may be so blessed as to be able to look past the All Mother into the Abyss of Stillness and know the bright and shining wisdom of all the worlds to come," he instructed.

"Then what am I to think about White Lynx? What moves her?" I questioned.

"That is not for us to decide. Each is deserving of respect for every choice they make and we must forgive if their choices cause us confusion or pain. I believe she has yet to choose which path she will take in her life. At times, the two-spirited reject the part of themselves they fear the most and remain out of balance by choosing to go completely to the opposite side. I believe White Lynx must have begun learning who she is in her heart when Auntie brought her to the White Womb to heal her troubled heart. But in opening to the white-spirits, she may have only come to completely reject the female side of her soul. You must know she acts and dresses more like a man every day and has even begun to go out with the hunters as a bearer. You are her age-mate and live in the same Middle Camp? Are you gift-givers and companions with White Lynx?" he asked without accusation.

The Grandfather may not have accused me with his question, but I did so to myself. I felt the blood rush to my face in shame even as I answered, "No, Grandfather, I am not. But I have promised Auntie I will become a true Moon Blood sister to White Lynx in the future."

"Yes, Dear One. I see that to be friends will be good for both of you. As members of the Red Sisterhood you should help each other, be friends and gift-givers. I'm sure you know how lonely she must be with only men to talk to. That is so especially now that her older brother has joined the hearth of his new wife. White Lynx is alone in her lodge with only her ailing father. Why have you not done this before?" he asked as if he had just thought of it.

"Grandfather, I don't know why, exactly. I am ashamed to say it, but it's just that she is so strange and so different from all the other women of the Middle Camp. She smells bad too. I really don't know what to say to her. Besides, what will I do if she wants to join in sex with me? I am not attracted to women's bodies at all," I babbled on.

The Grandfather smiled, actually chuckled out loud, before answering. "What if she does? You are a woman and, no doubt, have refused to join in sex with many men. It is you and no other who chooses to join in sex or not. Why would White Lynx be any different? She is alone in the world and surely would benefit greatly from having another woman and age-mate to talk to. You would certainly benefit from making a new friend within the Middle Camp. As Seer, you will have to talk to, be compassionate with, and giving of your healing gifts to many who are either strange, different or both. Surely, even those who smell bad are in need of your friendship too? Some of those you help will want to join in sex with you just because you are kind to them. Will you then reject them and deny them your gifts of healing just because they might want to join in sex with you?" he concluded with a knowing smile.

"Yes Grandfather, I know. I have already been scolded by Auntie for not treating her as a Moon Blood sister should."

My eyes turned toward the ground in embarrassment.

"I'm sure you will be pleased to make a friend of White Lynx. She is sure to be grateful for your friendship and she may one day become a powerful shaman-of-the-hunt ... but only the Mother knows that."

The Grandfather's voice trailed off into far away places and almost forgotten Great Hunts upon the Plains of Summer.

Then, with more than a hint of sadness in his voice the Grandfather said, "Enough of that. We have much else to do this day. Let us continue on our holy round of the Red Lodge."

* * *

Once again taking the lead, I knew the next place of great spirit-power in the Red Lodge is only fifteen paces further on. The well-trodden path followed a wall that curved around, first, toward the northeast, and then, in a more northerly direction. As we made our way along the smooth stretch of stone that had become the south-eastern wall of the Red Lodge, we rounded a large outcrop of rock forming the right-hand portal of yet another deep side-chamber. Upon the left wall opposite the right-hand entrance of this wide crevice, the huge Animal of Dots loomed out of the darkness.

During the second round of the Red Lodge for the girls, this was the place where all were taught how to contemplate and to meditate. We learned to relax our minds and our bodies, to go into a waking trance and to allow the powers to come to us. The open area in front of the Animal of Dots was much more spacious than many other parts of the Red Lodge. The wall of the Animal of Dots was actually the left side of a wide entrance to a narrow chamber which opened up to the Red Lodge, the center of which was mostly filled with fallen rocks and jumbled stones.

Here, before the Animal of Dots, we initiates, the Mother of the Rites and her assistants all had enough space to sit upon our robes and the red-stained clay floor. We were all instructed to stare at the Animal of Dots without looking away until we began to go into trance. It is easy to see that one of the Ancient Ones had made the Animal of Dots by covering the palm of their right hand with red ochre and pressing it against the wall. A few finger marks could still be seen on some of the dots.

"Daughter, which animal do you see in the dots?" the Grand-father asked.

"Well, today I can see one of the great ones, a mother mammoth. But at my Moon Blood I could only see the bison. See? Its head is made up of those dots that also looks like the mammoth's trunk," I explained while gesturing toward the image.

At first look, it appears to be made up of randomly placed red dots but they are anything but random.

"Some said they saw a bear. I still have difficulty seeing the bear unless I stand close in. Why is it made to look different to each of us, my Grandfather?" I asked.

"It is three animals-in-one and one animal-in-three because we all must learn to allow others to see what they will. We must learn to allow whatever spirit-guide speaks to us to come freely, whether it is Mammoth Mother or Ant Mother without saying anyone is wrong because it is not what we see or what we hear or what we feel. From a different position one sees the bear, another sees the mammoth and another will see the bison. And yet everyone is correct. It also teaches us that all the animal-messengers—and the People too—are one with the Mother. All things *are* the Mother and the Mother is in all things. The Animal of Dots may show only three of the most important of the Nine Kin, but we and all the People are still one," he explained.

We began moving again around a jutting, ground-to-roof column of stone that made up the left-hand portal of the Animal of Dots. We continued on to the eastern side of the Red Lodge which had numerous stony curves and bumps jutting out from the cave wall. I could tell we were moving away from the southeastern part of the Red Lodge where the Red Womb and Animal of Dots were located. After many paces, the wall had gradually curved around and we were now moving in a northeasterly direction.

After many more paces, we finally arrived at the Rock of the Yellow Horse which had been made upon the most easterly wall of the Lodge of Red Spirits. Here, the only two yellow images in the whole of the Red Lodge were made. The Rock of the Horses had been painted with two horse heads in yellow ochre with a smaller horse head in red made just in front of them—three horses in all. Only the heads were showing, which was the sign that the three were emerging—being born—from the stony skin of the cave wall. Surrounding the horse heads all around were many red lines, rods, slashes and small dots made with the thumb or tip of a finger. The Grandfather and I stood side-by-side holding our lights up to better see the images and signs. We continued to gaze at them in the absolute quiet of the Cave for a long moment.

I find the silence of the Great Cave on this journey is very unnerving. During my Moon Blood, the Red Lodge had echoed almost continuously with much sound. That is, except for the times when everyone was supposed to be learning how to trance. Then, the Cave had been full of the giggles, chatter, chanting, and toward the end of the rites, the sound of young girls' voices in song accompanied by the flutes, rattles and drums of a dance circle. Now, the Great Cave was as silent as death. The only sounds that could be heard were of our breathing and an occasional drip of water from the roof of the Cave somewhere in the encroaching blackness all around us.

As we looked at the Horse Mothers, the Grandfather whispered in that voice which made one lean toward him in anticipation.

"May I ask, Dear One, during your Moon Blood, did you see or speak with a personal animal-messenger while in trance?"

And then, so anxious to please after the shame of my exposed poor treatment of White Lynx, before I could stop myself and hold my tongue, I lied to the Grandfather.

"Yes, Grandfather," I croaked in a small, high-pitched voice.

"And who, may I ask, is your animal-guide, my Daughter?" he prodded gently.

"Horse Mother, my Grandfather," I said, my face flushing hot with the lie.

Good thing it is so dark in here—the Grandfather would not be able to see the signs of false words on my face or in my eyes. I had grasped at the first spirit-animal before me and since I was staring at a horse, a horse-guide it is!

"Ah, yes," he replied and slowly turned toward me. "I see the yellow spirit-fire of Horse Mother boiling around you even now. Yours *is* the yellow power of the rising sun warming and nurturing, giving new life and healing to all. You already have the healing gifts of Horse Mother. Auntie has told me and I see that in you," he said, to my complete astonishment.

"But, but, but …" I stammered, trying to find the courage to tell him the truth.

The truth is that I have *never* heard Horse Mother's voice in my head. I have never seen her with my heart or felt her in my liver! My trances are always incomplete, my dreams unremarkable. I cannot make a melodious song or even a rhyming chant. And I certainly do not have the Mother's gift of seeing another's spirit-fire! The turmoil of shame inside told me I had to speak the truth to the Grandfather.

"Grandfather?" I began. "I have experienced the shimmering dots, the lines and zigzags and swirling colors of trance. But I have *never* heard *any* messenger's voice. I have never seen any spirit-guide. I'm sorry. I lied to you Grandfather," I confessed in a tiny voice.

"It is of no importance, Dear One. Do not be concerned," he comforted. "Your trances and dreams may not have been complete but I see that your spirit-fire *is* that of the healing yellow Horse Mother. I see it even now surrounding and shining from you. She guides you and protects you, though you don't know it yet. I also see the roiling green spirit-fire of the opening of your heart, Dear One. When it is your time, yellow Horse Mother will call to you in the Small Quiet Voice in your heart and you will answer—the green spirit-fire glowing all around you tells me so. In the meantime, your gifts are the gifts of the white spirit-powers. You know the way home after only taking the trail once. You can remember stories and songs with only one hearing and you learn with great ease the healing herbs and potions and the healing chants of the seers and shamans. Even at this moment, these gifts are awakening within you because you can give birth to spirit-images that have the living, healing power of the Mother in them. That *is* Horse Mother speaking to your heart even though you don't realize it yet. This is why you have been called by the powers through my dreams because I have not your Mother-given skill to make the living images of the animal-messengers. In time, the Mother will fully awaken within your heart and the gifts of thy intelligent head will be balanced by the gifts of thy life-giving liver and you will become a great Shaman of the Bear People, healing body, mind and soul," he said with loving tenderness and great respect.

"I feel there is truth in your words, Grandfather. But how can I possess a lion-eye and have Lion Mother's favor and now you say you see the yellow Horse Mother's fire about me when neither of these animal-guides have ever spoken or appeared to me? With such signs, how can it be that two guides can fail to come to one person?" I questioned.

"The powers come forth to those whose hearts are open to them. Only when the heart has opened can you receive them, feel their presence and hear their voices. Know that as many powers will reveal themselves to you as you are open to receive, Dear One. If it is guidance your soul desires for things of the body, a red spirit-messenger will come forth. For the things of the heart, a black spirit-messenger will manifest to you. For the things of the head, a white spirit-guide will come. One guide speaking to you does not preclude other animal-companions from coming forth if that is what your soul desires or what you need to be who you truly are," the Grandfather explained patiently.

"I begin to see, Grandfather. May I ask … have you other guides beside the otter-spirit who is your companion?"

"No, I have no other that has come to me. That is most likely because the otter is a guide which already bridges two worlds—the red-world of the land and the white-world of the surface waters. The otter-companion alone has been sufficient for one such as me. All you need do is continue to go within to that secret place in your heart where the worlds of the Above and the Below are joined as one. When it is the appropriate time for you to know them and to be guided by them, they will come forth for you."

"But Grandfather, how will I know when I am called? How will I know when my heart has opened and my animal-messenger is speaking to me?" I pleaded.

"It may be you will know at the moment when you look into the eyes of a living animal and see the Mother there in its eye glistening with understanding. It may be that you will feel it in your heart when you are looking into the eyes of a sister or a brother, a father or a mother and you see your own true self looking back at you. You may know it when you see certain signs and symbols around you and you know in your heart their meaning without having to be told by another. Many know their animal-guides are speaking to them by finding a special stone or by seeing a shape in a cloud or a color in a rainbow. Some see the Mother's guide as a voluptuous woman with heavy breasts, wide hips and dancing eyes. Look at your own woman's necklace, my Daughter. Gifts given to us by others may be signs from the Mother that she is speaking to us. Dear One, do you not know this is the necklace of a seer and a shaman?"

The Grandfather reached out to lift the necklace from my breasts.

"What do you mean, Grandfather? This necklace was given to me by my mother when I became a woman," I said, knowing how much my mother detested anything to do with seers and shamans.

He held the single leopard tooth in the center of the necklace between thumb and finger. "This *is* the necklace of a shaman, Dear One. It is the necklace of a seer. You must have already realized that? The leopard's tooth is the sign and mark of the Dark Mothers of the Lodge of Black Spirits, just as your lion-eye is a sign and mark of those powers. The polished bird-bone beads look to be those of a goose, a sign of the white bird-powers that carry seers and shamans in their flights of trance through the heavens. They are a symbol of Swan Mother, who bridges the worlds of water, earth and sky. But most telling are the horse knuckle bones made into beads for your necklace—they are not just for playing games of chance, my Daughter. These knuckle bones are a sign of the red-spirits of the earth and are a symbol of Horse Mother. Do you see? Leopard, swan and horse—the Three-in-One and the One-in-Three. Without any doubt, yours is a shaman's necklace regardless of the intentions of the maker. Was your seer-hating mother the maker of the necklace?"

Stunned, all I could say was, "Yes, Grandfather. But does it not anger you that my mother thinks of you and all other seers and shamans in this way?"

"Of course not, my Daughter. Each discovers the Mother in their own way and in their own time. Each has had experience to make them what they are and as seers we do not reject or judge what they do or say, even if it is unkind. There is nothing to be angry with in what your mother thinks of seers and shamans. Those are her thoughts and have very little to do with me—or with you. You will learn that such people are often the source of signs and lessons for us. This necklace of your mother's making is just the kind of sign we must learn to pay close attention to when we become seers and healers of the People. Have only love and respect for those who teach you with signs and oppositions in spite of themselves, my dearest Little Bear."

I had become dumb and speechless and could only stare blankly at the Grandfather who suddenly seemed to have gone to another world again. Eyes closed, he swayed slowly from side-to-

144

side with what looked like absolute ecstasy upon his face. He moved so effortlessly between the worlds it completely astonished me. Left without words, I waited again in silent awe for him to speak.

"I will have to sort out all of this later," I thought to myself.

After a few more silent, blissful moments, the Grandfather returned from wherever he had gone. He whispered, "Come, Daughter, let us complete our holy round of the Red Lodge. You will know what comes next," he said with a little smile and a wink.

* * *

I did know what was coming next—the one place in the Great Cave that would have given poor White Lynx another screaming fit. As we followed the easterly wall of the Red Lodge, we moved around more stony outcrops, bulges and deep crevices. In no more than twenty paces we had come around to the most northerly wall of the Red Lodge and the last collection of images in its holy round. Painted on a smooth wall, there appeared a scattering of images beginning with an antlerless deer. Most likely a red deer or reindeer doe, by the look of it. If it was intended as the sign of the Reindeer Mother of the north, she was in her proper place on this northern wall of the Red Lodge, but she was not made in her proper black color as she otherwise should have been. I could see that this red Deer Mother also acted as an entrance marker. To her left, in the direction she was looking, lay a collection of red dots and some engraved crosshatching. Some of the crosshatched squares were filled in with black, yellow and red—the colors of the four directions all in one image, if you consider the white engraved lines as one of the four colors. There are also a lot of red rod shapes with a rounded protrusion at one end. They look like penises with man-eggs to me.

The most curious thing about this part of the Red Lodge is that the floor here is hard, white and wet with water dripping from a high ceiling in front of the wall of the colored signs and Deer Mother. The only ground that is dry and red, like the rest of the Red Lodge, is right next to the wall immediately below the painted images. The red color here is probably from the red ochre bags carried by the uncountable girls who have chosen to drop some of their substitute moon-blood in this place. Directly in front of this wall with its many red marks, signs, and its colored Net of Life, big droplets of water slowly fell from the roof to land on top of many white stone penises of different lengths and thicknesses.

"All different sizes and lengths. Just like the real things!" I thought to myself.

The white stone penises stood right up out of the floor of the cave. To complete a holy round of the Red Lodge, it was necessary to pass between the colored marks and images on the cave wall and the patch of white penis rocks on the ground. This is the place where the rite of the Hymen Stone is performed at the end of the girl's third, and final, round of the Lodge of Red Spirits. Thus, to be reborn as women. The hymen stone itself is rod-shaped with flattened sides. It is made of the most finely polished, dark green— almost black—stone I have ever seen. It is about the length of a small penis. My guess is it is flattened so that it is easier to insert the oiled stone into every initiate's pute as the culminating ceremony of the Moon Blood. As the eldest female shaman of the Bear-kin and the Mother of the Rites, my Auntie is the guardian of the hymen stone. I have been shown the holy stone on more than one occasion.

I can see why the stone might be frightening to any girl who has never had a man or boy put their penis or their fingers inside her pute. Besides, you would think that every girl has at least put her own fingers inside herself. This stone should have been nothing to be afraid of. Often a girl's hymen is broken and she bleeds a little from playing with the boy cousins or by putting her own fingers inside her vulva. Showing a girl the hymen stone should not have been capable of creating hysterical convulsions as it did with White Lynx. I know it was an intensely emotional setting and the embarrassment of having my own Auntie insert the stone could almost have caused *me* to fall into a fit. But it seems only White Lynx was *that* terrified of the hymen stone.

Every girl is expected to submit to this rite in order to become a woman and complete her Moon Blood initiation. When it was my turn, I just squatted in front of Auntie, she performed the rite while I sang the Women's Song to Dispel Fear and it was over. The stone rarely penetrates even half of its length because it has to be held in the Mother of the Rites' hand, which of course, covers much of the penis-shaped stone. The stone does have a penis head inscribed around the end—it definitely is made to represent a man's most singular member. And the hymen stone has fourteen short inscribed lines that run over the smoothly rounded top ridge. I know there are fourteen lines because I once counted them. They are very fine lines so they cannot be felt when the stone is inside. Actually, with fourteen marks on one side of the little ridge and fourteen on the other side, there are twenty-eight marks. Auntie says these are made to remind us of the twenty-eight days of a woman's moon-blood circle, which is also the same number of days as a complete moon-circle from new moon to new moon.

Everyone knows the rite of the Hymen Stone is intended to teach the girls that for us to give birth to a child, the man's penis must put his white essence inside the pute and no other body opening. A fact some girls, surprisingly, had not learned from their mothers before they were subjected to the hymen stone. Maybe because White Lynx was without a mother or a true auntie even, she was never taught about such things. If so, she was probably never told that even though a man gives you his essence in your pute, a baby is not always the result. Only the Mother knows why receiving the essence of a man sometimes results in a baby and at other times it does not. All I know from the Hymen Stone is that a man must put his essence inside my pute to make a baby. And unless we want to marry a man to our mother's hearth, we should never allow him to put his essence into that body opening.

As I thought about White Lynx, it occurred to me that without a mother to care for her and teach her, she may have been more vulnerable to abusive older men of the camp who may have wanted to join with a young girl in sex. I did not like to think that her older brother, or even worse, her father might have ill-used her in such a way. I truly began to feel sorry for White Lynx and I began to wonder what my life would have been like without a kind mother or a beloved Auntie to teach me and care for me. I am determined to make good on my promise to be a friend to White Lynx when this is all over.

I thought I should at least confirm with the Grandfather what had been taught to me before moving on so I said, "Grandfather, when I came here for my own initiation no one said very much about this part of the Red Lodge. Except that the Hymen Stone is to remind us it is the man who gives his essence to the woman and the male essence must be placed inside the womb before the Mother will send new life to come forth."

"What else is there to tell, then?" he smiled his reply. "That is all true and you can know the truth of it by looking at the wall in front of which the penises stand. See how the crack in the wall over there appears as a vulva when the torch is moved to its left side? All the red signs, the Net of Life with its different colored squares and Deer Mother appear to be coming out of it. The Cave *is* the Womb of the Mother out of which all life comes. But creation of that new abundant life is only possible when it is harmonized and infused with the male essence. This is so because, whether male or female, we are all part of the Net of Life and must honor and accept whatever is in our hearts, as I have said. Even in this place of the overwhelming red spirit-power of women, the white spirit-power of men is still present and must be recognized and honored—remember the full and crescent moon, my Daughter? Let us now move between the wall of red-creation and the stone penises of white-creation upon the Middle Path. This will take us between the male and the female to the end of the round and to your destiny as Seer of the Bear People. Do you have any more questions before we move on into the Lodges of the Hunters, my Daughter?" he asked.

"No, Grandfather," I said flatly.

"Well then, I have one more question for you before we complete this holy round of the Red Lodge."

I looked up at him with lifted eyebrows in anticipation of his question.

"See here—just beyond the signs and spirit-animals? There are thirteen large red dots? Did you receive the meaning of the sign of 'thirteen' in your Moon Blood, my Daughter?"

I peered closely at the red dots that were clustered in little groups of two and three. In fact, if viewed from a few steps back, the dots appeared to be made as the sinuous curves and meanderings of a river ... or a snake.

"As we completed the trial of the Hymen Stone, we were told that thirteen is the number of transformation. It is the number of our transformation from girls into women. Is that correct, Grandfather?" I said with the same raised eyebrows in expectation of an answer.

"Yes, my good apprentice. That is exactly what it means. As we move into the White Lodges of the Hunters and beyond, you will see many 'thirteens' and they will always point to some change, some shift or transformation of the body, of the mind or of the soul. Shamans are transformed into their animal-guides, boys are transformed into hunters and you will be transformed into Seer. Now let us proceed to your own transformation, Dear One."

We turned to pass between the opposites of male and female, past the thirteen dots of transformation to follow a curving path along the wall for another ten paces to the end of the holy round.

This ending was marked by the only black spirit-animal in the whole Lodge of Red Spirits.

CHAPTER 6.
THE ABYSS OF THE SILENCE

THE HEAD OF THE DARK LION MOTHER stared out of the stone, gaping with the maw that eats back all of the worlds to the Source from which they come. This, the only, black spirit-animal in the Lodge of Red Spirits appeared on what is the Eastern Portal of the Third Entrance. The image is made right at eye-level and could not be missed by any initiate passing by this spot even in the weak glow of an oil lamp. The face was so round and so darkened with black paint it looked more like a black leopard than a tawny lion, but Lion Mother it is.

The Western Portal of this Third Entrance, where we had entered to begin our holy round of the Red Lodge, was nearly lost in the charcoal darkness, beyond even the reach of the Grandfather's torchlight. We had come to the end of our circling of the egg-shaped Lodge of Red Spirits. Now the Grandfather would have to take the lead because none of the women's initiation rites in which I took part were conducted beyond this place. The gap of the Third Entrance opened into the Lodges of the Hunters somewhere out there in the utter blackness.

"Daughter, do you know why the face of Lion Mother only appears at the end of the rounds of this lodge of the new, blood-red life of the body?" his voice sounded from behind me.

I knew the answer to this question!

"Yes, Grandfather. I know. It means that all things come to an end. Even the red-life of our own bodies ends just as the red-lives of the animals that give themselves to us come to an end. Life pours from the Red Mothers in abundance and all is taken back by the Dark Mothers. Everything is eaten by something else to complete the circle and return to the Mother. And I know this is the holy Face of the Hunter, the ravenous Dark Mother who eats everything without ceasing. She even eats herself beginning with her tail, eating and eating and eating until only her face and open jaws remain," I recited, remembering the old tale.

I was completely entranced by the Dark Mother's open-mouthed face emerging from the stone wall only a few finger lengths from my own.

"Yes, Dear One, all things come to an end in their time. All things must, in time, pass away. But you must remember that it is only the red-life of the body that ends and returns to Earth Mother. Always there is a new beginning to follow every ending. Nothing important is really destroyed, it just appears that way. The spirit-powers of the All Mother move and live within all things and never die, even when the red-life is eaten by another of the Mother's children and shifts its shape into that new thing. Only the shape and form of things are forever changing. The Mother is eternal and never changes. As Seer, you will teach that all life moves in circles just as we move in our holy rounds circling the Lodges of the Great Cave. But the true life, the spirit-power, the life-fire within all things, goes back to the All Mother for rebirth, just as the red-body is returned to Earth Mother and Sky Father to be born again into another shape and a new form. To be ungrateful for the red-life that is given to us, no matter how long or short it may be, is to break the great round of gratitude and to stop the return of that abundance to us. *That* is the meaning of all the Red Mothers pouring their life into the world at the beginning of the round of the Red Lodge and the Dark Lion Mother at the end eating her own children back to herself. The Mother gives life to us all just as the Mother kills us all so that we may return to our Source. Do you remember what the gap of the Third Entrance between the Red Mother at the beginning and the Dark Mother at the end represents?"

"I have walked all three holy rounds of the Moon Blood, but I cannot remember what it means. Will you instruct me now, Grandfather?" I tried to ask humbly because I really did not know what it all meant.

I was beginning to feel a little overawed by everything being heaped upon me in such a short amount of time. The weight of it in my head was becoming ever more burdensome, like an over-loaded pack about to burst open to spill all its contents upon the ground.

"I could not know what you may already have been told," the Grandfather began. "But unless your Auntie has given you private instruction in the mysteries of the shamans and seers, you would not have been given these teachings during your rounds of the Red Lodge. This is knowledge only seers are given so they may instruct, heal and bless the People by this wisdom. The Chant of the Silence, which I will now teach you, may be shared with anyone you feel is ready to hear and to understand. Know that all the mysteries of the Ancients and the deepest wisdom of the All Mother lie within this chant." And with that the Grandfather began to chant:

Spiraling out of the Silence
The Power of One.
Out of the One,
The Powers of Two.
Out of the Two,
The Powers of Three.
Out of the Three,
Come Four Mothers of all things.
And all things
Return to the One.
And all things
Return to the Silence.

"My good Apprentice, give your close attention to the colors and numbers of the spirit-animals and signs you will encounter in every part of this Great Cave. They will reveal their mysteries to you and only to you and in your own way as you contemplate them. Giving close attention to the numbers and colors of the images will give you hints and clues to what is to be experienced in each lodge or womb of the Great Cave. Remember always that the hearing and the seeing with the eyes and ears of your head is only the first part of what all seers are to do in this holy place. Never forget that becoming aware of the powers within your heart and soul is the final goal of all you see and hear and experience in this place. This will be so not only for yourself, but for all others who enter this Great Cave under your tutelage. All of this you must know in the very center of your heart should you ever be given the gift of teaching and initiating others as Grandmother of the Bear People. If you open your heart to the spirits in each space of power within the Cave, they will give you the wisdom you will need to instruct the People. You will then have the wisdom to guide them through the initiations, trials and troubles of life both inside the Cave and in their daily rounds after they leave this holy ground. Do you understand, Dear One?" he asked with slightly raised eyebrows in anticipation of an answer.

My head was spinning with the echoes of the unfathomable Chant of the Silence and the Grandfather's words of instruction. I tried to see it all in my head as a single picture: the great red Rock of the All Mother is the sign of the Five Mothers giving birth to the world of red-blooded creatures and all else! But what are the Powers of Two? What are the Powers of Three? What is the Silence? I struggled to put it all together and soon I found myself in a whirlwind of confusion and panic.

"Help me to understand, my Grandfather. I am so confused," I begged, my voice cracking with emotion. "Is not the All Mother the source of everything? How can there be Five Mothers when the One is the Mother of All?" I pleaded.

I was beginning to lose all self-control. Overwhelming apprehensions thundered through my head and gut in a great stampede as if a multitude of hoofs and horns were rolling me in the dirt in complete confusion.

"Open your heart and clear your mind by closing your eyes and taking the Breath, my Daughter. Relax into the wonder of the Great Cave and all will be made known to you in its time. As you open your heart, the powers of the Above, which are so strong in you, will yield to the powers of the Below to reveal all things to your head and your heart through the intuitions and feelings of the liver. Let go of thinking, breathe deeply and try not to take it all in at once. A feast of any kind should be eaten slowly and savored. Remember that each is given only that which they can know and accept at the moment of hearing. Few will ever understand even as much as you do now, Dear One," he said comfortingly.

I tried to breathe slowly and hold back my galloping dread.

But the confusion persisted and the pitching anxiety in the pit of my belly increased. I was frantic with the urge to flee and I began to be very afraid to go any further into this terrifying darkness. Just as I thought I might regain control, a new whirlpool of fearful, confused thoughts flooded over me, drowning me. Uncontrollable panic began to rise up again. What had been slow and measured breathing turned into rapid panting. A rolling terror in my belly began to make me queasy and I looked furtively around for a place where I could run, hide and empty my stomach. So nauseous was I becoming that if I had any food in my gut I would certainly be retching it up right now.

What I have learned from all of this is that it is one thing to come into the Cave with many others and to be guided through the initiations of the Moon Blood with age-mates, friends and close kin. But it is entirely something else to be by myself with only this old man to assist me. I was in such deep, turbid waters. I was in way over my head and drowning.

"I'm afraid, Grandfather. I don't understand! I can't do this thing you ask," I blurted and began to sob uncontrollably.

"Come to me, Daughter of my Heart," he whispered.

The Grandfather took the lamp and placed it carefully on the ground so I could cover my face with both hands and weep behind them. Then he put his arms around me and let me cry into his white bearskin-covered shoulder until the tears gradually began to ebb.

"You are stronger and closer to the spirit-powers than you know, Dear One. When you are ready, let us move to the Center of the Silence. There I will instruct you with knowledge few seers ever come to own."

The Grandfather spoke with such complete concern for me that the raging urges to flee began to subside along with the sick feeling in my belly. After a few more moments, still whimpering and wiping my tears, I picked up my lamp. I followed as the Grandfather moved fifteen or so paces out into the middle of the Third Entrance. He planted his torch in a soft patch of reddish earth, took the lamp from my hands and placed it next to his torch. The Grandfather lowered himself stiffly to the ground and, sitting cross-legged, faced out into the unimaginable blackness of the Plain of the Bear Mother and the Lodges of the Hunters somewhere out there in the dark.

"Come, sit by my side and we will talk about the All Mother and her Great Cave," he said, gesturing toward the ground next to him.

Sitting here in the center of the Third Entrance, the torchlight is just bright enough that I can make out the Eastern Portal off to our right where the Dark Mother's head gapes. There is also enough light to see the Western Portal to our left where the ochre-drenched Rock of the All Mother loomed out of the darkness. We truly sat in the space between life and death, between the beginning and the end.

"Dear One," he said when my whimpering had finally ceased. "Let us take a few more calming breaths before I begin. This time, as you hold the Breath, place your tongue on the roof of your mouth and slowly exhale. That will calm you even more."

Breathing deeply in unison with the Grandfather, I did as he directed. Then he began to speak in a quiet and measured voice.

"The powers speak to everyone with a different voice. When a hunter's spear strikes its intended target, the Mother is speaking. When the newborn cries for the first time, the Mother is speaking. When the sun rises every morning and the fish return to feed the People and the flakes drop from a finished point, the Mother is speaking. When the last reed is woven into the basket, the rabbit is snared and the shaman in trance utters words meaningless to our ears, the Mother is speaking. When a song of your beloved rises up within your throat, the Mother is speaking. When one dreams of an animal brother or sister, or if you see a living creature and your eyes meet with recognition and affection, the Mother is speaking. The Voice of the Mother comes to us every day. And yet, you will only become aware of it in your own way and in your own time.

Do not be afraid that the Mother has not spoken to you in words to your ears, with visions to your eyes or dreams to your mind. And do not think the only way to hear the Mother's Voice is in a trance-vision or through a dream, for the Mother of us all speaks to each in a different way every day of our life. Those ways are as numerous and varied as there are the Mother's children upon the Plains of Summer."

"Yes, Grandfather. I see the wisdom of it," I whispered in a small voice, my eyes cast down toward the ground.

"As I have said, those with eyes to see and ears to hear may find the Mother in many different things. Perhaps in the face of a beloved wife or husband. We all see the Mother moving in our lives in different ways, but we will only become aware of the All Mother's presence in the world when we have first found her dwelling within our own hearts. Can you understand that, Dear One?"

"Yes, Grandfather. I am beginning to," I replied.

And I was, because the roiling fears were subsiding as the measured breaths returned my self-control and my head began to clear.

"Few are ever able to know the Abyss of Silence for it is the Unseen Power beyond all sound and light. The Silence cannot be spoken with words. It cannot be seen in dreams. It is beyond all our understanding and experience. It is beyond even the All Mother herself."

"How can anything be beyond the One who is Mother of All Things, my Grandfather? That I will never understand," I stated flatly.

"You must be patient with yourself and know that you will understand more as you have more experience of the Mother's plentiful life. You will learn from your mistakes and experience will ignite true understanding of things you cannot now grasp. You are still very young to be learning the deepest secrets of the seers and shamans. Just know that even the greatest hunter sometimes misses his mark. Even the most skilled hide scraper will sometimes slip and cut a hole in the skin. Everyone, from the most powerful shaman to the greatest hunter to the kindest mother, makes mistakes and understands imperfectly. Be patient with yourself and you will learn patience with others who do not even begin to have your own understanding and wisdom."

"Grandfather? Have you ever heard the Voice of the Silence?" I blurted before I realized I already knew what his answer would be. I am beginning to sound like my own mother, asking questions I already know the answer!

"The Silence has no voice and yet has all voices within it. The Silence has no shape and yet has all shapes within it. I cannot say I have heard the voice of the Silence with my ears, but I have experienced a blissful union with the Silence while in the deepest of trances near to death. After the long life I have lived, I am more aware of it daily in everything I see and do, but I know I am only seeing the pale reflection of the Silence. I see it not only while beholding the rising full moon or touching the rough bark of a tree. Yes, I even see it in the face of my good Apprentice," he explained patiently, nodding his head in assent to his own words.

"You see the Silence in *my* face, Grandfather?" I said and turned to look into his eyes.

"Yes, Dear One. In *your* face. As Seer, you will learn that the Silence is most readily found in the stillness of things. It is to be experienced in the spaces between things. It is found in the blackness between the stars, in the silence between two breaths, in the dark space at the center of the eye of your beloved and between the beats of your own heart. Whether waking or dreaming, you will only experience the Silence when the ear finds nothing to hear, when the eyes find nothing to see, the tongue finds nothing to taste, the nose finds nothing to smell and the hands find nothing to feel. Do you see the wisdom of it, Dear One?"

"How can the All Mother be in the blackness, Grandfather? There is nothing in the blackness but emptiness," I said, simply stating a fact.

The Grandfather smiled at me broadly and began to chuckle under his breath. "Dear One, that is only your head speaking. But if you open your heart and look within, you will know that the Silence can only be found in the stillness and formlessness of things and not with the five senses of your red-body. Remember your experience at the Rock of the All Mother? In the space between your hand and the hard stone, you touched the Silence out of which the All Mother comes to meet you as the Power of One. It is the space between things which the Mother uses to create all there is."

"How can that be, Grandfather? I still do not understand," I said.

"Think of it this way, my Daughter. The great blackness before us is one of the holy lodges of the Great Cave we call the Bear Mother's Plain of Bones. But without the space between the ground and the high roof, there would be no Plain of Bones. There could be no Great Cave at all. How could we be sitting here if there were no space of the Silence for us to sit within?"

The Grandfather was clearly appealing to my head for an answer. I began to nod in agreement as the whole idea of it began to make sense to me. I slowly moved my head up and down in understanding and the Grandfather continued his instruction.

"If spirit-powers appear to us with a shape and a form or speak to us with words in a dream, it is the All Mother speaking. The Silence has no shape or voice or color for it is the Silent Abyss within which all the worlds float and which is in and through all things. The Unseen Power cannot be heard and cannot be seen or touched except by searching within, to your own heart, wherein the red and white-spirits are become one as if they are joining in sex. If, in all four directions, you are aware of Horse Mother dwelling within you and moving you, then for you *that is* the All Mother through which the Unseen Power is seen and heard and experienced by you. We will never hear the still, soft voice of the Unseen Power with our ears; we will only *feel* the quiet voice within. We will only be able to experience its voice as gentle as a little girl's whisper when we have stilled the chaos and confusion of the thoughts of the World of Light within our heads. Remember what it felt like holding your hand above the Rock of the All Mother while feeling your own spirit-fire rising from within you? If you contemplate on that feeling, then you will begin to know in your heart the truth of what I am saying. Can you understand that, Dear One?" he asked.

Again I nodded my head in agreement while gazing intently at the silent blackness that enveloped us completely. I was still struggling to take it all in.

"Know also, my Daughter, that one cannot seek the Unseen Power. It only comes to open us according to the needs of our soul to learn and experience all of life. And when the Unseen Power does come forth, it will always be unbidden and unexpected. The coming forth of the Unseen Power will always be as the Trickster surprising us and sending us off in some other direction we never anticipated. And we must accept and be joyous in it whatever shape or form it may take. The sad irony of it all is that the more we seek the Silence with our heads, the more difficult it is to find because it can only be discovered in one's own heart. Relax into the beauty of the World of Light, let the urges of the liver balance the thoughts of the head and through that joining, live your life according to the desires of your heart. Only then will the Unseen Power reveal itself to you in a way in which you will become aware within your whole being that it is the wordless Voice of the Silence. If any seer or shaman tells you they have seen the shape or heard the voice of the Unseen Power, do not believe them. They are deceiving themselves and the People if they say such a thing," he warned.

"Then what *is* the All Mother?" I asked.

"The All Mother is the maker of all things and emerges out of the Silence of its own creative power like a great swan's egg containing all there is. To our eyes and our ears she reveals herself as the Mother of All. But in truth, she is also the Father of All and contains the father-power within her as well. How else could the Mother be the Power of One if she did not include all shapes and forms within her? Because our minds cannot comprehend what cannot be spoken with the mouth or seen with the eyes and because all the worlds pour forth from the Mother as if she is giving birth, to us, the Unseen Power appears as the mother-power and so we call her *All Mother*. But when she shows herself to you, it will be as I have already explained—in your own way, in your own time, in a shape and a form that you, and only you, will understand."

"Grandfather, do you mean that when I see the shape of the All Mother I will recognize it?"

"Yes, Dear One, depending on your willingness to see. Some women will experience the Mother as their lovers, in the form of a man they desire with their bodies and their souls. Some men see the Mother in dream and trance as a beautiful woman spreading her thighs, inviting them to join with her in sex. Children will see her as a loving mother spreading her arms in affection and offering her ample breasts to nourish them with her mother's milk. The rites of the Great Cave can help us find her, the teachings of seers can help us find her, the songs and dances and dreams can help us draw near to her. But she is already in everything and she *is* everything, so you do not need to come to her Great Cave or have a dream to find her. The Mother is everywhere you look and she is in all you do. Search for her within your own heart, open the Single Eye of Wisdom and you *will* see her in all things."

"I will think on the wisdom of this, my Grandfather," I said with real humility and a growing respect for this strange and wonderful old man.

"Always remember that the Mother can only show herself to us according to our own understanding and willingness to open our hearts to her. Be patient and gentle with yourself and you will gradually become aware of the Mother working through you and within you every single day of your life. Whether in dreaming or in joining in sex or making a beautiful lamp or singing a song that touches the heart or receiving the gift of an animal's life or even when burning with fever and returning to the Mother, she is always showing herself to us. When the trance dancers are spinning toward blissful union with the One, when you are singing the healing chants and giving the healing herbs, the Mother is showing herself to you. Do you not see that all of it *is* the Mother and the Mother *is* one with all things? The All Mother is the spirit-power of oneness and joining and completeness out of which all things come and back into which all things go—the All Mother *is* the Power of One," he instructed.

"I am sorry, Grandfather, but if the Mother is all and all things are the Mother, then how can two come out of the one?" I asked, remembering the words of the chant.

"My Daughter, it may be hard to understand, but you must also learn that whenever any thing is created and moves out of that Place of the One, it enters into the worlds of contradictory things—that is how the Mother makes everything we see and experience in the World of Light. The Powers of Two appear as the inside and the outside of the Egg of Creation, but they are still the one Egg of Creation. Meditate on this, Dear One, and you will see the wisdom of it. If all things remained uncreated as the One, then there should be no opposites and we should have no choices to make. There could be no choice of which trail to follow or which path to take for any of us. We should have no experience of being separate and different from one another. We should have no experience of the Three Worlds of Light at all because we should not be free to choose what our bodies will do and what our heads shall desire. We would also not be free to experience the consequences and blessings of the choices we make. Remember, in choosing any path, all things move in circles. Every thing comes back around to the opposite side from where it started. Without choices between contradictory things we would not know joy or sorrow, we would not know love or fear. And we would never know the bliss of joining again with the Mother had we never been separated from her," he explained.

"So by things being different from one another we can know and make choices between the two?" I asked. The light of my wisdom was beginning to dawn.

"Yes, Dear One. Do you begin to see that when the Mother pours the worlds out of herself like the rivers of life-giving water and salmon swimming through the All Mother's Eye, to our eyes she appears to separate into male and female, left and right, light and dark, hunter and hunted, dead and alive, up and down, before and after, liver and head, argument and agreement, hate and love, summer and winter, giving and receiving, Earth Mother and Sky Father—the opposites of the Three Worlds are endless! These are the innumerable Powers of Two which come out of the One, and in separating, become all the worlds. Remember that when the All Mother pours herself into the red-world of our five senses—the World of the Five Mothers—she separates into the opposites that are already within her. For every mother-power we are aware of, there will be a hidden father-power as her counterpart. For every father-power we are aware of, there will be a hidden mother-power as his counterpart. The Powers of Two are within and around all of us. Whichever power seems to our eyes to predominate in a thing, we refer to it with such words as 'Father' or 'Mother'. It is the maleness or the femaleness of the thing that appears dominant within it and which is being shown to us."

"Do you mean two-spirit people like White Lynx?" I asked.

"Yes. And so it is with every other kind of opposition we experience in the World of Light above. This holy space behind us is the Red Lodge of the All Mother. It is a place of transformation, rebirth and spiritual nourishment for women, and so the signs of the father-power will not appear on these walls. But they are still here. Remember, the Womb of White Spirits is here within the Red Lodge. Also, the field of white stone penises appears before Reindeer Mother and the Red Net of Life here in the Red Lodge. They are the signs of white-spirited powers hidden within the red. Between those two opposites did we pass in our round of the Red Lodge, did we not? As Seer, know that each of the Four Mothers has a male spirit-counterpart which you will encounter in their full power in other parts of the Cave—for the yellow Horse Mother, a white Horse Father; for the black Reindeer Mother, a white Reindeer Father; for the red Bison Mother, a white Bison Father; for the red Mammoth Mother, a white Mammoth Father. And finally, you and your eventual husband, as equals to the red Bear Mother and white Bear Father at the center of your own coupled lives, will be one pair of opposites engaged in the dance circle of the red-life. As you live this life, you will learn that the Powers of Two are always the inside and outside of the same thing—two aspects of the one. Because that is the truth of all things in the World of Light, as seers and shamans we should all be slow to make judgments about any of the things outside of ourselves. That is because we can never be certain which side of the Egg of Creation we are on—the inside or the outside?" he explained carefully.

"Why is it the waters of the Below are of the Mother while the waters of the hot springs and the rivers of the Above are holy to the Serpent Father?" I interrupted.

"All the living waters of the World Below belong to the mother-power. But the waters that rise up to the surface from the watery abyss below to bring life to the Middle World become the waters of the World of Light and so are of the father-power. Regarding the life-giving waters of the World Above, this is an example of the Powers of Two active in the World of Light because these living waters of the Above and the Below are just one pair of opposites spiraling out of the All Mother. The white rain and snow fall from the clouds to give moisture to the grass-sister and tree-brother. The waters of Sky Father fill the rivers so the salmon-sisters may come once again. Drinking springs of sweet water bubble to the surface so that all the Mother's children of the Middle World may drink and live. These are all the life-giving waters of the Above which all are full of the father-power, but all of which, in their source, come out of the One. Sky Father's storms bring life-giving moisture to Earth Mother just as a man gives his white essence to a woman's red womb to bring forth new life. So, you see, the hot waters coming to the surface of the World of Light are holy to the father-power. My Daughter, have you never seen the 'snake' of a man? How it curves and bends like a river?" he said with a sly smile.

I felt the warmth of a blush begin to color my throat and cheeks.

Becoming more serious again he continued. "Like the All Mother, who is One, we all have male and female powers within us—remember White Lynx and Bison Father's horns hidden within Moon Mother's round face? Which of any particular pair of opposites will be dominant in one's soul, and thus become what we show to others, is of our own choosing. And whether the two halves will be in harmony and in line with one another or not, that is a matter for each to discover as we come from the All Mother into the World of Light from between our mother's thighs. So, as the pairs of opposites struggle with each other, as they circle and dance with each other, when they join, when they align with each other by finding the Middle Path between the pair of opposites, the Two in harmony give birth to the Powers of Three—the Three in One and the One in Three. The Powers of Three are the liver, head and heart in harmony and moving as one. The very lamp that guides your way through the darkness has three wicks and combines three powers into one thing: the flame of spirit-power, the stone of earth and the oil of the living animal-messengers—three-in-one, one out of three. Do you see, Dear One?" he asked hopefully.

Completely enraptured by these ideas, I nodded my head and the Grandfather continued.

"The man gives his essence to the woman; the woman receives it and gives birth to the child. The animal gives itself to the hunter, the hunter receives its body-life and the hunter gives again to sustain the red-bodies of the People. The stages of the red-life are three: childhood, adulthood and old age. The healings of a shaman-of-healing are three: of the body, the head and of the soul. The shaman-of-words converses in love and mediates between two angry and injured people and finds the Middle Path of peace and harmony between two opposites raging against each other. The Three Worlds: Above, Below and Middle; our very souls: liver, head and heart—these are all the shape and the voice and the way of the Powers of Three. In every direction we look, we can see the Three in One and the One in Three if only we will. If only we open the Single Eye of Wisdom, we will see the Powers of Three within us and all around."

"And out of the three comes the Mothers of the Four Directions and all other things. My own necklace is three-in-one!" I volunteered eagerly.

I was beginning to grasp what the Grandfather was telling me.

"Yes, my good Apprentice, that is correct. The world of the Four Mothers is the red-world of the body senses, the world we can see and touch and hear and smell because all things are made of the four substances of earth, air, fire and water. It is the red-world of the First Mothers of each of all the animal, bird, bug, tree, grass and human tribes as the four substances—the Four Mothers—spin to the right in the creation of all things. It is the chaos and confusion and joy and sorrow and loss and abundance we see around us every day."

"Grandfather?" I said, bringing his lesson to a stop. "I have a question."

"Yes?" he replied. "What is your question?"

"If few are instructed as seers and shamans, how can the People ever be expected to see the Mother in this confusing world of so many different powers in conflict with each other?" I asked, truly puzzled.

"Each sees the Mother active as part of their daily lives with the opening of their hearts, as I have said. Without any seer's teachings, many of the People are able to see the Mother working in their lives by finding their special animal-guides through which they may own the Mother's wisdom. Many hunters become aware of the All Mother as the Five Mothers and the abundant Net of Life. The Fifth Mother is the Mother of the Center as you, yourself, have said. It is the sign of the life-giving, Fifth Substance which is of the black spirit-power. That fifth substance is the myriad of spirit-powers surrounding us, living within us all part of the One. We are all connected as one through this Fifth Substance, even though our red-bodies made of the Four Substances appear to the senses to be separate and different. But we know that the animals, the trees, the very rocks themselves are alive with the spirit-power of all there is. All these are the Mother's children that by this fifth, unseen power are connected as one in the Net of Life. *That* is the Fifth Mother's presence in the World of Light. Some can understand and can see the Powers of Three in the world, but fewer are able to see the One moving in the world and within themselves as the Powers of Two. The oneness of things is difficult to comprehend if we are looking at two battling rhinos or two bison wrestlers ferociously going at each other, struggling and fighting. As Seer, you will come to know the Powers of Two *are* one and you will see all things as in a dance with each other— sometimes fighting and at other times embracing each other. Even though all we see appears to be controlled by and acting as the Powers of Two, greater powers are always at work beneath the surface display of difference and conflict. Even if some do not see it, each of us is, in truth, Three in One regardless of the appearance of conflict and discord. All that is necessary is to take the Middle Path between the opposites to become the three-in-one. Do you see, Dear One?"

"I see more clearly all the time, my Grandfather. Is that why the two-spirits among us are so revered?"

"Yes, Dear One, that is precisely why two-spirits are so respected. The two-spirited combine for all to see the opposite Powers of Two into one body. For this reason we believe the two-spirits among us are especially close to the All Mother, and like the rhino-power, actually show us the powers of three-in-one. Two-sprit men and women are honored because they can more readily hear the Mother's voice to bless the People whether they are initiated shamans or not. More than almost any of the People, the two-spirits among us accept and honor the two opposite powers within us all. And more than most, the two-spirited can balance and harmonize those powers which are part of every one of us. When they cherish that power within which gives them great insight and awareness of the Powers of Two in the world, then they know the bliss that comes from finding the Middle Path, the Path of the Three in One, for their own souls. And when they have joined the opposites within their hearts and have brought the contradictory powers within to align with their opposites, they can bless and heal the People in many ways. Few of the People, few shamans and seers even, will ever directly experience the Power of the One as I have said. Few among us will ever see with the Single Eye of Wisdom and few of us will feel in our souls that the myriad of all things *are* one. So, Dear One, do not be concerned if you do not understand everything completely and all at once. Do you see that no matter what it is you do or no matter what it is you experience, in one way or another it is the All Mother? It matters not whether you can identify the thing as Powers of Three or Two or One, only that you know that all of it is of the Mother."

"I begin to understand, Grandfather. Thank you for being patient with me. I will do my best and do as you ask. I see now that yours is the Voice of the Mother for me at this time and in this place," I said with real conviction.

I began to think I really was starting to comprehend something of what the Grandfather was saying to me.

"That is very good, my Daughter. Are you now ready to move on to the White Lodges of the Hunters and your destiny?" the kind old shaman asked brightly through his gap-toothed smile.

I stood up, helped the Grandfather to his feet, handed the torch to him and picked up my lamp.

"Yes, Grandfather. I am ready. Do you still want me to go ahead?" I offered bravely thinking it would actually make me less afraid of the unknown trail that stretched out into the blackness.

"No, I will lead the way, Dear One. The path through the Bear Mother's Plain of Bones to the white-spirited Lodges of the Hunters beyond is a winding and confusing path. It is unlike the holy circles of the women's Red Lodge where the round is simple and the way easy to find. There is deep wisdom in this. You will learn that a woman's path in life is easier to find and follow than the path of a man and a hunter. The winding, zigzagging path of seers and shamans is even more difficult to follow. It is the reason this path beginning here, in the Center of the Silence, is called the Winding Way of Seers," he said.

With that, the Grandfather began leading the way out into the black void that is the vast Plain of the Bear Mother.

CHAPTER 7.
BEAR MOTHER'S PLAIN OF BONES

THE GRANDFATHER HELD HIS TORCH UP HIGH to
make the path called the Winding Way of Seers through the Plain
of Bones easier for me to see. Even with his torch held above his
head, I could just barely make out the enormous dome that was
the roof of this grandest lodge of the All Mother's Great Cave.

The trail began to turn and twist among the bear bones, winter
den hollows, white penis-shaped rocks emerging from the ground,
shallow pools of water and boulders that had fallen from the roof,
as a path called "winding" should. The trail turned back, and in
some places, crossed over itself like a marriage dancing line. It was
a true maze of confusing pathways and rarely walked trails. In one
place it circled completely around the bones of a mother bear
whose little cub had died beside her during their winter sleep.
Curled within the mother bear's protective embrace, the bones
were still connected with bits of fur and dried skin.

The meandering path was like following the blood trail of a
wounded animal out on the summer plains, or so I imagined. I had
only heard hunters tell their stories of tracking bleeding animals to
finish the kill, thus returning the suffering children of the Mother
gently and quickly to her welcoming embrace. Even when I have
accompanied my father or Uncle Bright Wolf on a winter hunt to
the nearby hills, I was never permitted to go with them for the ac-

tual killing of a wounded animal. I have always been told it is not pleasing to the Mother that a woman should take part in the letting of the lifeblood of her animal-messengers. We women are the watertight baskets in which new life is carried and we should never do the shedding of the living blood of the Mother's children. If a snared rabbit must be killed, it is done by twisting its neck so blood is not released from the animal-messenger of the Mother's power by the hands of a woman, who *is* the Mother in her power to give birth. I have often thought I am indeed fortunate not to have to let the blood of the Mother's children as all men must do every day of their lives as hunters.

I sensed we were gradually moving toward the northwest. But I could not yet see a western wall of this great cavern, so convoluted is the trail and so huge the Plain of Bones appeared.

"A straight path across the Plain would have taken far less time to reach the other side," I muttered quietly and impatiently to myself as we made our tortuous way.

But it would have been very disrespectful for us to step over any of Bear Mother's bones or to walk through one of the winter sleeping dens by taking a straight line across Bear Mother's own holy lodge. I realized that much.

"You know the women's Song to Dispel Fear?" the Grandfather asked.

Most likely, he was thinking I might be getting anxious again because I was saying nothing as we walked our seer's winding way into the unknown within the darkness.

"Yes, Grandfather. I do know the song," I answered.

Without any further encouragement, I began to sing. With the rhythmic singing, my feet began to dance a simple dance along the sometimes dusty trail. The tan-colored clay floor of what is the largest and driest of all the lodges in the whole Cave, stretched out far beyond the little circle of our torchlight. This path called Winding was only a faint trail to follow, unlike the well-trodden paths we had traveled in the Red Lodge. Since the boys always took the left-hand path along the western wall from the Skull Portal, that would be the well-beaten path here in the Plain of Bones. This way was definitely little-used and, I am guessing, would only be used by seer-initiates. Otherwise, I reasoned, it would have been much easier to see and to follow.

After circling around and around in too many paces to count, we finally reached the western wall of the Plain of Bones. The point where the path we were following comes together with the well-beaten trail of the boy-initiates along the western wall is marked by one large red spot high up on a part of the wall that bulges out into the Plain.

"The Power of One," I thought out loud.

Since the Grandfather's teachings of the Silence and all the different Powers, I began to count the dots and signs and spirit-animals which were sure to begin appearing in greater and greater numbers the further we got into the Great Cave.

"Yes, Dear One, it is the Power of One. If we had entered following close to the western wall, as the boys do, this red dot would be a sign of the beginning of the White Lodges of the Hunters. Mark this place well because five pathways meet at this big red hand-dot. It is the only sign or image upon the entire western wall of the Plain, so whenever you see it, you will know exactly where you are," the Grandfather instructed.

He pointed up to the round red blotch above our heads with his torch.

"If you were one of the initiated hunters leaving the cave, you would come from your trials along this same western wall of the Plain. Further in, this wall eventually becomes one side of the Passage of the Butterfly." Again he pointed with his torch to deeper parts of the Cave somewhere out in the darkness.

"Your female seer's path today will not follow the usual path for male seers because they will have already been initiated as men and as hunters. I want you to see what lies ahead before we cross back over to the entry side of the Passage of the Butterfly where your hunter's initiation will begin," he said enigmatically.

I was ready to go on, but the Grandfather continued to gaze up pensively toward the Red Dot for longer than I thought necessary for such a simple sign. Without further instruction, the Grandfather suddenly took a sharp right turn and began leading me along the western wall. The wall began to wave in and out in a series of smoothly curving rock walls, protruding curtains, thick and thin tree trunks of stone stretching from ground to roof and many stone pendants hanging from above. After many, many paces, the wall began to curve around to the northeast and then dead ended. The Grandfather kept following the wall that curved back around to the south forming a shallow side-chamber protruding out into the solid rock of the western wall of the Plain of Bones. This side-chamber was very shallow by comparison to some of the others I had already encountered within the Red Lodge.

"Dear One," the Grandfather said casually as we made our way out of the side-chamber toward a thin stone curtain which dropped abruptly from roof to ground.

"Think of this side-chamber as a left arm of the Mother extending out from the Plain of Bones."

"Yes, Grandfather. A left arm?" I asked without getting a response.

The Grandfather just kept plodding on into the Cave and in ten or fifteen paces we had come around to the other side of the narrow wing of rock If this side-cavern is a "left arm" sticking out from the cave wall, this curtain of rock jutted in to form an "armpit." I could see that the western wall continued on the other side of the "armpit" running almost directly north.

What is most striking to me is that not a single claw mark, spirit-animal, sign or handprint has been made on any of the flat stone surfaces along our entire trek of the western wall of the Plain of Bones, except for that single Red Dot. It is just as the Grandfather said. In both directions from the place of the Red Dot there had been many flat, easily accessed rock surfaces which were completely unmarked and unpainted. Even Bear Mother's claw marks are absent here.

"You may now take the lead, Dear One," he said. "Just follow the trodden path along the western wall and tell me what you discover there."

"Yes Grandfather," I said and moved around him to take the lead.

As I rounded the narrow blade of rock which dropped straight down from the roof of the cave forming the "armpit", a wall full of spectacular spirit-animals came into view. First, a trinity of large red bears drawn with simple, elegant lines ambled toward us from the complete darkness of a corner in the wall behind them. My mouth opened involuntarily in awe at the perfection and movement of the creatures as our lights played across the simple red lines of the spirit-animals.

"Rebirth through the Powers of Three," I thought silently.

Behind the three bears, on the flat wall that formed the other side of the corner, two red ibex with huge horns curving over their backs had been painted. The ibex were moving in, toward the corner, while the three bears were moving out of, and away from, the corner. Below the paired ibex were two red lions, also moving in toward the corner. The little procession was moving along the western wall toward the left arm, the Red Dot, and eventually, to the Skull Portal and the mouth of the Great Cave far behind us.

"Hunter and hunted. The Powers of Two. The Powers of Three spiraling out of the pairs of opposites. The beginning of things!" I whispered in amazement.

Bringing up the rear of the awesome procession, there appeared a single red horse—the Mother of abundant new birth—in a line behind the paired ibex and paired lions.

"It is the healing, life-giving Horse Mother as the creative Power of One. The fecund source of all life," I said to myself in a reverent whisper.

"Yes, Dear One. The Mother is indeed speaking to you through these images," the Grandfather answered quietly.

He stood behind me, still holding his torch up high so that I could see the marvelous spirit-animals.

"Powers of Three spiraling from the paired opposites, which are the Two, spiraling from the One in the great act of the beginning of all things. The Cave *is* starting to speak to me!" I thought to myself in wonderment.

Behind Horse Mother, a large split in the stone had been emphasized by the Ancient Ones with two black lines—or rod-shapes—on either side of the crack. Beyond the black-lined crack, the unpainted cave wall curved around to more flat rock where another big red spot had been made. And beyond this new red spot, out of the darkness loomed a red spirit-leopard painted in the middle of an expanse of overhanging stone suspended from above.

Leopard Mother was almost completely covered with spots made from thumbprints—except for her stomach. She held her long tail and head low, getting ready to pounce in the direction of Horse Mother, toward the entrance of the Great Cave and the World of Light beyond.

But overarching and standing above Leopard Mother, the huge head and body of a gigantic red Bear Mother had been made with just a few deftly painted lines. Curiously, this Bear Mother had Leopard Mother's spots pressed with thumb and finger marks onto her head and humped shoulders. I have never seen a spotted bear. What could it mean? I looked even more closely at the scene and explored the stone in front and behind the Bear and Leopard Mothers. Bear Mother stared intently toward deeper parts of the Cave hidden in darkness. Except for the Bear and Leopard Mothers, the whole procession of astonishing spirit-animals appeared to be emerging from the black-lined crack in the cave wall.

"This is certainly the dividing line between the Plain of Bones and the Passage of the Butterfly beyond, is it not, my Grandfather?"

"Yes, my good Apprentice, it is. This red spot marks the beginning of the Plain of Bones but only if one is coming from deeper inside the Great Cave, which is just the path initiated hunters take when leaving the Cave."

Less concerned with the meaning of this new red spot, I was transfixed in front of Leopard Mother. I gazed at her intently while clutching the leopard fang hanging between my breasts from my woman's—my seer's—necklace.

Seeing me hold the fang with one hand so reverently is why, I'm sure, the Grandfather asked, "What do you see, my Apprentice? What are Leopard Mother and Bear Mother saying to you? What are they saying to each other?"

Without hesitation I replied, "Bear Mother is saying: *This is my own holy Lodge, Leopard Mother. Here, you are my servant.*"

"Yes," the Grandfather said in a hush close to my ear. "The Mother of all Good Mothers is saying: *I contain thy spots within me. Thou and I are one in the game of life.* And Leopard Mother is agreeing: *This Cave is thy Holy Lodge, Bear Mother. I am thy servant in the game of life.*"

"Come, Dear One, let me show you something else," he said in full voice as he motioned me closer to the spirit-leopard. "Tell me what you see."

The Grandfather began moving his torch from right to left and then left to right, only a few hand-widths away from the spirit-leopard's belly. To my astonishment, the moving shadows revealed impressions in soft brown clay just beneath Leopard Mother's belly. As if the image of the great red-spotted bear surmounting the leopard were not enough to make it clear that this *is* Bear Mother's own lodge, a living bear had pressed a single muddy right paw-print into the soft clay just below the belly of the leopard. It is just as we might press our own handprints onto the Cave's walls with ochre-covered hands or fingers. It didn't occur to me until later that the Ancients may have made Leopard Mother in a place where Bear Mother showed them with her paw-print to make the image.

"I see all five claw-fingers of Bear Mother where she has pressed them in brown clay onto the stone!" I bubbled with excitement.

I peered as closely as I could at the miracle without touching it.

"Bear Mother is always speaking to Leopard Mother and both of them are always speaking to the hunters among us," the Grandfather whispered over my shoulder as I continued to gaze at the images.

"Bear Mother always says: *This is my Holy Lodge. I am the giver and nurturer and protector of the All Mother's red-life. You are only the Dark Mother's servant who takes the red-life back to the All Mother.* As hunters and killers, we of the human tribes, together with the lions and leopards and wolves and hyenas and all the other eaters of meat, are all servants of the Dark Mother. We do the work of the Dark Mothers when we send the All Mother's animal-messengers back to the Source which gives life to all things. As Seer, you will teach this lesson repeatedly to the men. Just as the leopard and lion are doing Dark Mother's work, so they, as hunters, are also doing her work in the World of Light as they go forth to shed the blood of the Mother's children. As the new men complete their initiations and pass this portal in their leaving of the Cave, they must never forget that life and love and light always triumphs over death and killing and fear of the darkness. Whenever there is an ending, there is sure to be a rebirth that follows because all of life moves in circles. What Bear Mother is saying to us is what we have already heard in other parts of the Cave, have we not?"

"Yes, Grandfather. That lesson has been shown in other places already. But what is it about these images that tell us life triumphs over death?"

"That it is a good question, Little Bear. When an image or a sign is made above another, that means it is stronger or is dominant in the clash of opposite things. Because Bear Mother is made above and over Leopard Mother, that is a way of saying that life always returns, life always survives, life is always triumphant. The paired ibex further on are also made above the paired lions, which is the same message," he murmured quietly in as much awe as I.

"Now, Dear One, get down and look beneath the overhang," he directed.

I got down on my knees, sat down, and tilted my head back so I could peer at the underside of the great overhanging rock upon which Leopard Mother and Bear Mother had been made.

"It's another red Lion Mother!" I called out in amazement. "That makes a threesome of hunters, does it not, my Grandfather?"

"Yes," Dear One. It is the three-in-one of the ending of life in the jaws of the Dark Mothers and upon the spears of the hunters. You will learn in your life that the ending of things is always painful. But never forget that every ending is followed by a new beginning. As I have said, life forever returns and triumphs over the ending of things. As Seer, you will always remember this teaching no matter what it is you do or where you go. Here, the Three Powers of the Return are seen to be led in a great procession by the Three Powers of New Life. The creative powers of new life are all seen to be coming from the crack in the stone with black lines on either side, which is a sign of the All Mother's great vulva giving birth to all there is. The death of the red-body is never the end of things. It is always followed by a rebirth and renewal," he sighed wistfully.

I removed myself from beneath the overhanging rock and stood up. Then I remembered my question. "Why is the red spot here made before the break in the wall, in front of the Three Dark Mothers?" I asked.

"This red spot is the sign of the beginning of a new holy round. It is 'before' the crack when you are coming from the spirit-leopard and her companions. I have said that this red dot marks the end of the Passage of the Butterfly and the beginning of the western wall of the Plain of Bones. If you were a new man leaving the Cave by way of the western wall of the Passage of the Butterfly, this red dot would mark your return to the Plain of Bones as an initiated hunter. As a new man, the first procession of spirit-animals you would see being reborn from a black-lined split in the rock would follow the Dark Mothers—Bear Mother, Leopard Mother and Lion Mother. Today, we have taken the round in the opposite direction, but that is for your instruction only. Come, we will return to the Red Dot and I will show you a secret of the Plain of Bones that only seers and shamans may know."

We turned back on the path to retrace our steps along the western wall, past the scene of creation, then to the armpit and the shallow side-cavern that is the Mother's left arm. We stopped again at the Red Dot.

"Here is another secret of the Plain of Bones that will help you, as Seer, to find your way and guide others through the Great Cave. This will also help you to understand why we walk the rounds of the Plain in the manner we do," the Grandfather explained.

"Dear One," he began his next lesson. "Stand with your back against the western wall beneath the Red Dot."

I did as instructed and he continued with his instruction.

"Now stretch out your right hand with your palm down."

I looked down at the splayed fingers of my right hand as the Grandfather continued his explanation.

"Do you see the direction your thumb points?" he asked.

"Yes, Grandfather. It points in the direction of Leopard Mother and her hunter companions, and the procession of creation," I answered.

"That is correct, Dear One. I have already explained that Leopard Mother is the sign of the new men's portal of exit from the Cave after their trials and initiations are complete. Your thumb, therefore, is pointing to the exit side—the western side—of the Passage of the Butterfly. From here, at the Red Dot, the entrance side of the Passage of the Butterfly on the eastern side of the Plain is reached by taking the path which is called 'Straight.' It is the path which corresponds to your first finger—the finger you might use to point at something. This is the path initiated hunters take from the Red Dot on the western wall to take them to the eastern side of the Plain of Bones on their way out of the Cave. Uninitiated boys will not take the Straight Path but instead will always take the 'second finger', which is a meandering, zigzagging trail to the eastern side of the Plain. Your second finger—the center finger—points to the path called the Maze of Boys. We will now take the same trail the boys follow from the Red Dot to the eastern side of the Plain of Bones as they come in from the Skull Portal. As seer-initiate, you will take the Maze of Boys to the other side of the Plain where you will enter the Red Womb of Hunters. Then we will move on to the entry portal of the Passage of the Butterfly. Do you understand?"

"Yes, Grandfather, I begin to see it. But what, then, is this third finger?"

"The third finger is the path we have just walked from the center of the Third Entrance of the Red Lodge of Women to the Red Dot of the Hand where you now stand. I'm sure you noticed the path called Winding, the one we followed to get here, is little used. This is because only seer-initiates ever walk it. Seers know this White Lodge of the Plain of Bones as the Hand of the Mother because the five trails which converge at this Red Dot are like the fingers and thumb of the right hand. The path called Winding corresponds to your third finger, the one next to your little finger. Your little, fourth finger, of course, points to the path the boy's take from the Skull Portal to this Red Dot of the Hand. I'm sure you now understand why the Plain of Bones is sometimes called the Hand of the Mother, do you not?" he concluded.

I continued to study the back of my hand, mapping out the Plain of Bones upon the little veins there. "Yes, Grandfather, I think I understand. Boys enter from the Skull Portal and follow the path along the western wall to the Red Dot—a trail represented by my little finger. Again, where do the boys go from here?" I asked.

I was not quite sure it should be by the second or third finger because of the confusing paths we had just taken.

"When the boys are brought to this spot, they will cross back over to the eastern wall by way of the second finger upon the path called the Maze of Boys. They are not taken to the Leopard Mother and her companions until their final journey out of the Cave as men. I'm afraid I may have confused you by taking you to see Leopard Mother first. Let me say that upon reaching the eastern wall, the boys will make a brief visit to the Red Womb of Hunters so the boys know they can come back to that place to quest for an animal-messenger if they so choose. From the Red Womb of the Hunters the boys will be led directly on to the entrance portal of the Passage of the Butterfly—the path you will now follow. Just remember, only initiated hunters will ever take the path called 'Straight.' And you, Dear One, are not a hunter yet!" he said with a lift of the eyebrows, a little nod and a smile.

"You are talking about the thumb and first finger. Am I correct?" I asked again. That was the only part I was still not clear about.

"Yes, Dear One. Initiated hunters will exit the Cave by coming out of the Passage of the Butterfly along its western wall to Leopard Mother and her hunter-companions. From Leopard Mother, the hunters will follow the path of your thumb to the Red Dot, just as we did to return to the place where we are now standing. To exit the Cave, the new men will take the path called 'Straight'—your pointing finger—back to the eastern wall. From there, they will exit the Cave along the eastern wall of the Plain, moving to the left in the sun-wise direction. There they will join again with the new women at the Third Entrance of the Red Lodge to leave the Cave together. Each new man is taken by the path called 'Straight' for the first time only after the completion of his trials and initiations of the Cave. Taking the Straight Path for the first time is a sign of the beginning of their new lives as hunters and as men," the Grandfather concluded.

"May I ask another question, Grandfather?" I said politely.

"Of course, Dear One. It is the question you have in your heart that will give you insight and deep understanding."

"Why is this path of the second finger called 'Straight,' my Grandfather? Does it not turn and change direction like the Maze of Boys and the Winding Path of Seers?"

"No, you can tell from its name it is not a winding path. The way from the Red Dot to the other side of the Plain is straight and without turns, twists and meanders as the other paths of the Hand of the Mother do. This is to teach that the life-path of all initiated men *is* the narrow and straight path of responsibility and duty to one's own heart, to one's kin and to the People. The way of a hunter is narrow and straight because the boys have become new men and they have lined themselves up to all go in the same direction as their hunter brothers by enduring the trials of the Mother's Great Cave. The man's life-path as a hunter and a killer of the Mother's animal-messengers is not a path for unruly children who may do as they please. New men are not ducklings who run about in confusion avoiding a hawk. They are to cooperate with each other and not behave as bull bison or rhinos who are always contending with one another. They must be of one mind and heart if they are to live as men. As hunters exit the Cave as new men, every hunter's life-way has been set, just as a woman's own narrow and straight path is set by the flow of her first Moon Blood as a giver of life. Do you now see why the Plain is sometimes called the Hand of the Mother by seers and shamans, my Daughter?"

"Yes, Grandfather," I said, still enraptured by the back of my own hand.

"You may ask further if you wish?" he said with a pause of anticipation.

"No, Grandfather. I think I understand. Wait, just one more thing. How much is explained to the men about these matters during their rounds of the Cave?" I asked as an afterthought.

"Explain nothing unless you are asked," he advised. "Do follow your heart in telling all initiates the meaning of the signs and spirit-animals, but only if they ask. Each must desire to know the answer or it will not find a secure lodge in their heart, never to be forgotten. What you tell others without their asking may find a place in the head, but it may not lodge in the heart and will soon be forgotten. This is why your questions are so important for your own initiation. In showing the meaning of the Great Cave to those who have eyes that can see and ears that can hear, your own heart will guide you as to how much should be revealed. Do not concern yourself with how much of your teaching will be accepted and how much will be rejected. Above all, do not waste your wisdom on those who will not hear you or who are not ready to receive the wisdom of the Mother. For the final exit from the Cave, it is usually sufficient to tell all the new men they have now become hunters like the Lion, Leopard and Bear Mothers. You may also say the procession of spirit-animals following the Dark Mothers is a sign of their rebirth as men whose life-path is now set as hunters of the Mother's children. For anything else, you should wait for one of them to question the deeper meaning of the signs and spirit-animals. Do you understand?"

"Yes, my Grandfather, I do understand. I will remember what you have taught me," I replied, full of conviction.

"That is well, my good Apprentice. It is good and very good. Now, allow us to continue your seer's initiation by following your second finger along the Maze of Boys to the entrance of the Passage of the Butterfly and beyond to the White Lodges of the Hunters."

With a satisfied smile, the Grandfather pointed in the direction we should go.

* * *

If I must go through a man's initiation before becoming a seer, I couldn't help wondering what might be involved in the woman's initiation of a male seer? I will have to ask Auntie if the Hymen Stone is shoved up the apprentice's rear end the way it is put into each girl's pute! I wonder if any of the men panic the way poor White Lynx did? I could not keep myself from smiling at the thought. The Grandfather continued his instruction without regard to my wandering thoughts and the pleased smile on my lips.

"As Seer, you will become one with all the People as you become one with the spirit-powers, the animal-messengers, the earth, the sky, the Above, the Below and all there is between. To continue your seer's instruction, we will now walk the same path the boys follow in their initiations as men," the Grandfather intoned his latest directions.

180

Having stated his intentions, the Grandfather turned sharply to take a well-beaten path in almost the same direction as we had just come upon the Winding Path of Seers. This Maze of Boys took a meandering path back across the Plain and was only slightly less convoluted than the trail we had just taken in the opposite direction. I could see where some of the skulls and piles of bear bones had been pushed to the side to make a more direct route to the eastern side of the Cave possible without showing any disrespect to Bear Mother in her own Lodge.

After many, many twisting and turning paces, the eastern wall was reborn by our torch light out of the darkness. The trail ended and the Grandfather halted our little procession at the entrance to a narrow, low break in the wall near the ground. I must be getting accustomed to all of this because I did not have to sing the Song to Dispel Fear a single time the whole way from the western back to the eastern wall of the Plain!

"Daughter, this is the Chamber of Fingermarks. All apprentices should enter this small cavern on their own to place their personal mark before entering the other lodges of the hunters. After you have asked permission to enter as a seer-initiate, go inside and place a single thumbprint on the roof of the chamber. You will know where to put the ochre mark when you enter," he said without emotion.

"Yes, Grandfather," I said compliantly.

I bent down almost double to get into the passage—any lower and I would have had to crawl in. So low was the roof here that my little lamp could easily illuminate the concentric circles of red thumb-marks surrounding a small pointed stone descending from the flat, overhanging roof.

"Another penis?" I wondered under my breath. "Well, penises always point up and vulvas point down. That's how one can tell whether masked and robed dancers with three-cornered patches over their organs of sex are supposed to be male or female spirit-powers." I reasoned silently in words as I dug the ochre packet from my satchel.

"Since this is a special entry place for seers into the men's parts of the Cave, it probably *is* a penis—too sharply pointed though," I mused out loud about the pointed stone hanging from the ceiling of the chamber.

I found the packet and placed the flickering lamp on the hard stone floor. I opened the Mother-ochre and then I began to sing. "Oh, Great Bear Mother, hear my words. I am Little Bear. I ask permission to enter this holy Lodge of the Hunters to be initiated as Seer of the Bear People. And I know permission is already granted," I improvised in an important voice.

I carefully placed a single thumb-dot on the outside edge of the many red finger-dots crowding and surrounding the pointed white stone. After adding my personal fingermark, I looked around the tiny chamber. There were no other signs or spirit-animals any-where to be seen, just the marks of many, many fingers or thumbs on the ceiling of the chamber.

"How many seers have come this way to place their thumb mark here?" I wondered in a whisper but got no answer.

I did not have time to count all the thumb marks in red ochre, so that's a question I will never know the answer. I rubbed the ex-cess ochre off my thumb with a little dry clay from the floor. Then I rejoined the Grandfather waiting at the entrance of this tiny cave within the Cave.

"Well done, my Daughter. Now you will enter the Red Womb of the Hunters, a very special lodge among the several Lodges of Hunters," he said, nodding in approval.

We moved several paces further along the eastern wall to a place where a narrow side-chamber stabbed into the darkness like a gigantic spear point. A large, red rhino head looked at me full-faced out of the stone to mark the entrance to this side-chamber called by the Grandfather the Red Womb of Hunters. The slender cavern ran in a northeasterly direction—I could tell that much. It also had a high ceiling and was very deep, reaching far beyond the light

"This has to be the All Mother's 'right arm'," I reasoned si-lently.

"I know you will be counting spirit-animals, dots and signs, my good Apprentice. But I want you to also give your close attention to which way the animals are going and the special points of spirit-power from which the animals emerge or those crevices into which they disappear," the Grandfather instructed.

I tried peering as far as I could down the narrow side-chamber. I could not see much else but more darkened stone.

"If you feel moved to linger, to sit down and commune with one of the spirit-animals, or even if you have the desire to touch them, please feel free to do so. Remember that the Hand of the Mother will come to meet yours at the living barrier of the Cave wall whenever you place your own hand against the stone. Do as your heart tells you, my Daughter. You must enter and leave the Red Womb of Hunters naked and alone, just as you emerged from your own mother's womb into the World of Light."

"What is this chamber used for, Grandfather? Is it only for the initiation of seers?" I asked as I prepared to enter.

I put my lamp aside so I could remove my things. I knew stalling for time before going in by myself was futile, so I dropped the bearskin robe and un-slung my oil horn and satchel. Besides, what could be so frightful in yet another side-chamber?

"No Daughter, this Womb is shown to all hunter-initiates because it is a place of the red spirit-powers within the White Lodges of the Hunters just as the White Womb is a place of the white spirit-powers within the Women's Red Lodge. Beginning with this Red Womb, the boys should be encouraged to become aware of the red-spirited, female part of themselves, which most boys do not know is there within their hearts. That red-spirited, feeling place within their bodies must be accepted and honored if their hearts are to be in harmony with all that the Mother has made and if they are to become true men and successful hunters. As Seer, remember that the spirit-animals appearing in this Red Womb will be the first any of the boys will have experienced within the Great Cave from the time they entered on to this point. Some may be overwhelmed by the red-powers suddenly becoming known to their hearts."

"Grandfather, you have said that women are more aware of the red-powers than men. Why is that so?" I asked.

"Yes, Little Bear, I believe that is the truth of things. Women bear children from their own bodies and nourish them with milk from their own breasts. As a matter of course, all women are more aware of the desires and needs and feelings of the red-body because of that. Men must, above all, use all the skills of the head to be successful hunters and so men are more likely to press down the red-powers that are within each of them because those feelings may get in the way of the thoughts and intentions of the head. Men must learn to guard their feeling hearts so as not to become incapacitated by their love for the Mother's children whose blood they must shed daily as hunters. Because the compassionate, feeling red-powers are often walled off by a hunter's training, and by the example of other men, they must be more deliberate than women in becoming aware of their heart-feelings and of opening their hearts and souls to others. Above all, the boys must learn to balance the feelings and desires of the many different organs of the red-body, which are always in conflict with each other and in a constant struggle with the thoughts of their own heads," he explained.

"That is very confusing, Grandfather. Please tell me more," I asked.

"I know it is confusing, my Daughter. But as with your friend White Lynx in the White Womb, some initiates—especially two-spirit boys—will be drawn back to this red-spirited lodge when the time comes for their solitary quests. Questing girls may also be brought here directly from the Women's Red Lodge—the Third Entrance lies further along this path here running next to the eastern wall of the Plain. As Seer, you must always listen carefully to the initiates and encourage them to go where their very souls are urging them to go. Were any of your Moon Blood sisters brought through the Third Entrance to quest here in this Red Womb?" he asked.

"White Lynx was taken from the group, as you already know, but she went to the White Womb within the Red Lodge. Why would one of the girls be brought here?" I asked.

"As I have said, the powers come to whom they will, when they will, and reveal themselves in the lodges of the Cave as they will. Some girls fall into very deep trances during the Moon Blood and are drawn to a lodge of red-spirits, unlike White Lynx, whose mind would have been even more terrified by being brought here. Girls who have such deep trances upon first entry into the Great

Cave may eventually become seers or even shamans. No girl is brought here as a matter of course as they are shown the Womb of Red Spirits within the Red Lodge. Some boys, who are not two-spirits, will also be drawn back to this place just as some girls are. Some will even desire to come to this chamber without even having been told there is such Red Womb within the Lodges of the Hunters. As Seer, the thing to remember is to allow everyone to go where their hearts take them to quest and commune with the spirit-guides of their soul's desire. You will soon see that few red spirit-animals or signs have been made in any of the Lodges of the Hunters from the Passage of the Butterfly on into the deepest parts of the Cave, so if a Womb of Red Spirits is desired, this is often the place you will bring them. You will soon learn from experience and from listening to your own open heart to recognize when it is appropriate to bring an initiate here. To know what is in this Red Womb, and so as to better guide others, all seer-initiates, male or female, will enter and walk its holy round. Some Apprentices find their animal-guides here and some will descend to encounter the monsters of their own dark abyss within this chamber of red-powers and will return as Thrice Born. For this reason, this chamber is called 'womb'. Follow the right-hand wall in as far as you can go, then take the opposite wall back out. I will be waiting for you on the other side," he instructed.

"Yes, Grandfather," I said.

I began my entry into the chamber called the Womb of Red Spirits.

* * *

"Just a red rhino head in profile, horns pointing toward the entrance," I said aloud as I passed the image.

I moved carefully along the wall, cautious not to trip or spill the lamp.

"It is like a big red dot but with two long horns. A red dot is the same as a red animal head and marks the beginnings of things and the beginnings of circles," I decided, speaking in a low whisper to myself.

"Still, a rhino is the sign of the Powers of Two. Maybe that is the meaning? Strange, I do not feel any colder without my robe," I rambled on to myself as I moved past the red rhino head and on down the passage. In truth, only my feet were really cold.

I was trying to concentrate on not tripping over something on the uneven ground. But as marvelously made images multiplied, I began to bump my toes and bang my shins in distraction. Just beyond the rhino head there appeared a red mammoth followed by a bewildering array of signs. First, a single red line like a short rod had been made. It was followed by groups of five and then three short red rods. Many of the rods had what looked like a pair of man-eggs at one end. I had begun to see red penises everywhere! I suppose I should have counted the little man-rods, but four marvelous mammoths appeared before my eyes followed by four lions and then three bears, all made with just a few cleverly drawn red lines. The lines were few but they had perfectly captured the power, the character and the movement of each animal.

"What skill the Ancients had, to be able to make a spirit-animal come alive with only a few strokes of a brush or an ochre-covered finger!" I said out loud in astonishment.

The spirit-animals on my father's oil horn had been made with many delicate and finely etched lines. Here, only a few boldly drawn lines were used to make the animals come alive before me. The moving lamp light also made it appear that the images were moving—living spirit-animals all. I was really counting everything now. I noticed most, if not all of the animals, whether fully emerged from the skin-wall of the Mother's stone-cold womb or not, were heading for the entrance through which I had just come. The profiled head of the rhino at the entrance also faced in the same direction: going out of the side-chamber.

"The Mother pouring her abundance into the red World of Light. The language of the Cave is known to me!" I whispered out loud.

The passage narrowed quickly. After twenty or so paces, the left-hand wall and the spirit-animals there became visible in my faint lamp light. For just a moment, I imagined I would turn to follow the left-hand wall back to the entrance. But I thought better of doing that because I could not guess what wonders might yet lay ahead that I should not miss. So, I followed the Grandfather's directions and moved on as far back into the passage as I could go. I began to be more and more curious about what was even deeper in this chamber when suddenly the passage turned sharply to the left and narrowed into one big crack.

A big crack! An obvious sign already repeated many times on these walls. Toward the back, just where the passage turned to the left, another group of red signs marked what I thought might be the end of the Red Womb. The red signs actually marked the turn to the left. At the very end of this extremely narrow place lay a small opening at ground level. I got down on my knees to try and see what was within. I could hear the faint tinkling and splashing of running water. Almost immediately, I became very thirsty. Since I had not been told to go through any openings at the bottom of cave walls, I turned around and began my journey out of the Red Womb of Hunters. The outbound wall had fewer animals and, like the spirit-animals on the opposite wall, they all had their heads facing toward the entrance. All of us were moving toward the opening of a huge woman's pute and birthing into the red-world.

"It *is* the Mother's Red Womb," I said to myself aloud.

My animal-companions on our way to rebirth included one magnificent bear, a mammoth and then two more bears before I came to what I immediately knew marked the end of the passage—the black, round, open-jawed face of the Dark Lion Mother.

I also knew I had reached the exit to the holy round of this Red Womb of Hunters because there were no more stone walls to follow. There was only absolute silence and oppressive blackness before, behind, and to either side of me. So overpowering was the encompassing blank wall of blackness looming up before me that my lamp seemed not to be shining into the darkness at all.

Worst of all, the Grandfather and his torch were nowhere to be seen. I waited in the heavy silence for what seemed a lifetime. Without the thick bear robe, I wrapped my arms around myself and shivered in the cold. The panic began to rise up again from my gut, no doubt, from the very center of my liver.

"Can I find my way out of the Cave if the Grandfather has abandoned me?" I began to wonder in a whisper.

I have no tallow horn to add oil to the lamp. But the remaining oil, though low, might be sufficient to get me out. Especially if I douse one or two of the wicks. Less light, I know, but surely enough oil to get me out of here to safety. I began to make plans to find my way out of the Cave.

I took a deep breath trying to calm myself. After repeating the Song to Dispel Fear a few times under my breath, the panic began to subside. I knew in that moment, *somehow* I could find my way out. I had a picture in my head of exactly where I was as if I had drawn it out in the sand. I knew I could feel my way in the dark, if necessary, all the way back to the Portal of the Mother's Mouth. There were no pits or holes to fall into, only a flat floor, and mostly smooth stone walls, from here all the way to the Third and then the Second Entrance of the Red Lodge. From the Second Entrance I could feel my way to the Skull Portal. And from there, I would be able to see my way to the entrance of the Cave, or if it were night outside, I could feel my way to the mouth of the Cave. I might have bruised toes and scraped shins, and I would be naked and freezing cold, but I knew I could find my way out. With one or two additional long, deep breaths, the panicked breathing slowed and a self-assured calm returned. My fears of being lost in the Cave melted away. I knew exactly where I was.

Suddenly, out of the darkness a huge black shape with flames for a head rushed toward me with a great roaring GRRRRR! Completely startled, and spilling my lamp in terror, I filled the cavern with echoing screams, even though I knew it was only the Grandfather.

"Don't do that! You nearly made me pee myself!" I complained loudly.

All protests were drowned out by fits of my own laughter *and* the Grandfather's laughter at my expense. He had all but fallen down with laughter and could barely hand me my bag and horn. Still chuckling, he lifted the bear robe to wrap it again around my shoulders in blessed warmth.

"Well done, my good Apprentice!" he exclaimed when he could stop laughing long enough to speak. "You should always wait here to test the apprentice's mettle. Some initiates will begin to scream for help just before they realize they really can find their way out if no one is waiting for them at the end of the round. I am proud of you that you began to sing the Song to Dispel Fear rather than panic and start crying out for help."

"I did not sing out loud, Grandfather. How could you have heard that?" I asked.

"Even the smallest whisper can be heard in such silence, my Daughter. And even if I could not hear you, the Mother hears every sound and will always come to your aid. Never forget that in the darkest of nights when those who believe they are nothing more than their red-bodies are overwrought, suffering and thinking they are alone, the Mother lies stretched in smiling repose ready to enfold us in her arms and suckle us at her ample breasts. Remember this lesson, Dear One, for it will serve you well throughout this life and in all the worlds to come," he said mysteriously.

"But *why* would you scare me like that?!" I blurted. I had started to calm down somewhat, but then I became angry again at being made a fool so easily.

"Daughter, here is another great lesson. This Great Cave is a fearsome place, but it is not a place of fear. All those who come here must learn to overcome their terror of the Cave and all it represents to them. For all who enter here, the Cave is uncertainty and change and transformation. It is leaving one's accustomed and comfortable place in life to move to another which is unknown and unknowable. All people fear such uncertainty and resist such change with great vigor. They resist because they are not in control of what lies, unknown, around the blind corner. But know that all corners are blind and no one knows what will happen tomorrow. Worrying about what may or may not happen tomorrow only brings anxiety and fear. To allow the fox-spirit of the Trickster to enter helps us all to release our fears of what might happen tomorrow. We should never take ourselves, and what we think to be so important at the moment, too seriously. In our darkest moments, the Trickster should be invited to make us laugh and love and enjoy the beauties of life, even when we are mourning those we love who have returned to the Mother. It is the Trickster who brings joy to a remembrance of the Returned as we don their clothes and impersonate them. Surely you know that, my Good apprentice. It is the Trickster makes us laugh and think of the Returned with fondness and love. And so it is for all of us."

Still, I was so peeved at being made to look foolish that I refused to speak, my mouth turned down in a sour frown.

"Let me ask you this, Dear One. Do you remember what the women were doing when it came time for you to leave the Red Lodge of your Moon Blood?" he asked, thinking to divert me from my rage.

"Yes, Grandfather, I remember it all so clearly," I replied, giving up some of my pique.

"After the three rounds were completed, the mentors helped us to trance in groups and by ourselves. We also sang the songs and danced the dances of newly discovered animal-companions. We told the stories we loved most to each other. Some composed and sang songs of love we would one day sing to our lovers or beloved husbands. We had flutes and drums and rattles and bull-roarers to accompany the singing and dancing around the hearth before the Rock of the All Mother. Mostly, we just danced and laughed."

My ill humor had dissipated completely.

"What else did you do?" the Grandfather asked with apparent interest.

"We talked with the auntie-mentors and the other new women. We made friends among our Moon Blood sisters and some pledged companionship as lifelong gift-givers. We became Sisters of the Moon Blood swearing to be friends and to help each other always. Some went off to other parts of the Red Lodge to become even better friends, if you know what I mean," I said with raised eyebrows and sidelong knowing glance.

Here I am, nattering on about the private business of the women's Red Lodge as if the Grandfather didn't know anything. But he seemed not to take any notice.

"Yes, Dear One. And when you left the Cave as initiated women and friends-for-life, were you afraid of the Cave and the *terrible* spirit-powers that lodge here?" he questioned.

"No Grandfather. No one was afraid of the Cave or of the spirit-powers. Including White Lynx," I realized out loud.

"And so it is with the initiation of boys. When they undergo the trials and revelations of the Cave, they will no longer be boys, but men and unafraid. They will be unafraid of the Cave and unafraid of a hunter's life that will always be full of uncertainty, fearsome change, disappointment and suffering. They will be unafraid of tomorrow and the unexpected lurking around the corner."

Interrupting his lesson, I broke in. "But how did you do that? How did you come out of nowhere to frighten me so? Why did I not see your torch's light, my Grandfather?" I asked with real curiosity.

Laughing out loud again he said, "Come over here, my Daughter. I will show you how it is done."

Grasping me by my left hand, he led me around the narrow point of rock that held the Dark Mother's face to a crevice in the wall on the other side.

"Place your torch or lamp inside this niche, then open your arms and block as much light as you can with your robe. Like this."

The Grandfather held out both arms of his beautiful white robe like the wings of some great white bird to cover the crevice and the torch within.

"The initiate on the other side looking at the Lion Mother's black face will have enough of their own lamp light in their eyes to keep any stray torchlight from their sight. Then you can run at them with a great shout to startle them," he explained.

Then, leaning in, as if imparting some ancient secret, the Grandfather whispered, "But learn patience, Dear One. Do give the initiate plenty of time to move past their panic and fear and to think out their predicament in their heads. If they are extremely frightened, then it is probably not a good idea to rush out of the darkness at them. If they are already so terrified that they are crying out, you could make their hearts stop beating!" he chuckled at his own little joke.

The Grandfather's face grew serious. All signs of his little smile vanished.

"Dear One, the Cave *is* a terrifying place. But it is the one best place for initiates to learn to overcome their fears of being alone with the inner light and love of the All Mother. This awe-inspiring and Holy Cave is the one best place for each to quest each for their own true selves and to allow personal animal-guides to come forth. Can you understand that?" he said, smiling sweetly.

"Yes, Grandfather. I can see the wisdom in it," I answered with the same smile.

"You have done well, as I knew you would, Daughter of my Heart. Now, let us continue with our own holy rounds of the White Lodges of Hunters," the Grandfather said approvingly.

CHAPTER 8.
PASSAGE OF THE BUTTERFLY

A WELL-WORN PATH led from the place where I had nearly peed myself in fright. The trail passed by the crevice where the Grandfather had secreted his torch on our way toward the entrance to the Passage of the Butterfly.

"We will continue to move along this wall against-the-sun to begin our holy round through the Passage of the Butterfly. Remember that moving to the right is the direction of the Red Sisterhood and so is the direction of the red-powers. It is the spiraling of the red-body coming in and the going out of being. Until we move beyond this passage of transition, we will continue to take our rounds to the right, against-the-sun. But as we move into the lodges of the white spirit-powers beyond, we will begin to make our holy rounds to the left, moving in the sun-wise direction. Circling with the sun is the direction of the white spirit-powers," the Grandfather rambled on as we walked.

"Is this the entrance to the Passage of the Butterfly?" I pointed at a large pute-shaped pendant with red signs that descended from the roof nearly to the level of our heads.

"Yes, this is the entrance portal. Come closer, my Daughter. Let us examine the images painted on the pendant and then we will enter."

The pendant stuck out from the wall and upon its left side there appeared a small cross of red with four equal arms. Just below and to the right of the little cross, a small cross-like object had been made. It looked like it had wings and a tail but no head. Above the two cross-like signs, a large red bird or butterfly with a rounded tail stretched out its rounded wings to hover over or shelter the two smaller images.

"What do these signs say to you, Dear One?" The Grandfather resumed the instruction of his good Apprentice.

I held my lamp close and looked carefully at the three signs. These were unlike any butterflies I had ever seen. But I reasoned that since this place is called the "Passage of the Butterfly" then butterflies they must be. I also noticed the big butterfly image had been painted so that it appeared to be coming sideways out of a dark vertical crack where the pendant joined the rock wall. Two long, red lines had been drawn on either side of the break to draw attention to the slender split in the stone—just like the crack in the stone with two black lines at the end of the Passage of the Butterfly where Leopard Mother lurked.

"I think these are butterflies that are changing their shape into the red All Mother's cross," I stated flatly.

"That is a very good answer, my Daughter, for the butterfly *is* the sign of change and transformation from one shape to another. What you may not see, however, is that the three parts of the creature, two wings and tail, should also remind seers of the oneness of all things—the three-in-one—as should the All Mother's cross of the four directions and the four substances of creation. They are the same sign and they are made as if emerging from the All Mother's womb—the two red rods on either side of the vulva-shaped crack where the pendant joins the rock wall. I am sure you have noticed that. This Passage *is* the place of transition from one way of being to another, from one way of thinking about oneself to another way. It is also the connecting passage that lies between the Red Lodges and the White Lodges of the Great Cave. This Passage is a bridge between two parts of the Cave and is a sign of the bridge between the worlds. All the signs and spirit-animals we will see here should remind us of that. Now, let us enter the Passage and begin your own transition from woman to hunter. And from earth-bound woman to high-flying Seer."

The Grandfather finished speaking and without asking any spirit-power's permission, led me on around the pendant to what lay ahead. Beyond the reach of our firelights stretched a long, narrow cavern with a very high roof covered with all sizes of long and short pendants and slim, wavy wings of stone. The gently curving, nearly straight up-and-down, right-hand wall of the Passage had many ribs and waterfall formations of red, white and yellowish stone. Some of the dry rock appeared to be dirty frozen water flowing down the walls from roof to floor. Stone ribs formed overhangs above door-shaped flat areas all along this expanse of cave wall. Stone ice sickles stuck out past the door-shaped openings from above like sharp teeth surrounding some monstrous creature's gaping mouth.

The first large door-like area of mostly flat stone we came to had seven red butterflies of different sizes painted within the "door posts." Some of the seven butterflies had slanted straight rods drawn on either side of their wings. The straight rods reminded me of the pute-crack we had just passed with two straight red lines on either side of the crack.

"There is another meaning in these butterflies that is only shared with seers," the Grandfather said quietly.

He stood beside me staring at the seven red butterflies for a moment. Then he leaned in to whisper in my ear as if his secret would be overheard by someone hiding in the dark.

"Come closer to the Red Seven to better see what the hidden meaning is," he said beckoning. "These seven butterfly signs in red, each slightly different in size, were purposefully made by the Ancients in a different shape than the bird-like butterflies on the entry pendant. The big butterfly at the portal has rounded wings and a tail, but no body in the middle where the wings of a butterfly would usually be joined. These images here all have wings made with sharp points. None have bodies joining the wings and they have no tails. The two three-cornered wings of each of the Red Seven meet at a single point in the center. Do you, my good Apprentice, know what these sharp-pointed signs should say to us as seers?" he asked, gesturing from image to image with his finger.

"No Grandfather, they are just seven pointy-winged butterflies to me."

"My Daughter," he said, announcing the beginning of his next lecture. "The butterfly is also a sign that speaks to seers and shamans of the twin spirals of trance. You will have learned to open the holy spirals when you were taught how to go into the place and time of trance-dreaming within you. How much do you remember of the two spirals of trance?"

"In the Moon Blood, Auntie told everyone that preparation is always required whenever we attempt to trance. Or even when we sit in contemplation for long periods of time, for healing or for seeking guidance. We practiced the preparations as Moon Blood sisters in our meditations at the Animal of Red Dots. And again before the Rock of the All Mother," I stated simply.

More was coming back to my head now, so I continued.

"I know that before opening ourselves to the Mother, and to prevent those powers we do not desire from joining with us, we must always imagine our spirit-fire spiraling first down into the earth to bind us and protect us with the powers of Earth Mother and the powers of the Below. Then we must imagine our spirit-fire spiraling up to the sky so the powers of Sky Father and the powers of the Above will protect and guide us. Is that what you mean, Grandfather?"

"Yes, that is exactly what I mean, my good Apprentice. Your memory is truly remarkable!" he said while looking at me through the slightly squinting eyes of disbelief.

"Do you also know why the butterflies are seven in number here, my Daughter?" he asked, testing me again.

"I think so, my Grandfather. There are seven butterflies because they represent the Seven Cow Sisters. Is that right?" I replied.

The Seven Star Sisters, what the Grandfather calls "the Red Seven" is the most important "seven" for all of the Bear People. Every child knows that when the Sisters begin to rise on the eastern horizon, very early in the morning, the time to return to the Valley from the Plains of Summer is approaching. And, when the Cow Sisters begin to leap off the hunting jump of the western horizon in the early evening, it is time to prepare to leave the Valley to follow the herds north upon the Plains of Summer again.

"Easy question, easy answer," I thought to myself.

"Right again! I see your Auntie has prepared you well for this initiation. What she may not have taught you is that the Star Shaman of the Hunt, who chases the Cow Sisters in the winter sky, also has seven great stars. This is also called the 'White Seven'. Look closely into the night sky and you will see the Great Star Hunter is also in the shape of a butterfly, its great wings in the shape of two imperfect three-corners. The three grand stars of the Star Shaman's belt is a butterfly's rod-shaped body to which the three-cornered wings are attached. As Seer, know that every shaman in trance sits at the central point of transition between the worlds of the Above and the worlds of the Below. That central point *is* the middle star of the Star Shaman's belt. All seers must learn that each shaman's body in trance *is* the Middle World linking the three worlds as one. When in trance, you will learn to put yourself in that central place when you wish to commune with the powers of the Above or the powers of the Below in order to serve and bless the People of the World of Light. When in dream or in trance, we go where our animal-guides take us, which powers are either of the Above or Below worlds—the white or red-worlds. But healing powers come forth from all the worlds: white, red *and* black; above, in-between and below; mind, body and soul."

"Grandfather, I have a question. If I become Twice Born Seer, does that mean I may not heal the soul of another as shamans do?"

"Yes, Dear One, you are correct. Seers who have not taken the shaman's journey to the center of their own soul can hardly be expected to go into the Void to heal and rescue another soul. If you are ever to become Thrice Born Shaman of Healing, treating and healing mind, body and soul, you must open your liver, head and heart equally in harmony and oneness. That is what it means to be 'Thrice Born.' When you will have taken the shaman's journey to the abyss of your own soul the holy joining of the Three Worlds within you will allow the appropriate spirit-powers to come forth. Whether that power is of the Above or the Below or is of the union of the Two Powers in the center of your own heart, it will matter not. Having been three times reborn, to heal all those who come to you with whatever ailment of the body, mind or spirit, you will yield to the appropriate spirit-power coming forth from your own soul. You will move yourself at will from one world to the other and back again as is necessary to heal and bless. This ability to move easily between the worlds at will is the one true power of every seer and shaman. But as I have said, the shaman's journey is not one that can be sought, neither can it be taught. As Seer, you will be content to bless the bodies and minds of the People. I hope you will be content to wait on the Mother for your shaman's journey if you are to also heal and bless the souls of the People. Did your Auntie discuss such things with you?"

"Not exactly, Grandfather. But she always says the spirals of trance must be properly opened for a shaman to perform a healing of the mind or the soul," I answered.

I tried to remember what else she might have told me.

"Auntie has taught you well, my Daughter. Now listen and learn even more that will serve you whether as seer or shaman of the People. Seven is a number of great spirit-power. It is the sign that a season of great change or transformation is coming or is just passing away. It is the change of the two seasons announced by the Seven Cow Sisters as they come and go. It is the transformation which comes as the Mother gives birth and takes back. It is the ever-changing moon making its complete round in four periods of seven nights each. We all know the women's moon-blood circle is also of twenty-eight days in duration. The four parts of the moon's round, each of seven days in duration, are therefore the signs of the Mothers of the Four Directions and the Four Substances of the coming forth of new life—earth, air, fire and water. These are all changes and transformations in the world around us that are forever before our eyes and divided into periods of seven days each. Upon your initiation, the Red Seven of the Star Sisters and the White Seven of the Star Shaman appearing in the night sky will be a constant reminder of your honored place among the People and your holy duty as Seer and Healer. Even now, the Star Hunter has chased the Cow Sisters to the western horizon signaling the time when the whole People will leave again for the Plains of Summer, as you well know."

"Yes, Grandfather. I know and I understand. The last great hunt of the winter season is now underway upon the Plain because the Sisters have begun their leap from the western horizon."

"Listen well, my Daughter, and add to all you have already learned with another secret of the seers and shamans. Within the great Star Shaman of the Hunt the spirals of trance are also hidden. The middle star in the Shaman's belt is the holy central point joining the upper and lower spirals which are the male and female three-corners of the butterfly's wings. The stars of the belt are three, but the central star should be seen as the third point of the upper, female three-corner as well as the third point of the lower, male three-corner. The three stars of the belt are separate to our eyes and yet they are three-in-one and one-in-three. Some fly to the Star Shaman in their dream-visions. They have told us that as they look upon the three stars of the Star Hunter's belt from a different point-of-view, the three stars of the belt become as one, leaving only the single central point to join the two spiraling wings of a spirit-butterfly. The middle star of the belt is thus the sign of the central point of transition and so is also the sign of the joining of the Two Worlds, the joining of woman and man as upper and lower three-cornered wings. The central star of the Shaman's belt is thus the sign of the shaman's gift to move between and connect the worlds of the spirit-powers, to move between the pairs of opposites of up and down, in and out; male and female; dreaming and waking. Having heard these words, when we leave the Cave and you have become Seer, the night sky itself will remind you of everything you have learned and experienced in your initiations. Think well on all these things, my Daughter. Remember so you may give others this great wisdom of the Ancients to the People," he concluded.

My head was spinning with so much wisdom and knowledge, but I continued pulling it all into my head as eagerly as a hungry hunter gobbles his stew.

"Now we will move forward along this wall to the next lesson in stone awaiting you," the Grandfather said as he began moving off into the darkness.

Other of the door-shaped spaces had very few, if any, signs or spirit-animals contained within them until we came to one in which a big black bison appeared. It was facing us as if moving toward the Seven Cow Sisters, the Red Seven or whatever they should be called, and the entrance to the Passage. This black bison is so memorable because it is the first black animal I have seen in the whole Cave—except for the Dark Lion Mother's face at the end of the two holy rounds of the Red Lodges. The Grandfather barely paused long enough for me to even notice that the black bison—maybe an aurochs—was there. Then he brought me to a stop before another flat space on the wall. This unique area is lined on all sides with rib-like stone. Ice sickles of rock surrounded and divided two big red images into their own special spaces.

I had never before seen such unusual signs. The first was a bug-like creature with twelve legs—a caterpillar, perhaps? The bottom half of the rounded, elongated body had been filled in with red ochre. The top half had a flat head where the lines of the legs crossed the unpainted rock in the center of the body making it appear somewhat like a net. The second image, to the left of the caterpillar and enclosed within its own curved-top frame, appeared to be another big red bird or butterfly. It was almost exactly like the one on the entry pendant to the Passage, only much bigger. Maybe it is a moth? A bird? I just could not be sure.

As I looked more closely at the two images, the many-legged creature and the butterfly brought to mind a cicada bug. Cicada bugs crawl up tree trunks out of the ground. Before they start screaming your ears deaf, they turn into flying bugs that appear to have no head. At least their heads look flat to me. Either kind of bug is still a sign of changing shapes, I am certain of that. Whatever they were meant to be an image of, both signs were painted on an unusually flat and narrow stretch of wall well-separated from any other images. The surrounding ridges and ribs of white stone seemed to be flowing from the roof to enclose the signs side-by-side within two elongated square frames, the tops of which curved inward from both sides to meet at the top in rounded arches—roughly the shape of the ends of our winter bark lodges that contain the door flaps.

"Daughter?" the Grandfather said, catching my attention to give more instruction. "As I have already said, the butterfly or night-flying moth is the sign of the change and transformation of the red-body. When a girl's body begins to give forth her moon-blood each moon, her body has been changed. When the boys come out of the Great Cave as hunters, their bodies have also been changed with new body-marks and shorn hair. But the butterfly is also a sign of change from one way of thinking to another—from boy to man, woman to seer, from red-body to white-spirit, death to life and life to death. In every change one must die to the old and be reborn as something new, just as the caterpillar dies to its old form as a creature of the earth, is hidden for a time within its cocoon and re-emerges as a butterfly, a creature of the sky able to fly like a bird. All of the Mother's children are like caterpillars—we all combine two kinds of things into one which are often hidden from view. All of us contain both red and white spirit-powers within and so we are all holy and full of the Mother's spirit-power. These signs and images are all different ways of saying the same thing: the act of changing from one condition or way of thinking to another is holy," he lectured on with many fascinating ideas new to me.

"Why does this caterpillar have only twelve legs, my Grandfather? Caterpillars have many legs," I observed, having had much practical experience with caterpillars.

"Could this be the image of a cicada bug just crawling out of the dirt and up a tree trunk before flying away?" I asked without giving the Grandfather a chance to answer my first question.

The Grandfather nodded his head up and down slowly in thoughtful agreement.

"I suppose it could be a cicada bug, my good Apprentice. As many times as I have seen these signs, I have never once thought of a cicada bug. I would praise your intelligence again, Dear One, but I fear your head has already swelled up enough! What I am certain of is that both butterflies and cicadas are signs of transformation and change. You may well be correct in this, Dear One," he said with a broad, gap-toothed smile.

· I too grinned in the sunshine of the Grandfather's praise of me.

"Still," the Grandfather continued, "the creature has twelve legs and the shamans-of-time tell us twelve is the number of one complete circle of the sun encompassing the two seasons of winter and summer. This is because the sun-round can be divided into twelve parts of thirty days each. Use of the sign of twelve is one way of referring to the sun-round or to speak of a completed circle of any kind. Think of it this way: the change from caterpillar to butterfly to caterpillar again, takes one full sun-round and encompasses both seasons. Whether of the ending or beginning of a sun-round, the number twelve is the sign that one circle is ending, another beginning. For each boy, one circle of their young life is ending and another is beginning. And so it is for you, my good Apprentice."

"Is that why the boys are brought to the Cave to become men in their twelfth season, my Grandfather?" I asked.

"Only in part," he replied. "Most boys are well-grown enough to become men after their twelfth summer. Some wait until they grow taller and heavier. But yes, twelve is the end of the circle of childhood and the time when boys should become men," he concluded.

"Why are girls not initiated after their twelfth season, Grandfather?" I queried again.

"That is because the moon-blood gives no heed to the number of seasons a girl has lived. One whose moon-blood was early in coming should know that, do you not?" he asked, tilting his head playfully toward me.

I wondered how the Grandfather knew so much about me. It must have been Auntie who discussed my initiation with him long before anyone else.

"Yes Grandfather, that is true. I was initiated ahead of one of my cousins of the Lower Camp because my moon-blood came a season before hers. My brother, Little Ibex, will become a man at the Great Gathering this very season. Although, I think he has seen more than twelve seasons. As they plan for his initiation, both he and my father are more animated and talkative than I have ever seen them. They seem absolutely happy and excited."

"Yes, Dear One. Men are always very happy and excited to take their sons or nephews into the Cave to become men. For a man, it is the highest, most honored place of their lives as hunters to do so. But let us continue on through this Passage of the Butterfly. There is much more to be seen and learned here."

Not many paces on past the bug and the butterfly, the wall jutted out before us and ended in another large pendant with only blackness beyond. Without stopping, we continued on around the pendant. Yet another long, almost flat stone wall stretched out before us for many paces beyond our lights. Here, the high roof is also hung with many large and small pendants, waving wings of stone and stone ice sickles. But from top to bottom, the entire right-hand wall appeared to be divided into three long, narrow sections of very smooth stone. The top level is very thick and is actually the roof of the Cave curving downward to the sidewall. The second level is narrower in thickness with the center of this second band of stone about the height of our heads. This second level is an overhanging continuation of the top level, but in a contrasting color. The third level is a very smooth wall curving back under the overhang to give the appearance of a third band ending at the more or less flat floor. Each long, level section has a different color—dark tan and grey on the top, yellow and light tan in the middle and tawny brown with patches of orange and red on the bottom level. By far the most astonishing is the middle—yellow and tan—level, which stretches away into the darkness. It curves up slightly in the center like a rainbow and it is covered by red spirit-animals in a long procession for as far as I could see. The whole line of images headed in the same direction as we were going—deeper inside the Cave.

"Come, my Daughter," he said. The Grandfather grasped my hand to pull me gently along the three-colored rainbow wall from the place where I was frozen in fascination.

As we slowly made our way, I could not pull my eyes away from the seven full-faced heads of Lion Mother in red ochre stretching out in a line next to each other. Three indistinct full-bodied spirit-animals—bison, aurochs or deer, I could not be sure—walked behind the seven lion heads. All were moving forward in a single-file line, except for one of the full-bodied animals, who was heading back out of the Passage.

"Let us move to the center of these marvelous spirit-animals and signs where their meaning will become known to you, Dear One," the Grandfather said to encourage me along and keep me moving.

The Grandfather led the way along the wall across a hard floor to a pile of thin flat stones that had been stacked up to form a low seat. The makeshift seat had been piled up at a point along the rainbow wall where the line of seven lion heads gave way to one full-bodied Lion Mother. Red Lion Mother, her head pointing inward to the deeper recesses of the Cave, had a straight line of nine little finger-dots beneath her front paws and a curious arc of little red dots coming out of her mouth. In front and above the arc of dots, two red handprints, with all the fingers showing, had been pressed onto the stone. Above Lion Mother's head, and almost standing on her muzzle, appeared just the rear end of a red horse. The headless horse was pointing toward the seven lion heads and the rest of the Cave behind us. No doubt the spirit horse was on her way out of the Cave into the World of Light. All she had to do was get past this formidable pride of red lions. It looked like they had already half-eaten her!

What is most extraordinary to me about this line of images is that to the left of the handprints, and further ahead in the line, appeared two rhinos who were also facing in the same direction. The lead rhino's horns pointed forward toward an odd red sign shaped like two half moons placed side-by-side with the round halves down.

"It's shaped like a pair of naked buttocks sitting down!" I chuckled quietly to myself.

Beyond the double half-moons appeared three more rhinos for a total of five. They all tilted their heads down and pointed their extraordinarily long double horns in the same direction—deeper into the Cave. It was as if they were running away from the lions coming up hard on their heels. Why they weren't turning to fight the lions, as rhinos are wont to do, is a mystery to me.

"Come sit here by my side, Dear One. I will tell you what you will not know about becoming a man and being a hunter of the White Brotherhood," the Grandfather said in kindly tones.

While I had been looking closely at the spirit-animals, the Grandfather seated himself upon his little perch of stacked up stones facing the lion with the red dots coming out of her mouth. He motioned toward the ground next to him. I settled in cross-legged facing toward the strange butt-shaped sign of simple red lines. Intrigued and without a word of questioning, I waited for the Grandfather to begin speaking from his high place. It was a high place from my point of view, sitting as I was upon the ground looking up at him.

He wedged his torch between two more of the flat stones which appears to have been placed in front of his seat as a torch-holder. I placed my lamp next to his torch on the hard stone floor of the Passage and waited for him to speak. The placement of the torch below and slightly in front of us made the light shine up at our faces. The flickering light from two sources of flame cast strange shadows from the Grandfather's nose and eyebrows up-ward at an odd angle. He sat quietly gathering his thoughts for a long moment.

Soon, the Grandfather began my instruction in the mysteries of the world of men.

"Dear One," he said. "The coming of your moon-blood made you a woman and a vessel of the Mother to bring new life into the red World of Light. No rites or initiations were really necessary to make you a woman. This is why it is said the woman's path of the Red Sisterhood is easy and straight, while the men's path of the White Brotherhood is crooked and difficult. The ways of all men and boys are forever changing and hard to follow. A straight path must be deliberately chosen and walked by every boy if he is to become a man and a hunter, in line with the Mother's ways. As a woman, you do not seek the transformation of the moon-blood. It just happens to you. The Mother sends it to you as a gift of the red-life. Your girl's feet are set upon the narrow and straight life-path of a woman with the coming of your first moon-blood. Still the women's rites are required because every girl must learn within her heart that, as a woman, she stands at the center of the life of the whole People with powers to give birth and nurture life from her own body. Each must recognize that these powers are those of the All Mother herself. The life of the hunters and of the whole People circles about you in one, great, holy round. Those gifts to bring forth and nurture new life are the creative red-powers of the All Mother embodied within you. As a woman you must realize this about yourself and live your life always with that knowledge within your head, liver and heart. You already know from experience that your woman's initiations are to make the three holy rounds of the Lodge of Red Spirits, to receive the Hymen Stone and to sit and contemplate upon what it is you have become. These women's rites of the Moon Blood are intended to teach that you *are* the Mother, if you learn nothing else. Hopefully, you will also find your life's guiding companion-animal as you go through the initiations of the Cave. In the end, for your initiation to be truly complete, you must know what and who you are as a woman of the Red Sisterhood."

"Yes, Grandfather. I do understand. But why are boys any different?" I asked, truly puzzled.

"Boys grow, their bodies become of full seasons and they are grown men. But because they do not have a change in their bodies such as that of the coming of the first moon-blood to make of them men and hunters, each boy must be deliberately transformed into a man by the trials and revelations of the Mother's Great Cave. Each boy must be taught how to be a hunter in his heart just as he must learn how to make points and blades with his own hands. Each boy must learn to throw the killing spears that take the red-lives of the Mother's animal-messengers. At the same time, each boy must learn what it means to line himself up with the heart of the whole People. None of these things come to any man without much learning and practice. Above all, in the boy's rites the powers of the head must be made the leader of every hunter's soul. If a hunter is unable to control the strong emotions of the liver and the heart with the clear thoughts of his head, it will interfere with the necessary acts of his life as a competent and successful hunter."

"Grandfather," I interrupted. "Do we women not have to learn to control the urges of the liver as the men do?"

"Yes, Dear One, but not to the degree that men must put the head as leader of their lives. A large part of becoming a man and a hunter is learning to control the strong emotions of the liver with the disciplined thoughts of the head. Otherwise, a boy will never become a man and a hunter. This, each hunter must do as he sheds the blood of the Mother's children with his own hands or he and his family will not survive. But at the same time and even while the urges of the liver are controlled by the head and harmonized within the hunter's heart, each man must never allow the head to utterly kill the urgings of the liver and the tender feelings of the heart. If that happens, that man ceases to be the servant of the Mother altogether and serves no one but himself. Such a man becomes a thoughtless and uncaring murderer of the red-life. This is the winding and difficult path every boy and every man must take between feeling his emotions and pushing them down. And the true man must learn to open and close his heart as he goes out to the hunt and returns to his family crazed with the bloody lust of the hunt. Without the rites of the Sand Animal to close the heart and the rites of the Division to open it once again, the men we live with would all be mad and forever brutish and violent without ceasing. But when the hunter finds that middle path and puts himself in line with it, it becomes the Straight Path every man must walk in his own heart and he will be able to open and close his heart as is necessary to live the life of a good and honest hunter of the People. The winding, contradictory, childish path is the Maze of Boys whereupon all who would be hunter must first walk. In walking the labyrinth of their initiations, they will come to the center of their own hearts and will find balance and harmony between head, liver and heart. In the puberty rites, each boy must begin to find his solitary way to the center of the heart and soul of the man that he truly is. And when they do find the path to the center of their own souls, it will be the myriad faces of the All Mother that they will find there. The struggling, contradictory thoughts of the head and the powerful emotions of the liver must be balanced and harmonized in each man's heart just as they must be brought together and harmonized in the hearts of all women. Let me ask you this, Dear One. There are many rhinos made on the walls of the Mother's Cave. Do you know what the rhino is a sign of?"

"No Grandfather. All I know is that they are a sign of the Powers of Two. Please teach me," I answered without feigning ignorance.

"The rhino-spirit is among those of the Mother's children possessing the most father-powers. Rhinos, like boys and like men, are constantly competing against and fighting with one another. I believe I have mentioned this before, but because the rhino has two horns on one head, it can also be a sign of the Powers of Three. But that is only so if the liver, head and heart have been brought together in harmony and alignment with each other. You will already know that rhinos are very ferocious and will fight with each other as easily as they will chase after us human hunters to protect their calves. Here is the wisdom of Seers in this: with any two opposing things, with any two things struggling and fighting against each other, there are only two possible outcomes. Either the one will dominate and destroy the other or the second will dominate and destroy the first. That will always be the situation unless the two, who are struggling against each other, take the Middle Path of cooperation between the conflicting pairs of opposites. The Middle Path *is* the Straight Path of hunters and is the way of harmony and joining. Through the ordeals and insights of the men's rites, and then in the daily rounds as hunters, each man must recognize that which appears to be two struggling against each other is really one in the Mother. They must see that which appears to be two spirits fighting within one heart is really one. Do you understand, Dear One?" he asked, his eyebrows lifted in anticipation of an answer.

"I begin to understand, my Grandfather. But how is such harmony accomplished between opposing sides, between the hunter and the hunted? I can hardly bear to kill a salmon or a rabbit let alone a big and powerful animal-messenger. How can any man be taught to do this thing without having his heart break with every kill?" I asked with all the concerned sincerity I had in me.

I had never before even given a single thought about what the men had daily to do upon the hunt to bring back the meat and hides that are their gifts to supply the red-bodies of the People.

"The trials and revelations of the Cave are the means by which this is accomplished. What is experienced by the men in the Cave opens their eyes and their hearts and teaches them unfailing respect for the Mother's children, all of which possess powers the human tribes do not. The salmon gives birth to thousands, the mammoth is a mountain of abundance; the eagle sees from great distances and can fly into the skies. When the men open their hearts, they come to know that they too are one with the Mother and they too are doing the Mother's Work of Life even when they kill the animals which give themselves to us as the Mother's holy messengers. One way this is done is to teach every hunter to be unfailingly thankful for the red-life given as a gift of the Mother's children. Every hunter must also learn to honor the feeling, nurturing, female part of himself and to forever express gratitude for the All Mother's unending bounty. We are to be happy wherever we are and we always give thanks for the red-life that is given to us. Our gratitude and respect are the greatest of all gifts we can give back to the Mother's animal-messengers who have given their red-lives to us. Thanksgiving is what our rites of the eating of the beloved's liver and the returning of the messenger's blood to Earth Mother are all about. We eat some of the liver as a sign of respect for the red-life of our beloved kin who have returned to the Mother. We do the same as we return some of the blood of the animal-messengers to the Mother. By taking the meat of the Returned within, it works inside us to make of us one with the red-life that came from the Mother to bless us. And so every hunter must learn to bring the thoughts of his head into balance and harmony with the hidden needs and desires of his liver. Such harmony is difficult to achieve and many men excessively push down their strong feelings of love, compassion and respect for the Mother's children. Cutting off their feelings of compassion for the other is a detriment to his soul, his kin and to the whole People."

As the Grandfather spoke, I could not help but think about my own father as one who excessively pushes down his feelings.

"Men who run away from or push down their kind and loving feelings for the Mother's children will find themselves unable to outwardly express kindness and love of any kind. But for those men who have opened themselves and accepted the thoughts of the head along with the feelings of the liver, these two powers are joined as if they are married like husband and wife within the heart. This is the ferocious bull rhino with the two horns of its red and white spirit-powers under the control of the rhino's heart that ceases to fight with everything and everyone around him and lines up with the Mother upon her Straight Path. When that part of a hunter which is one with the All Mother is recognized and awakened, that is what the People call the White Brotherhood of Initiated Hunters, without which Brotherhood the People could not survive for even a single season."

"Yes, Grandfather," I said. "I can see that is how it must be. We depend so much on the hunting skills of the men, especially in the winter season."

"Yes, my Daughter, you are correct. The very being of the whole Nine Kin depends on the boys becoming honorable, dutiful men and skilful hunters. And so the All Mother, in her wisdom, has made this Great Cave for the seers and the spirit-powers to transform the boys into men so they may willingly become the providers and protectors of the People. They must willingly become the walkers of the way called Straight. I have already said being a hunter means we must shed the blood of the animal children of the All Mother for all our lives and without ceasing. This is no easy thing to do and always tears at the tender feelings of every hunter," he said sadly.

"Is that why an un-initiated hunter is not allowed to shed the blood of any of the Mother's animal-messengers? Is that why women are never to kill any animal by means of opening the veins?" I asked.

With the Grandfather's weary nod in answer, I continued.

"Yes, Grandfather, I know what you mean. It is difficult to strangle the fox-brother or the rabbit-sister when the snare does not do the killing for us. I love all the Mother's children," I said, equally sad as the Grandfather.

I truly love the animals and the fish and the birds we must daily kill, butcher and cook. My mother always gets very exasperated with me when I take food from the hearth or the storage pits to make friends with the ravens, squirrels and jays. Once I befriended a fox-brother who had made a winter den near my mother's lodge. I was careful to see that no snares were set anywhere near the fox's den. I always try to find such animal friends near the Middle Camp, but there are few young animals easy to befriend during the winter season. But upon the Plains of Summer I sometimes rescue baby magpies or crows that have fallen from their nests. I feed them with my chewed-up food just as their own mothers would have nourished them. I carry them in makeshift nests in the top of my pack frame. Some of them have survived long enough to grow strong and perch upon my shoulder or head. Inevitably, they would fly to join their own tribes again at the end of summer. I was so sad to see them go, but always glad for their gentle company while it lasted. My mother says loving the Mother's children so much only makes it more difficult to kill them for food and fur. She says I should take care to separate my tender feelings for them, but I could not or would not listen. It is true. I am too tender-hearted when it comes to the Mother's animal-children. But if ever I saw the Mother looking back at me, it was through the eyes of these living animal-companions of mine.

"I'm sure you love all the Mother's children, Dear One," he said with complete kindness. "That is why the women are also taught the Song of Gratitude to be sung whenever anything has to be hunted, cut down, dug up, snared or netted. What you will not know is that if a hunter does not open his heart and realize in this Great Cave that in hunting and killing the animals he is doing the work of the Mother, he will never be at peace with himself nor with the souls of the animals he must kill for the People to live. A hunter who goes out with an angry, fearful heart, devoid of feelings of gratitude and kindness for the abundance of the Mother's Net of Life, or if he is a hunter who is out of harmony with his family, his kin or the powers, he is the hunter who will come back empty-handed, injured or dead. As Seer, this is the chief lesson you are to teach the boys as they are transformed into hunters in this Great Cave."

All this talk of killing the animal-messengers made my head roll with visions of my father and brother and all the other men, even at this moment, risking their lives in the hunt and spilling the blood of the Mother's children so our red-bodies could continue to live. I have never seen a wounded large animal tracked, killed and butchered close up. I have played the parts of spotter and runner upon many a hunt, but the men would never allow me to approach while those with spears and knives actually killed the prey. The baskets and bags of meat and organs, hides and tusks are brought to the camps for the women to tan and cut and cook for our families. But I have never killed anything larger than a salmon with my own hands. Salmon do not look at you with the terrified, staring eyes of fox-brother screaming and struggling against the snare. A root dug from the ground does not squeal and flail its legs like a living rabbit-sister as it is strangled. The work of the Mother *is* difficult, bloody work. It is almost always the men who must do it and I am glad of that.

"What of White Lynx?" I asked, suddenly remembering her. "Is she allowed to shed the animal-messenger's blood?"

"No, but she will be allowed to join the hunt as runner, tracker, spotter and butcher. She may even be allowed to draw the sand-animal to prepare for the day's hunt or to throw a light spear as un-initiated boys are encouraged to do. But before she is initiated as a hunter, White Lynx will not be allowed to kill the wounded with a heavy spear or cut the veins to shed the living blood of the Mother's animal-messengers. Neither will your younger brother until he is changed into a man and a hunter. Our duty, as seers of the People, is to transform all unruly, uncaring boys—and some women—into dedicated, mature, honorable and compassionate hunters—to set them upon the Straight Path of the White Brotherhood. To successfully do so, we instruct them and pass them through trials and tests in order to awaken within them the awareness of their oneness with the Mother," the Grandfather explained.

"How can we, as seers, teach anyone to wake up?" I asked, sincerely wanting to have an answer.

"The boys 'wake up' and become men by learning to respect and love the animal-messengers of the All Mother as their brothers and their sisters. The way this is accomplished is for the boys to learn that when they look into the dark space within the eyes of their dying prey, they will see the Mother looking back at them. From this they will learn to show their gratitude because giving thanks for the Mother's abundance is the one best way to wake up to her presence in all things. When a hunter is fully aware of what it is he does, he will love and honor the animal-messengers even as he must return them to the Mother by killing their red-bodies. Hunters must also call forth and commune with their personal spirit-companions to fully wake up to who and what they truly are. They must feel the Mother's presence in their animal-guides and so love them and respect their guidance. Only by awakening and bringing forth the black spirit-powers and becoming one with the Mother in their hearts can the boys become men and successful hunters who will continue to bring the Mother's abundance in to bless the People. Finally, a hunter must have strong bonds of friendship, trust and love for his companions of the White Brotherhood. The men must become gift-givers and lifelong friends during the hunt and fight along side each other in times of trouble."

"What are 'times of trouble', my Grandfather?" I asked, completely baffled.

"When I was a boy, some of the Others of the Plain not of the Nine Kin came to our Valley," the Grandfather began. "The Mammoth-kin and the Bison-kin, whose camps, as you know, are sited where our River flows out on to the Plain, sent runners to all the camps of the Bear People that their men should come and protect our home from the intruders. Some of the Mammoth-kin's women were captured and four hunters killed before the whole Mammoth-kin fled to the north bank of our River to take refuge with the Bison-kin. Without the ties of marriage and the bonds of gift-giving, friendship and cooperation between all the Nine Kin of the Bear People in our Sisterhoods and Brotherhoods, we would not have been able to drive the intruders from the camps of the Mammoth-kin. They, along with the Bison-kin, stand guardian to the whole Valley of the Bear Mother to this very day. It was a terrible time, Little Bear," he said with a scowl.

"Storage pits were looted, lodges burned and many lives were lost in the fighting between the People and the Others. The honored father of your own grandmother was one of those who were returned to the Mother by the spears of the Others. Without the unbreakable bonds of gratitude and love between the Mammoth-kin and the rest of the Bear People that are made within the Great Cave, they would all have starved or been killed and their camps and hunting grounds lost to the Others of the Plain. The Bison-kin would have been attacked next, cutting the whole Nine Kin off from the abundance of the summer Northland."

Completely taken aback at the thought of men killing other men, I asked, "Grandfather, why do we not tell these stories to the People? Should not everyone be warned of such dangers?"

"Dear One. This story is only for you as seer-apprentice to know that killing another of the human tribes is even more difficult and more likely to cause guilt and grief even than the killing of one of the Mother's animal-messengers. It may be that the People will have to defend our Valley with slings and spears one day, but as seers, we are not to unnecessarily frighten the People. Though we do not dwell on it, the men must realize that in times of trouble, every hunter must be prepared in his heart to stand shoulder-to-shoulder with his beloved brothers and kill another of the human tribes in order to protect the lives of the People. Do you understand, my Daughter?"

"Yes, Grandfather," I replied, "But why was I never even told this story of my grandmother's father?"

"We do not speak of such things for the same reason women do not retell the stories of those who die in childbirth or the stories of young children who return to the Mother. The words we speak will always come back to us—good for good, ill for ill—so we must carefully guard the words of our mouths. As Seer, you will teach the People only to speak words of abundance, life, gratitude, love and respect into the Mother's ear. The Great Cave is the best of all places to teach these lessons," he reassured me.

"In truth, the boys must die to their old ways as sons of their mothers and be reborn from the Cave as sons of their fathers—hunters and protectors of the Nine Kin. The ordeals, teachings and revelations of the powers in this place you must also experience and endure so that you may someday be capable of passing on this life-giving wisdom to the People, to your own daughters and to initiates who have not your wisdom. The Great Cave is the means by which the Mother changes us and the 'thirteen' of transformation, wherever it appears in the Cave, is always a sign of this change."

"Yes, Grandfather. I can certainly see the wisdom of it. Is the Great Cave the only place where this wisdom can be learned?"

"It is not the only place, Dear One. But opening our hearts, hearing, seeing and experiencing the powers in dream and in trance is much easier to achieve in this dark place far from the distractions and noise of the World of Light. The Cave is separated from the red and white Worlds of Light and is very close to the black spirit-powers of the Below where these truths must be realized in each heart in one way or another. When we leave the Great Cave it becomes much more difficult to quest for dream-visions or to go into trance. As healings are performed in the World of Light, the powers are not so easily called forth to assist us, even with the help of our wise animal-guides. That is why shamans-of-healing must sometimes use the moon flower, seeds and leaves of hemp or mistletoe and abstain from taking food and water in order to bring a trance for healing," he explained.

"Yes, Grandfather, I understand. Auntie sometimes uses the trance-plants. And I know she often does not eat or drink before a healing ceremony," I offered.

"See the sign of the Mother's abundance given to her children on the wall here before us?" he said, gesturing toward the red buttock-shaped lines on the wall before us.

"This is the sign of the Mother's ample breasts that give suck and nourishment to all her children with the milk of the red-body."

"Ah, it is the sign of the mother's *breasts*. Of course!" I thought in words to myself. Realization dawned as the Grandfather continued his speaking.

"A mother's breasts are large, heavy and full of milk to give the new life's body the abundant nourishment of her own red-body. We make lines and ivory carvings showing Earth Mother heavy with fat, huge-breasted with milk and with great hips and legs like no mother of the human tribes are ever seen to possess. The lines of power are made upon the shoulders and arms of the images of the animal-powers and upon the Mother to show the spirit-fire flowing down as water. But here, this is a sign of the Mother's love for all her children. It is a love which nourishes our souls with the spirit-milk of her great, all-giving heart."

"Yes, Grandfather I see that now. I thought it was a pair of bare buttocks!" I laughed.

Chuckling to himself he continued. "Yes, I can see how one could misconstrue such a sign! What is more important is to see how the two rhinos on one side and the three rhinos on the other side of the sign are nourished and put into line with the Mother's abundance. See how on the other side of the breasts, having found harmony and peace with each other, the two are transformed into the three-in-one leading the entire procession? No longer are these rhinos dueling and fighting with each other but they are all upon the path called Straight and are in line with the abundance of the Mother's great, overflowing breasts. The Earth Mother *is* the Mother of All and gives red-birth to all the tribes of animals and people, squatting in the birth position with her pair of male and female lion attendants to support her on either side. The Mother then suckles the new life with milk from her very own breasts of unending plenty. As Seer, you should see a deeper meaning as well. The All Mother is also the Source and Mother of our very souls, of our hearts. Boys enter this Red Passage of the Butterfly as children of their mothers. They have long since ceased nursing their red-bodies at their mother's breasts, but the boys are still dependent on their mothers in many other ways. This is why the sign of the Mother's breasts are here: to remind the boys of those mind, body and heart connections they have to their beloved mothers. For seers, the five spirit-rhinos are to teach us that the contrary Powers of Two, as I have said, are always present in the uninitiated and the untransformed. When we are nourished by the All Mother's love, we are changed, each of us, within our hearts and so changed within our very souls. This harmony of the mind and the heart is what places the struggling Powers of Two in a line with the Mother's love for all her children. In other words, the unified heart awakens the harmonious Powers of Three within us. Like the five spirit-rhinos here, we cross over the Bridge of Rainbows to our own true selves. Having done so, we may not cross back again to the children we were before. Having awakened to our true selves as soul-children of the Mother, there is no going back."

The bridge-like middle level of stone did have only a very few spirit-animals who were heading against the general direction of the long procession of lions and rhinos and breast-signs. I could see that much.

"Grandfather, I have a question," I broke in.

"Yes?" he said simply. I had clearly interrupted his lesson.

"The few spirit-animals going against the procession? Are they ones who have chosen not to be initiated? Have they changed their minds and gone back on their promises of initiation? Having come of age, does anyone ever choose not to be initiated as a woman or a hunter?"

"You always have such insightful questions, my good Apprentice. I think we could say, perhaps, that is the reason for, and meaning of, those few spirit-animals who are turning back and running against the general flow that is moving toward the wisdom of the Mother that is to be revealed to them within the Great Cave. All are free to choose whether to go to the Mother or to reject her wisdom and go the other way. For me, your Guide of the Powers and your mentor, the important thing is that this is the lesson your own heart is gathering from these images. I am very pleased with you, my very intelligent Apprentice."

The Grandfather's compliments seemed to me so profuse and undeserved I felt a blush begin to rise up my neck.

"To answer your question more fully, let me say I have never known an initiate to turn around and quit the rites before completion because they are too difficult. There are those whose hearts are not opened to the lessons of the Cave and who will just go along with the herd because it is what everyone else is doing. It is what their kin and their cousins and their friends expect of them and so their heads will follow, but not their livers or hearts. A hunter may come to reject the lessons of the Cave and, whether he wishes it or not, he will be a poor hunter for the rest of his life having cut himself off from the abundance of the Mother. If you give indifference to the Mother, indifference is what you will receive back from the Mother—it is simply the circling way of all things. For those who would become Seer, there is a much narrower path of higher power to walk. A boy can become a hunter with only half his heart, but the way of the seers must be freely chosen and willingly taken by those who would walk it. This is because it will transform you not only for this time and this place. It will change you for all the worlds to come because your very soul is made larger."

"Grandfather, do you mean that I can still choose not to take this path in my life?"

"Of course, Dear One. This is why I have repeatedly asked if the Seer's Path is the way you freely choose to follow. For when we have passed through this place of transition and have gone through the trials and revelations of the Great Cave, there is no turning back. It is just as there is no turning back once we have put the things of childhood behind us. None of us can become children again once we have taken the path of honorable adulthood and service to the People. Whatever has passed is past and can never, therefore, be changed. Only what we are doing at this very moment, only the choice we make at this moment, makes any difference and changes any path. Because of the choice each makes, regardless of their awareness of the choice, the boys leave this holy place as sons of their fathers and hunters, having been transformed by the initiations and ordeals of the Mother's Cave. Once this Bridge of Rainbows has been crossed, there can be no going back to being a baby at the mother's breast any more than one who has returned to the Mother can cross back to the World of Light. By these initiations, our hearts are awakened and our souls are transformed and nourished by the Mother as surely as our red-bodies are born from between our mother's legs and nurtured by her breast milk. Just so, you have entered as a red-blood woman and you will leave Seer of the Bear People—your body, head and soul enlarged and transformed. No matter how much you might regret it later, you may never alter this decision for all the worlds to come. You will have put all childish ways behind you and you will have put all things that are not of the Mother behind you. You will then be able to nurture and bless the People with the gifts of great power that only you are given. Are you ready to be transformed, Daughter of My Heart?" he said, looking directly into my eyes.

I only hesitated for a moment before replying, "Yes, I am ready Grandfather."

It was far too late to turn back now.

* * *

The Grandfather led me from his little stone seat to stand closer to the great red Lion Mother before us so I could see the image better.

"Count the small red dots beneath her feet, Dear One," he directed.

"There are nine dots, Grandfather. What is the meaning of 'nine'?" I asked.

"It is the sign of the coming of the Mother's power into the World of Light, just as the Nine Kin were dreamed into this, our Valley. Now count the red dots coming out of Lion Mother's mouth."

"There are thirteen!" I said, astonished.

"Yes, my good Apprentice, there are thirteen. But what appears to our eyes as red Lion Mother is actually a hunter in trance who has completely transformed into his red-spirited lion-guide. Red spots or spouts of blood coming from the mouths, noses or anuses of spirit-animals are signs of a shaman in trance or of a hunter who is in the process of changing into one or more of his animal-guides. The two red handprints in front of the arc of red spots tells us this spirit-lion—in a hunting crouch preparing to leap at the spirit-rhinos running away from her—is a boy who has been transformed into a man and a hunter. It is a new man whose lion-guide has come forth, a hunter who has completely transformed into red Lion Mother in his dreams and trances—the nine red dots of blood under her feet tells me that. You will see other partially and fully transformed shamans and hunters as we move into the deeper lodges and wombs of the Mother's Great Cave. As Seer, understand that these thirteen red spots are the same sign as the thirteen red dots at the end of the holy round of the Red Lodge where girls are transformed into women. For the boys, this is the point at which the transformation from boy to man truly begins because from this time forward, there can be no turning back to childhood. Please count the spirit-lions and the spirit-rhinos here that cross the Bridge of Rainbows from the Red Lodges to the White, the same crossing that you will now make," he directed.

I began to count and with astonishment found there were, again, a total of thirteen.

"Again it is the 'thirteen' of transformation, Grandfather!" I cried, completely elated by my discovery.

"Yes, it is, my Daughter. Now to see and understand the wisdom of the grand design of the Passage of the Butterfly, think on the first 'seven' we encountered at the beginning of the Passage. It was the Seven Sisters as star-butterflies, signs of the spirals of trance and signs of the coming and going of the People to this Valley, was it not? But I will tell you now that these seven hunter-lions are the 'seven' of the Star Shaman of the Hunt, forever pursuing the Sisters across the night sky in an endless round of hunting and being hunted. From the beginning to the end of this Passage, every sign and spirit-animal speaks of the change of one thing into another, from a transformation of one shape to another, from one way of thinking to another and from one way of being in the World of Light to another. Here, in the very center of the shapeshifting of one thing into another, is the holy place for every hunter-initiate to learn the Thirteen Holy Syllables of Transformation," the Grandfather concluded dramatically.

"What are the holy syllables, my Grandfather?" I asked in utter awe of his suddenly and inexplicably towering presence.

"Dear One, I will now speak to you the Thirteen Syllables of Transformation. These words will be repeated as we cross from one lodge of the Cave to some of the others as part of your initiations. But when you shall leave the Great Cave as Seer, you may repeat the Thirteen Syllables whenever a change in your life comes that is difficult to bear or which change brings you great joy. The Thirteen Syllables will remind you that you are never alone and whatever is happening around you is only temporary. As with all things, whatever you are doing, it too will pass away. No matter how sorrowful or joyful. The Holy Syllables will forever remind you of who you truly are in your heart and soul."

"What are the Thirteen Syllables, my Grandfather?" I asked, the thoughts of my head diverted again by another new secret.

"They are the seer's Words of Power, Dear One. They are the words that transform us utterly if we truly feel and accept their meaning in our hearts. During the hunter's rites, each mentor will whisper the Syllables to his initiate in this place. The initiates will then speak the Words of Power aloud before leaving the Passage of the Butterflies to enter into the Lodge of the Mother's Heart. The Heart Lodge is where the trials and revelations of manhood will truly begin. The mentor who has given the initiate the Holy Syllables in his ear will follow him through the portal into the Heart Lodge. But it is here, before this transformed hunter-lion, that the Words of Transformation will be learned by each boy. Now they will be given to you, dear Little Bear, my good and beloved Apprentice."

"Thank you Grandfather. Is there more that I should learn of the Words of Power? How much of this is to be explained to initiates?" I asked.

"I can tell you now, as with all the other teachings of the Great Cave, it is not necessary to explain the meaning of the Syllables to any initiate. Each will hear and understand what they are able when and if their hearts are open to the wisdom of the Thirteen Syllables. Most will not understand them for many seasons after leaving the Cave even while they are repeating them aloud in times of fear and need. Some may never open themselves to the Words of Transformation their whole lives. But as Seer, what you must remember is that all words of healing and wisdom have great power when they are spoken from the mouth, for they are spoken into the ever-listening ears of the Mother who will never deny us her abundance and her plenty. These are the most powerful of all the healing words known to the seers and shamans of the Nine Kin. Are you willing to hear and to learn this wisdom of the Ancients?" he said, looking directly into my eyes.

"Yes, Grandfather, I am ready to hear and learn the Holy Words. I am ready to be transformed," I said with a slight catch in my throat.

"Very well, my Dearest One."

The Grandfather took a deep breath and leaned in close to whisper in my ear:

I am the Mother's child. I and the Mother are one.

With so many thoughts and words already stuffed into my head, my mind began to reel again, and not in the trance spirals. Just trying to take it all in was making me feel dizzy. Perhaps it was because I hadn't eaten anything. In how long? I could not remember.

"I'm beginning to feel light in my head, Grandfather," I said weakly.

I hoped against hope the Grandfather would just stop speaking for a moment. I needed desperately to catch my breath and clear my mind and settle the tight queasiness gathering in my belly.

"Yes, I can see you may need to drink some water again, my Child. Let us move on to the Lodge of Living Waters. There you can quench your thirst before continuing on to the Heart Lodge," he said mercifully.

Without waiting for a sign of assent from me, the Grandfather led the way past the two rhino-powers, the sign of the Mother's

221

Breasts and the three rhino-powers leading the whole procession further into the Cave. The last of the five, or I should say, the first in the line, had huge, long curving horns pointing forward and down. The two horns almost touched a red zigzag sign—like water flowing down from the skies—made to cut across the Bridge of Rainbows making a barrier, of sorts, to the darkened chambers beyond,

"Grandfather?" I said signaling that I had a question.

"Yes, my Daughter. Do you have a question?"

"I see the first in the line of rhinos is pointing at this red zigzag line. What is the meaning of this sign, my Grandfather?"

"See how it crosses the Bridge of Rainbows as a barrier to what lies beyond? It is a sign of the Gate of Forgetting through which the souls of all the Mother's children pass on their way to rebirth in the World of Light. It is the Gate of Forgetting because all memories of lives that we have lived before are forgotten as we enter the World of Light like life-giving rain falls from the heavens. Similarly, we pass through a Gate of Forgetting when initiates cross this Bridge of Rainbows to their new lives as hunters and as men. The initiates are to forget their former lives as boys. Count the number of points on the zigzag, Dear One."

"There are seven points, my Grandfather," I reported, almost past any counting.

"Yes, seven is the sign of a completed circle and is the sign of movement into another circle of higher spirit-power. Initiates who pass this way are completing the circle of their childhood and are moving into the circle of manhood, a higher spirit-power wherein they must forget their past as children dependent on their mothers and become the sons of their fathers, as I have already explained. This sign is just another way of teaching the same lesson. Shall we move on further into the Passage?"

After the zigzagging sign, there followed yet another red sign of the Mother's Breasts. Following on from the breast sign, there appeared another spirit-animal made with a few simple black lines—the only black animal since the black bison, how far back? I could not even make a guess, so hazy and far away it all seemed. Yes, I remember. It was the first black spirit-animal I saw in the Passage after the big red butterfly-bird. Finally, this black spirit-bison's nose pointed to one last sign of such bizarre design that even if my head were clear I could not have guessed its meaning.

"Grandfather, what is this odd sign here?" I asked pointing to the image.

It had been engraved into the white rock immediately before another pendant-like stone. This pendant is void of any signs or spirit-animals and extends nearly to the ground.

"Dear One, it is the sign of the end of the Passage of the Butterfly and is the first sign of the White Lodges of Hunters that are to be found beyond the pendant-divider."

This strange sign was ball-shaped with engraved lines indicating it was spinning in a sun-wise direction. And it seemed to be suspended above a fountain of left and right-curving lines of spirit-power.

"Yes, Grandfather. But what is it a sign of? What is its meaning? I am feeling faint and my head will not think clearly."

"I can see that you are unsteady, Dear One. But I will answer your question directly so we can move on and quench your thirst. This is the left-turning sphere of spirit-fire to be found in great abundance in the White Lodges beyond. The fountain of white spirit-power supporting the ball of spinning life-fire is the equivalent sign to the red fountains of spirit-fire that we have already seen upon the Rock of the All Mother. The black bison almost touches the white ball of spirit-fire. This signifies an initiate who is preparing to harmonize the white and the red spirit-powers. It is one who is on the verge of his initiation as hunter in the White Lodges within."

In a swirl of signs and images I realized the black animal at the entrance to the Passage had been heading out of the Cave—a transformed initiate heading for the World of Light? I didn't have anything left in me to do any further thinking about it. All I could comprehend was this black animal is at the head of the procession and is heading in, toward the deeper parts of the Great Cave. And so, it seemed, am I.

I had reached the end of a completely astonishing procession of spirit-animals and signs within the Passage of the Butterfly. As we moved forward around what appeared to be a long pendant, it actually turned out to be a narrow wall-like partition between the

Passage and another side-chamber hidden in the shadows beyond. Without thinking, I began stumbling along the wall wherever it led me—always deeper and deeper into the blackness. The smell and sound of trickling water seemed to be coming from somewhere ahead in the shadows. I am uncontrollably drawn toward it.

My little flame first shone upon three stenciled handprints upon the wall I was following into the depths. They had been made by blowing red ochre from the mouth on to the back of someone's hand pressed against the stone. My head was too fuzzy to count the two clusters of red dots that followed the hand stencils. I fumbled on toward the sound and smell of cool, refreshing water. Soon I encountered two black spirit-animals: a horse and a mammoth going in the same direction as I, further and further into the blackness of this ever-narrowing side-chamber. The slender passage at last made a sharp turn to the left and disappeared into the darkness. I could smell the clean scent and hear the faraway tinkling sounds of fresh running water coming from the back of the narrow passage. I followed the sounds and the scent of water, my lips dry from wanting it so desperately.

I came to the end of the little passage that led to nowhere. When the roof became so low I could no longer stand up, I turned around to follow the opposite wall back out, frustrated I had not found the elusive source of the clear spring water. I had been so close! As I turned around to go back the way I had come, almost immediately my lamp cast its feeble light upon my very own namesake—a little bear made skillfully in red lines by ancient hands. Its snout pointed toward the opening of this side-passage where the Grandfather waited patiently for me to rejoin him.

"Dear Little Bear," the Grandfather called to me. "Come this way to enter the Lodge of Living Waters."

In my increasingly dazed condition I had stopped following the Grandfather's lead to enter the narrow side-cavern and there to find my namesake. I was feeling more and more disoriented and confused. The splashing waters sounded like the slapping of dancing bare feet against flat, wet rocks. In the sounds of some hidden babbling brook were the singing sounds of happy, high-pitched, children's voices. It was only the Grandfather calling my name that brought me back to my senses. I quickly rejoined him where he stood at the right-hand portal of yet another large side-chamber.

"This is the entry portal to the Lodge of Living Waters at the end of the Red Passage of Butterflies. The Rainbow Passage, which we have just walked, is the place of transition where red and black spirit-animals are seen together coming and going from the Cave—coming from and going to the Mother." The Grandfather gestured back toward the images we had just passed but were no longer visible.

I looked dumbly in the direction the Grandfather pointed. Everything was becoming blurry, my feet unsure. I looked back to the water-filled chamber we were standing before, its right-hand portal marked by the single black line of the back and trunk of a mammoth without tusks. Mammoth Mother again. The mammoth was coming out of a big chamber which resounded with the sounds of splashing, falling water. The scent of watery ice was overpowering. Still, as thirsty as I was, my head knew that a mammoth of any color indicates the southern side or end of a wall or chamber. This wall must be on the southern side of the water-filled Lodge we were about to enter. None of that mattered anymore. All I could think of was my dry throat and tongue. But still, the Grandfather's good Apprentice would not go in until he said I could proceed. Just at that moment, the Grandfather began to speak into the darkness.

"Oh, Swan Mother of the Living Waters, hear thou the words of my mouth. I am Flying Otter, Grandfather of the Nine Kin. I am honored to bring Little Bear, thy Daughter, as seer-initiate. We ask permission to enter thy Holy Lodge to slake our thirst and purify ourselves. With thy Holy Waters we awaken and cleanse the white-spirits of our souls. And we know thy permission is already given," he chanted.

"Come, Dear One," I thought he said to me. "We will purify ourselves with these living waters of the Mother's Cave before entering the White Lodges of the Hunters, just as we purified our red-bodies in the Serpent Father's springs before entering the Red Lodges. I can see you are very thirsty." The Grandfather's voice came to me from somewhere far away, my mind in a complete haze.

Without any more hesitation the Grandfather led me by the hand into a low chamber dripping and running with small streams of water. The blessed liquid emerged at the roof and trickled noisily to the ground in a lovely, burbling cascade. The streams of white, splashing water pooled and then disappeared into unseen fissures in the hard stone floor of the chamber just as they had done so long ago before Mammoth Mother, so very far away in the Red Lodge.

"Drink all you need, then wash your face, hands, body and feet, Dear One," the Grandfather's disembodied voice called to me from some distant place.

In a dream, I put down my lamp, divested myself of the black robe, bag and oil horn. I knelt on the hard white floor of the cave to drink. I stepped into a shallow pool to wash myself in the icy waters.

CHAPTER 9.
THE WATERS OF LIFE

COLD CLEAR WATER NEVER TASTED SO GOOD, nor had cold, clear liquid ever quenched my thirst so completely. The pure, icy waters on my face, breasts and belly revived me with a start. Truly the Waters of Life! The icy little falls and shallow pools felt so good and invigorating that I washed and drank, washed and drank, then washed and drank some more. Finally, my thirst was truly and completely quenched.

I tried to scrub the red paint from my face, breasts and inner thighs. But the oily Mother-ochre did not come off completely in the cold water leaving many red smudges and smears. The Grandfather, also down on his knees drinking deeply from cupped hands, was struggling to get to his feet. I moved to help him up.

"Thank you, my Daughter, I was truly as thirsty as you," he said in a voice sharp as the icy waters.

"It is nothing, Grandfather. I am here to serve you," I said meaning every word.

My head cleared instantly as I felt the chilling fluid moving through me like a sparkling fire. I began to think I had imagined seeing a herd of rhinos being chased by lions and the Grandfather saying, *Swan Mother*.

"Grandfather, did I see a herd of rhinos and hear you say that this is the Lodge of Swan Mother? Why is this place so deep in the

Cave and so full of water called the place of Swan Mother?" I asked in disbelief.

"Yes, you saw five rhinos in a line showing the way to transformation. But that would be a *crash* of rhinos, Dear One, not a *herd*," he joked, correcting my words.

"And this is the Lodge the Living Waters, the holy Lodge of Swan Mother, the mother of all water birds. This is her special place, my Daughter," he said with a smile and a one-eyed blink.

"Swan Mother's Lodge is here in the depths of the Great Cave to remind us that all waters that come from the Mother—whether her tears, sweat, saliva, birth-waters or blood—are holy and life-giving. Water birds, like the swan, embody all the holy waters, as does the great Eye of the Mother through which our River flows. Shamans speak of water birds as three-spirited because they move without effort between the three worlds of earth, water and sky. Many shamans fly on the wings of water birds in trance and certainly you know the flutes of the dance circle are made of hollow swan leg bones. The head of my shaman's staff is a swan and I carry one of her holy feathers in my staff-bundle. Some may prefer vulture bones as heads for their staffs or for making high-pitched flutes, but my soul's desire is for birds of the watery world."

"But why is it the swan and not the duck or goose, Grandfather?" I asked.

The practical questions of my head were returning with the invigorating waters. Goose and duck leg bones are much easier to obtain than those of the swan.

"What you will not know is that the Mother has made this Lodge of the Living Waters in the shape and form of a swan to teach us that all the Living Waters are one in Swan Mother," he explained as if I were hearing a child's tale and knew nothing at all.

"The shape of a swan?" I asked, still incredulous.

"Yes, Dear One. But we do not have time now to explore this lodge fully. We have much to do before we are ready to leave the Cave. Let me tell you that the place where we are standing, facing the cascade of water, is within Swan Mother's ruffed up wing. It's as if we are standing on her back made of white, bubbling, feather-like water. See the passage to our left that runs out into the dark?" he asked.

With a nod of my head he continued.

"That is Swan Mother's tail pointing up and backward. The shape of the passage over there to our right? The opening which we can barely see from here is a long, narrow passage that turns to the left. It is Swan Mother's long neck, atop which, of course, is her head and beak. All the passages there are very wet and narrow with low roofs so that one has to crawl into the Swan Mother's head. But let me assure you that even her eye is present in the form of a slender trunk of white stone from roof to ground. And, if you look over yonder behind us, to the side opposite of her 'wing' where we are now standing, there is an even narrower passage that is the Swan Mother's legs and webbed feet. The feet open up into the end of the side-chamber that lies between the Passage of the Butterflies and the Lodge of Living Waters. That is where you will have seen a little red spirit-bear. The side-chamber of your name-sake is the usual place to trance and quest in this very wet lodge, which is considered to be one of the White Wombs of the Cave as it lies beyond the sign of the ball of white spirit-fire at the end of the Rainbow Passage. The side-chamber is so close, and is actually connected to Swan Mother's feet, that the much dryer and adjacent Womb of the Little Red Bear is the preferred place to sit for long periods of time while questing. In such a place of transition as this, it is only fitting that a red and a white-womb should be so closely connected for those who are moved to quest here. Do you have any further questions of this lodge?"

"Will my brother Little Ibex be brought to this lodge or are only seer-initiates allowed to drink of these waters?" I asked.

"This is one of the lodges to which very few are led by their animal-guides for questing, but it is for all hunter and seer-initiates to purify themselves here before entering the White Lodges of the Cave. Besides, all the boys are as thirsty as you when they arrive here. If not allowed to quench their thirst, many would faint away into dreams!"

"Yes, Grandfather. Ironically, I too have my own experience of nearly fainting," I said. As if the Grandfather could possibly not have noticed I was about to collapse.

"All who are preparing to enter the White Lodges will cleanse themselves with Swan Mother's living waters. Certainly, all seer-initiates who would purify themselves here are to release all old thoughts and beliefs that they may have about the powers within before they enter into the White Lodges. As Seer, you must keep all things held in balance, harmony and oneness. It is why we perform the purifications of the red-body by means of Sky Father's hot springs before entering the Red Lodges. Now we cleanse the white spirit-powers by means of Earth Mother's cold springs before entering the White Lodges. What is most important for you to learn from this Lodge is that, ultimately, the Mother is the one source of all the waters flowing into the World of Light. These waters emerging from the unseen world of the Below give life to our white-spirits just as the waters of the seen world of the Above are holy to the All Father and give life to and purify our red-bodies. Even the tears that flow from the Mother's Eye as our River are tears of joy and abundance, sorrow and mourning all in the same moment. We might as well call the Eye 'the Mother's Mouth' because it is also shaped like a mouth and runs with the Mother's life-giving saliva. And as with all things of the Mother, the Eye is also the Mother's Womb bringing forth new life from her birth-waters and blood as the vast numbers of salmon swim upstream to feed the People. Just as you slaked the thirst of your red-body with these moving waters, here so you should slake the thirst of your soul with these Living Waters. We are all to enliven and awaken the white swan-power that is within our hearts. The swan-power will join the unseen Powers of Three within you as the Power of One if you are drawn to this place to quest for your animal-companion. You should be able to explore this part of the Cave on another occasion when you have more time," he concluded.

We stood looking at the bubbling waters and listening to the magic sounds of tiny splashing streams cascading over white rocks. Now I could see that this little rocky wall of falling water formed Swan Mother's fluffed-up wings as she might arch them up during the time of mating.

"The White Lodges of the Hunters and our adventure together beckons," the Grandfather spoke in plain words.

He turned to lead the way out of Swan Mother's Lodge to what lay beyond.

* * *

"Our purification is complete. After we pass through the portal here, we will enter the first of the White Lodges of the Hunters: the Lodge of the Mother's Heart. It is the very center of the Great Cave and is the holy lodge where initiates gather with their mentors to undergo the trials and revelations of manhood," the Grandfather explained.

We came to an abrupt halt just beyond the portal of entrance to the Swan Mother's Lodge, or I should say, the portal of exit. On our right, a stretch of stone wall extended several paces before it curved around and out of sight. This must be the entrance portal to the Lodge of the Mother's Heart.

The flat piece of wall we stood beside extended almost straight down from roof to floor and contained only two blown-ochre hand stencils. Framing each hand, delicate black lines had been made hinting with the most minimal outlines at a horse and a mammoth. I had to look very close to see the barely discernable horse's hind quarters enclosing the right-handed stencil. If the horse spirit had forequarters, which it did not, I would be staring directly at it because it was heading out of the Cave, the direction of birth into the World of Light. A mammoth with no tusks had been made below and to the left of the horse. The mammoth image was made with many more lines than the horse and had a left-handed stencil upon its flank. When I looked more closely at the thin line that made the mammoth's tail, back, hump, head and trunk, the trunk was extended out and pointing toward the entrance of the lodge that lay just around the corner.

And painted between the mammoth's pointing trunk and the unseen entrance portal around the corner, were a group of big red dots. I was immediately reminded of the sinuous clusters of thirteen dots at the end of the rounds of the Red Lodge, and with good reason. Sure enough, when I counted the dots, there were exactly thirteen.

As a maker of painted images, the blown-on hand stencils were fascinating to me. They looked as if the maker were inside the yellowish-white stone reaching out to the World of Light, pressing their insubstantial hands against the bare rock.

"Daughter?" the Grandfather said in the voice that always gets my attention. "This is the entrance portal to the Lodge of the Mother's Heart. We will ask permission to enter, as always."

Without a pause the Grandfather began to intone, "Oh, Mother of us all, hear the words of my mouth! I am Flying Otter, Grandfather of the Nine Kin, Thrice-Born of the Bear People. I have brought my Apprentice, Little Bear, to be initiated with the rites of a hunter so that she may serve the People. We are grateful and know thy permission to enter on our journey has already been granted."

He finished singing but did not move to enter the darkness beyond.

"Know thou the meaning of the blown hand prints and the thirteen dots appearing as a red snake, my Apprentice?" he asked formally.

I answered just as decorously, "No, my Grandfather, I know not."

"As Seer, in addition to 'transformation', the thirteen dots should always remind you of the thirteen moon-circles of the moon-year corresponding closely to the twelve periods of the sun-year, as I have explained before. The number thirteen is the 'twelve' of completion plus the 'one' of change and new beginnings—the thirteenth being the beginning of the next circle. Thirteen may also be a sign of the thirteen nights of the waxing moon or the thirteen nights of the waning moon. To this, add the two nights of darkness, when the moon does not appear at all in the night sky, and that gives us the full twenty-eight days of the moon-circle and the twenty-eight days of a woman's moon-blood. It is a continuous transformation in the moon and in the red-bodies of women that is always before us for our instruction. Here, the snake-form of dots is to remind us that within the White Lodges of the Father, the powers of the Mother are always present, just as the powers of the Father are always present in the Red Lodges of the Mother. Here, at this crossing place, the right hand of Earth Mother and the left hand of Sky Father come forth to meet you as stenciled right and left palms within Horse Mother and Mammoth Father. Do you understand the meaning of these images now?"

"Yes Grandfather, I now see the grand plan of this Portal. The very images are beginning to speak to my mind as if they are spirit-guides," I responded.

"Yes, that is very good, Dear One. I see that you continue to learn much and quickly. Our purification is now complete. The powers of our livers and heads have been ignited and we are now fully prepared to enter the Heart Lodge to begin your initiation as hunter. After we pass through the corridor to the right of the Portal here, we will enter in to the very center of the whole Cave, the Lodge of the Mother's Heart. This is the holy place where the boys gather with their mentors to undergo the trials and revelations of their initiations as hunters of the People."

"Before we enter, may I please ask another question, Grandfather?" I said meekly, trying to delay the inevitable.

"Of course, Dear One. What would you ask of me?"

"Will my brother Little Ibex be brought here too? Or is this lodge only for seers?"

"Of course your brother will be brought here, just as all who would become men and hunters will enter the Lodge of Living Waters to first purify themselves. The Heart Lodge is the place of transformation for each and every hunter who enters the Great Cave. So it will be for you on your journey to become hunter and then Seer. In this Lodge of the Mother's Heart you will die to your old self. The woman known as 'Little Bear' will be reborn as hunter and then as seer with a new secret name. As you enter here, you leave the red-world of the rising and setting of the sun, of the waxing and waning of the moon, the limits, boundaries and differences of the world of the waking senses of the head, as well as the hidden senses of the liver and of your dreams and trances. In passing through this portal, you come into the eternal, all-giving, timeless, limitless, formless Heart of the Mother. Here you will begin to bring forth the white father-powers of the hunter that are within you," he said solemnly.

I could feel my eyebrows clenching together in worry. An unwelcome but familiar stirring in my gut began to rise. Anxious waves began moving through me even as the Grandfather continued speaking.

"When you leave the Great Cave you *will* be born again to serve and bless the People. You will bear the marks of a seer who has entered the Dark Mother's Lodge in your body. You will have become Twice Born Seer, Healer and Teacher of the Bear People."

And with these words, surging ripples of panic began to rise again from the very center of me, from my liver and up to my heart to clutch at my throat in a suffocating lump. My hands and feet were still shivering from the freezing waters and I began to feel very ill at ease from head toe.

"Why are so many spirit-rhinos made to appear in the Passage of the Butterfly, Grandfather? Again, why is twelve the number of a completed circle?" I scrambled for more questions to ask.

Playing stupid, I grasped at the only questions I could think of to delay my inevitable entry into the place of terrors I imagined to be just around the corner.

"I believe I have already explained that rhinos embody both the Powers of Two and the Powers of Three because both bull and cow rhinos have two horns combined into one animal and both bull and cow rhinos are very contentious and love to fight each other. Six refers to one-half of the sun-circle, and when combined, encompass the two seasons of the year. As I have said, twelve of anything refers to the limits or boundaries of the thing. As such, the twelve parts of the sun-circle is the complete round of our comings and goings from the Valley to the Plain and back again. Upon our return to the Valley at the end of each summer season, the first five days after our arrival are spent resting. Certainly you must already know that no hunting, collecting of food or repairing of lodges is allowed. These five days complete the sun-circle and are five days holy to the Five Mothers. Only dancing, singing and chanting songs of gratitude and thanksgiving for a safe return to our Valley are performed by the Nine Kin during these five holy days. That is why five spirit-rhinos are made upon the Bridge of Rainbows as a sign of the People's return to the Valley. The seven lions is the sign of the Star Hunter who endlessly pursues the Sisters, just as the hunters endlessly pursue the Mother's children. The shamans-of-time count the days and nights of the sun-circle and those of the moon-circles and they tell us that five extra days are needed before the new sun-circle and the new winter season may begin and the moon-circle and sun-circle are aligned with each other again. Does that answer all of your questions, my Daughter?"

The Grandfather paused and then really looked hard at me standing there shivering in the cold.

"I think you have asked these questions before, Dear One," he said skeptically. "Are you again attempting to delay your journey to our shared destiny?"

Certainly the Grandfather was beginning to see the concern and worry gathering like a dark cloud before me, if not the sheer terror that flew up into my face from some dark place deep inside. Looking down at the ground I nodded in agreement, acknowledging my feeble attempt to delay what could not be delayed. Before I could open my mouth to ask another question, he grasped my wrist and held me in place for a few moments. He closed his eyes and mumbled a brief chant under his breath. The Grandfather opened his eyes to look into mine with complete caring and compassion. I knew he could see the trepidation building behind them.

"Fear and questioning is to be expected at this point of no returning, Dear One. Even the bravest are terrified before crossing such a threshold," he whispered gently.

Still I could speak no words. All I could do was look toward the wall and continue to stare, frozen, with big eyes at the red-ochre hands, the horse and the mammoth and the thirteen dots snaking toward the entrance portal of the Lodge of the Heart.

"If your fear is too great, you should not enter and complete the initiation, Dear One," the Grandfather said comfortingly.

"We have not yet entered the Heart Lodge so this will be your one last opportunity to turn back from a hunter's initiation, if that is what your heart desires."

The Grandfather turned me by my shoulder to again look straight into my eyes.

"Dearest One, if your soul does not desire this, there is no shame in turning back. I will respect and honor you and the Mother will love you and be with you always no matter which path you choose to walk in life. The path of Seer must be chosen freely and from the heart or all will be for naught. Do you understand that, Dear One?"

Turn back now? The thought of the shame of it made me shudder. How could I disappoint everyone? How could I turn a cowardly tail and go back just before the real adventure begins? I reasoned with myself frantically to regain control of my raging terror of what lay around that dark corner.

"No, Grandfather, I will continue. I will become Seer of the Bear People and I will do what you ask of me. But help me in my doubt and my fear of what lies ahead," I pleaded again on the verge of tears.

I took in a long, silent breath and held it for a long moment before letting it out slowly. Still I struggled to get my feelings of dread under control again … to endure whatever it was I was to endure.

"Very well, Dear One. The Mother is always with you and will give you the courage you need to complete any ordeal," he said with great kindness.

The Grandfather reached for and pressed my left hand gently, lovingly, like my mother or Auntie would have comforted me.

Then, motioning toward the hand prints on the portal wall he said, "Go, Dear One. Place whichever of your hands you will upon the Mother's hand that comes to meet you from the Unseen Worlds. Behind these walls of living rock the Mother is waiting, always, to welcome you and to embrace you in comforting repose. Know always that the Mother will give you both solace and the strength to suffer what must be suffered. In so doing, you will learn what must be learned in this place."

The hand prints were unlike any of the others I had seen in the Cave. They obviously had been made by blowing red paint from the mouth onto a right hand and then a left pressed against the yellow-white patch of flat stone that was this portal to the Cave beyond.

"Good thing that we are so close to plenty of sweet water to clean out the maker's mouth!" I thought to myself trying to divert my head from the fearful thoughts washing over and around me.

I had never made any image by blowing paint. It must really taste terrible! As I peered at each of the hands more closely, I became ever more fascinated with the stencils and how they had been painted on these walls so very long ago. After blowing the paint,

when the ancient maker's hand was removed, the remaining outline of a white stone hand was surrounded in a little cloud of
blood-red ochre. It *did* appear to be the Mother's hand—at least an
ancient maker's hand—reaching out of the darkness of the Unseen
Abyss to touch the inside of the invisible barrier between the
worlds of the spirit-powers and our own World of Light. The skin
between the worlds certainly *is* very thin in this holy place. That
much is certain. Touching the Mother's Cave helped me before,
why not now?

I took another deep breath, held it for a long moment, and
then slowly exhaled as I had been taught. Even before the next
breath was taken, I felt moved to press a palm against one of the
red-outlined hands. I put my right hand against the one on the
back-end of the Horse Mother of new life and healing. With a re-
flexive jerk I pulled my hand away. The handprint did not feel
cold! It was as warm and soft as any mother's hands rubbed against
a child's chilly palms. Wanting that kind of comfort and support
desperately, I cautiously pushed my freezing fingers against Horse
Mother and the stenciled handprint upon her rump. It really did
calm my heart and give me strength to face I knew not what.

"Here Grandfather," I said in a dreamy voice. "Please take my
lamp that I may place my other hand against the Mother."

"Yes, Dear One. I see that your heart is already calmed and
your courage has returned. When you will have placed both hands
upon the stone, speak the words of the Thirteen Syllables into the
ear of the Mother," he whispered to me.

I was already in a blissful half-trance but I did as the Grandfather suggested and placed my left hand against the Mammoth
Mother's flank. I began to speak the Words of Power:

I am the Mother's Child. I and the Mother are One.

I stood transfixed with both palms pressing the very Hands of
Solace for a very long time. The Grandfather, evidently deciding
that I had absorbed enough courage, broke the spell.

"Come, Dear One. Your destiny and mine await us. Let us
pass through into the Mother's Heart."

* * *

The Lodge of the Mother's Heart is roughly egg-shaped, much like the Lodge of Red Spirits, only smaller. A fitting place for rebirth and transformation, I suppose. I could not see the whole chamber from where we had entered, but from what I could see, the small cavern looked quite ordinary. Without a lofty roof, the Heart Lodge's walls curved down to the floor, in places, at an angle that made it impossible to walk a round of the Lodge right next to the cave walls. The faint but distinctive acrid scent of burnt human hair mixed with pine-smoke hung on the cold, stale air of the Lodge of the Mother's Heart. Without any explanation, the Grandfather immediately began to lead me on a sun-wise circle around the left-hand wall of the Heart Lodge. He began where the lines of a red bull-mammoth with big tusks marked the southern end of the chamber.

"A sign of the red father-powers within a lodge of white-spirits," I said aloud to myself.

We began to follow a well-worn path along the unmarked flat walls rising up above the damp floor and rounding into a domed roof. Unable to walk next to the walls, it was still easy to see that there were no other spirit-animals painted there. As the southwestern wall curved and jutted to become a western wall, we reached a large bench-like stone protruding out of the upward curving roof-wall. Upon the bench lay a pile of kindling and wood to feed the fires of the lodge's hearth. Now visible off to our right, kindling was already laid in the little hearth to light a blaze in the very center of the chamber.

Upon the stone bench there were additional pine torches— bark strips cut and bound, sticky side out, partly wrapped in bark paper and ready to light. And, curiously, a long fresh-cut willow branch, its bark stripped off to reveal the white rod within, had been placed next to the torches and firewood. A large wooden bowl was also part of the cache of supplies on the stone bench. The Grandfather picked up the bowl before I could see what it contained.

"Apprentices or seer-assistants must have come into the Cave to prepare for my initiation by bringing in wood for the hearths and these other things," I whispered quietly to myself. I wondered whether or not I would ever be sent into the Cave to prepare for an initiation?

As we continued along the western wall to what should be its northwestern corner, except for a large red dot marking a sharp drop off into another chamber below, there were no spirit-animals made upon the walls at all. I had learned well enough that a red dot like this one is the sign of a starting point for the rounds of another lodge waiting for us somewhere out there in the blackness. The Grandfather passed by the red dot and led our way on around an outward-curving drop off that divided the high-roofed chamber into two parts—one part with the hearth and the other out there in the darkness. At the furthest point in the curved shelf, a large flat block of stone had been placed to make a single deep step down into the next chamber.

The Grandfather passed by the step without going down. We continued moving around this northern limit of the Lodge of the Heart, and a few paces on, to our right, there appeared a large, very wet area. Sparkling white stone completely covered over the tan clay floor beneath. And just like a similar area in the Red Lodge, it was dotted with many stone penises of different heights and thicknesses sticking up from the hard ground. Without comment, the Grandfather took our little party around the edge of the chamber to what would be an eastern wall where three large red dots appeared in a row—the three-starred belt of the Star Shaman? I would have to ask the Grandfather.

These three red spots were made at eye-level where the high, ribbed roof of the Heart Lodge curved down into a smooth stone sidewall and then dropped to the light brown floor below. Immediately in front of the three red spots—where the sidewall was about the height of a man's head—what was, at one time, a green branch had been propped upright. A small heap of stones had been arranged around the bottom of the rod-like branch to hold it in place. It was now leaning over precariously and looked just about to fall. The fairly thick sapling had been stripped of all side branches and leaves except for a couple of twigs and a few dried and shriveled leaves at the very top of the staff-like wooden rod. The branch was begging to curl to the side from drying out and a cross-piece made of another short twig dangled from near the top of the rod where it had originally been bound into the All Mother's Cross.

I said to myself in the faintest of whispers, "What a forlorn, sad, white Tree of Life this is!"

The Grandfather stopped and stood facing the branch and the three red dots on the wall behind it. He began mumbling something under his breath that I could not hear. When he was finished with his unintelligible chant, he led our way in a tight circle that brought us completely around in the opposite direction. We now stood facing the red dots and the White Tree of Life across the central hearth. We were in almost the exact center of the Lodge of the Mother's Heart.

"Thou mayest light the dancing fire within the Hearth of the Ordeals, Dear One," he said with such formal words as only an old shaman speaks.

"This will be the fire of thy initiation as Hunter and Seer of the Bear People. Ignite, thou, this fire from thine own lamp just as the spirit-fire within thy heart will be kindled in this holy place of the White Cross of the All Father."

I had guessed correctly that it was a white-spirited cross, but the excessively honorific words of the Grandfather were somehow unsettling. Clearly, they were part of the words of the hunter's initiation rite, but being addressed as a "thou" always makes me very uncomfortable. Whenever the Grandfather addressed me so, I had the urge to look around to see if it were someone else he was speaking to.

I retrieved some firewood from the stone bench and began to light the fire. While I was busy with the tinder and kindling, the Grandfather began to speak.

"For your initiation, it will not be necessary to retrieve the ashes from this holy hearth for the making of white body paint before your flames of initiation are ignited. The ashes have already been taken from the hearth beforehand. We will use some of the oil from your horn to mix the ash paint in this bowl that I have brought from the stone bench."

"Very well, Grandfather. I will mix the ashes when the hearth is burning high," I said.

My attention was on the fire but I heard all the words he continued to speak.

"As Seer, you should know that as part of the preparations for the initiations, assistants will bring in and prepare firewood for the Hearth of the Ordeals. But before they lay the kindling, they will scoop the ash that remains from the previous season's hearth fire into this large wooden bowl to be mixed with bison tallow to make the men's white body paint. Only these holy ashes may be used for the boy's rites just as your own Mother-ochre was specially made for you. The assistants have prepared some of the ashes for our use and the ashes that remain from the fire of your initiation will be gathered for the coming rites of the Great Gathering," he explained without need of any comment from me.

As the flames began to leap up, the firelight revealed almost the whole chamber from the entrance on our right, with its red bull-mammoth, all the way to the white penis rocks on our left. The crackling flames also illuminated the three red dots, the shriveled Tree of Life before us and the stone bench behind us. The firelight also shone upwards to the chamber's high, domed roof.

"Grandfather, it looks like the ribbed roof of my mother's lodge!" I said, looking up in amazement at the rounded ceiling of the Lodge of the Mother's Heart.

And it *did* look like the curved roof of a winter lodge, except they have bent saplings that support the bark shingles. Here, the ceiling was made of ridges of rock arching overhead like the ribcage of some great beast bigger than a mammoth.

"Yes, my Daughter," he replied. "Our bark lodges shelter the body, but this Lodge of the Heart supports and shelters the mind and the soul. This is the holy lodge where the All Mother and her counterpart, the All Father, are reborn in our hearts."

"Why does the Heart Lodge smell like burnt hair, my Grandfather?" I asked, my nostrils irritated by the unpleasant odor.

"There is the scent of burnt hair in this lodge because if you were a boy being initiated as a man, everything that is part of your childhood would be stripped off—just like your boy's clothing is taken away. Were you a boy, removing all that belongs to childhood would include cutting off your hair. But since you are a woman being initiated as Seer, cutting your hair and burning it in the hearth of the Heart Lodge will not be necessary. That is only for the initiation of boys," he explained.

"Well, I know that the new men coming from the Great Cave all have awful hair cuts. But I had no idea what happened to their hair!" I said, laughing and feeling sorry for the boys at the same time.

"Some mentors are better at cutting the hair of the boys than others. That is for certain." The Grandfather added his chuckle to my own.

"My own father tried to shave my head and I came out looking like a half-butchered rabbit," he said with a little sidelong smile, clearly thinking fondly of other times and other people in his long, long life.

I stared at the Grandfather and tried to imagine what he might have looked like as a boy with a badly shaved head.

"The boys are all shorn of their children's hair during the initiations. When they come out of the Cave as men, they begin to style their hair to their own desires and not according to their mother's wishes. It is only fitting that a man should decide to shave the sides of his head or put his hair into matted braids, don't you agree?" he asked.

"Of course, that is how it should be, Grandfather. It's just that I've always wondered, as the boy's came out of the Cave, what happened to their hair? Now I know. Thank you, for telling me, Grandfather."

"It is only what you will have to know if you ever preside over the rites as the Grandmother of the Bear-kin. As Seer, you should also know that at the time the hair is cut, the boys are also blessed and anointed by their mentors with white paint made from the hearth's ashes. The words of the blessing are much the same as the girls receive from their mentors in the Red Lodge. But in this rite, the hunter-mentors, who are also naked except for their bison robes, will also mark and decorate each other with stripes and circles of white paint which they will wear until they leave the Cave. This rite marks the beginning of the boy's initiation into the men's group, the White Brotherhood of Hunters. Please mix the paint using the ashes in the bowl and oil from your own horn so that I may bless you as a hunter-initiate, Dear One."

"Yes, Grandfather. What should I do with the excess? There seems to be more than enough ash in the bowl for marking one apprentice."

"To whatever ash paint remains when we leave the Cave will be added all the ashes that are in the hearth when the assistants come to prepare for the boys' initiations. There should be ample ash paint to mark all the initiates and their mentors as I am sure you will see when I have finished blessing and marking you."

I picked up the bowl from which protruded a short stick to use in mixing. As if I were mixing paint for making animal images, I tipped small amounts of oil from my father's horn into the ashes, stirred them and added more oil until the right consistency was achieved. I held out the bowl of finished ash paint to the Grandfather.

"Please remove your robe, my Daughter. I will mark and bless you with the ash paint of the powers of the hunter's Lodge of White Spirits."

The blessings were almost exactly the same as for the woman's initiations. Soon all the red ochre marks I had received in the Red Lodge—partly washed off in the Swan Mother's watery lodge— were covered over in white ash paint. My forehead and nose, both cheeks, my throat to my navel, around both nipples, knees, and, of course, a big white three-cornered pute covered up all but a few stray streaks of red color here and there.

"Now you may use your own fingers to apply stripes or spots to any part of your body you wish," the Grandfather directed.

I dipped my fingers in the ash paint and began drawing stripes across my upper arms and forearms. Then I made more stripes across my thighs and shins. I had an idea to put spots in a place I could not reach.

"Grandfather? Will you paint some spots on my back? I want some leopard spots there but I cannot reach it."

"Very well. Turn around. Do you wish to have large spots or small spots?" he asked accommodatingly.

"Small spots. Like Leopard Mother and spotted Roe Bear from the Passage of the Butterfly," I directed for a change.

After the white paint had been applied, I pulled a piece of soft chamois skin from my bag to wipe my fingers. I passed the skin to the Grandfather so he could do the same. I was now painted and ready to carry on with the initiation.

"Now, my Daughter, leave your bag and oil horn behind. Don your robe and let us begin our rounds of the Lodge of White Spirits. I will explain it all to you as we go. We must be sure to leave enough time to complete all we have come to the Great Cave to do," he cautioned.

As we prepared to go, the Grandfather added his almost spent torch to the hearth fire. The remaining pine gum in the stump ignited and flared up with sharp popping and crackling sounds. The rapidly burning torch also added the far more pleasant scent of pine resin to the noxious, heavy air of the Lodge of the Mother's Heart.

CHAPTER 10.
THE HUNTER'S LODGE OF WHITE SPIRITS

I FOLLOWED THE GRANDFATHER as he turned toward the western wall of the Lodge of the Mother's Heart. He replaced the bowl of leftover ash paint and picked up a fresh pine torch from the stone bench. He held it to my triple-wicked lamp until the flames caught hold.

"Dear One, when you carry a torch for light in the Cave, always be respectful to the Mother and her spirit-animals. Be careful to wipe the tip of the torch upon the ground when the flame needs to be renewed. Never put your torch to the walls where claw marks, signs or spirit-animals have been made by the Ancients," he cautioned.

"Yes, Grandfather. I will be careful not to mar any of the images or signs of the Ancients with torch marks."

I had seen a few black lines and marks made by torches in various places along the way already. I decided they must have been made by the Ancients themselves. Surely none of the People would be so disrespectful to Bear Mother by putting random marks on the walls of her Great Cave.

The Grandfather walked along the western wall toward the red hand-dot in the northwest corner of the Lodge. I already knew it must mark an entry point into the unknown world of the white-spirits of the Cave somewhere below in the darkness. Surely that is where we are going now. As we reached the red palm-dot, the Grandfather answered the thoughts of my head without having been asked out loud in that way he has. It sends chills up and down my spine every time.

"My Daughter, you have seen the red hand-dot and you know it marks the beginning of another holy round. It is actually the beginning of the triple rounds of the Lodge of White Spirits that all the boys take in a single-file procession. The triple rounds are three dance circles of the white spirit-powers which are to be experienced and brought forth in these White Lodges of the Hunters. Like the winding trails in the Plain of the Bear Mother, these holy rounds are meant to represent the twisting and turning life-path of the White Brotherhood. The hunter's path is one that can turn and change direction at any moment. In that, it is like following the blood trail of a wounded animal. The triple rounds are also a sign of the Mother's Net of Life experienced as a confusing maze. The rounds also are a sign of the joining and oneness of the red and white spirit-powers awaiting each initiate at the center of the maze of each boy's heart. Walking these three rounds is intended to bring the boys to an awareness of that. As I have already explained to you, there are three worlds of our knowing in the World of Light: the world of the Sky Father above, the waters of the Earth Mother below and the middle world of the Five Mothers. The red spirit-powers of those three worlds were encountered by walking the three holy rounds of the Red Lodge. Likewise, there are also three rounds here corresponding to the white spirit-powers of those three worlds: Above, Below and Middle."

"Yes, Grandfather, I remember."

"I have said before that the Mother's Cave is a place of fear. But every boy must begin to learn fearlessness in this Great Cave by singing and dancing their way around all three circles just as if they were singing and chanting around a dance fire in the World of Light above. In all the rites to initiate a hunter, as Seer you should remember that a fearful hunter is a disrespectful hunter and a disrespectful hunter is a hungry hunter. When all is spoken, there are only two kinds of thoughts and two kinds of things in all the worlds: thoughts and things of fear, and thoughts and things of love. Every thought at its heart is one or the other and brings with it the children which are born of that way of thinking. If fear, then its children anger, hatred, discord, loss and starvation will come. If love, then its children joy, abundance, kindness, cooperation, generosity and plenty will come. Do you understand this teaching, my good Apprentice?"

"Yes, Grandfather. I understand. What we give to the Mother is what we get in return. Is that not the same teaching?"

"Yes it is, Dear One. As Seer you will also learn that all these rites that we perform are intended to bring the ideas of our heads in line with thoughts of joy, abundance, kindness, generosity, joining and cooperation one with another. Whatever the thing is, the white powers of our minds think it and put it into the ear of the Mother by means of our words and deeds and that is what will surely come back to us whether we desire it or not. As Seer, always remember that abundance, joy, concord and success in the hunt come out of the sure knowledge that the hunter is doing the work of the Mother. Hunters must always go into life with singing, rejoicing, cooperation with their brother-hunters and unceasing gratitude no matter how frightful the situation may be. If any hunter thinks to face the dangers of the hunt with fear in his heart, he is lost already and all his kin with him. The boys will begin to learn these lessons by leaving their mentors in the Heart Lodge and following the Grandfather of the Rites in taking the three holy rounds here while they dance and sing the Song of Abundance together. When the triple circles of the White Lodges have been walked and we have completed the necessary rites at the Heart Lodge, the hunter's initiations will be completed. You and I will then enter the Black Lodges of the Dark Mother to complete the further trials and revelations of your seer's initiation. This will be the order of your initiation as a hunter and then as a seer."

"Is there anything beyond the Dark Mother's Lodge, my Grandfather?"

"No, Dear One. Those are the deepest caverns of the Great Cave. The Lodges of the Dark Mothers are the places in the Great Cave where few are ever prepared in their hearts to go. Even the bravest of hunters shrink from entering there. But that is where we will meet our destiny, Daughter of My Heart." A large lump formed in my throat which I had great difficulty in swallowing.

The Grandfather handed me his torch, turned around and began to lower himself over the steep drop to the floor of the Lodge of White Spirits hidden in the blackness below.

"Help me down this ledge by giving me your hand, my Daughter."

"Yes, Grandfather. Just one moment while I put down the lamp and torch."

I put both lights on the ground and grasped his hand to help him lower his legs into the charcoal-black shadows at the edge of the drop-off. Without warning, his hand slipped out of mine and the Grandfather disappeared into the blackness with a fading shout as if he were falling into the Great Abyss itself!

My heart jumped up to replace the lump in my throat and stopped its beating. I grabbed the torch and quickly stepped to the edge of the drop off to see where he had fallen. Holding the torch out in front of me I leaned over to look down into the utter blackness.

In that instant, the Grandfather leaped up at my face with another great shout of GRRRRR!

I cursed loudly and then began to laugh when the Grandfather said, "The Trickster comes again!"

Of course, the ledge had been a much shorter drop than he made me think it was. I handed the torch down to him. I set my lamp on the edge of the drop off, and, still laughing, I slid over onto the flat clay-covered ground.

"You really have to stop doing that, Grandfather! So much for a solemn walking of the triple rounds!" I chided him.

"Never, my Daughter! The Trickster should always be our third companion and the triple rounds should never be so solemn," he chuckled out loud and took the torch from me.

"We can begin the first round just over here." He gestured with his torch toward the stone wall to our left.

The Grandfather only took a few steps across the hard, glittering white floor before the first spirit-animal appeared: a single large bear. It had been engraved into the soft clay-like stuff that covered all the walls here exposing the white stone beneath. Motioning me to go ahead along a stretch of almost flat wall, I felt we were moving toward the northwest. The Grandfather walked slowly behind while beginning my introduction to the Lodge of White Spirits. As he spoke, I gaped in amazement at an incredible procession of engraved, "white" spirit-animals that began to emerge out of the darkness, all coming toward me.

First, two mammoths with tusks appeared. Then an astonishing crash of twelve rhinos covered the flat wall. Behind the rhinos another single mammoth appeared, then two aurochs, six more mammoths, four more rhinos, four horses, and at the far end of the procession where the wall turned abruptly to the north, two black bison had been made up toward the top of the wall. One bison faced in the same direction as all the other spirit-animals on this wall, but the other faced in the opposite direction, rear haunches to rear haunches.

"All the white spirit-powers on one wall!" I said out loud in true astonishment.

"Yes," the Grandfather said under his breath with a little chuckle. "Did you also notice that this amazing herd of white spirit-animals is made in three long sections? There are only a few signs and a few spirit-animals above and below this grand procession of white and black spirit-animals. Except for the black aurochs, almost all the spirit-animals are lined up and moving out of the White Lodge toward the Heart Lodge for the rebirth and transformation of their souls along the center section. Would it surprise you to know that there are twenty-eight spirit-animals in the center band of this procession all moving in the same direction?"

"Of course, Grandfather! It is a white-spirited Bridge of Rainbows!" I exclaimed with a flash of realization.

"Three worlds in one. The Powers of Three again. White-spirits aligned and all moving in the direction of rebirth into all the worlds," I said under my breath, repeating the lesson to myself.

I studied each detail of this huge wall full of skillfully made white images. Some were made with doubled trunks, tusks, horns and backs which, as our flickering lights played across them, made for an astonishing display of lively movement. It was if they were tossing their tusks and trunks up and down as they ran across the white Bridge of Rainbows toward the Heart Lodge.

I lost myself among the carefully engraved spirit-animals while the Grandfather began his next lesson.

"The winding and circling paths we have taken through the Lodges of the Mother's Great Cave are the winding and circling paths we take in our daily lives. All of those holy rounds have brought us to this jumping off place into the white-spirited world of men and hunters. We have already made our way through the lodges and wombs where almost all spirit-animals and signs are made in red ochre signifying the red-world of the flesh-and-blood life of the Red Mothers. I will explain again that the red-world is the world of here and now. It is the world in which we live our waking lives. It is our very bodies and all of the unseen desires and needs of the liver rising up to move us in one direction or another. Red signs are for the lifeblood of women and of all the myriads of mothers giving birth to flesh-and-blood animals in abundant herds and flocks of birds. Only a small reminder of the Dark Mother's place in all this exuberant red life appeared in the Red Lodge. That is to bring to mind even in the midst of the plentiful life of the World of Light that all those lives must come to an end and all must be eaten back to the All Mother. It is the fate of all and none may choose otherwise. All blades of grass, every bug, every tree and every mammoth, every one of the human tribes from the least to the most honored, the end of our red-body is all the same. In the midst of this turmoil, change and movement of the red-life, we must all learn to rejoice and take pleasure in living our lives to the fullest every single day because our end is all the same. No one knows the moment of their Return and so each day is to be lived as if it is our last. And never are we to live with any regret for paths we have not taken or the mistakes we have made. Here, in the White Lodges, spirit-powers come forth which are the unchanging, unchangeable, eternal powers of the white spirit-powers. The white-spirits are the thoughts of the head that come and go but never die as the red-body dies. The memories of loved ones, of injuries, of missed marks, of kindnesses performed are forever alive within us. All we have to do to bring them back to life is to remember them. Women and hunters alike know the Song of Happiness and we sing this song around the dance fires before every hunt begins or before we go out to gather the bounty of Earth Mother. We will sing this song, too, as we move through the three holy rounds in this Lodge of White Spirits. In this place, the

Song of Happiness *is* the song of the light-filled, eternal, unchanging White Spirits of the Above. You have heard the song many times, have you not, my Daughter?"

"Yes, Grandfather, I know it well," I said.

I began to sing it softly as I continued to stare hungrily at the wall full of engraved spirit- animals:

> *All is joy*
> *All is health*
> *All is abundance*
> *All is freedom from want.*
> *I am happy wherever I am*
> *I am happy wherever I am*
> *It is a good day to live*
> *It is a good day to die.*

"Yes, Dear One. It *is* a good day to live and it *is a* good day to die!" the Grandfather began to sing along with me.

After a few verses of the song, the Grandfather ceased his singing and released a weary sigh with *such* longing in his voice as I never before heard a man's mouth make. I paused my singing and he continued with his teaching.

"We have left the hearth fire of transformation in the Heart of the Cave. As Seer, know that the Heart is the mid-point between the Women's Red Lodges and the Men's White Lodges, together and within which we live and move and perform these rites of your initiation. As I have said, the Red Lodges are those of the red, female spirit-guides. But these lodges are the worlds of the white, male spirit-guides. These lodges are especially holy to the white animal-companions and guides with which many shamans and hunters fly in their trance-dreams. Because this is the Lodge of White Spirits, many of the spirit-animals here possess their horns and antlers—signs of the predominant male powers within them. You can see that many of the spirit-mammoths here also have their gigantic tusks where they were completely absent in the Red Lodges. Just as the spirit-animals and signs of the Red Lodges signify the powers of our livers and of our body-urges and dreams, so are the images of the White Lodges the signs of the powers of our heads and of our waking thoughts and conscious choices. Brought together with the red-powers in harmony, the joined white and red-powers give us a full and abundant life that is to be discovered in each heart. This marriage of the white and red powers is the birth of the black spirit-powers within our souls. Do you understand what I'm saying, Dear One?" he said plaintively.

I shook my head up and down in agreement and so he continued.

"To find the spirit-companion of a hunter's heart, he must cease thinking only with his head. He must also learn to acknowledge and honor the feelings arising from the liver, the organ of the hidden senses and of the strong urges of the red-body. The liver is also the organ of all our secret feelings and dreams. Dear One, I have already taught you that when the head and the liver are in harmony, compassion and perfect kindness is born in the heart, which is the organ of oneness, cooperation and harmony. Harmony comes when the heart opens to the descent of the active, creative, giving powers of the Father to meet and join with the arising of the receptive, quiet, feeling powers of the Mother. When they come together in the heart, it is a joining of opposite powers that bring new life and love for all of the Mother's creations," he expounded.

In spite of the Grandfather's many-worded explanation I was rapt with attention and hanging on his every word. I barely even noticed that he had again begun to speak with the Mother's Voice. Awe-struck, I listened while the Voice reverberated off the stone around, below and above us in otherworldly tones.

"I transform White Spirit into Red Form, shape transforms into shape, Red Form transforms again into White Spirit in the One Life of my ever-giving Womb. My ever-nourishing navel pours life into the Three Worlds and my ever-abundant breasts give suck to all my creation!" The Grandfather's, I should say, the Mother's voice rumbled with words I could hardly comprehend.

"Behold, I make all things anew! My One Life pours into innumerable shapes and forms and I take them all back unto me!" The Voice echoed one more time and then fell silent.

I waited a long moment, not quite sure what I should do. And just a little unnerved by the awesome display of spirit-power.

Chapter 10. *The Hunter's Lodge of White Spirits*

"Was I speaking with the Mother's Voice, my Daughter?" he asked in a quavering whisper.

"Yes, Grandfather," I said quietly, not just a little afraid he would slip into the terrifying, unearthly Voice again.

"From here we will begin the triple rounds of the Hunter's White Lodge. We will circle the Navel of the Cave in a sun-wise direction beginning from the Navel's left side just over here. We will sing the Song of Happiness as we go. You may also dance this holy round if you wish, Dear One," he said.

The Grandfather turned to lead me out into the darkness without further comment.

What we began to circle was a vast hole that dropped straight down from the surface of the cave floor into the blackness. The bottom of the Navel was barely visible even when I cautiously held my lamp out over the edge to peer into its depths. If the Grandfather or I were to fall into this giant hole, neither of us would ever be seen again, I am sure. We made our happy but careful way around the circular edge of the dangerous pitfall.

As we two-stepped and sang our round of the Mother's Navel, white, engraved spirit-animals began to appear on the stone pendants and flaps descending from the very high roof of the Cave to within reach of the ancient makers. First, a lone ibex showed itself, then a single bear. One mammoth and then one reindeer appeared in turn. These spirit-animals were followed by a finely engraved herd of nine spirit-mammoths, after which appeared a single Owl Mother. Maybe since it appears in this white lodge, it is Owl Father! All the People have been told from childhood that Owl is the frequent companion of seers and is the knower and seer of all things of the powers. That's because owls see and hunt even in the darkest night. Owl's head was turned all the way around as she looked at us over her shoulder. Her, or his, big round eyes glared above a feathered back.

I was sure now that one of the feathers in the Grandfather's staff bundle was from an owl so I thought I should ask a question.

"Grandfather?" I stopped my singing to ask the question, "Is this spirit-owl a sign of Owl Mother or Owl Father?"

"It is Owl Father, my good Apprentice. It is the sign of the wisdom of the white-spirited powers that is to be experienced in this White Lodge. Does that answer your question, my Daughter? If so, let us continue on with our holy round of the Navel."

"Yes, Grandfather. That answers my question," I said and we continued on with the first round of the White Lodge.

Further on from Owl Father, three spirit-horses emerged into the light. Then nothing more was seen as we rounded the Navel to our point of beginning.

"Grandfather," I said, "I think I know why there are mostly only single spirit-animals appearing above the Navel. Is that because the Mother's Navel is the one source of all things? I even understand why there would be three Horse Mothers, Is that because the three worlds are one in the Mother and so on? But why are their nine Mammoth Mothers in a herd above the Navel on its southern side? What does the number nine mean?" I asked without giving him a chance to answer.

Having counted carefully every group of spirit-animals that I saw, this was the first group of "nine" that I had encountered in the Cave thus far. The only other "nine" had been the nine little red dots under the feet of the lion-shaman in the Passage of the Butterfly.

"Yes, the Mother is the one Source of all things. And 'nine' is the number of the All Mother pouring herself into all that she makes. It is the Powers of Three added to the Powers of Three added to the Powers of Three, which is another way of saying 'all the powers of the three worlds.' The All Mother nourishes all the worlds through her great navel just as we come into the world connected to and nourished by our own mother's red-blood through our umbilical cords. Our own navels are but a reminder of the cord that once attached us to our mothers. So should this Navel remind us of our connection to our Source, which *is* the All Mother."

"Grandfather, is not nine the number of moon-circles that a woman carries a child in her womb?" I realized in a flash of white-spirited insight.

"Yes, my Good Apprentice, that is correct. When one of the human tribe is born, it is the Mother pouring her life into the red-world and nourishing the new life through her Holy Navel, which is the navel of every child being born. Nine is also the number of kin-groups that were led to the Valley by Grandmother Red Bear through the powers of Bear Mother herself, as you well know. The Nine Kin are often said to have *descended* into our Valley just as the Mother pours herself into all the worlds flowing like water in descent from the high mountains of ice and snow. Here, on the southern side of the Navel, the nine white mammoths are the sign of the emergence and the coming forth of the white spirit-power of the All Mother's abundance into our hearts. In this White Lodge, it is the sign of the coming forth of the All Father within each of us to nourish our white spirit-powers as through a great spirit-navel preceding our rebirth and transformation into hunters. As Seer, know that the powers of abundance do not 'descend' from any place away from or apart from us. The powers come forth from the All Mother and the All Father who are within and surround all things—and that includes *you*, Dear One. The white spirit-powers of the Father of the Center are to be born, they are to come forth, and they are to be experienced in these White Lodges. Here, our souls are born anew and our liver-senses and urges are to become harmonized with, directed and controlled by, the white-spirits of the Above. We have had this lesson before, but as Seer, you will instruct and encourage all men to put the white spirit-powers of the Above in control of their body-emotions without utterly killing their kind and feeling hearts. The revelations of this Lodge will begin that opening of the heart for all who walk the holy rounds here. As seers, we bring the boys to the edge, to a jumping-off place, of the union of the red and the white. But in the end, each boy must take the final step for himself. That is true of my good Apprentice as well," he said with a pointed look in my direction.

I saw the look and replied, "Yes, Grandfather, I know that is true of me too."

I smiled a big grin at the Grandfather and he continued his teaching.

"Whether any of the boys become aware of it or not in this place, the All Mother continuously nourishes with the abundant spirit-power of three, plus three, plus three Mammoth Fathers. The Nine Mothers or the Nine Fathers are a sign of the Mothers and Fathers of the Three Worlds to which we should always be connected: body, mind and soul. To have noticed this 'nine" means you are very observant, my good Apprentice," he said fondly.

Then the Grandfather said, apparently spontaneously, "Dear One, I am so pleased with you. I am honored and gratified to be your mentor and I love you as the Daughter of My Heart."

The Grandfather's words were spoken gently and with deep feeling. Brimming tears filled my eyes because I have always longed to hear such words from my own father's mouth. But like so many other men, it is not my father's way to speak of the thoughts of his heart to such a one as me. I could not but think that control of such soft and kind emotions is just part of the training of a hunter and of a man. Still, my heart sang with these kind words of the Grandfather and I longed even more to hear them from the other men in my life.

* * *

We had returned to our starting point on the western side of the Navel, just opposite the White Bridge of Rainbows with its twenty eight engraved spirit-animals. But instead of following the same path around the Navel, the Grandfather moved along the western wall in a northerly direction toward a long line of great stones that seemed to have fallen from the roof. The jumbled rocks formed a sort of barrier running west to east across the White Lodge. As we approached the barrier of fallen boulders the edge of an astonishing circle of bear skulls at least fifteen paces from side-to-side came into our view.

Singing the Song of Abundance once again, we began to do simple dance steps around the left side of the amazing circle in the sun-wise direction. The skeletal snouts of all the pure white bear skulls pointed in toward the circle's empty center. The skulls were so white that they could only have been whitened with chalk paint. Only the vast darkness of a high roof covered with pendants, waving curtains of stone and stone ice sickles hung high above the ring of bear skulls.

I would have said the bear-spirits were in a dance circle, but no hearth fire appeared in the center to dance around. I suppose the unseen, white-spirited powers have no need for an actual flaming hearth. Nevertheless, we danced and sang our way around the edge without once stepping inside the circle of bear skulls. I counted the skulls as we went: twenty eight in all. A truly awe-inspiring dance circle!

"Are the White Bear Fathers dancing, my Grandfather?" I asked.

"Yes, Dear One, they are," he replied. "And when the boys are brought here, they sing and dance their way around the circle just as we do. It is a somber thing to see so many skulls because white bones are a reminder of the Return. But the dance of life and the Song of Happiness reminds each boy that there is always joy and the love of life even in the face of killing, the death of the body, and returning to the Mother. Each hunter must learn to live now. They must live in this day, at this moment. They must never agonize about mistakes made upon the last hunt. Nor should they fear what may come tomorrow upon the next hunt. It is always a good day to live. It is always a good day to die. All hunters and all seers must learn this lesson to live a happy and abundant life even while they kill and are killed by All Mother and All Father."

As we came full circle on this second of the triple rounds, the Grandfather led us again toward the western wall where we were able to move through the barrier by a gap between the scattered boulders near to the western wall of the chamber. The path between the great fallen stones had been marked on either side of the gap by two magnificent inscribed reindeer with full sets of branching antlers. One facing east, the other facing west, they stood in their proper place at the most northerly point I had yet reached since entering the Great Cave.

Then, astonishingly, we moved twenty paces on and began a third sun-wise path that led around yet another astounding circle of bear skulls. They had been placed with their snouts facing inward toward the center just as the other skull circle of equal size had been laid out. Four of these dancing spirit-bears placed at the four directions of the circle were painted in red or black stripes and spots like bison-wrestlers. The whole of this spectacular skull circle had been placed in the bottom of a shallow depression. The path for dancing lies on the outer edge of the circle and is raised up on a low terrace just one low step above the circle of skulls. The most astonishing thing was yet to be told, for in the center of this third circle lay a large block of stone shaped like Bear Mother. She had a red-striped, whitened skull placed upon the stone just where Bear Mother's head should be. The stone Bear Mother's skull pointed toward some, as yet, unvisited lodge hiding in the darkness of the northern side of the Lodge of White Spirits.

After a long pause to take in the astounding sight, the Grandfather led on to dance and sing this third of the triple holy rounds of the White Lodge. Counting skulls as I went—again there were twenty eight bear skulls—we completed the round. He then followed a well-worn path leading in a northerly direction away from the western edge of the breathtaking circle of dancing skulls. This trail led up to a flat area above the terrace of the third dance circle. The beaten path ran almost right up the middle of the huge Lodge of White Spirits in a northerly direction. I could see that this was the only way to enter whatever lodge lay beyond, because an already low roof sloped down in a gentle curve to both the eastern and western sidewalls. I could see that yet another large cavern stretched out into the blackness before us.

"Is this the place where the stone Bear Mother was pointing with her nose, my Grandfather?"

"Yes, my good Apprentice, she is looking toward the Portal of the White Net and a white womb beyond."

From the terrace of the third circle, a soft clay floor sloped up in two low terraces to an even higher level of the Lodge of White Spirits. The well-trodden path led up to a pair of big white stone pendants facing each other with only charcoal blackness showing between. They descended from the roof almost to the ground and looked every bit like entrance posts to a gigantic winter lodge made of white stone. A flap of stone above the pendants hung like a lintel post across a lodge's entrance way. I started to climb the terraces to enter the cavern that lay between the two pendants.

"Dear One," the grandfather called from where I had left him far behind. "Let me catch up. I want to speak a few words before you enter this Womb of the White Net."

"Of course, Grandfather. How impolite of me to go ahead. Let me help you," I replied.

Still anticipating a new adventure, I stepped back down the terrace to assist him in whatever way I could.

"Dear One, these are the entrance and exit portals to the White Womb of the Net. The roof is very low so you will have to stoop over from the portals for many paces toward the back of this Womb."

"Grandfather, because you are calling this lodge a 'womb', am I to assume this is a place to quest for white spirit-powers?" I asked directly.

"You are certainly beginning to understand the signs of the Cave, my good Apprentice. I am only guessing, but I feel that you will find this simple chamber for solitary questing of the white spirit-powers familiar and very comfortable. As you might not expect, only white spirit-mammoths and the Mother's White Net of Life will be found upon the walls here. This is the most northerly part of the Cave and the White Net made here by the Ancients balances and harmonizes the Red Net in the Red Lodge, the most southerly part of the Cave. You may now enter this White Womb. There is only one path in and one path out. Take all the time that you need, especially if your heart is moved to meditation by any of the powers of this place."

"Grandfather, will you be waiting for me here, at the entrance portal?" I asked suspiciously. I was wondering if he was going to hide somewhere and frighten me again.

"I will be waiting at the place where the upper terrace of the third skull circle meets the eastern wall of the White Lodge. There is nothing to sit on here and I do want to rest while you are questing."

He looked into my face. "And I promise I will not jump out to startle you again, Dear One," he said with his little smile.

I climbed the last of the two terraces and after asking permission to enter, I began moving toward the two big portal pendants. Above the low, door-like opening, upon the stone lintel, appeared a delicately but beautifully made black musk ox. At least black was the right color for "north". But I should have thought a black reindeer with branching antlers more fitting a sign for this place. There seems much the Cave has left to teach, so I will just have to think more on this.

Upon the left-hand pendant, no spirit-animals appeared at all. There were only a few incised lines in a more-or-less square shape. The right-hand pendant did not even have incised marks. But it did have a fascinating collection of small finger-dots toward the bottom of the door post-like stone. The flat side of the pendant-portal facing out to where the Grandfather stood watching me, had seven red finger-dots. And to the left of the red spots, there appeared two groupings of black dots. I began to count. There were seven black dots in one group, and just below what I immediately recognized as the sign of the Seven Sisters again, appeared thirteen black dots in a vaguely snake-like shape. I could see it was meant to be equivalent to the Red Net at the opposite end of the Great Cave, only in black.

"No black reindeer here. But there are plenty of other black signs and images for a northern chamber. The Mother continues to give up her secrets," I whispered to myself as I stooped over and began making my way into the White Womb of the Net.

It was fifteen or twenty paces, humbled and hunched over like a musk-ox, before the chamber's roof became high enough for me to stand up. Another mystery solved as to the absence of a black reindeer at the entrance! I guess the stooping musk-ox should have warned me to humble myself in this lodge of white spirit-powers.

So low is the roof on either side of the chamber that the side walls could not have been reached until I had gone further in for fifteen or twenty paces more. One would have to crawl on hands and knees to get into this narrow place if the somewhat higher roof down the middle of the chamber did not exist. I could not help but think again how the spaces between things are what make it possible for the Mother to enter and to create.

What is even more unusual about this Womb is that, in spite of the uncomfortable hunching walk I had to use to get in, I did feel strangely at home and at ease here. The floor of the entire chamber from the portal-pendants all the way to the back of this chamber was also very unusual: the ground here is hard, sparkling, reddish-orange rock.

"It is the mother-power within the father-power's own lodge," I said out loud to myself.

I searched but could find not a single spirit-animal or sign until I reached the very back of the high-roofed middle passage. The further back I went, the more the overhead rock began to slope down into another very low roof. Here, upon the back wall of this chamber, there appeared four white mammoths engraved in a net-like jumble of tusks and trunks and legs and backs as if they were four creatures merged together as one. This marvelously inscribed image was made just at the point where the roof became so low that I had to get down and lay on my back to see the whole thing.

"Possibly, they are bull-mammoths fighting and struggling against each other?" I questioned myself out loud.

The tusks and trunks of some of the bull-mammoths were doubled and even tripled giving the impression that they were swinging their gigantic heads and tusks back and forth in battle. Maybe that is so because, after all, this is a lodge of men. We all know how men like to struggle with each other to see who will win the contest or who will be the leader! I decided these mammoths were made to be a sign of the active, white, male powers of four bull-mammoths fighting with each other. The net-like impression the image left made me think that perhaps this *is* the White Net. But then off to the left of these spirit mammoths, made on the western side of the chamber, the White Net appeared. I extracted myself from beneath the bull-mammoths—always wanting to be on top, men are—and I went to a part of the end of the chamber that had the only smooth, up-and-down wall-space where you didn't have to crawl on all fours to reach it.

The White Net had been scratched upon the most northerly part of the entire Cave in the middle of a large protrusion of rock bulging out from the western wall of the chamber. I realized with a blaze of insight that the Net of the Mother in the Red Lodge had been placed in the southeastern part of the Cave. Just as the Grandfather said, this is to balance and harmonize the red-spirited powers with the powers of the White Net here in the most north-westerly part of the entire Cave. The Ancients had made two opposing Nets complete with red and white "thirteens" in exactly opposite directions from each other.

The main difference between the two images was that this Net had none of the square spaces colored in. The White Net of Life began on the bulging overhang and ran out of sight under the lip. Again, I had to get down on my knees and lay down on my back to see the whole image! The Mother's White Net actually consisted of bear claw marks upon which one of the Ancients had used their fingers to scratch crossways of the claw marks into the fine clay covering the walls. Actually, the White Net *did* look like the hemp-cord nets we make for the salmon weirs and traps that guide the fish near to the bank where they can be easily caught with round drum-nets or speared. I know the stories of the Net and how we and all things are but one cord in the Mother's Net. Here the very White Net itself was before me!

The words of the song we all learn from childhood ran through my head as a lay on my back to see the White Net more easily. Something within me wanted to sing so I began to hum the tune and mouth the words:

> *The Net of Life is all that comes from the Mother*
> *We are part of the Mother's Net.*
> *The trees, the fish, the birds, the animals*
> *We are part of the Mother's Net.*
> *The rocks, the rivers, the sky and the earth*
> *We are part of the Mother's Net.*
> *What we give or take from the Net*
> *We give or take from ourselves.*

Not only hunters but the smallest children of the Nine Kin are taught never to kill a pregnant animal or any creature that is not used for food or clothing. We are taught not to catch all the fish in the river neither should we take all the eggs from a duck's nest. Killing the Mother's children when it is not necessary for our own needs offends the Mother and damages her Net with greed and disrespect. In sending greed and disrespect to the Mother, we cause the Mother's abundance to cease returning to us.

I do believe what we do to the Net comes back to us in one great circle as the Grandfather has said. At least I won't have to ask him the meaning of *this* marvelous work of Bear Mother. I lay there letting my head wander around the World of Light that seemed so very far away, which it was. I thought of my mother and little White Fox in her lodge. I was with my father, Little Ibex and Uncle Bright Wolf out upon the Plain. I thought of Auntie and wondered what she was doing at this very moment. I do have a special warm feeling in what I imagined to be my heart from just laying here quietly looking at the crossed lines and singing the Song of the Mother's Net to myself. I would have loved to stay here and sing myself into a trance-dream but I knew the Grandfather waited and there were even deeper parts of the Cave I had yet to visit. Still, I could not make myself get up to leave just yet.

After staying for an amount of time that surprised me, I reluctantly got up and began moving back down the middle of the chamber toward the twin pendants. Soon I was hunching over like a musk-ox and then I stood up outside the White Womb of the Net, full of spirit-fire and ready to continue with my adventure.

The yellow glow of the Grandfather's torch at the eastern wall of the White Lodge clearly outlined the dear old man sitting on a block of stone. Even at this distance I could see his silhouette looking up at something on the wall.

I thought this might be my only chance to even the score between us. Along the terrace curving around from the portal pendants to where the Grandfather sat, there were several large boulders that I could hide behind. I crept silently from boulder to boulder with my most quiet feet. Unconcerned about my lamp, I thought the Grandfather's torchlight was so much brighter that he would never notice my feeble light. As long as he did not turn around, I knew I could sneak up on him.

I crept slowly with all the stealth and silence of a leopard until I could peek from behind a large rock very close to where the Grandfather sat. His back to me, he gazed up at a single engraved horse that must mark the beginning of another part of the Cave. I put down my lamp behind the boulder as gently as I could so that it did not make the slightest sound. I gathered myself to make a loud yell and to leap forward toward the unsuspecting Grandfather.

"Ah, it is you, Little Bear," he said, without turning around and not the least bit startled.

I had used my softest footsteps in an effort to sneak up behind him but to no avail.

"Yes, Grandfather, it's me," I said, not a little dejected. I had not been able to surprise him as he has frightened me more than once on this, our wondrous journey together.

"Come, Dear One, and we will return to the Heart Lodge by way of this eastern wall of the Lodge of White Spirits. I think you will be pleased at what you will see," he said calm as a summer morning.

The Grandfather got up and began making his way along the eastern wall of the White Lodge. I followed. We passed by some shallow pools of water, behind one of which was made a single white aurochs. This spirit-animal was followed by one white horse, which in turn, was followed by two beautifully engraved white ibex made in the hollow of a small, but sharp, outcrop in the wall.

I sensed that we had reached another end point. I could not see anything beyond the sharp outcrop of rock, so black and shadowy the wall behind it was, but something of import was coming. The Grandfather's nonchalant manner told me so if nothing else did

The Grandfather turned to face me.

"This is the end of the Lodge of White Sprits and the beginning of the Lodges of Black Spirits. The wall that lies beyond will take us to the entrance of the Lodge of the Dark Mother and our shared destiny. Let us continue on, but wait until we reach the entrance to the Dark Lion Mother's Lodge before you ask your questions," he said with dramatic foreboding of what was to come.

* * *

Now, I am becoming accustomed to the Grandfather's little shaman's tricks of voice and manner, so I was completely unprepared for the astounding collection of black-painted animals that stretched out on the wall before us as far as our torchlight could shine. So enraptured by the carefully shaded and lifelike images did I become that I barely noticed that the grand circle of painted skulls—the third holy round of the White Lodge—was just behind us and well within the glow of the Grandfather's torchlight. I had been so astonished and awed by my first sight of the circle of skulls and so focused on it during the third round, this incredible wall full of black spirit-animals had gone completely unnoticed.

Chapter 10. *The Hunter's Lodge of White Spirits*

For thirty paces or more the spectacle of a veritable flooding river of spirit-animals opened up to my senses. I could see them painted on a stone wall but it was as if I could hear the thunder of their myriad hooves as they fled in panic. I could hear the scream of struggling animals being brought down by lions upon the Plains of Summer. I could smell the manure-laden dust, the blood of fear, and the urine and sweat of terrified animals fleeing in every direction for their very lives.

All the hunters and hunted here had been made with charcoal or paint made from ground up black-rock. It is difficult for experienced painters to distinguish between the two types of black paint that we use. And so it was here on this masterpiece of black spirit-animals, but deciding out how the images had been made and with what kind of paint was the last thought on my mind. What is so unusual about the images here is that many of the spirit-animals have been made with subtle shading to produce the most astonishingly lifelike and gigantic herd of spirit-animals I have ever seen. The limbs and faces and bodies appeared to be rounded like living animals, and not at all the outlined, flat-looking images found in the rest of the Great Cave.

Some were running toward us and away from the still-invisible entrance to the Dark Mother's chamber. Many ran away from us in the direction of rebirth into the World of Light. Perhaps they were running away from us toward the Dark Mothers' chamber. I realized without being told that the direction toward the entrance of the Dark Mother's Lodge was the direction of the Return. The whole wall is filled to overflowing with all the chaos of milling, moving, running, mixed herds of the hunted chased by crouching, leaping, chasing, flesh-and-blood hunters, all made in the black color of the powers of the Dark Mothers.

The first animal to appear in this Lodge of Black Spirits was a single black horse marking the beginning point. Not very much further along appeared a large mixed herd of astonishingly beautiful animals. The surface of the cave wall had been scraped so that it was very white and upon that surface this amazing herd, mostly of reindeer, had been made. I peered closely at each image with my awestruck mouth hanging open.

"Dear One?" the Grandfather's low voice prompted from behind. "Count the reindeer you see within this herd of spirit-animals."

There were thirteen reindeer, certainly not to my surprise. What is more interesting is that more animals had been made above the thirteen reindeer. They formed an arc like a rainbow above the reindeer. This arc of animals included two red-deer stags with great, branching horns standing back-to-back in the middle of the herd. To the right of the stags a beautiful aurochs bull was made facing away from the entrance to the Dark Mother's chamber that still lay far beyond the limits of our torchlight. Below the aurochs bull, another red-deer stag with huge antlers faced the same direction as the aurochs above it. The red-deer stag had a big red stripe coming out of its anus—a shaman shifting his shape into his animal guide.

I pointed to the red stripe, "Another shaman in trance, Grandfather?"

"Yes, Dear One," was all he had to say in reply.

On the other side of the two stags, there appeared a strange creature—a half-horse, half-bison monstrosity.

"Grandfather, I know you told me to wait, but I must ask one question."

"Very well, my good Apprentice, ask your question," he said with his little smile.

Surely the Grandfather knew I would not be able to hold my questions.

"What is this half-horse, half-bison a sign of, my Grandfather?"

"To answer your own question, what is the predominant spirit-power of the horse and of the bison? Answer that and you will know the meaning."

Without answering the Grandfather out loud, I thought to myself: the horse is full of the mother-power and the bison is full of the father-power. It is a sign of the joining of the two opposites as one; the transformation of the Powers of Two into the Power of One once again!

I smiled at the Grandfather and he gave his knowing smile back to me. No further words between us were necessary.

As I moved from herd to herd and group to group along the wall, astonishment came upon astonishment. Herds made up of four horses, four mammoths and four more horses appeared. Single horses were made here and there among a herd of three mammoths, six more horses, a single bear, a group of six reindeer, four more horses and finally a deep niche with three lions crouching at the back of the crevice ready to leap out at us. Groups of aurochs and bison, horses and reindeer crowded the niches, outcrops and flat spaces in an astonishing, uncountable stream of the exuberant life of the animal-powers.

One of the most interesting images to me appeared on a wall to the left of the crouching lions in their little niche. It was an astonishing creature made of an aurochs looking left—away from the lions in their niche—superimposed over a horse head also facing left. These two merging animals then appeared to be transforming into a lion that was facing to the right, toward the crouching lions in their niche. No doubt this was a shaman transforming into the hunted and into the hunter again by means of eating the aurochs and the horse! Nearby, to the left of the transforming trio of hunted and hunters, an amazing bison had been made with eight legs and a doubled back line. This image is so full of movement that I could feel the panic as the bison scrambled to run away from the lions as fast as bison legs could carry him! So many astonishing, life-filled scenes of the hunt!

All these spirit-animals looked alive compared to the line-drawn or engraved red and white animals in the other lodges of the Great Cave. I was completely captivated, speechless and overwhelmed. I moved up and down, back and forth along the wall getting as close as I could, touching the images, peering at them. I marveled at how the very bumps and rises and depressions in the rock had been used by the ancient makers to create these truly enspirited, living images. So overcome I became by the staggering display that I was ready to burst into tears and laugh all in the same moment.

"Grandfather!" I called out in excitement. "These images have truly been painted by the spirit-powers themselves!"

"No, my Apprentice, they have been made by the hands of the Ancients. They have been painted by seers and shamans like you and me," he said quietly and with great reverence.

Having seen them many times before, the Grandfather was still held in respectful awe by these spirit-animals and their long gone makers, just as I was.

"Come, Dear One and I will show you even more wonderful things when you have seen enough of this part of the wall," he said in a voice made small by my excitement.

The Grandfather too gazed intently at the magnificent display of the Mother's Life before us.

After I had peered closely at the astonishing spirit-animals to my fill, the Grandfather once more motioned me toward a rock further along the wall. This new space of stone wall was full of even more magnificent spirit-animals to the height of two men. The flat wall of rock the Grandfather showed me was a veritable cascade of aurochs and horses and bison and fighting rhinos. The black images seemed to fall down the rock from above where bear claw marks could be seen at the very top of the amazing outpouring of spirit-animals.

"Bear Mother, standing on her hind legs to mark the stone, showed the ancient seers where to paint the spirit-animals—and they changed their minds in the making of them too," the Grandfather said, answering an unspoken question of my head.

"What do you mean, changed their minds, Grandfather?" I blurted.

My eyes and hands continued to play over this spirit-herd, not quite sure what to focus on next, so abundant and full of life each spirit-animal appeared to me.

"See the faint outlines of that rhino?" he said pointing with his torch. "It has been painted over with the aurochs and horses. And here! Here, a red mammoth has been re-painted in black as is fitting for this entrance to the Dark Mother's Lodge!" he said excitedly.

I looked toward the place on the wall of beautiful, living animals to which he pointed and it was so. One of the Ancients had changed their mind and painted over some images and replaced them with others.

"Spend all the time you wish now with the messengers of the All Mother in this place, my Child. We will not return here after you have completed your initiations. As Seer, know that there will be other occasions for you to contemplate before any of the spirit-animals here just as the boys are always encouraged to do during their initiations," he said, his voice very quiet again.

"Thank you, Grandfather. I am already overwhelmed by all of this. No one could see and experience it all in one journey through the Cave," I replied.

I continued to run my hands over the astonishing creations of the Ancient Ones, tracing with a finger the graceful, lines made by another hand so long ago. The paintings are all so perfect that I really understood why no one is allowed to mark or paint over them except Bear Mother herself.

I was lost in my own excitement and the sheer amazement of the black spirit-animals until, as if in a dream, I heard a faraway voice say, "It is time to go, Dear One."

"Yes," I said reluctantly. "Yes, Grandfather, I am coming," hardly able to make my feet follow him and leave this place of wonders.

The fact that I would be expected to make a new image on these very walls was so far away in its possibilities that I could not bring myself to even think about ever doing such a thing. Having the magnificent herd in front of my eyes made it easy to push such thoughts away.

"Grandfather, does every initiate find their spirit-guide in the rites of manhood with such astonishing spirit-animals to commune with?" I asked, suddenly curious.

"Did you, Dear One?" He paused to let me think and then continued. "As seers and shamans in the Mother's service we can only point the way. We can only bring others to the edge of the Abyss. Each soul must desire to hear and commune with their animal-guides before the powers will answer and come forth to meet them. The beauty or simplicity of an image does not change that and only helps to bring the soul along to its own moment of transformation. Just as you reached out your hand to touch the Mother's hand and just as you reached out to touch the spirit-animals here that moved your heart, we must, each one, reach out to the powers as our hearts prompt us. But if a heart has not yet been opened, it will be difficult to find one's animal-guide here before this spirit-herd or in any other place."

* * *

The Grandfather led our way past the almost perfectly round entrance of what I knew to be the mouth of the Lodge of the Dark Mother. We passed close enough to see a large red dot marking the left-hand portal of the round and rather narrow opening into the deepest part of the whole Cave of the Bear Mother. After passing by the entrance, the Grandfather followed a path that turned to the right at a point where engraved white spirit-animals again began appearing on hanging flaps of rock above our heads. We had completed the Grand Round of the Hunter's Lodge of White Spirits and the beginning of the Black Lodges of the Cave. Now we are on our way back to the Navel of the Cave. I know exactly where I am!

If we had walked the path to the right, against-the-sun, around the Navel, we would never have seen the engraved spirit-animals that now appeared above our heads. First to appear was a single white mammoth, followed by one of the only red images in the White Lodges—a single red bear—then another white mammoth followed by a white reindeer. Soon, we stood again at the edge of the great Navel of the Cave just at the point where the nine white Mammoth Mothers had been made. We had come back to the beginning point of the first holy round of the White Lodge.

But instead of following the edge of the Navel, which would have taken us back to the western wall, the Grandfather began following a trail that turned sharply to the left. It led us to the single stone step up into the Lodge of the Mother's Heart once again. We made our way past the patch of white penis rocks and on around to the bedraggled white Cross of the All Father and the three red dots. Finally, we ended our long, winding way before the central Hearth of the Ordeals in the middle of the Lodge of the Mother's Heart. We truly had come full circle through an incredible maze of trails and holy rounds overflowing with the white spirit-powers.

"The hearth-fire is only a few coals, Grandfather. What should I do now?" I asked.

"Why, reignite it of course, my Daughter. Then we will continue with your initiation," he said simply.

He sat down in front of the hearth looking in the direction of the leaning cross and the three red dots on the eastern wall. I busied myself with relighting the fire from my lamp and stoking the hearth with more firewood from the stone bench.

"When you finish rekindling the fire, please sit and prepare yourself to commune with the powers of the Cave by removing your bag and horn and by placing your lamp in front of you facing the hearth and the Powers of Three,"

I did as I was directed and when I was seated, the Grandfather began to speak.

"This is the place where the boys are taught how to trance and commune with the spirit-powers of their hearts just as the girls are taught at the Animal of Red Dots in the Red Lodge," he began slowly. "Let us begin by concentrating on the three dots that, in this Lodge, represent the long-body of the red-life of the hunters as boys, adults and elders."

I knew what this involved. Staring intently at the three dots, I began taking the slow deep breaths of trance. A few boys and girls may have had some experience entering a trance and some may have had powerful dreams before initiation. Still other may have had the powers come upon them during the dance or in a fever. But I already had considerable practice in breathing and sitting still for very long periods of contemplation because of my Auntie.

"Good, I see that you know how to begin," he commended my preparations to trance.

Then the Grandfather began to speak his next lesson softly, the easier to guide me into trance.

"In the middle place between the worlds of the red-powers below and the white spirit-powers above, we shamans in trance leave our bodies, transform ourselves into our spirit-guides and travel to all the worlds. But we must be protected whither we fly," he said.

I thought this was my signal to start spinning my own spirals of protection. I was actually very good at this by now having trance-chanted with my Auntie many times as she prepared for healings. But before I could begin, the Grandfather continued his instruction.

"The fathers or uncle-mentors sit behind the boys. The White Brotherhood will always sit in a semi-circle facing east toward the red Powers of Three and the white Tree of Life in the center of yonder wall," he began while I continued my breathing.

My eyes had quickly tired of focusing on the central red dot and were now closed listening intently to the Grandfather's every word.

"The mentors may assist the boys in learning to trance, but the Grandfather or Grandmother of the Rites should always use their own companion's voice to guide the boys into this first trance. I will begin when my guide is ready to speak through me," he explained.

After only a few deep breaths, silent contemplations and just a little mumbling, the Grandfather began chanting with the voice of his otter-guide—a distinctive rustling sound in his voice like that of rushing water. I suppose I must be getting used to different voices coming out of the Grandfather because the otter-spirit's hissing voice did not startle or frighten me in the least. What was a surprisingly soothing sound quickly had me spinning to the right down to the earth and then spinning to the left up to the sky. In no time at all I was far, far away in a warm, swirling cloud of flashing dots, zig-zagging meanders and rolling, multi-colored light. I climbed threads of white light amid the sounds of rushing waters. The Grandfather's voice seemed so far away.

Time and place truly have no meaning in the trance-dream. So when I heard the Grandfather's voice urging me to come back and to open my eyes and be awake, I had no idea how much time had passed.

"May I know what you saw on your dream-journey? What you may have heard, Dear One?" the Grandfather said, still worlds away.

I looked around. I was having trouble focusing on things and remembering where I was, let alone remembering what I had seen. The Grandfather could see I was confused and having difficulty because he took out a bottle gourd from his bag, unstopped it and held it to my lips.

"Here, Dear One," I thought I heard him say. "You have flown very high, my Daughter. Take this Water of Life. It will help you return and will hold you again to Earth Mother," he said gently.

I sipped from the gourd.

All I could think to ask was, "Where did the water and the gourd come from?"

"I went to the Lodge of Living Waters to prepare it for you, Dear One. You have been in trance for a very long time. The cold water always helps those who fly so high and so far to return to the World of Light," he replied. "Here, take these as well."

The Grandfather handed me three pieces of the roots that my mother had packed in my bag. I chewed on them and drank the water. Soon I began to feel more clear-headed.

After a few more moments the Grandfather asked gently, "Do you remember anything you saw or heard or felt while traveling in the many worlds of the powers, my Daughter?"

"Yes," I said and I told him everything I could remember about the glowing, flashing lights and the dots and the meandering colors and the sounds of rushing water.

The Grandfather's disappointment could not be masked when he said, "You saw no visions of Horse Mother? ... of Lion Mother? Did any other messenger come to you, my Daughter? Bison Father?" he asked with fading hope.

"No, Grandfather; I'm sorry," I apologized, not quite sure for what.

"No, no," he replied quickly. "Do not feel sorry or apologize. The powers come forth to those they will and when they will. We cannot direct or even ask for their appearance or the hearing of their voices. I think we should both rest a while—there is much left for you to endure, Dear One."

With no argument in me, I lay down right where I had been sitting. I tucked my legs in and rolled up in the bearskin robe against the chill, my bare feet towards the little hearth fire. I was so full of spirit-fire and excitement that I did not think I could rest let alone sleep.

The last thing I remember before I drifted into dreamless sleep was the Grandfather adding more tallow oil to my lamp. It sputtered silently where it had been placed near my head.

CHAPTER 11.
TRIALS AND REVELATIONS

HOW LONG I SLEPT I cannot say. As I opened my eyes, still snugly wrapped in Bear Mother's thick black fur, the Grandfather was tending the hearth to keep the small fire alive.

He turned, saw me watching him and said, "Ah, good. You are awake. Are you ready to continue your initiation, my Daughter?"

"Yes, Grandfather, I am ready. I feel wonderful!" I blurted. Suddenly I felt awake, alive and full of spirit-fire.

The Grandfather hesitated with brows furrowed. I could tell he was reluctant to go on.

After another moment of hesitation he said, "Very well, my Daughter. Don your robe, stand and I will teach you the Hunter's Song of Dispelling Fear."

He began the song—in its words very close to the Women's Song of Dispelling Fear—pausing only long enough for me to sing each line after him.

Fear not the stabbing horn
It is only the Mother's embrace.
Fear not the trampling hoof
It is only the Mother's embrace.
Fear not the bloody fang
It is only the Mother's embrace.

Fear not the winter storm
It is only the Mother's embrace.
Fear not the summer drought
It is only the Mother's embrace.
Fear is the killer of a peaceful heart
Therefore, Oh Noble One,
Let go thy terror of what is to come
Let go what has gone before.
We and the Mother are one
It is only the Mother's embrace.

"Keep singing the song in your heart as we begin this first trial of your initiation," he said comfortingly.

The Grandfather moved to the stone bench behind us and brought the willow rod back to the Hearth of the Ordeals where I waited patiently for him.

"Come around to the other side of the hearth and face the white Tree of Life and the red Powers of Three," he instructed while trying to hide the small willow rod behind his back.

"You should know that a freshly cut sapling will be brought in for the coming initiations, but this shriveled Tree of Life will serve our purposes."

While I moved around the hearth to the opposite side where the Grandfather stood, he bent down to prop the dry branch in a more upright position. He moved the stones of the pile around to hold it up and re-tied the short cross-arm that was about to completely fall off. Then the Grandfather turned to face me with the forlorn little cross and the three red dots at his back.

"Neither hunters nor seers know pain," he began. "Hunters have no fear of body-pain or suffering so you must not cry out as you receive the Nine Lashes of the white willow rod. It is the very willow whose bark eases pain—the inside and the outside of the one thing. Please remove your robe," he said with growing sadness in his voice as I dropped my bearskin robe to the ground.

Now, this is something I never expected. Nobody told me about this! My father has never beaten me or even slapped me, which is more than I can say for many men in the camp and the

women and children of their lodges. In fact, I have only seen my
father strike my mother once in my whole life. It was completely
unlike my father to do anything violent to any of us. These and
other thoughts rambled around in my head waiting for the first
blow to fall.

But instead of the whistle of the willow branch, the Grandfather continued speaking.

"Daughter, as a woman, you will know the pain of bringing
new life through the bearing of your children. But we men will
never know such suffering of the red-body in order to bring forth
a new life. As Seer, you will find that many of life's lessons must be
learned through painful experience. Pain and the suffering of life
must be accepted as a matter of course by all of us. Because the
boys must also learn that suffering and pain are always part of
bringing forth any new way of living or thinking, each boy must
experience the Nine Lashes as part of his rebirth as a man and a
hunter. A man can never know what that is for a woman and how
close to returning to the Mother every woman comes every time
she gives birth to a child. The Nine Lashes of the willow rod will
help the men open their hearts to the women in their lives in compassion for what childbirth is to a woman. The boys must receive
the Nine Lashes at the hands of their own fathers or unclementors in order to become men who can show courage in the
face of pain. All hunters suffer and endure much to bring the
Mother's abundance to feed the People and this is the first lesson
of manhood for every boy. To receive the Nine Lashes with courage before their brothers in the hunt is to ignite the white spiritpowers of the head as the leader and guide of the urges, hungers,
desires and pleasures and pains of the red-body, whose one goal is
always to avoid pain of all and every kind. To receive the Nine
Lashes without showing any feeling or reaction is to become the
son of one's father and no longer to be a little child crying in pain
at the mother's knee at every small injury. In turn, each initiate will
grasp the white Tree of Life with both hands to fully expose the
boy's naked back to the willow rod."

"Grandfather, if I may ask a small question?" I broke in. "Is
the holy branch of willow or laurel?"

Stupid to be asking such trivial questions at a moment like this!

"It is laurel, my Apprentice, as laurel is the most holy of all the tree-sisters to the All Mother. The laurel not only gives us outer bark to cover our lodges, but provides her inner bark for food and bark cloth, wood for our cooking fires and even large seeds to fill our bellies. There is no more holy tree than this and so it is made into the white Mother's Cross of Life."

"Thank you, Grandfather. The remaining leaves are so shriveled and are so few on the Holy Branch I could not decide what kind of tree is used."

Again I was trying to forestall the inevitable with irrelevant questions I already knew the answers for.

"The cross of laurel is a sign of the Mother's Tree of Life. It is cut afresh for each season's initiations, as I have said. Each boy firmly grasps the rod giving him courage and straightening his back in the pride and honor of a manhood fittingly earned. The lash is willow stripped of its green outer bark to reveal the white rod within. Each mentor whips their initiate in turn, in full view of all the other age-mates and mentors. As Seer, you should know this rite is also to teach that everything the Mother has made can be used to harm or to heal depending on our choice. The same willow that soothes pain in the hands of a healer now causes pain in the hands of the boy's father. The boys are to learn courage in the face of suffering and must never cry out. To cry out is to bring great shame on the boy, on his mentor and on his close kin," he said solemnly.

I was so stunned that I was about to be whipped by the Grandfather I could not speak. All words had flown from my half-opened mouth. All I knew was that I had to do what I must to get through this with my dignity and honor in tact. Without even thinking, I began to sing to myself, running the fear dispelling song of the hunters over and over in my head.

"My Daughter, you will not grasp the Holy Branch as the boys do. Please cover your breasts with your arms. And pull your hair up to fully expose your back," the Grandfather instructed with perfectly controlled emotion.

I pulled the horse tail of my hair around and let it fall between my breasts to cover my woman's necklace of bones and teeth. I folded my arms across my chest. I looked up into the brimming sad eyes of the Grandfather who stood facing me, his back to the Tree of Life and the Powers of Three. As he pulled his arm back, I closed my eyes and grasped my arms around my body as tightly as I could just waiting for what was coming.

The first blow stung like a thousand wasps. The supple willow rod wrapped around to lash all the way from the back of my upper left arm across my naked back to my right arm folded protectively across my breasts. I winced reflexively and gasped in pain, but did not cry out. The words of the Song to Dispel Fear began to rush through my lips in a whisper. The words of solace were a fast-flowing stream, splashing loudly in my head and blotting everything out.

I tensed every muscle as the second searing lash raised welts across my back. It may have broken the skin too. But when the third lash whistled through the stillness with the shriek of a bull-roarer, the very voice of the All Mother, my soul had already flown. The remaining lashes were no more to me than donning a doeskin shirt. Still, it took all the determination I had not to scream out loud with each blow.

I did not cry out, but the racking sobs that accompanied each stroke of the willow now echoed from the walls of the Heart Lodge. Only after all nine strokes had finished lashing my bare skin did I realize it was not I who cried out in agony.

It was the Grandfather who wept at lashing his imagined Beloved's flawless back so cruelly. It was over soon enough, but the Grandfather could not cease his pitiful wailing and begging my forgiveness.

It was no mystery to me why, between his tortured sobs, the Grandfather kept repeating, "Forgive me. I was not there! Forgive me. I was not there!"

I should have just sat down and waited quietly until the Grandfather regained his composure. But I could only think how humiliated he must be. Weeping in front of a mere girl, seer-initiate or not. My heart went to him. My soul went to him.

I don't know why I did it, but I reached out to touch his hand and speak words of comfort.

"Dearest Grandfather, there is no need for you, of all people, to ask forgiveness of me. Even if I were your Beloved, you did nothing to harm or offend me in any way. *If* I were she, I would have long since forgiven you for something you did not do, and could not have changed, my dearest Grandfather."

Between the gasping sobs he managed to get out, "No, no ... I do have many regrets ... much to be forgiven. I did not say fare-well. I did not tell her that my heart would always be one with hers. I did not tell her I loved her above all others. We could not com-plete the circle of our life together. I was not there to protect her as an honorable man should protect his family!" he wept uncontrol-lably.

I knew any further words would be useless and that he would just have to shed enough tears to drain his heart of all the sorrow he had carried for so long. I continued to hold his hand even while I clenched my jaws and pushed the dull throbs of pain from the lashing out of my thoughts.

"Forgive me for shaming myself in front of you," he said after finally regaining control. "I am the Grandfather of the Bear People and should never behave this way."

He spoke to me in a hoarse whisper, the tears still streaming down his cheeks, choking his words.

"My beloved Grandfather, I promise thee, there is nothing to forgive. I know why thou weepest. And I know the Mother weeps with thee at thy sorrow," I said, trying to comfort him with honor-ific words that came unexpectedly and spontaneously from my own mouth.

I pulled the black robe back up over my shoulders to cover my nakedness. The welts and small cuts immediately began to send sharp jabs through me as the bearskin transferred its salty residues to my wounds from how many sweaty, bleeding backs I could not guess. My tears brimmed and almost flowed over but, ironically, the rising pain in the welts on my back was the only thing that kept me from crying aloud. In truth, I was almost weeping, not for my throbbing back, but for the overwhelming sadness in my heart for the Grandfather's suffering of the soul. The Grandfather is, after all has been spoken, a man like any other.

The Grandfather looked into my eyes, saw I was about to be-gin crying myself and said, "Come, my Daughter. I will dress your wounds as a hunter dresses his companion's wounds while upon the hunt. It seems that this good Apprentice has taught the Grandfather a great lesson in the Mother's Cave this day. It is a lesson that could be learned in no other way and taught by no other teacher. You are truly the Daughter of My Heart and I thank you, Dear One."

I was confused and could not reply, not to mention how embarrassed I felt at hearing such words from one of the Thrice Born. The Grandfather instructed me to drop the robe again and turn my back to him. I said nothing as I turned around to show him my bruised and bleeding back. As I stood waiting, the Grandfather withdrew a bone container of what I knew would be yellow ochre from his bag. He turned me slightly toward the hearth fire, the better to see places where the skin had been broken. He began to apply small amounts of the healing powder to his finger and then to my broken skin. After the yellow ochre had staunched any bleeding, he unfolded a packet of willow bark salve from his bag and began to apply the soothing balm to my livid welts.

The yellow ochre powder had the faint smell of the healing steam from the hot springs of Serpent Father. Everyone knew yellow ochre could staunch bleeding and prevent wounds from festering. And so every hunter carries his own bone container of the yellow Horse Mother's healing ochre upon every hunt. But most hunters had to obtain the willow bark-infused salve from a healer because the making of it was no simple process. Fluffy, pure white fat for such balms must be rendered in very hot water, I have learned from my healer-Auntie. A lot of willow bark must be collected, chopped up, pounded and the oil pressed from the mashed up bark. The resulting oil gives the salve a slightly green color and the scent of willows growing along the river.

"I wonder if the salve to soothe my wounds came from the bark of the very tree or willow bush from which the rod was taken?" I thought in words to myself as the Grandfather gently smoothed the healing balm on each lash mark.

As the salve was applied with a soft touch, the Grandfather slowly regained his composure and began to speak again as my Mentor.

"In the initiations of the boys, such wound treatment is strongly encouraged. But many of the mentors will not have prepared any willow salve. As Grandmother of the Rites you will have to bring it for them. It is good and healing that the mentors treat the wounds of the initiates they have bloodied. It is also good that the wounded forgive their mentors for inflicting such pain as you have already done without being prompted. A hunter should never lose control of their emotions as I unfortunately did just now. Please forgive me for not honoring you with my self control."

"There is nothing to forgive," I replied. "No one can hold such great grief inside forever, not even the Grandfather of the Bear People. Thank you, Thrice Born, for treating my wounds."

"That is well, my good Apprentice. It will not happen again."

The Grandfather spoke matter-of-factly, without emotion and intent on covering all my welts with the numbing willow salve. Good and healing for both of us, so it seemed, because his tears dried and he had completely returned to himself by the time the last welt had been soothed.

The application of the soothing salve completed, the Grandfather turned me around to begin a new blessing with both arms held out toward me, palms held up to the Mother.

"The Mother is with thee always, Dear One," he declared. "Come thou and receive the marks of thy kin as a hunter of the People of the Bear Mother," he intoned formally.

Taking one of my hands in his, he guided me back to the other side of the hearth to sit, once again, upon the bearskin robe cross legged. I sat, facing forward and without emotion toward the red Powers of Three and the white Tree of Life across the Hearth of the Ordeals.

* * *

"Those are the words you should speak to each initiate after the rite of anointing of the wounds with yellow ochre and willow salve is completed. Just as we have done, the mentors will come back around the hearth to their initiate's place to prepare for the marking of the 'new sons' with the father's kin-marks. As an initiated woman of the Bear-kin, you already have Bear Mother's marks in red on your right shoulder. But now you must have your red marks re-cut in black as a sign to all that you have also completed the trials of the hunter's initiations and have become one with the White Brotherhood of hunters," he explained apologetically.

I had always wondered why the men's kin-marks were in black while the women's were in red. Now I know. The agony of the whipping had begun to subside, but my pain-energy was pumping so rapidly I knew I would feel nothing of the marking.

"Yes, Grandfather. I am prepared. Let it be so," I said, giving my permission for him to proceed.

"Stand with thy two feet upon Earth Mother and bare thy right shoulder, ye Hunter of the Bear People," the Grandfather intoned as I stood and pulled the robe back to bare my right shoulder.

He wasted no time withdrawing from his bag a newly chipped white flint blade with a tiny, sharp point at one end. He turned me toward the fire to light my red shoulder mark. The color had already begun to fade and must have been barely visible to those poor old eyes. But the fine scars of the mark would always be there to the touch. The Grandfather began making a series of tiny cuts over the old red lines and scars: half of an egg-shaped circle with three straight lines between the outer half-circle to represent Bear Mother's five-clawed paw. By the time the Grandfather began rubbing finely crushed charcoal into the oozing cuts, a tiny rivulet of blood had reached my elbow and was just about to fall off in one big drop.

"Allow thy lifeblood to drip upon Earth Mother," he said in the most formal way when he noticed the blood running down my arm.

"Thou mayest also wipe your blood with thy finger and place it upon Earth Mother as a thank offering," he said distractedly in the same high-flown words.

He continued to dab and rub the charcoal into the fresh mark of the Bear-kin to completely obliterate the red in favor of the black of the hunter's body marks. His grisly task completed, I wiped the remaining blood off my elbow onto the ground, again covered my shoulder with the robe and sat down facing the hearth fire. The flames had begun to wane so I got up and added some wood to the blaze as the Grandfather sat cleaning my blood from his marking blade. He seemed completely recovered from the sadness and tears of the lashing.

"My Daughter," he said, holding up the little flint blade he had used to mark me. "The flint awls used by the mentors for marking their initiates should be newly made and very sharp. Otherwise, it will be more painful and bloody than is necessary. Flints used in the White Lodges should be of the finest white stone that can be obtained. Those that break or are no longer sharp should be left in the Great Cave as a thank offering to Bear Mother," he instructed further.

"How are you feeling, Dear One? Is there much pain?" he asked with real concern in his eyes.

His duties as Grandfather of the Nine Kin evidently were completed.

"There is no pain, my Grandfather," I said lying again.

I really had to stop this lying just so the Grandfather would feel less guilty at doing what was only his duty.

"I know all of this seems strange to have to put the boys through. But they all must undergo these ordeals without crying out in front of their fathers, uncles and age-mates to begin learning control of the hidden senses of their red-bodies by their heads, as I have said. Upon the hunt, every hunter must make the thoughts of the head his leader at all times. Otherwise, else how should he know—when he sees a thing out upon the Plain—to go towards it or to run away for his safety? It is true the eyes go searching for that which pleases the secret senses of the liver. But a shaman-of-the-hunt and all hunters must put their full attention upon what they are doing in the moment they are doing it and send the eyes searching for those things that are needful in the moment. A hunter's very life and the life of his companions and kin depend upon it. He cannot be thinking of injuries and pains of the past; he cannot be fearful of injuries or failures that may or may not come in the future, he must be looking for every sign and signal of what the partially hidden shape before him is. Is it prey or is it predator? Is the hunter to eat or be eaten? Upon seeing a thing or smelling a thing or hearing a thing, it is the head which will tell his liver to have fear. It is the head that tells the legs they are to run away. It is the hunter's eyes that will see the bent blade of grass, the hoof print or the broken twig that tells his head what hides in the tall brush ahead. It is his tongue that tastes the dung to tell the head whether it is a male or female creature he is following. It is the head which tells the arm to throw the killing spear. And finally it is the head that tells the heart to have kind feelings of love and gratitude for the animal-brother who is giving itself to him, even as the hunter's fevered body chases and slaughters without let. Those tender feelings of love for the Mother's children cannot be allowed to interfere with the work of the Mother. But they *must* be given full expression once the kill is made if the hunter is to let go his fearfully violent spirit-fires and return to himself as a hunter of the White Brotherhood and one of the human tribes again. Do you see, my Daughter?"

"Yes, Grandfather. I do understand. But how do the Nine Lashes accomplish that for the boys?" I asked.

"The brave acceptance of the Nine Lashes begins to build a door flap between the tender feelings of the heart for the Mother's children and the thoughts of the head. Men must learn to open and close that door flap in a proper way. My behavior just now was not proper as a grown man acting in the place of the Grandfather. Such displays of emotion are never proper in the midst of the hunt when the animal-messengers of the All Mother's spirit-power must be returned in order for the People to thrive. In fact, it can be very, very dangerous to be distracted by kind feelings for the animal-messengers we must kill. The men must also be assisted by other rites in their going out to slaughter and coming back to the every-day world of living with their beloved kin and friends waiting for them within the camps. As a healer and Seer of the People, you must learn to separate your feelings, your desires and urges from the thoughts of your head just as every hunter must do. "

"I do not understand, Grandfather. In speaking the words of healing am I not to love the other and have compassion for them? How can I close my heart to one who is suffering and who requests my assistance?"

"That is the delicate and difficult task we all must undertake as seers and shamans, Dear One. It is the Straight Path as narrow as a flint blade to know when to open the door flap to your heart and when to close it. In speaking the words of healing or giving the healing herbs, you must not see the illnesses and old injuries the sick one may be suffering. Nor should you see the beautiful gifts they may have given you. Neither should you see the kind and loving or hateful and angry words they may have spoken to you in the past. Like every hunter, you must have your attention focused completely on where you are and what it is you are doing. You must be entirely concentrated upon the healing words you are speaking and not what the future outcome of your healing may or may not be. You must only put your attention completely on what you are saying and doing because you are speaking to the Mother who is there within the sufferer in all her health and beauty and compassion. The Mother's bones are not broken, the Mother is not feverish; the Mother is never in pain. When you truly see the Mother in everyone you treat, they will surely be healed. As Seer, having truly seen the Mother in the faces of those you bless with your healing words and herbs, if they then choose to return to the Mother, then it will not injure your heart with thoughts of failure and loss. This is the first lesson of every seer who would heal the body or the mind of another. It is never a thing that is concerned with you or your feelings or your desires or what you have done or will do. Your focus should only and always be the Mother that dwells within the ailing or within the animal-messenger that is giving their red-life to us. Do you understand, Dear One?"

"Yes, Grandfather. I begin to see and understand what you are telling me. But how does the experience of pain in the body accomplish that?" I asked.

"The Nine Lashes is only the first lesson in deliberately, and with forethought, opening and closing your heart at a time that the white spirit-powers within tell you they should be opened or closed. It is a skill which is to be learned here and practiced for the rest of one's life before the door flap can be opened and closed at will. Think on this thing because then you will understand how doing such things as grasping the rod or covering your breasts and chanting the songs to dispel fear allows the white spirit-powers of the head to even control the pains and thirsts and desires and hungers of the red-body. One last thing, my beloved Daughter: do not build a lodge wall where the door flap of your heart should be. Many men do so and many women as well. To build an immovable wall there is to shut your soul off from the black spirit-powers of the Mother's Heart. That is to close yourself to the abundance and love and joy that comes from the joining of the head and the liver, as we have already discussed. Before we move on, do you have further questions, my good Apprentice?" he asked with eyebrows raised in anticipation.

"Well," I said, still thinking of how to word my next question. "If the Nine Lashes teaches us how to close the door flap of our feelings, what teaches us to open it?" I asked, pleased with my concise wording.

"This is a question from an Apprentice who is really thinking!" he complimented me with a smile.

"Let me explain it this way: When women are together do they not find it easy to talk of their own feelings and other matters of the heart, liver and head? I believe you do and I believe it is because you are women and have so much in common with each other. The abundance of the red spirit-powers in most women also gives you much ease in opening the door flap to your hearts. Women are close to and open their hearts to other women because you are with each other in your daily round. You talk to each other and you are mothers to all the children of the camp without restriction. But men are much more solitary creatures and must spend much of their time outside the lodges and away from their families as part of their daily round of hunting. Because of this, the men must be taught, and they must practice, opening up their hearts to other men. This is especially true for those gift-givers, close companions and close kin with whom they share the dangers and joys of the hunt. Upon the hunt each hunter must be able to trust, cooperate with and rely completely on his brothers, not only for success in the hunt but for the protection of his very life."

"How can that be done for men, my Grandfather?" I asked. "My father is as close-lipped as a mussel when he is in my mother's lodge."

Even as I finished speaking, I realized that the rare times when I had felt very close to my father, and those times he seemed to be more talkative with me, were those occasions when he took me with him on winter hunts for ibex and chamois in the mountains near the Middle Camp.

"Even bravely enduring the marking and the Nine Lashes is not enough to make a boy fully a part of the White Brotherhood and a hunter in harmony with and bound to other men for life. These trials of the red-body are just a beginning. The ordeals bring the hearts of the new men to a place where they will benefit greatly from the next revelation of the Heart Lodge," he began. "Are you willing to be taught, my Daughter?"

"I am your Apprentice, my Grandfather. Teach me what you would have me know," I said, giving my assent to hearing teachings that promised to be things known only to men.

"Daughter, as I have already said, no man hunts alone. Each hunter cooperates with and depends utterly upon the others of a hunting party for their very lives. Do not believe the stories of the shaman-of-the-hunt who, by his own powers, can easily charm the animals to lose their heads and follow the shaman to the waiting hunters unaware. Every hunt is difficult and dangerous and the hunters must be of one liver, one head and one heart if any hunt is to be successful. This is the lesson of the Bridge of Rainbows and the five rhinos who were seen to have ceased battling one another. They have aligned themselves in cooperative actions with the selected Leader of the Hunt. Because of the very nature of the hunt, the men must balance the liver and the head within the heart just as any woman must do. And we men must also learn to control our hidden hungers and secret senses with the clear thoughts of the head and to join them in harmony and balance within the heart just as women must do in appropriate ways and in their proper time. These things we must learn to do for our very survival and this involves creating close ties of the heart between the hunters. It is from that we come to respect and love and trust each other as brothers of the same Mother without reservation. It is the joining of the hearts of hunter-brothers that makes of these new men the White Brotherhood with whom they may share all things of the heart, head and liver without shame. All strong feelings of love or grief may be shared with hunter-companions freely and without dishonor. Even the tears of grief and loneliness may be shared among initiated hunters without shame. Without these close bonds between the hunters, they will not love and respect each other as brothers of the same mother. Neither will they love and respect the animal-messengers as children of the same Mother even while they give their red-bodies to be killed and become the life of the People. Can you understand that, my Daughter?" he asked.

"Yes, Grandfather, I begin to understand," I replied.

I was thinking of the gift-givers and companions of my own father, Roe Bear, and Auntie's husband, Bright Wolf—the two hunters of the Middle Camp I know the best. I knew not how life-friends behave differently upon the hunt from those who do not have such bonds between each other. But I do know, among hunters who are life-friends, that marriages are often proposed between their close kin, their gift-givers and hunting companions. I certainly could understand why hunters needed other men to talk to. How could any man live a happy life and not be able to share their feelings, fears and hopes the way we women do with someone? If I could not speak of my hurts and fears to other women I think I would burst open with sadness!

The Grandfather continued. "In the rites of the Red Lodge, you know that through the ordeal of the Hymen Stone the girls begin to recognize their oneness with Earth Mother as a receptive vessel and as a river of new life. In the initiations, the boys must also recognize their oneness with Sky Father as active, giving agents of their white-essence in proper ways. They must also learn to play their part in the creation of new life as they go through their trials and initiations of the White Lodge. During the boy's first guided trance here in the Lodge of the Heart, it is common for many of them to have erections."

"When do boys *not* have erections?" I blurted out. "What is so unusual about boys having hard penises in this place when they are always trying to hump everything that moves wherever they are?"

The Grandfather began to chuckle softly. "Yes, my Daughter, that is the way boys are."

"But Grandfather?" I stopped him in mid-sentence. "Do all men have erections while in trance? I have never seen a naked seer or shaman in the midst of a trance. Besides, how could anyone see a stiff snake under all those furs and clothing anyway?"

"Most men will have hard penises at one time or another in their trances. It often depends on how deep the trance is," he explained. "You already know how young men can get erections in the middle of blinking," he said with a little smile and a nod.

"What is more important—should you ever become the Grand-mother of the Rites and be obligated to conduct the men's initia-tions here—is that the boys must learn to connect their nature as givers of male essence to create new life and being receivers of the bodies of the animals to sustain the lives of their kin as one great circle of the red-life of the World of Light. To do that, all of the boys and their mentors should be encouraged to stroke themselves and spill their essence upon the ground in honor of Earth Mother. The spurting fountains of the white essence from a man's snake is the sign of the white spirit-powers moving over and giving their life to the red-spirits in the act of creating all the worlds," he ex-plained as my jaw dropped in amazement.

"The boys rarely need any encouragement to do this. Many of them will rub their penises spontaneously during trance completely unaware of who is around them," he said, telling me more than I wanted to hear.

Now *that* was an idea which shocked me even more than the idea of the boys putting their man-essence upon the ground. Nei-ther boys nor girls like to be seen by others when joining in sex or playing with themselves.

"Grandfather? Do you mean they all stroke their snakes in front of each other? Why is that so important?" I asked incredu-lously.

"It is part of creating the ties of friendship and trust between the men," he answered, perfectly serious.

"After the Nine Lashes and the giving of kin-marks, many of the rites are intended to encourage the boys to befriend who they will. They are encouraged to become lifelong companions of the heart with at least one other boy or Uncle of the camp who is not their father. Some men and boys may become companions during the initiations and create gift-giver friendships during the men's rites that will last their whole life. These friendships may or may not include joining in sex whenever they are together. Many such companions share a tent or sleeping skins at Gatherings and many more share their bed rolls during the hunt. That is something for the open heart of each hunter to decide for themselves. It is never for any others to try and prevent such connections of the heart to form between the hunters."

I had not a word upon my tongue. My head was spinning with visions of my own father joining in sex with his gift-givers and hunter brothers. The Grandfather, too!

"If you are called to lead or assist in these men's rites of the Heart Lodge, you should not be embarrassed and you should never reject them. Otherwise, the men will have no heart-bonds as you women do who share the moon-blood, who work daily with each other in the camps and share all the trials and pains of child-birth and who are the mothers of the camps in their Red Sister-hood."

Seeing that I was completely unnerved by all of this, he continued speaking.

"Dear One, I know it is difficult for female seers to understand this, but this is all necessary to help the boys open themselves to the spirit-fire of their hearts whether the powers come forth during the men's rites or later in their life. And, if a boy is two-spirited, this is often the time he discovers that about himself."

"May I ask a question, Grandfather?" I had recovered enough from my surprise that more respectful words came out of my mouth again.

"Yes, of course, Dear One. Ask whatever you will," he replied.

"I have heard of women my age, younger girls, and even some of the boys who have been forced to join in sex with older men," I said matter-of-factly.

Actually, I had no direct knowledge of such a woman or girl in our camp, but I had heard stories and had to ask.

"How do the boys avoid being forced to join in sex with older, stronger men during the initiations?" I queried.

"Daughter, that is exactly why these rites are performed before the whole White Brotherhood of the boys and their mentors. With the boy's fathers and uncles present, the boys know they are free to do what they will and with whom they will and will never be forced. Some stay in the Heart Lodge wrapping up together in their robes with one friend for mutual warmth and private conversation. Some go to other parts of the White Lodges or to the wall of black spirit-animals, to quest and to be alone with each other. Some make no friends at all and yet others become gift-givers and will join in sex with several of the boys and men during the initiations. The only restriction placed upon joining between the men is that they must spill their white essence upon Earth Mother as you were required to put your blood upon the ground."

The Grandfather, hopefully, concluded his instruction in the private ways of the Brotherhood of Hunters.

But that was not to be and the Grandfather went on.

"After the boys have spent their desires for sex and most have returned to the Heart Lodge, the final phase of the rites will involve solitary quests to whatever part of the Cave each boy is drawn to. Each will be taken by his mentor to the lodge where his heart leads him. There he will be left alone to contemplate, and hopefully, to commune with his personal animal-guide, mostly for the first time in his young life. Each will have learned the Hunter's Song to Dispel Fear and most will get a good deal of practice reciting the Song when their lamps go out—you already know how easy it is for the flame to die and leave you shivering with fear in the overwhelming darkness. The boys must learn to overcome their fear of being alone in the dark with the powers of the Great Cave. Finally, the mentors will gather the boys back into the Heart Lodge to tell funny stories, to watch the unmasking of the bison wrestlers and to spend more time exploring the Cave alone or with their new brothers or gift-giver companions. They are encouraged to dance the dances and sing the songs their personal animal-guides may have taught them in their dream-trances and to sing and recite the stories they have learned to the rest of the mentors and new men. That is the usual order of the rites for the initiations of the hunters. But the journey you will now take is one very few new men ever choose to experience."

"What do you mean, my Grandfather?" I asked, the dread rising to choke off any more words.

What could possibly be more fearsome that few men would ever choose to do than what has already been done to me?

"Daughter, do you remember how White Lynx was taken to the Womb of White Spirits and how a girl who has a powerful appearance of her red companion-spirit is taken to the Red Womb of the Hunters for solitary contemplation?" he asked.

I said, "Yes, I understand why that would be so."

"Well, the Lodges of the Hunters all have places where those boys who are powerfully drawn by certain powers can go for solitary quests and contemplation, as I have said. Two-spirit boys, by their very twin souls, bridge the worlds and so they are likely to be drawn all the way back through the Butterfly Passage to the red-powers of the Red Womb of the Hunters. Yet others will be drawn to the powers of the Womb of the White Net, which you have also experienced. But only a very small number of the most courageous boys will be drawn to the Lodge of Black Spirits and the wombs of the Dark Mother to be found there. Even the hearts of many shamans and seers are not prepared to enter those deepest parts of the Great Cave. But, for you, Dear One, my dream-vision has shown me that you must enter the deepest part of the Great Cave, which is the Lodge of Black Spirits. That is our place of destiny and the special lodge of power of our greatest adventure. Are you ready to enter the very womb of the black spirit-powers, my Daughter?" he asked portentously.

"Yes, my Grandfather. Let it be so. I know the way back to the entrance and I will lead the way," I said in mock courage.

My heart raced, thumping in my neck with the anticipation of the unknown and what might be encountered within the deepest part of the Cave.

* * *

Having already walked the three holy rounds of the White Lodge, the way back to the entrance of the Dark Mother's cavern would be easy to find. The Grandfather did not object when I led out from the hearth fire of the Heart Lodge in a straight line skirting the edge of the white stone penises. I went directly to the rock step leading into the next chamber and went down into the Navel of the Cave.

"Slow your steps, my Daughter. I cannot keep pace with you," the grandfather called out from far behind.

I went back to the step to give any needed assistance. Of the white spirit-animals that could be seen when coming from deeper inside the Cave, only the staring Owl Father and the nine white Mammoth Fathers on the southern side of the deep hole that is the Navel were visible. I then led the Grandfather along the rim of the first ring of bear skulls which lay just outside the entrance to the Womb of the Dark Mother—a fact I had not noticed before. As we passed by the edge of the skull circle to stand facing northeast toward the charcoal-black entrance to the Black Lodge, the Grandfather's voice brought me to a halt.

"Daughter," he called. "Come back a few paces and tell me what you see."

The Grandfather raised his torch high. The flickering light revealed several black dots, rods and a small black cross next to a large black butterfly painted on some folds of rock a few paces back and above the round entrance to the Lodge of Black Spirits. This wing of stone with its images and signs in black was only visible when coming directly to the entrance of the Black Lodge from the Heart Lodge. I hadn't seen these signs the first time we came this way because we were coming from the other direction.

"I see the female dots and male rods of trance, a black cross of the Four Mothers and a butterfly of transformation—the spirals of trance," I said, listing rapidly what I saw with my eyes.

"Yes, Dear One, but because the image is black, properly, it is a *moth* of transformation," he corrected. "It is a sign of the union of red and white powers into a black moth that only comes out in the dark—a sign of the opening of the heart to the red and white powers. The meaning of the Mother's cross of black is also different from the red and white crosses we have already seen. Notice how all four arms are equal in length? They are unlike the Cross of Red in the Red Lodge and the Cross of White in the Heart Lodge both of which have one long vertical arm."

The Grandfather reached up to run his finger over the black sign.

"What do you think that means, my intelligent Apprentice," he asked playfully.

"I think you will have to give me another lesson, my wise Grandfather," I teased in return.

"Then come, let us sit and I will instruct you before we enter the Black Lodge of the Dark Mothers, Dear One."

And so we sat together I, again on the ground, and the Grandfather, sitting on a large rock only a few paces from the gaping darkness that was the entrance to the place of deepest mysteries.

"The black moth indeed represents the twin spirals of trance and of movement from one world to the next. But the Dark Mother's Lodge and the black wombs found within especially signifies that single point where the spirals come together—within the heart and within the shaman flying in trance. As Seer, the black cross with equal arms will also remind you that there is always the Fifth Mother of the Center within your own heart. This is where the All Mother's creation comes together again after their separation as Powers of Two. The Lodge of Black Spirits contains the holy lodges of the black Lion Mother and is the place of the union of all the worlds—the three Worlds of Light of our experience, but also of all the worlds that have ever been or are yet to come. And more than anyone else who may be drawn to the Dark Mother, this is the special place of those upon whom she has placed her holy mark in their right eye, Dear One," he said pointedly looking directly at me.

"This is why you have been chosen for this great work and why you have been brought to this place at this moment," he said, still staring at my lion-eye.

The thought of a Dark Lion Mother within *me* sent a chilly shudder up my spine.

"The Black Lodge is the Womb of All the Worlds. It is a sign of that place out of which all white-life and all red-life comes and it is the sign of the Abyss of the Silence back into which all life goes. The Dark Lion Mother's lodge is the place of the coming together of that which was separated. It is the re-joining of all the Powers of Two into the One. It is the oneness of life and death, male and female, hunter and hunted, above and below, light and dark, earth and sky, yesterday and tomorrow," he explained in hushed tones.

We both gazed intently at the river-like herds of black animals rushing out of and back toward the equally black entrance to the Black Lodge. The entrance yawned like a vast mouth eating back and giving birth to the world simultaneously. We watched as the marvelous herds of black animals spilled out of the entrance, stampeding into the darkness beyond our torchlight. From this vantage point, some of the spirit-animals were also rushing toward the entrance. In a jumble of legs and horns and haunches and humps, they rushed toward the opening in their awesome Return to the Mother. I was beginning to be overwhelmed again, but listening closely to the Grandfather's words helped distract me from the vastness of it all.

"Now, my Daughter, hear the words of my mouth, for I will tell thee the greatest secret of the Mother's Great Cave. It is why the Ancients made their spirit-animals here and not in some other cave," the Grandfather began.

"Yes, Grandfather," I said with rapt attention. "I am willing to learn."

"As hunter-initiate, you have now walked every part of the Cave except this deepest chamber. And while we may feel we are coming into a deep cavern in the ground from the middle World of Light above, we have actually come into the very body of the All Mother lying on her back. She has poured the wordless Silence of the Void into these spaces here so that her body-form is laid out in the various chambers as a teaching for seers and shamans. In doing so, the Mother has made for the People a most holy place for our rites of initiation and transformation. By coming into these spaces between the solid stone, we have come into the very entrails of the Mother. But before you ask, let me explain and you will understand because one of your many gifts is finding your way and feeling the directions in which you have traveled," he said.

"The entrance to the Great Cave is the mouth of the Mother and so is called the Portal of the Mother's Mouth. We came in to the Cave just as food might be eaten and water drunk. Just as with the images of the Mother we make, the Great Cave has no head or the face is a blank and veiled face. But the whole World of Light where we see and hear and taste and smell and think with our own heads *is* the very head of the All Mother, which is the 'head' of this Great Cave. From the mouth of the Cave, the passage of entrance to the Skull Portal is the Mother's 'throat'. The two red and white chambers of the women's Red Lodge on the right, and the Plain of the Bear Mother on the left, are the Mother's great 'breasts' nourishing both our red and white-spirits just as our mothers give us their milk to nourish our bodies. The Mother has two arms just as we of the human tribes each have two arms. Her 'right arm' is the Red Womb of the Hunters jutting out from the eastern wall of the Plain of Bones. Her 'left arm' is the side-chamber sticking out from the western wall of the Plain of Bones. The Mother's 'left arm' goes from the single red dot to the three red Bear Mothers of creation. Thence to the Rock of the Leopard Mother, the powers of ending and beginning joined as one, is at the level of the 'heart' just beneath the Mother's 'left armpit', where your own beating heart resides. The Mother's 'gullet' is the Passage of Butterflies that connects the Red Lodges and the White Plain of Bones to the 'heart' of the Mother from which we have just come. The great hole at our back is the Mother's 'navel', a sign of the connection to our Source, which is the All Mother, just as we our bound to and nourished by the mothers of our red-bodies. The Mother has two legs as well. Her 'left leg' is the Womb of the White Net at the northwestern end of the Cave. The white Mammoth Fathers and the White Net of Life there are where her 'feet' would be. But the All Mother has only pointed legs and no feet to connect her to the Earth for she *is* the Earth Mother and stands upon herself. That is why, when the All Mother is depicted in human form, she never has feet, as you must already know. The 'right leg' of the Mother at this northeastern end of the Cave is this Lodge of Black Spirits which we are about to enter. The opening to the Black Lodges where we now sit is the very 'vulva' of the All Mother, the great mass of black animals here, her 'pubic hair'. This Great Cave is the holy place of the All Mother to which the People were dreamed and which has made of us one People of the Bear Mother. The Great Cave is the Mother's very body-form laid out in the stony flesh of the earth and filled with the life-giving waters of the Below and blessed with the emptiness of the Silence of the Abyss," he concluded.

In stunned silence I saw it all in the eyes of my mind and knew the Grandfather had revealed to me a great mystery.

"Do you now understand why the Ancients made the spirit-animals as they have, where they have, in this most holy and special of all caves to instruct us in the ways of the Mother? Do you now understand why the Ancient Ones were dreamed to this Valley and not another? Do you know why we are the People of the Bear Mother and not some other?" he asked quietly.

Almost speechless, all I could say was, "Yes, Grandfather. I see it all and understand."

* * *

"Do you see it with your head, my Daughter, or do you see it with your heart?" he asked gently.

"I don't know, my Grandfather. What do you mean *see it with my heart*? I think I only know how to see with my head."

"Let me ask you one question and I will be able to explain it better. You learned much about being a woman at the Rock of the All Mother and through the trials of the Red Lodge, but have you, as yet, experienced a joyful joining in sex with a man, my Daughter?"

The Grandfather's strange question rolled around my head searching for its answer.

"Why, yes Grandfather," I answered honestly and without hesitation. "The cousins of the camp always want to touch my pute and my breasts. I have played with them and have allowed them to put their penises inside me too. Is that what you mean?"

I hesitated to say any more because I knew that was not what the Grandfather was asking.

"No, my Daughter. That is not what I mean. What I mean is, have you desired with the hunger of the secret senses to join in sex with a full-grown man? An initiated hunter? Have you joined with a man that made your heart sing? A man whose touch made your skin quiver and your heart jump inside your chest in ecstasy?" he pressed.

I was being coy and withholding what must already have been known to the Grandfather. Nothing happens in the camps between any two people without everyone knowing about it before the sun goes down. No more lying to the Grandfather! Besides, I couldn't begin to imagine what joining in sex with Brown Bull could possibly have to do with this Cave and my initiation as Seer? In truth, for one summer and one winter season now, I had forced Brown Bull's memory from my head. It was all too painful to even think about.

"Yes, Grandfather," I relented. "I have joined in sex with Brown Bull of the Bison-kin. It was during the last Great Gathering."

"I know of the man," he said. "His father is an honored hunter, well-respected by many. Brown Bull was initiated a few seasons before you became a woman. I remember him for reasons that will soon become known to you. I also know that he has become a powerful bison wrestler, is a good and honest hunter and a skilled tracker," he praised my erstwhile lover.

It did not seem that the Grandfather was aware of the other things Brown Bull was renowned for. Just the sound of his name brought it all back to me in a rush of passionate joy, heartache and disappointment. I had worked so long and so hard to build a lodge wall to my heart whenever thoughts of Brown Bull came in. It seems I have only managed to make the barrier to my heart an open door flap.

"Can you tell me more of your time together?" the Grandfather probed.

"Yes, Grandfather, I will tell you of our meeting," I said, considering what I should tell and what I should not.

I could tell him every tiny detail of our meeting as they were all coming back to me in a great wave of memory and pushed-down emotion. Still, I couldn't understand why any of this mattered to the Grandfather.

I first saw Brown Bull as people crowded around the wrestling ground at last year's Great Gathering. As the bison wrestlers always are, he was naked except for a tiny wrestler's loinskin and pads of leather strapped to his knees and elbows. He wore black and red paint on his body and face, a big sign of the Bison-kin drawn on his wide, strong back.

The women love to watch the wrestling because we all get to see the strongest, most handsome men at the Gathering—and almost completely naked. What better way to compare the body and man-rod of a husband or lover to the wrestlers? It was also much easier to meet a new lover or prospective husband among the crowd of spectators. If fortunate, one might even meet one of the wrestlers. It was always a time of the fox-trickster when women tell jokes and make fun of the men and their endowments—or lack thereof!

No one made fun of Brown Bull. He was too handsome, strong and had a man-rod as big as his namesake. Or so we all decided as the loinskins loosened—which they did during almost every match—allowing the man's snake to flop out if it were big enough! He looked so strong to me with his massive legs and buttocks from all the walking and running of the hunt. His shoulders and arms bulged with strong muscles from throwing spears and, obviously, from all of this wrestling. He was the most beautiful man I had ever seen. I had never before felt a hungry feeling in my pute when looking at a man.

I worked my way around the edge of the crowd nearest the wrestlers and did everything I could to catch this particular wrestler's eye. At one point, when the two wrestlers were grappling with each other, heads nestled into each other's necks trying to get a hold that would allow them to throw the opponent on his back and win, he looked directly at me and our eyes locked. This momentary distraction allowed his opponent to pick him up and throw him down. He landed on his back with a great "o-o-o-o-mph" and a cloud of dust. I cared less than a single blink of my eye that he had lost the match. As he dejectedly left the wrestling circle caked with dirt, blood dripping from a battered nose, bison robe and leather satchel over one arm, loinskin askew, his manhood flopping, he motioned with a little toss of his head and a crooked smile that I should follow him.

Follow I did. In only a few paces I caught up to him as he walked the little path leading toward the hot springs of the Serpent Father. No one could have failed to notice us leaving the wrestling circle together, but I did not care. Besides, the Great Gathering is the best of all times for young women and men to meet each other and to decide if they are suitable for each other as mates. There are few other times of the winter season when the unmarried men and women from all the Nine Kin are in the same place at the same time and can even meet each other face-to-face. Even those marriage matches that are proposed by mothers must be agreed to by those who will marry and so some meeting between the prospective mates must be arranged. The Great Gathering is almost the only time of the whole year when the whole People can do that with ease.

"I met Brown Bull at last season's Great Gathering when he was wrestling. We went to the Serpent Springs together," was all I actually shared with the Grandfather.

"And what happened at the hot springs?" he asked, knowing full well what happens to young men and women when they go to the Serpent Springs together.

As I joined him to walk the trail together, Brown Bull turned around abruptly and stopped short in the midst of the path bringing us face-to-face.

He opened his smiling lips to ask, "Will Little Sister greet the Mother in me?"

To which I said, "Of course, Elder Brother."

I pressed my forehead to his in greeting.

The smell of him, the sweat, the dirt, and the body paint made an excited knot form in my stomach. The knot proceeded to run up and down my body between pute and liver—or heart. He grasped me by the shoulders and held me back at arm's length to catch me with his penetrating gaze.

He must have seen the lion-eye, and so to break that steady glare and his grip on my shoulders, I looked down, stepped back and asked him what his name was. Then I asked all about bison wrestling. He asked my name and in no time at all Brown Bull was holding my hand leading me down the trail.

He led me toward the very spot and the same flat rock where the Grandfather had taken me to bathe and purify ourselves before entering the Great Cave.

Whenever Brown Bull would look at me, he always held my gaze for what seemed like forever. He would not look away even for a moment. And I could not look away from staring deeply into those dark blue eyes either. I knew even then that with those dark blue eyes I was being pulled inexorably into the depths of a bottomless pool of blue-black water. Those darkest of blue eyes were the color of the eastern sky just before the first bright star appears—almost purple in some light. A narrow ring of black color surrounded the blue and impossibly thick, dark lashes emphasized the blue-blackness of his eyes.

Even then, I knew that I would never, ever forget those eyes no matter how hard I tried to build that lodge wall to my heart to shut him out.

His very light, almost blond, brown hair was obviously the reason for his rather odd hunter's name. Bound in a horsetail for the wrestling match, the ends of white-blond hair were almost completely untied with loose lengths of hair falling onto both shoulders and down the back of his neck. Below a line that probably marked the edge of a fur cap, his light brown hair had been whitened by exposure to the sun giving him two-colored hair—light brown near the scalp but white-blond toward the ends. His hair was also thinning a little in the front, unlike most men with his relatively few seasons.

I wonder, do all lovers remember so much of a first meeting?

"Little Bear, will you please help me untie my elbow pads?" Brown Bull coaxed with a broad smile showing his cloud-white teeth.

He pulled the leather tie out of his hair to let it fall to his shoulders. I untied his elbow pads. He untied his own knee pads. My heart and liver swelled up into my throat and my face burned hotly as he untied his already loose loinskin and stood completely naked in front of me. His hair was full of dirt and bits of leaves and grass, but every hair was perfect and beautiful to my completely bedazzled eyes. I had already dropped my own bison robe to the ground next to his. Peering as deeply into my eyes as anyone had ever peered, he began to unlace my doeskin shirt without looking away or even paying any attention to his finger tips loosening my laces.

In no time I was naked too and he was leading me into the steaming waters by the hand. Face-to-face, waist deep in the scalding waters we began to slowly wash each other. The oily paint, dirt, blood and leaves began to come off and drifted away on the surface of the gently moving water. I moved my hands over every single part of his hard, muscular body, ostensibly washing the paint off. I just wanted to touch every part of him.

"Will you get the ash-water soap from my bag, Little Bear? It is the only thing that will loosen this body paint of oil," he cooed, never breaking our gaze.

Every word from his lips sounded like an invitation, a seduction. Brown Bull seemed to like saying my name. I certainly loved to say his. The sound of my name on his lips was a melodious lover's song coming from his perfect mouth.

"I would be pleased to get the soap for you, Brown Bull," I said with a crooked smile.

I loved the feel of his name on my tongue and wondered what his skin would taste like. I got out of the pool, his eyes following every movement as I searched his bag for the lump of ash-water soap. A drawstring bag full of soap flowers and chopped up soap root also contained the lump of ash-water soap. I brought the whole bag to the water's edge and handed the lump to Brown Bull. He began soaping the oily wrestler's paint from his chest and arms. I would be the one to scrub it from his back.

As Brown Bull began washing, I added the soap flowers and ground soap root to the little depression in the stone near the water. The shallow dish had been made here, in the solid rock close to the water, for just such a purpose. The addition of a few handfuls of the Serpent Father's hot water and we had fragrant suds to finish our soapy bath. He raised his arms so I could soap him there too. In spite of the steaming water, a chill ran up my spine as my fingers played across the hard little muscles that looked like ribs under the smooth skin of his perfectly muscled flanks. I was in pure ecstasy washing every part of his body. Then using his hands and tongue, and turning my body around at will, he did the same to me even though I had no paint to wash away.

All soil and paint removed, we stood face-to-face in the gently flowing water. Brown Bull looked at me with that paralyzing gaze, never looking away. He spoke with those blue-black eyes all I had ever desired to hear from the lips of a lover. He peered first at my right eye. Then he looked at my left and back to my right eye. Any doubts that he had failed to see my lion-eye were gone. The sight of that eye seemed to excite him and when he pulled our naked bodies together to kiss my mouth I could feel his hard sex pressing against my belly. It moved urgently and slid against me in a way that set my whole body afire—this was *nothing* like playing with my boy cousins.

"We bathed in the water and washed each other clean," I said to the Grandfather, leaving out virtually the whole story.

"And what then, my Daughter?" the Grandfather asked, with a knowing look under one raised eyebrow.

The soft hair of Brown Bull's chest reached from the sign of his first-kill just beneath his throat—a reindeer—all the way down to his man-rod. His snake stood straight up and reached, astonishingly, almost to his navel. I remember thinking at the time that it was very attractive for a penis, but not as large as it might have been judging from its soft appearance. And from Brown Bull's name! I wanted him inside me more than life itself and told him in just so many words. He wasted no time lifting me up in his sturdy arms above the steaming waters. He carried me the few paces to the flat rock where our bison robes lay. He quickly spread out his robe, fur side up, and I lay down on my back to get lost in those darkest of blue-black eyes all over again.

The boy-cousins who had put their little rods in me as play did not have hair on their chests. They barely had any hair above their penises. I had not bled when any of them played with or entered me. Besides, there were usually other holes in my body they wanted to explore too. Neither had I bled when the Hymen Stone was inserted in my pute during the Moon Blood. But I *did* bleed when Brown Bull entered me for the first time. There was no pain because I had opened head and heart and legs to him completely. Both of us were oozing with slippery fluid after he slid his tongue from lips just kissed, between my breasts to circle around my navel and down to my pute. My back arched to meet his tongue and lips involuntarily. So it was that he slid inside my pute without the slightest effort or discomfort. He entered me again and again and it was at that moment I knew that I would have him as my husband or would have no other.

"Brown Bull entered me with his penis. We joined several times after that during the Great Gathering." I cut the story so short it made me feel as if I were lying to the Grandfather all over again.

One thing that I would never tell the Grandfather was that Brown Bull noticed my first blood on his penis after he excitedly climbed the peak of his ecstasy and spilled his essence.

"Little Bear, have you never joined with a man? Did your first-blood not come with the Hymen Stone?" he had asked in rapid succession.

I could tell that having a woman's first hymen-blood excited Brown Bull because he immediately got hard again. Again he hungrily explored all my hidden places with his fingers and tongue. Again, I could not help but arch my back in ecstasy to meet his tongue as he drew a line from lips to pute, licking the blood from me where it still oozed slightly. At the touch of his tongue inside me, my own ecstasy burst for the very first time while joining with a man. Now I know why it is called "climbing the mountain of bliss"! Completely distracted by the unimaginably euphoric sensations that were flooding my whole body, I was still able to answer his questions in a halting voice as his tongue touched parts of my pute that had never been so stimulated before.

"My ... boy cousins ... tiny rods ... the hymen ... stone only ... inserted ... little way," I stuttered.

And then I spoke no more as he entered me with his penis and my body began to explode like flying stars all over again.

During the remaining days of the Great Gathering we would visit the hot pools, sneak away from watching eyes into the trees or into my mother's empty lodge many more times. We went anywhere and everywhere we could to find a place to be alone with each other. We wanted our privacy even though no one at the Great Gathering cared in the slightest who anyone else was joining with in sex. Those coming upon a couple joined in sex at the hot pools would discretely find somewhere else to go.

I had re-lived this time with Brown Bull many times since then, touching myself and making the ecstasy of the soaring birds fill my body once again. I was reliving the whole experience here and now.

Since he left, night and day, I dreamed only of Brown Bull for one long summer and one long winter season. I knew the Great Gathering would come again and with it the chance to see him again. That time had finally arrived but in my secret heart I knew he did not want me. At our parting, the sight of his back walking away from me is burned into my memory as is the cool, non-committal farewell that flew casually from his lips. He offered no words of hope that he would come again to see me, to be with me. He left me with nothing to hold to.

Somewhere in the darkest depths of my soul I knew I would never be with Brown Bull ever again. Still, since the last Great Gathering, I continually hungered to join with him only to force all thoughts of him from me as too painful to bear. It is clear to me now, as I re-ignited that brief time with Brown Bull, that I had not been able to cut him off and shut him out of my heart, head or liver! The narrow chance I would be with him again, somewhere, somehow, was always there no matter how many times I tried to close the door flap forever upon those desires of my very soul.

"My Daughter?" the Grandfather said, yanking me back rudely from some far away place.

"Clearly, you have not been given a child as a result of joining with this man," he said, stating the obvious.

"Did Brown Bull withdraw his penis and spray his man's essence upon your belly?"

The Grandfather's question brought my waking dreams to an abrupt halt.

Astonished that he could know such a thing I asked rudely, "Why yes, Grandfather. How could you know that?"

Shaking his head slightly in disbelief at my pretended innocence he said, "Surely, my Daughter, you delude yourself and refuse to accept what I know you must have learned about joining with men, if not from your mother, then certainly from Auntie. Can you possibly need more instruction to know that if you are to have a new life grow within you the man must put his essence inside your womb through the vulva? I thought you had learned the lessons of the stone penises in the Red Lodge, but perhaps not? Have you ever seen a mating bull spill his essence on the cow's back?"

The Grandfather began laughing out loud at my feigned ignorance.

I was so ashamed to be caught lying to myself, let alone trying to mislead the Grandfather, that I turned my eyes to the stony ground. The Grandfather was right. I was only lying to myself now. I was willing, there was no doubt, but Brown Bull clearly had no intention of becoming a husband to me. If he had, he would have put his essence into my pute as he did into my other openings as we played away the days and nights of the Great Gathering joining with each other.

Without waiting for my unworthy, embarrassing answer the Grandfather said, "It is of no great importance, my Daughter. Even if you had been given the gift of a child, no mother would do anything but welcome the new life to their lodge, whether an additional hunter for the lodge was to come with the child or not. I am sure you have learned much from your joining with this man. It is enough to know that you have felt the overpowering hunger for such a well-grown hunter and to have experienced the life giving heat of liver-passion for another. I am sorry to ask, but Brown Bull did not ask your mother to become a son of her hearth, am I correct?" He asked but already knew the painful answer.

"No," I said dejectedly. "Brown Bull did not even hint at it."

* * *

My mother has been very annoyed with me ever since I became a woman. I am getting old, but I would have none of the hunters who *have* asked to join my mother's lodge as my husband even before I met Brown Bull. Since joining in sex with him I have determined I will take no man to my mother's lodge except him no matter how long I have to wait and no matter how dry and old my womb becomes.

"After Brown Bull, I will have no other," I said stubbornly to the Grandfather.

"That is unfortunate, my Daughter," he said, all humor gone from his voice.

"What do you mean, *unfortunate*, Grandfather?" I shot back rudely, pained irritation in my voice.

"Dear One, do not be offended. I only meant that your mother will only have your happiness at heart in these matters of a husband to make your own hearth. Her only concern will be to see that you have a suitable husband with whom to make your lodge. If you listen to her advice she will find a mate of the head who does not beat you and who is a good and honest hunter as provider for your lodge. She will certainly choose a man who will care for you, give you children and one who will respect you. In time, you will become one in your heart out of the kindness and respect sure to be given you by a good and honest hunter and worthy husband of your hearth. Listen to your mother's good council if you are able, my Child," he advised sensibly.

"I know my mother loves me and cares for me, Grandfather. But she also cares for herself and she cares that any son of her lodge will be acceptable to *her* regardless of my desires. My grandmother did no less with my own mother and that is why I have determined to take no other but Brown Bull as husband," I said bitterly.

"Then listen to the advice I will give you, Dear One. I say this as one who loves you and cares for your happiness. I also speak as one who is uninterested in whom you choose to bring to your mother's lodge. The passions and urges of the liver are the most powerful we will ever experience, Dear One. But this hunger of the organs of sex for each other should never be the reason you take someone as the husband of your lodge. When there is no joining of the heart or the head between two people, the inevitable pleasures of joining in sex cloud the judgment of both the head and the heart. Those blissful clouds soon dissipate and so one must always choose carefully to share their lodge with a companion of the head *and* the heart and not a companion only of the organs of joining in sex. Everyone is free to choose their own mates, but having chosen, if they then separate and the husband returns to his mother's lodge, that brings great dishonor and shame to both families. You will already know that couples only go apart for the most serious of reasons so that among the People it is almost never seen. It is far better for your soul to enjoy each encounter with another for what it is and not to try to make it into something it is not nor ever could be. Wishing something to be what it, by its very nature, could not or should not be, is the path to disappointment, sorrow, disillusionment and unhappiness."

"But I love Brown Bull, my Grandfather. Can't you understand that?" I blurted before I realized what I had said.

If anyone knows about heart-love that can cross the worlds, the Grandfather does. He did not react to my crude and unfeeling words and just continued his speaking.

"I'm sure you do love him, Dear One," he replied without the slightest rancor at my disrespectful outburst.

"Did Brown Bull ever speak the words of love to you?" he asked with a pained concern showing in his eyes.

"No, Grandfather, he never said the words of love to me, nor I to him," I admitted.

A stabbing feeling ran like a spear point through my heart, through my gut.

"I know you will not agree, but that is probably for the best. Many men may say the words of love to entice a woman to give them what they want from you. If the tongue speaks words of love to you which are not matched by acts of kindness and respect, then that is the worst kind of love there is. At least Brown Bull respected you enough not to put his essence within your womb when he had no intention of joining your mother's lodge. Listen to an old man when I say there are many different kinds of love and you must learn to distinguish between them if you are to see into your own heart and not confuse the one kind of love for the other. First, you must know who *you* are before you may become one with another and live a contented life together in a happy lodge," he said.

"What do you mean, Grandfather, *different kinds of love?*" My puzzled look encouraged him to continue.

"There is the passion of the liver which is concerned only with satisfying the body-hunger of the organs of sex—and only for the moment. The eyes go scouting for a shape and an image which will satisfy the desires of the body and the organs of sex. And when the eyes have discovered that shape, the organs of joining in sex are drawn to it to satisfy those powerful desires. The enjoyment the organs of sex feel is only for a short time until your lover, perhaps, moves on to a different, newer, more exciting set of genitals they have not had the pleasure of rubbing together with their own. If this is the *love* of which you speak as possessing for Brown Bull, it will be fortunate for you to take it for what it was, enjoy the moment and do not pain yourself with thoughts of future meetings with such a lover. They may never come to you again no matter how much you may desire them. Should such a lover, who only desires to join with your red-body, say words of love that entice you into believing the joining is more than a passing hunger and you take him into your lodge, those words of love will hang in the air like a curse. Those false words will be a poisonous smoke in a lodge that should be full of genuine kindness and respect between the two of you. Before you give your heart and soul to a husband, make sure his words match his deeds. If you make sure that deeds of love come with the words, then you will be using your head to lead you in the choosing of a husband of your lodge. At the very least, deeds of pure kindness and respect should be present even if the words of love are never spoken. Do you find my meaning in all this, my Child?"

"Yes, Grandfather. I can see the wisdom of it," I said on the verge of tears mourning the loss of a man I never had.

"Do not be discouraged, Dear One, for there is a second kind of love—the love of the head. Your mother's choice of husband for you is a love of the head because her eyes go searching for the kind of man she believes will treat you well and provide abundance for you and your children. There also is a mother's love like no other when it comes to the happiness of her children. I'm sure she will also try to find you a husband who you would also enjoy rubbing your sex organs against," he said, the familiar smile returning in an unsuccessful attempt to chide me into a better mood.

"Yes, Grandfather, I'm sure my mother is acting out of love for me. But surely there is something else, something of the heart?" I said, beginning to lose hope.

"You are right, Dear One, there is. I was just about to say that if the *love* of which you speak as having for Brown Bull is that image which the eyes go searching for to make welcome to the heart, then that is a love which can connect two souls as one in this and all the worlds to come. It is the true joining and marriage of the Powers of Two that have been separated but are now one. Bodies can never become one, but the hearts and souls of two such lovers can become one. This kind of love is born only if both lovers look into that dark, still space at the center of each other's eyes and see the Mother there looking back at them. That is what is called *heart-love*. The Mother *is* this kind of love and this kind of love *is* the Mother. If you do not see the Stillness of the Abyss in each other's eyes then it is bound to be an attraction between two rutting bodies in heat and nothing more. If, when your bodies are separated, you still feel their soul's presence and that calms and satisfies you, then that is the heart-love that will cross lifetimes. If, when your bodies are separated, you only have sorrow and longing, then happiness and heart-love can never result. Have you ever thought about Brown Bull in this way? What if you are never with him again, Dear One? Will you live your life waiting for your joy and happiness to begin but never living and enjoying the love that is here for you in this moment? I can think of no worse fate for one as beautiful and blessed as you, Dear One. This is why I used the word *unfortunate*. I meant no disrespect for your feelings for this man. Can you forgive me for saying such a thing?" he concluded.

I sat once more in stunned silence realizing the Grandfather had not only asked my forgiveness again, but he had answered questions I had never voiced out loud to him or anyone. Certainly the Grandfather knew Brown Bull was well past the age when the hunters of our People usually marry. Did he also know that Brown Bull had not yet married because he was more than fond of seducing every girl, and some of the married women, from every camp he could find some reason to visit? My own father had mentioned, just as an off-hand remark, that it was Brown Bull himself who had come from the Bison-kin as a runner to all the other camps of the People to give word that the herds had arrived again upon the Plain for the last Great Hunt of the winter season. That Brown Bull had not taken the occasion to look for me pained me deeply because I was completely possessed by my desire for him. In spite of all my efforts, I continued to long for his touch and speaking of him and of our short time together only made me yearn for him once more.

I would not allow myself to think about it and no one knew how it made my heart, liver and soul ache when I learned Brown Bull had come to the Middle Camp and had no desire to even see me. Who had he dallied with here in the Middle Camp? Why was it not me? I know now that many others are just as obsessed by this man as I am. But after a full sun-round without so much as seeing the back of his head, how could I be so self-deceiving that Brown Bull would ever come to me again? To imagine I could ever bring such a man to my mother's lodge because of a momentary passion of the organs of sex was the silliest of childish fantasies! What a painful revelation to see oneself as deluded and naive—one who is in the midst of her initiation to become Seer of the Bear People!

It is time to put such unworthy, childish thoughts behind me.

After much thought, I replied. "No Grandfather. You were right to discuss this with me. I know I am young and inexperienced, but you have answered many questions for me. I most humbly thank you, my wise Mentor, for all of that. I will try to listen to my mother more and I will put this man out of my thoughts and out of my heart. You are right, Grandfather, it may be that I never see him again. I should not agonize so much over something that will never happen even though I desire it with my body."

And desire it with my very soul, I thought to myself.

When I was with Brown Bull I truly believed I had seen the Mother looking back at me from the depths of his darkest-of-blue eyes. But clearly Brown Bull had not seen that in my eyes or he would have wanted to be the husband of my lodge. He would have desired to see me once again if the joining with me in sex had been satisfying and enjoyable at all!

"Come, Dear One, I think you are ready for the rest of our adventure," the Grandfather said as he struggled to his feet.

I was in a half-stupor unable to stop running the whole experience with Brown Bull through my head. In a daze, I rose to my feet and picked up the lamp anyway.

"I *am* ready to move on toward my destiny!" I forced myself to say over and over in my head.

As we moved toward the entrance of the Dark Mother's Lodge I heard what sounded like someone else very far away ask, "Grandfather, what does joining in sex with a man have to do with this place of the Dark Mothers?"

"This is the Black Lodge of Oneness, my Apprentice. It is the place of the reunion of those things which have been separated as the Powers of Two. You have joined your woman's body in the heat of passion with a man's body and have felt the bliss of the touching of two skins. That feeling of oneness in the heat of passion is as close to the ecstasy of joining with the All Mother that most will ever experience in their lives. You will understand more as we move into the Lodge of the Lion Mother. It is the Black Womb for the re-birth of shamans, my Daughter."

I was beginning to come back to my senses, preparing myself to face what was coming.

"It is all so mysterious, my Grandfather. What is *in* this place?" I asked.

"Only what you take with you in your heart, Dear One. The Dark Mother's Lodge is our final destination. It is my dream-vision and the reason for your meandering journey that has brought you to this place today. My heart tells me you are ready for our great adventure, so let us now enter the Black Lodge of Lion Mother where we will meet our shared destiny."

We had arrived at the unfathomable mouth of the deepest part of the Great Cave of the Bear Mother.

CHAPTER 12.
LODGES OF THE BLACK SPIRITS

THE LEFT-HAND PORTAL OF THE ENTRANCE to the Lodge of the Dark Lion Mother was marked with a large red palm-dot, just as the starting points of so many of the other holy rounds of the Cave have begun.

"The Power of One, again. It is the beginning of things," I thought to myself.

"If you have no further questions, please prepare yourself to enter the Lodge of Black Spirits by kneeling before the entrance."

"I have no more questions, my Grandfather. I am prepared to enter. Let it be so."

I knelt down on the hard rocky ground facing the black hole which was the entrance to the Black Lodges.

"Now, my good Apprentice, extend both arms and look up to the black sign of the All Mother's Cross there above the entrance." He pointed toward the black signs with his torch.

Kneeling, I put my lamp down and extended my arms straight out to either side. I looked up at the black cross, dots and signs appearing on the wing of stone hanging down and over the entrance like a door lintel. These black signs were only visible to us as we had come to the entrance directly from the Heart Lodge. They had been invisible to us when coming in the opposite direction and so I knew this was the proper point of entry even though the Grandfather had not said as much. I have ceased asking questions for which I already have the answers.

"My good Apprentice, thou art about to enter the womb of thy transformation as Seer of the Bear People. The woman called Little Bear, thou wilt no longer be. Thou art a new creature altogether. Speak ye now the Thirteen Syllables of Transformation three times before thy Mentor asks permission to enter. Art thou prepared to enter the Black Lodges and become one with the Dark Mother, Little Bear, Hunter of the Bear People?"

"Yes, my Grandfather, I am prepared to be transformed. Let it be so now," I said with a tiny catch in my throat.

I began to chant the Holy Syllables:

I am the Mother's child. I and the Mother are One.
I am the Mother's child. I and the Mother are One.
I am the Mother's child. I and the Mother are One.

As I completed speaking the Thirteen Syllables of Transformation, the Grandfather turned to face in the same direction as I. Speaking into the dark round entrance open like the gaping mouth of the face of Lion Mother that signaled the end of the rounds of the Red Lodge, the Grandfather began to ask permission to enter.

"Oh, great Lion Mother of the worlds below, hear ye the words of my mouth! I am Flying Otter, Grandfather of the Bear People. I am come to initiate thy willing daughter, Little Bear, as Seer of the Nine Kin. We ask permission to enter thy Holy Lodge and we know it has already been granted," the Grandfather intoned.

We passed quickly by the red dot on the left portal. It could just be seen from outside the entrance because it had been made toward the outer edge of the curving rock that folded smoothly into the opening like lips surrounding a mouth. The lodge's roof became very high after passing through the low entrance. The passage itself was very rough and so narrow here that we could only make our way into the Black Lodge by walking single-file down the middle of the chamber. There was no true holy round to be walked here. So many of the other wombs and lodges had been walked by following one wall in and leaving by following the opposite wall out. In this black lodge, the way in was the way out.

Just inside the right-hand portal, invisible to anyone standing outside the entrance, a black big-antler stag had been made at an angle that made its antlerless head point up to three black wavy lines like water-waves above it. The head also pointed in the general direction of the entrance portal, which was now behind us. This big-antler not only announces the beginning of a holy round, it is on its way out of a chamber that I felt in my hollow gut is the entrance to the very Silence of the Abyss.

Oddly, as if riding on the big-antler's rump, a single black line formed the long horn, head, back and rear haunch of a rhino. Its single horn pointed straight up to the three black wavy lines and the high roof above.

"My Daughter, this is the Passage of the Big Antler, the first of the Lodges of Black Spirits," he said, again startling me with his full voice.

"The big-antler stag is often found on the right-hand portals of womb chambers, as I am sure you have already observed. Can you remember the meaning of the big-antler appearing at the entrance of such a lodge as this?" he asked.

So much had happened and I had heard so much already, for once I had to say, "I think I have forgotten, my Grandfather. Will you instruct me?"

"Very well," he said, beginning another lesson. "You know that the big-antler deer is a creature of the Great Plain of the Mammoth Mother. Its gigantic, spreading antlers are so huge and are so wide that a big-antler bull cannot escape the wolves—and our own hunters—by running through the trees. You know that a large big-antler has such gigantic branching horns that he would not be able to enter this very passage while he still carried them, let alone run through a forest of closely set trees. The message of the hornless big-antler appearing at the entrance of any womb-chamber is that we must leave behind all that we think we are, all that we think we want and all that keeps us separate and apart from the Mother, her animal and human children, and all that the Mother has made."

"Forgive me, Grandfather. But how can I leave antlers behind that, as one of the human tribe, I have not?" I asked smiling.

"Dear One," he replied with a smile growing on his own face. "The human tribes have other things to leave behind if they are to gain the wisdom of this lodge. A man who enters this place must leave behind all he believes makes him a man. A woman who enters this place must leave behind all she believes is female about herself just as the big-antler deer must let go of what keeps him from running easily through the birch trees. This is the lodge of joining and of oneness with the All Mother. By holding on to the things and thoughts we believe define who and what we are out there in the World of Light—which are always one-half of some pair of opposites—how could we ever find union with the Mother let alone with the mind and heart of another of the human tribes? When male animals with big distinguishing antlers or horns have shed them, they cannot be distinguished as male or female. We say they have let go of what separates them and are neither male nor female. In their hearts and souls they are *both* male and female. As Seer, you will soon notice there are many spirit-animals in the Dark Lodge that are the signs of oneness and of joining together as one. Do you remember why the big-antler deer without antlers appears at the entrance of womb-chambers?" he asked again.

"Yes, Grandfather. I remember now. But why is this rhino here sitting upright on the big-antler's rear haunches?"

The Grandfather gestured at the rhino sitting on the rump of the big-antler with an up-and-down motion of his fingers.

"Rhinos, both bulls and cows, all have two large horns. But in the Great Cave, sometimes we see one-horned rhinos like this one, or like some of those in their line crossing the Bridge of Rainbows. They are the sign of the Powers of Three-in-one, as I have said before. Take a closer look at the line that makes the upright rhino and tell me what you see, Dear One."

I did as directed and began to closely examine the line painted in one stroke by an expert and practiced hand.

"There is a kind of wavy short line that crosses the rhino's humped shoulder just behind what looks like an ear," I reported. "It looks like a cross with a long vertical arm under the 'ear'."

"Yes, Dear One. The upright rhino with its head and single horn pointed toward the sky, its haunches sitting upon the big-antler—already the sign of the union of opposites--signifies the oneness of the All Mother's Cross of Black. In other lodges you have already seen, and will see many more times, that rhinos are sometimes painted with a wide band of dark color around their heavy bellies. This divides them into three parts and is another way of saying rhinos that are not fighting with each other are signs of the Powers of Three—three-parts-in-one, as it were. Many rhinos have no such belly-bands or are seen fighting with one another horn-to-horn. Most often, such rhinos are the sign of an un-transformed initiate. I think the grand plan of the Ancients will be made known to you if we look closely at that wall just inside the entrance portal." The Grandfather gestured toward the wall opposite to where we stood at the entrance.

Nodding my head in agreement, I moved to the wall across from the big-antler with a rhino standing on its rump. It took a few moments to decide what the engraved white lines there were intended to represent.

"I think it is the back, hump, head and trunk of two big mammoths, my Grandfather," I finally decided.

"That is correct. You will also notice that they are white-powers without tusks. But pay close attention to the half circle-shaped lines that seem to be spraying out to either side of the mammoths. Have you seen anything in the Cave before that reminds you of these images?"

I thought for just a moment before I enthused, "It is the All Mother's Rock of the Red Lodge with its cross and liver spouting streams of red lifeblood! It is the fountain of spirit-fire supporting the sphere of spinning life-fire at the end of the Passage of the Butterfly!"

"That is only as I would expect my good Apprentice to answer," the Grandfather said smiling his pride for me to see.

"Yes, you are quite right. These images to the right and left of the entrance are equivalent images to that of the Cross of Red in the Red Lodge. It is also the same sign as the laurel Cross of White in the Heart Lodge. Here, the abundant white powers of Mammoth Father—without their great tusks--are joined again as one with the red-powers within a Cross of Black in the form of an upright rhino. Do you see what a marvel the Ancients have made to bring us into this Lodge of Black Spirits, my Daughter? Have you any questions about this portal of transformation and oneness?"

"No Grandfather, you have already answered my questions so completely that I have none. I see that the same teaching is repeated in different parts of the Great Cave. Is that not so?"

"Yes, Dear One that is so. It appears that you are prepared to move on to your initiation as Seer."

The Grandfather led the way up the center of the narrow Passage of the Big Antler.

* * *

The first pair of rhinos we encountered had been painted on the left wall not far from the two mammoths at the entrance. The rhinos faced opposite directions with one behind the other. The rhino behind and just above the other was just a single line showing the back and single horn pointing toward the mammoths and their spouts of white life-essence. The rhino in front was skillfully painted with a wide band of black around a bulging belly, pointed "spirit" feet, two horns and the same wavy line just behind the ear as the upright rhino of the Cross of Black on the opposite wall of the passage. At least these rhinos were not fighting one another as other pairs had been seen to be dueling with each other outside this passage!

The further in we went, the narrower and steeper the passage became. The roof was coming down in height except where small niches and side-chambers with flat floors spiked away from the main passage into the left and right-hand walls exactly opposite each other. A short drop just past the twin rhinos let us down into the first of these doubled side-passages.

Within these narrow passages no images had been made except for the first right-hand niche, at the back of which a large black lion appeared. Her head held low, she was coming out of a crack in the niche behind her. She crept disconcertingly toward us as if ready to pounce.

The ground was sloping down but still relatively flat until we came to the inside wall of the second set of side-niches. The passage narrowed in front of us to form yet another portal into the blackness beyond. Here, on either side of what became an entrance to the rest of the Black Lodge, three, three-cornered putes had been made. The two vulvas on the right side were painted in black but the single vulva on the left side of the portal had been engraved into the white rock.

The design of the Passage appeared to be white mammoths and vulvas on the left side and black vulvas and images on the right. Just below and between the single white vulva and the left portal, a white Lion Father had been carved into the stone. His muzzle almost touched the white vulva and his muscular shoulders were covered with vein-like cross-hatching—lines of spirit-power that are often scratched onto the images of the Great Cave and engraved upon the shoulders of some spirit-animal ivories.

The Grandfather stopped, but I already knew what he was going to say.

"My Apprentice, the three vulvas here marks the end of the Passage of the Big Antler and indicates the entry portal to the Womb of the Dark Mother, the deepest chamber of the Cave. Just beyond the next short drop the steepest, most dangerous drop off in the Great Cave is to be encountered. Everything you see from this portal onward *is* the very Womb of the All Mother. Any place may be used for solitary questing or meditation by the brave initiates who dare to enter and commune with the Black Spirits. The stony surface of this chamber is the skin of the Mother's life-giving womb, and at the same time, is the mouth of her life-receiving maw. This is the very place out of which the life-force of the powers come to transform us just as new red-life passes through your woman's vulva to be born into the human tribes. This *is* the mouth of the very Silent Abyss back into which life goes in its return to the Mother. Because it is both entry and exit, we will see spirit-animals coming from within and going out of this Lodge of Black Spirits."

"Yes, Grandfather. I see the wisdom in it. Shall we go in now?" I asked boldly.

"There is a short drop just beyond the vulva portals, my Daughter. Take care as you move through this entrance." He let me go ahead so that I could help him down the thigh-high drop into the blackness.

Beyond the second drop off of this passage, the sloping, flat clay floor of the passage began to widen out the further in we went. The Grandfather again took the lead and began moving toward the right-hand wall.

"In entering the Black Womb below, we will take one holy round in a sun-wise direction beginning after we descend into that deepest part of the Cave. You will have noticed that the big-antler at the entrance of this passage was made on the right side of the Cave and so, as Seer, you should consider that the round of this passage is in by the right-hand wall and out by the opposite. This is the proper order of the round even though we found it necessary to walk the center of the passage because of its narrowness. As the only way down is also found on this right-hand wall, initiates will take the path against-the-sun to enter the Dark Womb below, the Grandfather explained as we moved the last few paces from the second drop off beyond the vulva portal to the right-hand wall.

An astonishing array of spirit-animals emerged into the light. On this right side of the chamber, two pairs of part-black, part-engraved rhinos appeared. Of each pair, one had been made above and behind the other like a similar pair of rhinos on the left-hand wall near the entrance to the Passage. The rhinos in front and below both had black belly-bands and were heading out of the Womb—their seer's initiations complete, no doubt. The two rhinos above and behind were made with only one simple line and had been made as if heading deeper into the Cave—their transformations were yet to come?

Just in front of the two pairs of rhinos, the simple lines of two black ibex had been made. They both had the gigantic curved horns of males and both were headed in toward the blackness of the Dark Womb beyond. In total, six spirit-animals.

"Grandfather, why are the banded rhinos heading out of the passage and the others without belly-bands heading in?" I asked just to confirm my interpretations of the signs.

"The rhinos heading in are those initiates who have not yet been transformed. A belly-band on a rhino is the sign of an initiate who has realized that they are the three-in-one and have realized their oneness with the Mother and all things. Here at this entry place, they are those who have awakened to their true selves and have become seers and shamans having joined white-spirits with black-powers as one. They are the guides of the unitiated," he answered.

"There is a very steep drop to the deepest part of the Black Lodge just beyond the two ibex, so be careful, Dear One. Below the ledge of the drop off on this right side of the passage there is a shelf running deeper into the Womb along the right-hand wall. Below the shelf is a large boulder which slants down to the floor that we can climb down into the Black Lodge," the Grandfather explained and then pointed toward the dark edge of the drop off just ahead of the two ibex.

I was not paying close attention to his words, so engrossed was I in the details of the six spirit-animals before me, but he continued with his directions anyway.

"Initiates will be led down the drop off from this right side of the Passage. When they leave the Dark Womb, we bring them out again here and then take them to the opposite wall for the exit. Let us move across the passage to the other side to see the images that have been made there before returning here to descend. This part of the Cave is dangerous in many different ways," he cautioned.

Without giving a word of assent, I simply began following behind the Grandfather as he moved straight across the passage to its left-hand wall. I could see the black edge of the drop off falling away into the darkness beyond.

"Tell me again, how do we get down this very steep drop off, my Grandfather?"

I moved a couple of paces toward the edge and stood on the lip of the ledge holding my light out to see if I could tell how deep it really is.

"The drop off might higher by half than a man is tall," I said, a little dismayed.

The drop appeared nearly as deep as the Great Navel. How would the Grandfather ever be able to climb down such a steep cliff?

"Yes, it is steep but do not concern yourself. I will be able to climb down. Come this way, Dear One. Join me here where the ledge meets the left-hand wall. Upon the completion of their initiations in any of the Black Lodges below, hunters or seers will be brought up and out by the right-hand wall because that is the only way in or out. Then they are to be brought here before exiting through the Passage of the Big Antler. Come see the images that they will see as they move out of the Dark Lodges."

This time I heard his instructions and marveled again that he could answer questions I had not yet voiced.

"Yes, Grandfather. I am coming," I said.

I turned away from the edge of the drop off to rejoin him where he stood looking up at an astonishing mixed herd of black animals. They were all running away from the darkness before us as if to leave the Dark Womb. All of these images had been painted with charcoal. I knew that because of the small heaps of charcoal powder that collected in little piles at the base of the wall beneath the spirit-herd above. I counted six horses, two full-bodied bison, two big-antler deer without antlers and a pair of little rhinos facing in opposite directions, one painted above and behind and the other as we had seen at the beginning of the Passage. Neither of these rhinos had belly-bands that I could see. Signs of the unitiated, the un-transformed, even after the initiations of the Dark Womb?

But what was most curious about the whole herd was a pair of big-antler deer that had been made at the top of the wall. One was bigger than the other and had been painted with a thick black band around its long neck. Surely this was the sign of a transformed initiate leaving the Cave? The smaller of the two big-antlers had no neck band and was facing in toward the drop off and the Black Womb below. But even more peculiar, the big, black banded big-antler was being mounted from the rear by one of the horses!

The Grandfather saw me counting the spirit-animals and said, "You will be interested to know, my good Apprentice, that there are twenty eight spirit-animal images in this Passage of the Big-Antler from the entrance to the place where we now stand. There are few new men who choose to enter this black-spirited lodge and most of them go no further than this herd of black animals in their personal questing. Few dare to descend any further. But for us, we must go even deeper into this Abyss of the Dark Mother."

"Yes, Grandfather. I understand. Let us go on, then," I said, ever more curious about what I would find below.

We made our way back to the right-hand wall and I peered over the edge. Sure enough, about hip-high below the ledge there was a fairly wide shelf of flat stone that ran level along the right-hand wall out into the darkness. Another short drop from the shelf would take us to the top of a fairly flat boulder sloping down to the brown clay floor below.

"Do you want me to go first, Grandfather? You can hold the torch for me and then hand it down to me at each giant step," I said cheerfully trying to calm my fears of going down what were very steep and dangerous stair-steps of stone.

"Yes, you go first, my good Apprentice. You can help me down to the shelf and then to the sloping stone."

I put my lamp on the edge of the drop off and hopped over the ledge to the shelf below. I moved my lamp down to the shelf then reached up for the Grandfather's torch. He turned around and lowered himself over the ledge to the shelf, after which he sat down on the shelf and swung his legs out above the sloping stone. Then he let himself down to the top of the sloping boulder while I held his torch for him.

"Hand me the torch, Dear One," he directed, obviously having climbed down these rocks many times before.

I picked up my lamp and carefully slid over the short drop to the sloping boulder trying not to spill any oil. The Grandfather shuffled ahead of me in small sideways steps down the rather steep slope of the big stone steadying himself against the ledge that was already considerably above our heads. To my horror, as he sidled down the sloping boulder, the Grandfather slipped on a muddy patch of clay, his legs went out from under him and he fell heavily onto his right hip with a loud cry of pain.

I was frantic to get to him and help him up. I hurriedly scuffled down the sloping stone spilling lots of lamp oil on the way. I had to be sure he was not seriously injured. A broken hip bone for any one of the People is the equivalent to an announcement of your Return to the Mother.

"Grandfather, Grandfather! Are you all right?" I yelled in panic as I reached him where he lay on his side near the bottom of the sloping stone.

"I am fine, Dear One," he said. He sat up stiffly while I retrieved his torch that had fallen to the clay-covered floor of the Dark Womb.

"I think this thick bearskin robe cushioned the fall, my Daughter. Do not be concerned. I will be bruised for certain, but I am just fine. Help me down and we will continue on," he said as if nothing had happened.

My heart was still pounding, but I helped the dear old man with a hand under his elbow to limp heavily back toward the right-hand wall from which we had just descended.

"There are more images made upon this wall just above the shelf we used to descend. Take the lead and when you come to the end of the line of animals above the shelf, turn and cut directly across the chamber to the opposite wall. There is a faint path for you to follow."

Without acknowledging his directions I took the lead across the nearly flat, clay-covered floor to the right-hand wall beneath the shelf. As he rejoined me, his torch revealed a procession of spirit-animals just above the shelf. All of them were moving in the same direction in a line—deeper into the blackness. First, nearest the drop off, a white-engraved bison head emerged from the ledge as if entering the chamber. A white spirit-power as yet untransformed by the Dark Womb it was about to enter? Or is it just a round sign like a red rhino head to mark the start of another holy round? Just ahead of the white bison, the lines of a single, very large, black bear appeared. In front of the black bear, three lions—one above the other in a line--made their appearance. Just ahead of the three lions, the black lines of three rhinos appeared, again made one above the other—another holy "seven" I realized.

"Grandfather? Is the white bison head meant as a sign of a new holy round?" I asked simply.

"Yes it is, my good Apprentice. It is a sign of the transition from the white lodges of the hunters at the end of the Passage of the Big Antler and the beginning of the Lodge of Black Spirits, which is a higher, more powerful expression of the All Mother which is to be experienced in this place. I'm sure you will have counted the spirit-animals following the white bison head," he said with a wince as he put his weight on his bruised hip.

"There are seven, my Grandfather."

"Yes, seven is the sign of the end of one way of thinking and the beginning of another, a more enlightened way of thinking and being in the World of Light. I see that you do understand these signs and symbols, my very good Apprentice."

Without acknowledging the Grandfather's compliment, I slowly made my way below this procession of seven spirit-animals until the little-traveled trail turned sharply to the left in the direction of the opposite wall. Long reddish pendants hung from the high roof and one big tree trunk of white stone descending from roof to floor was smudged with red blotches. The red smudges were so high up they could only be part of the chamber's rock and not added by human hands. Either way, it clearly is a sign of the red and white-spirits that are to become joined in this deepest and blackest of all the Cave's lodges.

Fifteen or so paces took us to the opposite side of the chamber and a nearly flat, westerly sidewall. There, a headless horse with a big belly was beginning to disappear into the rock as it dashed out of the chamber toward the ledge of the drop off. Just behind the horse, a big-bellied, black-banded rhino frantically fled the disembodied head of a lion just opening its jaws to bite the rhino's tail.

Only a few paces on, and following a stretch of flat wall marked with many bear claw marks, the rear ends of a pair of huge lions appeared out of the darkness. Side-by-side and drawn without paws, the astonishing likenesses floated above the ground as most spirit-animals are usually portrayed. That's how you can tell they are spirit-powers or dream-visions and not red-bodied animals: they don't have feet. Or so I have been told.

The two big lions were almost identical and stood as if guarding the exit of the Black Womb. The male, in a half-crouch slightly above and behind the female, made it appear as if he were to the female lion's left. He was also made to be much bigger than the lioness. He was so much bigger that his body and head almost completely enclosed her body and head. Between the two, a hazy red line seemed to outline the ear, shoulders back and rump of a third lion in between the other two. But I noticed the red line more closely followed the back and rump of the male—the female powers within the male? A third red-spirited lion between the two? I could not decide which. Two black lines of spirit-power ran across the female's shoulder down toward her invisible front paw. Many finger-engraved wavy lines of spirit-power seemed to be issuing from the two great lions' mouths.

No one would have guessed the bigger lion was a male without looking beneath his gracefully arching tail. I could tell it was a male lion because two small man-eggs had been painted there. Both lions lowered their heads in perfect unison as if getting ready to pounce upon something in front of them at the same time. The pair twitched their long tails and stared intently in the direction of the darkened chamber ahead, a cavern whose final depth could not be fathomed with our feeble lights.

"Do you recognize who the two spirit-lions are?" he asked after I had scrutinized the magnificent pair for a long time.

"No, Grandfather. Who are they?" I replied.

"They are the two lion-guardians of the All Mother assisting in her great work of life as one. The red line between them is a sign of the Mother of Life, her two attendants serving to return all to the Mother by hunting and eating the Mother's children. I'm sure you have seen ivories of the Mother of Life with one female lion-attendant supporting the Mother at her right and a male lion-attendant at her left as the Mother squats to give birth to the all creation. These two *are* those Lion Powers of the Return. As I have said, they attend to Dark Mother's work as they eat back to the Mother all there is," he whispered in awe.

The hair stood up on the back of my neck and along my arms at the thought, so alive and full of lion-power these two images appeared to me.

"They face inward toward the herds of spirit-animals coming from the Mother in the form of her Great Vulva at the very back of this chamber. Come, Dear One and we will enter this deepest part of the Great Cave—the Lodge of Black Lion Mother," he whispered reverently.

We turned away from our gazing at the two lion-guardians. The Grandfather led us on into the darkness.

* * *

What marvels next appeared on the left-hand wall of this chamber truly astonished my eyes and made words of description fail me. As I discovered more and more of the astonishing scene that stretched out before me, deep feelings began to stir in the pit of my stomach and flooded my face like the rush of embarrassment that turns one red. Facing the two lion-guardians, beyond the stretch of wall marked only by finger-engraved lines and claw marks, there appeared a big rhino with a broad white band around its fat belly. The rhino faced the guardian lions as if to run past them and out of the Great Cave having been transformed within this chamber. Three long, thin waving lines of spirit-power over-arched the rhino as if to protect it: two black lines below and a long single red line above. Behind and beyond the rhino stretched a vast abundant hunting ground full of black-painted animals. With the Grandfather's torch showing the way, the astonishing herds were visible all the way back to a huge vulva-shaped rock hanging from the roof. From where we stood, the big pendant was barely visible in the gloom at the back of the chamber.

From what would be a high rocky outcrop upon the summer plains of the World of Light, four lions placidly gazed out over the broad back of the belly-banded rhino. From their lofty place, they peered intently toward the twin lion-guardians of the entrance. The black-banded spirit rhino appeared to be caught between an entire pride of black spirit-lions. The heads and shoulders of three of the lions had been marvelously made with black shading and stippled whiskers. They had been made ahead and slightly above each other so that they all faced in the same direction. I approached them closer and could see that originally there had been five lion heads made with red lines. They had been over-painted with four black ones by some Ancient maker. The fourth lion of the group, its huge head held out over the middle lion's disappearing shoulders, had also been over-painted in black.

Most significantly, this fourth lion head in profile had a rain-bow-shaped arc of thirteen big red dots completely overarching it. The back end of this Bridge of Rainbows ended just in front of an astonishing herd, that is, a crash of rhinos. Most of the rhinos were in a vertical line behind the four lions and facing in the same direc-tion—toward the entrance of the chamber. There might have been thirteen rhinos in this crash but it was difficult to count them as their horns were doubled and triple-lined to create the feel of movement. A few without belly-bands ran toward the back of the chamber while the line of rhinos with belly-bands appeared to be tossing their long curved horns into the air as they stampeded toward the four lions in front of them. Something inside told me that they were transforming into the lions as they ran. As I looked closely at the fourth lion, I became certain that was just what they were doing. Astonishingly, the lines of the fourth lion's head and shoulders changed into the rear haunches of an aurochs or reindeer with six legs! I could tell it was some kind of animal like that because of the shape of its deer-like hooves.

And between the rear end of this six-legged monstrosity and a black-banded rhino in the center of the line of rhinos, another arc of thirteen tiny red dots arched from above the rhino's twin horns to the rear of the six-legged, lion-headed creature ahead of it. My head began to swirl trying to take in all the wonders of this herd of spirit-animals. In my excitement I knew that I had only just begun to discover its mysteries.

Below the four spirit-lions on their high vantage point and behind the crash of rhinos stretched a vast plain full of an enormous, roiling, mixed herd of bison and rhino and horses and mammoths. Further back in the direction of the Vulva Pendant—becoming more and more visible as we approached it—this magnificent spirit-herd was being chased and stampeded by another whole pride of lions! As I stood before the amazing scene picking out all the details I could take in, I realized that the pride of lions running behind the herds were transforming into bison before my eyes. The further toward the back the lions were, the more they looked like lions. But as I moved my eyes across the herd from back to front, the further forward they were, the more they looked like bison! Astounding and astonishing does not adequately describe what I saw with my own eyes before me painted on the walls of this holy lodge.

This amazing wall was covered by an entire herd of spirit-animals transforming one into the other before my very eyes. And all of this shape-shifting was taking place without the killing and the bleeding and the open-mouthed gashing of lion fangs and the slashing of lion claws. The lions, all with closed mouths, were peacefully running with the herds of bison and transforming into them as if they were one animal. The vast herd, partly obscured by clouds of dust, thundered across the stone walls toward us in groups of two, three, four, five and six mammoths, horses, bison and rhino. I could hear the pounding of hooves, the braying of horses, the bellowing of bison; the trumpeting of the mammoths. I could smell the dust, terror-sweat and manure and I could taste it all on my tongue, so alive this spirit herd appeared to me.

"Dear One," the Grandfather said in reverent tones from behind me. "Take the torch and examine the great herd as much as you wish. But first, step away from the wall and tell me what you see between the rear of the crash of rhinos and the single great bison at the head of the transforming herds behind him."

Almost in a daze and without comment I exchanged my lamp for the Grandfather's torch and turned back to the awe-inspiriting wall of black-painted animals. The heads or forequarters of some animals emerged from shadows and folds in the rock while others disappeared into the cracks and crevices of the cave wall leaving only their hindquarters visible. I backed up a few paces and focused my attention on the big, beautifully shaded bull bison and the transforming rhinos ahead of him. The bison's nose almost touched the tip of a three-cornered niche in the wall with its wide end terminating in the flat, clay-covered floor. Above the tip of this three-angled niche, a three-cornered, pute-shaped flap of rock descended from the roof and ended just above the bull-bison's upward curving horns.

"Grandfather!" I shouted, unable to contain myself. "It is the Star Shaman and the spirals of trance!"

"Yes, my good Apprentice. The Cave is speaking its wisdom to you once again."

I could hear the approval in his voice and was so fascinated by the spectacle unfolding before me that I didn't even turn around to acknowledge the Grandfather. I had seen something else I felt compelled to look at much more closely.

I came back to the wall and began peering closely at a creature like no one has ever seen before. It was made just to the right of the lower, male, three-cornered spiral, its bizarre head just beneath the bull bison that I now recognized as the bison shaman-of-the-herd, the Leader of the Herd. The three-cornered spirals of trance, the bison shaman and this creature had been made in almost the exact center of the great boiling display of transforming life with its four lions in front and its pride of transforming lions to the rear. This monstrosity appeared to have a head with the rounded profile of a human but with the four legs and bulbous feet of a mammoth or rhino. Curiously, the feet appeared to have three-toed bird claws within them too. The shadowy three-toed talons of an eagle grasped a ball of something to make the bulbous feet of this chimera. The creature stood almost upright like a human, but it had the body and tail of a lion. This was undoubtedly a shaman in trance. It had to be a shaman transforming into his animal-guides and running with the herd—the three-into-one, the many-into-the-one and the one-into-the-many.

Upon closer examination of the head, I saw that even it was a mixture of different animals. Standing a few paces back, the head looked human. Close up, it seemed to have the hooked beak of an eagle, or maybe an owl, which would explain the bulbous, clenched talons that served as the creature's feet. When I got as close as I could, the distinctive trunk of a mammoth stretched out from the head reaching to touch the edge of the lower spiral of trance.

Just behind the shaman-creature, and separating it from the herd of bison transforming from lions, what looked like a string of seven, maybe nine, or even thirteen, round beads separated by bundles of feathers or grass appeared. Smudges and lines making up the arcing lines of the "bundles" made it difficult to tell exactly how many "beads" were intended. The feathers, or grass, whichever it was intended to portray, pointed up and could have been spraying out like fountains beneath the round "beads." In a flash, I knew it was an extended version of the ball of spirit-fire supported by arching fountains of spirit-force that I had seen before!

At the top of these stacked up, black spheres spouting the spirit-fires—as if the whole rod-shaped image were some kind of shaman's staff—a bundle of what definitely were long tail feathers of some kind topped the straight-as-a-rod stack of beads. At least it looked like a string of beads when viewed close up. I stepped back and one of the beads near the top, beneath the spray of feathers, had two fuzzy black balls to either side becoming the horizontal black line of a cross with a long arm pointing down. It was just like the other crosses of the All Mother seen in other parts of the Great Cave, only this one is made of black spheres of spirit-power.

"Grandfather?" I said, preparing him for yet another question.

He cocked his head toward me and raised his chin and eyebrows in anticipation of my question.

"This is a very strange sign, my Grandfather. Can you tell me what is it the sign of? I have counted the round objects but I can't decide if there are seven, nine or thirteen of them."

"The number of round balls of life-fire is only important for the one who is viewing this image, for this is the sign of the Gates of Forgetting and Remembering. Each will see the number of spheres of spinning life-fire as has meaning for them. You will have noticed that the talons of the transforming shaman grasps with its claws four of these spheres of spinning life-fire. These are to represent the four spirit-substances of creation: earth, air, fire and water, which the shaman rides to the worlds of dream-trance. The spouting lines at the bottom, between some of the balls of life-fire and at the very top of the Gate are equivalent to the spouting red life-forces we have already seen upon the Rock of the All Mother and the white life-forces spouting at the entrance to the Passage of the Big Antler. But here, the sign is made in black, which is the sign of the Gate between the worlds which is two gates-in-one. It is one portal through which shamans pass as they embark upon their journey into the Abyss. That is the Gate of Remembering because as we leave behind the world of the senses we remember our true selves within the Abyss. It is also the Gate of Forgetting through which the shaman passes back into the World of Light, and in that process remembers little of what has transpired during the dream trance. If the spirit-fire is seen to be spinning to the left, it is the Gate of Remembering, the Gate of the Going to the Mother. If the spirit-fire is spinning to the right, then it is a sign of the Gate of Forgetting, the Gate of Coming In from the Mother. As Seer, learn that this is also the sign of the same two gates that all the Mother's children pass through as they come into the World of Light forgetting all that went before. The Gate of Remembering all that went before is the gate we pass through when we return to the Mother. They are two-gates-in-one depending on which way you are passing through them. They are the inside and the outside of the one thing. Can you understand this, my good Apprentice?"

"Yes, I see it now, my Grandfather." I said thoughtfully.

I knew that he spoke the truth because I had already noticed how the Gates were placed between the shaman-in-trance on the left-hand side and the fully transformed bison on the right-hand side of the staff-like barrier between the worlds. Further back from the shaman-creature and the Gates of Forgetting and Remembering in the very center of the lions-becoming-bison, an odd animal stood out from the surrounding herd. It had a pointed nose and a long, sleek body. I would have said it is a wolverine running with the herd but the snout was too pointed for a wolverine. It had to be an otter? Otters don't run with herds of bison transforming into lions any more than wolverines do. But then, otters don't fly either, unless you ask the Grandfather!

I was truly overwhelmed by the stunning spectacle of it all and could only stand open-mouthed in amazement for a very long moment.

"What is the monster in the center of the herds, my Grandfather?" I asked, pointing at the creature to the right of the lower spiral of trance.

"It is a vision of the shaman-in-trance whose spirit-guides merge and join with the shaman as one creature. It is the shaman appearing in the shaman's own dream in complete unity with his companion-animals and running together with the herds. It is a sign that everything is part of the abundance and mystery of the All Mother's Oneness," he answered, eyes wide as mine with wonder and awe.

I was utterly transfixed by the spectacle of this left wall of the chamber—the hunter's wall—with its fantastic, boiling profusion of spirit-animals engaged in the play of life. Some spirit-animals headed for the mouth of the chamber on their way to rebirth in the red-world of flesh and blood. Some were running toward the back of the chamber giving their body-lives to the Mother's human and animal hunters in the Return. The Return is the joining again with the Mother as One—red-bodies given back to the Mother in the endless round of life and death, eating and being eaten. But it is also the transformation and re-birth of our spirits and our souls, as the Grandfather has said many times. The Great Cave was speaking to me in the Mother's own voice!

Overwhelmed and inexplicably on the verge of tears I cried aloud, "What life, Grandfather! What abundance!"

So overcome I became that I actually staggered backward to be caught by the Grandfather. He stood behind me, bearing me up. I continued to hold the torch high so I could see the whole spectacle of the Dark Mother's life spread out before my eyes. It *is* the Mother transforming into new forms and shapes and then back again in one great circle—all without the shedding of a single drop of blood. This *is* the very world of trances and dreams and transforming souls and bodies becoming one in the heat of the passion of living and then separating again when the dream ends, when the trance is completed; when the red-life is ended.

"Yes, Dear One. I know," the Grandfather said quietly in my ear. "The first time it is experienced, we all feel the sheer life of the Mother in these spirit-animals. It is awe-inspiring and overwhelming, I know. Take what time you need and when you are ready, this will be a good time to teach you the Song of the Mother's Abundance. Listen well and let my words speak to your heart as you run with this magnificent spirit herd in your soul," he said gently.

After I had exulted in the beauty and power of the herd of transforming spirit-animals and had searched out all the fine details, the Grandfather began to speak quietly his new teachings from where he stood behind me.

"A seer must understand that fear comes always from the constant uncertainty of what is yet to be. Fear is also the reluctance to accept the Mother's abundance thinking that we are not worthy of it. When we are fearful, we will reject the Mother and her wisdom becoming afraid that the abundance will cease. Fear of an unsuccessful hunt, fear of sickness, fear of loss, fear of unkind words and deeds, fear of returning to the Mother—fear of any kind—is always the rejection and denial of the Mother's love for all her children which she pours forth without favor. Fear is denying the Mother's abundance and is always a withdrawal from the Mother's bounty and wisdom. Everything moves in circles so when a hunter goes out to the hunt in joy and with a heart full of gratitude for the gifts of the Mother, he returns with abundant game. When the hunter goes out with angry thoughts and a heart full of failure and scarcity and fear, he has already rejected the Mother's abundance and will return as empty-handed as he went out. The abundance of the Mother constantly flows through us and unless it is stopped with fear and thoughts of hunger and empty meat bags, the Mother's abundance will come to us forever in an endless holy round," the Grandfather expounded as I continued to search the wall for more astonishing detail.

"Are you ready to sing the Song of Abundance, Dear One?" He waited for my answer.

"Yes Grandfather, teach and I will learn," I said, still entranced by the wondrous herd of spirit-animals spread out before me.

"The Song of the Mother's Abundance is sung and danced by the hunters before they leave the camps for the hunt as part of the rites of Going Out. It is sung to women as they bring forth new lives and it is sung to those returning to the Mother. It may be chanted at any time the flow of the Mother's abundance appears to have stopped for any reason or whenever we wish to have the Mother's abundance come to us," he said softly.

I turned away from the wall of spirit-animals, ready to learn the song. The Grandfather also turned away from the spirit-herd and began to sing into the darkness at the back of the chamber where the Vulva Stone hung from the roof.

In harmony with the passage of the Mother's love through us
We follow the path to abundance and life.
Out of line with the flow of the Mother's love through us
We follow the wrong tracks,
We go where the blood trail runs out,
Where the animal sign stops.
In line with the flow of the Mother's love through us
We live in love,
We live in oneness,
We live in respect,
We live in sympathy with all others.
The trail is always clear, the animal sign abundant.

All the Mother hath flows unceasingly.
I shall live life to the full.
I shall sing and dance and be glad.
I am happy wherever I am.
Today is a good day to live.
Today is a good day to die.

After a long moment of silence as the echoing notes of the Grandfather's voice faded, he turned back to me.

"Come, Dear One, let us move on. The end of the Dark Womb and the great Vulva Stone of the All Mother awaits us."

* * *

We took a few more paces along the wall where the spirit-animals dwindled to just a few. Following behind the great herd, a small musk ox ran out of a large niche that marked the back end of the great herd. On the other side of the niche, the forequarters of a bison bull emerged from it in the direction of the Vulva Pendant only a few paces further on. The bison stepped forward with a front hoof to stand upon the nose of another lion facing toward the little musk ox and the rest of the pride on the other side of the niche. The head and shoulders of the lion's mate appeared below and to the right. And above them all appeared the last spirit-animal in the incredible procession that had begun with the two guardian lions at the entrance.

This last, or maybe I should say, first spirit-animal—because it was the one closest to the great stone vulva—was another huge full-bodied rhino. It emerged out of a narrow ridge of rock which jutted out from the astonishing wall of spirit-animals just to the left of the suspended rock called the Pendant of the Mother's Vulva. The narrow ridge divided the western wall of the Dark Mother's Lodge with all its magnificent spirit-animals into two parts. One part lay before the Vulva Stone with its herds of transforming animals all the way to the entrance and its two lion-guardians. The second part extended behind the Vulva Stone as part of the western wall. This last black spirit-rhino of the part of the western wall before the Vulva Stone was different from all the many others that I had seen. I recognized it as a rhino-shaman in trance because it had fountains of red blood spouting from its eyes and mouth. Some shamans in the deepest of trances are sometimes seen to bleed from their noses and mouths, even from their eyes, just as the Grandfather has said.

From this vantage point at the very back of the herds, the rhino-shaman seemed to be the first in the entire conglomeration of spirit-animals emerging from the huge, hanging vulva-shaped stone behind it. The bleeding rhino-shaman had the black lines of a belly-band but the band itself had not been filled in with black paint like some of the other belly-banded rhinos. Neither had there been any clay to scrape from the yellowish stone all around to make for the rhino-shaman a white belly-band. The big-bellied rhino stood upon a large patch of reddish stone that was not the blood-red color of the spouts coming from its mouth and coloring its two horns and a half circle of red behind its eye. The half-circle was probably meant to indicate the cross-arm of a black All Mother's Cross. It curled oddly where the rhino's ear should have been. All-in-all, it was a truly astonishing image.

"Grandfather, is this bleeding image a rhino-shaman? Is all that we have seen here in the Black Lodge a shaman's dream-vision?" I asked with a dawning realization.

"Yes, my good Apprentice. That is exactly what it is. This shaman transformed into a rhino-guide dreaming the dream of the Mother's life of all the worlds. The shaman's trance-vision is, in turn, being birthed from the Mother's great Vulva Stone. Before our very eyes the shaman is dreaming himself into the midst of the Mother's vast herds of spirit-animals. The shaman is running with the herds as they emerge out of the Dark Lodges into the World of Light to become transformed—in his soul—as Thrice Born. The Mother *is* speaking to you through her Great Cave, Dear One," he said quietly.

We were both still exulting in the rolling spirit-fires that seemed to fill the whole cavern in wave after wave washing over us. We both stood contemplating the bleeding rhino-shaman and the spectacle of the spirit-herds stretching out along the wall all the way to the two guardian lions now in deep shadow at the entrance to the Black Lodge.

Now it is time to turn to the Pendant of the Mother's Vulva.

* * *

The Mother's Vulva Stone, from which all this astonishing life was coming forth, is a great rock shaped like a woman's pute hanging from the roof of the cave. It dropped toward the floor with its pointed end coming down to about the level of my breasts. There is a gap of two or three paces to the dividing ridge of rock on the western wall just to the left side of the Vulva Stone. The dividing ridge extends down the wall and then along the ground, reaching almost to the Vulva Stone. It forms a low platform or step up to a narrow passage running behind the Pendant.

The Ancient Makers must have stood upon this step to paint some of the lines that ran high up from the Vulva Stone itself on to wings of stone hanging from the roof of the Cave to the side and behind the Pendant. The Vulva Stone was not joined to any of the surrounding outcrops or walls which left a gap all around it—it hung free from the chamber roof. The western wall continued behind the dividing ridge and disappeared into a narrow and shadowy passage of undeterminable depth. I could see that a few spirit-animals were painted there too. The first of which, just behind the dividing ridge, is a beautifully painted black horse facing out toward the Vulva Stone.

"Look at the painted lines upon the Vulva Stone and tell me what you see, my Apprentice," the Grandfather whispered over my shoulder.

I was beginning to have fun with the Grandfather's little shaman's game but I was truly excited to discover what new and hidden things I would find there. If there were enough torchlight, one could have stood before the two great lion-guardians at the entrance and looked directly at one face of the Vulva Stone—the side I am looking at now. This Vulva Stone is definitely the focal point for every other image and sign made within this chamber. The heavy black paint of the image makes it perfectly clear what it is and so I answered the question without hesitation.

"It is the wide hips, pointed legs-with-no-feet and the female sex—the vulva—of the All Mother," I said, describing the figure. It loomed up right in front of my face and covering one whole side of the pendant.

The huge three-cornered pubic patch included a heavy vertical line in the center that was clearly the cleft of the vulva. It was so large and black that it fairly jumped off the stone. The Ancients had prepared to paint this image by scraping clean the pendant of its thin, light-brown clay layer to expose the white stone beneath. Outlines had then been made with a charcoal pencil. I could see that much. The oversized vulva had been almost completely filled in with black paint from a brush.

"Maybe the pubic hair of this gigantic pute was dabbed on with a piece of fur?" I speculated quietly to myself.

It was difficult to decide exactly how the image had been painted, but the maker had represented curly pubic hair perfectly. The torso above the wide hips ended in blank stone—the figure was all hips and legs with no upper body. The All Mother's huge breasts, her arms and head were completely missing.

"Grandfather, why does the Mother have no breasts or head or arms?" I asked.

"Are you sure the Mother has no head or arms? The stone has four sides and some of the lines run around the pendant up onto the roof. Follow the black line on the left of the stone—the Mother's right arm as she lies upon her back—around to the back side of the Pendant. Remember, the Great Cave *is* the All Mother lying upon her back and so is this image. Follow the line and tell me what you see," he replied.

"Yes, Grandfather. I will go where the lines go and I will tell you what I see," I said with a broad smile of anticipation.

With my eyes I began following the black lines from the topless torso up and around the left side of the Pendant, one side of which faces the western wall behind the great hanging stone. The thin black line ran up to the roof and then down onto a thin wing of stone that hung down behind the Pendant. There, the lines became the back, the profiled head and one front leg and paw of a lion. The spirit-lion looked out from behind the Pendant in the opposite direction toward what would be the eastern wall of the Black Lodge.

"Oh Grandfather!" I exclaimed with real surprise. "It's Lion Mother!"

"Yes, my Child. Now, go all the way around the four faces of the Vulva Stone and tell me what spirit-animals you find there," he replied with genuine glee.

On all four faces of the pendant engraved marks in white and painted lines in black had been made. There was not a single image in red. Below and encompassed with Lion Mother's back and front paw, I found two more lions. These two smaller lions were looking toward the western wall of the chamber where the hindquarters of the bleeding rhino-shaman drew near to the Pendant of the Mother's Vulva. If one were to stand in the middle of the Black Lodge and look toward its western wall, the spirit-animals painted on the wall behind the Pendant would be seen to continue the panorama of the spirit herds onto the other side of the dividing ridge of rock. On another flat wing of stone that descended from the low roof behind the pendant, three more lions appeared. All three of these spirit-lions were looking deeper into the narrow passage which disappeared into the darkness behind the Vulva Stone. Below the three lions, who were heading out of the narrow passage behind the Pendant toward the spirit-herds and the prides transforming spirit-lions, the beautiful all-black horse had been made.

"Grandfather? Where does this passage behind the Vulva Stone lead?" I called out in an excited voice.

"It is the passage that leads to the Womb of the Mother's Foot where some initiates will be led to quest for their companion-animals, Dear One. Continue on around the Vulva Stone, come back to the front of the Pendant and then you may explore that womb of black spirits if you wish."

Without any acknowledgement of the Grandfather's directions, I continued moving around the Pendant peering closely at all the images that had been made there. From where the two small lions looked across toward the three lions on their little wing of rock, I came to the open jaws of the Dark Lion Mother's round face. This familiar image was followed by the head-on white engraving of a mammoth without tusks, a white Mammoth Mother within the Black Lodge. The image had been splayed across the dividing ridge between two of the faces of the Vulva Stone. The white-spirited Mother of Abundance spanned the gap between the ending and a new beginning of things. On second thought, maybe it is a Mammoth Father with no tusks? I will have to ask the Grandfather. One-half of the mammoth's head was on one side of the ridge and one half on the other as if its head had been skinned and laid over a rock to dry.

"A bridge between two sides of the Pendant? Between the beginning and ending of things?" I guessed aloud.

There are always so many different ways to interpret the signs!

What followed on the next face of the Pendant confirmed my guess because after the white Mammoth Mother, several short rod-shaped lines, engraved with a finger in some un-scraped soft brown clay, had been made. These engraved, "white" signs were then followed by a black horse head. As I moved around to what would be the eastern face of the Pendant, there appeared a confusion of black lines and engraved crosshatching that must be a sign of the Black Net of the All Mother. Some of the lines of this Net of Life wrapped around the edge of the tapering pendant to run over and onto the reclining All Mother's left hip and thigh. I had come full circle in a sun-wise round of the Great Vulva Stone to gape in astonishment at the Grandfather. He smiled broadly as if he had just presented his most beloved friend with the most valued gift he had ever given.

"Now, come all the way around the Pendant and go back behind the Vulva Stone and follow the passage to the Womb of the Mother's Foot. If you wish, my good Apprentice," he said with twinkling eyes.

"Follow the passage behind the Vulva Stone into the deepest part of the entire Cave," the Grandfather said cheerfully.

* * *

The narrow passage behind the All Mother's Pendant is a continuation of the left-hand, western, wall containing the great spirit-herds. Behind the big black horse running toward the bleeding rhino-shaman, a mammoth's forequarters emerged from a deep cleft in the rock just before the passage widened and turned to the left. This is, no doubt, the left-hand portal of that side-chamber called the Womb of the Mother's Foot. This side-cavern has many sharp ice sickles and pointed curtains of stone hanging from a very high roof. It was a relief to find it had a flat, easy-to-walk floor.

The left-hand portal to this side-chamber is also marked by an amazing group of spirit-animals.

Facing out of the side-chamber on the left portal, a huge black lion overarched two black horses painted one above the other. The top horse faced out in the same direction as the black lion, while the bottom horse faced in toward the Womb of the Foot. I wondered if the right-hand portal of the Foot also had images?

I walked the ten paces it took to reach the right portal to see what might be painted there. On this right-hand portal, another huge black lion overarched two black horses painted one above the other, just like the left portal. The only difference between the two portals is that within the body of this lion, another smaller lion had been made—three lions in all on the two portals of the entrance to the Mother's Foot.

A vision of this great Black Lodge burst into my head: two great lion-guardians with a third red-lion between at its entrance facing in, and two great lion-guardians with a third small lion painted within one of them, at this portal facing out. And in-between, a most astounding herd of transforming spirit-animals all coming out of the Mother's Vulva Stone. But even more astonishingly, above the lion-within-a-lion, there had been made a red big-antler deer without any horns—the only completely red spirit-animal I had encountered in the entire Lodge of Black Spirits. This right-hand portal clearly was the way to enter this womb for questing. I will have to remember this if ever I become the Grandmother of the Rites.

Just as I prepared to enter the side-chamber, I noticed a gap between the eastern wall of the passage behind the Pendant and the north wall of the right-hand entrance to the Foot. The gap is most likely a passage to another chamber below. But the jumble of boulders and rocks that I could see with my lamplight stepping down into the darkness would not have been easy to descend so I decided not to try it. Besides, the Grandfather only mentioned the Womb of the Mother's Foot.

Between the images of the right-hand Portal of the Foot and the entrance to the gap, two spirit-animals had been made. Facing toward the entrance to the Foot and the guardian-lions of the right-hand portal, there appeared a mammoth—without tusks—

made with both painted black and white engraved lines. Rump to rump with the mammoth, a black rhino made in expert brush strokes faced out toward the gap, certainly an indication that another side-chamber lay within.

I turned back to enter the Womb of the Mothers Foot by its right-hand portal. Within I found five smaller side-chambers and niches radiating out from the high, wide entrance above an easy-to-walk clay floor—a foot with five toes! Or so it seems!

"Little wonder this chamber is called the Womb of the Mother's Foot," I said out loud to no one but myself.

"Has seer-apprentice Little Bear found the All Mother's missing foot?" I chuckled to myself.

The largest of the "toes" was the middle chamber, which quickly got very narrow and soon ended completely. I knew I was now in the very deepest, most northeasterly, part of the entire Cave of the Bear Mother, a black-spirited womb for solitary questing and trancing. Since I could go no further, I turned around and walked down the center of the Foot, through the entrance portal to the flat eastern wall of the passage behind the Vulva Stone.

As I moved out of the Mother's Foot along the wall opposite the beautiful black horse—the eastern wall of the narrow passage behind the Pendant—I realized the Vulva Stone actually could have been a continuation of this eastern wall of the narrow passage behind it. But the Pendant hung clear of this wall and was separated from it by a narrow space which had allowed me to circle the Vulva Stone completely.

"Come, my Daughter. Pass through the gap between the passage wall and the Vulva Stone. There is much more to be seen upon the other side of the narrow passage's wall," the Grandfather called to me, unseen, from the opposite side of the Pendant.

Only a few paces were needed to skirt around between the Pendant and the end of the passage's thin stone wall to its opposite side. And there, made on the flat surface of the stone, appeared the most magnificent spirit-bison I had yet seen in the entire Cave. I backed up a few paces into the chamber to take in the entire scene. I opened my mouth in astonished awe at the spectacle of one huge, black, bull bison with elegantly curved horns staring in the direction of the Vulva Stone. What is even more astonishing is that the snout of the bull bison was almost nose-to-nose with the spirit-lion head that wrapped around the Vulva Stone.

The left front leg and hoof of the beautifully detailed bison staring toward the Mother's Vulva had been made to merge into the rear haunches of a second bison that, strangely, had no front legs, hump or head at all. There was a crack in the stone out of which the two bison might be emerging from and entering into, but it was not otherwise marked to draw attention to it. What was a third bison's rear haunches blended skillfully into the head and shoulders of the bull bison looking toward the Vulva Stone resulting in a jumble of three bison with only one skillfully painted head, hump and front quarters. Very strange and beautiful—a bison with one head and three hind quarters! The one-in-three again? I shall have to ask the Grandfather! More bewildering still, below the three-in-one bison, another bull bison had been made facing the opposite direction from the single head and three hind quarters above it.

"Grandfather? Is this a bison or a musk ox? It has the body of a bison but the down-turning horns of a musk ox?" I turned to ask the Grandfather standing and smiling from cheek to cheek.

"It is what the seer of the image sees in it, Dear One."

Clearly I would have to decide which it is myself! This creature, whatever it is, faced in the opposite direction from the bison head above it toward the eastern wall of the Black Lodges. But the bison that was one head and three bodies was far more interesting. The single head of this amazing bison had a staring white eye, a gaping mouth and a lolling tongue. Bison Father tossed his head and bellowed in the direction of the Mother's Vulva Stone. He was obviously preparing to mount and join in sex with her across the gap between their respective stones. A truly amazing sight! So astounding were these images that I forgot to ask the Grandfather my questions.

Still more wonders were to be revealed before all of the images of the Black Lodge would show themselves. Three profiled horse heads in a line had been engraved behind the three bull bison. The line of horses went all the way back to the corner of the chamber. And in this corner, a gap opened up with stair-step boulders leading up—up to the Womb of the Mother's Foot, no doubt.

So quickly was I moving to see everything that I almost missed the tiny white shell that made one of the white Horse Mother's eyes. I could barely contain myself.

"Oh, Grandfather! Oh Grandfather! The Three Fathers in One! And the Three Horse Mothers too!" I called in sheer excitement. "

I moved closer to touch the magical images and to run my hands over the swelling in the rock suggesting the bison's great hump. I tried to work out how the Ancients had made such an image so full of spirit-fire and with what brush or drawing skills? I could see faint outlines that had been done with a pencil-stick of hard charcoal. But the wooly, coarse fur of the triple bison's massive head and ruff must have been made by dabbing on finely crushed charcoal paint with a piece of fur. Maybe the Ancient maker had used a wad of flax cloth? As I peered intently at the spirit-bison, I realized Bison Father's head had been drawn around, and centered on, a small, round object—a small clamshell from the river! The tiny white shell was embedded in the rock and made the white of Bison Father's staring eye just as with the white Horse Mother near the corner of the chamber. I was completely astonished!

"Daughter," the Grandfather murmured over my shoulder so as not to startle me in my reverie.

"Can you make a spirit-bison that has this great bull's life-fire?" the Grandfather asked in a whisper.

I held the torch up so that I could examine every detail of the image.

"Yes, Grandfather, I can. But I am a mere girl ... the spirit-powers of the Ancients ... I would not presume ..."

He cut me off in mid-complaint.

"Do not believe the stories that the spirit-powers have made these images. They were made by the gifted hands of the Ancient Ones who heard the song of the Mother and made these images to bless and instruct us. They were made by the hands of seers and shamans just like us."

It is true the hand and palm prints are clearly made by people, however ancient they may have been. And I had already seen the spirit-animals that have been obliterated and others painted in their

344

place. I knew the Grandfather spoke the truth. This Great Cave *was* painted by gifted and skilled hands filled with the Mother's spirit-powers. But they were human hands, nonetheless. I saw that some of the images were very crude—any child could make such drawings. But most were made with such skill and power that the animal could have come down from the wall and ran away.

"But what would you have me make for you, my Grandfather?" I pleaded. "I have not seen your dream? I have had no trance-visions? I have not taken the shaman's journey! How can I do what you ask when the Mother does not show me what she would have me make upon these walls already so full of spirit-fire?"

"Dear One," the Grandfather said gently. "You have learned much, seen much and your wisdom has grown since we entered the Mother's Great Cave. But your initiation is incomplete. First, become Twice Born Seer of the Bear People, and when you are fully initiated, you will answer your own questions. You will settle your own doubts and release your fears."

"Very well, my Grandfather. I will complete the seer's initiation," I replied in acceptance of my destiny.

I just wondered what could possibly remain to complete a seer's initiation?

CHAPTER 13.
A SHAMAN'S JOURNEY

THE GRANDFATHER LED ME a few paces out into the center of the Lodge of Black Spirits where we sat at an angle to the All Mother on her Vulva Pendant and Bison Father on his wall. From this vantage, Bison Father was only partly visible because the wall behind the Pendant slanted in to the corner where the gap led up to the Womb of the Foot. As we sat facing the Vulva Stone and Bison Father, only now did I notice a charcoal hearth near my right hand filled with large and small chunks of the blackest, finest pine charcoal.

It was easy to tell this was a special hearth for making charcoal. It is always made by covering the smoking pine logs with dirt. If left to blaze up like cooking or dancing fires, the logs will completely turn to ash. I could see this charcoal-making hearth was very, very old because not a single flake of gray ash was anywhere to be seen. I also noticed other piles of crushed pieces and powdered charcoal heaped at the base of the wall beneath the three-in-one Bison Fathers. It was a much larger pile than would have been left over, or could have fallen, while the Ancients made the bison images on the wall above.

So taken was I by the beautiful, power-filled bison that I had not even noticed the little heaps of charcoal beneath them! I am sure now the presence of this holy charcoal made by the Ancients is the reason the Grandfather did not mention bringing my own powdered charcoal into the Cave. All along he intended for me to use the charcoal of the Ancients already piled here in the depths of the Mother's Cave.

The Grandfather looked directly into my eyes.

When I held his intense gaze and did not look away he said, "Dear One, the Mother has spoken to me in dreams and visions. This is thy destiny and this is thy life's great adventure. Open now thy heart and be one with the Mother, for this is the Lodge of Union and of the rejoining of that which has been separated—man from woman, hunter from hunted, light from dark, above from below, one from another. Learn thou the Song of the Joining to guide, comfort and strengthen thee always as Seer of the Bear People."

The Grandfather began to sing:

> *The Mother makes all things of herself by herself*
> *Becoming the thing that she makes.*
> *I and the Mother are One.*
> *The Father takes all things back to himself by himself*
> *Becoming the thing he takes back.*
> *I and the Father are One.*
> *The Mother joins with the Father*
> *I join with my opposite*
> *I give birth and I eat back.*
> *The Mother that lives within moveth me*
> *I and the Mother are One.*
> *The Father that lives within moveth me*
> *I and the Father are One.*
> *I am a fountain of life*
> *The blood of life flows through me*
> *I and the Mother are One.*
> *I am an eater of life*
> *The spirit of life flows through me*
> *I and the Father are One.*
> *I am the Beginning and I am the Ending*
> *I am the Mother-power and I am the Father-power.*
> *I Am All There Is*

Beside which there is no other.

Tears were streaming down my face before the Grandfather finished his song and I did not know why. I certainly am not sad about anything. To the fading sounds of the Grandfather's chant, all the images round about seemed to swirl and spiral around me in a great rush. I remembered every word of the chant with this single hearing. I knew in that moment that I would sing the Song of the Joining to myself in times of despair and loneliness for as long as my red-body would live in the World of Light.

"Thank you, my Grandfather," I said. "Thank you for giving me the heart and courage to do what you and the Mother ask of me."

"It is well, Dear One," he said, speaking with as much compassion in his voice as I had ever heard.

"Repeat back to me the Song and you will then be prepared to meditate and trance. You will then be prepared for the final solitary journey you must take into the darkness of your own soul and enter the Black Womb of the Seers."

I looked around the chamber in all directions trying to see any opening or crevice that had not yet been explored. The gap in the corner only led to the Womb of the Foot. Where could this Black Womb of the Seers be? I could only see one small opening, far too small and too high up for anyone to climb through, just beneath the roof of the chamber's northeast corner, opposite the trinity of Bison Fathers and the gap in the corner.

I thought to myself "Surely that can't be the entrance to the Black Womb of the Seers? It is far higher than a man's head and too small for even me to crawl through!"

I was baffled. So I just decided to relax and let the Grandfather surprise me. The Trickster in him so loved his little surprises!

"Are you ready to open the spirals of trance, Dear One?" he asked.

I nodded in assent and the Grandfather began to intone the opening of the two spirals of protection as we breathed the Holy Breaths and chanted the Song of the Joining together. As he began intoning the spirals of protection I removed my robe and unslung the oil horn and satchel. Then I lay down next to the ancient charcoal hearth wrapping myself up in the warm, black bearskin robe. By the time the Grandfather asked the All Mother to come forth to show me his dream-vision and spoke the words, "We thank thee, Mother and we know that it is already done," I was deep in trance.

* * *

Flying and floating through swimming colors and billowing waves of spots and flashes of bright light, time means nothing in the trance. Place melted into place, moment melted into moment and there was only the Cave, the spirit-animals, the Grandfather; the silence—nothing else. I no longer even had a name, as if the girl called "Little Bear" had died and ceased to exist altogether. Still I saw no spirit-messengers. I heard no Voice. My Horse Mother guide did not show herself to me and no half-animal half-human monsters came to tear and rend me to pieces. All I heard was the sound of rushing, falling water. All I saw was the beautiful spinning colors and lights interspersed with the utter blackness of the Great Cave.

An eternity of floating in the rainbow, fluid brilliance soon melted away as the morning fog before the sunlight and all I could see was the face and the blue-black eyes of my Beloved. Only his lips and tongue and skin and probing manhood could I taste. All I could hear was the sound of his voice laughing, his moaning and grunting and gasping as he thrust himself inside me again and again. All I could feel was the gentle touch of his hands, his lips and both of us at last reaching the highest peak of bliss in the same moment. All I could smell was the scent of his perfumed sweat, the pungent fragrance of his essence between our sweating bodies gluing us together in an unbreakable embrace. Rising to the peak again, his white-essence filled me with light, expanding me, exploding me into a myriad of shooting stars. My scattered body of rainbow light and spinning flame rejoined, my heart and liver and vulva pulled back together as a body of ice crystals and fire.

Now joined as one with Brown Bull forever—my body, his body; my mind, his mind; my heart, his heart. My soul, his soul. Where did my skin leave off and his begin? Where did his soul leave off and mine begin? Only in his blue-black eyes, sun-filled hair, flawless skin and smooth, sweet lips could I find this ecstasy of trance. Only there could I find my bliss.

This is all I saw or heard or touched or felt until the far-off voice of the Grandfather called me to a reluctant return in a floating ascent back to the World of Light.

I opened my eyes blinking. I sat up to look about the chamber.

The Grandfather sitting beside me asked quietly, "Did the Mother come to you, Dear One? Were you given the vision of what you are to make upon on the holy walls of the Mother's Cave?" he asked plaintively.

And then, unable to help myself, I lied to the Grandfather once again.

"Yes Grandfather. I saw the vision."

The Grandfather sighed with complete relief and held the gourd of sweet, clear water to my lips. He let me drink and clear my head for a few moments without speaking.

"Rest, my good Apprentice. When you are ready I will show you the entrance to the Black Womb of the Seers. Leave your lamp here and take a fresh torch with you."

I sat sipping the water and eating a few of the roots that the Grandfather handed me until my head began to clear. Still half-dazed, the Grandfather handed me his, then withdrew a new torch from his bag. He unwrapped the top and touched it to the torch I held in my hand.

The new torch caught the flame and he handed it to me.

"As before, you must enter this Womb naked. You will take with you only your open heart and this vision the Mother has given you. The way is so narrow and the roof so low you will have to crawl on four legs. You must squeeze through narrow passages just as you forced your way through your mother's vulva to be born into the Light World of red blood and red flesh. But this birthing will be the coming forth of the black spirit-powers of oneness and union within your heart. You will follow the red spots, black torch-marks and images found in the passage to the very end of this black-spirited Womb of Seers. As you re-emerge from this journey it will be the end of Little Bear and the beginning of your new life as Seer of the Bear People. This is your final step on a new and winding path to your own heart. As you force your way through these narrow passages you will die as a woman and be reborn as Seer of the Bear People. Come now, and you will take your last journey of transformation into the black Entrails of the Mother."

"Yes, Grandfather. I am ready to take this journey. Let is be so," I said with determination.

And I am ready to go because I truly feel in my heart that I am no longer a woman called "Little Bear". I am another creature, somehow reborn of my blissful trance and dream of Brown Bull, my Beloved.

* * *

When I was well-recovered from my flight of dreams, the Grandfather led me back towards the drop off and the sloping stone. We walked along the chamber's bare eastern walls until we came to what looked like a gigantic boulder protruding from the wall. The top of a rounded overhang stretched out toward the drop off where it gradually flattened out into the shelf we had used to come down into the Black Lodge. At the bottom of the protruding rock, a wide, but very low, opening had been marked in its center with the only image on the entire eastern wall of the Lodge of the Lion Mother—the three-cornered, completely blacked-out Vulva of the All Mother.

"In you must go, Dear One. The Mother will guide the way," he said pointing to the opening.

I sloughed the robe from my shoulders and handed it to the Grandfather. Then I got down on all fours and began to squeeze under the huge boulder while holding trying to hold the torch out in front of me. A few red rod-shaped marks on the rock I kept bumping my head on showed me the way. As if I could go anywhere but in the direction the long and ever-narrowing passage took me!

I crawled painfully, bare knees on rough stone, for what seemed a great distance before the roof raised up high enough for me to stand. The right-hand wall at this spot was marked by a single Bear Mother scratched into the stone—the only white spirit-bear that appears in all the Lodges of the Dark Mother.

"Bear Mother is the protector of new life," I whispered to myself.

"White Bear Mother, hear the words of my mouth and protect me now!" I said out loud.

The dots and torch marks appearing from time-to-time along the wall were hardly necessary to guide me through this passage. There is only one way to go in this narrow, narrow place! Just when I thought the passage couldn't possibly get any tighter, it did. The narrowest point in the passage had been marked by an engraved Mammoth Mother. I pushed my way through her tight vulva as well.

Beyond that tiny opening, the cavern expanded out again in all directions. The Cave was now full of a jumble of boulders and rocks over which I was forced to climb down in a descending passage, after which I had to go up and over a flow of wet, white stone. Then the path led down again through more narrow cracks and passages, some so narrow I was sure anyone larger than I am was certain to get stuck forevermore. I forced my way through the narrow places and felt as if the entire mountain was crushing me. I tried not to panic. I chanted every song to dispel fear that I could remember.

The passages were narrow, but the roof was very high in this part of the cavern, rising up far beyond my torchlight in many places. The caverns were really just big cracks in the stone. As I reached a small flat area covered with blessedly soft clay, I thought I could see a faint glow coming from an opening in the left-hand wall above me higher than a man stands. I shielded my torchlight behind a large boulder to cast the left-hand wall in full shadow.

Now I am *sure* a faint light is coming through an opening in the stone!

Fallen sloping rocks to the right side of the passage allowed me to climb up to a kind of platform. There, a yellow light shone through a small opening in the solid stone. I inched forward to the opening, cold rough rock against my naked belly, breasts, elbows and knees. To my amazement I looked out upon the entire Lodge of Black Spirits! I was peering out of the small opening in the Lodge's northeast corner directly across from the three Bison Fathers and the little gap to the Womb of the foot!

I could see the entire western wall of the Black Lodge from the paired lion-guardians at the entrance to the herds of transforming animals in the middle, all the way to the Mother's Vulva Pendant at the back, and beyond to the great Bison Father directly across from me. I could also see the Grandfather sitting cross-legged and facing the All Mother on her Pendant. My oil lamp was on the ground in front of the Grandfather, but he had also lit three pine torches. He had placed one in front of the paired lions at the entrance, one in front of the great herd of transforming spirit-animals and one close to where he sat, the third torch shining on the Vulva Pendant and Bison Father. The torches lit up the whole chamber in a warm yellow glow. The flickering light made the transforming herds and the very walls of the Black Lodge come alive with movement as they fled toward the entrance away from their source in the Mother's life-giving black vulva.

I could not see much of the All Mother's Vulva. The face of the pendant upon which it was painted faced more toward the entrance and the lion attendants than it pointed in my direction. But I could just make out her left hip and one corner of her oversized, charcoal-blackened vulva. As I took in the astonishing scene, my eye was drawn to Bison Father whose great shaggy head with his eye of shell loomed to the right of the Pendant. The great bull seemed to be looking with his staring white eye at a large un-painted section of the Pendant just beyond the Mother's left hip and pointed left leg as she lay upon her back.

I knew in that moment what image I would make there.

I called out, my excited voice echoing around the chamber, "Grandfather! Grandfather! I made it! I made it!"

All that the Grandfather said, as he turned toward me smiling, was, "Come back, Dear One. Be reborn as Seer of the Bear People."

* * *

The narrow passages of the Black Womb of the Seers seemed eas-ier to squeeze through and the return path seemed much shorter, so anxious was I to get back to the Grandfather where he waited for me before the All Mother's Pendant. As I emerged from be-neath the overhanging boulder marked with the Mother's black three-cornered pute, the Grandfather was waiting there to help me up. He enfolded me in the comforting warmth of the bearskin robe.

I had completely forgotten that I was naked and very, very cold. My body, hair, hands and face were smudged with streaks from the muddy passage floor and walls. My elbows and knees were bruised and scraped from crawling through the narrow rocky caverns, but I did not care. All I could see in the eye of my mind was the spirit-image I would add to the Mother's Vulva Pendant.

"Well done, my Daughter!" the Grandfather said warmly.

He put a comforting arm around my shoulder and led me back to the place before the All Mother's Vulva Stone where my bag, oil horn and oil lamp had been put aside.

"Now come, thou, and receive ye the marks of a Seer of the Bear People," the Grandfather said in formal words.

I knew what that would involve. But I was so excited and full of joy, spirit-fire and satisfaction with myself that I did not care what was to come.

"Come, Dear One. Kneel before the All Mother's Pendant and I will make of thee Seer of the Bear People," he intoned.

The Grandfather then led me to kneel upon the stony ground to look up at the All Mother's Vulva. As I knelt, the Grandfather fished in his otter bag for the marking flint. Finding it, he turned me slightly so that the nearby torch would shine more directly on my face. Then he went to the wall of the bull bison-in-three and scooped a small handful of the powdered charcoal from the pile beneath the image. He came back to where I knelt, my face still upturned and waiting for him.

"Hold out thy palms to carry the All Mother's charcoal as thou wilt carry her spirit-power with thee for the rest of thy life," he said solemnly.

He poured the charcoal powder from his hand into my upheld palms.

"Dear One, sing the silent song of thy heart while I mark thy face with the sign of the Mother's Tree of Life to make of thee Seer of the Bear People," he said respectfully.

I began to hum very softly to myself and he began to make the marks.

"By the All Mother who is thy Source, I mark thy left cheek as Seer of the Bear People with the White Tree of Life," he chanted softly as he stabbed the All Mother's cross into my left cheek.

"By the All Mother who is thy Source, I mark thy right cheek as Seer of the Bear People with the Red Tree of Life," he again spoke quietly.

He worked intently to make the tiny cuts of the second of the two crosses I would carry for the rest of my life.

To divert myself from the pain I was feeling, the first song that came to my mind was the Song of the Joining. As I hummed the song and said the words in my head, the music seemed to gather at the base of my spine. It began moving up the center of my body to fill me with the warmth and ecstasy of joining in sex with Brown Bull all over again. I was in such bliss, and my skin so chilled, I barely felt the multitude of tiny stabs of the pointed white flint. The Grandfather finished making the shaman's marks quickly, stopping only long enough to rub tiny pinches of the Bison Father's charcoal from my palms into the oozing cuts.

When the Grandfather finished with the flint and the charcoal, he raised me up to stand before the All Mother's Pendant. He stood back slightly to one side so as not to block my view of the Great Vulva. He began to chant the song of my initiation—the Song of Abundance—while occasionally moving back to rub more of the powder into the two crosses where the blood continued to seep out.

These cheek marks would announce to all who saw me as an initiated Seer for as long as I walked in the World of Light.

Just as I thought the rite had been completed, the Grandfather began to speak more words of my initiation.

"Little Bear, woman of the Bear People, give ear and hear the words of my mouth. I, Flying Otter, Grandfather of the Nine Kin, make of thee Twice Born Seer of the Bear People with the holy charcoal of Bison Father. I mark thee with the Two Holy Trees of the All Mother at each eye that thou mayest see the truth of all things of the worlds of the Above and the worlds of the Below. Oh Great Mother of all there is, hear now the words of my mouth and accept thy daughter Little Bear as thy servant, who shall henceforth be known as Yellow Lion, Twice Born Seer of the Bear People. And we know that thou hast already accepted her and now gift her with the sight of thy Holy Eye as Seer.

Overwhelmed at hearing my new secret name, I nevertheless knew to thank the Mother for her gift of sight with the words, "I thank thee, Mother, and I accept."

And with the Grandfather's final words, "Thou art Twice Born, Dear One," the ordeal was over.

I had been marked and given the secret name that should never be revealed to anyone, except the spirit-powers or to another seer or shaman. Not even to a husband would this secret seer's name ever be given. With this seer's name I would not choose a new woman's name at the time I bring a husband to my mother's lodge. For the rest of my life in the World of Light I will have no personal name to any of the Nine Kin, not even to the man I will someday bring to my mother's hearth. I would forever be Auntie or Mother to those younger than I, Sister to those who are my age-mates, and Daughter or Twice Born to those older than I.

If I am fortunate, my future husband will call me "Beloved" but the name "Little Bear" will never again be heard by these ears of mine coming from another's mouth. I am sure that will be so, except when my family or close friends get angry at me and they are forced to be disrespectful to the great Twice Born Seer I have become. Certainly, my Thrice Born grandmother would have been pleased with me this day. I wonder if I have all *my* bones? Am I missing one that might prevent me from taking the shaman's journey one day? That would certainly not please that honored ancestor of mine! I just hope I do not learn of missing bones and such as my dear Auntie did!

At long last, I begin to understand why my mother was so unhappy to see me come to this initiation. Her daughter, formerly known as "Little Bear," has died. I have been born a second time as Yellow Lion, Seer of the Bear People, a name my mother will never speak or even know. That does make me very sad for my mother.

* * *

The making of the new spirit-animal took no time at all.

A large flat stone moved beneath the western face of the Vulva Stone gave me just enough height to reach almost to the top of the great Pendant where it joined with the cave ceiling. The empty space on the Pendant, upon which I would make my new spirit-image, had long been scraped of its fine layer of light-brown clay. Even that small amount of preparation of the rock surface to receive my paints was unnecessary. All I had to do was select a piece of hard, partially burned, charcoal from the ancient hearth and sharpen it a little with the Grandfather's holy marking flint. With that ancient pencil, I could make the guidelines as fat or thin as I required. Using Bison Father's beautiful ruffed head on the wall to my right as a model, the sketching of the head of the new spirit-animal was accomplished with just a few quick strokes of the charcoal.

It only took a few more moments to outline the forequarters and back of a sprit-bison overarching the torso and vulva of Lion Mother as Bison Father prepared to mount and join with her in sex. The left front leg of my new Bison Father lay across the reclining Mother's right leg and ended, not in a hoof or a point as spirit-animals are usually made, but with a man's five-fingered hand. I made my spirit-bison's left leg end in a human hand the way that masked bison-dancers always leave their left arms bare and painted to make it known that they are human beneath the mask. My new Bison Father caressed the inner thigh of his Lion Mother with human fingers as my own lover might put his hand on the inside of my thigh. I made a half-man, half-bison joining in blissful union with the body and soul of the half-lion, half-woman Mother of us all.

The Grandfather watched with rapt attention while I worked.

All that remained to finish the image was to use pieces of the softer charcoal from the ancient hearth to draw in and fill out the bull's open mouth, staring eyes, flaring nostrils, flying spittle, his bison beard, and gracefully curving horns. The finished image showed Bison Father mounting Lion Mother in the heat of body-passion just as my own Brown Bull had mounted me in my dream-vision.

I decided the best way to imitate the wooly, curling fur of a bison's head and ruffed hump would be to mix some of the ancient charcoal with some of my lamp oil. I mixed the oil and powder in the grinding stone from my bag and then I began to dab it on with a piece of fur from my satchel.

The effect was perfect and identical to the Ancient bull bison which had been my model.

Perfect, except for several lines from the ancient painting that now looked out of place on my new bison's hump and shoulder. Before dealing with that, the charcoal-and-oil mixture remaining in my grinding stone—when thinned a little with more oil—would provide the paint for the bison's penis. Since I had never seen a bison bull's penis in the act of joining with a cow, the only thing I could do was make a human penis modeled after my own lover's rod and man-eggs. It was only fitting that the bison-man possessed more than a left arm that was human if he was about to join with his lion-woman in sex!

This was a task for a paintbrush. I had brought several of different sizes with me and they had already been laid out ready for my selection of just the right-sized brush. I played with the idea of giving the bull a penis as big as Brown Bull's, but this image was only a fraction of the size of a living bison, or a living man for that matter, so I made a penis that better fit the size of the spirit-image. I hope Lion Mother will be pleased with it anyway!

The Grandfather watched in silent, open-mouthed amazement as I worked rapidly to complete the image. He pulled his brows together in puzzlement as I cleaned the remaining charcoal paint from the grinder and then began searching one of the damp walls still covered by the fine coating of soft brown clay near the floor of the Cave.

"What are you doing now, my Daughter?" he asked. "Bison Father is beautiful, powerful, and complete. The long, curving horns are identical to the spirit-bison of the Ancients. You truly have a great gift of the Mother," he praised me with true enthusiasm for the image I had made.

"I will show you, Grandfather. Just wait one moment while I scrape these walls of their soft clay," I said.

I scraped the walls with the fingers of one hand and wiped them into the grinder until I had collected enough of the moist brown clay to complete the making of my new image. I added some spit and mixed it in to make the clay more fluid.

"Watch what I do to cover the old lines that confuse the new bison image," I said.

With a wad of flax cloth, I began to daub and rub the light-brown clay onto the bison's shoulders, hump and back to cover some of the ancient lines that were now out of place with the new image. Then I applied the tan clay down the bison's left arm to obliterate the fine, ancient lines of Lion Mother that appeared there. All of this made it appear that Bison Father was on top of Lion Mother, ready to impale her giant vulva on his man-rod.

"It is finished, my Grandfather!" I said, standing back out of his way so that he could see my work.

"Yes, Dear One, this *is* my dream-vision," the Grandfather commented thoughtfully as he peered closely at the finished bison-man.

"It is the very joining of Bison Father and Lion Mother, the joining of the pairs of opposites that have been separated. My good Apprentice, do you know this image that you have made is the very giver of the People's bison dances of the White Brother-hood?"

I was more than astonished at this because no such dream-vision had come to me. No spirit-guide had spoken to me of what image I should make upon the Vulva Stone. I had just looked at the images that were already there before my eyes. Until this very moment I truly had not even thought of the well-known story of the human girl who married a bison-shaman. My stunned silence was taken as agreement and knowledge of what he was saying. Then the Grandfather began to weep.

"I thought this is what you wanted, my Grandfather?" I said in a frantic attempt to comfort him.

"No, No, my Daughter, it is more than I ever could have imag-ined or asked for. The Mother *is* with you. You *are* blessed with the Mother's spirit-power. The Mother speaks to you through your brushes and your paints! Do you not see that the Mother works through you to be a powerful blessing to the whole of the Nine Kin for all the worlds to come for what you have done this day?"

I was made dumb by the Grandfather's words but I still managed to get out a weak, "Thank you, my Grandfather."

I didn't know what else to say, so overwhelmed I became at his words.

Half embarrassed by such high praise, I looked down trying to find something more to say scratched in the brown clay of the cave floor, but I found nothing there.

The Grandfather put his rough, crooked finger under my chin and lifted my head to look into my eyes for a long moment.

"Dear One, you have done very well this day," he said lovingly. "I am so pleased with you. The Mother is greatly pleased with you and will bless you all your life long as a healer and gift-giver for the whole People. What you have done this day will bless and instruct the Nine Kin for as long as there are people who come to the Great Cave and for all the worlds to come. Take comfort and honor in that, Daughter of my Heart."

At such words, I could not prevent the tears of joy from welling up. They spilled over to track down my new Seer's marks wetting the patches of dry charcoal powder that still adhered to the livid marks. Charcoal powder cannot staunch teardrops as it does red blood.

This was the moment I really felt I had become, in fact, Seer of the Bear People.

Quite suddenly, I began to feel very, very tired.

"Thank you, my Grandfather, for all you have shown me and taught me in this place. I will remember it for as long as I am in the World of Light," I said with real humility. "But may I ask a question, Grandfather?"

"Of course, Dear One," he said. "Always ask what you do not understand."

"I can see how the spirit-image I have made might make you think of the Marriage of Bison Woman, but I saw no such thing in my trance-vision. I only saw Bison Father on his wall with his shell eye looking toward the Vulva Pendant as if to mount the Mother. That is what I made. How is it that my looking at Bison Father and your dream-vision could be the same, Grandfather?"

"Dear One, that is because there is only one Mother who sends visions and spirit-companions to all. The Mother is always present and forever speaks with one Voice from within, but she speaks through many mouths. You have heard that Voice today and it may be many seasons hence before you realize it in your heart. But realize it you will, one day. I have never been so sure of anything. But let us now complete your initiation, my good apprentice."

"What remains to be done before my initiation is complete?" I asked wearily, hoping against hope the ordeal was complete.

"One trial remains, Dear One," he cautioned. "But this rite is entirely of your choosing. If you choose not to do this thing it does not alter your power or place as Seer of the Nine Kin. Should you choose to mark your left shoulder with the sign of the Dark Lion Mother, your honor and standing among the seers and shamans, indeed, of the whole People, will be that much greater."

"Yes, Grandfather, I understand that. But how could one more mark upon my body give me greater honor than having these two crosses upon my face?"

"As Seer, you will learn that the powers signified by our body marks, the close connections to the spirit-messengers indicated by our pendants, charms, necklaces of teeth, bone and rare stones, all increase our power as seers, healers and shamans in the eyes and hearts of the People. The mark of Lion Mother upon the shoulder is the sign of the Dark Mother's spirit-power coming forth from within you. It is a choice to be closer to Lion Mother and to have her at your left hand always as you already have Bear Mother at your right hand wherever you go. Do you have another question?" he said, a query clearly showing on my squinting, upturned eyes and furrowed brow.

"Yes, Grandfather, I have another question," I said straight out.

As I began to ask my question the Grandfather glanced sidelong at my lamp. The oil was getting very low in the little bowl. Even as I spoke, he unstopped his horn and poured the last of his oil into the lamp

"Of all the women seers and shamans I have ever seen, only Auntie has Lion Mother's marks upon her left shoulder. None of the other seers or shamans of my acquaintance have the Dark Mother's marks on their left shoulders. If they entered the Black

Lodges but have the marks of other spirit-guides, why would this be so?" I asked.

"Twice Born," he began. "You have been initiated Seer of the Bear People by entering the Black Womb of the Seers. It is now your right and your honor to have her marks placed upon your left shoulder. This reveals to one and all and whoever sees your marks that you had the courage to descend to this darkest and deepest of the Black Lodges for your initiations. Most shamans choose other Lodges for their initiations but a very few are directed by their own spirit-guides to the Black Lodges as you have been brought to enter the Black Womb of the Seers out of necessity. The Dark Mother speaks to the hearts of only a very few of us and always each apprentice is allowed to choose the lodge or womb within the Cave that speaks to their own heart. Whichever lodge that is, it becomes their own holy lodge of initiation with the powers of that place speaking to their very own soul. Do you understand?" The Grandfather paused for my response.

After thinking about it for a moment I said, "Yes, Grandfather, I understand. But you said that some male seer-initiates take their trials here and that even some of the boys choose to enter the Black Womb of the Seers during their puberty rites. Is that not so?"

"Yes, that is so," he answered simply.

"Then, if I were a man and if I were drawn to enter this deepest and darkest of all the lodges of the Cave, would I not be marked in any way to show *my* courage to enter such a fearsome and powerful place?" I asked.

"Yes, you would, my good Apprentice. All the men who fear not to enter here are also marked. But male seers, or even new men who enter to commune with the powers of this place, are not marked with the Dark Mother on their shoulders."

As he spoke, his voice lowered to a much more somber and serious tone. I leaned toward him in rapt attention, the better to hear him. I had the feeling I should not have asked this question.

"Women shed blood with every circling of the moon and they shed even more blood in the pains of childbirth. With every new birth a woman draws very near to the Dark Mother and many women return to the Mother during childbirth. But men, as I have already explained, do not have an experience of that kind to join

362

them to the powers of the Dark Mother in their hearts. Because of that, every hunter initiate, male seer or shaman who chooses to commune with the Dark Mother here, in her most holy of lodges, is marked with the Lion Mother's fang marks in his penis. Each male initiate will shed blood from his foreskin onto the earth of this Dark Mother's Lodge," he whispered in hushed tones.

I knew I shouldn't have asked. I paused for a moment, thinking about what the Grandfather had just said. I tried to imagine the pain involved—a man's penis is so tender and easily feels much pain. I was completely unable to decide how such a thing could be done without permanent damage to that most useful and enjoyable of all male appendages.

"How is that done, Grandfather? Isn't it painful?" I blurted.

"Yes, it is painful, my Daughter. But experience of pain and suffering is the purpose of it. It is also to teach the lesson to the men that blood and pain are always the result of getting a woman with a child in her belly. By this, they are led to understand that the little pain and bleeding they go through in this is nothing compared to bearing a child. Come, I will show you how it's done."

My eyes got big as bowls and surely were bulging out of my face. He fumbled in his bag for a moment then withdrew a very slender ivory needle. It was the longest awl with the finest, sharpest point I had ever seen on anything, including a newly made spear point. To my utter embarrassment and horror, the Grandfather began to unlace his trouser drawstring.

"What are you doing, Grandfather?" I called out in surprise just as his red leather trousers dropped to the ground around his ankles.

Thank the Mother he has his loinskin on! Now, I do not think I am a silly little girl in such matters. In fact, I have already seen the Grandfather naked and I know what his penis and his man-eggs look like. It is just that I am not prepared to see the Grandfather's man-rod skewered on that needle like a fish roasting over a fire!

"Calm yourself, my Apprentice," he said laughing. "I am not going to impale my penis just to show you how this is done."

Yet again, the Grandfather had seen my thoughts upon my face and answered before the question could be asked.

"Besides, it might help to know that the penis is not run through. Only the foreskin," he explained. As if that somehow made a huge difference.

"It is unlikely you will ever have to do this to an initiate in this Black Lodge. But in the event you are made the Grandmother of the Bear People, you must know how this can be done without forevermore ruining the initiate's joining in sex!"

The more uncomfortable his words made me, the bigger the Grandfather's smile became.

"Very well, my Grandfather. If it is necessary to know, I will learn," I said cautiously.

"Here, take the needle in your right hand," he said handing me the slender shaft of ivory.

My instruction began in earnest as he pushed his loinskin aside, pulled out his penis and held it in his palm. I'm sure I grimaced a little when I noticed his big testicles hanging down his leg in an oddly disgusting way. I waited for further instruction hoping it would all be over soon.

"You use your right hand the most, do you not? Place your thumb on the flattened end and hold the needle as you would to stab downward at something, not as you would to make a hole for sewing." he continued.

I nodded in stupefied agreement.

"Now, with your left hand grasp the very end of my foreskin firmly between your thumb and first finger. Pull it out as far as it will stretch," he said offering his penis to me with a side-to-side shaking movement of his hand.

I hesitated for a moment, distaste almost certainly showing on my face. I grasped his foreskin.

There was absolutely *nothing* enjoyable about this, but I began to pull the Grandfather's foreskin toward me as I had been told. All the while, I was thinking I might be hurting him.

"I can't believe I'm doing this!" I said in a low whisper.

Even as I muttered the words I felt a rush of incestuous shame run through me as if I were touching my own father's penis.

"Go ahead," the Grandfather said. "Pull and stretch it as much as you can. It doesn't hurt!"

I pulled harder and the skin began to stretch to the point that his massive man-eggs even began to rise up his leg little.

"Now, my careful Apprentice, place the needle point just beyond the tip of your thumb. But don't push it through. I do not need to have my foreskin pierced anew!"

When I placed the needle as I was instructed, the point lay exactly over one of the faded charcoal marks on the top side of his foreskin—one of the marks I had glimpsed at the hot springs.

"It is the same mark as on Brown Bull's penis!" I realized with words and a bright light blazing up inside my head.

"Quickly push the needle through both layers of foreskin, top and bottom. Then pull the foreskin all the way back down the penis before applying powdered charcoal to the bleeding punctures. In this way you will leave four black spots in the initiate's foreskin—two on top and two on the bottom of the penis. All four spots will only be visible when the foreskin is pulled back to pee ... or when joining in sex," he concluded.

"You needn't show me the spots on the underside, Grandfather. I think I understand how this is done," I said with not a little disgust.

I found my thoughts effortlessly flying elsewhere and I began to wonder, "Are any of the little black spots in the Cave meant to signify these penis marks of the Dark Mother?"

I almost asked the question out loud but I had become so exhausted I was ready to collapse to the ground. I just did not want to have to think about anything or count any more dots or marks on the walls of this Cave. But that was not to be and the Grandfather went on and on.

"Should you ever perform this rite and make these marks in a man's penis, remember to use your strength to pinch the dry foreskin as tight as you can. If you pull it out toward you as far as you can, when you suddenly push the needle through, the point will surely puncture all four layers of skin. Make sure the needle is as sharp as you can make it. And ask the initiate to lean back against a wall or sit on a boulder so he cannot flinch and pull his foreskin out of your fingers just as you stab. Also, never warn the initiate that you are about to puncture his foreskin or he might pull to the side when you plunge the needle through. Just grab the foreskin,

tell him to turn his head, bring out the needle and do it quickly before he realizes what is happening and all will be well. The Mother
will guide your hands and the needle as it makes the four fang
marks of the Dark Lion Mother in the penis of the initiate. Now
you can let go my foreskin, Twice Born," he concluded with an
amused smile.

I quickly pulled my hand away and absentmindedly wiped non-
existent substances from my fingers onto the bearskin robe. Unconcerned, the Grandfather stuffed his genitals back into his loinskin. He tightened the loinskin, pulled up and tied his trousers.
That ordeal was over!

Then he signaled readiness to continue further by saying, "If
you are now willing to have the Lion Mother's marks made upon
your skin, lie down on your side and bare your left shoulder, Seer
of the Bear People."

The Lion Mother's incredibly sharp penis-stabber was used to
make her marks on my left shoulder instead of the flint. But before
the Grandfather began to make the many, many stabs of the needle, he withdrew from his bag of shaman's tricks a small piece of
hard leather with a circle cut into it. It was a stencil to guide the
punctures into a perfect circle. Inside the circle, the needle stabbed
four dots in a square—the four lion-fangs of the Dark Mother.

I knew without the Grandfather's telling me these four marks
will speak to one and all that this woman braved the terrors of
Lion Mother's Black Lodge. This new Seer, however young and
inexperienced, now brings that spirit-power to the People. I have
inexorably taken the seer's path and there can be no going back.

Bison Father's holy charcoal was rubbed into the wounds and
it was finished.

As I rose to gather my things, the Grandfather took another
sidelong glance at the oil in my lamp. It was quite low as the remainder of his oil had not begun to fill the bowl.

"Our time in the Great Cave grows short. It is time to go, my
Daughter."

"I have more oil to fill the lamp?" I offered.

"That is not necessary, my good Apprentice. We have now
completed all that I intended for us to accomplish in the Great
Cave and we have completed all the rites and ordeals of your initia-

tions. It is time to leave the Cave and return to the World of Light."

The Grandfather picked up the torch from where it had been stuck to light the marking of my shoulder and turned to go. As we moved back toward the entrance of the Black Lodge, he picked up the second torch and doused it in the soft clay at the base of a large rock. He then led me on to the third torch that lit the paired lion-guardians. He doused that one too. Upon a dry, shelf-like rock near the sloping stone he laid the partially used torches alongside several other new pine torches that had been placed there. I had not noticed the little cache of supplies coming in, what with the Grandfather falling down and all. We reached the bottom of the sloping stone and the Grandfather began to instruct me how I could help him climb out of the Black Lodge.

"Dear One, please climb to the top and leave your lamp upon the ledge then come back down to assist me in climbing the sloping stone and the steps of the drop off."

"Yes, Grandfather," I said.

Before the words were even out of my mouth I was ascending to the ledge above. I returned and took the Grandfather's torch in my right hand. I gave him my other hand and assisted as he sidled along with his back to the nearly vertical stone of the drop off. He limped and shuffled up the sloping stone, stepping carefully across every spot that looked the slightest bit slippery until we reached the big step up to the shelf. He placed both hands on the edge of the shelf and, in a surprisingly quick and agile move, boosted himself up. I climbed to the top of the drop off, put down the torch and gave the grandfather both my hands to help lift him up the much higher step to the top of the ledge.

The rest of the way through the Passage of the Big Antler was relatively easy. Still, it pained me to watch the Grandfather's hobbling limp. When we, at long last, reached the entrance to the Passage of the Big Antler, the Grandfather turned completely around so that the red dot of the entrance portal was again on our left and the big-antler with the upright rhino standing on its rear haunches was to our right. The Grandfather thanked the spirit-powers of the Dark Mothers for allowing us to come into their holy place to complete his dream-vision and to initiate a new Seer of the Bear People.

The giving of thanks was completed. We both turned to begin our final journey out of the Great Cave of the Bear Mother back into the World of Light.

CHAPTER 14.
THE WAY OUT

WHEN WE REACHED THE HEART LODGE, the embers of the Hearth of the Ordeals had long since faded.

"Shall I reignite the hearth fire, my Grandfather?" I asked, not knowing the order of the rites.

The Grandfather paused, looked thoughtfully into the cold ashes and began to speak.

"Had you been a male initiate coming back from solitary questing within any of the holy lodges, you would have returned here to rejoin your age-mates and their mentors. Here, you would have talked to each other as new men, told the ancient stories, sung the songs of your own making and danced the dances of your new animal-guides. This is always the time just to be with other men— our new hunter companions of the White Brotherhood. We share the stories of our experiences in the Cave and we tell our new brothers what plans we have for our lives as good and honest hunters among the People."

I looked down at the wide arc of well-beaten earth around the cold hearth darkened by countless drops of men's blood and sweat and semen. Suddenly my liver and stomach felt very heavy and I just wanted to be gone from this place. But more was to come. I could tell by the way the Grandfather paused and continued to stare at the burnt-out fireplace. Finally, after a long and thoughtful pause, he began to speak again.

"There is one last rite which takes place here at the Hearth of the Ordeals for hunter-initiates that you may someday witness. As a woman, you will probably not understand the ceremony," he said in that tone which always meant a great secret was about to be revealed.

I couldn't help but think to myself, "I have held the Grandfather's foreskin between my fingers, what other 'secret' could this cave possibly conceal?"

"Do we need to sit down for this, my Grandfather?" I asked with regrettable sarcasm.

"No. That is not necessary, my good Apprentice. I can explain the essentials of it to you quickly before we go. It is a rite performed by the men's White Brotherhood that you should be aware of as an initiated Seer of the People, if for no other reason," he began.

"Whenever we perform the masked dances of the bison wrestlers or the wedding dance of the lion and the bison or bring out any of the other holy masks or costumes, the initiated adults present all know the dancers are flesh-and-blood men and women. However, many of the children still believe the masked dancers *are* the spirit-powers, as children are wont to do without instruction. As Seer, you must learn that the power of the dance, as the Mother speaking through the rhythmic movements of our bodies, is diminished if the dancers are unmasked in the presence of the uninitiated. The initiated know the spirit-power of each mask unites with the dancer's own spirit-fire as they don the masks and dance the dances. Dancers become those animal-messengers while they are dancing. Do you see?"

"Yes, Grandfather. I see. Please continue," I said.

"During the dancing in the Heart Lodge some men fall into deep trances. A few may even take the shaman's journey for the first time in the very midst of the bison dance here in the Heart Lodge, so powerful are the music and rhythms of the dance. Putting childish beliefs behind us is part of becoming a man. It is part of the awakening of the white-spirits within every hunter to know that when you don the holy masks, you have become the spirit-powers of those masks and costumes. For a man to know that he and the Father, that he and the Mother are one, is to bring forth the power of the dance from within. But not all spirit dancers fall to the ground in the ecstasy of trance. Some just keep dancing endlessly until the dream-trance is ended! As a man of the White Brotherhood, you would be expected to act as a self-responsible adult, put on the dancing masks if you are moved to do so, do the All Mother's work in the hunt and put the things of childhood behind you."

"Yes, Grandfather. I know that only children believe the dancers are the spirit-powers in the flesh. The unmasking of a dancer is the quickest way to pull the mask of childhood from anyone."

"Yes, Dear One, that is very true. But there is another thing the boys must learn in this place and by a holy rite here at the Hearth of the Ordeals after their initiations as men have been completed. The lesson to be learned is that each man is in competition with every other as much as they are brothers and friends in the hunt and companions in gift-giving. For their whole life, each hunter will strive with his brothers for the extra share that comes to the Leader of the Hunt. The dueling rhino within every man's heart will always be there no matter how well the urges have been channeled. There is always a surface display of cooperation and unity within the hunting band, but all men vie for the honor that comes from striking the killing blow and doing the Dark Mother's work with their own hands. Here at the Hearth of the Ordeals, after the story of the origins of the bison dance is told and the dance is performed, the bison wrestlers will be unmasked before the initiates as a sign they have grown up and are no longer children. In this rite, they are to know in their hearts they have become hunters and fully grown men. They have put childish things behind them forever and there can be no going back. The unmasking of the two bison-dancers who come into the Cave both garbed as Bison Fathers is the last trial that all men and hunters must experience as part of their initiations."

He had my full attention now because this really *is* a secret that women do not know. I wondered why Auntie had never discussed this with me? She has always shared such secrets before?

By the time the Grandfather had finished his teaching I knew why Auntie had never told me of the ceremony of the Dance of the Bison Wrestlers.

The Grandfather began, "In this final rite of the hunter's initiation, after all the solitary questers have returned to the Heart Lodge to be together with their new Brothers and Uncles of the camps, two masked bison wrestlers enter. Their bare left arms, bare legs and any other exposed skin is painted in black and white stripes and spots. The two rush into the circle all at once with great bison bellows and grunts and making the lowing sounds of bison cows. As you will have seen at the bison dances of the dance circle, the masks are bison robes with the horns, head, ruff, hump and tail attached. The bison skin covers the dancer's back, and as you will have seen in the dance circle, most of the face of the dancer is covered too. One strip of the bison's right front leg skin remains as part of the costume to cover the dancer's right arm with bison fur. You will already know that the holy dance which the Bison Shaman Who Married a Woman taught the Ancients along with the telling of this story always precedes the wrestling at the Great Gathering. And so it does in these rites, with one important addition to the dancing and singing of the story.

"Yes, Grandfather," I agreed. "I have seen the bison dance of the dance circle. I have heard the story of the Bison's human wife many times before."

"Then you will know that the masked bison-dancers never reveal themselves as men in the dance circle when uninitiated children are present. But within the Holy Cave, when the bison-dancers throw off their masks and reveal the bison spirit-dancers as ordinary men, it can be a great shock to some of the boys. Many of the boys will have yet to identify themselves with the All Mother or even with any of her animal-messengers. If so, they will not have learned that the coming forth of the Mother is from within their own hearts and souls, but some will not yet be ready to acknowledge that in themselves. In this rite, the Trickster uncovers what is covered to reveal the truth of things to the newly initiated. This unmasking of Bison Father is an essential part of the rites and is part of every boy's essential training in the ways of men and of the White Brotherhood."

"But surely, Grandfather, even small children can see that a masked dancer is a man or woman in a costume even if the costume gives the dancer great spirit-power. There must be something else you have yet to tell that would make this rite of such importance besides the unmasking."

I really was beginning to understand how the Grandfather liked to teach his lessons—he always leaves the biggest surprises to the end the way a good storyteller does!

"Yes, my good Apprentice. You are correct, there is more to tell of this rite," he said smiling a knowing smile.

"The unmasked dancers, naked except for body paint, will then proceed to grapple with each other in what is made to appear as an actual bison wrestling match. They bury each other's heads in the hollow of each other's necks and struggle with each other, there, in the space between the Tree of Life, and the Hearth of the Ordeals over there."

The Grandfather pointed toward the red dots of the Powers of Three on the wall and the little Tree of Life in front, then back toward the cold hearth.

"The whole company watching the wrestlers begins to sing the song and do the slow, ponderous, heel-walking steps of the Bison Dance. It is danced not in a circle around the wrestlers, but each dances and sings in his place in their half-moon circle between the hearth and the stone bench—exactly where we are standing now. The only caution in arranging for this rite is that the bison-dancers must be carefully chosen or they will not be able to perform their proper roles."

"Why is that so?" I asked. "A bison dance is a bison dance. We all know how to do a bison dance, masked or unmasked," I said incredulously.

"That is true, my good Apprentice, but it is not for dancing or wrestling that the two are selected as those who will participate in one of the Trickster's most startling rites. That is because when the pre-arranged victor in the match throws his opponent to the ground, he then pretends to force the loser to suck his penis before the entire group of initiates and their mentors."

The jaw-dropping shock at hearing these words must have registered on my wide-eyed face because the Grandfather said to me,

"My Daughter, I told you this is a secret of the rites of the White Brotherhood that you might not understand. But I promise you as the Grandfather of the People, the boys always learn the lesson the Trickster teaches with this rite and they keep it all their lives. Every man must learn that sometimes he will win and sometimes he will lose in the great dance of life. Whichever it is, each man must know that whatever the outcome, it is only temporary and will soon pass. Upon the next hunt he will throw the killing spear or in the next contest he will win and another will lose. At times, each man will be the cow. Sometimes the bull. Do you begin to understand?"

"Well, yes. I, I ... think so, my Grandfather," I stuttered, still stunned and unable to sort it all out so quickly.

"What you will also not know, having never seen the rite, is that sometimes the victor will mount the vanquished as a bison bull humps his cow as they join in sex. Some bison wrestlers will mime the mounting, but others will actually enter the 'cow' and hump until they withdraw their penises to spill their essence on the dancer's back or upon the ground for all to see. Here, the Trickster's lesson is the same as that of the Hymen Stone for you women: until one is willing to join the lodge of another in marriage, the man's white essence should be spilled upon the ground. Or upon the skin of the woman. What will surely astonish you even further is that if any man or boy of the White Brotherhood watching the rite desires to do the same to the vanquished wrestler, they are encouraged to join the bison-dancers in the circle. There, they will have the defeated one suck their penises or even make the bison-dancer play cow to their bull. This frequently happens because men are easily aroused by watching the joining in sex of any two people. But then, as a woman you already know that," he said, his wry smile returning.

"On occasion, some of the watching boys or men will be moved to play cow to the victor's bull. My final word of advice to you is that you should be prepared for anything to happen because anything that is willingly done is acceptable during this final rite of initiation into the White Brotherhood."

I have to say I was so completely astounded and astonished by all of this that I was almost beyond all words.

Still, I managed to ask, "Grandfather, what hunter would ever agree to play the part of the bull? Let alone the part of the cow in front of all the other men?"

The Grandfather saw the bewilderment on my face and began to laugh out loud.

"I see the Trickster is paying you a visit as well, my Daughter! The answer to that lies in the souls of the men who willingly come forward to play the parts in the Trickster's unmasking of what the boys believe to be Bison Father and his joining in sex with another man. As Seer, you must learn this lesson well: all of us come from the Mother and one is no more honorable than any other. All will fail at times and play the cow and all will win at times and play the bull. As I have said, the lesson is that everything as it is now will change; it is only temporary and will pass away. Next time, you are just as likely to be in the opposite position once again. All of life *is* of the Mother, even this. This is an important lesson you must learn before you are able to give this teaching to the men. Things are rarely as they appear to our eyes. Know that in all things, beneath the skin, all of it *is* the Mother moving in the World of Light. Whatever happens, it must be accepted. All expressions of friendship, companionship and joining in sex between the men are as beautiful and acceptable to the Mother as are the expressions of companionship and joining in sex between men and women, or between two women for that matter."

"But Grandfather, who would agree to play the cow to another man's bull as part of these rites?"

"In practical terms, it is often a two-spirit man who agrees to play the part of bison cow. Still, many of the White Brotherhood who are not two-spirited will volunteer to play both the bull and the cow in these rites as they are moved by their spirit-guides to do so. As you might guess, two-spirit men are equally suited to enact the part of bull. This is one of the reasons why we believe that any two-spirit man or woman is so close to the Mother. The two-spirited among us, in their very bodies, bridge the contradictory Powers of Two into one as we have already discussed. Do you begin to understand that in your heart, my Daughter?"

I considered all of this for a long moment before I replied, "So much has happened to me that I am completely overwhelmed by it all, my Grandfather. Please give me some time to think on this and I will come to understand it better."

"Very well, my good Apprentice. You have a loving heart and in time you will understand all that is necessary for you to understand and you will see what is necessary for you to see. Just know there is so much good in what we think to be the worst of us and so much dishonor in what we think to be the most honorable of us that no one should pass judgment on another. Let me ask you this and your answer will probably reveal all to you. What do you think is the message of the story of the Woman Who Married the Bison Shaman that every one of the People knows by heart? Is it not the very image you were moved by the Mother to make in the deepest parts of her own Holy Lodge?"

"I'm not sure, Grandfather. I should understand this but my head is getting cloudy again. I am so exhausted I am having difficulty thinking clearly. Will you teach me?" I asked.

"As Seer, you can become your own teacher by telling the story as you know and understand it. Tell me now the story of the Woman Who Married the Bison Shaman and listen to your own words with the Single Eye and the discerning ears of an initiated Seer."

"I can tell the tale, my Grandfather, but we will have to sit down. It is a long story and I am growing very weary," I said, looking around for a boulder or something to rest against.

I *was* becoming terribly exhausted, what with so many spirit-animals, stories, songs and trance-visions still swirling around in my head, not to mention the dull throbbing of so many new body marks. I was having difficulty sorting everything out and keeping the stories from merging one into another as in a night dream.

"Very well, let us sit here in the midst of our way out of the Great Cave. You may have the last of the living waters of Swan Mother and whatever root foods you have remaining to revive yourself."

We both sat down cross-legged facing one another across the Hearth of the Ordeals.

"Now that we are both comfortable, please tell me the tale as you have learned it, my good Apprentice. I would see if the meaning becomes known to you as you speak the words of the story.

Then we will exit from the Great Cave, for all of your formal trials and teachings have now been completed."

* * *

The Grandfather planted his torch in the cold hearth to give us a semblance of a dance fire. I began munching on the rest of the roots and sipping the still cool waters of the Swan Mother. Slowly, my thoughts began to clear allowing the rather long story to come to my tongue. The Grandfather also took a drink from the gourd and passed it back to me. After one more sip moistened my tongue and the last bite of the food found its way into my empty belly, I began the story of the Woman Who Married the Bison Shaman.

As every good storyteller does, I sang the words of the characters in the tale. And I spoke the narrator's words in as dramatic a fashion as I could, even though I did not stand up to make the proper gestures and to take the usual dance steps of the story.

The melodious sounds of the tale began to issue from my mouth:

Long, long ago and far, far away, the People had gathered their roving bands for a final Great Hunt of the summer season at the Mammoth Mother's Rocks. Here, the best animal jump of the People's knowing had been made. Every summer the People gathered at the jump to send a great many of the Mother's children back to her welcoming arms. The rock, branch and rush-mat walls of the jump, made in the shape of the Mother's abundant three-cornered vulva, were sturdy and, to the eyes of the animals, solid-looking enough to fun-nel great numbers of them from the grassy Plain to the sheer cliff at the tail-end of the trap. The great herds giving themselves to the People in their return to the Mother leaped over the steep drop to the rocks below where the People waited to butcher the Mother's children in order to feed their families through the Dark Mother's cold and barren winter season.

On this particular late summer day, great herds of reindeer and aurochs and horses had all passed by the wide mouth of the jump. None had entered to be driven on to the long drop at the narrow tail of the trap. The shaman-of-the-hunt chanted to Sun Father for success in the hunt. The hunters had drawn the shape of each animal that approached in a circle of sand and they had chanted the words of calling the Mother's children in. All the hunters had thrown their spears into the sand-circle as the rising sun touched the animal drawn in its center. But no matter what they did to call them in, the Mother's children kept turning away from the mouth of the trap. First, they turned away to the left. Then the herds turned away to the right. Whatever magic the shaman-of-the-hunt performed, still the herds swerved away to avoid the mouth of the trap and the rocky cliff waiting for them below the narrow throat of the jump.

Early one morning, as the people began to complain that they were all hungry and beginning to starve, a large herd of bison approached the mouth of the trap from the grassy plain. The shaman-of-the-hunt put on a bison mask and came near to the herd lowing and grunting like a bison. The People took their hidden places along the sides of the trap in anticipation of a successful bison jump and full bellies. Everyone—young, old, man, woman, child—crouched down so they would not be seen by the herd approaching the mouth of the trap. They all fell silent and waited and waited and waited for the bison to come into the jump. If the bison entered the mouth of the trap, that would be the sign they had given themselves to us and the People would jump up, shouting and waving their hands and pieces of clothing in the air. If the herd entered the mouth, then they could be stampeded toward the end of the trap where, unseen, the steep cliff awaited them. The bison looked at the bison-masked shaman, snorted his wind, smelled him as one of the human tribe, put their tails straight up in the air and galloped back toward the safety of the grassy plain.

On the second morning, another herd of bison approached. This time the shaman-of-the-hunt went out to charm the bison into the trap without a disguise. He came right out in front of the herd where the Bison Shaman led his great herd as they grazed the plain, their big shaggy heads down in the tall grass. The shaman-of-the-hunt turned around and around in front of the whole herd and then disappeared into the thick grass. All the bison lifted their woolly heads to watch the shaman dance his magic dance. Having disappeared from sight, the bison walked toward the shaman trying to find this strange creature hidden in the grass because, as everyone knows, bison are very curious. Then the shaman-of-the-hunt jumped up again, turned around and around and around, all the while singing his magic hunting song. Unbeknown to the bison, each time the shaman jumped up and then disappeared, he moved further and further inside the mouth of the trap, leading them slowly to the leap at the end.

Some of the bison were curious just what kind of odd animal this was who kept jumping up in the air and disappearing again. They began to approach the bizarre beast that kept disappearing in the high grass. Before long, the shaman was dancing his crazy dance and singing his calling song well inside the mouth of the trap. The bison came closer and closer and closer and still closer. The herd came close enough to the shaman that he could spit upon their bison noses. But they looked at him, snorted his wind, smelled one of the human tribe, put their tails straight up in the air and stampeded back toward the Plain. The People were going to starve and everyone was terribly concerned. No one knew what to do, not even the shaman-of-the-hunt.

On the third day, very early in the morning before anyone in the camp was awake, Red Girl went out from her mother's tent, pitched at the bottom of the cliff, to get water for her family. She looked up to the edge of the jump and to her complete surprise she saw the herd of bison. They were just at the edge of the cliff, placidly grazing.

That was surprise number one. In her frustration at the appearance of the bison on the very edge of the jump just calmly looking down at her, she suddenly cried out, "Oh! If only you would leap off the cliff and give yourselves to my People, I would take one of you to my mother's lodge as husband!" In her disappointment and hunger, Red Girl had put these very words into the Mother's ear.

And what was surprise number two? The bison began to come over the cliff. They came jumping, tumbling and falling over the edge in great numbers. They heaped up in a great pile of bawling, flailing bison legs and hoofs and horns and tails at the bottom of the cliff. Red Girl began to be terrified at what she had done. But she knew that now the People would not starve this winter season.

Then came surprise number three! A huge bull bison, the Shaman of the Herd, had not been killed in falling over the cliff. In one great jump he leapt in a bound across the pile of dead and dying bison to land right in front of Red Girl! Red Girl was terribly frightened and tried to run back to her father and mother in the camp, but the great bull held her fast by the arm. The bull was the Grandfather of the Herd and in a terrifying loud bellow he said, "Come with me, Red Girl!" and he began to drag her away. "No, no!" Red Girl cried. She tried and tried and tried to pull away from him, but she could not loose his powerful bison grip. "Yes, yes, yes, my girl!" said the Grandfather Shaman of the herd. "You have made your promise. You have vowed that if my bison friends and relatives should jump that you would take one of us as husband!" the great bull bellowed. He shook his shaggy head and stamped his heavy sharp hooves in anger that Red Girl would even consider going back on her promise.

"See here, this great heap of dead bison before you! All my kin, our mothers, our fathers, our aunts and our uncles, all our children are lying here dead!

379

You will keep your promise, Red Girl! I am your bison husband now!" he said with a voice as loud as thunder. And with that he took her on his back and ran up, over the cliff and out onto the Plain.

There, the bison truly became Red Girl's husband in almost every way. When they were well away from the blood and carnage of the bison jump and the camps of the People, the bull bison joined in sex with Red Girl, humping her face-to-face as any married couple would among the human tribe. Red Girl's bison husband also mounted her from the rear as he would a bison cow. But to Red Girl's dismay, her bison husband always spilled his bull-essence upon her back or upon her belly. To be called a wife and not be treated as one made Red Girl very angry.

"My husband, how dare you treat me as one who is not your wife and only a plaything!" she complained long and loud to her bison husband. "Husbands of the human tribes must honor their wives by placing their white essence inside our wombs and not upon our backs or bellies!" Red Girl shouted at her bison husband in shame and anger.

"Well, your husband is not of the human tribe and I will do as I please," Red Girl's bison husband said dismissively. Clearly, the bull bison had no respect for Red Girl even though he called her "wife". Ignoring her pleas, the bull bison ran with Red Girl even further out onto the Plain. Red Girl was certain that she would never see her family again.

Meanwhile, back at the jump, all the People were so busy skinning and butchering the huge number of bison that had come over the cliff so unexpectedly that no one even noticed Red Girl was missing. When Red Girl's mother and father went to look for her very late in the day, they found her water bag lying upon the ground just below the bison jump. It was in just the spot where Red Girl had made her ill-advised promise to the bison shaman. Her footprints were all about and leading away were only the hoof prints of a huge bull bison. It was then that they all realized Red Girl had been taken by a bison—we all know how some young girls are!

Red Girl's mother was terribly upset when she found that her only daughter had run off with the bull bison instead of bringing him to her lodge as is only proper and fitting. Red Girl's mother began to cry and shout and rail at Red Girl's father for letting his daughter run away with a bison. "You have dishonored my lodge!" the mother of Red Girl berated her husband. "It is shame and dishonor that my daughter's bison husband has not been brought to her mother's lodge!" She screamed at Red Girl's father and complained all the day long. Red Girl's mother insisted that her husband should immediately fol-

low the trail, kill the bison that had stolen her daughter and bring Red Girl back.

Finally, Red Girl's father became so tired of listening to his wife's complaining and weeping, he picked up his spear, his bedroll and his water gourd. Red Girl's father began to follow the trail of the bison's hoof prints out into the Plain. Red Girl's father walked and walked and walked and walked until he found himself in the middle of the Plain in the midst of a confusion of bison hoof trails. He was getting more and more worried he would never find his daughter. Still, he did not dare to return to his lodge without the girl, so he continued searching and searching and searching for his daughter and her bison husband.

Red Girl's father traveled for many days and nights before he came to a clear spring with a mud wallow nearby. All the animals loved to come and roll around in the mud in this place, but on this day there were no bison to be seen near the wallow. Red Girl's father was very discouraged. He could not decide what to do to find his daughter so he sat down to think. As he sat by the muddy wallow thinking and considering what he should do, a beautiful black raven circled three times above his head. Since Raven was his animal-guide, Red Girl's father called up to the shining black bird soaring over head. "Oh my brother and friend, you are wise and can see everything from up there. Come as my brother, then, and help me in my need!" Red Girl's father cried pitifully to Raven. Raven continued to circle a few more times and then cawed down to his human friend below, "Yes, brother, we have been companions all your life. I will help you."

Raven dropped straight down to alight upon the ground next to Red Girl's father. Iridescent rainbows of dark blue and purple glinted from Raven's head and folded wings as he rocked his head from side to side, making clacking noises with his big beak. Clever Raven nodded his head up and down and fluttered his wings slightly as he spoke with his Brother. "What are you doing here in the middle of the Plain so far from your camp and all alone, my Brother?"

"My daughter, Red Girl, has run off with a bison and her mother is grieving terribly. I have looked and looked and looked but I cannot find my daughter. Will you help me, my Brother? As you fly about, please look around and see if you can find my daughter," pleaded Red Girl's father.

Raven loved his human brother and began to feel sorry for the man. His brother having lost his daughter, Raven knew the man's wife would be ferociously angry, just as his own wife would be if something like this happened to him. Raven said, "Why, there is a beautiful girl with a herd of bison just *across the ridge over there. I can fly to her and give her a message. What would you have me say to your daughter?" asked Raven.*

Red Girl's father thought very carefully. "Well, I think you should tell my daughter that her mother is very angry and she is demanding Red Girl restore the honor of her lodge by returning immediately. Tell my daughter her father is waiting for her here at the wallow. But be very careful not to allow any of the bison to hear you speaking to her, especially not her bison husband!" Red Girl's father warned.

"Why should I be so cautious and quiet, my Brother? Should a father not be able to give a message to his own daughter?" Raven asked. "Brother, if my daughter's bison husband should find me here, he will surely kill me!" "Very well," said Raven. "I will do as you ask, and I will be as discreet as I am able, my Brother."

Raven flew off toward the bison where the herd had gathered around with Red Girl in the midst of them. He saw the young woman sitting among the dozing herd placidly chewing their cud and barely aware of anything. Raven quickly decided on a plan to reach Red Girl without alarming the bison. Raven lit on the ground not far from Red Girl. Then, pretending that he did not see her, Raven began picking around at little things on the ground the way that ravens always do. Turning his head first this way and then that, Raven peered at the bison. When Raven saw that the bison had their eyes closed, he took a few steps in the girl's general direction, weaving in and out of the sleeping herd. Raven lumbered, his big black head rocking from side-to-side with each short-legged step. Slowly, ever so slowly, Raven began to make his nonchalant way closer and closer to the girl.

Raven was very careful to keep looking toward the dozing bison, and then away, and then back at the bison as if he didn't care about them or Red Girl. When Raven thought that none of the bison were looking his way or they had their eyes closed, he began hopping his rapid sidelong hop to sidle up close enough to speak to Red Girl without any of the bison hearing.

When Raven was close enough to whisper, he said in his softest clicking, clacking voice, "Your father is waiting by the wallow, Red Girl. Your mother insists that he bring you back to her lodge immediately." "Shhhh! Be quiet Raven," Red Girl said in a loud hiss so as not to awaken her sleeping bison husband and the rest of the herd. "I will have to find a way to go to my father without endangering both of us. Please go back and tell my father to wait at the wallow until I can decide how to find a way out of this terrible mess. The bison will kill both of us if they find me running away with my father after I have made my promise!" "Very well," Raven said and flew away with the message.

Presently, Red Girl had an idea. She got up and went over to her husband, who was just waking up from his long bison nap, and said, "Husband, give me one of your horns and I will fetch you some water from the spring." "Very well," the bison husband said. He broke off one of his horns and handed it to Red Girl. "I will return with fresh, clear water for my husband to drink," Red Girl reassured her bison husband.

Red Girl made her way to the wallow where her father waited. "Father!" she cried, glancing nervously around to make sure her bison husband had not followed her. Then she asked her father, "Why did you come here, my Father? We will both be killed if they find me trying to run away with you! I made a promise to come away with my bison husband if the herd would jump."

Red Girl's father replied, "Your mother does not know of your vow to the Bison Shaman and sent me to bring you back. The People are grateful that the bison jumped from the cliff, but if I do not bring you back, your mother will make the rest of my life miserable. She will nag me until I return to the Mother! You are her only daughter and you must come back with me to your mother's lodge. Bring your bison husband with you, if you will, but come home to your mother's lodge you must! Come, Red Girl, let us go," her father said and grabbed her hand to take her away with him.

"No, no! Not now!" she said frantically. "If I do not return with the spring water as I promised, the whole herd will pursue us and trample us both to death. Let me go back with the horn of water and I will try to sneak away after the darkness comes. Stay here at the wallow and wait for me, my Father," Red Girl pleaded.

Red Girl's father agreed and she went back to where her bison husband was still dozing. Red Girl handed the bison horn full of water to her husband and he took a drink. Then the Grandfather of the Herd took a sniff of the water and shouted, "Aha! I snort the wind of a man nearby! I can smell his stink in this water you have brought me from the wallow!"

"No, no dear husband. There is no man of the human tribes here!" Red Girl protested. Then the bison husband took another sip of the water, just to be sure. "Yes!" he cried. "I sniff the wind of a man nearby in the water you have brought me!"

Red Girl, trying to protect her father, said again, "No, no dear husband. I would not lie to you. There is no man of the human tribes here!" But in her *liver and in her heart she knew she had not told the truth to the bison shaman, her husband. And the bison shaman-of-the-herd knew it too.*

The bison husband took a third swallow from the horn just to be certain his human wife was not lying to him. But he shouted again so all the herd could hear, "Yes! Yes! A man is here! I can snort his wind in this water you, my human wife, have brought to me!"

Red Girl's husband began to bellow his angry bison bellow. It was a frightful sound and Red Girl truly began to fear for her father. At the Bison Shaman's roar, all the bulls of the herd stood up, raised their tails in the air and shook their great horned heads from side-to-side throwing spittle in all directions. They stamped their heavy hoofs throwing up great clouds of dust and bellowed back to the Bison Shaman in answer. Then they all ran off in the direction of the wallow where Red Girl's father was hidden.

When the herd found Red Girl's poor unfortunate father, they trampled him with their sharp hooves, crushed him with their massive foreheads and they gored him with the sharp tips of their horns. The bison hooked him with their curving horns to toss Red Girl's unhappy father high into the air. As Red Girl watched and wept loudly, they stomped and trampled him again and again until there was not even one tiny piece of his body or a drop of his blood that could be seen. He had been completely crushed into little bits and tiny pieces and had disappeared altogether in the mud of the wallow. Red Girl, seeing the carnage, began to wail and weep even louder at the complete disappearance of her beloved father who was only doing her mother's bidding to bring her daughter home.

"Well this is a fine state of affairs!" said Red Girl's bison bull husband disgustedly. "Now you are crying and mourning for your daddy!" he said with great sarcasm. "What about our fathers and mothers, our brothers and sisters, our children and all our many kin hurling themselves over the cliff to be slaughtered by your people?!" Then, thinking it was an impossible thing to do, the bison husband said to Red Girl, "Unlike your human tribes, I will have pity and compassion for you and your father. You will only have one chance, but if you can bring your father back to the World of Light, I will release you from your promise and you may return to your mother's lodge."

"Very well, my bison husband. But only if you will do one thing that I ask," said Red Girl quickly ceasing her weeping. The bison husband looked at his human wife with suspicion. "I don't know what you are planning to do, Red Girl my wife, but I will agree to grant you a single favor. But I will grant

only one favor to bring your father back to the World of Light," said Red Girl's great bison bull husband.

"Very well, my husband, it is agreed. I will only ask of you one favor," Red Girl said smiling a knowing smile. Red Girl then spoke to brother Raven who had been watching the whole sad affair while circling above hoping to find some tasty morsels of daddy-meat to make a meal. Red Girl held out her arms to Raven and said in a loud voice, "Brother Raven, hear the words of my mouth! Have compassion for me, pity me and help me! Help your own brother-companion, Oh thou holy Raven!" Red Girl pleaded.

Raven looked down at Red Girl. Still circling, he was very upset to see his own brother so cruelly trampled to death by the bison. "I will help you Red Girl, daughter of my soul-brother. What would you have me do?" Raven said in a cooing, kindly raven cackle.

"Go and search in the mud where my father was trampled to pieces. Try to find some small bone from my dear father's broken body," she begged. "Very well," said Raven.

Raven flew to pick about in the mud and broken grass with his sharp beak. He searched and searched and searched but could find no part of Red Girl's father, however small. When he found nothing, Raven side-hopped quickly back to where Red Girl and her bison husband waited. "I am sorry, Red Girl, daughter of my brother. I have searched and searched but I cannot find even one piece of your daddy's skin," said Raven to the girl who began weeping again. "Oh Raven, brother of my father, please keep searching! All I need is one little piece of bone. Please help me, holy Raven!" she cried piteously.

"Your father was my spirit-brother so I will search again," said Raven with a loud caw. Raven went back to his work of looking for some small piece of Red Girl's beloved father. Raven scratched in the dirt. Raven turned over tiny stones. Raven dug in the mud with his beak, but still he could find nothing left of Red Girl's father. Raven returned to Red Girl sad and dejected.

"I am so unhappy that I have been unable to find even one small piece of your daddy," said Raven when he came back to give Red Girl the bad news. Red Girl was inconsolable and, with streaming tears, begged Raven to go just one more time to search as hard as he could search to find the smallest part of her beloved father. Raven reluctantly agreed to search through the mud one more time.

Presently, and to his surprise, Raven found something hidden in the mud. Raven began pulling and pulling and pulling at it with his big, strong beak.

What Raven had found was just one tiny piece of backbone from his human brother's shattered body.

Elated, Red Girl cried, "That one little vertebra will be more than enough! Thank you, honored Raven, spirit-brother of my father!" Red Girl then put the piece of bone on the ground. When she had covered it with her own bison robe she turned to her bison husband who was watching with great curiosity at what Red Girl was doing.

"I will now ask you to do the one thing that you promised to do. Did you not agree to grant me one favor, my husband?" "Yes, Red Girl, I am ready to do anything you ask of me for I have promised you that I would," said her bison husband.

Red Girl's bison husband may not have treated her as an honored wife, but at least he was an honest and truthful bison who always kept his promises. While he watched, Red Girl removed all of her clothes. She lay down on the robe completely naked and then she said to the Bison Shaman of the Herd, "Thou art my honored husband. Join with me now in sex and put thy white-essence inside my vulva. I am thy willing wife. Do not further dishonor me by withdrawing thy great bison-rod from inside me to spill thy bull-essence upon my belly or my back as thou hast been wont to do until now!" Red Girl demanded in the most respectful of words.

The bison husband was happy to comply and promptly mounted his wife. And, as Red Girl had demanded, he spewed his white-essence inside her three-cornered vulva. Red Girl got up, and with some of the bison husband's semen still dripping from her vulva onto to the robe that covered the tiny piece of her father's backbone, she began to sing her song of great power, a song of rebirth into the World of Light. After only a few verses of the song, Red Girl lifted the robe to look. Her father's re-born body was lying there, but it was not yet moving, as if it were still dead.

Red Girl again covered her father's lifeless body with the semen-stained bison robe. Once more, she began to sing her holy song. Presently, she lifted the robe to look again. "He's breathing," she said. "Just a few more verses are needed." She covered her father once more with her robe and Red Girl began singing the song of great power again. In that moment, her father stood up to wrap the robe around his renewed body, white and naked as a newborn child!

The bison-people were all completely amazed! A startled Raven flew up to circle around and around, cawing and cawing and setting up a great clatter. "We have seen the Mother's great power here today!" said the Grandfather of the Bison to the rest of his herd. "The red-body of the man we trampled to death, the man who we gored and tore into pieces, has been made alive again! The spirit-power of the human tribe is truly great and holy! The Mother dwells in their hearts as she does in our own! I release Red Girl from her promise!" declared the bison husband.

Then he turned to Red Girl and her re-born father and said, "Before you return to your mother's lodge, we shall teach you our bison dance. You must never forget this dance for all the worlds to come. For when you shall have driven our kin and our loved ones over the cliff and returned them all to the Mother yet again, you shall sing your song and do our dance and we shall all be made alive again."

"This we promise forever more to do," vowed Red Girl and her father. Then the bison all began to dance their bison dance. They began to sing Red Girl's song of great power, their hooves thumping on the ground like the many drums of a dance circle. Red Girl and her reborn father followed the slow, solemn steps, so ponderous and deliberate a dance it is, until they had learned every step and every movement of head and hand and foot.

"Oh ye of the human tribes, hear the words of my mouth! Keep thy vow and never forget this bison dance!" bellowed the bison Shaman of the Herd. "Remember always to do the heel step to mimic our bison hooves and we will forever come again and again to be willingly sent to the Mother by your hunters. Teach this dance to all your human tribes and dance it with the horns, head and skin of Bison Father so that you may always remember which of the Mother's messengers has given you this great wisdom," the bison herd all shouted together."

So after learning the bison dance and singing the Song of Gratitude, which is the song of great power sung by Red Girl to bring all things new life, Red Girl and her father returned to her mother's lodge. There they told their tale and taught all the People the bison dance and the Song of Gratitude.

To this very day, every time any one of the animal-messengers is returned to the Mother, we always sing this song. And to this very day, we still dance the holy bison dance. We dance this dance and the wrestlers of the Great Gathering wrestle as bison because Red Girl and her father were returned to the People. The People of the Bear Mother now dance the bison dance and sing the Song of Gratitude to bring joy and abundance and happiness forever more in one Grand Round of the Mother's endless life.

"I know what the story is saying to us, my Grandfather. It has all become so clear to me in its telling," I said quietly.

I truly felt spent and wrung-out like a wet chamois skin. But at the same time I felt satisfied and full in my heart for having told the whole tale without leaving anything out.

"You have done so well, my excellent Apprentice. You have told the story just as I would have told it and just as I taught it to your own Auntie. My teachings live on in all the worlds to come through you, my Dearest One."

"Thank you, Grandfather. I will always be your Apprentice. I will always learn from you" I said, humbled by the weight of the very idea of all the worlds to come.

"Now, let us make our way out of the Cave. The time to re-enter the World of Light has come," the Grandfather said with a palpable feeling of completion.

I helped the Grandfather to his feet. I turned to leave the Heart of the Cave, initiated Seer of the Bear People.

* * *

"Take the lead, Yellow Lion. You will know the way back to the Skull Portal," the Grandfather said.

I stood there dumbly not responding to my new secret name.

"Oh, that's me!" I said with a chuckle. The Grandfather added his high-spirited laugh to my own.

As we left the Lodge of the Mother's Heart we approached the portal of the Lodge of Living Waters.

"May we enter again Swan Mother's Lodge, my Grandfather? I think I am going to faint if I do not get some water."

"Your ordeal has been long and arduous, my Apprentice, Yellow Lion. It has been more difficult than those of any hunter, and for that, your courage is greatly manifest. From here, the new men will always follow the right-hand wall of the Passage of the Butterfly to the rock of Leopard Mother on their exit from the Great Cave as hunters. But I am very thirsty too, so continue on ahead and we will satisfy our thirst once again.

Just the permission to go in gave me tremendous relief because my head had begun to spin again. I was suddenly so disoriented I felt I might stumble and fall. I passed by the hand-stencils on the wall to my left and could hear and smell the waters of Swan Mother's lodge coming from the darkness ahead. I just moved in the direction of the sound and the delicious smell of crystal clear waters. I drank again at the cold pools without even thinking to ask permission or anything, so suddenly and unquenchably thirsty I was.

"Excellent idea, my Daughter," the Grandfather said as he got to his knees and drank deeply of the invigorating waters.

"I always forget to drink enough water while in the Cave—it's all of the excitement of the spirit-powers. You are wise to drink whenever you can. As Seer, you should know that initiates can become ill and feverish for want of water," he advised between gulps taken to his mouth by cupped hands.

I could feel dried blood and clumped charcoal on my face and began to fill my hands with the refreshing water to rinse my face. The Grandfather stopped me with a gentle warning.

"Dear One, take care not to wash the dried blood and charcoal from your seer's marks until we reach the hot pools of the Serpent Father. There, you may cleanse yourself of everything that comes from the Holy Cave."

"Yes, Grandfather, I will wait until then," I replied.

Suddenly longing to be warm once again, I imagined the feel of the steaming waters of the hot springs upon my feet. Soon we were on the return path through the Passage of the Butterfly again.

"Dear apprentice," the Grandfather said in a kindly tone. "Cross over to the right-hand wall of the Passage and make your way to Leopard Mother and her companions."

"Yes, Grandfather," I replied.

Without stopping, we crossed back over to the exit wall of the Passage of the Butterfly and made our way to Leopard Mother still cowering beneath the leopard-spotted, "roe" Bear Mother, above her. Then it hit me: this great spotted bear was the namesake of my own father. I had always thought it a strange name for a man, Roe Bear. My father's selection of his new hunter's name must have been inspired by this very spirit-image. I stood lost in thought, connected to my father in a new, unexpected way, until the Grandfather began to speak.

"Before we take the Hunter's Way along the path called Straight back to the eastern side of the Plain and our final exit, there is one last secret of the Cave I wish to show you," the

Grandfather said looking off in the direction of Leopard Mother's place.

"I have already revealed the secret of all secrets in telling you the Mother's Great Cave is in the shape of a woman lying on her back. Leopard Mother and her companion-images are the sign of the ending of the hunter's holy rounds of the White Lodges. It is the sign of the completion of their initiations as men and hunters of the Bear People."

"Yes, Grandfather. You have already shown this to me, have you not?

"Yes, Dear One, I have. But I wish to emphasize it one more time as we leave the Great Cave in the manner of the initiated hunters. As is fitting for the end of such a grand round, Leopard Mother, Bear Mother and Lion Mother—all hunters themselves— are the equivalent sign of the face of the Dark Mother made at the end of the holy rounds of the Red Lodges. These signs of the Dark Mother of Hunters are also made here, on the Mother's left side at the level of her heart, because these are the signs of a joining of spirit-powers and an ending. This ending is followed by a space without spirit-images or claw marks. You know by now that such an empty space is a sign of the Silence back into which all things go. Following the empty space of the Silence, as with all life, there follows another beginning, as day follows the night. Just beyond the space of the Silence, you will remember that there are made signs of the Power of One followed by the signs of the Powers of Two, which are, in turn, followed by the signs of the Powers of Three all in one grand, right-handed spiral of creation. All these signs are made here at the very end of the Hunter's rounds of the Great Cave. These signs and images are intended to teach the New Men that the ending of every life is followed by a joining as one in the Silence, and, in turn, the Silence is followed by another begin- ning, a rebirth. These teachings all come together in this place be- neath the Mother's heart where every child is carried. The Mother carries all of her children within her heart whether in their begin- ning, during their lives in the World of Light or at the ending of the red-life of her children's bodies."

"Grandfather, am I to understand that the act of returning the Mother's children to her in the hunt is an act of creation and re-birth?" I asked.

"Yes, Dear One. The New Men are to see these signs and know in their hearts, not in their heads, that the act of killing and eating is every bit as much an act of creation as a mother giving birth to a child. Understand that the bringing forth of any new shape or thing is as a mother giving birth to a child. For both mothers and hunters, it is a shifting and a changing of one shape into another. The men must know in their hearts they are equal to the women in their holy gifts to change one form into another. They must know in their hearts that to bring forth new life from what has been killed and eaten is the Mother's work they do. Can you see with your seer's eyes and your seer's heart the truth of it, my apprentice?"

"Yes Grandfather. I see all of that and much, much more."

The Grandfather placed his hand affectionately on my shoulder as I continued to gaze up at Leopard Mother, the spotted Bear Mother—my father's namesake—above the spirit leopard, knowing that the Lion Mother of my own new name lay hidden beneath the lip of the great rock before me.

"How much of this teaching are the new men to be given as they pass by this place on their way to the exit?" I asked.

"As Grandmother of the Rites, tell them only that the hunting spirit-images here are a sign of the ending of their trials and revelations of manhood. Tell them as hunters and as new men, they have become as the bear, leopard and lion in doing the Mother's work. You may also tell them that the space without images is a sign of the Silence into which all things go in their return to the Mother. Make it known to all new men that every ending is followed by a new beginning, as I have said before. Those new men who have had deep trances or a profound joining with their animal-guides during their trials and initiations may have questions, which you should, of course, answer according to your understanding. Just remember to wait for the questioning hearts to ask, for they are the ones who are ready to hear. At this point in their initiations they are all exhausted and are not likely to remember much of what is said anyway—unless they have the heart to ask as you do, my good

Apprentice. As Seer, remember that those who have eyes to see and ears to hear will not need to be told anything. They will see it, know it and often will not ask any questions of you at all. With experience, you will be able to look into their faces and see the clear eyes of understanding. You need say nothing to such initiates and apprentices, or to great souls like yourself, Dear One. Just know that as Apprentice you are now being taught to be a teacher to the others so I am giving you much more than even you will remember," he said smiling and patting me softly on the shoulder.

"Yes, Grandfather, I am feeling very exhausted myself. Is it yet time to exit the Cave?" I asked. My spirit-fire truly was beginning to fade.

"It is time to go, Dear One. Take the 'thumb' back to the Red Dot and from there, follow the 'first finger' of the way called Straight," were his simple instructions.

* * *

The path of the thumb to the Red Dot was not very long—only thirty or forty paces. After passing by the blank stone wall of the Silence and then to the Powers of Creation, we passed from what is the left "armpit" of the Mother lying on her back on our way toward the Red Dot. By going directly across, instead of following the wall of the left arm, in and all the way out again, we reached the Red Dot quickly. Without stopping, we made our relatively short way on the Path Called Straight toward the eastern side of the Plain of Bones.

I realized in a flash of light that this is the exact spot where the Grandfather had concealed his torch to frighten me as I emerged from the Red Womb of Hunters. I assumed we would follow the left-hand wall to the exit, but the Grandfather began to speak before I could confirm this is the way out.

"The new men leave the Lodge of the Mother's Heart and come back into the Plain of Bones by following the right-hand wall of exit through the Passage of the Butterfly. You should always stop at Leopard Mother, as we did just now, because it will be the only opportunity the New Men will have to encounter those important hunter-counterparts before they exit from the Great Cave. The usual order is to bring the men back to this eastern side of the

Plain along the Straight Path of the 'first finger' to where we now stand on their way to the Skull Portal. From this place, we will leave in a sun-wise direction by moving to our left along this eastern wall of the Plain. You may follow the well-beaten path that runs along it," he directed.

It was many, many paces from the Red Womb of the Hunters to the eastern portal of the Third Entrance of the Red Lodge and the Void of the Silence. How long ago had I cried uncontrollably in this place as the Grandfather sat so patiently to instruct and calm my fears? I could not tell. All the experiences of the Cave had begun to merge into one timeless, seamless whole. Without stopping in the center of the Silence, our feet fairly flew to the western portal of the Third Entrance to the Red Lodge. The Grandfather called a halt to our little procession.

"There is one last instruction for completion of the puberty rites, my Apprentice," he said bringing me to a stop. "When the hunter's rites have been completed and they are ready to leave the Cave, the Grandfather, or Grandmother of the Rites, will bring the new men here. This is where the new women will join the hunters to leave the Cave in procession, side-by-side as one and all together," he explained.

"Yes, Grandfather, I remember my Moon Blood. We were dancing and singing and drumming together before the All Mother's Rock when you suddenly appeared and announced it was time to leave the Cave. How do you know when it is time to go, my Grandfather? Does your spirit-guide tell you?" I asked.

"Daughter, only the seers and shamans know the secret of when to come out of the Cave. But since you are now Seer of the Bear People and my good Apprentice, I think it will be acceptable if I share the secret with you," he said with that oh-so-familiar conspiratorial smile.

"You were watching as I filled your lamp from my oil horn," the Grandfather began. "The secret lies in the amount of tallow you bring and in the kind of lamp wicks you use. My horn's oil will last for three days and two nights if triple wicks of twisted tree moss are used. When the last of the tallow oil is poured into the lamp, it is time to begin making your way back to the entrance of the Cave and the World of Light. If it takes longer to leave the

Cave than you anticipate, it is of no consequence. There will still be plenty of oil left by the time you reach the Skull Portal if one or another stage of the initiations are delayed, or if there are many questions to answer," he explained.

"As Seer, you should remember that these little tricks the shamans learn and do not share with the People have a very important use. The seers and shamans must live among the People, but they must not be *of* the People in every way. This is part of a seer's or shaman's apartness from the things of the World of Light. The People must believe in their hearts that we have the power to bless and heal because without their belief, they cannot be blessed. To encourage that belief, demonstrations of our gifts before the People are sometimes necessary. As I have already explained, the People are sometimes resentful of us. And you will learn, Dear One, that seers and shamans who use their great power for selfish or harmful purposes will always be greatly feared. Sometimes, such wicked shamans are even driven away. We are fortunate here in the Middle Camp to have the Shelter of the Solitaries for those who cannot live comfortably among the People."

"Yes, Grandfather. I understand what you are saying," I said, thinking of our terror of the Grandfather's sudden appearance in my mother's lodge so very, very long ago.

"But what do you mean by 'demonstrations' of a seer's gifts and 'little tricks'?" I asked.

"Many seers and shaman have clever hand tricks they show to the People to put them in awe of the powers."

"Hand tricks? Do you mean like making a short leather thong increase greatly in length? Making it shrink again to a short thong and then making the whole thong disappear within the mouth?" I asked.

I had seen with my own eyes such a magical thing performed by a shaman once.

"Yes, Dear One. That is the kind of hand trick I mean. These are performed as tricks partly to entertain the People at their leisure. But often the tricks are shown in an effort to make the People fearful. Such magic tricks will always encourage the fearful to keep their distance from the shaman. Some seers and shamans can use their skill to pull glowing spheres of their own spirit-fire out of their bodies to hold the shimmering balls of light between their hands. These spheres can be made to appear as the spinning balls of light portrayed in the Black Lodge as the Gates of Forgetting and Remembering. Do you remember the balls of life-fire portrayed upon the Gates, my Apprentice?"

"Yes, Grandfather. I see what you mean about the Gates, but I have never seen anyone hold a ball of light in their hands. Can that really be done?"

"Yes, it can. But only if the shaman has a specially prepared clearwater crystal and a piece of rough chamois skin in his hands," he said with a knowing smile.

"Be assured that used wisely, such hand tricks and gifts of the Mother can benefit the People. Just as our abilities to see and to trance and to have dreams are all to be used to heal and bless, so may hand tricks be used to heal and bless the People. Seers and shamans are not to simply amuse or entertain with such tricks because it is not good to keep the People always in fear of us. Never forget it is not we, the seers and shamans, who do the work of blessing the People. It is always the Mother within each of us who performs the healing. The Mother's healing magic is the magic of love for another. It is never of fear and never comes forth out of fear or anger."

"Will I have to learn such tricks to fool the people into believing I am Seer?" I asked. Rightfully so, because I had none of those hand tricks.

"No my good Apprentice. You will not have to perform tricks of the hand. Your gifts are already demonstrated by the making of spirit-animals of paint and charcoal to which you give life-fire. And your gifts are already demonstrated by your knowledge of the healing herbs and potions that heal the red-bodies of the People. The true power of every shaman and seer lays not in performing tricks but in concentrating all of our attention upon the task, upon the person, or upon the thing, which is at hand. We cannot allow our concentration to be diverted by what happened yesterday. You must never be distracted from what you are doing in this moment by what might happen tomorrow. If you are to make a spirit-image, set a broken bone or mix a brew to cool a fever, your full attention must be placed upon the task at hand. I saw that you were completely concentrated upon the making of your marvelous new spirit-bison. Nothing the Mother has made could have distracted you as you performed your magic upon the Mother's Vulva Stone. Do not be distracted by anything when you are demonstrating your gifts. This is the very purpose of the healing songs, chants and trance-visions—to bring your full attention to the healthy, unbroken, abundant All Mother within each person who is to be blessed. As I said, this is exactly what you did when you made your living spirit-image upon the walls of the Black Lodge. This is what you will continue to learn to do as the Apprentice of two Thrice Born shamans, your Auntie and myself."

"I do not quite understand, Grandfather. Is the shaman-of-the-hunt or the shaman-of-storms or of time or of words, are they all just playing tricks on the People? What hand trick is it to control the winter storms?" I asked in confusion.

"No my Apprentice, do not be deceived. The powers of a shaman are never simply hand tricks whenever spirit-power is being demonstrated in any way. Even a magic trick is a cunning and clever use of the shaman's hands whose purpose may be to bring forth the Trickster. Even a hand trick can be of the Mother if it is performed to heal and to do good. Whatever brings good, whatever brings healing and togetherness is of the Mother, whether or not it appears to be just a hand trick or a funny story. "

"But Grandfather, how do I judge if a trick is done for good?" I asked.

"The only test of its goodness is whether the trick is being used to harm or to heal. No further judgment is necessary, and even that must be withheld because the end result often cannot be seen. You must understand that the powers brought forth by any seer or shaman are entirely a result of what it is they are putting their attention upon. Always ask yourself, 'What is it I am concentrating all my thoughts and words and deeds upon?' If you are holding those spirit-powers in place with your full concentration and you are bringing blessings and healing, then you will have no need of hand tricks to show the People to make them afraid of you."

"I can see how controlling a storm would be a good thing, but how can that be a hand trick? How can thinking about a storm make it do anything?" I asked skeptically.

"Think of it this way: the shaman-of-storm probably does not hear the Father of Storms speaking to him as a spirit-guide. All the shaman-of-storm has to do is be aware of his surroundings and pay attention to the signs in the morning or evening sky given him by the powers of storm. The same signs are given to all but only a few will pay heed to them. Have you never noticed that all the famous shamans-of-storm are either of the Mammoth-kin or the Bison-kin?" he asked.

"We have only traveled a few times with those who are said to be able to predict the coming of storms. But you are right. Both of them were Mammoth-kin. Why is that so, my Grandfather?"

"As I have said, it is all in what you make yourself aware of and what you pay close attention to, my Daughter. The camps of the Bison-kin and Mammoth-kin are at the edge of the Great Plain. So, if a shaman is in harmony with the Mother and aware of the clouds on the horizon and if the shaman is holding the image of the storm in place by his attention, he will be able to tell the People when a storm is coming. It is just that simple and is no more of a magic trick than that. When you open your heart to the powers and pay attention to where you are and what you are doing, you will be able to look at someone and read the signs of illness on their faces or feel the places of pain and sickness with your fingers. They will tell you what is troubling them, where their pains are and how you can heal them if you but pay attention to the signs and to what they are saying to you. By paying attention, you will be able to heal as surely as if you were a shaman aware of the signs of storm in the skies. The shape of anything you hold with your attention is real enough as an image in the head. But never should it be thought of as a thing in and of itself."

"What do you mean, Grandfather? The image in the head is not a real thing?" I asked.

"Think of it this way, my Apprentice. The image of a coming storm in the head of a shaman-of-storm is just as real as the image of a spirit-animal you are thinking about painting. Neither the thought of a thunder cloud coming up on the horizon signaling a storm, nor the shape of a spirit-image in your mind is ever a thing of itself. It is only what you think it to be in your head. Do you understand?"

"Yes, Grandfather, I see what you mean," I said. "Then, are our necklaces, charms, talismans and healing songs all hand tricks, my Grandfather?"

"The skull and tooth necklaces, the shaman's marks upon our faces, the spirit-animals of the Great Cave, the shaman's staff and even your herbs and ochres, all these things are intended to focus *your* thoughts. They are also intended to lead the People to become aware of their own spirit-powers working through you to bless and heal them. As seers and shamans, we must become one with the Mother and sense the healing power of the Mother flowing through our painted images, our words and herbs and songs. If a fevered person does not believe in their heart that the powers are working within you, then when you speak the healing words, give the healing herbs and sing the healing songs, they will have no effect. Do you see that this is the way of the seers and shamans, to bless the People and not just to fool them with our tricks or to inflate our own importance? Do you see that it is the Mother within and not herbs and singing that does the true healing, Dear One?" he asked gently.

"Yes, my Grandfather, I see the wisdom in it."

And with those words I saw my solitary destiny as a seer among the People of the Bear Mother. For just a moment I was not sure it was a life I truly wanted to live. But how could there any turning back now? My straight path as Seer is already set. In my mind I could see it stretching out before me as narrow and undeviating as the "first finger" of the Hand, the path called Straight.

When we began to move along the path of exit again, the Grandfather spoke once more.

"As we now leave the trials and revelations of your initiation, you will formally become my Apprentice. I will continue to be your teacher in the ways of the seers and shamans for as long as I remain in the World of Light. There is still much for you to learn, Dear One, and I will be there to explain what it is your heart does not know of its own accord. My time in the World of Light is short and your vow to pass my wisdom on to those who come after you has given my heart great peace. Thank you, my good Apprentice. I will be with you now and in all the worlds to come."

Again I was left speechless by the Grandfather's words in the way only he can make my tongue so thick it will no longer make words.

Still, I managed to croak out a feeble, "Thank you, my Grandfather."

The path is wide and well-beaten from the western portal of the Third Entrance to the Skull Portal. Uncountable generations of men and women have walked this way before and now I am very rapidly approaching my rebirth into the World of Light as Twice Born Seer. Whether I am prepared for it or not.

The trail is wide here because the new men and new women, and now the Grandfather and I, walk side-by-side as equals before the All Mother as they leave the Cave together. As frightened boys and girls we entered the Cave in two separate lines—boys on the left taking the left-hand path along the western wall of the Plain, and girls on the right departing along the right-hand path to the Second Entrance of the Red Lodge. As we leave the Cave, the new men and new women come together again walking side-by-side and in a line one behind the other—aligned with the Mother for the rest of our lives as People of the Bear Mother.

The eastern wall of the Plain of Bones took one last turn to the left and we approached the Skull Guardians on the way out of the cave of my initiation as Seer of the Bear People. Our eyes had been so long in the dark that even the dim light flooding in from the entrance far above our heads and around a corner blinded us. But the white light of that world outside the Cave still seemed so far, far away. As we passed between the Skull Guardians and crossed over the cold fire of my initiation, the Grandfather turned to face the darkness of the vast cavern from which we had just emerged. I turned with him and together we raised our arms to the blackness and the silence of the Holy Cave.

We stood in silence and soon the Grandfather began to sing the song of our exit from the Great Cave of the Bear Mother.

"Oh, Great Mother of us all, hear thou the words of my mouth! We thank thee for allowing us to come into thy Holy Lodge to initiate thy beloved daughter, Yellow Lion, Seer of the Bear People, through whom thou wilt bless the People with joy and abundance and health and love. Oh, Great Mother of Us All, hear thou the words of my mouth!"

We slipped on our grass sandals still waiting for us near the cold hearth. The Grandfather took his staff from the wall where he had left it and doused his torch in the sandy dirt of the entrance passage.

Then the Grandfather turned toward me and said, "Daughter, blow out the light from your lamp and pour the remaining oil upon the ground as a thank-offering to Bear Mother."

I poured out the rest of the oil and cleaned the bowl with sand from the ground. I wrapped the lamp and its stone lid in its fur covering, stowed them in my bag and we were on our way out of the Cave and up into the World of Light.

As we turned the corner to face the radiant sunlight coming in through the entrance it grew brighter and brighter until we reached the Portal of the Mother's Mouth. The brilliance almost painful, I had to turn my head away from the blinding light. We squinted our eyes tightly and waited for them to adjust again to the brightness that blanked out everything in the radiant sunlight of a new day.

As our vision slowly returned, a spectacular view of our blessed home spread out before us. The sun's morning rays were just reaching the valley floor and touching the rounded roofs of our bark lodges at almost the exact time of day as the Grandfather and I had entered the Cave three days and two nights ago. The dank air of the cave was forgotten as I breathed in the crisp, fresh air of a new morning washed clean by a passing late winter storm. The whitest billows of fluffy clouds I have ever seen soared into the bluest sky I have ever seen. My nostrils and lungs filled with the perfume of fresh rain, wet sage, budding crocus and pine. The soft scent of sprouting leaves and grass filled my head as we began to make our way down the path still dotted with small pools and puddles of rain water left over from a rapidly moving shower.

I felt more alive and full of blissful joy than I ever had in my life. But I knew the World of Light would never look the same again. No matter how well-adjusted my eyes became to the brightness and clarity of everything.

CHAPTER 15.
GOING INTO THE LIGHT

STILL DAZZLED AND HALF BLINDED by the blazing morning sun, the Grandfather and I made our squinting way slowly down the trail that led from the mouth of the Great Cave back to the hot pools of the Serpent Father. The unrelenting moist chill of the Cave had taken much out of us both, especially the Grandfather, who limped and hobbled more slowly than ever.

"I can hardly move, my Daughter," he complained. "I can't wait to soak these old joints."

"Me too Grandfather!" I replied, trying to help him move along faster. "I am *so cold*!"

And I was cold. Every part of my body seemed to either be aching or rubbing on something. I was itchy, uncomfortable and sore from head to foot. When we finally reached the big flat stone next to the hot pools—holding even more memories for me now—it took me no time at all to doff the bearskin robe and grass sandals. I helped the Grandfather with his clothes and assisted him down into the blessed warmth of the steaming pool of waist deep water.

In the full sunlight I was shocked to see how scraped and muddy and bloody and smeared with charcoal and smudges of red ochre and white ash paint my whole body was. It was not until I lay back into the near scalding waters that every cut and scrape and welt came alive with searing, cutting pain. But it just felt so good to finally be warm again that nothing else mattered at that moment. I let go of everything and allowed the pain to be part of the heat until the healing waters of the pool began to do their work. Soon, the aches and cold and the excitement from the Cave finally began to melt away. I drifted into dream-like oblivion.

"Daughter!" the Grandfather called loudly so I would pay attention. "I forgot to tell you. When you begin to wash yourself take care not to rub your new marks. Try to leave as much of the dried blood and charcoal on the marks themselves as you are able. They will heal faster and more color will remain if you don't rub them now."

When I did not respond, he shouted, "Yellow Lion!" trying to rouse me from my blissful stupor.

The Grandfather seemed to be calling to another so I did not answer. I did not want to answer to anyone or any thing. I floated like a weightless, bobbing cloud in a sky of healing, warm water, the sunshine on my face, just drifting and drifting and drifting in this wonderful world of bright, bright light and buoyant, warm liquid. I would not allow the Grandfather to irritate me with any more words.

The Grandfather gave up trying to speak to me and both of us just soaked in the soothing waters until my skin began to wrinkle like a dried fish. I began to hope his joints had relaxed enough that he would be able to easily climb the hill back to the Shelter of the Solitaries to bring an end to our great adventure together. I just wanted to go home to my mother's lodge to sleep.

"Have you soaked enough, Grandfather? Are you ready to go?" I asked, suddenly longing for the comfort of soft sleeping furs.

And just like our first time in the hot pools, he had the same answer.

"No, let me soak a while longer, my Daughter. You get out of the pool and dry yourself. I will come along soon enough."

I quickly dunked my head under the water to rinse out my hair. I tried to wash off the mud, ash and ochre paint still adhering to my body, but the oily paint was not coming off well without soap. I was being very careful not to rub the new marks. Yes, I heard the

Grandfather's directions about how to care for new body marks. But I had to do something about the smears and smudges of red and white paint that still adhered.

"Maybe there is some old soap flower soap in the stone dish? Old soap root will be better than nothing!" I whispered to myself.

I got out of the water to scoop whatever soap remained in the dish and used the suds to remove the worst of the red and white smudges from my breasts, belly, pute and knees. I got out of the water again and wrapped myself in the bearskin robe to wait for the Grandfather.

By the time the Grandfather got out of the pool I was completely dry except for my hair. I huddled under the bear robe squatting to keep my back and feet warm. The bright sunlight warmed the rest of me as I ran my fingers through my hair trying to comb it out a little.

I put my grass sandals on thinking to myself, "At least we won't have to walk barefoot up the hill."

I helped the Grandfather with his loinskin, trousers and tunic and then tied his grass sandals for him. After hefting the thick white robe around his shoulders, we were ready to make the climb back up to the Shelter of the Solitaries.

* * *

At the entrance to the Shelter, we were met by my mother, Auntie, and it looked like every person of the Middle Camp except the hunters who, my mother informed me, had yet to return from the Plain. Only my little brother was not there, or so it seemed. Still in a daze and hardly able to distinguish waking from dreaming, I was nevertheless aware of the awe-struck faces of those who were my close cousins, age-mates and aunties of the camp. They all gawked at me as if I were some shape-shifting monster from the Great Cave. Which, when I thought about it a little more, I am.

I pulled the bear robe closer about me so as not to reveal any more of my nakedness to these suddenly strange people than was absolutely necessary. The Grandfather was met at the entrance by a big two-spirit boy a few seasons older than me. The boy—at least he looked like a boy to me—spoke to the Grandfather in a quiet voice and rubbed the fingers of his gnarled hands affectionately.

The two-spirit boy I know is named Red Dawn, gently guided the Grandfather with a strong arm about his waist and disappeared into the darkness of the Shelter of the Solitaries.

One on each arm, my mother and Auntie, to my great relief, led me past the onlookers clustered outside the entrance into a dark, quiet chamber toward the back of the Shelter. There, they loosed the claw-ended ties of the bear robe and let it fall. A collective gasp escaped their lips as they took in the full extent of my bruises, cuts, scrapes, welts and raw initiation marks. Auntie immediately opened her bag of healing charms and remedies to rummage in it for something. My mother began to weep.

"I'm all right Mother, it doesn't hurt. Please don't cry," I tried to comfort her, in spite of the fact I was the one needing comfort and was, in fact, in great pain.

I thought to myself, "Here I am in pain and still I feel the urge to comfort my mother!"

The nurturing Bear Mother is prompting me, no doubt. Perhaps it is my yellow Horse Mother guide? How am I ever to tell the difference? How will I ever become a true Seer and Healer to my people if I cannot hear the voices of my animal-guides?"

I calmed my fears with the thought that at least until the Grandfather and Auntie return to the Mother one day, I will be the apprentice of two great shamans. Until then I will not be forced to rely on my own skill or judgment. My life should not be very much changed, should it? But one day I will be left alone as Seer and Healer and what will I do then?

"What have I done? What have I done?" was the question that would roll over and over in my head endlessly.

Soon, my gentle Auntie brought out a bone tube of yellow ochre and a small packet of what I knew would be willow salve. My mother's shock and concern showed heartbreakingly on her face. She gave me spring water to drink and the first solid food I had tasted since those few roots in the Cave. My mother fed me the pieces one by one with her fingers to my mouth as if I were a baby—very comforting, somehow.

I could not think how many days ago I had eaten those tiny bits of food in the Cave? It was only now, as I began my return to the World of Light, that all the terror, excitement and overwhelming emotion that *is* the Mother's Cave began to subside. As the excitement and fear ebbed, my numerous cuts, scrapes and wounds began to throb in dull aching waves. I could see a few of the livid welts of the Nine Lashes under my right arm where they tracked, one below the other, down my ribs. The willow rod had wrapped completely around my body to make these welts. One stroke had even broken the skin under my arm. Thank the willow-sister for my Auntie's healing balm!

As the willow salve and yellow ochre did their soothing work, my own tears started to flow. I began to weep uncontrollably, finally collapsing into my two mother's arms in the quiet shadows of the Lodge of the Solitaries where we three wept as one.

This was the true moment of my second birth as Seer of the Bear People, a moment that would shape and guide my soul's journey for all the worlds to come.

But then, that is exactly what the Mother made the Great Cave for, did she not?

* * *

Days passed in the cool, dark, healing solitude of my mother's lodge beneath heaps of soft, warm sleeping furs. The familiar smells of wood smoke, food cooking on the hearth, old rush mats and dry pine needles comforted and soothed my body and soul. At times awake, sometimes asleep—mostly in a half-trance—I could not always tell if I were awake and dreaming or asleep and dreaming. I seemed to be sleeping in the belly of some great ribbed creature. The experiences of the Cave, my whole waking and vision life all merged into one ever-present dream.

Auntie came often with healing herbs and oils. She brought fragrant teas and food like carrots and cattail roots. These and other foods she said would help to pull me back to the Middle World from the airy heights of the Above where I had been flying so high and for so long. My mother must have sent White Fox to another lodge, probably Auntie's, to give me some restful quiet. It was so peaceful without him running around and screaming in play. I found myself wishing he would stay wherever he is forever. I didn't even ask my mother where he had gone. That seemed strange because I really do love my little brother with the grass-blond hair and eyes of bluish-gray.

I now realized Auntie was already well along with my training as a shaman-of-healing. There would still be much to learn about ochres and charms and herbs and teas and animal parts with healing powers in them. Mostly, I still had to learn how to heal through the speaking of chants and the singing of powerful songs. Above all, I must learn how to trance for healing. With such complete skills, I would become more than a seer and healer. I was now certain of that. Could my own shaman's journey be far behind?

I have learned that treatment of wounds, the setting of broken bones and bringing in babies are all skills of the yellow Horse Mother of the dawn. I see now these are all gifts of the head and that I do seem to have real skill in healing the red-body. I may not have heard Horse Mother's voice or ridden her back on the shaman's journey, but Auntie is teaching me all I will ever need to know to become a famous and welcomed healer among all the camps of the Bear People.

Auntie had already begun to take me with her to different lodges and camps to deliver babies long before my initiation as Twice Born. Before entering the Great Cave, I was already spending more time with Auntie than with my own mother, to my poor mother's dismay. All of this had long seemed to be a barely concealed bone of contention between my mother and father. Neither before nor after my initiation could I fully understand why, but I was getting more clues all the time.

So, it probably was not for the better that Auntie was caring for me in my mother's lodge when the hunters returned.

The Great Hunt had been more than successful and they came in with heavily laden dragging poles and carrying baskets full of dried and fresh meat, fat, organs and hides. And even part of a mammoth tusk. An already dead mammoth must have been received by the hunters because the Great Ones are too thin at the end of the winter season for the men to risk a dangerous mammoth hunt. At this time of the year only the reindeer are fat. But then, reindeer seem to be able to get fat on nothing but snow and ice.

Imagine my father's shock and surprise in returning from a Great Hunt to find his daughter's beautiful face marred with the terrible marks of the Twice Born! The first time he saw my face, he fell back as if he had been pushed. That fearful withdrawal of others I had been warned of had begun. Still, I never expected it to start with my own father.

"My daughter a seer! How did this happen? You indulge your daughter too much, woman!" my father railed at the both of us even though his words were directed at my mother.

When the initial horror of seeing my face wore off, his arms flailing, Roe Bear angrily questioned my mother in a muted hiss clearly audible from the sleeping platform where I lay. Auntie had made a hurried departure from my mother's lodge upon my father's arrival—she obviously knew what his reaction would be. That left me and my mother to confront my father with the unalterable fact that a Seer of the Bear People had materialized, as it were, out of the very smoke of his own lodge.

I covered my head with sleeping furs trying to shut out their hushed but very angry voices. Other bits and snatches of their almost wordless exchange were overheard. But I was still so distracted with my own problems and still in such a dreamlike condition I couldn't pay close enough attention to catch the whole back-and-forth between them.

"Not enough that his son … Auntie must rob me … my own daughter … never forgive …" my father ranted on and on.

He was more furious than I had ever seen him. But as my father raved on, hardly any words of protest or argument came from my mother's mouth.

"Why is my father so angry that I have become Seer?" I asked my mother after he had stormed out of the lodge in a huff to attend the division of the hunt. My mother only had some vague answer about how my father thinks our lodge is already too full of the Mother's power, that the lodge should be more balanced with the Father's power or something like that. I was never quite sure what the two of them were saying, but having learned many lessons of the Cave, and more importantly the stories of my family, I began to put the scattered flint chips back together.

I had rarely seen my mother and father quarrel. They never raised their voices to each other. But neither had I ever seen them show any affection for each other, even in the privacy of my mother's lodge. I had only seen my father slap my mother once in the midst of one of their almost silent arguments. My father was unlike so many other men who hit their wives and children with closed fists. Both of them have always been a mystery to me. How could they live under the same lodge-roof and still treat each other as if the other weren't even present with cold, unspoken sadness?

I never heard them joining in sex in the middle of the night when they might have thought my brothers and I were asleep. In fact, I can't imagine how my mother could possibly have had another child so long after Little Ibex was born? What with them sleeping under different skins and my father's taking every possible opportunity to be away from the lodge hunting or mining flint or whatever else the men do when they are out of the camps.

Come to think of it, my mother *does* indulge me shamelessly. Not forcing a husband on me for so many seasons after my Moon Blood is only one of the ways she spoils me. She always gives me my way in everything. And yet Auntie told me once that my mother is anxious for me to bring a son to her lodge, that sometimes my mother wishes that any one of the boys I have been with will put a baby in my belly. But to me, it is as if she does not want me to bring a husband to her lodge at all! Did she intend to keep me always as her daughter? A desire to keep me as a girl by allowing me to refuse so many suitors is one reason to let me have such freedom. I am sure of that now that I have become Seer. My mother all but said as much in as many words before I entered the Cave.

And my mother does not know anything about my desire for Brown Bull, apart from the fact that we were together at the last Great Gathering, and have joined in sex. She would probably reject him too as not good enough for her only daughter and the inheritor of her lodge when she returns to the Mother. But that is all for naught. Even if Brown Bull had put his essence in me and asked to become a son of my mother's lodge, she probably would still have rejected him as unsuitable—his family is not honorable enough for her only daughter or some such nonsense. My mother should know better for all her experience with her own mother!

That is still my greatest sadness when I think of Brown Bull, I suppose—that he never asked my mother to become the husband of my lodge. She must know that Brown Bull rejected me to my utter shame. It is my greatest pain and I still do not understand how I can hate Brown Bull and still want to see him again at the same time. Even Auntie says my mother is spoiling me by giving me a completely free choice of husband no matter how long it takes. It is certain now that Brown Bull will never be that husband of my mother's lodge no matter how many seasons I wait. Having once rejected me, why would he ever change his mind?

Perhaps that is why my father and my father are so distant from each other. Perhaps my father resents it that he has not another hunter within the lodge to hunt with him? He always seems so impatient with me and only wishes to spend his time teaching my brother Little Ibex to hunt, to make flint blades and spears. He leaves me to learn only the work and skills of women. Perhaps my father is anxious that a husband of his only daughter should be his hunting companion instead of teaching sons to be hunters who will just go to other lodges. The man I bring to my mother's loge will certainly be one with well-honed skills and close ties of affection and cooperation with other hunters. But who will that be?

Actually, I have no idea why my father does anything. But I think the lessons of the Cave are beginning to give me some very good clues to explain his behavior. It has not always been this way between me and my father. As long as my elder brother, Big Ibex, was in the lodge, my father paid his little girl almost no attention— much as he treats me now. Then, he had a son in Big Ibex to take with him on his little journeys and to the Great Hunt upon the Plain. Now that Little Ibex is old enough and big enough to go everywhere with him, my father is back to almost never speaking to me. I might as well be invisible as the Silence.

It was that in-between time I remember with so much warmth and fondness in my heart. The time after Big Ibex married but before Little Ibex got old enough to attend the hunt. Then, I was like another son to my father. He took me with him on short winter season hunts into the nearby hills for deer and into the higher mountains for ibex and chamois. He always said that my lion-eye gave me the best eyesight of anyone among the whole Nine Kin. In truth, I could spot a hiding ibex in the crags all the way across a wide chasm when none of the other hunters could. He and his hunter-brothers pretended to fight over who I would go out with as spotter. Those were the most joyful and happy times of my life.

To my endless delight, I always went with my father as spotter and tracker. And we shared a travel tent on those short hunts. He even had me draw the animal figure in the sand or the snow to be touched by the rising Sun Hunter and stabbed by the men's spears to prepare for the day's hunt. The spirit-power of the Mother is brought forth when a hunter draws the sand-animal. But the hunters believe that rite is much more powerful hunting magic when a woman draws the sand-animal. The Great Cave has revealed to me why I was at least good for that in my father's eyes!

What I loved the most was being around the little campfires at night with my father and the other hunters. Everyone, including my father, would sing songs and tell stories of the hunt. I would tell the stories and sing the songs of the Nine Kin I had learned from Auntie and in the dance circle. My telling always involved standing up and miming the different animals in the story. I always tried to give the listening hunters an exciting performance with songs and loud shouts when the story called for it.

I always did a little dancing with the telling, too. Mine is not the best voice for the songs, as I told the Grandfather, but it is acceptable. Everyone enjoyed my telling of the Nine Kin's stories in those long nights circled all around by the darkness beyond the campfire. My father especially loved to hear me chant and tell the stories. His pride of me shone from his face like the mid-day sun warming me to the heart. But those were the only times I ever saw my father laugh and sing and dance. He was like an altogether different man when he was with his hunter-brothers than when he was in my mother's lodge. Having now been initiated as a hunter, I begin to understand why.

I never wanted those days with my father upon the hunt to ever end. I see now it was one reason why I did not wish to take a husband to my mother's lodge. I think I was trying always to remain my father's "third son." Those wonderful days and nights with my father and the other men would end if, and when, I brought a husband home to my mother's lodge. Still, I would have brought Brown Bull to my mother's lodge without a second thought had he only been willing. And if he had loved me in his heart the way I was certain I loved him.

It makes me sad that I should have to become Seer in order to understand my father better. To understand his obsession with the ibex. I still call my older brother "Big Ibex" because I have never become accustomed to calling him by his married name. "Black Eagle" sounds so pretentious for a brother. Besides, it is a name I never hear from any of my family so I am not accustomed to using it at all. Sons marry, they choose a new name and they go away to their wife's lodge and only occasionally return to visit. I am happy that Big Ibex and his wife will be coming to the Great Gathering this season. This will be the first time I have seen or spoken to either of them since we traveled together two seasons ago upon the Plains of Summer. He has always treated me well and in spite of his high-flown name, I do love my older brother too.

To say the least, my father was more than delighted when my older brother met and mated with one of my Moon Blood sisters of the Ibex-kin, even though he would be leaving my mother's lodge. She is very pretty and owns the most beautiful and melodious married woman's name I have ever heard. Dawn Star Rising is her lovely name. My brother is fortunate to have found such a beautiful woman from among those "poor, upriver Ibex-kin"! Of course, there was no hesitation on my father's part to marry his eldest son into a lodge of the Ibex-kin. Now I see. Now I understand.

My elder brother, of course, chose his own name as a married man. I wonder if "Black Eagle" was an acceptable name to my father? But then, childhood names and adult names are always completely different. And parents play no part in the choice of the adult names for their children, just as my mother and father played no part in the giving of my own adult name, my secret seer's name. I had no choice in that and look at the adult name that was chosen for me!

Now that I am Seer, I will be called by my secret name only by other seers and shamans. Even when I bring a husband to my mother's lodge, I will not choose a new married woman's name. Little Bear is gone forever. Yellow Lion is never to be spoken. And so I will be called "Sister" by whatever husband of whichever of the Nine Kin I may someday have. If I am fortunate, perhaps he will call me "Beloved". Why does that make me so sad in my heart?

The Ibex-kin are still thought of as poor and as skeptical as the winter night is long. I wonder if my mother had any objections to her eldest son going to live among them? I would never dare to ask her if my grandmother ever voiced the reason for her rigid opposition to One Doe's marriage to my father. When she is angry at my father, my mother sometimes hints that she could have done better in a husband than he. Only now does that make any sense to me.

But I never cared about any of that. All I know is that I love my father no matter which of the Nine Kin he comes from. The only thing I desire more than hearing the words "I love you, Little Bear" from Brown Bull's lips are the same words of love from the mouth of my own father. Now I see there is little chance of ever hearing those words from any man who truly means them in his heart. In any event, I am now Twice Born of the Bear People and I know my prospects for finding a husband at all are even more narrowed than before. Now I may even have to look to the poor, up-river Ibex- kin for a husband to bring to my mother's lodge. A match certain to please my father and distress my mother!

But the Trickster is always present and hiding around a dark corner to jump out at us unexpectedly. So much to my surprise I would learn that while many may draw back from me, others would find me even more attractive having become Seer of the Bear People.

* * *

The return of the hunters with such heaps of meat and hides on this last Great Hunt together with the sign of the Seven Cow Sisters leaping from the western horizon meant the winter season was rapidly coming to an end. Soon, the Nine Kin would be scattering to the four directions out upon the Plains of Summer. But the ending of the winter season also meant another Great Gathering and the new summer season's puberty rites would soon be upon us. So great is the fame and prestige of the Cave that the mentors of all the Nine Kin of the Valley of the Bear Mother desire that their boys become men and their girls become women in the Great Cave and in no other holy place. Another opportunity to meet new lovers and exchange gifts with friends will also soon be upon us.

The Middle Camp of the Bear kin may already be the largest of all the camps of the Nine Kin, but during the Great Gathering, the traveling tents of many of those coming for the rites will be pitched here. All these visitors will more than double the size of the Middle Camp. The close kin, gift-givers and mentors bringing their boys and girls to be initiated will greatly outnumber the Bear kin of the Middle Camp for the nine days of the Great Gathering. So many will come that some will be forced to pitch a tent at the other camps of the Bear-kin and walk to the Middle Camp for the initiations, dances, games and gift-giving.

"Nine days of the Great Gathering," I thought aloud.

That is the number of the coming of the Mother's spirit-power into the World of Light. I had never wondered or even cared why the Great Gathering was nine and not ten days in duration before my initiation. Now it seemed significant, somehow more important.

The temporary lodges of guests are always set up below the half moon of the south-facing bark lodges of Middle Camp. Visitor's make their own half moon of north-facing traveling tents to make the camp of the Great Gathering one grand circle with a central hearth, roasting pit and dancing circle in the round space between.

The downhill side from the central dancing and wrestling grounds are the least preferred lodge sites as the seasonal frosts and freezing air rolls down the slope and collects in the bottom of the Valley where the River flows. And there are more trees on the downhill side. The trees shade the ground and prevent the winter sun from warming the lodges during the day, so many come early to get the best camp sites with the most sunshine. Regardless of location, for the nine days of the Great Gathering, no one ever complains and, more often than not, the weather is clear and beautiful and warm. Certainly, the shamans-of-storm will be consulted to predict good weather for the timing of the Great Gathering that marks the end of the old winter season and the beginning of a new summer season.

While the Grandfather of the People and the assistant seers and shamans are conducting the coming-of-age initiations within the Cave, those that have come for the Gathering will eat and dance and sing and give gifts. We will tell stories and meet old friends or kin and compete in different games and contests. The unmarried, indeed, some of the married men and women, take the opportunity of the Gathering to meet someone to take into the bushes to see if they would make an acceptable wife, husband or lover, as I well know. Mostly, the Gathering is just to have fun, to make friends and new acquaintances and to renew old ties. Bonds having been formed, a joining ceremony for newly matched couples is always the last rite of every Great Gathering to be held before everyone returns to their own camps. To see old friends and enjoy themselves is undoubtedly the reason my older brother, the erstwhile Big Ibex and his pretty wife, Dawn Star Rising, are coming this season. All of this excitement of the Great Gathering will take place just before our Valley and all the camps of the Nine Kin will be entirely abandoned for the Plains of Summer.

And lest anyone forget, it is the time for the young men and some of the women to compete at bison wrestling—my favorite, of course—and foot racing, throwing spears, slinging stones, throwing bird bolas and tossing the knuckle bones in games of chance. It is a joyous time for all who attend. But it is the last time for all the People to be together before the traveling bands of several lodges each move down the River and out upon the Plain to follow the herds to the Northland.

For some of the People, this will be the last time they will be seen or heard in the World of Light. It may well be the last time they can enjoy one another's company, and so everyone is full of joy and happiness and singing at the Gathering. The summer season of constant wandering is difficult and hard. Moving camp once or twice or even three times in a moon is wearying. And there are many biting flies and mosquitoes that can only be partly repelled by oil and ochre paint or long hair and beards that cover the face and neck or by wearing face nets of loosely made flax cloth. The sudden, soaking lightning storms and the difficulties of cooking, cleaning and preparing hides on the move makes the summer season a difficult time, especially for us women. We women truly mourn the leaving of the winter camps and our warm, dry lodges of bark and bent saplings. On the other hand, the men do not seem to mind that the lodges of winter are being left behind. Out on the Plains of Summer, the men are completely in charge of everything and they seem to like it that way.

"Pairs of opposites in conflict with each other," I thought to myself. "Bark lodges stay in one place and are female. Summer lodges move constantly and are male."

The men do not seem to mind the fact that upon the Plain there are the ever-present hyenas, lions, wolves and bears, who, even with sling stones and heavy spears, are not easy to keep away from a kill reeking of blood and entrails. These other hungry tribes of hunters are equally difficult to keep away from the camps where meat is always out drying and skins are being worked. All of this, in addition to the usual dangers of the hunt, makes leaving the Valley a bittersweet time for everyone, more especially for us women.

The teachings of the Grandfather bubbled up continuously without having to even think about them. The lessons of the Cave are beginning to make things clearer to me in many ways, there is no doubt about that. I nodded to myself with some degree of satisfaction with it all. Perhaps what I have chosen to do is the best path for me after all?

I could not help but ponder how leaving the safety and plenty of our Valley only makes our return—when the Seven Cow Sisters again climb up onto the eastern horizon—a truly joyous homecoming. The women always yearn for our return to this beautiful Valley of the Bear Mother with all its abundance, shelter from the storms of winter, and the closeness of many friends and kin. I think secretly, that even the men are happy to return to the Valley and rest from the continuous summer wanderings. Though you could not tell from how excited they are to leave the Valley!

The last Great Hunt of the winter season is undertaken partly to have plenty of food for the Great Gathering. But the feasting of the Gathering also helps to clean out last season's larders and storage pits. Nothing edible will be left behind to rot over the summer season. It will all be eaten or turned into traveling cakes by the time we turn our backs on the Valley to enter the Plains of Summer.

All in all, this is the best time of the whole year when gift-givers can exchange their gifts and renew their old friendships. Those bringing fine skins or swan or vulture bone flutes or rare flint and amber from far away can exchange their gifts for our fine spirit-carvings of ivory or stone. And there is always our fine flax and hemp cloth and hemp string bags for which the Bear-kin are famous. Don't forget our famous stone lamps. It is always a time of great abundance and singing and dancing.

And I, of all the People, know it is also the time for excursions to the Serpent Springs with a new lover or a new husband.

* * *

Now that the hunters have returned, it is time for me to raise myself just as Red Girl's father was raised from the dead. There is much to be done in this World of Light to prepare for the Gathering and the hoped-for meeting of an old lover or a new husband. It seems a lifetime ago, but it was only last season when I met the husband of my heart.

"Maybe Brown Bull will come again. Maybe it will be different. Maybe *he* will be different this season," I whispered the wishes of my very soul into the ear of the Mother.

In my heart I shamelessly begged that the Mother would make of Brown Bull my husband in spite of my deepest fear that I would never be with him again. Pulled this way and that, my wounded heart still would not let the hope of him be banished forever.

My father and Little Ibex returned from the division just as the sun had begun to move from the center of the sky. That meant we all had a great deal of work to do preparing the skins and butchering the joints of fresh meat that were the share of my mother's lodge for one hunter and one bearer. First, we had to strip useful sinews and separate meat from fat—the fat would either be rendered immediately or used to cook with later. Excess fat and meat adhering to the skins had to be scraped in preparation for tanning, bleaching, staining and softening.

Few of these late-winter season skins would be made into furs because many of the animals have already started to shed their hair for the summer. Reindeer skins are still thick and full, but few of the others will make warm, soft sleeping furs or robes of the highest quality. The skins which are to have the hair removed will be soaked in the rotting pee of my mother's clay-lined urinal basket. The return of the hunters is always a busy, messy, smelly time for everyone. And when the work is completed, everyone loves to go bathe in the hot, cleansing waters of the Serpent Father.

My father always takes the occasion of a division like this one to teach Little Ibex how to flake the simple blades and scrapers we will all use to accomplish our work of preparing the Mother's gifts. Everyone works together at one task or another chanting to ourselves, if not singing out loud. We sing the hunter's Song of Gratitude and others of our favorites. Singing and chanting always makes the work go faster. This was the first time I had helped with the everyday work of my mother's lodge where I truly gave thanks for it all and understood what the words of the songs really mean.

That blasted Cave and all it has taught me is always crowding my thoughts now no matter what I am doing.

The work progressed rapidly with all four of us doing what needed to be done. By nightfall, cuts of meat had been wrapped in dry grass and stored in the bottom of our still-frozen storage pits. Some of the meat was cut into strips for smoking and drying over the fire that had been lit outside, in front of my mother's lodge. The same activities were going on everywhere in the Middle Camp and soon the whole of our Valley was full of the smoke and the smells of drying and cooking meat mixed with the pungent odors of fresh organs, meat, hides and urine. By nightfall in my mother's lodge, sinews were already pulled and drying, some of the skins had been staked out on the ground near the lodge or were stretching on frames. Hides were soaking in urine and much of the first scraping of the other skins was already completed by the time the sun went down.

Even my pesky but lovable little brother, White Fox, helped by watching the rendering pan of clay-covered wicker to make sure it did not get too hot. Each lodge had a joint roasting outside and the sweet, delicious smoky smell of fresh meat cooking made everyone's mouth water in anticipation of the feasting to take place at the end of the day. Each lodge was careful to reserve a couple of fresh haunches to be slowly cooked during the Gathering in the large, common roasting pit near the center of the camp.

The hunters actually eat very little of their kills during the hunt. The eating of some of the liver as part of the returning-of-the-blood rites in the Ceremony of Gratitude removes some of the offal and meat to be carried back to the lodges. Almost everything else is brought back. The hunters also consume marrow from the large bones and some of the organ meat that will not keep. Marrow does not travel well and cannot be dried so it must be eaten or it will be wasted. Besides, a little marrow from cracked bones gives a hunter great strength and stamina—so I have learned myself in those delightful hunts with my father.

Because many of the animals had been killed toward the end of the hunt, luckily, a good deal of the organ meat had been brought back. Everyone enjoyed this part of the hunter's return the most because fresh liver or heart would be fried or cut up and stewed with roots from the storage pits and mixed with the fresh greens and herbs already sprouting near the River to make delicious stews. When rested, and having begun our feasting, there would be much talk of the last Great Hunt of the winter season. There would also be much talk of all that had happened to me since my father left. That is, if he is still not too angry with me and my mother to speak to us at all.

Later that evening, my father was still angry, but a little less so than earlier in the day. As we all sat about the hearth after a long day of hard work, our bellies full from a well-deserved feast, I found myself trying to find a way to bring up the subject of Brown Bull with my father. I decided, after a long silence in the general conversation, that it was just best to be direct. After all, I am Seer of the Bear People now and deserve *some* respect.

"Father?" I said cautiously

When he looked up, said "Yes, my Daughter?" and did not bite my nose off like a hungry hyena, I continued.

"Did you happen to see Brown Bull upon the Great Hunt, my father?" I asked casually and with feigned nonchalance.

"Yes, Daughter," he said with a frown. "Your *lover* hunted with us this time," he sneered sarcastically.

Taken completely aback by the poison in his voice, my face flushed ochre-red. I looked over at my mother. She had put her sewing into her lap and sat staring down into the hearth fire without saying a word. My liver heated with embarrassment and anger and I could not hold down my words.

"Why are you so angry with me, my Father? What have I done to make you hate me so?" I pleaded on the verge of tears.

"I have only done what all other unmarried women do! And as far as these marks on my face are concerned, I have only done what the Grandfather has required of me!" I shouted in anger at my father for the first time in my life.

He looked up at me, clearly taken aback by my outburst. He could not have failed to see my brimming eyes above those fearsome marks. My father's face softened with compassion for what his only daughter had been put through and for what reasons he knew not.

"I'm sorry, my Daughter," he said. "It has been such a surprise to come from the hunt to find you so bruised and your beautiful face so scarred. I forgot myself. Forgive me. You are the daughter of your mother's lodge and I only speak for you all the abundance of the Mother," he said apologetically.

I took my father's apology for the sincere one that it appeared to be. At least he had not used my old name to address me all day, knowing that it was respectful and proper to refer to a seer by one's relationship and not by their childhood name. The marks of the All Mother's Cross had power and received respect even from the likes of my father.

"To answer your question with honor, Twice Born," my father began respectfully. "Brown Bull indeed was upon the Great Hunt. He was very courageous and successful but he was injured by a broken branch as he ran after a wounded reindeer," he explained in more detail than I cared to envision.

Suddenly, I was the concerned and unhappy one. "Is he all right? Can he walk? Will he live? Will he ever wrestle again?" I blurted a rapid string of questions.

Everyone in my mother's lodge started to laugh. Then I did too, harmony restored by the Trickster at my expense. The exuberance of my questioning and worried look on my face was enough for my father to see how concerned I really was for Brown Bull. My father spoke again, but this time with a semblance of a smile.

"Don't worry, my Daughter, he is well. It was only a minor wound. But he probably will not be wrestling at the Gathering this year because of it. Too bad, he is one of the best wrestlers among all the Bear People," he commented distractedly.

With an antler pick against his trouser-covered thigh, my father took a few flakes from a large spear point he continued to work as he spoke.

"Did he ask about me, my Father?" I couldn't resist asking further.

In anticipation of my father's answer my heart pounded into my neck and pulsed into every new mark or scratch I had suffered.

"Yes, Daughter, he did," my father replied tersely and said no more.

I patiently waited for more explanation. My father skillfully took another tiny flake off the spear point, the little stone chip landing in the hearth. It seemed like a whole season had passed without any more words from my father.

In sheer exasperation I blurted, "Father! What *else* did he say?"

"Well," he hesitated, taking the time to flick another chip toward the flames before answering.

My father stopped working the point, looked at me directly and said casually, "Brown Bull asked if you had taken a husband yet," and went back to his spear point.

Incredulous, I cried, "Is that all he said?"

"Yah, that's all," my father said distractedly without the slightest interest, all words of honor and respect for me gone from his terse reply. "What else would he be saying?"

My father must never talk to my mother, or anyone else for that matter, not to know who his only daughter had been out rutting with in the bushes during the last Great Gathering. Either he doesn't know or he doesn't care. Either way, it made me very angry all over again.

I could not hold back from speaking.

"Do you mean to tell me that you don't know that Brown Bull and I visited the hot pools many times at the last Gathering?" I asked without the slightest pretense of respect for the man who is my father.

"Do you mean to say that you do not know that I am in love with him?" I asked, in complete disbelief.

"Yes, I do know," my father replied without emotion. "Women of your age are expected to find a husband on their own if they refuse the advice of their mothers. Hunters hump whomever they please," he said rudely.

My face flared up in embarrassment and rage but he only fed the fire with more accusing words.

"You must know, my Daughter, a hunter will only marry one whom the mother accepts as a son of their lodge. And hunters have more to be concerned with than who wants to play with them in the bushes until they are ready to join a woman's lodge as husband," he said with ice in his words.

"What's more, hunters do not boast and tell stories of the woman they have taken to the hot pools with the woman's father," he said, rising irritation in his voice

Not the slightest hint of a smile remained on my father's face.

"Did Brown Bull ever speak to your mother about a marriage match?" he asked pointedly looking directly into my eyes.

I looked over at my mother's downcast face, turned my own face down toward the hearth in shame too.

"No, my father, he did not," I said as sadness and disappointment rushed throughout my body.

"Well then, what do you want me or your mother to do about it?" he asked.

And that was the end of that.

* * *

I did not sleep well that night. I tossed and twisted in my sleeping furs as images of Brown Bull kept running through my dreams in the shape of a light-brown bison bull who dodged and darted away from me as I pursued him across a grassy plain. I tossed light spears at him but always missed. White Lynx and the promises I made about her also kept running through my dreams. So, the next morning I decided it was time, at least, to make good on promises regarding my erstwhile Moon Blood sister.

"Mother?" I said, broaching the topic.

"I have not been a good friend to my Moon Blood sister, White Lynx, as I should. Auntie has already promised to take me with her the next time she goes to care for White Lynx's father, which is today. Will you help me? I would like to have my own mother there to help me make amends," I explained.

"Of course I will," my mother said unreservedly. "I am happy to help you. I will prepare a small gift for you to bring to White Lynx."

My mother immediately went to the basket of my brother's out-grown leathers. She selected a plain, long-sleeved hunter's shirt and a pair of men's drawstring trousers. Both pieces were in the light-brown color favored by hunters seeking to become invisible to their prey upon the Plain.

Holding the leathers up one-by-one my mother said out loud, but obviously thinking to herself, "White Lynx is wearing men's clothing now. She is not as tall as Little Ibex but is as big and strong as he."

She held the clothing up to my body and said, "Do you think these will fit? If the trousers are too long, I can easily shorten them for White Lynx."

"Yes, I think they will fit," I said.

But I really did not have any sense of how tall or how "strong" White Lynx is, so little notice had I ever taken of her.

"They will be fine gifts for such a sister as White Lynx," I said, without having to give too much away about how little I actually knew of her or her life.

Evidently, the preferred dress and hunter's way of life of my Moon Blood sister was no secret among the Bear-kin. Later in the day, the three of us made our way to the lodge of White Lynx, which lay to the east of the central dancing ground.

Auntie scratched at the unadorned and raggedy door flap to announce our arrival.

"Sister White Lynx! It is I, your Auntie come to treat your father," she called through the flap.

And just so White Lynx would not fall down in surprise to see all three of us standing at her door, Auntie added, "I have also brought Sister Little Bear and her mother, One Doe, to assist me.

She wishes to pay a Moon Blood sister and a gift-giver's visit to you."

I thought never to hear that name again. But certainly, Auntie had no other way to identify me to White Lynx except by using that name of mine so recently discarded.

White Lynx pushed her squinting eyes and disheveled hair around the edge of the tattered entrance flap. As her eyes adjusted to the bright afternoon sunlight, they got big and round as bone plates when she spied the new seer's marks upon my face. Clearly in awe, and not without emotion, she pulled back the flap quickly.

White Lynx looked fearfully down toward the ground and said, "Welcome, Sister. Welcome, Twice Born," she corrected herself as if I were her only visitor.

"Thank you for your hospitality, sister White Lynx," I replied politely wondering at the same time what she could possibly have prepared to entertain any guests.

I entered first. White Lynx and I pressed our foreheads together in greeting followed by Auntie and then my mother. The stink of a bloody-handed, sweaty, dusty, unwashed hunter was almost overpowering. The smell of her made my stomach flip over in revulsion. As White Lynx greeted each of them, I wondered how Auntie and my mother could stand the odor.

The three of us stood in the darkness of the lodge, our eyes adjusting to the gloom. White Lynx went to busy herself with stoking her hearth fire and adding a few cooking stones. Eyes now adjusted to the dimness of a bark lodge, we found ourselves standing in the entry of a lodge much like all the others in the camp. However, one side of the draft screen was beginning to collapse—only the stiff rawhide of the screen seemed to be holding it up. My nose curled up with the stench of rotten food, dust, rodent droppings and the acrid smoke of burned meat.

And, from the back of the lodge, which completely lacked any curtain for the sleeping platform there, came the unpleasant mixed scents of sickness, human and mouse urine, dirty clothing and filthy sleeping furs. The muffled sound of her poor unseen father's coughing was the only sound to be heard. I was so appalled by everything I saw and smelled and heard that I stood paralyzed waiting for Auntie and my mother to take the lead.

"Thank you for welcoming us to your lodge, Sister White Lynx," Auntie finally broke the silence. "We are honored that you entertain us without any warning. My wish is that you also welcome your Moon Blood sister and Mother One Doe to your lodge," Auntie said.

"Yes, please come in," White Lynx said feebly.

Insecurity and embarrassment in her voice, she mumbled something I could not hear. She then busied herself with putting stones into a cooking basket to heat water for her father's herbs. I hoped the heating water was entirely for her ailing father because I did not want to have to drink anything from any of the filthy cups or baskets piled in a heap on the rickety work table between hearth and draft screen.

"You are all welcome to my lodge, Sisters," White Lynx said in a tiny voice, making every attempt at proper manners.

"I am so sorry for the disorder. There is only myself to hunt, clean and cook for my father. Please disregard my poor lodge and be my honored guests," she apologized nervously.

I had the strange feeling that I had been in White Lynx's anxious and frightened position once before. Yes, it was that morning that seemed so long ago when the Grandfather had come to my mother's lodge unannounced. The Trickster turns us back upon ourselves to see who and what we really are!

"Please sit in the honored seat, my Auntie. I will prepare the poor herb water. I have only been able to collect these herbs by my own hand while upon the hunt. I know these herbs do not make the best tasting teas. Please excuse my lack of preparation to honor you as I should," White Lynx explained, her eyes still downcast.

Her words only made me feel more pity for her and more ashamed of my treatment of this, my Moon Blood sister.

"Thank you, Sister White Lynx," Auntie said politely.

"Thank you, Sister White Lynx," I echoed Auntie's words not knowing what else to say.

In spite of my strong desire not to walk around this lodge in bare feet, we had politely removed our boots at the screen while trying not to touch it lest it fall down completely. Auntie took the honored seat before the hearth facing the door. Auntie motioned me to the seat on her left and my mother to the seat on her right.

We sat upon dirty, well-worn rush mats without even a single sitting-fur anywhere to be seen.

The hearth fire was burning much higher now that White Lynx had stoked the flames. The rising heat began to draw in some fresh air around the shabby doorway, carrying too little of the stinking air of the lodge up and out the smoke-hole above the entrance. The fresh air floated around the draft screen like a perfume bringing some limited relief from the unrelenting stench of White Lynx's lodge. That little draft of fresh air was the only thing that kept me from bringing up my morning meal, I swear by the Mother! Without it, I would have had to rush out to avoid soiling the already fetid lodge with my own vomit for sure! I felt dirty just sitting in this poor girl's home.

White Lynx finished steeping the herb water. And, I'm sure to everyone's surprise, she brought each of us a beautifully carved wooden bowl of the unexpectedly fragrant tea—no finely woven cups to entertain guests in this lodge. That was just as well! She ladled her own tea into one of the small, finely made bowls with a large chip on the rim. White Lynx then sat in the place that had been reserved for her between Auntie and my mother. I looked across the hearth to where White Lynx sat, her head still down. I began to speak the words that Auntie had prepared me to speak.

"Sister White Lynx," I began. "I am your age-mate and sister of the same Moon Blood. I beg your forgiveness for my failure to give you the honor every sister is due from another of the Red Sisterhood. Please forgive me, Sister White Lynx. Please give me the honor of becoming a friend of your gift-giver circle."

White Lynx was clearly astonished at my words because she looked up at me open-mouthed and wide-eyed. Her head even rocked back slightly in surprise at my apology and offer of friendship. My mother and Auntie looked on with approving smiles as White Lynx sat up straight for the first time since we had arrived. White Lynx looked into my eyes and spoke directly to me in very polite and formal words.

"There is nothing to forgive, my Sister. I am overwhelmed by your generosity and I happily accept you into my gift-giver circle ... which now consists of one sister," she said, sincere pleasure spreading across her face in a beautiful smile full of perfect, white teeth.

White Lynx had made a joke! We would soon learn the Trickster dwells within that shy, retiring heart and many stories full of wit and laughter would be told. But in that moment, it broke my heart to hear her words. I got up and moved around the hearth to hold both her dirty hands in mine and to press our foreheads together as Sisters of the Moon Blood and gift-giver friends.

"Thank you, Sister White Lynx," I said, choking back the tears of shame and pity all mixed into one brimming flood.

"I have brought you a gift, Sister White Lynx. It is a poor first gift of friends and I hope you will accept it."

My mother handed me the chamois-wrapped bundle of clothes and I passed the package to White Lynx with both hands as all gifts are given. I moved back to my seat while White Lynx opened the package of hunter's clothing. She beamed even more broadly and then began to cry when she realized they were men's hunting leathers.

"Oh, thank you! Thank you, dear Sister! You do not know how the hunter's make fun of me for the women's clothes I have had to wear as bearer and tracker. My honor will grow among the men with these beautiful clothes for the hunt," she gushed as she hugged them to her breast.

"Sister White Lynx, it is my mother and my Auntie you should thank for the hunter's leathers. My mother has made them and Auntie has shown me how to be a true sister to you," I said with as much remorse for my poor treatment of her as I could muster.

"Yes, yes. Thank you, dear Auntie. And thank you, Mother One Doe! I am so grateful for these wonderful gifts! Please forgive me that I have such poor gifts of return to my honored Sister and friend," she said apologetically.

Leaping up abruptly, White Lynx began rummaging among the litter of moth-eaten sleeping furs and crumpled clothing upon the single sleeping platform behind my mother against the western wall of the decrepit lodge. I looked around. It seemed that every corner and unoccupied space was full of broken baskets, pack frames and other unidentifiable objects fit only to serve as kindling. Her sleeping furs were ragged skins chewed by rodents. A heap of dirty, bro-

broken bone plates and woven baskets with stale and rotting bits of leftover food threatened to topple from the work table. My heart truly sank as White Lynx found what she was looking for. She brought it to me holding it out with both hands.

"Please accept this gift of a hemp string carrying bag made by my own hands. I know it is a poor thing, but I am now a gift-giver of your circle and I am so grateful for the abundance you have brought me, Dear Sister."

With that, I accepted the gift with both hands. Before I could say a word of thanks, she darted away again. This time White Lynx went toward the leaning pile of cooking and eating utensils on the work table. From beneath the table she pulled two more of the finely carved, highly polished wooden bowls and formally handed one each to my mother and Auntie.

"Thank you, sister White Lynx," spoke my mother and Auntie in unison, clearly stunned at the quality of the carefully polished bowls of colorfully grained hardwood. The gift bowls were even more finely made than those she had used to serve the tea.

After another long and awkward silence, thankfully, Auntie spoke.

"Please allow your Sister to assist us in preparing your father's herbs, dear White Lynx," Auntie said, recruiting me as assistant healer.

"Sister White Lynx, will you be so kind as to welcome our further visits to give you the gift of a woman's helping hands with your lodge?" my mother said in a prearranged request.

"We know that since your mother made her own Return, you have been the only woman in your lodge. Because of your father's illness and inability to go out, you have been forced to spend much time as the hunter of your lodge as well. Please allow us to assist you as friends of the Red Sisterhood," my kindest-of-all Aunties requested formally.

* * *

Over the next few days, my mother and I made many visits to the lodge of my Moon Blood Sister, White Lynx, in addition to those visits made by Auntie with me in train as assistant to treat her ailing father. There was much to do in just removing all the broken baskets and rodent nests from the darkest corners of White Lynx's lodge. My mother cleaned and repaired all of the old sleeping furs and threw away those that were too tattered to be of any use whatsoever. To shelter White Lynx's feelings, my dear mother was also kind enough to replace all the furs she threw away with others, pretending they were not gifts of new furs for old.

White Lynx more than repaid us with her delightful wit and her funny stories of the Trickster. When she told it, it was the first time I had ever heard the story of the wife who had never joined in sex with her new husband before bringing him home to her mother's lodge. We all laughed and laughed at this funny story and the many others White Lynx told. This and other stories were only to be told among women, but I could also imagine a happier, more open White Lynx telling the tale to her hunter-companions around a campfire for a hearty laugh as well.

It is my favorite funny story of White Lynx and it goes like this:

Once upon a time, there was a girl who was so stupid that she had never joined in sex with her new husband before bringing him to join her mother's lodge. Because of this she knew nothing of men and of their hard bones and rods and what a woman is expected to do with them when joining in sex. On their first night together, the girl's mother had given the new couple the privacy of her sleeping platform behind the leather drape at the back of the lodge. Dumb Girl was so nervous and unsure about joining with her new husband in sex that she kept running out of the sleeping area to be reassured by her mother and ask questions. Her mother tried to calm her fears by saying, "Don't worry, Dumb Girl. Your new husband is a good man. Go back behind the drape and he will take care of you. Meanwhile, I will be heating some herb water for the two of you."

So Dumb Girl went back in and when she got behind the curtain her husband had already taken off his leather shirt to expose his hairy chest. Dumb Girl shouted in surprise and ran out to her mother and said, "Mommy, Mommy, my husband has a hairy chest!" "Don't worry, Dumb Girl," says her mother. "All good men have hairy chests. Go back behind the curtain and he will take care of you."

Dumb Girl went back in and when she got behind the leather drape, her new husband had taken off his trousers exposing his hairy legs. Again, she ran back out to her mother. Dumb Girl cried, "Mommy, Mommy, my husband took off his trousers and he's got hairy legs!" "Don't worry my daughter! All good men have hairy legs. Your new husband is a good man. Go back behind the curtain and he will take care of you," her mother said.

So for the third time, Dumb Girl went back in to her new husband and when she got there, he had unwrapped his feet and she saw that he was missing three toes on one foot—they had been completely chopped off. Dumb Girl saw this, she ran back out and cried, "Mommy, Mommy, my new husband's got a foot and a half!" Dumb Girl's mother got up and hurried toward the drape and says, "You stay here and make the tea!"

No one, least of all I, would ever have guessed that poor, dirty, shy White Lynx could have ever told such funny, funny stories of the fox-trickster!

My father was even persuaded to come and rebuild the sleeping platforms of the disintegrating lodge of White Lynx. My father, Uncle Bright Wolf and my brother, Little Ibex, all came to help repair the holes in the rush walls, replace the leaking bark shingles and fix the rickety draft screen. I taught White Lynx how to wear a woman's moon-blood belt and what kind of animal wool or flax cloth to use as padding. We went to the hot springs together to wash each other's backs with soap flowers. The first time we went to the pools together she touched the almost healed welts on my back with such unexpected kindness and gentleness that I felt them completely healed in that moment.

White Lynx soon began to look and smell like a woman should, which was a great relief to me because she had always stank like an unwashed hunter fresh from a bloody kill. As we began the "rebirth" of White Lynx, her hair had been so matted and snarled that I was forced to cut it as short as a new man's hair. In fact, White Lynx discovered that she liked her hair short. Once she learned how to clean and wash herself, she was really very pretty, even with short hair. Her straight hair was much darker than my own—almost black—and she possessed the most expressive, big round eyes. White Lynx's beautiful eyes were less and less covered with sadness as the days went on. The centers of her dark gray-brown eyes were encircled by a thick band of black color, just as Brown Bull's eyes had a black band encircling the dark blue.

White Lynx and I became sisters and true friends. We spent much time together combing each other's hair and listening to each other's stories of my entering the Great Cave and her following the men on the hunt. Other than hunting stories, we did not talk of men very much. And, to my great relief, she never once tried to get me to join with her in sex. She never even hinted at it with words of mixed meaning in the way that men always do when they want to entice you into playing with their man-bone.

My mother came often, as well, to teach White Lynx how to cook and take care of her clothing and how to keep her lodge clean and orderly. White Lynx did not want to learn how to cook because she said it was "woman's work", as if there were something less-than-honorable about being a woman and doing the work of women! How like a man she had become by going out with them all the time! But when my mother told her that learning to collect and cook tasty food upon the hunt would greatly enhance her honor among the hunters, she became an avid learner of the skills of cooking. My mother is so very wise in her own way.

As the days passed waiting for the beginning of the Great Gathering, I became healer to White Lynx's father. Auntie showed me his herb mixtures and then entirely handed his care over to me—my first patient as Healer. Auntie often came along to speak the healing chants in trance, which I had not even begun to master. But other than that, I was completely responsible for his care.

To my great satisfaction, with the foul odors of the lodge eliminated in favor of clean mats and sleeping furs, freshly made eating and cooking utensils, White Lynx's father began to recover. Within a few days he was able to sit outside the lodge in the warm sun carving and polishing the beautiful wooden bowls that were his most precious gifts. It was not long before both my mother's and my Auntie's lodges were well-stocked with his lovingly made handiwork. As he became more and more healthy, he was also able to hunt more often. That also helped bring more abundance into the lodge of my Moon Blood sister and gift-giver friend, White Lynx.

And thus began a lasting friendship and a true sisterhood. White Lynx and I—two outcasts for different reasons—became fast friends. I discovered that in White Lynx there was one who would love me and care for me regardless of the marks upon my face, and I her, regardless of her man's short hair and hunter's clothing.

* * *

By the time people started arriving for the Great Gathering, my seer's marks—there for all to see—had mostly healed. My brother Big Ibex, now known as Black Eagle, arrived with my Moon Blood sister of the Ibex-kin with the beautiful name to lodge with Auntie and Uncle Bright Wolf. My older brother is a good bison wrestler and, no doubt, will be wrestling with a big black-and-red ibex painted across his rather narrow, but muscular back. It is unfortunate that my father will probably not get to see his eldest son wrestle. That is because he will be mentor to Little Ibex in this season's initiations.

Both Big Ibex and Dawn Star Rising had eyes as big as bowls when they first saw my seer's marks. The scars were still very dark from scabs and bits of charcoal still adhering to them when they arrived for the Gathering. Because they were so fresh, the marks were especially noticeable, unlike Auntie's and the Grandfather's, whose marks had faded to a murky blue. Big Ibex and Dawn Star Rising drew back visibly and tried to look somewhere other than my face as we greeted each other and talked about how long it had been since we had seen or spoken to one another. The stiffness and hesitance in their touching of foreheads was noticeable and it made my heart ache.

With the friendship of White Lynx having barely been mid-wifed into being, I would be going out to watch the competitions of the Gathering as a young, unmarried Seer of the Bear People by myself. Also, my friend White Lynx had decided to wrestle this season. Preparations and practice for the bison wrestling kept us entirely apart these last few days. The isolation of the Twice Born had begun in earnest.

After the initiates, their mentors and the assistant seers and shamans had entered the Cave for this season's puberty rites, I thought it was time for me to venture out and watch the competitions and, perhaps, to participate in the dance circles. Next to the hot pools, a dance circle is the best place to meet and get to know new lovers and prospective husbands. The day is sunny and warm, so neither I nor anyone else will have to lug heavy bison robes around.

My mother's lodge is on the west side of the Middle Camp. I went first to the throwing ground that had been set up on the far western edge of what had become a huge ring of permanent and temporary lodges with the dancing, wrestling and feasting ground in the center. At the throwing grounds, the younger boys were slinging stones and tossing bolos. Here also, some of the older boys were competing with the young hunters without first-kill marks to be the best of the light spear throwers and the fastest of the runners.

Little Ibex would have been among the spear throwers if he were not in the Cave, but it had been a cousin of the camp who asked me to paint the targets—an image-making task I now felt a bit over-qualified to do as an exalted Seer of the Bear People. Since all the other seers were busy inside the Cave with the initiations, I was left to perform my first service to the Nine Kin by painting spirit-animals on the boys' targets.

The slingers had set a short tree trunk into the ground fifty paces away from the edge of the encampment for their target. The light spear throwers, on the other hand, had stretched an old piece of rush matting around a bundle of reeds and grass for their target so as not to damage the precious spear points by hitting something as solid as a tree. Upon the tree trunk I painted Lion Mother's head full-faced and with gaping jaws. I thought it might help to prepare the boys in their hearts to someday sling stones at a lion or hyena in order to keep it from a kill.

Upon the rush mat target, which was at least eighty paces back from the edge of the lodge circle, I painted a full-sized reindeer's forequarters in a side view. I made it without hooves or rear quarters, but with a magnificent rack of antlers. I painted the left leg of the reindeer as if it were stepping forward to expose what, even the youngest of the Bear People know, is the killing spot every hunter aims for. If the spear strikes too far forward, it will hit the animal's shoulder and likely will hit the bone there and bounce back. If the spear strikes too far back, it might hit a rib, or worse, the stomach, spilling the bitter contents of the stomach and gall bladder onto the meat. Either too far forward or too far back is not a killing wound.

But if the hunter hits the place just behind the extended leg, it is the throw that will send the point straight to the animal's heart and lungs avoiding days of tracking the suffering, bleeding animal. It was important for every hunter to focus all their attention on the killing spot and not to be distracted by anything else—that much I had been told by my hunter-father. And having received that same teaching about focusing one's attention in the Cave, I knew the truth of it.

"Out of the Great Cave mere days and here I am already teaching the boys to be hunters," I thought to myself, with just a little self-satisfaction and pride in my choice to become Seer.

After inspecting my handiwork, I watched the boys throw their spears and sling their stones for a time. I also flirted with some of the young hunters, giving them little looks and smiles with hidden, yet transparent, meanings. In seasons past, the new men without first-kill marks, hunters with kill marks and even some of the big-ger boys would have flirted back. They would have talked and joked with me, a pretty girl of the Middle Camp.

But now, every one of them tried to avoid looking directly at me. The fearsome shaman's marks on my face kept all but one brave and handsome young hunter with a Reindeer-kin mark upon his shoulder from flirting. Reindeer-boy approached me with flash-ing eyes and smiling lips, his mouth full of compliments for my beautifully painted reindeer target enticing me to speak to him.

Shortly before Reindeer-boy came toward me grinning from ear-to-ear, he had stood in a little knot of his brothers whispering and looking in my direction, their slender throwing spears all held skyward in a tight circle. I knew he was proving to his less coura-geous companions that he was enough of a grown man and un-afraid to approach a woman with shaman's marks upon her face. I really had no interest in teasing the boy, the young man, I should say—he seemed like such a boy to me. All I wanted was to go where the strong men were bison wrestling on the dancing ground at the center of the camp. Maybe I could see White Lynx wrestling there too? He approached, greeted me, and I asked him if he wanted to go with me to see the bison wrestlers.

Reindeer-boy answered, "Yes, Thrice Born. I would like that."

I started to laugh, but held my tongue. How could he know that I had never taken the shaman's journey? How could he know that I was merely Twice Born Seer of the Bear People? I could not help but hurt a little inside as this brave young man of the Reindeer-kin walked and talked with me on my way to the wrestling ground where I would look for my brother Black Eagle. And perhaps look for someone else, who, so it seemed, was never out of my thoughts.

As we walked toward the wrestling ground together, Reindeer-boy did not mention my face marks even once, although he could not look me in the eye for staring at them. I have never felt so alone while in the presence of other people in my life. My heart wept silently to think this would be my life hereafter and forever more. My feet moved aimlessly toward the large crowd laughing and singing and cheering the wrestlers on. My lips mouthed vacuous words without meaning in some kind of mindless conversation with this handsome Reindeer-boy.

"What have I done?" I thought to myself over and over again.

The camp had grown enormously with many temporary lodges having sprung up like saplings on the half of the cleared area of the Middle Camp on the river-side of the large dancing hearth. After the dance circle, and of course, going to the hot springs, bison wrestling was the most exciting activity of every Gathering. Having done what I have done inside the Great Cave only made me more aware of how important the bison dance and bison wrestling is to my People. I wondered what everyone would think or say if they knew exactly what I had made with my paints and charcoals inside the Holy Cave?

When Reindeer-boy and I drew close to the wrestling ground, many people were already circled in a knot around a pair of bison wrestlers painted in oily black and red paint. I spotted my brother Big Ibex—I still cannot think of him as Black Eagle—and Dawn Star Rising in the front of the crowd. They were very close to the pair of grappling wrestlers each struggling to throw the other to the ground. I casually strolled up to the inside of the circle and began moving around toward where my brother stood while pretending I wasn't looking for anyone in particular.

Reindeer-boy was lost in the crowd. I had not even said, "Farewell and good fortune in your contests," so rude am I.

Neither the two wrestlers stirring up great clouds of dust nor any of the other painted wrestlers who were waiting to have their own matches had the red and black sign of the Bison-kin. I knew he would not be wrestling, so why was I looking for the sign of the Bison-kin? Still, my heart sank with disappointment.

"Perhaps, since he was injured and could not wrestle, he did not come at all?" I speculated to myself.

My eyes scanned like a stalking wolf around the circle of shouting, singing and laughing spectators. Instead of nearly naked, painted red and black and sweating against another man's heaving muscles as I had first seen him, Brown Bull stood on the edge of the circle of onlookers just beyond Big Ibex and Dawn Star Rising. Everyone was watching the match and shouting encouragement to the wrestlers locked in combat but I could only look in one direction.

"What a shame, what a waste! Brown Bull is a far better wrestler and far more handsome naked than either of those two wrestlers," I almost spoke out loud.

As I stared at him, my gut emptied completely with angry pride and unfathomable longing all in the same moment. Then Brown Bull looked up at me.

Our eyes met and locked across the grappling, grunting, heaving, dust-covered wrestlers, who just seemed to simply vanish into the air. Even from that distance all I could see was the black abyss in the center of Brown Bull's dark blue eyes and I could not look away. I wondered what was showing on my face of the churning whirlpool of feelings that were pulling me to pieces. I was certain my expression revealed nothing but forced apathy—no love, no anger, just ice.

A puzzled look of recognition crossed Brown Bull's face. Without looking up, down or to the side, he began to move around the circle toward me. He moved past Dawn Star Rising and then passed Black Eagle at the edge of the wrestling circle. My brother dodged right and then left as Brown Bull passed by, the better to see the struggling wrestlers unobstructed just in front of him.

As a hunter trained to be dispassionate and practiced in concentrating and taking everything in at all times, Brown Bull's hunter's eyes visibly widened as my freshly made seer's marks registered somewhere in that handsome head of his. He was coming toward me, edging in front of the onlookers. I deliberately broke his intense gaze by looking over at the wrestlers still pushing and struggling against each other. I pretended I hadn't seen him.

All the while, I wondered, "What it is that I intend to do now?"

I turned slowly toward him as he placed his hand on my shoulder. I pretended to be surprised with fake, wide eyes that it was his hand touching me.

"How stupid of me to pretend I don't see him. I am not deceiving anyone," I thought to my foolish self.

Then I looked into those night-blue eyes. I am lost all over again.

CHAPTER 16.
THE GREAT GATHERING

UTTERLY SURPISED, Brown Bull called out my old name. "Little Bear?" he asked with an astonished little boy's voice.

He was staring at my new seer's marks, livid and dark-stained.

"When?" he mumbled. "Where? How is this possible? I, I, … you?" he stammered incoherently, unable to comprehend what it was his eyes were seeing.

It was the only time I had ever seen him so confused, surprised and with such a thick tongue he could hardly speak. Again taken aback by the suddenly alien sound of my old name on anyone's lips, I looked again into Brown Bull's blue-black eyes.

That was my first mistake. With the arrogance I thought would be fitting one who is Twice Born and a great Seer of the Bear People, I spoke to him.

"My name is no longer Little Bear, my Brother. I have a new secret name. As Twice Born Seer and Healer of the Bear People, you may call me Elder Sister," I said pretentiously, knowing full well he actually had more seasons than I.

My ridiculous act didn't fool Brown Bull even a little. With laughing eyes, he beamed back a radiant smile of ivory white teeth—all of them still intact. But something was different about his face … it is the dimples, and moustaches with shaven cheeks! At that moment, I wondered who had shaved his face so closely for him this very morning? Unusual for any man to be this vain and impractical as to shave his whole face when he isn't even wrestling. Come to think of it, on our first meeting his face was not covered by a beard either. Bison wrestlers will either wear long beards or they will shave just before a match—wrestlers dislike stubbly beards as prickly as hedgehogs on their opponents as much as women do on their lovers. Too much exuberance with the delicate skin of either and we come away as if burned by fire.

Last season, at our first meeting, beneath all the mud and greasy ochre from a wrestling match, dimples would have been easy to miss. After all, I was so concentrated on his eyes, arms, legs, chest, and man-club I could hardly be expected to notice something as insignificant as dimples! But these newly discovered dimples charmed me even more deeply into his magic spell. Suddenly, I wanted more than life to be the one asked to shave that handsome face.

Unable to hold my hurt and anger from the past and unable to hold my pretended high place as Seer, we both began to laugh at my ridiculous pretentions. He took my hand to lead me through and away from the crowd, toward the up-slope bark lodges. The hot pools would be too crowded today with other couples for him to want to take me there again. I just decided to follow where he led. That was my second mistake.

"Oh, great Seer and Healer of the Bear People," he chuckled aloud. "I have need of your services," he mumbled quietly while narrowing his eyes in that sly, sidelong grin.

Somehow, the feel of my hand in his and that smile made it impossible to remember all my suffering for want of him. So certain was I that this was to be just another roll in the sleeping skins with a convenient pute for Brown Bull to poke and play with—and thinking about Auntie's warning of the loneliness of the seer's life—I brought him to a halt by stopping in the middle of the trail, grabbing his hand tightly and spinning him around to face me.

"Where do you think you're taking me, Brown Bull?"

In the bright sunshine, the black rod of my lion-eye must have been in full bloom, because he looked at it, then his eyes shifted to the shaman's marks. First to my eye, then to the marks, then back again, his eyes went from one to the other with genuine curiosity. He then speared his penetrating gaze to my right eye again.

With more teasing sarcasm than I could ever muster he said, "I have been wounded in the hunt, Elder Sister. I am in great need of your healing skills. And of your other gifts as well," he said with a lift in his eyebrow.

Brown Bull spread that flashing smile and popped those dimples once again. Suddenly, I didn't care if this was only to be another afternoon of body-passion I still wanted him inside me more than life. Come what may.

I said softly in reply and with a lift of my own eyebrow, "I will treat your wound, Brown Bull."

Never did I turn my gaze away from those deep, deep blue pools he calls his eyes.

* * *

We climbed the slope in the direction of my Auntie's lodge thinking it would be the closest lodge or tent most likely to be empty. Auntie was in the Cave conducting the girl's Moon Blood as the Mother of the Rites. Uncle Bright Wolf was probably watching the wrestlers or exchanging with his gift-givers. Of course, there were no children in Auntie's lodge who might burst in on us. Though they had their sleeping furs with Auntie and Bright Wolf for the Gathering, we had just left my brother Big Ibex and Dawn Star Rising at the wrestling circle.

I thought of taking him to my mother's lodge since my father and Little Ibex are in the Cave. But I had no idea where my mother and White Fox are or when they would return. Auntie's lodge it is. I could not wait to get inside the lodge and join with Brown Bull again. My heart raced much faster than my feet!

But as we approached my Auntie's lodge, we could hear voices coming through the flimsy rush walls and bark roof—men's voices. The muffled sounds were those of two men grunting and moaning as they noisily joined in sex thinking no one was about to hear them. It appeared my Uncle Bright Wolf is presenting some gift-giver of his acquaintance a different kind of gift altogether! We both covered sniggering mouths with our hands and without saying anything out loud, I pointed to my mother's lodge just across the way. Still fairly close to the rutting bulls in Auntie's lodge, I spoke very softly so as not to alert whoever was there to our presence. As if any sound would ever be noticed by Uncle Bright Wolf and whoever he was humping!

I whispered into Brown Bull's ear, the scent of his hair bringing everything back in a flood of memory.

"My brother, Little Ibex, is being initiated today. My mother will have taken my youngest brother to see the excitements of the Gathering. We will be alone for as long as we like in my mother's lodge."

"Do you know when they will return? Should we find another place to be undisturbed? My traveling tent?" he whispered back.

His warm breath on my ear made me dizzy.

"Just to let anyone know who might disturb us that we are within, I will hang your shirt outside the door flap," I suggested as we reached the entrance to my mother's lodge.

I really just wanted some pretext to get his shirt off as soon as possible. But placing it outside where anyone coming to the lodge would see it just *might* deter them from coming in on us. I entered first and held back the flap for Brown Bull. I removed my boots on the mat-covered area of the entry and waited for him to remove his. Then I led Brown Bull by the hand around the draft screen into the darkened, empty lodge toward the fur-covered seat of honor before my mother's hearth.

The hearth had only a handful of banked coals that were barely alive. They glowed beneath the thin, flat baking stone that had been pushed off its four supporting rocks toward the work table. The angled stone directed the warmth and the glow of the hearth back in the direction of the seat of honor. Our eyes quickly adjusted to the only real light that was coming in through the south-facing smoke hole beneath the lodge's curved roof.

After brushing off the grass boot stuffing adhering to our feet I said, "Give me your shirt."

I waited while he undid the laces before helping him pull it over his head. Brown Bull's glorious bison wrestler's chest emerged from the soft leather sheath of his shirt. Just holding the shirt in my arms and smelling the rising perfume of him started a rush of heat. It moved down my body, from the lump in my throat to the knot of body-hunger in my pute. He just stood there smiling his sidelong smile, eyes burrowing into mine.

I forced myself to break his gaze and went to the entry, his shirt carried over both forearms like a gift. I took it outside and hung it on a peg that supported one of the paired ibex horns above the door flap. No one coming to my mother's lodge could fail to see it at the entrance. Brown Bull's leather shirt would stand guardian to our passion. I came back to where he stood waiting for me upon the sitting furs at the hearth facing the door. The seat of highest honor in any lodge could be the only fitting place for us to be together at this moment.

"Without my shirt, I am cold. Will you not come greet me as a guest in your mother's lodge? Will you come and warm me, beautiful Sister," he teased.

Brown Bull stood with his feet planted wide, his massive arms folded across the hard muscles of his wrestler's chest.

I thought to myself, "He certainly knows how to show off what he has to his best advantage!"

As I looked at him, taking in the sheer masculine splendor that seemed to emerge from every pore and hair, I noticed a faint, other-worldly white glow around him. Brown Bull seemed to radiate light within the darkness of the lodge. It took my breath away.

"It is only the sunlight coming in through the smoke-hole under the curve of the roof," I explained the apparition to myself.

Stray sunbeams or not, I was absolutely transfixed at the shimmering beauty of this man-creature. He stood before me, unmoving, and yet seeming to glow in the darkness of the surrounding lodge.

"Yes, Brother, I will greet you. But first let me stoke the hearth so you are not so cold," I teased back.

I have visited other lodges of the Nine Kin while assisting my Auntie. None have the richness in furs and skins as do the lodges of the Bear-kin. My father says it is because of the Cave and the many rich gifts brought to the seers and shamans who oversee the rites and perform healings. My mother says it is because of the fine gifts the Bear-kin have to exchange with their gift-givers. I don't know about any of that, but I do know the mats of most of our lodges are covered in heavy sitting furs on top woven rushes with fragrant pine boughs beneath. Because of the many furs on the floor, one can sleep anywhere in my mother's lodge you care to place your sleeping skins and not just upon the sleeping platforms on either side and at the back of the lodge.

"Brother, while I am stoking the fire, please bring that pile of sleeping skins from my platform there." I gestured toward the women's sleeping platform against the right-hand wall of the lodge.

"You can use them to warm yourself if the skin bumps begin to arise," I said with another sidelong smile.

And so this is where we would dance our little dance and play our little game together. It mattered not in the slightest where this joining might take me or what joy it might bring. Neither did the pain that might also come deter me in the least.

* * *

"Will you look at my wound, Dear One?" he asked in a little boy's voice.

Such an endearment coming from Brown Bull's lips startled me for just a moment before I regained my composure.

"Yes, Dear One," I responded in kind. "I will look at your wound. But I must be free of these doeskins to do a complete and thorough examination," I said with the biggest, most seductive smile I could make.

It took him no time at all to remove my shirt and untie my leather kilt. I stood completely naked in front of him except for my loinskin. The flickering flames of a revived hearth fire danced glowing shadows against our bare skins. The passions of my liver rose with the rising flames of the hearth fire and soon I felt feverish from head to toes. We stood looking into each other's eyes and, without touching him with a single finger, it was clear to see he was already fully erect and hard beneath his soft doeskin trousers.

"Will you not greet me and welcome me into your mother's lodge, Elder Sister," he said.

The words were said in jest, but the look in his eyes could not have been more serious.

Our eyes still locked in a dreamlike embrace I replied, "Of course, Younger Brother. Where are my polite manners? Where is a proper greeting for a guest?"

Brown Bull grasped both my arms to pull me toward him in the forehead-to-forehead greeting of visitors. The gesture of welcome slipped easily into a long kiss on my mouth.

"May I look at your wound now?" I said, looking down at the bulge that rose almost to his trouser-top.

"Yes, my beautiful Shaman, but *that* is not it," he said with a droll smile.

He untied his trousers and let them fall, but the waist tie caught on his sex as hard as an oak branch.

"Let me help you with that," I said smiling broadly.

I reached out to pull the trousers from the end of his man-rod. It was already oozing with clear, slippery liquid.

After he stepped out of the trousers and tossed them aside, I said with my most seductive smile, "I will look for the wound since it doesn't seem to be there between your legs, my Brother."

I began slowly running my fingers over his lips, down his neck, tracing around the first-kill mark at his throat, across his chest, up and down both arms pretending to look and feel for a scar or a wound of some kind. He quivered under my fingers and tiny hairs stood up at my almost-touching of his skin. I made snake-like trails with my fingers across his flat, hard stomach, just grazing the tip of his rod. Already aroused, it jumped even higher at the touch. I watched, fascinated, as the liquid oozed from his foreskin to drip slowly down the front of his penis, the livid red head just peeking out from its glistening hiding place. I would search for the black marks of the Dark Lion Mother later.

Then I drew closer to kiss his delicious lips and run both my hands lightly up his back. Hard muscles rippled, moving and responding to my every touch. I pressed my bare belly and full breasts against him. Once again I ran my hands down the hard muscles of his back, over his solid half-moon buttocks and down onto his massive legs.

I whispered, "Oh ... here is the wound. It is upon your thigh."

The injury had been bound with a strip of flax cloth so I could hardly have missed it. I kneeled down in front of him to unbind the injury.

"Is this the *terrible* wound that we have all heard so much about?" I teased.

Still on my knees, I looked up at him, my eyes slowly drinking in everything about this man that I loved with heart, head and liver above all others. His huge, hard, dripping sex stood up as if it had a spine of its own. Never mind that everyone says a man's rod has a mind of its own! And then I saw what I had not paid much attention to the first time we were together: two black dot-marks on the underside of his penis. Brown Bull *had* been pierced and marked in the Lodge of Black Spirits. I knew that when I eventually looked, there would be two more black spots on the upper side of his glorious man-club.

But now, there were other, more interesting sights to be seen and paths to be taken. The trail of soft, light brown hair that flowed up past his navel and over the hard ridges of his chest to his throat and shaven cheeks would be a most delightful path to take. And above all, over all and always, there were those blue-black eyes! I all but gasped out loud at the sight and smell and taste of him.

But it was his enticing voice humming, "Well, what is the great Healer and Seer's diagnosis?" that brought me out of the stupor of my own liver-passion.

A liver-passion to have this man inside me again is certainly what I am feeling in this moment. Is there anything beyond that? I hope not because I fear I will not survive his leaving me again.

"The Seer's diagnosis is: beautiful man, perfect, complete and arousing as any man could be. The other wound is healed," I said enigmatically.

I spoke the words teasingly, but the words actually voiced the song of my heart, if not entirely the song of my liver. How is it I could not voice those words as a song of my heart as lovers do to each other? If I have gifts, why do I not have the gift of singing a song of my heart as others do?

"I am too afraid he will not sing those songs of love back to me," was the coward's reply echoing back inside my head.

The leg-wound itself was hardly more than a big scratch from some branch or thorn. It had already been treated with yellow ochre and was almost completely healed. I could chide my father for calling this a serious injury, but I suppose any scratch or cut received during the hunt can be very dangerous. Otherwise, the hunters would not keep a bone tube of yellow ochre always at hand.

"The scratch is healed. Since you are no longer in need of a healer, Little Brother, what would you have me do now?" I taunted him.

"Only this," is all he said to me.

Brown Bull grabbed both sides of my head by the hair and pushed my willing mouth over his sex. He shoved his penis down my throat as far as it would go, but slowly so that I would not gag too quickly. He began to moan. I worked the slippery man club in and out of my mouth. Thrusting rudely, he bumped the back of my throat uncomfortably and then he put his head back, no longer looking into my eyes, impaling someone or something else altogether. Brown Bull was no longer humping me. That was for certain.

Soon he began to groan with a deep, rough voice. He thrust between my lips faster and faster. I thought he would put his essence down my throat at any moment. With my tongue, I could feel the low scars of the marks of Lion Mother and just as I thought he would erupt into my mouth—a thing I was aching to have happen—he pulled out of my mouth altogether.

Brown Bull got down on his knees to face me. He looked deeply one more time into my eyes, gently ran his finger tips over my shaman's marks and began to kiss my mouth. Then he lightly pressed his lips against each eye lid and ever-so-gently outlined each shaman mark with his tongue of lightning. Searing ecstasy flooded my body from the single point of his moving tongue. As he kissed my mouth again and then my neck and then both my breasts, twirling each nipple on his tongue, his hand went down to pull my loinskin loose. It too was wet with my own oozing liquids.

Without ever once breaking that steady blue gaze, he laid me on my back atop the pile of soft sleeping furs. Brown Bull pushed my bent knees wide apart and entered me easily, smoothly, slowly.

Just as he had done the first time we were joined in sex like this, his eyes held my gaze without ever looking away even while he moved in and out of me in long slow strokes. Both of us squirmed with every sensation. I moved, writhing under him to allow his sex to go as deeply into mine as possible, seeking out every secret corner of my pleasure and my bliss as high as the heavens.

"Is this what a shaman feels when joining with a beloved animal-companion? Is this the bliss of a shaman's journey? If so, they are correctly named "the Ecstatic Ones" I thought to my heart in hazy words.

Amazingly, Brown Bull never once looked away with those eyes of the Dark Mother's Abyss until he began to thrust harder and faster as his powerful orgasm began. He was completely unlike any other man or boy I had ever joined with in sex. They had all closed their eyes from beginning to end. They almost never even looked at my face, let alone gazed so deeply into my eyes and into my very soul as this.

If ever I saw the Mother's Face in another, it was within the black, black circle at the very center of Brown Bull's incredible eyes.

As I pulled him down to bury my face in the crook of his pulsing neck, I pressed my breasts against his sweating chest and locked my legs around his waist. It was at that moment my own orgasm began, pulling every part of him ever deeper into myself as his white, creative essence filled my red-womb to overflowing. As soon as I finished climbing my own mountain of joy, he collapsed atop me gasping for breath. Still moving slowly inside me, he gently rubbed his hairy chest against my soft, wet breasts and belly.

The two as one—at last!

* * *

I don't know how long it was that we drifted together in the enfolding mists of the blissful trance of each other's dream. But all too soon, he rolled us over onto our sides without pulling out of me. We faced each other, my head resting on his strong right arm. He just lay there—inside me—without speaking or moving. He never once looked away until his penis softened and slithered out like a slippery snake to drip slowly onto the fur between us.

He rolled onto his back. I just lay there looking at him. Neither of us spoke for what seemed an eternity. At this moment, I only desired to drink in the utter bliss of feeling all I had ever wanted from joining in sex with this man. I never wanted it to end.

A little sleep was next for both of us, so utterly poured out I felt. Before we drifted off I used the flax cloth bandage to wipe him and then myself and the sleeping fur beneath us. I put my head against his chest. The sweat was already drying and we both were beginning to feel the chill. Brown Bull pulled a soft sleeping fur over the two of us. I drifted into a sublime dream of Brown Bull, Brown Bull, Brown Bull and nothing else.

I was awakened by the strange, but exciting, feeling of my pute being entered from the rear. During our little nap, I had rolled over so that Brown Bull was holding me in my sleep, my back tight against his chest. How easily had holding me like that turned into humping me again! Before he climbed his mountain again, he had me up on all fours rutting and moaning like the Bison Shaman had undoubtedly humped his wife in that old story that held so much meaning for me now. With a few great thrusts and what sounded like a laughing bellow—I am sure it can be heard all the way to the dancing ground—he collapsed on my back making silly grunts and snorts like a rutting bull. Once again he had not pulled out before spilling his essence inside me as he had done the first time we joined so long ago. I wondered at its meaning. My hopes began to rise that this joining would, indeed, be different for us.

I thought to myself, "He really is well-named. Here is a bull able to mount his cow again so soon! But then he is young and in his prime, that is certain!"

Soon we were face-to-face again. This time he lay on his back, his head nearest the hearth. I straddled him and sat on his rod, the light from the opening above the entry shining more brightly on my face. With more light, I knew he would be searching for my lion-eye. While Brown Bull toyed with me by slowly working his hips up and down, I ground my pute down against him in rhythm with his every move. I wondered, does he see the face of Lion Mother in my lion's black pupil? But how could I ever ask such a thing of him directly? Given the position we were in, me sitting atop him, I could not hold myself back any more. Besides, it is always best just to be direct, especially when you are on top!

"Tell me of your journey to Lion Mother's Black Lodge," I blurted impulsively.

"How do you know I was ever there?" he teased, biting his smiling lower lip and ramming me hard a few times.

"I am Yellow Lion, Seer of the Bear People. I know all and see all!" I teased back and in doing so revealed to him my secret name.

With the sounds of my holy seer's name barely off my lips, he stopped moving inside me.

Brown Bull locked those deepest-of-blue eyes on mine and in all seriousness said, "My lovely Yellow Lion, you have the marks of Dark Mother upon your left shoulder. From that I know the Grandfather will have told you how all men who dare to enter the Womb of Dark Mother are pierced and marked in their foreskins. Being Seer has nothing to do with it!"

He smiled and rammed me a few more times with his delightful man-rod.

"Dearest One?" he asked. "Would you have had the courage to thrust the needle through *my* foreskin?" The dimples reappeared.

Again, such an unexpected endearment from the mouth of Brown Bull stopped my words for a moment.

Then I said with cool detachment, "Not now that I know your foreskin so well, Dearest One."

I watched his face for a reaction at my returning his endearment kind-for-kind. His only reaction was to look deeper into my eyes. In so doing, Brown Bull spoke everything that needed to be said between us without a single spoken word.

I slid backward off him, his sex flopping forward and slapping against his belly with a wet thwack. I reached to caress his penis and slide the foreskin all the way down so the two marks could be clearly seen on the underside in dark blue. I ran my finger over the two low, round scars and looked back up into his eyes once again.

"Yes," I said analytically. "I see two black marks on this side, but where are the other two, I wonder? Maybe I should take a closer look?"

I pulled his penis back up to me where I could place my mouth over it again, tasting my own pute in the process. Brown Bull loved to play these little sex games and so did I. Incredibly, all Brown Bull had to do to get ready to climb the mountain again was to see his rod going in and out of my mouth. Ask as many times as I would, but Brown Bull would not tell me exactly what it was that excited him so much about this one particular act of joining in sex. Perhaps he did not know himself. He is another man, like my father, who just will not talk with words about anything that is close to his heart. I have learned that much about him. Only with his eyes would he ever speak of such things. The difficulty with that is, I am always one to hear the words of the mouth before my heart believes.

I could never hazard a guess why this one act excited Brown Bull so much before entering Lion Mother's Lodge. But now I think I begin to understand. I could only imagine what it must look like from his point-of-view—gazing into my lion-eye, his penis in my mouth between the two shaman's cheek-signs of the All Mother. It must be like a male river snake sliding into the Eye of the Mother, into the Mouth of the Mother! I only know that when we join in sex in this particular way he is not really humping me. He closes his eyes, puts his head back and his soul flies far, far away. When he is with me, *truly* with me, he looks into my eyes and does not look away. Nor could I ever look away from his when he is piercing me with his eyes as only he can do.

"Brown Bull," I said in a whisper. "Tell me what you see when you look into my lion-eye. I have tried many times to see what it is that others see by looking into still pools of water. But I can never see it. What does it look like, Dear One?" I asked.

He took my face between his hands and peering closely into my right eye he said, "Your magic lion-eye is the same fawn-brown with yellow and red-ochre flecks as your other eye. Your lion-eye is a dark rod of black color that runs from the center spot to the dark grey circle around the outside of your eye. When the center dark spot is large, as it is now in the dim light, your lion-eye cannot be seen. But when you are in bright light, the center shrinks to a tiny dot and the magic lion-eye appears. I will search for you always my beautiful Lion Lady. I will search for this lion-eye in all the worlds to come," he whispered in my ear.

I knew from the ebbing and flowing feelings in my heart that Brown Bull had said something very important, but the very thought of "all the worlds to come" left me without words. He continued to gaze into my soul with his own eyes of the Mother's blue-black Abyss. Whenever he spoke words of never-ending love with those eyes, our twin spirit-fires drifted to some secret place far, far away that could never be told or described with any words.

At that very moment he began to sing a song of love to me, the first any man had ever made just for me. In this moment I knew Brown Bull had heart-love for me because it was a song he would never be able to sing to any other because it had been made for his lovely Lion Lady alone.

Brown Bull would say no more about what he saw in my eyes that he should gaze into them so intently every time we joined in sex. If ever he saw the Mother there, he never told me so with words. And even with this beautiful song of love for me, the words I yearned with my soul to hear from his lips were never voiced, just as they had never been spoken by my father, Roe Bear. Neither could I bring myself to say those words to my Beloved, so afraid was I that he would go away again as he had done before. I would have made a song for him as he had done for me, but still there were no songs upon my lips or in my heart. Not even for Brown Bull would they come forth.

When, in time, he did come back from that far, far place of ecstasy, he made me sit again on his man-club and work my hips back and forth until he spilled himself into me again. The pulsations of his own orgasm would often bring mine, so again we lay spent—breast to chest, his softening snake finally slipping out again. In sheer bliss at this joining as one, I truly could not say where my own skin left off and Brown Bull's began. I felt I would surely return to the Mother if he were ever to leave me again.

After I slipped off to lie beside him, the sweat of our passion began to dry and cool us again. But I could not leave him alone so began to gently stroke his chest, belly and limp rod with my hand and then with my lips and tongue. To my utter amazement he started to get hard again. Because I was intent on pressing him to speak to me more of his heart-feelings, I let go of his sex and pulled the sleeping furs over us again. This was not the way to encourage him to talk instead of hump!

"Brown Bull, my Beloved," I cajoled. "Tell me about your initiation and what the spirit-powers showed you in the Great Cave."

"Not now, Dear One," he put me off. "I want to hump you again and then sleep a little, not talk."

He was so reluctant to talk about anything of his feelings or of his experiences in the Black Lodge. I could tell the door between his liver, head and heart was a strong wall, not easily opened. But with a little more encouragement to talk to me, some of the story would eventually be told. Then he could get back to what he was really interested in: me playing cow to his bull.

One of the few things he did tell me was about the Nine Lashes administered by his father, a well-respected hunter of the Bison kin. Only a few things about his experience in the Great Cave would he ever give to me and this was one of them. Never would he speak of why his heart had been drawn so strongly to the Black Lodges. What wisdom he may have taken away from that place Brown Bull would never share with me.

As he told his abbreviated story, I wondered to myself what Brown Bull would think of my addition to the Vulva Stone? That was a secret I was sworn to keep and I would never break that promise to the Grandfather. While I might have given my secret name to Brown Bull, that was purely by accident. I would never reveal the true reason for my unexpected initiation as Seer of the Bear People or the task my own journey to the dark heart of the Cave was meant to accomplish.

"Did you also make special friends and companions of any of your gift-giver circle?" I asked idly, trying to draw him out

I certainly was not considering how the answer to this question would shape the rest of our lives or how Brown Bull's answer should have alerted me to what would come.

"Yes, of course," he said, suddenly getting very talkative. "Several, in fact, including your uncle, Bright Wolf, the husband of your famous Auntie," he revealed.

It was then that I realized he did not know it was Uncle Bright Wolf who we had heard humping in my Auntie's lodge this very day. He must never have come to Auntie's lodge so how would Brown Bull have known which was my Auntie's lodge?

Without any further encouragement from me, Brown Bull continued with his story, a story I was less inclined to hear the more he told.

"Bright Wolf was one of the Trickster's bison wrestlers the season of my initiation as a hunter," he continued talkatively to my utter surprise.

"We have also played the Trickster's bison wrestlers in the rites of the Cave together since my initiation. It was good to hunt again with him on this last hunt of the season—and with your father, too. The Bear-kin and Bison-kin do not often hunt the Plain together. I asked both of them about you, you know?" he rattled on and on.

"Yes," I replied, trying to put it all together in my head. "My father told me you had been injured," I said cautiously.

I was speaking about my father and Brown Bull's hunting injuries, but my mind was spinning with images of Brown Bull joining in sex with Uncle Bright Wolf like he had just joined with me. I could not prevent my mind from thinking it could possibly have been the other way with Brown Bull playing the cow to the Trickster's bull! I had no idea what to think. So stunned was I that I was afraid to ask which parts Uncle Bright Wolf and Brown Bull *had* played.

Finally, to force the images from my mind, I had to tell myself several times over, "This is the way of men. This is the way of the hunters in the Cave. It is all of the Mother. It is *all* the Mother."

The words Brown Bull then spoke to me blotted out all else and were all I had ever dreamed of and asked the Mother for.

"I will ask your mother to become son of her lodge as soon as the Great Gathering is completed," he said quietly, earnestly.

"Will you have me as husband, my lion-eyed Seer of the Bear People?" he pleaded with those blue-black eyes that could not be denied.

* * *

Of course I said, "Yes". No other considerations were of the slightest importance. I could not even think about any of the practicalities involved, such as, whether to live in my mother's lodge or build a new one? I needn't have worried about such things because the summer season would soon be upon us and all the Bear People would be on the move again. There would be a whole summer season to sort out living arrangements for the winter return to the Valley.

All I am sure of is that we must find the time and place to be alone whether we are in my mother's lodge or sharing a tent in a summer band. Whatever it takes, I will not have the heat of my passion always where others could hear, let alone see. How can any couple have the kind of impassioned joining as Brown Bull and I have where others can hear us?

Our passion truly spent for the moment, we had managed to avoid any interruptions. So it was probably for the best that we heard my mother and White Fox coming up the trail speaking in unusually loud voices. They paused for an unnaturally long time outside the lodge before scratching at the entry flap.

We hurriedly put on our clothes. A muscular bare arm reaching out of the flap for its shirt was the signal my mother needed to pretend not to know who was in the lodge and what they had been doing. When we were both dressed, I went to the flap and pulled it back.

"Come in, my Mother," I said, in a sex-husky voice. "Brown Bull is just leaving, but he wishes to speak to you for a moment. In private."

I exited my mother's lodge and she entered with a look of either exasperation or faint hope, I could not decide which. White Fox was given to my care leaving the two of them alone to discuss our joining in marriage.

It took only a few moments and soon Brown Bull emerged from my mother's lodge with a big grin.

"I will come and get you later this evening. I will bring the marriage gifts of promise to your mother tonight," he said, gushing excitedly.

We pressed foreheads and then I sent him off with a knowing smile.

As we parted, he whispered so that only I could hear.

"I will hump you again tonight if you have no other suitors that steal you away from me," he said, still flashing his dimpled grin.

I grabbed my little brother's arm and pulled him toward the lodge. Brown Bull turned around, smiled and waved at me. The sight of Brown Bull's back going away ceased being such a painful image in my head.

* * *

"You could have any husband you choose, my Daughter!" One Doe exclaimed as we discussed Brown Bull's proposal.

"Why not someone we know from the camps of the Bear-kin or the son of Auntie's gift-giver of the Reindeer-kin?" she asked.

"No mother, I will have only Brown Bull!" I countered.

"Besides, people talk about him ... and his mother ..." she started in again.

I cut her off before I could hear any bad words about my Beloved.

"Never mind that," I said, more than irritated. "I will have no other man as husband, so if you want me to be a dry old cow in the Shelter of the Solitaries and give you no granddaughters to fill your lodge, then send him away!" I threatened.

"Very well," she relented. "But all the People wish to send their sons to the Bear-kin as husbands because of the richness of our camps and to more easily receive the blessings of the Cave. Only the most skilled hunter of the most respected lodge is a fit mate for the honored and beautiful young Healer and Seer that you have become," she expounded, starting the argument anew.

My mother would never know how her words cut me to the heart. She is implying that I had not been good enough for Brown Bull to ask for in marriage until I had become this fake shaman that I am. Her words hurt me to my very center because she could not have known—not even the Grandfather really knew—that I had never seen any animal-guides nor heard them speak either in my dreams or in trance. What kind of *seer* is that? What kind of *shaman* is that? Besides, I was so enraptured by Brown Bull that no argument under Father Sky could ever dissuade me. The image of the two of us together was ever-present whether waking or asleep.

And I knew in my liver Brown Bull had made me with child as a result of our day of joining in sex.

"Enough of this arguing! I will marry him whether you will or not! If necessary, I will enter the lodge of Brown Bull's mother and become her daughter if you oppose us," I shouted, beginning to get frantic and desperate.

"I meant no disrespect to Brown Bull or to you, my Daughter," she said trying to calm me.

"I did not understand the depth of the feeling you have for this man. Does he feel the same as you? Will he respect you when you are joined? You met him last season at the Gathering and yet he did not ask you then? What has changed?" she asked without giving me any opportunity to answer.

I was absolutely incredulous.

"What has changed? What has changed?" I shouted. "*Everything* has changed! Look at the scabby marks on my face and then *you* tell me what has changed!" I raved.

"Very well, then," she said quietly, trying to calm me down. "I was only concerned that he would not treat you well. But I see your head and liver are decided and only you can make this choice. I can see that you are enraptured of him and truly will have no other. I only hope the love you have for each other is of your heart. That is my only concern. I will agree to the match and I wish you the blessings of the Mother in it."

"You're saying *yes*? You're saying 'yes' to the match just like that? After all this argument!" I stammered, completely disoriented by my mother's abrupt reversal.

"Yes, my Daughter. I am saying yes." She took both my hands in hers trying to calm me further.

"But before you take this path, my dearest Daughter, listen to your old mother and hear the words of my mouth. They are the words of a mother who loves her only daughter. They are the words of a woman who has much experience of men. Will you hear my words and cease being so angry with me?"

I took a couple of deep breaths. I could see the concern in my mother's face and knew that she truly did have my happiness in her heart.

"Yes, Mother, I will hear your words. I will take them to my heart if I can," I said.

"That is good, my Daughter, for I will tell you what the seers and shamans will not at the Moon Blood. The men know nothing of a woman's life. No man knows anything of the desires of a woman's liver, how deep feelings arise from the act of joining in sex and how those feelings control the wishes of our heads and our hearts. A man takes his pleasure with a woman, and though she may also have pleasure in their joining, he goes away and has no second thoughts of the woman or of the fleeting enjoyment they have just had together."

"Yes, my Mother, I do have some experience of that as you well know," I said sarcastically, still angry.

"Yes, and you probably think that Brown Bull is not like other men. But I will tell you, as one who loves you, that every man is the same from the time of his initiation to the time of his Return to the Mother. Whether he withdraws and spills his semen upon a woman's belly or is willing to become a son to the mother's lodge and leaves his essence within the woman's womb, he is the same and remains unchanged by their joining in sex. Even though he sings songs and speaks words of love and even though he is sincere in his love and his concern for the woman, he is unchanged. Do not be fooled by words of love that have no actions to accompany them as longtime friends do who cling to each other in heart-love and real concern."

"But mother," I broke in. "Women are the same. They take their pleasure with boys and men at the hot springs and are unchanged."

"No, Dearest One, you are wrong. You may be able to take your pleasure with a boy and leave it off as nothing but an enjoyable day at the hot pools. But the day a woman joins in sex and feels her first love is the day she is cut in two. She becomes another woman on that day but her lover is the same after his first joining as he was before. Though he professes undying devotion, he is unchanged in his heart as we women always are changed because our hearts are opened by the joining of two bodies in sex. I believe that day has come for you, my only daughter."

"I must admit, I believe you speak truly in that, Dear Mother," I responded, my anger spent at her kind concern for me.

"Dear One, I wish you to always be happy wherever you are. But never forget that the man joins in sex for a night with a woman and he goes away unchanged in body or mind. Should the woman have a new life begin to grow within her womb from that joining of her heart and soul, she is another person altogether. She carries the sign of that joining forever as her belly grows larger and larger. For nine moons long, the new life grows within her very body and that new life continues to grow in her heart her whole life long in a way that it never can for her lover. Something grows into her life that never again departs from her. Please believe your old mother in this."

As my mother spoke, I could not help but think of the new life I was sure had begun growing in me. My mother continued her speaking with even more insistence than before.

"A woman is, and she remains, a mother even though her child leaves in the Return—even though all her children return to the Mother. You will carry the child under your heart and it will never go out of your heart ever again. Not even when the child has grown and is dead in its body, it will still be with you. None of this a man can ever know. Men know nothing! A man does not know the difference before love and after love, before motherhood and after motherhood and he can never know it! Only a woman can know that and speak of that. Dear One, you must learn that, as women, this is why we respect ourselves and will not be told what to do by our husbands. This is the only thing a woman can do: respect herself and keep her honor and choose a husband that will respect and honor her and her children as she does her own self. A woman must always be what she is: a woman before love and a mother after. Do not be blinded by the liver-passion you feel for this man if you are able, my Dearest One. Forever more you will be the mother of the children you bear, but your husband will never know how that changes you. He will leave you to bear that burden alone in body and heart if you do not choose the man wisely. I tell you this only because I do not have the passion for this man as you do and I am your mother who will always be your mother. I speak as one who will always want only the best and most compassionate man you can find. Can you understand my feelings and desires in this, Dear One?" she concluded.

"Oh Mother. Yes, of course I know that you only want me to find happiness wherever I am. But when I look into Brown Bull's eyes I only see the All Mother's heart-love there. I must now follow my heart in this no matter what happens or how little he may know my heart and soul. Please help me in this, my beloved mother. I love him so much I feel I would die if he cannot be a son of my mother's lodge and the husband of my heart. Can you not understand that?" I pleaded and began to cry.

"Of course I can, Dear One. I loved your own father with the same passion," she said shaking her head slowly, a broad smile so full of sadness on her face.

"Come," she said, holding out her hands out to me. "Dry your tears. Let me hug you and kiss your cheeks. You are my beloved daughter and my only wish is that you be happy and find the Mother's abundance with this man. You have experienced much and learned much in the Great Cave, of that I am sure. Now having said my words I will trust that you have learned even more and you are making the wisest choice of husbands as you are able."

"Besides," she continued. "What hunter does not want a beautiful Healer such as my daughter in their lodge to care for them? A woman who can mend their broken bones and bind their wounds when they return from the hunt? I will tell your father of our decision to accept Brown Bull as son of our lodge when he comes out of the Cave with Little Ibex. Of course, you will marry at the end of the Gathering?" she asked helpfully.

"Yes," I said a little too abruptly but finally calming myself and drying my tears.

"It is already agreed between us. After the Dance of Promise, Brown Bull will return to the camp of the Bison-kin to help prepare his mother's lodge to leave for the Plains of Summer. If my father agrees, Brown Bull's family will join us as a summer band. He will return this evening for the exchange of the Promise Gifts," I explained.

"It looks like you have it all planned out, my Daughter. It will be a busy time for all of us. But then, leaving for the Plain is always a busy time, is it not?" she said.

As we hugged, my mother kissed my cheeks and pressed her forehead to mine, all rancor forgotten.

* * *

As promised, Brown Bull returned to my mother's lodge that evening for a small feast and for the exchange of the promise gifts. He arrived at my mother's lodge wearing his finest, softest dark brown leathers, his hair smoothed back and bound in a horse tail. Grinning from ear to ear, his shining eyes gave off a purple light, or that is how he appeared to me.

I wore my best white dress, the same in which I had begun my initiation as Seer. My mother was also wearing the best of her best white leathers as befitted such an occasion. Brown Bull sat in the honored seat with me to his right, my mother to his left. White Fox fidgeted to her left. After my mother's delicious stew of fresh meat, new vegetables and spear-grass greens, White Fox began to squirm, unable to sit still long enough to get through the gift giving. Then, with some relief on everyone's part, he climbed up on the platform and went to sleep.

The exchange of the Promise Gifts followed.

"Mother of my Beloved's lodge," Brown Bull began in a formal speech. "I desire to become a son of thy lodge. These gifts are tokens and signs of my promise to become husband of thy daughter and son of thy lodge."

"Welcome to the lodge of thy Beloved's mother, my son. I accept thy Gifts of Promise and I welcome thee as a son of One Doe's lodge," she replied in the same formal words.

I sat quietly by without speaking because the whole affair was to be arranged between my mother and Brown Bull without any interference or interruption from me. Brown Bull opened a soft fur wrapping that enfolded three drawstring leather bags. He ceremoniously handed one of the bags to my mother with both hands.

"This Gift of Promise is for thee, Mother of the Hearth of my Beloved," Brown Bull intoned importantly.

The Bison and Mammoth-kin both are known for the richness of their gifts, many of which come from the far places of the Others that few of the Nine Kin ever visit. I was very curious to see what treasures Brown Bull had prepared for this Gathering. For an unmarried man to come unprepared, should they meet someone to marry, was unthinkable. It was clear to me he had come prepared to join someone's lodge!

My mother loosened the drawstring and pulled the bag open. She put one finger to the white crystals that filled the big bag to the top. She touched the finger to her tongue. My mother began to smile broadly at the incomparable gift of so much precious salt. This salt certainly came from the legendary Great Salty Waters of the south, to which the salmon are said to return every year. She held the bag out to me so that I could taste the pure white treasure. So sweet it was! Tasting and smelling of unknown plants and fish, the exotic gift pleased my mother so much that she beamed in complete approval. It is good to see such a smile on my mother's face.

"Thank you, Brown Bull, I accept thy generous gift as Son of the Hearth," she said with real sincerity.

The formalities of giving and receiving completed, my mother said with unfeigned affection, "This would have made a delicious addition to our stew, my Son. Thank you for such a great and wonderful gift!"

Brown Bull lifted, and my mother received, the second bag with both hands.

She prepared to open the bag after Brown Bull said, "This Gift of Promise is for the honored husband of thy hearth, my Mother."

The string of the bumpy-looking bag was loosened to reveal two large lumps of black, glistening obsidian. The facets of the partly worked stone sparkled and reflected the flickering hearth like smooth, black water. My mother held the obsidian reverently in her hands turning the treasure from side-to-side to better see the reflected yellow flames of the hearth fire. I knew my father would be ecstatic to have this finest of all stones to be found anywhere to shape into his famously beautiful spear points.

"I thank thee, Brown Bull, my Son. On behalf of the husband of my hearth, Roe Bear, I accept thy generous Gift of Promise as Son of One Doe's Hearth," my mother said with reverence for the magnificent pieces of shiny stone so rare among the Nine Kin.

I knew that a gift for me was hidden in the next, and last, leather bag.

"This Gift of Promise is for my Beloved, the Daughter of thy Hearth," he said simply.

Brown Bull passed the last bag to my mother with both hands.

"Here, my Daughter, take this Gift of Promise from the hunter thou hast chosen to become Son of One Doe's Hearth."

My mother passed the rustling, clicking bag to me with both hands. I opened the bag carefully as if something would escape if I were not careful. To my complete astonishment at such a lavish and rare gift, I lifted a full seven long strings of delicate white cowries from the bag. Another gift from the faraway Great Salty, no doubt!

The pierced and strung cowry shells unraveled like snakes being pulled from their leather lair. My eyes, my mouth, my whole body smiled at the unbelievable treasure I held in my hands. Smooth and pure white, with wavy serrated openings of pale lavender, the little replicas of a woman's pute glistened white with the same sheen of the obsidian. I was already imagining in what pattern I would sew these rare shells to my long white tunic. The Bison-kin truly are givers of great and wonderful gifts!

"Oh Brown Bull!" I exclaimed, not really concerned if it were proper to be so happy about anything in the midst of such a solemn ceremony.

"They are the most beautiful things I have ever seen! Thank you, thank you!" I gushed uncontrollably.

Then I remembered my good manners.

"Thank you, my Beloved. I accept thy generous Gift of Promise to be Husband of my Hearth," I said trying to contain my bursting heart.

All that remained to complete the exchange of gifts that would make Brown Bull and me husband and wife was the opening of my mother's gift to her new Son of the Hearth. The bundle she had prepared lay next to her. I knew it must be some of her famously beautiful clothing. I had not seen her bring it out or wrap it in the soft chamois skin that now concealed the Gift of Acceptance from view. My mother picked up the bundle ceremoniously and passed it to Brown Bull with both hands.

"Receive thou the Gift of Acceptance from these hands, Brown Bull of the Bison-kin. Thou hast now become Son of the

Hearth of One Doe of the Bear-kin," she said with the accepted words.

"Thank you, Mother of the Hearth. I accept thy generous gift and I accept the daughter of thy hearth as wife until we shall return to the Mother," he also replied with the accepted words.

We had become husband and wife in my mother's lodge. I did not know what else should be said, which is just as well, because no one expects the new wife to say anything at this point in the Exchange of Promise Gifts. I watched as Brown Bull fumbled with the cords on the bundle as if he were nervous. How could he not be nervous? I am terribly nervous! He unfolded the soft fur wrapping to reveal a sleeveless short tunic of pure white reindeer leather.

My husband, Brown Bull, held the shirt up, awestruck at the softness, the smoothness and the even, snow-white color of the doeskin. The tunic was unadorned except for pure white leather fringes in the same pattern as the long mammoth hair fringes of my own best dress. The opening at the neck was the same shape as my own tunic with white laces that could be let out or taken in to make the shirt fit better.

"I thank thee, One Doe, Mother of the Hearth. This is the finest tunic I have ever seen!" he said, running his fingers over the impossibly thin white leather.

He then lifted up the trousers folded beneath the shirt. They were also made of the same pure white, rabbit fur-soft reindeer leather.

"My Son," she broke in. "If the legs are too long, I can easily shorten them to fit you. I don't think you are going to grow any taller, unlike my true sons Little Ibex and White Fox. It will be safe to shorten them to your legs as you are now if need be," she smiled her little joke.

My mother was visibly elated that Brown Bull was so appreciative of the work of her own hands. But there was one final surprise at the bottom of the bundle beneath the folded trousers that was already a more-than-fitting new suit of marriage clothing. It was a long belt and two armbands of braided black mammoth hairs sewn into wide bands with a long fringe hanging from each armband and belt. The black mammoth hair would be truly spectacular against the whiteness of my mother's beautiful leather. And my lover's muscular wrestler's arms would be more than spectacular in the sleeveless tunic.

"I am overwhelmed by the generosity of thy gifts, Mother of My Hearth," Brown Bull said with more emotion than I had yet to see him display.

And with these exchanged gifts and those few spoken words, Brown Bull and I became husband and wife in the lodge of One Doe of the Middle Camp of the Bear-kin, my beloved mother.

* * *

It was another night and another day before the new men and the new women emerged from the Great Cave, half-blinded and stupefied as I knew they would be. They made their way from the Cave to the dance circle of the Great Gathering. There, they would dance and sing and chant themselves back into the world of red-flesh and red-blood and the warming sun of the World of Light. This Dance of Rebirth is always very brief for obvious reasons. So, after only three rounds of the dance circle, the initiates were mercifully allowed to drag themselves back to their lodges to sleep and eat and drink and heal the wounds of their ordeals of the Mother's Great Cave. The mentors and seers would also collapse with exhaustion for a time. The initiations always coming hard on the heels of the last great hunt were especially draining for them.

It was a tense but joyous time for everyone because the excitements of the Great Gathering and the initiations were always followed soon thereafter by preparations to leave the Valley for the summer. Everyone worked very hard at this time of the season, so Brown Bull thought it best to wait until my father had rested a little before he brought up the subject of traveling with his family as part of the same summer band. Being part of the same hunting band, the two families of newly made kin can get to know each very well indeed. It was now up to me and One Doe to tell my father of my marriage to Brown Bull hard upon his coming from the initiation of his son.

Both Little Ibex and he were so exhausted when my mother broached the subject of who it was I had chosen to take as my husband, all my father could utter was an exasperated, "Every time

I leave this lodge she does something like this! What will it be next?" Then my father rolled up in his sleeping furs and went to sleep.

Once the new men and women emerge from the Cave, the Gathering comes to a rapid conclusion and many lodges are struck so people can return to their camps to begin their own preparations to leave the Valley for the summer. Only those couples who have agreed to be married, whether just met or promised for some time, linger for the Dance of Promise with their friends and family who are present at the Great Gathering.

The marriage dance itself goes on for half the night around the large dancing hearth. Then the newly married couples go to the hot pools of the Serpent Father to bathe and purify themselves after which they spend their first permitted, or acknowledged, night together as husband and wife. It is almost *never* the first night they have spent together. Just as in White Lynx's favorite joke, who in their right mind would marry someone they haven't yet joined with in sex?

We would spend our "first night" in Brown Bull's traveling tent. I have seen the marriage dance before, but never had I understood and seen so clearly what the dance is and what it should mean to all the People.

To dress my hair for the dance, my mother braided cowry strands into the two long braids. She had also joined the ends of the strands of cowry that had not been braided into my hair to make a long, double strand of cowries. The leopard tooth of my necklace hung at my breast to complete my marriage necklace of three strands: two of cowry and one of my woman's necklace.

The Dance of Promise is a special one for which Lion Mother and Bison Father masks and robes are brought from their keeping places in the Shelter of the Solitaries. After feasting on fresh haunches roasted in the ground-oven near the dance circle, all Seers of the Bear People, including the Grandfather and Auntie, stand on the western boundary of the circle along with the drummers, flutists, rattlers and those swinging the bullroarers behind them. The seers and those making music all face east across a dance circle with the lines of male and female dancers weaving and twining about the central fire of the circle. The lines of dancers move in and out and around each other in a glorious display of feathers and fur and the finest white doeskins and decorated tunics the marriage partners possess. Each line is led by a masked dancer—a Lion Mother and a Bison Father—who each represent the men and women who are coming together in a holy joining of the two who are now to become one.

The masks and costumes are astonishing. Bison Father's mask is a bison robe with the long curving horns, eyes and top of the head intact, his hump stuffed with grass. The bison dancer's left arm is exposed and unpainted to let everyone know this is a shape-shifting bison-man. Lion Mother's costume is an equally astonishing lion skin with the top part of the head and its huge upper fangs left intact. The lion dancer's right arm is exposed and unpainted to reveal a transforming lion-woman beneath the mask. Although, the actual dancer is almost always a man strong enough to carry and lead the dance with such a heavy costume.

The faces of the women joining in the Dance of Promise are painted white; the faces of the men are painted red. The married men and women follow immediately behind the masked leaders of the dance each in their own line. The lead couple—which is actually me and Brown Bull—each grasps the tail of the lead dancer. The ten or twelve other couples follow behind with their hand on the shoulder of the person in front of them. Following behind those who are promising, anyone of any age can join the two lines. The lines of dancers slowly move along like two great snakes with a simple two-step any child can dance.

My mother and father joined the lines of dancers too. They really seemed to be enjoying themselves, which made both me and Brown Bull very happy. Little Ibex joined the men's line far behind Bison Father at the head of the line of dancers. Even toddling White Fox tried to dance along while holding my mother's hand in the line behind Lion Mother. Soon, it seemed the whole People were part of one line or another weaving and intertwining in the Dance of Promise. All were singing the Song of Abundant Joining and dancing to the drumming of log and circle drums, the whistling of swan bone flutes, the clacking of rattles and the jingling of shell ankle rattles.

In unison, the lines of dancers sang:

Beauty and abundance above me
I and my beloved are one.
Beauty and abundance below me
I and my beloved are one.
Beauty and abundance before me
I and my beloved are one.
Beauty and abundance behind me
I and my beloved are one.
Beauty and abundance to the right of me
I and my beloved are one.
Beauty and abundance to the left of me
I and my beloved are one.
Beauty and abundance surrounds us
I and my beloved are one.
It is a good day to live
It is a good day to die
We are happy wherever we are!

As the women's line moved around the western edge of the dance circle, I two-stepped past the Grandfather and Auntie. They were both sounding their instruments and singing along with the lines of dancers moving slowly in front of them. Auntie thumped her round shaman's drum with a short piece of bone, the thrumming skin painted with a red Lion Mother. The Grandfather shook a rattle to the rhythm of the dancers. His rattle was an enormous bison horn curved like the new moon, filled with small pebbles or seeds of some kind and stopped with a plug of mammoth ivory. The horn rattle was deeply engraved with different animals I could not make out even if I had been inclined to do so.

I slowly danced past Auntie and the Grandfather and tears of joy welled up and spilled down my cheeks. I could feel them sliding down the crosses of the All Mother. Auntie smiled broadly, full of joy for me. The Grandfather nodded slightly in my direction with a wink and his little gap-toothed smile.

All is well and all is right in the World of Light.

* * *

The day after the Dance of Promise and our "first night" together spent in Brown Bull's tent, we went to my mother's lodge for the first time as a married couple. This was also the time for formal discussions between the men regarding summer traveling arrangements. Brown Bull would have to leave for his mother's lodge very soon to help prepare for the summer traveling. The final makeup of our summer band had to be decided very soon.

We arrived at my mother's lodge after Auntie, Bright Wolf, my brother Black Eagle and Dawn Star Rising were already seated around the hearth. Most of us had traveled together as part of the same summer band before so Bright Wolf would be part of the negotiations along with my father and, for the first time, Brown Bull. Black Eagle, the former brother Big Ibex, had traveled with his wife's family since they were married. This season he wanted to travel with his father's band to renew family bonds and allow us all to better know Dawn Star Rising of the Ibex-kin.

The men were seated around the hearth with my father in the seat of honor facing the entrance. The women were all seated behind the men—out of the circle, so to speak. My poor brother Little Ibex still had that dazed and disoriented look everyone has when they come out of the Cave. But he was far less battered and bruised and marked up than I was when I emerged into my new life. Since only married hunters would sit in the council, my younger brothers remained outside the half-circle of adults lolling upon their sleeping platform. As children of my mother's hearth, we always loved to just observe the ritual of negotiating the composition of a summer band. White Fox had already gone to sleep but "new man" Little Ibex watched intently as the council unfolded.

The formalities always begin by passing around the hemp reed. We women smoke the hemp less than the men. But when we do, it is done using a stone lamp with a little pile of the dried herb heaped up on an ember from the hearth, just as the men were now preparing to do. Auntie often smokes the hemp in preparation for healing ceremonies, but we women would not be taking any direct part in this most male of all councils, including the smoking of the hemp. In no time, the men were passing my father's beautiful stone lamp, sucking in the smoke through a short length of reed—

the very lamp of my initiation as Seer. The men held the smoke in as long as possible before exhaling it into the air. Soon, the hemp smoke filled the still, warm air of the lodge and began working its meandering way up and out the half moon hole above the entry. The whole lodge always smells like a badger, or some other equally musky animal, for days afterwards.

After the feasting and dancing the night before, and certainly after smoking some of the hemp, my father was in a much better mood. He actually seemed to be pleased that he would be traveling with Brown Bull and his kin this summer season. He could only be pleased that I had brought an honored hunter of his acquaintance into my mother's lodge. I'm sure he will be pleased to travel with his son again and his wife of the Ibex-kin. It promised to be a good summer season for my father.

Uncle Bright Wolf was the first to speak. "Roe Bear, husband of my wife's sister, I respectfully ask to join you for the summer traveling this season," he said with a minimum of formality.

"Yes, agreed." My father answered with an abrupt coldness that was a startling contrast with what I had assumed to be his good spirits.

I looked over in my father's direction with a question on my tongue, but thought better of saying anything.

Then my father turned toward my new husband.

"I have known your father for many years, Brown Bull, honored new son of One Doe's lodge. Yours is a family of honest and respectful hunters and I would be pleased to travel with you this season, and for as many seasons as you and my Daughter wish. I am pleased to have such a skillful hunter as son of One Doe's lodge. We will build a new bark lodge for you and my daughter next winter season if you find our lodge too crowded," he said with unbelievable generosity.

"Yes, father of One Doe's lodge, I will be pleased to travel with you this season," Brown Bull said simply, not quite having mastered the fancy polite speech of a council.

"If my son Brown Bull and Uncle Bright Wolf are agreeable, we will also have One Doe's brother of the Reindeer-kin traveling with us again this season," my father offered.

"Yes, I am agreeable," said Bright Wolf and Brown Bull in turn.

"I will also request that my eldest son, Black Eagle of the Ibex-kin be allowed to join our band. This will give us at least five experienced hunters in addition to new hunters like my son, Little Ibex," he said proudly.

"Yes, I am agreeable," Brown Bull said importantly. Uncle Bright Wolf simply nodded his approval.

"And that will also give us plenty of room to add other lodges who wish to travel with us," Brown Bull added.

My new husband sounded like he knew what he was talking about. But I knew this was his first such council as a married hunter making arrangements with other married hunters for the well-being of their kin during the summer travels. It was a new and grown-up feeling for both of us to be part of all this.

It must have been the hemp they were inhaling because very quickly all of the men seemed to have become old, dear friends. I was just happy to see everyone getting along so well and to have the plans for our life together becoming real so effortlessly.

Who would travel with whom as a summer band changes each season. It is rarely the same group of lodges, friends or kin, because always this person doesn't get along with so-and-so or that person used to get along but now they don't. There are always discussions of how that one hoards and does not share with others as they should and so on and so on. Women make the final decisions in almost everything that goes on in the winter lodges because the bark lodges and everything in them are the possessions of the women. We collect most of the food our families eat and we prepare it all year long, so it is women who make all the important decisions in the winter season.

But the movable summer lodges and all the hunting implements are the possessions of the men. It is always the men who guide the little summer bands of the People to follow the herds to the Northland. And so it is always the men who decide the makeup of the traveling companions in a summer band. It is they who decide all matters of the hunt, of course, and so the men make all the important decisions in the summer season. The twenty or thirty members of every summer band must get along exceptionally well together as the band's abundance and very survival is dependent on the extraordinary cooperation of each member. Just like the rhinos of the Bridge of Rainbows, we all have to be of one mind and walking the same path. No dueling rhinos are tolerated in the winter camps. And none are ever allowed in the summer camps which are so much more intimate.

Each summer band needs to have as many expert hunters and trackers as possible and at least a few expert spear makers and blade flakers. And every band needs experts in leather making and women who can sew clothing and repair shelter skins and who can find the numerous plant foods we always collect along the way. The number of needed skills for the summer travels is endless. Often the mix of people in the band is not ideal, but it is always the men that decide who will and will not be part of any given traveling band. It is a blessed summer band, too, that has a shaman or a healer as one of its members. That is always so because the number of seers and shamans among the People are few and they are mostly women.

"Our band will be fortunate this summer, indeed, with two Healers—Auntie and me," I thought to myself.

Small wonder that men like my father, who always seem to be diminished somehow by the overwhelming female presence and feminine spirit-power of the winter camps, are energized by the prospects of leaving the Valley. It seems especially so here, among the lodges of the Middle Camp of the Bear-kin. The men of the Middle Camp are always mindful of the ever-present All Mother's Cave above and the Mother's Eye below. I should think it is easy for a man to become resentful of the Mother's overwhelming presence in the Middle Camp. It almost certainly explains my father's feelings on the subject. My father's unusual animation and enthusiasm around planning to leave for the summer was noticeable, if not understandable, I began to realize. To say the least, not only my father but Brown Bull, Bright Wolf and Black Eagle were all clearly enjoying themselves being the center of everything for a change.

"Are there gift-givers or companions of your acquaintance with whom you would also like to travel and hunt, my Son?" my father asked, as part of the formalities.

"Yes, my Father," Brown Bull replied.

They are already calling each other *Father* and *Son*!

"My elder brother, married into the Musk Ox-kin is a good and honest hunter who wishes to travel with us this season if that is agreeable. If there is any question as to his skills and abilities, our Uncle Bright Wolf will be willing to vouch for him as they have traveled in the same summer band before."

Then, without waiting for everyone to agree, my inexperienced new husband went on.

"I am very pleased to see our Brother, Bright Wolf, already here as one of the hunters of our band," Brown Bull commented offhand.

Brown Bull leaned out slightly to better look directly at Bright Wolf sitting to the left of my father as if we all didn't know who he was talking about.

"Uncle Bright Wolf is my companion and gift-giver of many years," Brown Bull said formally. "He is a famous tracker and never misses the mark, but I am sure you know that already having traveled with our Uncle before."

My new husband praised Bright Wolf lavishly, thinking to give my father great honor by approving of his choice of traveling companions.

My father's smile immediately turned into a frown.

"Also, your Sister, Bright Wolf's wife, is a great and renowned Healer to whom your daughter is apprentice. It is a blessing to have one Healer on the summer journey; but we will now have two among our traveling band," my new husband concluded, echoing my own thoughts on the subject.

"Yes, that is true, my Son," a suddenly somber Roe Bear replied.

An uncharacteristic clenching of my father's jaw at the mention of Bright Wolf's name was visible even to me.

I had rarely been present for such negotiations between men. I usually preferred to be somewhere else when the hemp is being smoked and the men are talking back and forth so self-importantly. I sat quietly, my mother and me both watching the three men carefully. It was only when the subject of Auntie's husband, Bright

Wolf, came up that my father's jaw clenched tight and his eyes darted briefly in my mother's direction.

The Cave has taught me to pay attention to what is going on around me and that lesson, at least, seemed to have been learned.

What is this all about? I thought to myself. Why would my father object even slightly to Bright Wolf and Auntie traveling with us? We have gone to the Northland for many seasons together. Just then, my eyes fell upon my two brothers sitting side-by-side, their legs dangling over the edge of the sleeping platform. White Fox had stirred himself and both boys were trying to be interested in the men's business, though not doing a very good job of it. What was left of Little Ibex's ragged hair was dark brown like mine—and like my mother's hair. Little Ibex's eyes were light blue like my father's. My youngest brother, White Fox, was as dry-grass blond and grey-blue eyed as Bright Wolf, our Uncle and the husband of my dear Auntie. Even in our most intimate, warm and friendly moments as mother and daughter, when such secrets are often divulged and shared, my mother steadfastly refused to say anything about any of this—and not for lack of my asking. Neither would Auntie ever say anything of it. Whatever the connection had been between my mother, her sister and Bright Wolf, I most likely will never know. But having lost my senses over a man, I began to understand much. Without having been told in words, I began to see the truth of it.

The tension in the lodge when Bright Wolf was speaking, or was even named in my father's presence, went completely unnoticed by my new husband. He could be excused because I had never noticed it before either.

Brown Bull took my father's silence as assent and said, "So, it is agreed then. We will all travel to the Plain together and hunt together and share our lodges for a season."

"Yes, my Son, it is decided," my father said formally, without any feeling.

"Now let us ask Uncle Bright Wolf if there are any of his companions, gift-givers or kin who wish to join our band," my father said.

He turned to look directly at my Uncle with the glare of a sharp spear point.

Bright Wolf replied after taking another long draw on the hemp reed. "We have traveled with Auntie's gift-giver of the Lower Bear-kin many times and Auntie wishes that they travel with us again this season. The husband of her lodge is also a fine hunter and tracker."

"And," Bright Wolf continued before my father could reply, "I have agreed to present the Grandfather's request that he be allowed to travel with us this season as well."

"Great Mother of the Cave," I thought to myself.

That will be *three* seers and shamans in our little summer band! I wonder what my mother and father will think of that?

Without missing a single drum beat, my father turned to speak directly to Auntie where she sat behind Uncle Bright Wolf.

"Will not the other summer bands be jealous of us that we have so many powerful seers and shamans in our midst?" he said with barely veiled sarcasm.

As a famous shaman-of-healing always addressed as Thrice Born, Auntie could be spoken to as if she were a man in such councils. My father and all of us knew it was Auntie who was requesting the Grandfather be allowed to travel with us and not Uncle Bright Wolf of himself.

"The Grandfather has asked that he be allowed to join our band in order to continue the training of his new apprentice, your Daughter," Auntie answered him directly without going through Bright Wolf to make her reply.

Everyone knew, whatever the reason, the Grandfather would be allowed to travel with any band he chose. There's no arguing with the Thrice Born, as I know so well!

"Also," Auntie continued unexpectedly. "The Grandfather requests that his two-spirit companion, Red Dawn, be allowed to travel with us. He is skilled at tanning hides and stitching leathers and is also proficient at spear making, cooking and collecting plant foods," she said, anxious to justify the Grandfather's companion's presence among the band.

"And he is very strong and able to assist the Grandfather in walking," she added in afterthought.

My father just grunted in rude and reluctant agreement. He glanced at my mother again, took a long draw on the hemp tube and passed it to my new husband. Brown Bull took another long pull on the tube and then passed it back to my father. From Roe Bear's hands, the beautiful lamp and hemp tube was passed to uncle Bright Wolf. He then passed it on to my brother, Black Eagle, to seal the agreement.

I looked at the four of them smoking their hemp and getting happier and happier by the moment. Through it all, I could not get the image out of my head of Brown Bull and Bright Wolf dressed in bison wrestler masks, passing the hemp tube back and forth, then going in to the boy-initiates to perform the Trickster's dance of bison cow and bison bull in the Great Cave. Which had played the cow and which the bull I would probably never, ever know. I had not the courage to ask either of them.

"It is the way of the hunters. It is men being men," was all I could tell myself to calm my fears.

* * *

Preparations for the summer travels prevented my mind from straying too much and dwelling on such unpleasant and puzzling thoughts as who played cow or bull to whom. Besides, Brown Bull was still every bit the bull with his beautiful new shaman cow as often as we could sneak away to the hot pools or the concealing bushes. For the next couple of days, Brown Bull helped us clean, fold and pack in tightly woven baskets and net bags all the skins and furs that would be left behind. Floor skins, door flap, sleeping drape and some of the winter sleeping furs were rolled in rush mats and suspended from the lodge's supporting ribs. To keep everything from any marauding animals while we were away for the summer, bags and baskets were either suspended from the lodge's rafters or were taken up the hill to the Shelter of the Solitaries. There, the really fine furs and clothing to be left behind were sprinkled with mouse bain and suspended or stacked in one of the driest chambers of the Shelter for the summer season.

Only the bare essentials would be carried with us out upon the Plains of Summer. All of the food that remained in the storage pits had to be brought out and anything rotten disposed of. The remaining nuts, seeds, dried salmon and dried meat had to be ground into powder and baked into traveling cakes with fat from the last hunt. Any remaining fresh meat was cooked, dried or baked into traveling cakes, the easier to carry everything that was useful or edible with us. Some of the last of the fresh meat was always saved as a small feast to be made on the last night in the Middle Camp before departing for the Plains of Summer. Hunters always take traveling cakes with them on the hunt and now we would carry the last of the winter season food with us as such cakes. This dried and already-cooked food would sustain us until fresh plants, roots, berries, fruits and, of course, fresh meat and fat were given to us by the Mother's children out upon the Plain.

As we finished packing away what we would not take with us, Brown Bull left to help his mother and father finish their preparations to leave their winter camp. When he arrived in the lodge of his mother, he would formally announce to them that we would all be traveling together this season. His Bison-kin brothers and cousins returning from the Gathering will have told his parents of his marriage to me. That was equivalent to telling them we would all be traveling together for the summer season—always the custom for families newly joined by marriage so they can get to know one another better.

All that remained was for my father and Little Ibex to prepare dragging poles to carry some of our things and to use on the Plain. Good wood for tent poles is often lacking on the Plains of Summer. We waited for Black Eagle and Dawn Star Rising to return and join us as the Ibex-kin summer bands made their way through the Middle Camp toward the Plain. Upon their arrival from the camps of the upriver Ibex-kin, we would fill the back packs, bags and carrying baskets with all the things we would need for the season of summer upon the Great Plain of the Mammoth Mother.

After chanting our songs for protection and for the continuing abundance of the Mother, we placed the ivory Earth Mother from the hearth in the center of the entry to protect and watch over the lodge of my mother, One Doe. Then we turned our backs on the Great Cave, the Mother's Eye and the whole Valley of the Bear Mother to begin our trek to the Plains of Summer.

We made our way downriver joining up, as we went, with our other traveling companions from the camps along the way. We met my new husband and his family in the camp of the Bison-kin where we shared their final feast of winter. Early the next morning, the assembled band struck out in a line following my father, Roe Bear, Leader of the Summer Band, into the Great Plain of the Mammoth Mother.

The only difference between this summer season and last? This is the beginning of the winding path of Brown Bull and Yellow Lion's life together in this beautiful World of Light.

CHAPTER 17.
AN APPOINTMENT TO KEEP

I NEVER SAW THE LEOPARD in the dappled light of the grove. I had come alone to relieve myself and to be sick out of sight of the others. She dropped from a low branch to knock me face first to the ground and into instant unconsciousness as I squatted down to pee.

It had only been a few days since we arrived at this most favored and favorite of our early summer campsites. We always look forward to pitching our tents on this grassy knoll that backs up to cliffs of the same white stone as that surrounding the Middle Camp of the Bear-kin. This grove of giant trees huddles close to the cliffs and runs with abundant springs of clean, clear water. When camping here, we often visit this grove for firewood and as a latrine well away from the traveling lodges.

But never do we enter the trees alone, for reasons all too obvious to me now.

My soul fluttered skyward, no longer anticipating a long and abundant stay in such a lovely place so favored by the Mother. The campsite had its own splashing spring-fed brook flush with water cress and many other edible plants along its banks. The grass-covered hill of the camp looked out toward the rising sun and gave a long overlook of the entire Plain in a great arc from the north to the south. From here, it is easy to spot the herds below making their way among the glittering ponds and flashing streams meandering between lush green clusters of brushy trees. When I left our tent to go to the grove, I noticed that out on the Plain, pools of early morning mist collected in the low places waiting to be dispersed by the morning sun.

It was one of those calm and cloudless, achingly beautiful summer mornings offering unobstructed views to the distant horizon. One could almost see the Mountains of Ice on a day like this. It was the clarity of the morning air that had also made it easy to see the signal fire. The smoke had been spotted in the still of the early morning, rising up into a great white cloud-tree. The wispy white branches spread out to either side atop a tall, straight trunk, like some variety of gigantic mushroom. I remember thinking, that smoke-tree is the very All Mother's Tree of Life, its branches full of shaman's nests.

My Tree of Life had other creatures hidden within its dark green branches.

I remember going outside our tent to see it. The sight of the smoke-cloud made me nauseous at the thought of having to move the whole camp again after just the few days we had stopped in this marvelous place. Such a signal fire always means one of the summer bands of the Bear People—at least we hoped it was one of our bands—had been extremely successful in the hunt. Someone had made a great kill of reindeer, bison or maybe even a mammoth. White smoke is the sign that whichever hunting bands are within sight of it should also come and share in the bounty—and help with the butchering. A band had probably been fortunate enough to stampede many animals over a jump, returning so many of the Mother's children to her that others should come so as not to waste the abundance. Even bands of the Others would be welcome to share in such a kill and we would be reluctantly welcome at theirs. Often a tree of smoke attracted many bands to a brief summer Gathering with feasting, games, the meeting of new friends and lovers and the rekindling of old ties.

Upon spotting the cloud, everyone began busily pulling down the traveling lodges to move our whole camp to the tree of smoke. Amid the bustle of breaking camp I will probably not be missed for a long time. No one in the camp could possibly have heard a single sound as the mother leopard clamped her jaws on my neck instantly breaking it. My shredded, bloody clothing may be the only thing to be found if she carries me into a tree somewhere to eat my body.

Brown Bull and the other hunters left immediately for the sign of the smoke leaving the rest of us to follow later when the camp is packed. So even my husband will not come to look for what reeaten pile of meat and entrails? This is how all my People's remains are returned to the Mother anyway. Had he been within the camp, not even my beloved Brown Bull would have tried to track down what was left to the flies and maggots.

Should it have been he who came to look for me, Brown Bull would certainly have found my lion-woman pendant, bloodied and chipped by the leopard's powerful bite. The pendant lay half covered by the grass next to my bison robe which had been pulled from me after the leopard drove me to the ground. Perhaps my father or my mother will find the robe and notice the blood-covered pendant which has hung at my throat since Brown Bull and I were married, how many seasons ago? Fifteen, I think? I should like for my Beloved to have the pendant, all the better to hold a memory of me. But that is unlikely to ever be.

As it turns out, Brown Bull has a great gift for making spirit-animals of ivory and stone. He pours his soul into his ivories just as he gives his heart to his songs. He imbues each with a kind of full-bodied life that my flat paintings can never have. He carved two thumb-sized neck pendants from some of the very mammoth ivory brought back from the Great Hunt by my father. That was just before our joining in marriage—and just after my initiation as Seer in the Mother's Great Cave. It seems like another life of another person altogether.

Brown Bull made my pendant with a downward pointing, three-cornered pute—a sign of a human woman for the tiny ivory Lion Mother. She stood up on her two hind legs like one of the human tribe. Her right paw was clearly a woman's hand. Her arm was bent at the elbow, a hand resting upon her belly. Had she large breasts, the arm would have supported and lifted them. But lions don't have the big breasts of the human tribe and so she has none. The lion-woman's left arm hung straight down against her side.

Wavy lines of life-fire ran over both shoulders and down on to her strong upper arms. My Beloved's lion-man pendant had been made with a little three-cornered penis pointing up. His pendant was made with the same standing pose as my woman's pendant: left arm and hand of this miniature Lion Father carved, of course, as human, but with both arms straight at his sides.

The smoothly polished pendants had been a love-gift, a constant but unspoken, reminder of our love for each other. The pendants were also the signs of the spirit-powers that bound our souls together forever. For both of us, they were ivory images of the paired lion-guardians at the entrance to the Black Wombs of the Lion Mother. Will Brown Bull search for that bond in the worlds to come as he always said he would? Will he search for my lion's eye? Considering how I am returning to the Mother, maybe everyone has been wrong all my life? Could my lion-eye actually be the eye of Leopard Mother who I encountered so long ago in the Mother's Great Cave? I wonder if I shall recognize Brown Bull if we should meet again in some world that is yet to be?

I would be lying if I said I had no regrets. I regret that we let the strong feeling we had for each other fade. Boredom and the routine of our daily round crowded out conversations and reflection on the very things that had brought us together. But then Brown Bull never liked to talk of such things. It was his way to sing beautiful songs of love to me, even though no songs of love for him ever came to my heart.

My way was to speak words. But they were words that came from a wounded heart for so long that it is little wonder he never wished to give me the words I longed to hear.

The heat of the liver-passion faded very quickly with the coming of our children. Even his songs speaking of worlds to come and lovely lion-ladies came less and less frequently. And he ceased to gaze into my soul without looking away except on those rare occasions when we would join in sex face-to-face in the light. Joining in sex became routine too soon and only his infrequent urgings in the middle of the night ever made me open my legs to him. Even then, it was mostly from the back. How can you look into your beloved's eyes when they are humping you like the animals of the plains do their joining?

The everyday drudgery of moving from camp to camp on the Plains of Summer changed both of us that very first season. My mother once said the coming of children changes everything between two lovers because it changes everything for the woman. I have found that to be all too true. I was changed in every way by my love for Brown Bull and by my love for the children that were made by him in my body. My Beloved, however, was not so changed—just as my mother had tried to warn me.

But the heart-love we did have could never be taken away no matter how many or how few words were spoken between us. Even here in the midst of my returning to the Mother that heart-love I have had for Brown Bull from that very first season of a new love's excitement is still alive within my soul. It still remains in spite of everything. I know it. I feel it. Did we ever get to that place of cold indifference to each other that I saw in my own father and mother? Perhaps we did. But that only makes me love and appreciate my mother and my father even more.

In the end, and if I am to be perfectly honest now that it is all finished, I was as fearful as Brown Bull of the bright powers of Lion Mother that I saw whenever I looked into his dark blue eyes. In my heart, I pulled back from all of it as certainly as Brown Bull refused to speak of it. I was always drawn to and yet repelled by that blue-black space in the center of his eyes so filled with the stillness of the Silent Abyss. Attracted and drawing back in fear, both in the same moment—the inside and outside of the same thing. I have long since given up hoping he would see the stillness of the Mother in my eyes and open his heart to me, to tell me in words from his own lips that I am loved above all others. The words never came and until they did, my proud heart would never utter them either.

From that first season, his body was all he seemed to share with me. But then, what else did I share with him? The more I wanted of his heart and soul the less he seemed willing to give. I could never cease wondering what is it that I lack? What else could I have done to make him love me? What is wrong with me? What could I change that he would, at long last, speak his love for me?

Always there were these questions without answers. And now those answers will never come.

It is said among my People that when we see the Dark Mother approaching from afar she seems terrifying to us. But when she arrives, it is bliss. I now see that this beautiful, peaceful morning *is* a good day to live. It *is* a good day to die. And so it *is* bliss as I drift up like a soaring shaman-bird to watch the Leopard Mother drag away the bag of blood and bones I thought of as "me" into the underbrush.

The child my body carries will never see her father's blue-black eyes or know the joys of life in her mother's winter lodge in the Valley of the Bear Mother. And now my baby daughter, Many Waters, will have no mother to teach her the wisdom of the Grandfather or the compassion and healing skills of my gentle Auntie. It all ends here because Many Waters has seen only two seasons. She will grow and not remember me at all.

I see now that I have had a longstanding appointment with Leopard Mother ever since we met in the Great Cave so many seasons ago. More and more I think it is her eye that I have had all my life. It is the Trickster's final joke that the unforeseen coming of this unnamed daughter, so soon after the birth of Many Waters, would take me back to the Mother in this manner.

But I had grown so tired. I had no life left in me after trying to carry Many Waters at my breast, carrying my share of the traveling camp upon my back and this little unknown daughter beneath my heart to the summer Northland. I could blame it all on Brown Bull's insistence he always put his man-essence inside me whenever we joined in sex. But that would be unfair. I have long since found my peace by forgiving him of every real and imagined hurt. After all, it was *my* body. I was the only one who could have prevented what did happen from coming to pass.

It was my choice to bring Brown Bull to my mother's lodge. It was my choice not to send him back to his mother's lodge if I were unable to bear his never-ending unfaithfulness. It was my own laziness and the silly belief anything or anyone could protect me from the consequences of my own choice in taking the risk of an untimely child. It was I who allowed Brown Bull to put his semen inside my womb at a time I well knew was not appropriate. It was not he who was still carrying a new life in her arms. It was not he whose milk had stopped and whose moon-blood had returned before its time after the birth of Many Waters.

In truth, I was always pleased to take Brown Bull's white-essence into whichever opening in my body that pleased him. It was the only way I thought to hold him to me. It was that one time, almost five moons ago, when he pressed me to join in sex during the night and I was too lazy or too sleepy to take him into my mouth. The fact I was in absolutely no mood to take him anywhere else in my body is no excuse either. Neither could I ever utter the word "no" to Brown Bull. Not ever. I always thought he would cease to love me at all if I were ever to do anything counter to his wishes or ever to stifle the urgency of his desires for my red-body.

Sad when a woman thinks joining in sex is all she has to offer her beloved.

So it was on that one night I chose to allow him to reach his mountain top and finish inside me and to have his pleasure of me. And thus, he has given me another child too soon after the birth of Many Waters.

I smile now to think the words, "Could the Mother ever have given me a little less abundance? What harm would that have done to anyone?"

But that was not to be, however oddly amusing those words sound to me now.

It seems so clear now, though it was not so clear then, the part my decisions have played in all of this. My mother's milk has never been so copious that I had to find another nursing child to drain the excess lest my milk sour and putrefy within my breasts as Auntie always used to warn. My milk has always been sufficient to nurture my children. But this time it had ceased to flow too soon after Many Waters' birth. We women all know the womb of a nursing mother never starts a new life even if her husband's essence enters her pute while the child is still at her breast. Always, the moon-blood returns only after nursing ceases, or so I have always been told.

Still, I should not have been so careless. Or lazy. All women know how to bring on the birth-blood prematurely once the moon-blood has stopped flowing out so it may nourish a new life growing within. And all women know that sometimes the herbs do not do their work of bringing on the birth-blood. Besides, if one only discovers the new life after the summer bands have dispersed upon the Plain, that is the most dangerous place and time to try and stop the birth without also killing the mother. That much I do know as a healer.

I took the herbs and roots well before we departed for the Plain to avert the birth of this little daughter. But the medicines only made me sick and did not send the new life back to the Mother. I would have endangered my own life if I had tried the herbs a second time. This unknown daughter was determined to come into the World of Light through me no matter what I did. Or so it now seems.

There I was, sick and big-bellied, moving constantly and struggling to carry Many Waters and a share of the camp all the while. My dear mother, One Doe, helped me as she was able. But she is old and can walk and carry only her share of the traveling camp. It was impossible for my mother to carry Many Waters as well, struggle as she might to help me. My heart was also very burdened by the fear I would have the baby while still upon the Plain with only the assistance of my mother as midwife. I am the only healer or seer among our little summer band this season. There would only be she, and the even less experienced women of our traveling camp, to assist me in this birth. There would be no Four Mothers of the Birthing Bed—before me, behind me, to the left of me and to the right of me—to assist with bringing in this new life. So different from our first summer upon the Plain when our band had three seers, shamans and healers among us—the Grandfather, my Auntie and, of course, me.

And even if I survived giving birth upon the Plain, the baby would, inevitably, have to be abandoned to the Mother. I simply could not carry two babies any better than I could carry one. There was no one of our summer band who could even adopt the child. Every tent had its own children and share of the camp to carry. No matter what happened to me, this sweet little soul was doomed to return to the Mother before her life had even begun.

Had I managed to make it back to our Valley before giving birth, it might have been easier to find a lodge to foster her. At least my mother and I could have cared for her so long as we did not have to be constantly on the move. Such is the comfort and bounty afforded by our women's winter lodges within the shelter of the blessed Valley of the Bear Mother.

Now that is all for naught. It was all just too much for this one woman to bear.

Only now do I see clearly I have had this long-standing appointment with Leopard Mother of the Great Cave, whose very tooth I have held at my throat for my whole life. So many signs and symbols all around us. Still we refuse to see.

What I cannot deny is that my life as Seer and Healer of the Bear People has been good. It has been so very good! I have been happy wherever I am and it *is* a good day to die. In spite of Brown Bull's neglect of my heart with his constant sniffing after every willing woman—or man—he could seduce, I still do not count a life together with my beautiful blue-eyed husband as something that should not have been. He may have been married to me and the father of our children and an abundant provider for my mother's lodge, but he was also lover to many women. And he was companion to many more men than even my good Uncle Bright Wolf, the husband of the woman I loved most in this World of Light, my dear mentor, sister and Auntie. All of this was of my choosing and I refuse to have any regrets.

In marrying me and becoming one of the Bear-kin, Brown Bull was always where the People came together at the Great Gatherings to dance and to sing, to compete as a bison wrestler and to enjoy life as a generous gift-giver. Brown Bull was always there to see that he enjoyed as many as he could!

During the Great Gatherings while we lived together in my mother's lodge, I never even saw my husband, so busy was he in the bushes, the hot pools and various empty lodges of the Middle Camp. Even if I had not been engaged within the Cave during part of each Gathering as assistant seer, and later, the Mother of the Rites, I still would not have seen him during those days of fun, excitement and the chase after new and unfamiliar prey. In summer, Brown Bull was far less active than during the winter, for obvious reasons. When so many of the Nine Kin were settled in their respective camps he always knew where to go to practice his charming, beguiling ways.

Brown Bull also volunteered often as a bison-dancer in the men's rites of the Great Cave. I never witnessed him playing cow or bull there because I was never more than the Mother of the Women's Rites. I never had the place of Grandmother of the People overseeing the rites of the Heart Lodge. Still, during the initiations of the Red Lodge, I could never keep my head from wandering into the men's Lodge of the Heart. I could not keep my heart from imagining the beating of the drums, the chanting of the songs. And I could not keep my liver from wondering if he were, at that moment, playing one of the Trickster's bison-dancers.

Auntie did become Grandmother of the Bear People for a few seasons. So it was no surprise that neither Brown Bull nor Bright Wolf ever volunteered to play the cow and bull in the men's rites while she was there to witness their performances. It did not take me very long after the Dance of Promise to learn that my husband truly was well-named because he was bull bison to many cows.

But that is the way of men. It is the way of the hunters and it is *all* of the Mother. I became resigned to that or I would have gone raving mad. In truth, after torturing my heart so long with the sheer anguish of it, I am at peace and have been for many seasons now. Each must allow all others to be who and what they are in their hearts. This is one lesson that has been long in its coming and hard for me to learn. A few times, I tried to even the game with my humping husband by joining in sex with young men and hunters at the Gathering. I knew how to flirt with the men as I moved about the dance circle as well as anyone. And in spite of my seer's marks, I was attractive to many, even though I never thought of myself as beautiful or desirable.

But spreading my legs and giving my pute or my mouth to men for whom I had no heart-love left me colder than the Great Cave. To do as my husband did made me feel dead inside my heart and liver as if the Dark Mother had eaten them completely away. Such jealousy is the most poisonous of feelings which can arise from one's liver. I know that from the many long nights of tormented anxiety and desolate longing I spent while Brown Bull was playing his never-ending game of the chase for the unknown and the un-tasted.

I know the unquenchable anger that arises from a broken and pierced heart. Left there to fester and turn putrid, such jealousy can bring bitter rancor and utter disaster to an entire camp. I had seen enough of that kind of discord in the course of my healing travels. I made a choice that I would accept Brown Bull just as he is.

Indiscriminate joining with any man-creature that has a rod and two man-eggs certainly did not nourish my heart and did nothing to soften the ache or fill the gaping hole that seemed always to be my belly. I thought better of it for the benefit of my own soul if not for the good of my children and my honorable reputation as Seer and Healer. The good of the whole Bear-kin depended on banishing jealousy from my own heart and preventing the poison from spreading beyond our lodge. I have always remembered the Grandfather's advice that seers who do not use their power to harm have no need for hand tricks to awe the People. And I know now that a seer who would use her power to bless the People can have no place for anger and rancor for another who resides within the lodge of her very own heart. Without a forgiving heart, the seer's healing powers will disappear as quickly as a hand trickster can make a feather vanish.

Still, I became so disconsolate and angry at times I wanted to curse Brown Bull's captivating blue eyes, his perfect body and his hard, fang-marked member. Auntie, as always, brought me to my senses before I had sent out such fearful darkness as could only have returned to me increased in its bitterness and loneliness.

Better than anyone, Auntie understood what my life was like with Brown Bull as husband to a Seer of the Nine Kin. After all, she had Uncle Bright Wolf as the husband of her hearth. I well remember how Auntie had tried to warn me about the solitary path I was taking. But who among all the People could have ever refused the Grandfather? She had also tried to gently warn me away from Brown Bull for reasons I could never have understood or comprehended at the time, so intent was I on having Brown Bull as my husband.

My dear mother, too, had tried to do the same in a much more forceful way. But I was truly a woman possessed by my liver-passion and heart-love for this man. How could my head have ever listened to any warnings? How could my mind have ever taken control of my liver and my heart and gone contrary to their overwhelming desires? But in the end, it was I who made all the choices. This has been *my* chosen path, after all is said and done.

Through all of this, what I did gain was more understanding and love for my own mother. I have come to understand what it was that had driven her to do what she did with the husband of my childless Auntie. The feelings of the heart and soul truly do move and guide us whether we are aware of it or not. My mother is wiser than I ever guessed and it was she who tried to warn me of other pitfalls in the match with Brown Bull that I never could have imagined as a naïve young girl, shaman's marks notwithstanding.

For all my threats to become the daughter of Brown Bull's mother, I have known since our first summer traveling with his family that it was an idle threat. I could never have left my mother's happy home to become a daughter of that accursed lodge. My mother tried to caution me in marrying Brown Bull, but I cut her off and would not listen to a single word of it.

Only after that first summer did I realize it had been a warning about Brown Bull's mother, and not him, that my mother had tried to give. I could never have lived as a daughter of that woman's lodge, so vicious and foul-mouthed was Brown Bull's mother. She should have been named Snarling Wolverine as a much better reflection of her short temper and constant hateful words than her actual personal name might have indicated. She seemed always to be screaming in anger at everyone around her. She even cursed at me, who had never done her any harm or had never spoken back to her in anger. In all ways, I was a good daughter to Brown Bull's mother.

She was especially irritable and loud when the camp's moon-blood was approaching. The women in the summer camps have their moon-blood at the same time each moon, so we always knew when Brown Bull's mother was about to become completely insufferable. And what was even worse, she never had any words of praise or gentle speech of any kind for her own husband … or mine—her own son! I even saw her striking her husband and Brown Bull on more than one occasion. I was completely dismayed that either of them, as respectable men and hunters, would accept such treatment at the hands of the mother of their lodge. But then no one ever seemed to be courageous enough to face her down. I know I was never so brave.

I have to admit I was as cowed by her violent outbursts as everyone else in the camp. It got so disruptive and the summer band was so full of discontent and chaos the Grandfather found it necessary to take Brown Bull's mother aside where his words could not be overheard. I have always wondered what the Grandfather said to her. After that, Brown Bull's mother changed her mood sufficiently for the better so it was possible to get through that first summer season with some semblance of harmony in the camp. Auntie also stepped in to gather special soothing and calming herbs and roots. She taught me which ones to gather and how to prepare them for Brown Bull's mother's exclusive use. The herbs and roots seemed to help in addition to the words of the Grandfather.

It was with great relief that my mother and father both refused to ever travel with Brown Bull's mother again. Brown Bull was just as relieved as I. Certainly, I found more compassion for my Beloved after traveling with his mother that first season. We could, and did, take consolation with each other in that. In fact, because the summer bands were so small and made of up mostly of close kin, Brown Bull's desire to run about and find some new prey waned considerably during our summer travels. In spite of the hardships, the summer season was, ironically, the time when we were closest to each other. We ended up spending much more time with one another than in the winter season when so many "strangers" were close at hand. Let us not forget the Great Gatherings when I barely even saw his face the whole time!

I came to be utterly ashamed at the anger and jealousy that arose within me with Brown Bull's obsession to hump everything and anything with a hole in it. In my pride, I could not go to my mother or Auntie for comfort or consolation. Even in the winter season, daylight was never a time when I concerned myself with Brown Bull's whereabouts. My head was always full with the daily round of my children, the coming and going of those needing healing and the general work of the camp.

The nights spent alone in what should have been our shared sleeping furs, was altogether another matter. Many times I would roll over in the night, reach for my Beloved and find only cold and empty furs beside me. I always thought I could live my life and be all right if only the sun would never set to leave me alone in the dark. Instead, the anguished nights without my Beloved beside me were interminable. As I lay alone on our sleeping platform, all I could think of was which one is Brown Bull joining in sex with now? How long before he will tire of this new prey and return from this particular hunt? I agonized about what it was he was doing with them, whether it was a man or woman and whether he was singing the same songs of love he had sung to me.

I wondered if he looked into their eyes without turning away as he did with me. Or was that just another of his seducer's tricks?

In my deepest despair and loneliness, I turned to an unexpected source of love and comfort. The very girl I had shunned as odd and smelly became my heart-friend and a source of unfailing acceptance and perfect kindness in my times of greatest misery and emptiness. She will surely mourn my returning to the Mother. And I will miss her very much. She is certainly one my soul will search for in all the worlds to come. Will I recognize her? Will she recognize me?

The first summer season after I gave birth to my oldest son, White Lynx became my unfaltering friend and support. She traveled with us for every summer season after that until she met and became the hunter of her wife's lodge. White Lynx's beloved was a kind and generous two-spirit woman of the Horse-kin. She was very pretty too. And unlike White Lynx, always dressed as a woman and did not go out to the hunt. It made my soul glad that White Lynx had finally found a true heart-love of her own.

White Lynx's ailing father returned to the Mother only one season after we became gift-givers and true Sisters of the Moon Blood. Her father returned about the same time I gave birth to my first son, Many Spears. Her father's death left White Lynx alone in her mother's lodge, which, in spite of all our work on that old heap of bark, continued to slowly fall down around her. She confided to me that she was happy to leave the lodge of a mother she had never known and a place which held so many sad memories for her. Her body had been ill-used by both her older brother and her father. It is little wonder she would never allow any man to touch her or join with her in sex.

I had suspected as much. Though she made many of her funny stories about such an unhappy subject, it was clear to me that it was all in an effort to make such a terrible thing less than it obviously was in her life. She could always make anyone laugh at the story of the boy who came in on his mother and father while they were noisily humping like rabbits in front of the draped sleeping platform before the hearth fire. I would always remember this funny story the way White Lynx told it. It seems the boy was terribly upset by the sight of his father on top of his mother grunting like a bull. He was shocked and upset, he yelled at his father and said, "What are you doing?!" But his father just laughed at him and said, "I am doing nothing you need to be concerned about, my son!" The boy fled from the lodge in embarrassment and anger. The next day, the boy's father came to the lodge and even before he entered he could hear someone humping, making loud noises as they joined in sex. The father entered the lodge and there was his own son humping his grandmother. The father was extremely angry and yelled at his son who didn't even stop humping the grandmother when he was caught doing such a disgusting thing. The father cried in a loud voice, "What are you doing?!" The boy turns to his father and says, "It's not so funny when it's *your* mother, is it?"

To make light of such behavior abhorred by all the People and still make everyone laugh tells me it was a subject White Lynx could only face with funny stories. It was a great sign of trust in me and love for me as a friend that she would confide such horrible secrets to me.

In my loneliness and anger at my own husband, it was not long before we found solace in each other's smooth, rounded, soft bodies. But mostly we took comfort in the gentle conversation of cherished friends. Men's bodies are all angles and bones and hard rods and muscles—which I continued to desire fervently—but the touch and feel of another woman is incomparable in its gentle comfort to hearts bruised by the men who are their kin and lovers.

What a joy it was to touch another woman's skin and know exactly what she was feeling! Without words I knew exactly how she wanted me to touch her. So many secrets were whispered between us, naked and warm within our cozy nest of sleeping furs. It was she who was always able to comfort me with assurances that Brown Bull's unspoken words of love would never wound my heart as long as she were there to speak them. I love her still and I know I will search for the soul called White Lynx in whatever dream worlds may yet come.

It was White Lynx who soothed my soul with funny stories and clever words when I was in my deepest, angry and murderously heartbroken moods. She was able to tease a smile from me by making fun of my foul tempers with such words as, "Oh Brown Bull, I'm so miserable without you. It's almost like you're here!" Sometimes she would sing to me a trickster's mock song of love:

> *Heard your wife left you, Brown Bull,*
> *How upset you must be.*
> *But don't fret about it,*
> *She's sleeping with me!*

Always we would laugh and laugh and laugh until my anger and heartache had vanished completely. She was a shaman-of-joy if ever there was one. It was also she who would remind me that even though Brown Bull chased after many, it was I who he had chosen to bear his children. It was my own lodge Brown Bull had willingly joined as husband and not some other. White Lynx wisely told me to listen to the words of the only song of love that Brown Bull made that could never have been sung to any other of his companions. She always said that this song was even better than if Brown Bull had spoken the words, "I love you above all others" as I never ceased longing to hear.

The words of Brown Bull's song of love which he sang to me on the day he asked to be Son of One Doe's Lodge and my husband, still echoes in my very soul:

> *Oh Lion Lady mine,*
> *Eat thou me not with fangs of ivory white*

Devour thou me, instead, with yellow eyes of thine.
Oh Lion Lady mine,
Rake thou me not with claws that flash
Soothe thou me, instead, with slender fingers, fine.
Oh Lion Lady mine,
Rasp thou me not, with tongue so rough
Comfort thou me, instead, with sable lips, sublime.
Oh Lion Lady mine,
Accuse me not with words that slash
Forgive thou me, my gentle heart is thine.
Oh lovely Lion Lady mine

I still feel ashamed that I could never sing a song of love for him. That was never my gift. Certainly I reveled in those times with my Beloved when he would press his luscious lips to mine, then to my big belly and the new life that grew within. But no songs of love would ever come from that wounded and angry heart I called mine.

So many regrets. I could have felt joy in those sublime moments when he pressed his ear to my belly to hear his son's heartbeat and spread his rough hunter's hands to feel the kicking life within. Instead, I always looked ahead to the next time he would leave me alone to suffer the lack of his touch and the absence of his unmatchable blue eyes. I would not think on his coming to me as a loving husband, as White Lynx always said. Instead, I would look back to the time he had walked away from me as if I were just another of his kills, which of course, I was.

That was before my initiation as Seer, the event that changed everything for him when it came to me. Was it ever an angry face that I showed to my beloved that made him sing the song of love that came to his heart that could only be sung to me? How could any man brave Lion Mother's devouring jaws and then say to my lion-face the words of love that my soul hungered to hear? That I never truly forgave his first imagined rejection of me I will regret for all the worlds to come.

How delicious it was to sleep naked, back-to-back beneath our cozy furs, as a howling winter storm found the little gaps between the reeds to whistle a melancholy tune in to our bed. All the sweetness and the kindness the two of us did have together I squandered and rejected by always having my attention on something else. Will I ever find Brown Bull in some never-world to come in order to complete this circle of our life together? That I cannot say, not even here in this world of ever-brightening spirit-light.

White Lynx, my Sister of the Moon Blood, gift-giver and heart-friend, became an initiated hunter after several seasons of going out with the men. She confided once that the Nine Lashes, the shearing and the marking of the hunter's initiations were easier trials for her than had been the insertion of the Hymen Stone. She insisted this was so even though it was done at the gentle hands of my Auntie as Mother of the Rites. That was the only time we ever talked about her experience of the Hymen Stone, the wild screams and seizures that resulted, and the terror it caused in all the girls who witnessed it. It all seems so long ago and so far away as if it were only an ancient dream. But then, all of the ordeals and revelations of the Great Cave seem like dreams to me now.

My father never liked to have White Lynx around my mother's lodge. He knew the times when Brown Bull was out of the lodge for no good reason that I would be with White Lynx either within her lodge or in my mother's lodge. When I sought refuge with White Lynx in her lodge, I always left my children to the care of my mother. I could always depend on my mother, who always understood my heart and never complained or criticized me.

My father disliked it even more when White Lynx and I would sometimes share sleeping furs within my mother's lodge. I think that was the reason he refused to stand as White Lynx's mentor for her hunter's initiations when it was time for her to enter the Great Cave with the boys. But good old Uncle Bright Wolf was willing to stand in—yet another source of irritation for my father, I can only assume.

Of course, Bright Wolf had no son for whom to stand as mentor and so he was proud to take White Lynx into the Cave for her hunter's initiation. I think he was really doing a favor for me because everyone knew of our deep friendship with each other, including my wayward husband. Brown Bull never showed the slightest sign of any jealousy or rancor no matter what I did. He seemed to like White Lynx and never begrudged the time I spent with her. I learned much from Brown Bull in spite of myself.

I have struggled for so long against my destiny as a lone traveler and servant of the Mother among the Bear People. But I have long since submitted to the Mother and settled into the life I have made for myself. Day to day, I did find a great measure of joy and abundance in the life of a seer and a healer. Even though a spirit-guide never came to me, I always knew the Mother was with me even when I was apart from all others, alone only with my own thoughts and in the deepest despair. Who ever could have dreamed that my greatest comfort would be in the form of a loving sister with whom, at one time, I had been so terrified to join with in sex? The Mother truly has many faces and one of those had the form of one called White Lynx.

It turns out that the Mother's companionship within any face is companionship enough. Just as it is now, only it is the companionship of a mother leopard using my old body as prey to feed her cubs, to nourish the new life she has brought forth. That is only fitting and good.

But there is now to be no inseparable union of two bodies and souls as one for me and my Beloved. I will not find the perfect union of two hearts living across lifetimes as I believe the Grandfather had found. Surely Brown Bull will mourn my return to the Mother? I wonder what the Grandfather really felt for me in his heart? Was I truly his beloved wife in another world, another life? Or was I merely seer-initiate and a learner of his wisdom? Either way, surely the Grandfather would mourn for me if he were still in the World of Light?

Even as I had such thoughts, a vision of Brown Bull answered some of those questions. Though I could not hear his thoughts or feel his feelings, as I floated above, enraptured by the terrible scene of the leopard mother eating my flesh, I saw my beloved Brown Bull falling to his knees. He uttered a great cry of sorrow and grief as someone's disembodied hands gave him my bloody robe and chipped lion-woman pendant. I heard his weeping and tasted his tears.

In utter desolation I heard Brown Bull cry out the words, "I will search for you in all the worlds to come. I will search for you in all the worlds to come."

But still the words, *I love you above all others,* did not come from his lips, even at this parting of our lives together. What worlds are those? When will they come? How can one soul ever find another who is their very twin if we could not find it within each other's eyes in this life just lived?

After my initiation in the Great Cave, I thought many times about the Grandfather and his own lion-eyed beauty. I have learned that just because I feel my heart at one with another and I see the Mother within his eyes, it does not mean this is also in his heart. So hard it is to know another's heart let alone one's own. If my soul had actually been the short-lived heart-mate of the Grandfather then why do I not remember it? One would think that in this place where the soul has fled the body that such memories as being violently killed in another life would be remembered? But I have no such memories.

It appears that crossing the Bridge of Rainbows through the Gate of Forgetting to a new life blots out all memories of lives past. So how could the Grandfather recognize me as his lion-eyed Beloved? And yet he wept so bitterly to beat me with the Nine Lashes even though I was not the one he thought me to be. In truth, if I were that soul and had the Grandfather's strength, beauty and spirit-fire had attracted me to him in that lifetime, how could we have been twin souls and I not remember? How could he have seen the Mother in my eyes when I did not see her within his?

Yet, what a full and abundant life I have had! So blessed a life for one to take the Seer's Path with such little experience of the spirit-powers! I may never have become Thrice Born Shaman of the Bear People, but this life of mine has been so full and abundant! It has been full of our children, full of the life-giving and healing gifts of a seer, full of the initiations of the girls in their Moon Blood rites; full of the daily round of my blessed life among the Bear People! My life has been full of laughter and dancing and feasting and full, even, of the endless moving from summer camp to summer camp. Finally, it was always full of the winter season's return to the joyful reunion with friends and kin in the welcoming bosom and the abundance of the Valley of the Bear Mother.

I will never become Grandmother of the People now. All the teachings and wisdom of the Grandfather and my Auntie ends with me. I have failed in my holy promise to the Grandfather and to Auntie.

Ah, and there was always my beloved and ever-generous Auntie.

My dear Auntie returned to the Mother more than five seasons past at which time a cousin of the downriver Bear-kin became the Grandfather of the Nine Kin. But this new Grandfather had not the wisdom of Flying Otter and his apprentices, who are now *both* returned to the Mother. Regrettably, when I heard the new Grandfather instruct the Nine Kin with wisdom not that of Flying Otter, I did not speak up and teach what I knew to be the ancient truths of the Great Cave.

Always I told myself, "Each seer teaches according to his own understanding and this Grandfather is already very old. I will wait until I am Grandmother of the Bear People to make the truths of the Great Cave known to the many."

But now that day will never come. The truths of the Mother's Cave I vowed to pass on to my own daughters and to the People will never be spoken.

My heart still aches for Auntie, whose knowledge of herbs and healing chants and potions could not stop the thing from growing inside her. First it shut off her moon-blood and then drained her lifeblood away slowly and without ceasing, all the healing skills Auntie had given me notwithstanding. The Mother's Embrace for my sweet and gentle Auntie was neither sweet nor gentle. Difficult, it is, to think of my loving Auntie's Return as any kind of mother's embrace.

My own Return is much quicker and far easier. And yet we have both been embraced by the Mother in our own way. I cannot leave off from wondering who will mourn for me? Auntie certainly would have missed me and mourned deeply had I returned to the Mother first. But now, the last one who knows the secret of my adventure with the Grandfather in the Black Lodges of the Great

Cave returns to the Mother. This secret of the Great Cave goes out of the World of Light with me, never to be known again.

As Grandmother of the People after the new Grandfather's return to the Mother, Auntie had taken several into the Black Lodges for their initiations. She told me how all who saw Lion Mother joining together with Bison Father in sex marveled at the beauty and power of the spirit-bison I had made with my own hands and heart. I may have left a holy mark within the Great Cave for all the People to see, but this secret dies with me.

Somehow, it is enough.

My mother and father will surely miss me. Though old, they are still able to make the summer journey. Certainly they will love my children and care for them as I did for as long as they are able to walk, at least. My mother will surely care for and carry baby Many Waters back to the Valley and our winter home.

And I know my father will help her. In spite of his coldness, I know my father always favored me as my mother favored her youngest son, White Fox. Even then, a new lodge was never built for Brown Bull and me. Instead, the east and west sleeping areas of my mother's lodge were rebuilt and extended to make sleeping spaces for all of us. What my mother also did to accommodate the newly married couple in her lodge was to give the sleeping area of the father and mother at the back of the lodge to me and Brown Bull. It appeared not to be much of a sacrifice for either of them as she and my father had not slept under the same skins for many seasons.

No doubt, that is how my father knew White Fox was not the son of his essence, the son of his body.

"Is that why men do not change when they give new life to the red-bodies of their children? Does the white-essence only make the child's body so that we look like our fathers? Do we women change forever because the child is the child of our hearts, of our souls, as well as the child of our very bodies?" I spoke these questions aloud, in spite of knowing there was no sound to hear and no ears to hear it with.

My mother and father even took to sleeping each on the western women's platform and the eastern men's platforms of One Doe's winter lodge. They slept apart except when they were grudgingly forced to share their sleeping furs in the more cramped summer tents. My father snored like a herd of bull aurochs, but we all were used to that. I always loved him dearly in spite of that and all the other ways he disappointed me. I know he loved me too, even though it was not his way to say it in words as my mother often did.

What is it with the hearts of men that they are so stingy with their words of love? Do they all have the door flaps between heart and tongue stitched shut with heavy sinews? I know both he and my mother had only my happiness at heart when they tried to keep me from following Auntie's path and her shaman's ways. But I also see now that my destiny as Seer was already set the day I began to sketch spirit-animals in the sand which appeared to one and all to be alive.

As they grew older, my mother and father began sleeping together again. But I know that was only because of the return to the Mother of my beloved youngest brother White Fox. The Trickster is cruel and joyous in turn. Even then I knew the return to the Mother of my youngest brother was perhaps the best example of the Trickster having given a gift only to have it taken back again. White Fox was the source of so much joy and love and pain and sorrow all at the same time—the inside and outside of the same thing.

My mother was inconsolable when White Fox's badly broken leg festered in spite of everything Auntie and I could do. I know now that often there is nothing the most powerful shaman-of-healing can do to save a life when the shattered ends of a leg bone are sticking out of the skin. My Thrice Born Auntie was the most powerful of healers and the Grandmother of the Nine Kin, yet she could do nothing to save the red-life of White Fox to her utter despair and the sorrow of the whole Middle Camp. One day the boys are playing together by the River. One falls from a boulder and a whole camp is sent into mourning. Live for the day because it *is* a good day to live. It *is* a good day to die. This I know, *all* of it *is* the Mother, even as she gives us life only to devour us again with her cruel teeth.

Not only was my mother inconsolable, Auntie shared her grief completely as did Uncle Bright Wolf. My father shed not a tear.

But I know he secretly mourned the loss of the boy he had raised as his own in spite of everything. Who would have been so hurt, betrayed and angry and still have welcomed and fostered a son who was not his own? Only my father. Only my father whose heart was as big as he pretended it was small.

I still marvel at my own blindness at what was going on around me between those I most loved in the World of Light. It should have been as clear as the similarities in the names of Bright Wolf and White Fox, let alone the similar look of the two. To my long-suffering father, those grey-blue eyes and dry-grass blond hair with a touch of red must have been a constant reminder of my mother's betrayal. But I was just a girl and always intent on my own needs and desires and completely caught up in the pettiness of my own life. How could I be so callously unaware of what was in the hearts of those I love? But then, who is not mostly oblivious to both the joyous and the injured souls around us?

My eldest son, Many Spears, has already been initiated as a man and always joins his father on the hunt. Even though he has not yet had his first-kill, every man or bearer who joins the hunt receives a share as hunter. My mother's lodge will be well-provided for until Many Spears marries and joins the lodge of his wife-to-be. My father, Roe Bear, is one of the most skilled flint makers of the Bear-kin and he has taught his grandson Many Spears well. Many Spears will always be sought after to join the hunt and to make the summer journey to the Northland by his many friends and gift-givers. I have no need to hold any concern for him. The Mother will always watch over him even if I cannot.

My father and Brown Bull may yet teach my second son, Many Antlers, the same hunter's skills they possess. But Many Antlers has seen only seven seasons and with at least five more seasons before initiation as a man, it is a long, long time in the life of a boy of the Bear People—witness poor White Fox's end.

But who will teach my little daughter Many Waters the ways of a girl and a woman of the Bear People? Only my mother remains to do that and she, no doubt, will teach her everything she has taught me of how to be a woman. But my mother is not a seer and she continues to despise everything about being Seer or Healer. In that, my mother is like a man who does not change his heart. As sure as she tried to prevent me from following my grandmother and Auntie in following a shaman's ways, I know that she will do everything she can to see that Many Waters will not take the path so many other women in her family have followed.

But if Many Waters is not missing a bone, she may yet take the shaman's journey in spite of anything her grandmother does or says. Many Waters may yet surpass her mother who never took that journey and only managed to become a mediocre healer and a fake shaman. I know my mother will not live forever so it seems that my son, Many Antlers, and my daughter Many Waters, will both be fostered by another. I can only hope that Brown Bull's wide circle of "acquaintances" will be of some use in finding my children a suitable new mother.

All things work for the good and the All Mother will forever care for her children. That means my children too.

There are many other things I know and see so clearly at this moment but many things are as unknown and unclear as they were when I lived within that unmoving piece of bleeding flesh I still see within the leopard's jaws. I know my eldest son Many Spears did not cry out as his father whipped him with the Nine Lashes. I knew that not because any spirit-guide whispered it to me. I know it because he has his father's courage in the face of pain, as well as Brown Bull's flawless skin, his light brown hair and beaming smile. Although, Many Spears did not get his father's famous blue eyes. It's just as well. Those night-blue eyes have gotten so many into such trouble!

I also know that neither of my sons will ever see the work of my hands and heart in the Lodge of Black Spirits. As brave as my son Many Spears is, he had not the heart to face the Dark Mother within his own soul as his father did. How do I know this? Because Many Spears' penis was unmarked with the charcoal of the Ancients when he returned from his ordeals in the Great Cave to be soothed and healed by his mother's healing hands, oils and yellow ochre.

Whip them all you want. Make them bleed. Hear them cry out in pain to make of them sons of their fathers! They are still our sons and our sons they will always be, whether in this world or in those to come! My mother was so wise in this.

What is it that leads us to pull back from the spirit-power and the light of the Mother after we have seen and felt it? In the Cave I pulled back my hand in terror when I touched the warm palm of the Mother when I should have felt cold stone. And I have held back and closed my heart to the Mother as surely as Brown Bull has pulled away from me. We both have pulled away from the Dark Mother whose marks are still fixed upon my shoulder and pierced into Brown Bull's foreskin.

Strange and mysterious are the ways of the Mother and how unexpected and ironic the turns of our lives in this labyrinth called life. The Trickster is always hiding around the corner in the dark to startle us and send us off in a new direction. That my barren Auntie's husband should get a son of my own mother's body to create such discord among the two families was always a mystery to me. It was never spoken of by either of those two women who I love the most and the ones who taught me all I know of being a woman of the Bear People. Somehow I know it here, in this strange place of bright light between a leopard dragging something away below and a world of even more brilliant clouds above that now beckons to me.

The biggest joke the Trickster would play upon us all would be to make of my Auntie's lodge a refuge for one of my own twin sons, otherwise doomed to exposure and a quick return to the Mother.

My second son, Many Antlers, was the largest and strongest of twin sons born to our lodge barely six seasons ago. Because of these twin sons, I had already learned—out of my own hard experience—that mothers cannot carry or nurse more than one child at a time during the journey to the Northland. None should ever bear another baby before the older child is able to walk and keep up with the camp.

I have done both, and it is the end of me.

The smallest and weakest of my twin sons would have been sent back to the Mother except for Auntie and Bright Wolf's desire for a child to fill their lodge and their hearts. It was their willingness to take him in that saved my little son from exposure. Bright Antlers, their adopted son, thrives as does his twin Many Antlers. In due time, the two boys will be initiated together in the Great

Cave as age-mates. Bright Antlers will take the Nine Lashes at the hand of his adoptive father, Bright Wolf. Just as my son, Many Antlers, will take the Nine Lashes under the hand of his father, Brown Bull.

One of the reasons we continued to travel together to the Northland with all the tension between the two families—even after Auntie returned to the Mother—was so the twin boys could be together and get to know one another as the brothers they are. No, Bright Antlers did not get Brown Bull's blue-black eyes either. Nor did he get his mother's lion-eye, for that matter.

But all the more unexpected and mysterious were the ways of the Trickster when Auntie returned to the Mother only a few seasons on, thus giving back the care of both twins to me and to the hands and back of my ever-loving mother, One Doe. Bright Wolf, to give him credit, mourned Auntie's return deeply. He missed Auntie terribly but he was desperate to take another wife to tend his lodge and care for his baby son.

And in the way of the Trickster, the final irony was my uncle's taking of the Grandfather's two-spirit companion, Red Dawn, of the Shelter of the Solitaries, to wife. Together, they care for Bright Antlers. And Red Dawn cares for his husband Bright Wolf just as my dear Auntie always did.

In spite of it all, and maybe because of it all, Auntie loved my Uncle Bright Wolf well. In the World of Spirit Light, I see that the Mother's Net enmeshes us all with finely woven and endlessly entangled strings. All in all, I think the Grandfather would be pleased with me even though, among all my other falsehoods, I lied to him about seeing his dream-vision and hearing the voice of the Mother and the spirit-guides.

And there is always the Grandfather. His fear that he would not be long with us was well founded. The season of our great adventure into the Cave was very hard on him. So many days were spent in the Cave, fasting and staying awake for days and nights. And there was his falling and bruising his hip. All of that had been followed by the Great Gathering, the puberty rites again in the Cave and the Dance of Promise. It took all his strength from him. Through the kind care and gentle ways of Red Dawn, the Grandfather managed to keep up with us that first season. I had been so happy that he chose to travel with our band on what would be his last summer in the Northland.

What was even more delightful was that we all got to know Red Dawn as sisters. We loved him well for his respectful and gentle care of the Grandfather. The women of our summer band also welcomed Red Dawn for his strength and size. He helped us with many tasks that only a strong man can do. Red Dawn's caring and sturdy presence made life in the summer bands that much easier for us all.

It was in the following summer season when my first son, Many Spears, was still an infant carried at my breast that the Grandfather returned to the Mother. It was only two moons after leaving the Valley. Every day he had struggled painfully along far behind the main party of the band and even further behind the scouting party of good hunters and strong walkers. Even though Red Dawn, together with Auntie, White Lynx and I, all tried to help him along, he was unable to keep up. I assisted Auntie in collecting and preparing the herb waters to sooth the pains in the Grandfather's bones and to reduce the swelling in his joints. But after a few weeks of trying to keep up, nothing seemed to help and the Grandfather found it more and more difficult to go on.

When on the move, we would always straggle in to the camp of the night well after dark. By the time our little party came into camp, the fires had already been made and the food cooked. It was often the campfire light which directed us the last few dark and perilous footsteps to warmth and safety with our families. The Grandfather knew this was very dangerous for us to be doing—me with my first baby at my breast. He often told us to go ahead with the others where we would be safe.

And so it was that one day the Grandfather simply walked out into the Plain, sat down and refused to go any further.

The old who are blind or crippled in their arms or who can no longer hear, may not be fit to join the hunt. But they have great wisdom and knowledge and must be cared for during the long journey to the Northland and back again to the Valley. If an old one is unable to walk and cannot catch up to the band by the end of the day, they are doomed and often return to the Mother in the manner of our beloved Grandfather, Flying Otter. Auntie, Red

Dawn, White Lynx and I all wept loudly and begged the Grandfather not to give up. But he was adamant and ordered all of us to leave him to return to the Mother in peace. The Celebrations of Return are never quite as joyous and as full of happiness when someone leaves the World of Light as the Grandfather did.

And so will be the mourning for me, I suppose.

Without clothes and belongings to dress the impersonators, or even pieces of the beloved departed's liver to share, it is never quite the joyful celebration we all expect. The Grandfather could not have made it through the night before he was taken by some animal or another. The next morning, knowing that he was gone, the band moved on. It was a few days later, when we stopped at a good campsite, that we celebrated the Grandfather's Return. At the ceremonies, Red Dawn did as well as he could to fight back the tears long enough to tell a funny story of his life with the Grandfather—and to imitate Flying Otter's hobbling walk. I told and reenacted the story of how the Grandfather frightened me out of my wits and how I almost peed myself when he jumped out at me from the blackness of the Great Cave. I told the story of how he pretended to fall off a cliff during my initiation as Seer to terrify me once again. We all missed the dear old man so much. No one was happy the Grandfather had returned to the Mother in the way he had chosen to return. How could we be happy at that?

Have I chosen to end this body-life of mine in the same way? Can I truly say some part of me has not given my red-body to the mother leopard to feed her cubs just as the animal-messengers of the Mother give their lives to us? In the end, everything is eaten back to the Mother by some creature or another. This is why we always put the bodies of the dead out upon a sleeping platform of return or we put their remains into the rivers as food for lions, vultures or eels.

It matters little how the red-body returns to the Mother. If it were not so, how could it be that my body is now becoming the life of this mother leopard and her family of hungry cubs? In the end, it *is* all the Mother's embrace.

But how could I not want more life? How could I just walk out to be eaten by a leopard? How could I not want my only daughter, Many Waters, to live and love and learn the wisdom of the Grandfather and Auntie from me and pass it on to her daughters? How could I give myself to the leopard and have my body carried off where the People cannot place a piece of my liver into my mouth and cannot share some liver of my red-body themselves in a loving farewell?

Like the Grandfather, I will not be so honored by the ones who love me and who wish to carry some small part of my life-fire within them. In the end, it is all a mystery when and how the Mother calls us to return. But in the calling, we hear and we still choose to go.

And so, it seems, have I.

* * *

My soul did not, at last, flee my dying flesh until the leopard began to drag the bloody skin-bag up into a tree. A great white light began to envelop me and spin my soul upward in a left-turning spiral—the direction of the return to the All Mother. I became light as the air, beyond all pain and free of all sorrow.

I am the air! I am the light! But still I clung to the red-world I had just departed. I seemed to be watching from above as the bloody robe slipped away from some meat being dragged into the tree branches. The robe lay there like a shrunken, crumpled bison on the brilliant green grass of summer. They would at least find my old bison robe, see the leopard tracks and the drag marks and so know my fate.

I no longer wish to hold to this place. The white light begins to swirl even faster around and around in a huge sucking whirlpool. It is drawing me in to a deep cave of spinning white light, taking me where? I know not. The white light becomes brighter and brighter and causes such pain to my eyes that I turn my head away. The brightness of the light burns so fearfully hot!

In an instant I am surrounded by slashing, gnashing, part-human, part-animal, part-bird creatures of great power and strength. They stab at me with sharp spears and needle-like fangs. These horrific monsters chew me to red pulp and grind me with their ponderous mammoth feet into nothing! Vicious teeth and gashing talons tear at my body and pierce me in every part!

I am rended into pieces!

But even as I am shredded into nothingness I recognize these monsters. I know these ravening creatures. I have seen them painted on the walls of the Great Cave. I have heard Auntie tell me they are but dreams and visions and that I should fear them not. The Grandfather has taught, as Twice Born Seer, I control and call forth these monsters from within my very soul. These ravening creatures that tear at me are as illusory as the spirit lines drawn by me and the Ancients gone before me upon the stone of cave walls. They are painted and marked upon our bodies and on our clothing and on our lodges. They can be nothing to fear unless our minds fear them. They are made as charms and pendants to be hung about our necks and close to our hearts. They are fashioned into shaman's necklaces and oil lamps. They are carved into bison and aurochs horns.

In my soul, I know they have no life-fire of their own except I give it to them.

As I thought these thoughts, the words of the Thirteen Syllables of Transformation floated up, as it were, from some alien world far below. I began to speak the Words of Power with lips of fire and a tongue of light.

"I am the Mother's child. I and the Mother are One."

No sooner did I speak the Thirteen Syllables of Power that I realized this tearing of my flesh is not real. My eternal soul cannot be injured in this way! Toothed creatures cannot claw a body of light!

The fanged monsters that so cruelly ripped at me dissolved instantly into the Silence and the Nothingness from whence they came. Only then did the vision of the twin door posts of a great gate open before me.

Each astonishing portal was made of spinning spheres of iridescent, colored spirit-light floating on spraying fountains of the same spirit-light one above the other like beautiful stones strung on a necklace.

"I am standing on the Bridge of Rainbows!" I exclaimed in a voice of the same iridescent light. "This is the Gate of Remembering and I shall pass through it!"

My soul floated effortlessly through the door that I felt I had been looking for all my life. It had always been there before me and within me waiting to be opened.

In an instant I remembered everything. I remembered every life I have ever lived. One of those myriads of lifetimes *had* been lived as the Grandfather's lion-eyed Beloved. I *had* returned again to the Grandfather as Little Bear to complete the circle of our lives! As I contemplated the uncountable lifetimes my soul had ever experienced, three glowing human shapes began to approach me out of the all-encompassing, blinding light of unimaginable peacefulness.

The light grew impossibly bright. It was more brilliant than the light of the sun at the mouth of the Great Cave after three days and two nights of darkness with only feeble lamplight to show the way. When the fierce brightness did not cause me to look away, the first shape, a kind and gentle woman with smiling eyes, came forward toward me. She held the hand of a young man, his hair a radiant dry-grass blond with just a touch of red, his father's grey-blue eyes shining out to me in love.

The two beings of unimaginable radiance came closer to me out of the dazzling light, the woman holding out both her hands to me in greeting. There could be no mistaking my Auntie's loving, gentle presence.

The third figure, a man with white-light, shoulder length hair and a cropped beard, emerged from the brilliance of the brightness of all brightness. His deep voice speaking infinite wisdom to my heart was unmistakable.

"Well done, my good and faithful Daughter. Enter into the peace of the Mother of Us All."

CHAPTER 18.
TRAVELING WITHOUT MOVING

MY SOUL WOULD BE DRAWN BACK to live as one of the People of the Bear Mother many, many times. Often, I would visit them as a woman, in other lifetimes as a man. In some lives I died in childhood, some in childbirth. There were lives where I returned to the Mother as an old lady, honored and respected, cheerfully sent on my way by children and grandchildren around me with the rites of returning to the Mother the People of the Bear Mother cherish.

I would live many more lives as a woman among the Bear People. Always they were lifetimes full of freely chosen husbands, full of laughing children, collecting and preparing food and making clothing. Always they were lives of gathering the Mother's abundance with my own hands and loving, mourning, dancing and singing in gratitude for all of it.

I have also returned to the People many times as a man and a hunter. I have known the thrill in the hollow pit of my belly when the spear leaves the thrower knowing the sharp point will find its mark swiftly and surely, guided by the unseen hand and eye of the Dark Mother. I have known the swelling pride of bringing heavy-laden carrying baskets of meat and fat and hides from the hunt to feed and shelter a whole camp.

I have thrown the spear farther and have run faster than any other man among the People and rejoiced in the pride of winning such contests of men. I have known the exultation of beating another man at bison wrestling and I have taken the bloody pleasure of rubbing the loser's face into the mud just for spite.

I have thrust at a woman's sex with the passion of the demented caring only to take my pleasure, to press her into the dirt and then cast her aside. I have held a woman under my subjugation and control with the threat of my superior strength and reveled in it.

I have joined with a woman in heart-love with the tenderness and kindness and fidelity that my own soul longed for. I have pressed my lips to the growing belly of a beloved wife. And I have felt with a soaring heart full of joy and love, the jumping new life growing within her womb that was body of my body, flesh of my flesh.

I have mouthed the words of love to a woman when I did not mean them in my heart. And I have spoken them into the ear of one who I truly loved above all others. But never has there been a lover—man or woman—for whom my heart would ever bring forth a heart-song of love. The only songs I had to sing were made by others. The only music that moved me was that played by others. Are the walls I have built between liver and heart and head unable to be breached?

Every lifetime I have lived was, in part, a search for one who could tear down those walls. But never would I truly open my heart and soul to any man or woman. But I have known the bliss of the joining of minds and bodies that only two men can know when they have faced the danger of the hunt together. When the two friends have protected each other from the Dark Mother's deadly gaze and ravenous teeth. And I have huddled together with a brother for warmth and the healing comfort of one skin against another's beneath the same bison robe through the long, cold lonely nights of the never ending hunt for the red-lives of the Mother's children.

I have rejoiced in my heart when leaving the cloying women's winter lodges for the freedom of constant movement and the unchallenged authority of the men upon the Plains of Summer. I have laughed and joked and clasped my hunter-brothers in warm embraces around the sheltering blaze of a solitary campfire. My heart has been opened by the men's circles far from all camps and lodges of nagging, chattering women forever clutching at me and whispering words of love that I can never speak in return.

I have been trampled and wounded and terrified by the beloved object of my endless bloodletting pursuit, heart pulsing in my throat as if I would suffocate. What bliss to run down and return a mountain of flesh to the Mother with my own spears, with my own hands! And I have known the ecstasy of returning to the Mother by her many different embraces.

I have known the bliss of a beloved companion's rough but gentle hand dressing my wounds and comforting me in the way that only another hunter's body can in the face of so much blood, manure, dust, slaughter and isolation that is the Mother's work of life for us as men.

I have been lashed by my mentor's willow rod many times in the Great Cave. Many times have I witnessed the making of the bloody marks of the Nine Kin in my own shoulder. And I have rejoiced at the sight of my father's face glowing with pride at the making of the first-kill marks upon my throat as a grown man and a hunter.

I have stood overawed at the sight of the Mother's spirit-animals in her Great Cave. And I have trembled in terror as my lamp went out leaving me in the cold, hard, despairing blackness of the Mother's belly to be rescued in my darkest moment by the father of my body and of my heart.

I have spilled my semen upon the Earth Mother in the rites of the Heart Lodge. I have been shaved, sheared and painted to signal the beginning of a new life as a hunter and a man, my boy's hair and old life consumed by the flames of the Hearth of the Ordeals. And I have witnessed the unmasking of the bison-dancers with overwhelming feelings of betrayal, revulsion and arousal all at the same time.

At times I have even been moved with some unexplainable anger to rape the mouth and anus of the unmasked bison cow in the hidden rites of the Hearth of the Ordeals with a roughness and disgust within my heart I could not understand. I could not believe such hidden anger and darkness could come forth from within me. And I was baffled by my own actions when I took pleasure in spilling my essence, not upon the ground out of respect to the Mother, but inside the helpless, moaning cow-man.

I have watched as my sons have been born in a gush of water and blood. I have cared for them and laughed with them and danced and sung with them. I have taught them everything they must know to live the life of a hunter among the People of the Bear Mother.

And I have whipped the quivering backs of my sons and nephews, wide-eyed with pain and terror all to make a woman's child into the son of his father and to make of him a man and a hunter of the People. I have silently choked back the tears that stung my own heart with greater force than I could ever swing the willow rod against the wincing skin of my own flesh and blood.

All these lives I have lived among the People of the Bear Mother. But not one life was ever spent again as Seer or Healer who could bless the People with the Mother's greatest gifts. How completely did I reject the light and wisdom of the Mother that had been given me so generously! At last, the gift of making spirit-animals and painting their images on wood, stone or bone did I reject. Never again would I paint a spirit-animal nor would I draw an animal in the sand.

Even though in every life I ever lived, I was born with Lion Mother's mark within my right eye, never again would I enter the Black Lodges to gaze in reverent wonderment upon the bison-man and his lion-woman there—the very spirit-images I had made with my own hands and heart. And never would a trance bring forth from me any animal-guide to lead me through that lifetime and be my heart-companion to ward off the loneliness of being human in the World of Light.

I wonder? If I had been courageous enough to once again enter that Black Abyss of Union and Joining, would the work of my own hands and heart have spoken to my soul? Would the spirit-image of my own making have awakened a tiny spark of recognition within my heart?

No. I would forever fear, in some unfathomed part of my heart, to re-enter that Bright Lodge of the Soul ever again.

* * *

Inexorably drawn again and again to this abundant Valley and to this People of the Bear Mother, again and again I struggled to complete the circle of a life well-lived. My soul refused to fly elsewhere. At least not until that day came when the Mountains of Ice drew nearer and nearer, the air became dryer and dryer and the winter seasons became longer and longer.

Finally, after thousands upon thousands of seasons in the Valley, the Mother withdrew her abundance and the People began to dwindle. The all-giving River of the Bear Mother shrank to nothing. The great swarms of salmon disappeared, no longer able swim the dry stream through the great Eye of the Mother to feed her People.

At long last, the Mother closed the portals to the wellspring of her spirit-power, the very source of her bounty and her wisdom. After eons of uncountable visits, that day finally came when a great slide of rocks and dirt came crashing down from the cliffs above the entrance to close the entrance to the Mother's Great Cave. It was the sealing of the Great Cave which ultimately decided all the seers and shamans of the Bear People that the Mother had withdrawn her favor.

It was time for the People of the Bear Mother to leave the Valley forever.

And the People did leave the Valley, moving ever further east and south into the Plain of the Mammoth Mother. Their children even crossed the Great River where the People had never ventured before. The diminishing herds survived there, but so did the human tribes of the Others who resisted our coming with their lives. Now it would be the People of the Bear Mother who would bring times of trouble to the Others. It became an age of continual struggle and warfare between and among the human tribes. The People became hunters of men and we saw the shedding of human blood as we had never experienced before.

It was the end of living and the beginning of survival.

Having left the Valley of the Bear Mother and her Great Cave, the People no longer claimed her bounty and protection. We became another People altogether. We were re-born as the People of the Wolf, living and hunting continuously upon the Plain like packs of wolves or hyenas. Still, we followed the herds wherever they may have been directed by the Mother to go. But the People of the Wolf would always follow blindly wherever the herds would lead and had no bountiful winter home to return to.

Without the Great Cave to instruct us, to initiate us as men and women, the stories and the songs and the mysteries of the People were forgotten. The rites of passage from childhood to adulthood changed and diminished beyond recognition. But the Great Cave's melding of the Nine Kin into one People was too much a part of our very souls for us to completely forget. Always, within our hearts, in that tiny place where the Mother always dwells, we remembered.

In our souls we remembered, even as we passed through the Gate of Forgetting.

* * *

No longer called the People of the Bear Mother, we were still her children though we didn't know it. We had been lashed by the willow rods, marked with the stabbing blades and bound forever into one People with one heart and one mind by the revelations and trials of the Great Cave. We had been the People for so many generations it would forever be a part of our very souls. And so it is an inseparable part of my own.

In our scattered bands, the People still lived and moved—and often fought—as one. Uncountable generations had been taught the lesson: *I and the Mother are One* by the Great Cave of the All Mother whose own holy lodge it was and would always be. Hunting, moving, and yes, fighting and killing other human tribes, as if it were one continuous summer season, what was left of the Nine Kin would survive as a People only by coming together in a late summer Gathering. Once each summer season, the Wolf People gathered at the place where a mere trickle of the River of the Bear Mother entered the Plain. The Wolf People always gathered upon the very same ground the Bison-kin had once called their home, their Place of Abundance, although the People of the Wolf did not know it.

What was now an unnamed little stream wended its much-diminished way to the River of the Mammoth Mother. That much had not changed. From where the small stream joined the large, they flowed together to the Great Salty Waters as one river. The Great Salty had become the last remaining source of abundance and refuge for all the tribes and peoples of the Plain because the fierce winter storms blowing from the Northland and the Mountains of Ice still barely reached its endless expanses of salty water.

At this one of the few times of the year of relative abundance, all the bands of the Wolf People would gather to find wives and husbands and to initiate their boys into manhood. Only at this place did the initiations of the boys continue with the grasping of the Mother's Tree of Life. Only in these Gatherings were the Nine Lashes given and the hair shorn and kin-marks made while singing and dancing around a hearth open to the sky.

The dancing and singing of the Song of Promise continued, but there were no hot springs of Serpent Father to ease our sore muscles and our souls. Still, sweating tents gave forth billows of steam from heated rocks as a poor substitute for the Serpent Springs and were far better than no hot baths at all. And the bison wrestling, running and spear-throwing contests would continue. How could they not?

But without the Great Cave to stir our hearts and souls, guiding the many to trance-visions of their animal-guides was much more difficult to achieve. Endless dancing and singing, the trance herbs, fasting from food and water still brought the dreams to some. Those we still called "shaman." But too many of the songs and teachings of the Cave that reveal the meaning of the dreams and visions that came to those shamans had been lost forever.

A few bands of the Wolf People still ventured up the Bear Mother's River to hunt the roe deer, ibex, chamois and boar that continued to roam the scrubby forests around the Great Cave. There, a few bands would wait for the few fish that still made their way up the river to spawn at the end of summer. Those who ventured up the River saw and marveled at the great stone arch of the Eye of the Mother, although they no longer called it that. Somewhere deep inside their souls, in their very marrow, they saw and understood and longed for the Mother's Bountiful Place. The Wolf People pined for that place of endless abundance and eternal togetherness with the Mother and all their beloved kin that somehow seemed to reside in this particular valley.

Our roving descendants eventually spread along the shores of the Great Salty, always following the herds wherever they led. And so the People scattered far beyond the Great Plain that had nurtured them for so long. My wandering soul still followed them lifetime after lifetime. In their hunting bands they sometimes fought and sometimes merged with other peoples as far as the great, endless steppes of the north. There, the Mother still brought forth her abundance of mammoth and bison and reindeer. There, on the greatest plain the All Mother had ever made, trees were so scarce that shelters and initiation lodges were made of skins, dirt, mammoth skulls, tusks and bones. Our hearth fires upon the never-ending plains were fueled, not only with dung from the great herds, but with their very bones as well.

Roam we did, forever following the eternal herds. But never did we find a place as full of the All Mother and her abundance as the lovely Valley of the Bear Mother. In time, the Mountains of Ice would recede again; the winters would shorten. The trees and grass and abundant herds and flocks would return, but never as bountifully as they had been before. Above all, the rivers of fish would not return to the Valley of the Bear Mother in their vast numbers to support many camps of the People through the winter season.

Even when some of the People returned to the partially renewed abundance of the Valley, the Great Cave remained sealed and would never again be used to teach and test and reveal the secrets of the All Mother to her People. Other caves would be painted. Other caves would give shelter. Other rites would be performed. Other boys and girls would be transformed into hunters and women. But the All Mother's Great Cave would remain closed off and utterly silent except for unheard drops of water falling into its unfathomable darkness.

The Great Cave would remain completely dark, except for the light of a tiny opening that shone through to illuminate the entrance of the Great Cave as a den for bears and wolves. Only an occasional human visitor too terrified to go very deep into the darkness ever left their footprints in the soft, brown mud that had covered many of the bones of Bear Mother. The paths and the well-trodden trails which used to carry the multitudes of the People to the center of their own souls had been all but obliterated by flowing water and lack of use.

In time, even that opening would completely close, shutting out the mother bears seeking winter shelter to sleep and give birth to their cubs. Bear Mother withdrew her favor even from her own bear-children. The Great Cave ceased completely to reveal the Mother's secrets to any of the human or animal-tribes. Before the Cave was sealed forever, I would not visit the Place of Transformation again. Except, that is, for one last time.

* * *

"Climb up here to see the Mother's Mouth, the stream running through it and all that lies below," my father called to me, hands cupped around his mouth

He called down from atop a rock slide at the foot of the white cliffs behind our camp of skin lodges. It did not take long for me to clamber up the slope to join my father. We looked together out over the beautiful valley where our band had camped to wait for the fish to arrive. We would spear and smoke as many as we could. While we camp here, the women of the camp will collect the abundant nuts and roots that are found in this valley. And the men will hunt the boar and deer that also abound here. When the fish cease their coming, we will move down the river again back out onto the Plain for the winter season. The herd animals and flocks of water birds are more numerous upon the Plain, especially the great herds of fat reindeer. They can get fat on nothing but snow! Or so the hunters say.

"I want you to crawl inside this opening. It is just large enough for a courageous boy like you to squeeze through."

My father encouraged me toward a narrow gap in the tumbled boulders with a big, approving smile. I joined him next to the dark hole that opened amid a jumble of stones, dirt and broken tree branches. I wanted to see if I were, in fact, small enough to get inside.

I love my father dearly because I am the only one of our camp he always takes to explore the many caves in this valley. My older brother is initiated as a hunter now, but then he never wanted to come along when my father went exploring the caves. My brother has *more important* things to do. Or so he says. I think he is just afraid. The only sister of my father's lodge is also too afraid to go into the darkness of any cave.

I have never been afraid of dark caves. My father says I have the eye of the lion-powers. He says lions and leopards can see in the dark and that is why I am unafraid. But I don't think I can see any better in the dark with my lion-eye than anyone else. My father also says that his dark blue eyes are the deep color of the Mother's Abyss, so neither of us need be afraid.

The Thrice Born of our band has warned my father many times that the spirit-powers within the caves are powerful and dangerous. Everyone says we are foolish to go into such places for our amusement. But we never listen to them. We think we are well-enough protected—and experienced enough—so neither of us is afraid of Earth Mother's caves and caverns. I love to explore these dark, cool places with my father more than anything else because then we can be together. I am still too young to go out on the hunt with my father, so this time together exploring caves is very precious to me.

And we have found wonderful spirit-animals in the caves which no one has ever seen but us! I would do anything for my father. It is true that, of all the kin of our band, the two of us seem drawn to deep, dark caves more than any other. We are pulled to those caves in the same way others are drawn to quest for dreams and visions upon the open Plain in solitude. We have gone into many caves together, my beloved father and I.

"Yes, Father," I said. "I think I can get inside."

Always willing am I for such an exciting adventure into a dark cave, as any boy of my age should be!

I love to climb the many trees in this valley too—there are so few out on the grassy plains. And I love playing near the river catching frogs and water snakes. But what I love the most is exploring caves with my father. There are lots and lots of caves in this valley. We can see that some of them have been lived in by people, but some are only lived in by bears or wolves. Together we have explored almost all of the caves my father has found up and down this valley.

I knew there would be no animals that could hurt me inside a cave like this. The opening is too small for wolves or bears to squeeze through to make their dens within. Besides, my father has taught me not to take stupid chances inside any cave. I always take the easy paths instead of climbing up or down the rocks so as not to fall and break a bone. Above all, my father has taught me to always mark the walls and roof of a cave with my torch to find my way out again.

"I can feel cool, moist air coming out of the opening," I said.

We both knew that meant there was probably a large cavern within.

My father knelt down to make fire to light the pine torches he always brings along for our cave journeys together. I gathered a few dry twigs and leaves from the ground for him to use as tinder. I squatted down to watch him work. He struck a spark into the fireweed fluff and began to blow gently to nurture the tiny flame. I added the twigs when his tinder caught fire.

Two torches were lit which I held tight in one hand. A few others were packed into my bag and I began to squeeze my way into the narrow opening that seemed to have jagged rocks on every side. This is the kind of cave opening that made wearing a long-sleeved skin shirt and long trousers a necessity. I wore no boots or sandals as my bare feet were better to hold to and climb over the wet rocks and stones that were encountered in a cave like this one promised to be.

As I pushed my way inside the opening, I came upon only a couple of very narrow places I had to squeeze through. The hole soon opened out into a huge cavern stretching far beyond the limits of my torchlight.

"It is a fine, large cave, my Father," I called back to him.

I cupped my hand near my mouth and shouted into the light streaming through the small opening.

"Can you see any spirit-animals on the cave walls, my good Son?" he shouted, his voice already muffled by the narrow entrance.

"No," I said. "This is just an entrance to a very deep cave. I can only see that much!" I shouted back.

"Be careful, my son!" His voice echoed real concern through the rocky gap.

"I will spend as much time as my torches will allow. Do not worry about me, my father. I will be very careful," I called back to reassure him.

As my eyes adjusted to the complete blackness, a gradual slope of loose stones and rocks led down into the cave where it made a sharp turn to the left. At some time in the past a great flood had washed a good deal of water and dirt into the cave. I could see where the rivulets of water had once run hard down into the depths of the cave.

Several paces on, to my right there opened another passage, mostly filled with rocks. There was yet another passage directly ahead. The passage straight on was also mostly filled with rocks and dirt from the slope I had just descended.

"That leaves only one way to go," I reasoned to myself aloud. "I will go around the corner and to the left."

My astonishment was complete at the high roof of a gigantic cave that opened up before me. It's perfectly flat, clay-covered floor was dotted with many skulls, white bones and depressions in the ground where mother bears have spent their winter sleep. The dank air filled with the scent of water and the faint odor of decay hit my face like a breath from the cave. As if it were alive. A chill ran through me and I mumbled a prayer to the spirit-powers of this place.

"Good to have the second torch in a cave like this one," I whispered in awe of the gigantic chamber that lay before me.

I would be in big trouble if a single torch went out in a place like this!

Without thinking about it, I found myself asking the powers of the cave for permission to enter—always advised by my father when entering a place of spirit-power for the first time. And I began to sing the Song of Dispelling Fear to myself to calm my racing heart.

One skull--near the bottom of the scree of dirt and rock that had obviously come in from the blocked cave-mouth above—had been pushed out of its place by rolling stones and dirt. I knew it was out of place because directly across from it, on the left-hand side of the passage, was another skull with a big leg bone half stuck into the ground right in front of its snout. The two skulls had once faced each other across the opening to the larger chamber beyond.

"These two bear skulls must once have marked the entrance to the cave," I said to myself.

I decided I would begin moving along the right-hand wall of the cave. Without even thinking about it, my path was diverted out into the great cavern where I could better see some of the bones and bear hollows. I decided it was a cave that had never before been visited by people because there were only bear claw marks on the smooth cave walls and only bear bones and hollows on the ground. Neither trodden paths nor any painted or scratched spirit-animals could be seen. There was only a water-flattened cave floor of tan clay covered by a thin, crunchy layer of white, sparkling rock in some places and soft dirt suitable for making sleeping dens in other places. The whole place was scattered everywhere with animal bones and skulls as I had never seen before in any other cave. I decided this must be Bear Mother's cave for so many of her bones to be scattered here.

My torches flickered with little drafts coming out of the charcoal blackness like the breath of the bear-spirit on my neck, stalking me in the dark. A hard shiver ran up my spine. I stopped to listen. The only sounds I heard were my bare feet crunching on the crystallized ground, water dripping from the roof somewhere in the dark, my own rapid breathing and my heart thumping in my throat.

I had been in big caves like this before. So in spite of the churning anxiety in the pit of my stomach, I followed the almost flat wall to the right until I reached a large gap—the entrance to another large chamber. I moved over to the left-hand side of the entrance which was marked with a rod of red ochre made by human hands. There was certain to be more painted signs and animals beyond.

I skirted the wall around to the inside of the chamber. Following its left-hand wall, I came to a huge rock shaped like a woman's pute hanging from the roof. The whole thing seemed to be painted in red ochre hand-dots. I knew they were hand-dots because I could see some of the finger-marks besides the palm-marks. Everywhere I looked, the clay floor was blood-red too.

My astonishment increased as I made my way along the great red rock with images of red bison and other indistinct creatures, fearing all the while to touch it. I stopped before a mass of red ochre above which appeared a cross of red with great spouts of gushing, flowing fountains of blood spewing out from its base.

"This could only be the holy tree of the Mothers of the Four Directions. This cave must belong to them," I reasoned out loud to myself.

And then I felt compelled to place my hand against the mass of red ochre out of which the cross arose.

"It looks to me like ... yes, a liver," I said to myself.

I held my hand against the cool, reddened stone for a long moment. The distinct feeling that I had been here before puzzled me. My father and I most certainly have never seen this cave before.

My amazement would only increase as I left the great red rock and made my way to the edge of another, wider, opening. So wide was it that I could barely see the other side even with my double torch. It looked like another separate cavern was to be found beyond.

To orient myself, I followed the portal of the big opening around to see what lay on the other side. I took a few steps out into the same tan clay, bone-covered floor of the same cavern I had just entered. I followed the wall for several paces more until I was sure this could be another way back to the entrance of the cave. The high roof and numerous bear bones told me I was in the same cavern as I had come into the cave through. I turned around and followed the wall back to the big opening. I crossed it to its other side.

Upon this portal of the big opening there appeared a round, black, open-mouthed face of a lion. With an open mouth like that, it was certainly the ravenous spirit-lion that ate the whole world, including herself from her own tail up to her belly and to her chest and neck, leaving only her gaping jaws. The menacing black lion head seemed to be telling me not to enter here.

Instead of entering, I turned to follow the right-hand wall that curved around the edge of the portal into the same high-roofed chamber I had entered. Here, there were no painted spirit-animals. Only bear claw marks were to be seen high up on the walls, higher than a man standing on another man's shoulders could reach. It must have been a gigantic bear to have made claw marks so high up!

As I moved along this wall, I noticed it had sharp turns into both shallow and deep side-passages. I was careful to make swipes with the tip of the torch as I went so I could be sure to find my way out again. I continued to follow the right-hand wall until I came to what was a much narrower passage leading deeper into the cave. I could see across the passage. When I crossed to the other side, there appeared another black face of Lion Mother. Another warning not to enter?

I made my way around from the wall where the second black lion-head lurked. Soon I began to see many strange signs: red bird-like butterflies, black butterflies with pointed wings, a big red bug of some kind and another huge red butterfly-bird. Rounding a pendant of stone, I followed the right-hand wall further into the cave. What opened up to me was an amazing line of seven lion heads followed by a big lion with an arc of red dots coming out of its mouth. In front of the big lion, there stretched out a line of beautifully made, huge red rhinos walking head-to-tail toward deeper parts of the cave. An odd sign the likes of which I had never seen before had been painted in the midst of the line of rhinos.

"It has to be Earth Mother's great breasts. Or a pair of half-moon shaped buttocks!" I laughed to myself.

I rounded another outcrop and other spirit-animals appeared—and some hand marks with all the fingers too. Suddenly thirstier than I had ever been, I heard the sounds of running water. I willingly followed them into a small, low side-chamber running full of clear, sweet water. I had my drinking gourd with me but I had not even thought to drink from it. I was so enthralled and excited by my discoveries in this wonderful cave I had no thirst until I heard these sounds of flowing water. It is often so journeying into such dangerous and frightful places. The painted animals in some of the caves are so beautiful and alive they can bring even my brave hunter-father to tears. A little hunger and thirst is never of any consequence in our explorations.

I drank my fill of the chilly waters. Then I emptied my bottle gourd and re-filled it with the living waters of the cave—waters coming directly from a spring and flowing in a white cascade into a pool. These waters were certainly "living waters" and were sure to be full of the spirit-power of such a magnificent cave.

"My father will be happy that I bring the living water of this cave back to him. He will say it is Earth Mother's Water of Life," I said out loud.

The sound of my own voice echoing back to me from the dark silence all around startled me. It was all silence, that is, except for the splashing, tumbling waters of the side-chamber. The running waters gave out the high-pitched sounds of children singing and chanting. And there was something else in the sound too—the unsettling, high-pitched whirr of a willow switch flying through the air. Maybe it is the sound of the bullroarer singing in the darkness?

I kept trying to force the strange feelings of foreboding back down into my gut. But they bubbled back up and made my throat and mouth dry even though I had just quenched my thirst in the icy waters. My throat was suddenly dryer and scratchier than it had ever been in any other cave I had ever entered with my father. Something, I could not understand what, pulled at me and drew me on to see more of the wonders that I knew lay ahead of me. I entered the next chamber of the cave in spite of the clutching feeling in my chest.

The low-hanging flaps of stone in most parts of this and other caves allowed me to make backward swipes of my torch so I would be able to see them on the way out. That is one very valuable trick of cave exploring my father has taught me. It is a practice that gives me all the confidence I needed to find my way out of this or any other cave and back into the World of Light again—all on my own.

Still, the fearful feeling in my liver surged up into my heart and throat telling me to turn and run as fast as I could away from this place. As I moved on, following the right-hand wall of the chamber I had entered, I came to an ancient hearth in front of three red dots in a line. Only the hearth stones remained to surround a little fire pit without a single trace of ash. There may have been no ash, but I am certain I can smell burning human hair. And again, that disturbing feeling that I had seen this place before.

There are no spirit-animals painted on these walls—only the hearth and a little pile of stones on the ground below the red dots. The chamber's rounded roof with stone ridges was not so high that it was in complete darkness. It reminded me of the ribs of some huge animal bigger than a mammoth. The more I lingered in this place the more it filled me with some unspeakable dread.

Not wanting to stay in this place any longer, I made my way along the right-hand wall where it curved around to a patch of white, wet stones. They stuck up out of the ground like a little forest of man-rods. I could see that just beyond the white penises a big stone step led down to yet another large chamber. I went down this step and moved toward an owl-spirit staring at me from above a huge, darkly dangerous hole in the middle of the cave floor.

The large hole in the cave floor made it necessary for me to skirt around it, always staying within sight of the right-hand wall. I eventually reached what can only be described as a river of black spirit-animals so astonishing I could only look and wonder with my mouth wide open. All the caves my father and I have ever explored have not had as many spirit-animals as are painted on this one wall. And no cave of my experience has spirit-animals as full of life-fire and movement as these!

I was overwhelmed by the spectacle of this boiling river of black-painted animals, shaded so that their limbs, bodies and heads looked rounded in contrast to the flat outlines of spirit-animals in most painted caves.

I followed the astonishing mixed herds that moved and ran and jumped in my flickering torchlight until they finally stopped at a large protrusion in the rock wall. I continued on, following the right-hand wall around the protrusion. To my left hand an astonishing circle of bear skulls opened up to my view.

I stared at the circle of skulls for a long time trying to count how many skulls were in the circle. Several had been pushed out of their place making it difficult to see the whole circle. I edged around what I will tell my father is a dance-circle of bear skulls by walking along the edge of a line of big boulders that had fallen from the roof. The edges of two of the boulders made a gap to more of the cave beyond. And these portals contained two reindeer engraved into the white stone of the boulders. Each of them had giant, branching sets of antlers. They seemed to be pointing to something deeper inside the cave so I went through the gap in the boulders marked by the reindeer to explore further.

I moved straight out into the darkness and to my utter surprise the edge of a second dance-circle of bear skulls appeared. This circle pointed in toward a big block of stone upon which a skull had been placed where the bear's head would have been. I edged around the second skull circle where the floor of the cave began to slope up.

Ahead of me, I could see what looked like two massive pendants of white stone coming down almost to the cave floor like the portals of some huge door. I went through the entrance marked by a little black musk ox on a wing of stone above the doorway. Immediately, I had to bend over, the roof was so low. I went on until I could stand up and finally reached what had to be the back of the cave for I could go no further. The walls here were almost unmarked except for some bear some claw marks looking like a net at the back of the cavern where the walls were straight up-and-down. There was also a jumble of mammoths that seemed to be shaking their trunks and huge tusks back and forth the way mammoths do when they want you to go away and are about to charge. It was odd, but this jumble of mammoths looked like a crisscrossing net too.

"The Earth Mother's Net of Life!" I realized out loud in amazement.

I thought it unsafe not to return the way I had come for fear I would get lost in some jumbled maze of rocks. I needn't have worried because the roof was so low here that I could only go back the way I had come.

After passing through the big gate of white stone, I turned to the left to follow the edge of the amazing skull circle. Curious about the bear stone with its black and red striped skull out in the middle, I entered the circle and approached the rock with a skull resting on it. All about lay many bones and skulls of the bear-spirit.

Most of the skulls were in place so I could count them—twenty eight in all. Some of the skulls in the dance-circle had also been painted in red and black stripes and dots.

The more I saw of these painted skulls, the more anxious to be gone from this place I became. I felt I was trespassing upon the bear-spirit's lodge and should not be here at all. Certainly, I should not have come within this holy circle. Had I realized this was Bear Mother's holy lodge, I would have known to ask more proper permission to enter than I had. It was too late for that now as I had already encroached into the center of a dance circle of bear skulls without the Bear Mother's consent.

I looked up from the bear stone and saw the great herd of black spirit-animals stampeding in my direction. I knew where I was and I knew how to get out of this dangerous place.

I left the circle of skulls and went to the wall of black animals. I followed the herd of horses, reindeer, bison, aurochs and rhinos for a distance and soon found a couple of my torch marks on wings of stone above my head.

I had come full circle and it was time to leave this disturbing cave.

I was sure my father would be worrying about me since I had already been so long inside this cavern. I began to follow the black herds that would take me back to my father. As I made my way along the wall, I turned to my left as if being called or beckoned by a small whisper in my ear. There, a black-as-charcoal, round open-ing appeared in the wall of animals. The black spirit-animals seemed to be coming from this place that promised to be the deepest part of the entire cave.

My heart was beating so hard I could barely breathe. It pulsed wildly and so loud in my ears I thought there should certainly be echoes of its thudding sounds coming back to me from these terri-fying walls. But I had to go in. I had to know what was within.

As I moved toward the round black hole, my bare feet left fresh prints in soft brown clay that had not been trodden by any of the human or animal tribes for how long I could never even guess. Something unspeakable and unseen carried me forward into the dark as if in a dream-trance. I am being carried into a place where no living person has been for a long, long time.

The opening to this narrow side-chamber was the same shape as the Mouth of the Mother through which the river below this cave flowed. I was being sucked into it by an unseen current stronger even than the Mammoth Mother's great river upon the Plain.

Inside the entrance on the right-hand portal, a strange deer with no antlers appeared. I looked closer. To my surprise, the deer had a bizarre rhino sitting on its rear haunches, the rhino's single horn pointing to the cave roof above. Only a single big red dot marked the left-hand portal through which I had stumbled unable to stop myself from discovering what was at the end of this passage.

"What is at the end of all this? Why am I compelled to go further in?" I asked myself in a panicked whisper.

The narrow passage had a high roof, but the floor went down and down and down in big steps, one of which was marked on either side by women's putes—three of them. Then I came to a deep drop off that I would never have dared to climb down by myself, so steep it appeared. Painted animals on the right-hand wall seemed to be directing me to something so I went to investigate.

I held my double torches cautiously out over the ledge just next to the right-hand wall. Sure enough, there was a wide shelf a short drop below the ledge. And below the shelf, there was another short drop to a sloping stone that would take me down to the chamber's floor in relative ease and safety.

Reaching the bottom of the sloping stone, I could see some painted animals on the opposite—the left-hand—wall of this deep and dangerous cavern.

Then opened up to me the most terrifying display of lion-spirits I will ever see. One huge pair of lions gazed over the back of a banded rhino toward another pride of lions that appeared to be sitting on a high promontory. And behind them, another astonishing herd of bison and lions and rhinos opened up as if it were a herd running upon the Plain.

To my astonishment—in the middle of this swirling, moving, mixed herd of spirit-animals—appeared a fantastic monster with huge, round feet. One of the Thrice Born in trance, shifting his shape and running with his animal-guides, no doubt. I drew closer to peer at the vaguely human head. The hooked beak of an eagle or an owl appeared to my eyes as I stared at the black image. Then as I looked closer, the trunk of a mammoth reached out to touch a big gap in the stone wall in front of the chimera. Behind the monster, a line of round bead-shapes formed a kind of barrier to the bison and lions behind it.

The most astounding thing about this spirit-herd is that the pride of lions at the back of a great herd of bison, seemed to be transforming into bison even as I stared at them!

Finally, at the very rear of this awe-inspiring spirit-herd and its entranced shaman in the middle of it all, I came to another pute-shaped stone hanging from the roof of the cave. The whole mass of black spirit-animals seemed to be emerging from this great stone pute and running toward the entrance of the chamber guarded by the two enormous lions.

And painted upon the stone pendant, a gigantic woman's vulva had been painted. My heart was about to jump up through my throat. I began to sweat, my mouth as dry as the piles of ancient charcoal scattered on the ground. It was Earth Mother's pute, open and black as if ready to swallow me up and pull me into the darkness with all of her lions and bison forever. Above her pointed legs and wide hips, a great, black bison bull loomed. It was mounting her, its spittle flying over her, its eyes bulging in the heat of the rut.

Sheer panic rose up from my liver and all I wanted was to flee this place! I knew not why but I had to run! I just had to go from this place as fast as my legs would carry me!

In a cold terror I turned and retreated as quickly as I could from the darkness of this black chamber of lions and bison. I climbed the sloping stone to the ledge and jumped up the drop offs in the narrow passage until I reached its round mouth. Out of the mouth-like entrance my feet flew, following my torch marks on the flaps of stone above. I jumped up the single step, past the white penises and out of the chamber with the three red dots as fast as my bare feet could carry me.

I fairly flew past the cavern of thirst-quenching waters, past the big rhinos in a line, past the Mother's breasts, past the lion with spots of blood coming from its mouth and past the butterfly and the bug. My mouth is so dry! But I dare not stop to quench my thirst at the cave of living waters.

By the time I passed the skull guardians, I was running so fast I was fairly flying. I reached the sloping scree below the narrow entrance above and began clambering up frantically. With terrifying presences nipping at my heels and clawing at my back, I scratched at the loose stone and rock scrambling toward the blinding white light of the tiny opening I had used to come in to this accursed place.

Torches long since tossed aside, I pushed my way through the jagged tight opening, fleeing to the warmth and the light and my beloved father waiting outside the entrance.

Out of the narrow opening I struggled, panting like a hunted animal, feet and hands scraped and bleeding. My knees, shins and elbows bruised against the rough stones. Finally reaching the outside, terrified to close my eyes I shielded them with my hands from the blinding sunlight.

I fell into my father's waiting arms on the edge of unmanly tears. But with my father's sheltering embrace, the tears did start to flow. I began to weep uncontrollably like I had never wept before.

"What happened, my son?" he cried, holding me and letting me grip his waist as hard as I could.

"Are you all right? Have you been injured?" he asked, frantically feeling up and down my arms and legs for some part of me that had been injured or broken.

I may not have been initiated as a man, as yet, but I know a man never cries like a baby even if he is still a boy. But I could not cease from sobbing aloud even as the tears continued to roll down my face. I did not know, nor could I understand what it was I am so terrified of in this cave.

After all, it is just a cave like any other.

My father held me close and patted my back to calm and soothe me.

"My son, there is nothing to fear. I am here and nothing can harm you. Be my brave son. Dry your tears and tell me what happened to you in this cave," he comforted.

My fear finally passed. The tears dried and I could speak again.

My father asked with caring concern, "What did you see in the cave that so terrified you, my son? I was certain that you had been injured!"

"I don't know, my father. I don't know," I said my control returning.

"I have never seen you so frightened from going into a cave? We have done this thing so many times together, my son. What did you find in this cave?" he said, his famous blue-black eyes wide with concern.

"Nothing, my father, I found nothing in this cave. I saw nothing in this cave. It is empty. My torch went out and I just became frightened of the dark. There is nothing in this cave," I lied, utterly shamed in front of my father by my tears.

"There is nothing in the cave but some springs of cold water. I have brought you some of the cave's living waters," I said and spoke no more.

I handed my father of the darkest of blue eyes the bottle gourd full of the cave's clear, icy waters with both hands as if it were a gift.

EPILOGUE

IN TIME, THE MOUNTAINS OF ICE would disappear completely and along with the ice and snow, the great herds of animals. The reindeer and musk ox followed the snow to the far north beyond the Mountains of Ice because, as everyone knows, they can get fat on nothing but ice and snow.

Most of the great herds and flocks of birds upon the Plain of the Mammoth Mother just ceased to exist in the World of Light. Gone were the herds of bison and reindeer and mammoth and rhino and horse. The big-antler deer disappeared completely and the rivers and streams were no longer filled with flashing, jumping salmon. Only deer, ibex, boar, and, of course, the ever-living bears remained in the mountain fastness and in the spreading forests of a transformed landscape. Without the great herds, the lions, leopards, and hyenas also disappeared. Only a few of the wolf and human tribes endured to hunt the remaining animal-messengers of a much less giving Earth Mother.

Angry that the herds had returned to the Mother never to come again in abundance, the People of the Wolf forgot their songs and dances of gratitude and abundance.

And in due course, these remaining hunters of animals and birds, these collectors of plants, nuts and fish, gave way to those with strange new ways. These new peoples of the human tribes put seeds into the ground, waited for the plants to grow, and then cut them down for food. To feed their families, they keep captive herds of animals and flocks of birds to be slaughtered without ceremony or gratitude.

And these new tribes lived in lodges that remained in the same places all year long. In these vast heaped-up camps of mud, people were jammed together in such great numbers that the stink of one's neighbor was never out of one's nostrils. The stench of servitude was never far behind the settlement of one of these places. The most esteemed among them made rules for all to follow instead of each respecting the other and treating the other as they would be treated themselves.

The People of the Bear Mother were gone forever. But my soul longed for more life and more experience among those who had replaced and merged with them as new peoples of the human tribes. I suppose you could say that the People of the Bear Mother never really disappeared—they just changed their form and their way of living, as all the Mother's children do as they pass in and out of the World of Light.

What none of the new tribes knew, however, was that the disappearance of the People of the Bear Mother was the end of living as children of the same Mother and the beginning of a never-ending contest for survival. They did not know it was the beginning of the struggle against one another—and even against the Mother herself—to wrest her bounty from her with beggings and pleadings that the Earth Mother's abundance should come to them and not to another.

Do they not know that the Mother's abundance is always there and given alike to all, if only gratitude is freely given?

And so began my many lifetimes among the tribes who build gigantic lodges of earth and sticks and who stay always in one place. They are people who cage their animals for food and who use strange tools to make the earth produce food for them to harvest. These human tribes esteem some above others and divide the Mother's bounty unequally.

No longer respected as children of the same Mother, the animal-messengers became a lower form of life to be slaughtered without ceremony and without gratitude for the bounty of their body-lives. No longer honored as messengers of the Mother's spirit-power, the animal-guides became less-than-human slaves to be corralled and driven into captivity to await their unfeeling butchery into pieces of meat and fat. The animal-messengers of the Mother's spirit-power and many of the human tribes themselves became mere bodies to be given as bribe-offerings to the highly esteemed and the unseen divinities they served.

These are the human tribes who knew not Lion Mother or Bison Father. Nor did they know the revelations and trials of the Great Cave. These are the human tribes who honor some families above some others. They give to those who already have much and take from those who already have very little.

These are the human tribes who enslave not only the animal-messengers of the Mother of All, but even some of their human brothers and sisters, who they mistakenly think to be soul-less and undeserving of respect and honor. These are the human tribes who give the right to bigger lodges and more of the bounty of the earth to some and withhold it from others. These are the human tribes who allow their brothers and sisters to starve when they have more than they can eat.

But these are also the human tribes who know the All Mother in many of her other guises and forms. There are those wise teachers and lovers still among them who preserve the Mother's wisdom.

And so I will come again and again to seek this knowledge and wisdom among them. I will seek the Mother's face within their eyes. I will search for those souls whose circle of life has yet to be completed with me.

For it is *all* of the Mother, is it not?

ACKNOWLEDGEMENTS

Above all, I want to acknowledge the two wise guides in my life without whose teachings this novel would never have been conceived or written. First and foremost is Joseph Campbell, my intellectual mentor and inspired revealer of deep truths common to all of us. I was not fortunate enough to meet him and receive instruction at his feet, but through his enlightened writings on the mythology of the ages I feel as though I know him. I certainly know his soul.

My other great teacher is Dr. Sharron Stroud, founder of Inner Faith Ministries Worldwide and the Institute of Successful Living. She continues to open new vistas to me on the wisdom that can only be found within.

I am also deeply indebted to Ahriah Vocare, a true mystic for our own time. Without her gifts, the creative energies that have lain dormant within me for so long would never have been opened so that I too could hear the Song of the Universe and to write about what I hear.

I also want to acknowledge the everyday oracles in my life, both living and already passed. They are the friends, lovers, family and antagonists who have taught, each in their own way and in their proper time, so many lessons of life.

I especially want to thank those everyday oracles whose unfailing support and encouragement gave me the motivation to write this story. Because of them I know that I too am a wise teacher of ancient truths that show us all how to live a human life under any circumstances, in any time and in any place. These special friends are those who read and commented on early drafts of this book without which it would never have been written. They are: William E. Hubbard, Kathy Thompson, Terry Lynn Jones, Jan Alford, Douglas Lott, Charles Lynn Frost, Anita C. Bradford, Susan E. Schaffner and Camilla Anthony. Each gave tremendously important early feedback from very rough drafts and I will be forever grateful for their insights.

I want to acknowledge my editor, Teresa Jache, who worked tirelessly to polish and refine my first diamond-in-the-rough. I would also like to acknowledge the professionals at Writers Literary Agency and Eloquent Books for so ably and smoothly guiding this novice writer through the maze of the book publishing process. Also my gratitude goes to Mark Anderson of AquaZebra Graphic Designs for his excellent work on the map of the Great Cave.

The whole world is indebted to Dr. Jean Clottes who has so meticulously and lovingly excavated Chauvet Cave, this one-of-a-kind artifact of our common Paleolithic heritage. I am personally indebted to him for his generosity in allowing the use of some of the images from his beautiful book *Chauvet Cave: The Art of Earliest Times* which has so inspired me.

Finally, I am grateful to those ancient sages, shamans and inspired artists who heard the Song of the Universe in their own words, for their own times, and have so marvelously transmitted to us the wisdom of all the ages through their astonishing works of animal art.

T.D. Austin

LaVergne, TN USA
15 December 2010
208887LV00003B/8/P